THE HOUNDS OF HELL is the latest in a series of thunderous bestsellers by Jean Lartéguy. The others, all available in Avon editions, are THE CENTURIONS (filmed as THE LOST COMMAND), THE PRAETORIANS, and YELLOW FEVER.

<u>The New York Times</u> says of Lartéguy: "His books are all marked by an intuitive feeling for his subject. As an aid to understanding what has happened and what is still happening . . . for helping us to understand why it has happened, Jean Lartéguy has few parallels among contemporary writers."

Also by Jean Lartéguy

The Centurions

The Praetorians

Yellow Fever

THE HOUNDS OF HELL

JEAN LARTÉGUY

Translated from the French

by

XAN FIELDING

AN AVON BOOK

AVON BOOKS
A division of
The Hearst Corporation
959 Eighth Avenue
New York, New York 10019

Published in France 1963 under the title *Les Chimères Noires*
Copyright © 1963 by Les Presses de la Cité, Paris.

English translation Copyright © 1966
by E. P. Dutton & Co., Inc. and Cassell & Co., Ltd.
Published by arrangement with E. P. Dutton & Co., Inc.
Library of Congress Catalog Card Number: 66–12258.

First Avon Printing, July, 1967

Cover illustration by Don Stivers

Printed in the U.S.A.

This book was written in collaboration with my friend Max Clos who, as a special correspondent of *Figaro*, has closely observed the dramatic events that have occurred in the Congo during the last few years. It is none the less a work of fiction, all the characters in it are imaginary and so are the adventures it describes.

Jean Lartéguy

ACKNOWLEDGEMENT

The passage from *Anabasis* by St-John Perse, translated by T. S. Eliot, on page 387 is reprinted here by kind permission of Harcourt, Brace & World, Inc.

CONTENTS

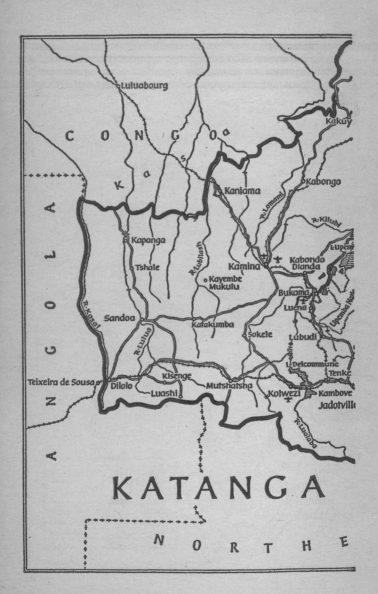

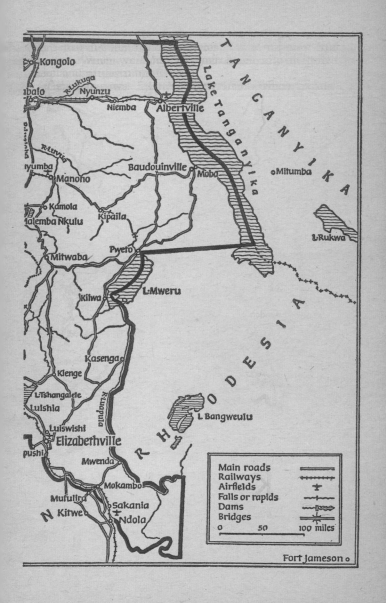

1. Julienne's Friends

Once again the space reserved for him in the Ecole Militaire car park was occupied and Colonel Chaudey did not know where to leave his little Citröen. This annoyed him considerably. He drew up beside a shed, but a policeman signaled to him that he was forbidden to park there.

Chaudey had had an office in the Ecole Militaire for over a year, but the sentries hardly ever recognized him, perhaps because he was always in civilian clothes, or else because, with his little paunch, his thinning hair, his chubby cheeks and his everlasting gray suit, he looked so much like thousands of other Frenchmen that he really could not be distinguished from any of them.

He eventually found a space beside a general's car, a black DS flying a pennant. The driver, a headquarters sergeant, winced at the way Chaudey ground his gears.

The colonel felt sheepish, angry and ill at ease. His awkwardness in everyday life, the acuteness he showed in the performance of his duties, the difficulties he felt in his relations with people whom he did not command had made him a timid and retiring character and at the same time gruff and brittle.

Whistling to himself, he climbed the three floors leading to his office. By the time the decision had been taken to install a lift in the moldy old building, he would have gone into retirement. He was fifty years old and had only two more years to serve—unless he was asked to continue, as a civilian, to deal with the same affairs. Even then he would remain the everlasting assistant: the command of the "dump" was a political post and "Uncle" Chaudey was only a technician.

The office allocated to him in the Ecole Militaire bore

the number 424. It was situated right under the rafters, at the end of a corridor with brown paint peeling off the walls.

Chaudey heaved a sigh of content as he sat down, then opened his briefcase and took out a cigarette-case and a yellow file inscribed at the top in a fine round hand "Lieutenant-Colonel la Roncière." He cut one of the cigarettes in half and lit it. The colonel had discovered this way of limiting his consumption to twenty cigarettes: twenty cigarettes cut in half make forty cigarettes.

His secretary, Madame Dustelle, poked her pointed nose through the communicating door.

She gave a cough.

"Come in," said Chaudey. "When I'm alone there's no need for you to cough to inform me that you're there. Since all my visitors pass through your office you always know when I'm busy; therefore there's never any need for you to cough."

Madame Dustelle had gray close-cropped hair, lovely eyes, but a gaunt face and, above all, huge flat-heeled shoes that were never polished.

Once again the colonel peered at his secretary's feet.

"It's impossible, by God, she must take size eight!" he reflected.

Conscious of Chaudey's gaze, Madame Dustelle stiffened. Her voice, which was not unpleasant with its slightly husky tone, now sounded sharp and impersonal.

"If I cough, Colonel, it's because I've got a cold. This place isn't properly heated, even though it's January. You're smoking already? . . . I thought your doctor told you . . ."

The colonel, when in a bad mood, was inclined to be stand-offish.

"That will do, Dustelle! Now, what's on today?"

The secretary went out fuming and came back with her spectacles on her nose and a sheet of paper in her hand.

She began to read in the same tone as a sergeant making a verbal report, doing her best to mispronounce names which she knew perfectly well.

"Verrier"—the name was Perrier—"telephoned. It's about the trouble the Assistant Military Attaché has had in Sofia. Cairo are asking for another radio operator . . . who must at least be able to speak Arabic. They were sent a Turkish specialist!"

"Falençon"—by which she meant Valençon—"wants to see you. He'll be calling at noon tomorrow. A certain

Thomas Fonts asked for you. He struck me as being somewhat uncouth: he called me 'little quail.' ''

Chaudey could not help smiling at this, which put his secretary in an even worse mood.

"And what did he say?"

"That it would not be long before you met him, for this meeting was inscribed in the stars. He's barmy! You must also ring up the Elysée, it's urgent . . . yes, that man Dumont."

Madame Dustelle hated Dumont, the Head of State's private secretary, whom she suspected of all sorts of turpitude, such as not really being called Dumont, which was true, having contacts with Iron Curtain countries, which was false, and being a man of loose morals, which for him was impossible.

Chaudey forthwith rang up the Elysée.

"Hello, Dumont? Chaudey here. You want me to come round at once . . . with Lieutenant-Colonel la Roncière's file . . . only la Roncière's? It's as urgent as that, is it? Of course I know la Roncière . . . like everyone else. All right, I'll be with you in a moment . . . just give me time to find the file."

There was a chuckle at the other end of the line.

The colonel put the yellow file back in his briefcase, took his overcoat off the peg and stepped into the adjoining office.

"Madame Dustelle," he said, "I shan't be in for the rest of the morning. Tell Perrier to deal as he sees fit with the Sofia business . . . there'll have to be a reprimand, of course. But we can't recall Moncel, he's the only member of our crowd who speaks Bulgarian. If there's anything very urgent, get in touch with me at the Elysée."

"What do you call very urgent, Colonel?"

"If my dog Tosca falls ill, if the Americans declare war on the Russians or vice-versa. . . . ''

"And what if there were a putsch in Algeria?" Madame Dustelle eagerly asked.

"That can wait. Anyway Dumont would know about it. Usually he's the one who organizes them."

"If you want to know my opinion of that fellow Dumont . . ."

"I don't."

Madame Dustelle sat down in front of her typewriter, an old Remington which had seen better days, and started hammering out a letter of refusal to the Head of Mission in Ankara who was asking for additional funds. She added a few nasty remarks of her own.

Dumont occupied an antechamber next door to the Head of State, which had been converted into an office. There was an Aubusson tapestry on the wall representing a hunting scene: a plump Diana aiming with a stretched bow at a stag that was already weeping.

There were also three Louis XV armchairs and a directoire desk. Behind this desk a tall, skinny, horse-faced character with a colorless mane of hair alternately neighed and whinnied. His extremely conventional blue suit set forth the red dot of his Légion d'Honneur rosette, but the tips of his shirt collar curled up and his spinach-green tie hung askew; his nails were dirty and his eyes sparkled with intelligence.

Chaudey lit another half-cigarette, sank back into an armchair and waited.

Dumont had opened the yellow file and was perusing it attentively. At certain passages he showed signs of agitation and the colonel was able to tell what point in the text he had reached.

La Roncière, like Thomas Fonts, was a character who fascinated Chaudey. But towards Fonts he felt an instinctive affection, perhaps because he represented a circumscribed and at the same time seductive type of adventurer, whereas he found la Roncière disturbing—a man who seemed to herald a world abandoned to technocrats. Chaudey dreaded a future which had the countenance of Lieutenant-Colonel Jean-Marie la Roncière.

Dumont was a mixture of them both. In common with Fonts he had an appetite for danger, scorn for conventions and ordinary laws, and loyalty in friendship; like la Roncière he showed a certain heartlessness, faith in statistics and contempt for human beings.

Jean-Marie la Roncière, one of the most brilliant officers in the French Army, Infantry Lieutenant-Colonel, former Major in the 3rd Foreign Parachute Regiment, at present awaiting posting.

Born 4 January, 1922, at La Rochelle. . . .

(Another Capricorn, Chaudey had noticed; although a Polytechnician and a good Catholic, the colonel believed in the stars when they provided a confirmation of his opinion.

Capricorn: unstable, tortuous, difficult natures . . .

14

proud, extremely prone to fanaticism: Stalin and Mazarin were born under this sign.)

A modest background: father a notary's clerk, mother the fifth child of small farmers; both of them Protestants.

Elementary school, school certificate, won an exhibition to the lycée, passed first part of the baccalaureate. After the 1940 defeat, at the age of eighteen, attempted to embark for England, failed twice, continued his studies, prepared for Saint-Cyr but before the examination joined a Maquis. Gave immediate proof of courage and maturity; was not amenable to discipline, however, and on two occasions, without notifying his superiors, organized raids which, moreover, were successful. Promoted to the rank of sergeant. . . .

The photostat of a confidential report was attached to this part of the file. It was Chaudey who had winkled it out from the archives of the FFI battalion in which the future colonel had served. This report had been drafted by a regular officer, Major Volbert, who for some time had commanded the unit. At the end of the war he had resigned from the Army. Major Volbert had this to say about Sergeant la Roncière:

An extremely courageous NCO under fire, capable then of the greatest daring, headstrong, intelligent, lacking in humanity but a good psychologist. Disturbingly proud in spite of his youth. Would have made an inquisitor in the Middle Ages or a political commissar with the Russians, for he feels he is in possession of the truth and is entitled to employ any means to make it prevail.

On several occasions he has made this sort of remark in front of his comrades:

"We are not obliged to obey officers who lost us the war. Under the Revolution they were shot."

Jean-Marie la Roncière intends to make a career of the Army. But, for the above-mentioned reasons, I do not hesitate to advise against his promotion, even on a temporary basis, to the rank of second-lieutenant.

This report was accompanied by a recommendation for a mention in dispatches, and a recommendation for the Médaille Militaire and Croix de la Résistance.

When this report first fell into his hands, Chaudey had reflected: "A pity this Major Volbert left the Army when he did. A pity his successor did not see fit to abide by his opinion. No one ever listens to men like Volbert and myself: we are suspected of common sense, and common sense has always appeared undesirable in every army in the world. That's why soldiers commit such startling blunders.

"In consequence our present-day Army has seen a number of disturbing characters take command of paratroop and Legion units while at the same time forming the nucleus of the staffs of the best divisions. These men dreamed of nothing but agitation and politics because they had the virus of these in their blood, but their agitation was disorderly, and their politics based more often than not on force rather than persuasion."

Chaudey darted a glance at Dumont who was still immersed in his file.

"They have imposed a régime on France. Without them this nitwit would not be here and his boss would not be occupying the adjacent office. But we should be still changing the government every month or so and our finances would collapse."

La Roncière, leaving the Maquis as a second-lieutenant, entered Coetquidan in 1945. His instructors were deeply impressed by the young officer's personality and fanatical military ardor. Only one discordant note: his comrades, though they obeyed him, did not like him. Cadet-officer la Roncière would not tolerate any form of opposition and during college rags gave evidence of absolute savagery towards the freshmen.

Passing out fourth, he chose the Legion. A volunteer for Indo-China, he was one of the first to join the Foreign Parachute Battalion shortly after its formation.

Légion d'Honneur, four mentions in dispatches as a lieutenant.

Thirty days' close arrest.

After an operation in which his unit, as a result of a faulty intelligence report, had fallen into an ambush and suffered heavy losses, he had publicly called the colonel in command of the sector an inefficient criminal.

The colonel was relieved of his command and sent

back to France, but la Roncière had had to wait six months before being promoted to captain.

According to a Military Security report, he used to make violent remarks against the traditional hierarchies of the Army. "This war," he kept saying in every mess, "is being waged by the subalterns and captains and will be lost by the colonels and generals."

As he read this passage, Chaudey had crowed with delight. He did not care for Military Security personnel, whom he considered mentally circumscribed and unnecessarily suspicious.

A few weeks later General de Lattre de Tassigny, who had just assumed command in Indo-China, made a similar declaration in public and every newspaper in the world published it.

It was to de Lattre that la Roncière owed his Légion d'Honneur rosette, for his conduct during the Vinh-Yen offensive. But by the end of the operation his company had been reduced to a handful of legionaries.

He already had the reputation of being prodigal with the lives of his men.

At his own request Captain la Roncière was transferred to the GCMA,* where he once more proved efficient and a sound organizer, but he demanded the impossible of his men.

There was a further Military Security report, accusing him of malpractices and also of Communist sympathies.

Dumont looked up and scratched his cheek, which with him was a sign of perplexity and interest.

"I say, Chaudey, la Roncière's accused here of being a Communist, of racketeering and drug-trafficking and, to all intents and purposes, embezzling his unit funds.

"Underneath there's a note: 'File closed,' and, a little farther on, a copy of yet another citation, this time for the work our bird accomplished in the GCMA. Can you tell me what it all means?"

"What does 'Communist' mean to someone as narrow-minded as the worthy Colonel Milletaille, who was then in command of Military Security in Indo-China? La

---

* *Groupe de commandos mixtes autonomes,* units entrusted with certain missions behind the Vietminh lines.

Roncière, an intelligent and efficient lad, was responsible within the framework of the GCMA for fighting against the Communist Vietminhs, forming resistance groups in their zone and inciting the population against them, that's to say doing exactly what the Vietminhs were doing against us.

"So he copied their methods, learned their rules and studied their books, and from this Milletaille at once deduced that he'd got hold of a Red. Anything the poor fellow doesn't understand is Red, and since he understands nothing. . . .

"When you have a job like this to do you need money, Monsieur Dumont, a lot of money. You know something about that. A resistance leader in Tonkin had two thousand piastres a month; on that he had to pay his agents, help his partisans. . . . Like many of his comrades, la Roncière found money where he could: he took over the Haute Région opium racket and, for the benefit of the cheese-paring accounts department of the Army, created bands that existed only on paper."

La Ronciére was seriously wounded at Dien-Bien-Phu while making his way back to the entrenched camp with his Maquis. One of the last aircraft to leave the camp brought him to Hanoi, where he spent six months in hospital.

On becoming a major he distinguished himself again at Suez, which earned him the Légion d'Honneur cravat. As second-in-command to the colonel commanding the 3rd Foreign Parachute Regiment, he took part in the Battle of Algiers and dealt in particular with the Communist network which was providing the *fellaghas* with bombs. In fact he was virtually in command of the unit, the colonel being a mere figurehead.

As a lieutenant-colonel he took part in the battle of the frontiers with the same regiment of which he had at last been given official command. He produced an exceptional "score" of killed and wounded, enemy prisoners and recovered arms, but his unit suffered extremely heavy losses: too heavy in the view of the Inter-Service Headquarters in Algiers. Fortunately they were legionaries.

Dumont closed the file and looked at his telephone as though expecting it to give him some advice.

"Chaudey," he said, "all that's in here we already know,

or more or less. I'd like you to describe the man himself, to tell me what you think of him."

The colonel assumed an astonished air.

"What exactly do you want to do with the fellow? Put him in jug or make him a general?"

"Don't be silly. You know perfectly well what it's about. Should we send la Roncière out to command the Katangese Army?"

Chaudey whistled through his teeth.

"Is it up to us to send him?"

"Don't play with words, either. Let's say we could facilitate his departure."

Dumont rose from his chair, and, as though the tapestry was a map of Africa, turned round and faced it.

"Here," he said, pointing at a plump and languid nymph, "is the Congo in the process of disintegration. Katanga alone stands fast."

With his finger he indicated the nymph's left thigh.

"To begin with I didn't believe it . . . but the Katangese régime is holding out and even growing stronger. The Belgians are former colonizers, so Kimjanga, the President of Katanga, can hardly ask for their support; he has to take certain African susceptibilities into account, but there's nothing to prevent him from appealing to France. General de Gaulle's decolonization policy has earned us great affection among the blacks. . . ."

With a slight gesture of impatience Chaudey indicated that he knew all this already and had no need to be lectured.

But Dumont was now in full flight.

"Furthermore, if Katanga eliminates the Belgians politically, she will eliminate them economically. Katanga means copper—ten per cent of world production—but it also means cadmium, cobalt, germanium, all the rare metals, the metals of the atomic age."

"Here we go," the colonel reflected irritably. "Power politics, the striking force, the Pierrelatte works, the little crackers they want to let off in the Sahara."

Still facing the tapestry, Dumont pursued his theme, on a confidential note at first, then with greater vehemence, sometimes even using the expressions or the very tone of his master:

"Certain financial interests closely concerned with the Government are wondering about the future of the . . . Union Minière. Black Africa with a French outlook—and the Congo is part of it—needs a central rallying point.

France already has the Communauté . . . while the UN go on committing blunder after blunder. . . . So here we have Katanga asking us for advisers, including la Roncière, of whom they have heard a great deal of good."

Dumont came and perched on the edge of the desk opposite Chaudey.

"So now you're in the picture. . . ."

The colonel wriggled in his chair.

"This little business of yours, my dear Monsieur Dumont, could be extremely dangerous. The UN are a wash-out, I agree, but it's best not to rub them up the wrong way just when we've got so many worries in Algeria. I'd very much like to know what Foreign Affairs think of all this."

"On the whole they're against our project, but we've decided to by-pass them. Africa doesn't concern them . . . yet."

"We shall have to play this hand carefully . . . reduce the risks. If you allow French officers to enlist in the Katangese Army, they must first hand in their resignation. I fancy it's more than just one colonel they're asking us for. So if there's any fuss—which is always to be expected in this sort of business—we could then bleat like innocent young lambs."

"Thanks for your advice, Chaudey. You may be sure we've put our minds to it. But to get back to la Roncière. Is he likely to succeed in this sort of venture? Is he the man for the job?"

"Technically speaking, you couldn't find anyone better. Intelligent, a good organizer, not liable to lose his head; he has broken loose from the narrow framework of the Army, in which he never felt at ease in any case. He's one of our best experts in revolutionary warfare. Like all men who are difficult to command, he'll see to it that he's obeyed. . . . In choosing him for this sort of mission, I can see nothing but advantages. . . . And yet. . . ."

"Come on, get it off your chest. You don't like la Roncière?"

"I can't stand inquisitors, and la Roncière's one of that breed. Like them, he's without weakness, disinterested, pitiless. In the name of God or an idea or a national policy he has embraced, he remorselessly burns all heretics."

"What is his God?"

"A certain idea he has in mind about the defense of the East. No doubt it occurred to him in Algiers, when he had to find excuses for torturing. Mere Intelligence duties were not enough for him. It's for this reason, I think, that he chose to tackle the Communist networks rather than the FLN. In his eyes Communism is the great danger threatening the East. Not the FLN. La Roncière will go and play the same sort of game in Katanga. That's what I don't like."

"You're against this operation?"

"Not at all. How many officers are they asking us for?"

"Twenty straight away. A hundred in a few weeks' time."

"For you, at all events, it's a good job, especially if la Roncière selects those officers. He'll take the ones like himself, the most dangerous. In this army, which has developed a taste for putsches, la Roncière sets the pace. As you probably know, the military don't approve of the slant General de Gaulle is giving his Algerian policy. Only there are no more than two or three hundred officers capable of pursuing their ideas to the end. Send them all off to Katanga with la Roncière! Then, on this specific score, the operation will be worth while."

"The anger of the Army has been exaggerated: it's only sulkiness. Now that the barricades are over, it won't do anything more. We've recalled the most impetuous officers from Algeria!"

"And dispersed them throughout France and Germany. Do you know where Colonel Godard is? In Nevers. His job? Sending colonial veterans for a cure to Chatelguyon to deal with their dysentery or to Vichy to deal with their livers, which keeps him busy ten minutes a day. Yet it was he who cleared the FLN out of Algiers, and with methods he never learned at Staff College.

"Trinquier is responsible for seeing that the raw recruits in Nice keep their nails clean"—here Chaudey cast a fleeting glance at Dumont's hands—"and their boots polished. Broizat is kicking his heels in Châlons, Argoult in Germany. Most of the activist officers are without a posting. You've put them on half pay, and half-pay officers plot together.

"Yes, send the whole lot of them out to Katanga, it would be a splendid idea. Furthermore, since they will have left the Army to join the service of a foreign country, you won't have to take them back again and, having made themselves mercenaries, it will be difficult for them to play the part of disinterested defenders of French Algeria."

21

"Thanks for this little course in politics, Colonel. The military can be very Machiavellian!"

"They know one another only too well. Look at the big fellow next door. As I see it, the choice of la Roncière is already made. I therefore have to perform my usual little duty. Needless to say, I'll need a man of my own out there . . . and one who carries some weight. . . ."

Chaudey assumed his sly expression and asked:

"You can't think of anyone, can you?"

"You're really exasperating, the way you make a mystery of everything—just like an old concierge!"

Dumont thumped the table.

"Like me, you're thinking of Thomas Fonts. As usual he made a nuisance of himself out in Guinea and once again I've got him on my hands. I don't want him to stay in France."

"Why not?"

"Because instead of merely making a nuisance of himself he may get into real trouble. Can you see him holding out much longer in this climate charged with dynamite—a born dynamiter like him? He's too cynical to believe in ideals, and not old enough to enjoy power! And what makes it more complicated, Chaudey, is that we at the Elysée are greatly indebted to him. He has been, is, and always will be a friend of mine . . . or else I shan't be worth very much!"

Chaudey and Dumont shook hands. The colonel retrieved his yellow file and left the room just as a furious voice from the other side of the partition let fly with the violence of a cavalry officer dressing down a recruit.

"All these military are a bloody nuisance. Instead of playing at politics they'd do better to have another look at Infantry Regulations . . . at least, it's well written!"

Dumont pondered for some time on the case of Colonel Chaudey who was not by any means a negligible character, for all sorts of strings culminated in his hands.

Was he reliable? Was he unreliable? The problem was more complex.

The colonel had once described himself as "a firm believer in law and order." He had smiled as he used this expression, of course. But Dumont had felt that he meant it at the time.

What did law and order mean to a man like Chaudey, if not respect for a certain form of ritual or rather a certain style of government? The "Gaullist" style was not his.

The colonel—and of this one could be certain—would

never involve himself in a plot against the State, but at the same time he would always refuse to identify the State with one man alone. He served de Gaulle, as he had served his predecessors and would serve his successors, on condition that certain rules, fortunately susceptible to fairly wide interpretations, were not violated too openly. Chaudey was loyal, but he would never become "a loyalist" or one of those men who in the army were referred to, with a certain amount of scorn, as "out-and-outers." Soldiers were strange creatures. They had never stopped screaming that they wanted a master worthy of the name, and no sooner did they have him than they tried to impose their own conditions on him.

All the same it was a pity Chaudey could not be made a general.

Fonts presented Dumont with another problem. Six months earlier he had had him appointed Vice-Consul at Konakry, giving him to understand that this modest post was merely a cover and that he was to apply himself tactfully to re-establishing good relations between France and Guinea.

What was one to do with a creature like Fonts, who was useful but at the same time dangerous? His career, in which he had adopted a succession of disguises—Special Services officer, colonial administrator, technical expert or vice-consul—had been a series of disasters and brilliant successes.

He had the intuition of a woman, an insatiable curiosity, the cynicism of a ponce, a lively and impatient mind and the cool courage of an inveterate drug-addict who has ceased to be moved by danger. With this went a complete lack of racial or class prejudice.

Dumont sometimes suspected there were two Fonts, the one on the verge of rising from the ashes of the other, from his strained nerves, sleepless nights and inordinate passion for danger, violence, disorder, whoring and drinking.

He hoped this rebirth would occur fairly soon and he kept watching for signs of it.

On the very day he returned to France, Fonts had come and seen him in this very office, as self-possessed as ever, rude and insolent by turns, but pleading his cause, which was a new departure for him.

Dumont saw that his nerves were strained to breaking point, but he had not been able to resist reminding him that they were no longer on an equal footing, that it was he who now held the reins of power and that Fonts, through his own fault, was nothing.

Hitherto their relationship had been that of two wrestlers who respect each other and who, each time they meet, feel an urge to measure their strength by exchanging cynical remarks and harsh references to their stormy pasts.

From being a wrestler Dumont had risen to the position of manager and it was while lounging in his armchair that he had listened to Fonts putting on his usual performance.

"You see, old man," he had said, "as soon as I reached Guinea I twigged straight away that Sékou-Touré was in the soup! The Russians had had a spot of bother; they took advantage of this to withdraw their stakes. The Chinese did their best to replace them. But with their meddlesome attitude, dogmatism and sour expressions, they soon rubbed the Negroes up the wrong way. Sékou-Touré, deserted by everyone, tried to get his chaps to work; things went wrong straight away. So he re-established forced labor but called it 'human investment,' the only sound idea the Chinese gave him!

"In Guinea, however, human investment didn't have the slightest result. Sékou-Touré had no other solution but to approach the good old French. It embarrassed him to make the first move. So I took a hand in it . . . and this is the result!"

"I can see what happened," Dumont had observed. "In spite of my advice you once again went blundering in like a bull in a china shop!"

"I palled up with a bunch of jovial African lads who thought it was in the bag, that they'd see good French cash pouring in again, with no strings attached—realists in their own little way. It's amazing what those soaks can put back. Nothing but champagne! My secret funds were soon swallowed up . . . and more besides. I owe the best part of a million to various restaurants and pubs in Konakry."

"You'll have to see Foreign Affairs about the money. . . What happened then?"

"My drunks were the Western tendency of the government. They talked too much. . . . The extremists of the Socialist revolution went and whined to Sékou-Touré. Just for the hell of it, the Russians and Chinese pitched in as well. . . . The local rags began to talk about neo-colonialist intrigues; and Sékou-Touré, fed up to the teeth, declared me *persona non grata.*"

"Was the Quai d'Orsay covering you in this business? I told you to have a word with the ambassador!"

"Have you ever seen the Quai cover anyone, least of all a little vice-consul who's a bit of a secret agent and has had a somewhat stormy past? Not to mention that I entered this Foreign Affairs museum by the back door! The ambassador I had was a stingy old fogy, who had never set foot in Africa before and was scared stiff. You should have seen the report he sent back! A tissue of lies and nonsense!"

"I had a copy of it."

"So what do I do now?"

"Lie low for a bit, my little Thomas . . . wait for the storm to die down. You ought to have a short spell at home in Catalonia . . . which would please your mother. Incidentally, she wrote to me. It's her only way of getting any news of you!"

"I love you, Marcel! Shall we have dinner together?"

"When you get back from Catalonia. We're not going to leave you in the lurch, but you've got to calm down!"

"Guinea's all set, I tell you!"

"No . . . that's why you're back here."

Fonts had maintained an insolent smile that would have estranged him forever from the régime, but he had nevertheless slammed the door on leaving.

Dumont pictured Thomas wandering about Paris, ringing up all his friends, having a drink with one, a drink with another, and, at three o'clock in the morning, gray in the face, leaning on a bar, begging a girl to come home with him so as not to be alone.

Fonts was frightened of being alone at night; he always left the light on, and Dumont, who had often lived with him, would hear him whimpering and sometimes screaming during the few hours he slept.

Fonts, he knew, would not be able to bear more than a few days with his mother at Elne. This evening he was like a bewildered fly trapped in a vinegar bottle.

Dumont would immediately have to find him an adventure fit for a man of his caliber: a brisk affair that would enable him to act on his own initiative.

The next day he rang him up at his hotel.

"Look here, old boy, before going home, what would you say to a trip to Katanga? . . . Well paid, no reports to make. . . . Just follow your inspiration. . . . and see that the officer you'll be with out there doesn't suddenly go off the rails!"

"Who is it?"

"Colonel Jean-Marie la Roncière."

"I know him."

"Chaudey will put you in touch."

"La Roncière's going to cut up rusty!"

"He has no choice."

"Thanks!"

"What for?"

"I was at death's door, at my last gasp, like a fish struggling in a leaking bowl. I can feel water again!"

"You'll have to stop one of these days!"

"Not yet . . . not yet. . . ."

Fonts's voice sounded almost suppliant and Dumont was overcome by a wave of affection.

"You know, Thomas, that business of yours in Guinea, it's not really so serious! But why did you have to put on an act for me?"

"What about the act you put on?"

Colonel Chaudey went into a little bar near the Elysée and ordered a coffee. He took three lumps of sugar, hesitating to take a fourth since the cashier was looking at him.

After each of his meetings with Dumont he tried to work out why he felt so uneasy. The man was by no means uninteresting; he was active and intelligent, but perhaps the colonel could not accept the fact that someone of his ilk should occupy a key-post in the Government of France?

A mixture of St. Joseph, tax inspector and Renaissance bravo, Dumont belonged to a new species that had recently burst into politics.

Like all his fellows, he was somewhat lacking in maturity for, although he could juggle with ideas and organize a plot or a conspiracy, he was a bad judge of men; he looked on them as rational creatures impelled by a lust for power, money or women. He forgot they could be lazy, disinterested, fanciful, and have likes and dislikes which had no bearing on reason or ambition.

La Roncière belonged to Dumont's world.

His gravity and ponderousness inspired immediate confidence. He was just the sort of officer that the new technocrats took seriously, because he resembled them.

Now Lieutenant-Colonel la Roncière had suddenly become an important card in a game of which Chaudey was not sure of the stakes. He had not seen him for a year and, although there was nothing he did not know about

26

his conduct during this stormy period, he could only hazard a guess as to his personal development.

In favor of the notion of a French Algeria—more for technical reasons than from sentiment, for it constituted a testing ground, and at the same time full of distrust towards the Algerian French—la Roncière had played an important part in the barricades affair. In the early stages he had induced the civilians to take action but very soon afterwards had reversed his policy and urged his comrades not to follow the movement.

He had suddenly realized that the Army, in spite of its hatred for General de Gaulle, through the need of some degree of law and order, the habit of a certain form of discipline, from laziness and fear for the future, would refuse any kind of adventure.

It was then la Roncière had come over to the side of obedience. He had nevertheless been relieved of his command in Algeria, albeit with the utmost courtesy.

Chaudey reflected:

"As far as I remember, this fellow la Roncière is touchy and extremely jealous of his authority. He must take Thomas Fonts with him without being too aware that I'm forcing his hand. They've worked together before, but on what terms are they now? At all costs I must avoid an official meeting in my office, introductions and all the rest of it. . . ."

He asked for a telephone counter, went into the glass-paneled box and rang up Julienne Roissy. The number was engaged.

What could Julienne be doing? It was eleven in the morning. Perhaps she had begun her man-hunt, restless female that she was, always on the prowl, never reassured. He pictured her lying in bed, nibbling a biscuit or smoking a cigarette and indefatigably ringing men up on the telephone, needing if not their presence at least the sound of their voices, their promises, to start living again and embark on a new day.

Whenever Chaudey thought of Julienne he felt disturbed.

Fonts had once said this about her:

"Julienne doesn't exist. Alone, she's a lamp without a light; she is listless, devoid of desire, incapable of switching on the radio, reading a book or pouring herself a drink. But the presence, however distant, of a man brings her to life: then our Julienne lights up, preens her feathers, discovers the world and converses about it without

27

talking too much nonsense, for Julienne never says anything that touches her personally. She is the splendid reflection of all her lovers. She's a man-eater, a vampire . . . she feeds on what we bring her."

Fonts had then given his peculiarly caddish chuckle.

"Julienne is the real big-hearted female who makes men behave like fools, but who also behaves like a fool for them, one of those rare women who leave you with pleasant memories. . . ."

Colonel Chaudey was with her on the boat which brought her back from Indo-China. A dance had been held on board. It was somewhere off India, at four in the morning.

The orchestra had stopped playing. A few streamers, which the seamen would presently sweep overboard, still littered the deck. The atmosphere, he remembered, was damp and salty with a promise of cooler weather. Julienne was drunk and looked perfectly lovely, with her thick tawny hair and close-fitting evening-dress.

She stood alone in the stern of the ship, weeping soundlessly, and it was only when he came close that he could see the tears streaming down her cheeks.

Clinging to his arm, she had said to him:

"I'm finished as a woman, I'm growing old, and I can't stand it."

All of a sudden she had ripped her dress from top to bottom, a dress from one of the leading Paris couturiers, which she had worn for the first time that evening, and flung it into the sea. For a few seconds the light-colored cloth had floated on the gray water, then it had disappeared in the eddy of the propellers.

Chaudey had realized that she had likewise thrown herself into the sea, with her memories of a forty-year-old woman who had loved too much, had taken too much out of life. Julienne now knew she could no longer continue this mad dance in the midst of wars, abandoning the suitor she had just left to the embrace of death.

Chaudey had seen her back to her cabin and, since something had to be done about her, he had slept with her.

In his own way he had loved Julienne, but he had been very frightened of her and the disorder she might bring into his life; he had been scarred by her before making her his friend, accomplice and benevolent agent.

Julienne was always in need of help, whether for herself, or for her friends, or for the career of her husband whom she did not like to see kicking his heels.

She loved being or appearing to be abreast of things, participating in mysterious encounters, in meetings at which, she believed, the destiny of the world was dictated in undertones. And Chaudey threw her a few crumbs of his secrets.

He rang up again. Julienne's voice, flat and dull at first, soon became lively and animated.

"How are you, my dear? It's a long time since we've seen you. Roissy was just saying . . ."—Julienne always called her husband by his surname and every other man under the sun by his Christian name—"you ought to ask Chaudey some time. Look, dear Pierre, couldn't you find him a post? Something or other far away where he wouldn't have anything to do? Otherwise he'll be getting up to his old tricks again."

"My dear Julienne . . ."

"My dear Pierre?"

"Have you seen la Roncière lately?"

No answer. Julienne must have seen la Roncière frequently but she tried to assume an indifferent, artificially social tone.

"I saw him at drinks with some friends the other day. He seemed in very good form. Are you interested in him?"

"Extremely interested . . . I'm not going to try and hide things from you. . . ."

"Katanga, isn't it?"

"You're better informed than I thought."

She gave the self-satisfied laugh of a woman whose vanity had just been gratified.

"I could arrange something for you."

"Dinner tomorrow evening, for instance. Your place would be best. . . . What about asking Dorat as well? He's just back from Katanga."

"Dorat, certainly, he's great fun, but not that little worm of a wife of his, Chantal. Guess what she did to me yesterday . . . Véronique rang me up after meeting Bernadette who had told her that Chantal . . ."

Chaudey adored this sort of gossip but he had no time to listen to it now. Regretfully he broke in:

"Look, my dear, this is a serious matter; forget your little squabbles. Anyway, I thought you and Chantal were on the best of terms. . . ."

"But I tell you, Chantal . . ."

29

"Did you know Thomas Fonts has just got back from Guinea?"

"Thomas? . . . He hasn't even rung me up!"

"I'd very much like you to ask him as well!"

"Ask him here? But, like you, Thomas doesn't need an invitation; he's quite at home in this house!"

"He's quite at home everywhere. Good-bye, my dear. Tomorrow evening, then, at half past eight. About Roissy, I may have something for him: we need a military attaché in Laos whose job is to do absolutely nothing. . . ."

Dinner was coming to an end. They had reached the cheese. Félicien Dorat was beginning to feel restless; he had come to deliver his little lecture on Katanga and had not been given the chance.

To show his bad temper, he spilled a glass of wine on the tablecloth and apologized with a growl. Félicien knew how to exploit his clumsiness, which had become proverbial, in order to settle his little scores. He noticed a glint of amusement in Fonts's eyes. Thomas was no man's fool!

"I say, old boy," he shouted across the table, "I hear you've got the sack from Guinea?"

La Roncière pricked up his ears and turned to Fonts.

"Really? What have you been up to this time?"

Fonts's handsome face puckered, as from the effect of a hypodermic. But he quickly recovered his composure.

"Once again I was misunderstood and had to deal with a lot of imbeciles!"

He turned away and switched his gaze to the women in the party. Julienne was a memory. Memories were sacred! One reverted to them only when there was nothing better on hand. Julienne's cousin sitting next to Dorat? She filled the gap whenever a spare woman was needed; in the morning she probably did the washing-up. Utterly uninteresting, ageless, and colorless. Chantal, Dorat's wife, to whom la Roncière was paying court? Fonts would have gladly dealt with her: vivacious and plump as a young quail, with good legs and a firm bosom. To him Chantal was the very model of an eighteenth-century woman of easy virtue. But her intolerable snobbery annoyed him.

In any case no woman was worth the promise of adventure that he felt was incongruously emerging from this unsuccessful dinner. Fonts had a gift for intrigue, an extremely acute sense of environment and the mastery of a chess-player for following each successive move of a scheme. Imperceptibly the atmosphere had changed. Old

Colonel Chaudey had leaned forward, with his chin in his hand, as though still hesitating before moving his first pawn.

With all his senses awake, Fonts turned toward him.

"Well now, my dear Dorat," Chaudey inquired, "what about this Congo business?"

Dorat settled back in his chair and cleared his throat as though he was about to spit.

"The Congo has never existed!" he observed.

"Long live de Gaulle!" Fonts shouted. "He doesn't exist either. That at least is what we're told by all our dear little soldiers in Algeria who think they invented him."

"Tch! Tch!" said Chaudey, shaking his head.

Fonts gave vent to a youthful, almost childish laugh.

"Come on, old Fifi, let's get going on your conducted tour of the Congo. That's why we're all here!"

Chaudey was thinking that Fonts and la Roncière might make a good team, their qualities and their faults were complementary. But it was time to butter up Dorat, who was sulking. Chaudey wanted him to perform his act before embarking on his own. He assumed a wheedling tone.

"Go on, Dorat, please do. I've read your articles on the Congo and Katanga; they were . . . remarkable . . . but one felt you weren't able to tell the whole story. The Congo doesn't exist. Go on from there."

Like one of those sea birds that have to run in order to take flight, Dorat resumed his monologue but did not recover his reassurance for several minutes.

"The Congo is . . . er . . . an incongruous collection of tribes and clans, none of whom speaks the same language and each of whom longs to wipe out the others in the name of ancient enmities, the origins of which are lost . . . er . . . in the mists of time. . . ."

Chantal felt uneasy; she was livid with anger whenever Dorat was called "old Fifi" in front of her and she felt he had started off on the wrong foot. He's going to commit a bloomer, she thought.

La Roncière showed hardly any interest. Colonel Chaudey was busy crumbling his bread into pellets.

"All these Bakongos, Luluas, Balubas and Batetelas follow their witch-doctors who are known as politicians: Lumumba, Kalonji, Kimjanga, Gizenga. . . . The whole thing is sheer burlesque. Do you know what their independence anthem was? A cha-cha-cha!

"The Belgians thought they could solve everything by giving these former cannibals the reassuring name of

31

'wards.' They reckoned the mental age of these Negroes was not more than a twelve-year-old's and that with enlightened care—their own—they would take at least a century to become adults. Abiding by this principle, they gave them an intellectual and technical education which did not rise above this level. It was to these children that one fine day, without the slightest precaution, they granted independence!"

"What about the raping?" the female cousin, who had so far said nothing, inquired in a sharp voice.

"The Negroes behaved like twelve-year-olds. To revenge themselves on their masters, they raped the white women and made the men go without shoes. There's been a great deal said about raping, not enough about footwear. To all the wards the symbol of the white man's power was his shoes. The first thing an educated black bought was a pair of shoes! He waddled like a duck, they hurt his feet, but he had taken a step up.

"For the slightest prank, however, he was made to take his shoes off and put his hands in the air. Once he was independent, he tried to do the same: humiliate the white man by making him lose face. He first of all made him go without shoes, then put his hands in the air, and finally he raped his wife."

The cousin could not restrain herself, much to Julienne's surprise.

"But wasn't anything done, monsieur, to prevent this raping?"

"It was mainly the work of the army which in the Congo was called 'the Force Publique.' So as to make their wards behave themselves, the Belgians had trained a lot of thugs to beat them over the head. That's what the Force Publique were: twenty-five thousand well-armed men who were used to beating-up fellow-creatures indiscriminately. . . .

"When independence came the thugs turned on their masters. Drunk on beer, they fell on the Belgian officers commanding them and then spread through the town with their weapons. Everything was grist to their mill, little girls no less than grandmothers, prostitutes as well as nuns. . . . Sexually, the wards were extremely adult. . . ."

La Roncière was drumming on the table. These stories of rape irritated him; he found them out of place at a dinner-table. To him this sort of talk derived from exhibitionism in bad taste.

"What did the UN do?" he asked.

"On their arrival the UN restored a semblance of law and order, prevented raping and looting . . . but subsequently they merely added to the general chaos!

"The UN are extremely divided between Afro-Asians and whites, partisans of the Communist *bloc* or the West. Everyone tried to impose his own political solution, but the Congolese, even though they were independent, were still twelve-year-olds."

"What about Katanga, Monsieur Dorat? Tell us something about Katanga!"

"On one point only, Colonel, are the Russians, Americans, Africans and Asians all agreed: they want to put an end to the secession of Katanga. . . . To their minds Katanga is above all the Union Minière, an intolerable survival of colonialism. This irritates them like a corn or an aching tooth!"

"Yet there's a lot to be said for Katanga, Monsieur Dorat. In Katanga law and order reign, while everywhere else there's chaos: Lumumba, the creature of the Communists and Afro-Asians, has been arrested. When they were given forty-eight hours to clear out of the Congo, the Russians and their satellites made no attempt to dig their heels in."

"Maybe they were only too glad of the opportunity," Fonts quietly observed. "It was the same in Guinea. Africa is too anarchic to accept their law and order. . . . Any form of organization collapses there at once; Marxism is reduced to mere palaver. The Russians don't like Africa!"

"No one likes Africa," Dorat interjected. "The whites, whether Communist or 'Imperialist,' are frightened of her. They don't know how to handle her. Africa disgusts and terrifies them. You know, the Americans have just sent a new ambassador to Leopoldville. He's an old acquaintance of ours, that fellow Ferwell, who served as the model for Graham Greene's *Quiet American*. Yes, the man who made such a nuisance of himself in Saigon, after Dien-Bien-Phu. . . ."

"American policy in Africa is absurd," la Roncière remarked. "Those people have never understood anything about that continent. They think they're fighting Communism and all they do is add to the chaos, which, in the long run, serves the Communists' interests. The game they're playing in the Congo is utterly crazy. . . ."

Colonel Chaudey was growing impatient. He interrupted:

"Well, Dorat, what did our old friend Ferwell have to say? Always as hot-headed as ever?"

"He's calmed down a little. In the first place, he's married and has two children, which has made him put on quite a lot of weight. Ferwell made a witty remark. 'You know,' he said, 'in Katanga I'm more the Unquiet American'!"

"How does he view the problem?"

"From the American angle . . ."

La Roncière broke in:

"I believe, Monsieur Dorat, that the only future for the Congo is Katanga, where white men and Africans co-exist without clashing. All that's needed is to endow that country, which has substantial financial resources, with a trained army and a sound politico-military organization so as to keep all those UN thugs in check. And for that, all that's needed is a handful of experts in revolutionary warfare."

"And these experts in revolutionary warfare are la Roncière and his little pals. . . ." Dorat concluded.

"La Roncière," he reflected, "who has never set foot in black Africa, is fascinated by Katanga . . . and this little blackguard Fonts who's just back from Guinea. . . . Old Fifi has been fooled; he's being used as a pretext for this meeting."

Furious at having been exploited without being warned, he counter-attacked vigorously.

"Colonel," he said, addressing la Roncière as though there was no one else in the room, "I'm going to tell you a story. It was in Leopoldville, in the summer of 1960, shortly after independence. Two Dutchmen decided to go and have a bathe in a swimming-pool just outside the town. They took a transistor and a towel with them. The towel was an indeterminate sort of color, somewhere between brown and green. They dived in, climbed out again, dried themselves on the towel. Then they did some physical jerks and listened to the news on the radio set.

"Ten minutes later three jeeps turned up crammed with Congolese soldiers armed to the teeth. They pounced on the Dutchmen, beat them up, then hauled them off to their camp. Luckily for the Dutchmen some British officers serving with the UN Ghana troops witnessed the scene. They collected a few men and made their way to the camp. The Congolese refused to hand over the Dutchmen. 'They're Belgian parachute officers!' they insisted. The British asked for evidence of this. It was provided straight

34

away: in the first place, the Dutchmen listened to the radio. This meant they had in their possession a sort of magic box which enabled them not only to listen to the news but also to transmit military information to Brussels. That wasn't all. They had brown towels. Now brown is closely akin to khaki. Finally, they did physical jerks when they came out of the water. Now, in the army, what are recruits made to do as soon as reveille sounds? Physical jerks! Who would indulge in such a useless activity but Belgian officers! Conclusion: they were guilty, so they were going to be shot. It's with this human material, these raving and rampaging Bantus, that you want to undertake psychological warfare, Colonel?"

Very pleased with himself, Dorat started laughing—a big belly-laugh, like a Negro's.

A slight flush came over la Roncière's lean handsome face.

"It seems, Monsieur Dorat, that for a good journalist like you one story is all that's needed to explain Africa and the conduct of a whole continent! You yourself and your colleagues went about it the same way in Algeria!"

"But tell me, Colonel, I thought you were far more preoccupied with the problems of Algeria than those of black Africa. . . . There was a lot of talk about you at the time of the barricades. . . . Is Algeria already forgotten?"

La Roncière's thin lips grew even thinner.

"Who says I've forgotten Algeria, the people who live in that country and my comrades who are still fighting out there? And what makes you think that the best way of helping them is not to allow an African country, with a healthy climate, immense possibilities and no feeling of hostility towards white men, to defend itself against foreign ambitions? Later on that country will be able to welcome the settlers as well as soldiers!"

"Because Algeria is lost?"

"Yes. The Army didn't waver at the time of the barricades; it will never waver again. But what we learned in Algeria and Indo-China might be useful to us in this new field!"

The party left the table for coffee. Colonel Chaudey took la Roncière by the arm and led him aside.

"My dear colleague, it was a great mistake to talk so indiscreetly in front of Dorat. He was only provoking you in order to pick your brains. . . . He's a crafty devil."

"He's a dirty sod!"

"No, he's not. He's doing his job just as we're doing

ours! Now that I've got you button-holed, I'd like to tell you something. As you know, the Présidence de la République and the Présidence du Conseil are both prepared to help you, provided, of course, you hand in your resignation to the Army: a mere formality!"

"I should have preferred to be given unpaid leave!"

"Foreign Affairs, my dear fellow! They're firmly opposed to the appointment of a French colonel at the head of the Katangese Army. At the Quai they're playing the UN game and courting Nasser.

"For the time being, hand in your resignation; later on we'll make the necessary arrangements. But do be careful: there mustn't be any publicity over the recruiting . . . I don't want to be accused of providing mercenaries. . . . The Quai . . . always the Quai. . . ."

And, in quite a different tone, Chaudey asked:

"The pay's not bad, is it?"

"I'm not interested in the money. I hope you believe me!"

"What! Ten million cash down, six hundred thousand francs a month! Of course I believe you!"

"I've managed to get civil as well as military powers: in fact, both the Interior and War, but of course with African figureheads. I can take with me . . ."

"I know . . . I know. . . ."

"I shall need arms, radio transmitters."

"We'll see to it. But keep your eye on the Quai!"

"They're a useless idle lot. . . ."

"They're grumpy old maids. . . . They don't like people kicking up a row when they're sleeping. Fonts made too much noise and he got into trouble." He jerked his head in the direction of the little Catalan who was obviously describing atrocities to Chantal since she looked as ruffled as a startled hen. "Fonts, whom I believe you know extremely well. . . ."

"We were in Indo-China together, in the GCMA."

"He's now available. In your team you need a good African specialist. Fonts is one of the best I know. We very much hope you'll take him with you!"

"I'd like to choose my assistants myself, according to my needs and their qualifications. Fonts isn't a soldier. . . ."

"He's played at being one long enough!"

"He's not a serious character . . ."

"But he's intelligent and courageous."

"He wouldn't make a good subordinate . . ."

"But he's got useful contacts. . . . Through him, I could be of greater help to you. You know, Fonts has some pretty good friends in the Elysée."

"I'll think it over . . . discuss it with him, see if my conditions suit him."

"I'm afraid I haven't made myself clear, Colonel. This Katanga operation is only possible for us if Fonts is involved in it. Of course, you can go ahead without us! On the other hand, and you know it, Fonts can be extremely useful to you. . . . Besides, like you, he needs a spell abroad. Excellent for his career, as it is for yours!"

The evening dragged on. Dorat and his wife were the first to leave. Scarcely had they stepped outside than they began to squabble in the cold drizzle falling from the overcast sky.

"You put up a pretty poor performance," Chantal declared. "I wonder how people can still think you're so intelligent!"

"Maybe because they read my articles!"

"Compared to la Roncière, you were pitiful. He knows how to talk. . . . Psychological warfare . . . revolutionary technique. . . ."

"Can you tell me what battles they've won with their revolutionary warfare? Indo-China? Algeria? Psychological warfare among the Bantus, why, it's ludicrous!"

Dorat finally managed to open the door of his old Aronde. He settled into his seat and left his wife standing outside. Furious, she hammered with both fists on the window.

"Let me in, you idiot!"

Dorat opened the other door with deliberate slowness. Chantal snorted:

"Look here, old Fifi, when are we going to get a new car? An Aronde's so dowdy and common. I'd like the next car we have to be a sports model. Marie-Hélène was just telling me . . ."

"To hell with you and Marie-Hélène," he said in measured tones as he switched on the engine. "I think I'm going to go and have a look at Katanga; there might be something interesting there. I must speak to the boss about it! French mercenaries in Katanga: it's a good subject. You could go and see your mother in Dordogne while I'm away . . . she may not be a very distinguished person, with those rough red hands of hers . . . but she can at least cook . . . and leave her husband in peace!"

37

"You oaf! . . . I hope the Balubas put you in a pot and boil you!"

Chaudey went home on foot, hoping his stomach would be grateful for this exercise.

Growling to himself, he kept stabbing at the pavement with his umbrella.

"La Roncière! How self-satisfied he is, that brute with all his medals! After reading two or three books of political indoctrination and coining a few slogans, he fancies himself in possession of the truth, which is not so serious, but he also thinks he's big enough to ram it down people's throats, which is. Dorat put him in his place twice. Julienne seemed depressed: her affair with la Roncière is turning out badly. I'll send her some flowers tomorrow." For her alone Colonel Chaudey never counted the cost!

Julienne had some difficulty in getting to sleep. Sadly she realized that Jean-Marie la Roncière had taken leave of her just like an ordinary guest thanking his hostess. On his arrival in Paris, being at a loose end, he had come, like many others, and sought asylum in her arms. But Jean-Marie had now recovered his self-possession; he no longer needed her to while away those long evenings when, after making love, a man endlessly reviews his life, his setbacks and disappointments in front of a silent, friendly and understanding woman.

"Let's go back together," la Roncière suggested to Fonts. "I've got something to tell you. I wish our meeting had not been arranged by Chaudey, I'd rather it had been due to chance or to my own initiative. . . . I'd forgotten you were so well in with the Government!"

"What about you? You're not in jug and you've kept your rank!"

They made their way in silence up to the Place de la Madeleine and went into Weber's, the only café that was still open.

The old-fashioned lamps shed a yellow light. On the red plush banquettes, under the gaze of as many waiters, sat a dozen or so customers, who hesitated to plunge into the icy darkness but avoided ordering further drinks.

In one corner a man with hefty shoulders and close-cropped hair—all that was visible of him—was talking in German to a fair girl with forget-me-not-blue eyes.

Fonts and la Roncière sat down side by side and managed to catch the attention of a sulky waiter, who brought them two brandies. The two men had not seen each other for a couple of months and they found some difficulty in picking up the threads. What they needed, for a few minutes at least, was a woman like Julienne with them, a woman with the same memories as themselves, who would have helped them to settle down together and then slipped off.

They talked about Algeria.

"In the Army," Fonts observed, "everyone talks his head off, everyone plots and schemes, but nothing serious ever comes of it."

"I'm just back from there," la Roncière sharply reminded him.

He could not bear a civilian presuming to pass judgement on the Army, even if it was Fonts, who was on friendly terms with a large number of parachute officers and had been through the war in Indo-China with them. In this respect la Roncière's attitude bore a close resemblance to that of many ecclesiastics towards the Roman *Curia*: they criticized it among themselves, but never in front of an outsider. But the colonel quickly recovered himself and made an effort to be pleasant.

"I'm sorry, Fonts, but we're both on edge. It's all very well to be reasonable, to tell oneself that the game's up in Algeria and look for something else to do. There are one's friends to consider. . . . What's more, I think I've persuaded a certain number of them to come to Katanga with me."

"Who?" Fonts quietly asked.

"Of course, I can't take any officers senior to me in rank . . ."

"Listen, Jean-Marie, we've been beating about the bush all night. If I'm not mistaken, you're recruiting people for Katanga. The Elysée is turning a blind eye on this or even viewing it with favor . . . but at the same time they want you to take me with you. Your hand's being forced, I agree, but on a job like this I could be very useful to you. . . . Remember the GCMA."

La Roncière did indeed remember the arrival of this little Overseas France administrator at the Hanoi rear base. Very smart in his white suit, lively and agile as a squirrel, exuding charm and wit, he had first of all seemed ridiculous to the few officers who were there. These officers were all too ready to assume a patronizing air.

Lieutenant Simon had asked him:

"Tell me, Monsieur l'Administrateur, aren't you frightend of soiling your hands, being with us?"

Fonts had looked him straight in the eye.

"You can call me captain, since that's my honorary rank, or if that sticks in your throat, Fonts, or even Thomas. I'm quite used to being addressed as captain, you know. At the age of nineteen I already had that rank . . . in a Maquis group."

Simon, who was forty, had merely been able to growl:

"We'll see what he's like on the job!"

They had seen what he was like. Indefatigable in spite of his light build and shortness of stature, Fonts, who had quickly learned the Haute Région dialects, had proved an invaluable assistant. He went into the firing-line if necessary, was a rapid and accurate shot, but he dealt above all with political affairs: winning over the local headmen, handling the minorities. He was popular with all the pirates on the China border, all those disillusioned cynical old opium-addicts who knew they were doomed but were resolved to make the best of their last years. He recited Baudelaire to them for his own pleasure and told them dirty stories for theirs.

The more he remembered and recollected, the more useful the colonel considered it would be to have with him a man endowed with such splendid imagination, such cynicism, but, alas, also such an exaggeratedly negligent manner. In any case he had no choice.

"I asked you a question," Fonts remarked.

"I'd like to take you with me . . . on one condition."

"Only one . . ." Fonts went through the motions of counting out money. "How much?"

La Roncière took the plunge and spoke with brutal frankness.

"Three million on enlistment; three million frozen in your name in a bank, which you can draw at the end of your contract; and five hundred thousand francs a month."

"That seems reasonable, but who's stumping up this money?"

"Katanga has a sort of unofficial agent, a man called Pimuriaux. A month ago Pimuriaux put me in touch with someone closely connected with President Kimjanga."

"Negro republics never give money away, they ask for it."

"Behind Katanga there's the Union Minière. . . . You know the Quai d'Orsay's against this operation. . . ."

Karl Kreis felt ill at ease sitting opposite this young girl who kept trying bashfully to smile at him. She had everything that appealed to him; she was a German like himself and had the long platinum-blonde hair of most Nordic women. When you plunged your hand into it, it felt as cool and soft as running water.

Her name was Lisel, a pretty name which recalled a pleasant memory: there had already been a Lisel in his life, but she had had short hair, cropped like a boy's. He had met her at the beginning of the war when the youthful German Army was breaking through the rusty gateways of ancient Europe. What had become of Lisel of Rostock? Raped by the Russians? Sold to an American sergeant? By now she must be fat, the mother of several children, and had almost certainly forgotten the boy in the Hitler-Jugend leather shorts to whom she had surrendered in a haystack.

Lisel, from across the table, touched his arm.

"Karl, this is our last evening together: tomorrow I leave for Frankfurt!"

She had the sing-song intonation of the Rhineland and there was something cat-like about her high cheekbones and rather widespread eyes. Kreis was fond of cats. But the astonished and suppliant expression in her eyes reminded him more of a fawning submissive dog.

Lisel was dressed in impeccably good taste, which was unknown in Germany under Hitler. That is what had first struck him when he caught sight of her in a café on the Champs-Elysées: her elegance. It had all happened extremely simply.

"My name's Kreis, and I was once German."

"My name's Lisel, and I'm still German, soon maybe European. . . . I've come to Paris for a few days . . . on business. I have a husband and two children in Frankfurt, and I'm very fond of them."

"I was a sergeant-major in the Foreign Legion. When my fifteen years were up (Indo-China, Morocco, Algeria) I left with the rank of second-lieutenant, French nationality, some meager savings and a pension which enables me to have a good meal once a month. I'm looking for a job."

"I'd like to go out this evening."

"Let's have dinner together."

Kreis had gone back with her to her hotel, amused but also touched by this frank and simple lust which reminded him of his dealings with young German girls during the war.

41

Their affair had lasted a week. Kreis could never have enough of this gleaming golden body. If the weather had been less cold, he would have taken her out into the country and tumbled her in the grass or the cornfields.

He asked her what Germany was like now. He had not been back since 1946, when he had made a quick dash for the Foreign Legion three days after escaping from an American camp where he had been imprisoned with a thousand former SS officers.

"Germany," said Lisel, in the earnest manner common to many German women, "is now a very fine country. No one thinks of war any longer or of recovering Prussia from the Russians and Silesia from the Poles. We live well, eat well, go to Spain or the South of France for our holidays, produce handsome children for whom there are big playgrounds. . . ."

Ex-Oberleutnant Karl Kreis remembered another Germany which, with her old men, children, hard-pressed soldiers and towns flattened by bombing, was still trying to fight the entire world.

"Come back home," Lisel had suggested to him one day. "You'll easily find a job. My husband's firm needs a commercial director who speaks good French: we do a lot of business with France. But you mustn't say you've been in the Legion—my husband is wary, when it comes down to business, of anything . . . romantic—or that you've fought in Algeria. . . . My husband's a Liberal . . . and he votes Socialist."

Lisel increased the pressure on his arm.

"Darling, this is our last night. Let's go back to the hotel instead of drinking here in this old café. Have you noticed? In France cafés can't grow old gracefully. In Germany we preserve them with loving care."

Kreis felt like yielding and following her, immersing himself once more in the cool stream of her hair, relaxing in her arms and wallowing in the warm clammy affection which girls of her race were so adept at providing.

In one gulp he drained his glass, and the weakness that had crept over him hardened into an anger which rose from the pit of his stomach and stifled his breathing.

He wanted to get rid of Lisel and rid himself of the man who desired Lisel, who was prepared to be sentimental about good old Germany, go home to the warm *Vaterland*, grow fat while smoking a pipe and drinking beer.

He could not resist the urge to insult her.

"Bed, that's all you can think of, isn't it? . . . You come

to Paris and have your fling, but back in Frankfurt you're the irreproachable little wife in an irreproachable little Germany . . . which has likewise forgotten the flings she has had all over Europe."

"What on earth's the matter with you?" Lisel asked in amazement.

She knew that men who enlisted in the Legion often had a stormy past and unexpected reactions when they drank. She had seen all this in films, she had also read about it in books. But this fellow Kreis had seemed so normal. . . . He was actually the first man she would have liked to keep as her lover. Healthy, sturdy, he did not bother her with endless questions about her life, which would have forced her to lie: her life was her own business, it did not concern her lovers.

In his love-making he was sometimes rough, but this was not unpleasant. He also howled in the night like a wolf, but a good psychoanalyst could probably cure him.

She noticed how his face had suddenly changed. His pale eyes had narrowed. They had assumed that milky color which all German eyes have when their owners feel an urge to kill.

On two occasions Heinrich, her husband, had had eyes like this: the first time when he had caught her in a hotel in Amsterdam with one of his Italian representatives. But he himself was with his secretary. They had subsequently come to an understanding.

The second time was when a drunken American sergeant had tried to kiss her forcibly in a *Weinstube* on the banks of the Moselle. Heinrich hated the Americans. All his family had been killed during the raids on Hamburg.

But Karl had no reason to have eyes like that.

At the adjacent table a self-satisfied character, pink as a piglet and with a decoration in his button-hole, was making a speech in the manner of Monsieur Prud'homme to his wife who was almost bursting out of a tight green dress.

"Agathe," he observed, "this war in Algeria has been going on too long."

He paused to see if there was any reaction from the other tables and raised his voice:

"This war is costing us human lives . . . but let's face it, Whitsun week-ends cause even more deaths. Money . . . but then a financial wound isn't lethal. . . . Above all it's affecting our prestige and on this score I agree with Duperret. Because of Algeria we're in danger of missing the bus in Europe."

Kreis sneered and said in German:

"Look, Lisel. Look at all these people who, like you, are catching the Europe bus as though entering a pastry shop. They're bloated and can only think of guzzling more. They're ugly. In our Europe they'd have all been sent to the gas chambers."

The blow landed right on the bridge of his nose. Lisel and dear little Germany could not tolerate certain remarks.

Kreis went livid with rage and yelled:

"*Raus!* Out of my sight! I don't allow anyone to lay a finger on me, least of all a woman, a whore. I'll give you ten seconds to get out of here, otherwise I'll bash your face in."

The whole place had fallen silent, the waiters discreetly drew closer. One of them went off to fetch the manager.

Lisel rose to her feet, snatched up her bag and rushed out. She was still running when she reached her hotel. She told the porter not to let anyone up to her room. If they persisted, he was to call the police.

"A double brandy," Kreis ordered.

"No," said the manager, who had just appeared. "You've had enough this evening."

With a gesture of his hand he waved the waiter away.

Kreis stiffened. He had lost all control, he only knew that he was going to tear this little man in the dinner-jacket limb from limb.

Yet the little man was rather touching with his smooth close-shaven cheeks, his impeccably knotted tie, his carefully adjusted white cuffs and the manner he had of throwing his head back to obliterate the folds of his double chin and give himself a more authoritative presence.

Kreis saw all this, but at the same time his muscles and nerves were stretched to breaking point while his heart pounded against his ribs.

Rage did not prevent him from realizing how ridiculous and odious his attitude was. He stood six-foot-five in his stockinged feet, weighed almost sixteen stone, and there was not an ounce of fat on his bones. With his vast shoulders, his huge clenched fists, he was already overpowering the brave little manikin who, in a trembling voice, nevertheless stood up to him.

"A brandy," he repeated.

During the forty years he had been in the business the

44

manager had learned something about men and their reactions when they were drunk. The most dangerous were those who did not say a word, made no threat, but struck. The hard-faced giant who stood before him belonged to this sort.

He was frightened, he was anything but tough, but he could not give in. The whole staff was watching. His prestige was at stake, and so was whatever self-respect he had earned since serving as a courier during the Resistance.

He did not even think of calling for the police.

"No," he firmly replied.

The fist was poised.

"Kreis!"

The name had resounded, sharp as a word of command; the fist was lowered. Kreis had whirled round on his heels.

"A fine automaton," reflected Fonts who had followed la Roncière. On the way he had seized a bottle from a table. An old reflex. More often than not, when it came to a fight, he had had to deal with men bigger than himself; so he defended himself or even attacked with whatever came to hand.

Kreis was still dazed but gradually his muscles untensed, his heart thumped less violently, while the blood subsided from his head and the red mist before his eyes dissolved.

"Colonel!" he finally stammered.

Standing with one hand in his pocket, eyeing him with a mixture of haughtiness, disgust and familiarity, la Roncière ordered him:

"Go and put your head under the cold tap, then come back and have a drink with us; this time they'll bring you your brandy."

La Roncière turned his lean face towards the manager.

"Won't they, monsieur?"

The manager heaved a sigh. He could not have gone on being brave a second longer. His legs were trembling, his hands were clammy.

"Of course, Colonel . . . of course. . . . And it will be a pleasure if you will have it on the house."

Kreis went off to the cloakroom. Fonts calmly put his beer bottle back on the table where they were preparing to catch the Europe bus, made a vague bow to the lady in green, then went back and joined la Roncière on the banquette.

"Who's that thug?" he inquired.

"Sergeant-Major Karl Kreis. Two years with me in Indo-China in a foreign parachute battalion, two years in

45

the Third Foreign Parachute Regiment, Médaille Militaire, Légion d'Honneur, eight mentions in dispatches, apart from the Iron Cross with clusters."

"How does the Iron Cross come into it?"

"Kreis distinguished himself particularly at Vinh-Yen. Without him the company would have been lost. I was wounded. My second-in-command, a raw little subaltern, had lost his nerve. Kreis, then a mere section leader, took command. When we got back to base, the subaltern tried to put Kreis in his place. He sentenced him to shit-house fatigue on the grounds that his rifle wasn't properly cleaned or his boots weren't polished. From then on Kreis began obeying orders like an automaton, without trying to understand, or rather by forcing himself not to understand. So when the subaltern gave orders, for a parade that was due to take place in front of the GOC Tonkin, that Number One dress was to be worn with full decorations, Kreis wore all his medals, including the Iron Cross. He was reduced to the ranks and given fifteen days CB. But four months later I promoted him to sergeant.

"He's the prototype of the German legionary, who'll never let you down under fire, hard as steel but absolutely pig-headed. And, what's more, one of the best instructors I've ever known."

Fonts was playing with his glass of brandy, twiddling it between his fingers.

"I'm not very fond of legionaries, especially if they're German. Kreis has the mug of an SS officer."

"It's quite likely he was one!"

Fonts was getting worked up.

"You see, the shooting of hostages, the concentration camps, the burning of villages and all the rest of it can't be explained by the need to make an example or even to exterminate a nation. We ourselves did some pretty filthy things in the Resistance, but out of hatred, good healthy Latin hatred. Your Kreis and his sort aren't capable of hatred . . . they're just priests offering their gods a human sacrifice. That's why it would have given me great pleasure to beat him over the head with a bottle."

Fonts hasn't changed a bit, la Roncière reflected. After a certain stage in the evening and when he had been drinking, he was inclined to indulge in metaphysics.

But it was then he showed himself in his true colors, more than when he was joking. To this Mediterranean type, war, like revolution, could only be an unbridled adventure which had to take place in an atmosphere of lawlessness, eroticism and enthusiasm. Anyone who made fighting his profession, who killed in cold blood and without apology, could not fail to be unattractive to him.

This anarchist could not understand the renunciation of the monk or the legionary.

La Roncière had likewise fought the Germans, and even more relentlessly than Fonts, but he felt no resentment against them; on the contrary, certain sides of their character, their strong sense of law and order and their discipline, appealed to him.

But it was not with them that a revolutionary war could be waged—they understood nothing about it—nor with Fonts and his sort; they were too sceptical.

Kreis snapped to attention in front of their table. He seemed to have sobered up.

"My respects, Colonel."

"Sit down," said la Roncière. "This is Thomas Fonts, he was in Indo-China with us. What are you doing here?"

"I've left the Legion. When my fifteen years were up, I didn't want to sign on. . . ."

His German accent was still fairly pronounced.

"Why not?" asked Fonts, who was interested in everything.

"In the foreign parachute battalions everyone dabbles in politics, and I joined the Legion to avoid ever hearing the word politics mentioned."

"Why the outburst just now?" la Roncière in his turn inquired. "That girl who was with you looked rather pretty."

Kreis hung his head.

"Everything's so difficult. I couldn't stay on in the Legion. But I don't seem able to settle down in civilian life either. Civilian life's so complicated; so are women. You've always got to talk, explain, bow and scrape. You want to work here? Then get down on your hands and knees. You want to make love to me? Then kneel down at my feet. Ach, how much better it was, the war! I haven't been able to find a job because I swore at everyone I went to see, and I swore at that girl, Colonel, because I was getting cramp from bowing and scraping so much."

The waiter brought a brandy, but Kreis waved it away and made as if to leave.

"Wait a moment," said la Roncière. "Maybe I've got something for you. How would you like to go to Katanga?"

2. *Uhuru* Congo

At Brussels Fonts almost missed the plane for Elizabethville. He rushed up just as the steps were being removed.

"What a girl!" he said to la Roncière as he fastened his
seat belt. "She had everything the others haven't got."

"What?" the colonel sharply asked.

"I was just saying good-bye to her."

La Roncière felt like reminding Fonts that he was his
subordinate, that it was thanks to him that he was leaving
for Katanga. But the little Catalan, taking advantage of
the colonel's recent worries, had imperceptibly transformed their relationship into a partnership between two
associates who had different activities, perhaps, but the
same rights.

"We'll straighten things out once we get to the Congo,"
la Roncière decided.

Kreis, sitting just behind them, felt more and more excited. He still could not believe he was actually leaving, although the enlistment fee had been paid into his bank
and, when he touched his breastpocket, he could feel his
passport.

He was now called Charles Créash, a native of Colmar,
and he had a foreman's contract with the Pétro-Congo.
Ach! A foreman, but still doing the same job—fighting.
Only now it was well paid and, though he did not care for
Fonts, he had known la Roncière for a long time and rec-
ognized in him a born leader.

La Roncière had envisaged another departure scene, at
le Bourget, surrounded by press photographers, after a
farewell celebration followed by a sort of parade: the
twenty officers who were due to leave all lined up in front

of the aircraft, with the Katangese badge, a bronze cross, in their button-holes.

The eighty officers who were to join them later would have gathered in a solid *bloc* and waved to them from behind the barriers. Then la Roncière would have made a statement for the radio and television:

"We are going to Africa to defend law and order against lawlessness, the right of nations to manage their own affairs and settle their own destinies against the pretensions assumed by certain irresponsible international officials who are consciously or unconsciously acting as the purveyors of Communism. Because of them, Leopoldville is in a state of complete anarchy; because of us, Katanga will continue to enjoy law and order and prosperity."

There had been none of this, there had been only this semi-clandestine departure of three men under false identities.

The whole recruitment operation had started extremely well, however. With the funds put at his disposal la Roncière had rented a flat in a quiet street in the Parc Monceau. A few notices in the Paris and provincial press, and also in the parachute regimental magazines, had made it known that Colonel la Roncière was looking for colleagues to go with him to Katanga.

Applications had poured in forthwith from Algeria no less than from metropolitan France.

It was Kreis, who had been engaged the day after his outburst at Weber's, who interviewed the candidates. He made them fill in a brief questionnaire and did not pass them on to la Roncière unless they could show the following qualifications: that they belonged or had belonged to either the 10th or 25th Parachute Division; that they were young and in tip-top physical condition; that they were commissioned but had not risen above the rank of captain or subaltern; that they had been engaged in the Army on duties other than those of a mere platoon or company commander, for instance SAS or SAU activity, Intelligence, Propaganda or Security. . . .

The colonel interviewed them in an informal manner, seated on a sofa. When he knew them he gave them a drink and told them what he proposed doing in Katanga. Then, if the job seemed to suit them, he promised to summon them again for a thorough examination of their situation.

"If we accept you," he pointed out, "you'll have to hand in your resignation at the same time as you sign the contract. It will be accepted at once. I have the Ministry's assurance."

By the end of the first week la Roncière had personally interviewed eighty candidates. Six hundred applications in writing had been sent to his office, including some from well-known colonels who had played an important part in Algeria and were prepared, albeit older in years or senior in rank, to serve under his orders.

His vanity had been flattered, but he had rejected these applications although he fully realized that the colonels in question, by volunteering as mercenaries, were making a last attempt to escape their fate of soldiers in revolt, praetorians discontented with the king whom they themselves had made. They would come to grief—it was quite likely —and end up facing a firing squad or in a military prison. All the same this was no reason to make room for them. For he knew his comrades extremely well: in spite of all their promises they would never have been willing to serve under an officer junior to them without trying to get rid of him. He would have done the same.

In spite of the advice of Fonts, who felt this sort of business ought to be conducted with a modicum of discretion, in spite of a word of warning from Colonel Chaudey whom Fonts had notified, la Roncière decided to hold a press conference.

Unlike some of his comrades, who liked seeing themselves in the headlines, la Roncière, out of pride, preferred to avoid all publicity. But he felt that in the present case the very rules of psychological warfare obliged him to "condition the public," and, for that, he obviously had to resort to the journalists.

A dozen of them, including Dorat, all specialists in black Africa or military affairs, had gathered at his invitation in a room in the Hotel Lutetia.

"You're making a big mistake," Fonts had told him, "but since you insist, at least do them proud! They might be grateful to you for the food and drinks."

Accordingly little sandwiches and the best champagne were served.

Glass in hand, so as to make this initial contact more informal, la Roncière had launched into a lecture on psychological warfare and its methods. His audience started yawning. Dorat revived their interest by rudely interrupting the speaker.

"Look, Colonel, we've already heard all this in Indo-

China, Algeria and everywhere else. . . . I'd like to ask you one or two questions."

"Go ahead," la Roncière had retorted.

"You're recruiting French serving officers for Katanga. Is this with the sanction of the Ministry of the Armed Forces?"

"Of course. How could it be otherwise?"

"Are you being sent on a mission to Katanga on behalf of the French Government?"

"Not exactly . . ."

"Yes or no?" another journalist insisted. "It's very important, Colonel. Up to now the French Government has abided by this official position: it does not recognize Katanga. Well, then?"

Chantal had continued to expatiate to her husband on the colonel's good looks and brilliant mind. So Dorat, who out of laziness would have let the matter drop, now resumed the attack on his own account:

"You have opened a recruiting office at 17, Rue Murillo, on the ground floor. You have had a certain number of reports published in the papers to inform the public of the kind of activity in which you are engaged. This is nothing more nor less than recruiting for a foreign army. Either the French Government is not aware of this, which is hard to believe, or else it approves of it, which seems to indicate a change in its policy towards the Congo and the UN."

Noticing the trap that was being laid for him and at the same time furious at Dorat's insistence, la Roncière retorted stiffly, as though to an impertinent remark:

"You will understand that I cannot answer that question."

The journalists were all laughing when they left and he heard one of them say:

"I thought our great specialist in psychological warfare was more astute. He fell into the trap like a novice. Really these colonels aren't what they're cracked up to be!"

The next day, la Roncière was able to see a short account of his conference in most of the big dailies.

Two papers only accorded it a certain amount of importance. One of them, an extreme left-wing journal, came out with the headline:

Factious Colonels Help Union Minière,

and inveighed against la Roncière, recalling the Battle of Algiers, the tortures and the barricades. . . .

The other, which was read by political experts and government circles and for this reason tended to assume the moral guidance of the country, asked the following question:

A New Slant to French Policy in Africa?

A press conference held in a big hotel on the left bank by Lieutenant-Colonel la Roncière seems to confirm the rumors current in circles connected with the Government, according to which a revision of French policy in the former Belgian Congo is being envisaged.

Colonel la Roncière refused to specify if the mission he is about to undertake in Katanga has or has not received official approval.

Questioned in the evening, the Minister of the Armed Forces confined himself to stating that Lieutenant-Colonel la Roncière had been retired from active service at his own request and that his journey to Katanga would take place on a purely private basis.

It is nevertheless a cause for concern that French officers—about a hundred, according to the information we have received—who were serving in the Army until yesterday, should be able to be recruited openly as mercenaries in the service of a government that is not recognized by France and is in a state of open secession from the Leopoldville Government which, until further orders, is the only legal authority in the Congo.

Colonel Chaudey rang up late in the afternoon, speaking in that paternal tone of voice that exasperated la Roncière.

"My dear colleague," he said, "your press conference has caused quite a stir . . . to put it mildly. There's been a lot of excitement, not only at the Quai d'Orsay but also at the Elysée."

"I don't see why, Colonel! I made no statement that wasn't true . . . and I confirmed nothing either."

"You couldn't have seen the evening papers and this article on the new slant to our policy in Africa!"

"I read it, of course. But I don't see how those few lines of stuff and nonsense can bother anyone."

La Roncière heard Chaudey clicking his tongue on the other end of the line.

"Tch. Well, I'll tell you the result of these few lines of stuff and nonsense . . . as you call them. The American Ambassador has rung up the Quai d'Orsay to inform them of the concern of his government which—as you know, I believe—is deeply involved in this Congo business. He asked for further details about the Roncière mission.

"The Quai has turned against Dumont, who was on your side, however. Didn't he make his friend Fonts available as soon as you asked for him? Dumont was hauled over the coals for having backed your candidature; and I've received the after-effects!"

La Roncière still refused to believe that his press conference could have had such serious consequences. It was in a choking voice that he asked:

"So all is lost?"

"Lost, no. Adversely affected, yes! To appease public opinion we're obliged to take certain steps, including the closing down of your recruiting office. We must also ask you—officially speaking, that's to say—to renounce your mission."

"But. . . ."

"Which means, my dear fellow, undertaking it this time with the utmost secrecy. Keep out of the limelight. Of course, there's no question of a departure with brass bands!"

"According to the terms of my contract with the Katangese Government, I have to report to Elizabethville within the next ten days!"

"There's nothing to stop you taking a plane for Rome or Vladivostok. Nor is there anything to stop you engaging civilians, who happened to be serving officers only twenty-four hours before, for some company or other whose main office could be in Brussels and the industry or mines it handles in Katanga."

Chaudey could not resist the pleasure of teaching la Roncière a lesson. His voice assumed a tone of deep regret. He sounded as though butter wouldn't melt in his mouth.

"What a shame, old boy . . . that such a brilliant specialist in revolutionary warfare, one of whose most efficient weapons is the press . . . the instrument for swaying public opinion—I think this is how you once described it yourself—should become the victim of this very weapon!"

"It was a put-up job!"

"Then why lay yourself open? Let Fonts deal with that sort of thing rather than you. He's a civilian, he's not involved. Allow me all the same to wish you a pleasant journey. You can always rely on our help so long as it can be given discreetly. . . . By the way, the police will be searching your place tomorrow morning. Don't let the list of the six hundred candidates fall into their hands. The Interior always like meddling in things that don't concern them. Have you heard from Julienne lately? What's that? She left for Italy? In January? . . . With her husband? Julienne's always full of surprises."

The police had searched the premises in the Rue Murillo on the following day. Some extremely formal and inquisitive inspectors had collected a few pamphlets and papers and placed their seal on the apartment, which had forced la Roncière, fuming with rage, to move to a hotel.

No reaction from Katanga. Only a telegram from Justin Pimuriaux asking Colonel la Roncière to cease recruiting and take the plane for Elizabethville on the agreed date with a skeleton headquarters staff.

As the Boeing took off from the runway in heavy rain, la Roncière recalled his first meeting with this jovial, mysterious and extremely self-satisfied character. Like all former lawyers, he liked well-turned phrases and would seize you by the arm as he uttered them.

What would Justin Pimuriaux think of the closing-down of the recruiting office?

In Paris Pimuriaux was always flanked by a big Negro—his African surety!—who spent his time gazing at his fingernails and by a certain Bernard Rivet who claimed to be a political journalist. This puny precious character had started defending the West as a member of the Milice during the occupation, and had continued to do so in an extremely right-wing organization.

Rivet had spent some time in Algeria. During a visit to the rear base of the 3rd Foreign Parachute Regiment, which la Roncière was then commanding, he had inquired at great length into the colonel's methods of warfare and pacification in order, so he said, to write a series of articles or a book about them.

His great project had been reduced to a short caption under a photograph in *Libre Belgique*.

Then Rivet had gone to the Congo and one morning la Roncière received a call from him. He did not know how the journalist had managed to find his address but Rivet prided himself on being well in with the Présidence du Conseil. He it was who had organized the meeting with Pimuriaux, on the first floor of a secluded restaurant in the Rue des Fosses-Saint-Bernard which was famous for its steaks and ham.

Justin Pimuriaux had unfolded his napkin with satisfaction and ordered lunch for himself and his Congolese without even asking the latter what he wanted to eat. He had chosen highly spiced dishes and full-bodied wine.

Rivet himself drank nothing but water and ate nothing but plain grilled meat.

The colonel, partly from bravado, partly for fun, only slightly by preference since he was extremely abstemious, had ordered the most expensive dishes on the menu.

Justin Pimuriaux was about fifty years old and beginning to put on weight. He had the ruddy complexion peculiar to beer drinkers. His gray hair was plastered carefully forward from the back of his head in a vain attempt to conceal his baldness. His pale little eyes were embedded in fat; his hands were chubby and in his buttonhole he sported a big black-and-purple rosette: the Order of Leopold.

Pimuriaux had waited till the meal was almost over before broaching the subject which had brought them together.

"We Belgians," he announced, placing both hands flat on the table. "are open and above board in our business affairs. . . . My friend President Kimjanga, who honors me with his confidence, and"—he indicated the guzzling Negro—"His Excellency Monsieur Adalbert Namango, who's a member of the President's family and one of our closest collaborators, can confirm this."

His Excellency lifted his nose from his plate, showed his teeth, gave a nod and dipped his nose back into his food.

"Well, now, President Kimjanga has entrusted me with a mission of the highest importance and this is what has brought us together here. As you know, Katanga is threatened by barbarism. Throughout the rest of the Congo they're killing, looting, raping. . . . With us, black and white work together in perfect amity. But we're being threatened by the United Nations . . . the *machin* as your President de Gaulle rightly calls it.

"What we want are some men capable of establishing a military and at the same time political organization which will enable us in the first place to resist enemy pressure, and secondly to extend our pacification throughout the

55

Congo and make that country a model for the whole of Africa, the symbol of multi-racial coexistence based on the essential values of the Western world."

He had then gulped down a big glass of wine and, having come to the end of his lecture, had immediately become less formal.

"My worthy friend Bernard Rivet who saw you at work in Algeria told me something about your methods and ideas. He also told me you were available at the moment. Katanga—as you no doubt know—is not without resources, but she lacks men with your qualifications. And so. . . . But first of all, do you think your methods can be applied to black Africa?"

La Roncière had given the condescending smile of the specialist to whom a layman puts a question that is pointless since the answer is obvious.

"My dear sir, these methods of warfare have proved themselves in Asia no less than in Egypt or the Mahgreb. They are universal since more or less all nations can be conditioned according to the same principles. Have you read the *Rape of the Masses* by Serge Chakhotin?"

Pimuriaux had not read the *Rape of the Masses*. He appeared extremely distressed by this lapse.

"What about the Belgians?" the colonel inquired. "From what I hear, Belgian instructors are still running the Katangese Gendarmerie."

"Oh, my dear fellow, those Belgians! They're recent arrivals and know nothing about the mentality of the African. Isn't that so, Your Excellency?"

His Excellency was dreaming of the *Folies Bergère*. He mumbled a few stilted phrases which might have been interpreted in any manner.

"The Belgians don't know anything . . . about Bantu psychology . . . or the evolution of geopolitics."

Rivet wriggled in his chair restlessly. He felt he was being forgotten and was anxious to point out that he too knew the President.

"Only a week ago," he said in his shrill voice, "the President told me: 'My dear Rivet, the Belgians in Katanga don't seem to realize we are now an independent country. They go on behaving as though they were still in a colony . . .' "

Pimuriaux interrupted him.

"Great changes are going to take place in the Army as well as in the administration. A new lot are coming to power. I can now tell you, Colonel, that President

Kimjanga's confidence requires me to fulfil some extremely important functions; in fact he is entrusting me with the reorganization of Katanga, and, what's still more important, the task of engaging from all over Europe the technical, administrative and political leaders that we lack. It was my idea to appeal to you."

"But what on earth do you want me to do?" La Roncière asked in utter amazement.

Rivet, in the course of his first visit, had been extremely vague. According to him, this dinner was to be confined to a mere establishment of contact.

Pimuriaux leaned back in his chair.

"Nothing less, Colonel, than to undertake the responsibility of Minister of the Interior and of War in the new State of Katanga."

"I beg your pardon?"

"You will not be a minister officially, of course: these posts have already been allocated to Africans, but you'll be adviser to these ministers with full powers of decision. Didn't you once write in the *Revue des Armées* that the first rule of revolutionary warfare was to unite both civil and military power in one hand?

"I've always been very interested in your various activities, haven't I, Rivet?" Resignedly, Rivet confined himself to giving a nod. "As I understand it, it wouldn't be difficult for you to bring out with you a hundred or so officers, trained in these methods, who could become full-time instructors in Katanga."

"But I'm still on active service; so are my comrades."

With a wave of his hand Pimuriaux swept aside this objection.

"I've seen certain people who are closely connected with the Elysée. I don't think any serious objections would be raised in that direction. I can also tell you that certain circles would be only too pleased to sce closer ties between France and Katanga. We've got mines, what! And then Abbé Fulbert Youlou is a great friend of our President."

"But one can't just shed the Army like an old suit of clothes," la Roncière observed. "One's pension . . . one's . . ."

"You mean financial assurances? We can give you those. We can promise you a high rate of pay as well as a substantial gratuity which will amply compensate for any loss you may suffer. Katanga is a rich country, believe me, and the President is a man who sets a proper price on merit. With your qualifications and experience, do you want to end your career in a little provincial garrison?"

"I've been offered a chair in the National Defense Institute of Higher Studies."

"Come along, now!"

And, lowering his voice, Pimuriaux had quoted figures.

Fonts did not wake up until the stop at Rome. He was in a bad mood and had a furry tongue.

"What are we playing at?" he asked la Roncière all of a sudden.

"You want a game of cards? You can't even open your eyes and we're just landing."

"I'm not talking about cards, Jean-Marie, but about what we're doing in this plane. Have you any idea how we're going to be received in Elizabethville?"

"By a chubby and extremely self-satisfied Pimuriaux. President Kimjanga will invite us to dine with him and the next day we get down to work, you take over Information and Security, and I the Police and Civil Affairs, both white and African. You also send back a few little reports to the Elysée, Dumont and Uncle Chaudey. But that part of the job is your own business, isn't it? In ten days or so the seventeen officers I selected among the first applicants will sign their contracts, get their plane tickets and join us in Elizabethville. Katanga is not like the Congo, it's a country of law and order."

"But Katanga is also in Africa, and in that bitch of a continent—that nigger-boy continent, as our friend Dorat calls it—anything can happen. Generally speaking, you're never bored there. But every day you have to start all over again what you've done the day before: nothing is ever achieved! You can get used to Africa, but you can't change her."

"All you need is method, the necessary means, suitable men at your disposal, and you can change anything."

Fonts shook his head.

"Not in Africa. I think I know it pretty well. When I got back from Indo-China I did a spell with the IFAN.* I made a study of the brotherhoods and fetishes. I learned how Islam had been digested by Africa. In Guinea I saw how Communism in its turn had been digested. Islam, Communism, Catholicism, Democracy, the whole lot pass through the great Negro stomach. When they re-emerge they're all an indistinguishable hotchpotch. Each time I

* *Institut français d' Afrique noir,* whose headquarters are in Dakar.

come back to Black Africa I feel scared. Of course, once I've dipped my nose into it I get used to the seething chaos, maybe because chaos suits me and I'm fond of the Negroes."

At Rome airport the papers were full of the assassination of Patrice Lumumba.

"What did I tell you?"

And Fonts shrugged his shoulders.

"You never know what's going to happen in those bloody countries!"

He studied the report more carefully.

On the night of 10 February, Lumumba and his two ministers escaped during a thunderstorm after overcoming the two sentries and tying them up. A black Ford belonging to the police escort had disappeared, no doubt stolen by the prisoners. It contained enough petrol for sixty miles; two rifles had also disappeared. . . .

On 12 February the three prisoners were found dead; their throats had been cut by the inhabitants of a small village. But the Katangese Government refuses to display the bodies. . . . The Minister of the Interior has calmly declared that the graves of the prisoners have been dug in a secret place so that they should not become an object of pilgrimage for their followers.

"A typical Negro story," Fonts exclaimed. "All the essentials are there, witchcraft, tribes and tribal rivalry, the whole lot washed down with beer, palm wine or spirits. Look, they've even issued a doctor's certificate to say that Lumumba's dead . . . but it doesn't say how he died."

La Roncière felt embarrassed and at the same time disturbed. He tried to apologize for his new masters.

"It's the Leo gang after all, Mobutu, Kasavubu and Co., who eliminated Lumumba and handed him over to the people of Katanga."

"Did they have to accept this gift? But it's such pleasure to revenge oneself on an enemy. Africa is the land of symbols and, to the whole world, that hysterical idiot Lumumba was the symbol of independence in the Congo. People were beginning to get used to him. Above all he had the support of those who decide on what is good or bad, who bless or excommunicate: the Communists and the

Afro-Asians. Even those on the opposite side are susceptible to this sort of game."

"I don't follow."

"Just think, Colonel. You find yourself by chance on the
other side. You must, on the psychological plane, exploit
this assassination against Katanga. What would you do?"

La Roncière discovered with astonishment that for the
first time in his life he was able without any difficulty to
put himself in his opponent's place. In Indo-China it was
impossible to put himself in the place of the Viets or, in
Algeria, in the place of the *fellaghas*. Now he was nothing
but a mercenary, a technical expert in a certain form of
warfare, who was engaged as other technicians are engaged to build a bridge.

He thought the matter over and came to this conclusion:

"If I were one of the people who wanted to put an end
to the secession of Katanga, I'd say that this assassination
had been organized by the big capitalist interests who want
to go on controlling Africa. It's true, Fonts, this business
could be a bit of a nuisance and I now wonder if President Kimjanga hasn't fallen into a trap."

Kreis had no idea who Patrice Lumumba was. A man
had been killed? What did it matter? Thousands of men
were being killed the whole time, for saying No when they
should have said Yes, for being white when it was better
to be blue or red, for having too much or too little fore-
skin or merely because they happened to be in the line of
fire.

An air hostess of a Scandinavian company who was
crossing the airport waiting room reminded him of Lisel,
of her warm body and soft skin. It was good to plunge
into women like Lisel; they wriggled like a fish trying to
escape from one's embrace until the moment, when, pin-
ioned and surrendering to one's thrusts, they moaned as
though they were about to die.

But afterwards they had to talk, to spoil the beauty of
what had just happened with idiotic or commonplace
remarks about love. Petty, futile creatures, designed for dis-
pensing pleasure, the divinest thing of all, and then immediately spoiling everything!

"Are you dreaming?" Fonts asked him all of a sudden.
"Have a coffee. Italy has been lucky enough to lose her
colonies. So you can get good coffee here."

Kreis was bewildered by Fonts. He spoke to la Roncière
as an equal; he could thus be ranked as a colonel. Yet he

looked extremely young, except when you had a close view of his tired face or when he had not shaved. His chin was then blue and reminded Kreis of those caricatures of "Spanish Reds" that were circulated among the Hitler-Jugend.

A few days after engaging him, la Roncière had said to him while talking about Fonts:

"Kreis, don't ever forget that Thomas Fonts is intelligent and dangerous, that he can be extremely useful to us but can also play us all sorts of dirty tricks. He isn't a soldier but he may have killed as many men as you have. Only he chose to do so, whereas you were merely carrying out orders."

Fonts, as Kreis quickly realized, had been one of those partisans who shot Wehrmarcht and SS soldiers in the back and who, when they were captured, spat in the face of their executioners.

"Still dreaming, you bloody old Hun?" Fonts asked him again.

With a blank look Kreis listened to the incomprehensible chatter of this little Southerner. He felt he talked far too much. Everyone talked too much, men as well as women, and this fellow talked for his own pleasure.

The colonel came back. He had gone to buy another paper.

"I'd very much like to know," he said to Fonts, "what all these Belgians traveling with us think about Lumumba's liquidation. Look at them, they've all got their long red noses buried in the papers."

"Why not ask them?"

"We'll see presently."

The Boeing took off. The steward announced: "Next stop Kano in Nigeria. Five and a half hours' flight, at an altitude of forty thousand feet."

"Coming? We'll have a look at your Belgians," Fonts suggested to la Roncière. "There's one of them swilling beer up in front, in that sort of bar behind the crew's cabin."

"I'll join you later."

La Roncière always disliked the first contact with strangers. It gave him an almost morbid feeling of embarrassment. This was one of the reasons why he liked the Army and, in the Army, the extremely circumscribed world of the paratroopers where everyone knew everyone else.

Strict formalities preceded any introduction and dictated

behavior according to certain more or less secret hierarchies which sometimes had no bearing on actual rank.

Fonts went up front, sat down next to the Belgian and ordered a whisky.

The Belgian, delighted to have a drinking companion, raised his beer-mug to him.

"To your health. You're French, aren't you?"

Dressed in light tweed and very pleased with himself, the Belgian appeared to have a sound digestion and not a care in the world.

"Is this your first trip to the Congo?"

Fonts acquiesced with a nod.

"Business, eh? What do you sell?"

"Sewing-machines . . . with instructions on their use. How are things in Leopoldville these days?"

"Better. Colonel Mobutu has got rid of Lumumba and those Russians. The Americans gave him a helping hand, admittedly. Lumumba has been sent off to E'ville."

"E'ville?"

"Yes. We old hands, you know, call Leopoldville Leo, and Elizabethville E'ville. But I believe Patrice Lumumba ran into a spot of bother at E'ville. He tried to make a get-away and the others. . . ."

"You're quite sure he tried to make a get-away?"

"No one can say for sure, it's a question of politics."

"This assassination is liable to have serious consequences: Lumumba had followers, mainly in the Congo, but also abroad."

"Maybe among the Communists abroad, but in the Congo he's finished! Look, monsieur, let me tell you something. Lumumba never governed anything in the Congo. He was a little agitator who had already been to prison for dipping his hands in the till. He knew how to read, count and knot his tie, but scratch a bit below the surface and he was nothing but a savage. You know what happened when Lumumba moved into the Governor-General's house? Well, every day he sent for the plumber to mend the bidet. No, it's not a dirty story; it's merely that Madame Lumumba thought the bidet was for pounding millet. So every morning she arrived with her pestle and started pounding the seeds. The porcelain cracked. The bidet was changed eight times. Lumumba concluded from this that Belgian material was of poor quality and that's why, they say, he wanted to give contracts to the Russians."

Fonts roared with laughter, summoned the hostess and ordered a beer for the Belgian, another whisky for himself. He clinked glasses with the Belgian and pointed out:

"You know, old boy, if Madame Lumumba didn't know what a bidet was for, maybe it's because you people never taught her. Now, in order to sell my sewing-machines, I have to give a course of instructions. And if I want to sell bidets. . . ."

The Belgian wept with laughter at the idea of this little Frenchman giving bidet instruction to fat black mammies who, until then, had always dipped their backsides in the swamps and were none the worse for it.

La Roncière joined them, enabling the hostess to admire his bearing, and asked for a fruit juice—in the tone which one would use to address a real hostess, not an air hostess.

He was shocked by the fat Belgian's noisy hilarity, for he attributed it to Lumumba's assassination. The more he thought about it the more he considered it an unforgivable mistake. It was a pointless job and badly carried out. If this liquidation was necessary it should have been left to the people of Leopoldville. In no circumstances should the inhabitants of Katanga have had anything to do with it.

"And then," the Belgian went on, "what made a complete shambles of the Congo was, of course, the wards trying to dispense with their guardians the whites and, having got rid of them, straight away trying to do what they had not been allowed to do for their own good: drinking *mbulu* and *bitaha,* beer and palm wine, and all of them starting to smoke hemp. Then they relapsed into the hands of the witch-doctors. They practiced *wwelaet* and *ngimbi.* They forgot everything they had been taught by the missionaries. These fine fellows, without bothering to marry or anything else, began making love like beasts on heat . . . like monkeys in the zoo who spent the whole of their lives doing nothing else. Because, as far as temperament is concerned, no one could say they were lacking in that line! Just ask any white woman who's been through it, eh! The Negroes are again dancing naked in the jungle, painted as though every day was a carnival.

"In other words, the place is finished for some time, unless the Congolese come to their senses and ask the Belgians, who understand and like them, to come back and help them restore law and order everywhere."

"With a horsewhip?"

"No, but with a firm hand. It's a rich country. Everyone could live happily there. And you, monsieur, what do you sell? Sewing-machines, like your friend here?"

"I sell law and order," la Roncière curtly replied, "but not the same sort as yours."

"With that thin face of his, he must be a Communist,"

the Belgian reflected as he gulped down his beer and hastily disappeared.

At Kano they were greeted by a heavy clammy heat smelling of decay and offal.

"The belly of Africa," la Roncière said to himself with disgust.

He too felt frightened all of a sudden and understood what Fonts meant.

Kreis, as he mopped his brow, thought of the icy nights in Russia and that village near Smolensk where it was so cold that when you fired a rifle shot the air was ripped apart like a piece of silk.

"The aim of revolutionary warfare," la Roncière began, to reassure himself, "is not to kill but to subdue the population. . . ."

While the aircraft was being refueled Fonts stood leaning against a barrier, recalling what a half-caste in Dakar had told him.

"The Negro believes only in force. Anyone who tries to explain things instead of giving orders is therefore displaying weakness. If he is weak he has no right to command, therefore he should not be obeyed."

A lovely Negress walked past with swirling skirts and heavy gold jewels in her ears and round her neck. Her pungent sugary smell, like a heady whiff of vanilla, reminded him of the fair-skinned young African girl he had known in Konakry.

He remembered her fiery loins, her splendid body with its full firm breasts: an obliging good-natired statue which he never managed to bring to life.

She was a Peuhl from Fouta-Djalon. When he was away she let herself be tumbled with equal indifference by the house-boy. But when he went back to France she had drunk some "devil brew" and tried to kill herself. Perhaps she was going to have a baby by him, unless it was by the house-boy . . . perhaps she loved him in her own fashion, like a very rare object which everyone envied her, a white man from the Embassy for whom the white women competed.

Three hours later the plane was circling over Leopold-ville. The town appeared through a gap in the clouds, white and imposing with its buildings on the banks of the huge Congo River in whose turgid waters clumps of wild hyacinth went drifting downstream.

"It's Algiers without the sea," said Kreis, who was glued to a porthole.

"The finest town in Africa," proudly declared a Belgian behind him, "and we built it."

"Why didn't you keep it?" la Roncière asked him in a gruff voice. "One fights for a town as one fights for a woman. One leaves it but one doesn't let someone else take it from one. . . ."

This was what Kreis liked about the colonel—the arrogance of the regular officer. It was to be found in certain Wehrmacht officers but not in the SS. There was greater opportunity in the SS but no tradition.

The plane circled above the river under the blanket of cloud and Brazzaville appeared, a little colonial town with squat houses.

Then Leopoldville came into sight again, the Boulevard Albert with its reinforced-concrete blocks.

Dorat had told la Roncière what Leopoldville had been like during the days following the proclamation of independence.

Mutiny had broken out in the military camp at Thysville, about a hundred miles from the capital.

The officers and NCOs had been beaten up without defending themselves, without firing into the mob; their wives and daughters had been raped. In the middle of the night all these panic-stricken soldiers had piled into cars and arrived in Leo screaming: "They're all up in arms; they're on their way, they're going to kill everyone! It's the women they're after."

Other officers, gray in the face with fright, had been seen to tear off their uniforms and borrow civilian trousers from their house-boys. Within one hour there was complete chaos. Thousands of men and women had rushed down to the wharf to cross the Congo and take refuge in Brazzaville. Hundreds of abandoned cars littered the streets near the port. Some of them still had their lights on. Suitcases and children's toys had been forgotten on the seats. Night and day the lights blazed in the abandoned shops and apartments.

Stupefied, the Africans could hardly believe their eyes as they witnessed this shameful flight. In these disheveled women and wild-eyed men they were unable to recognize the arrogant self-assured whites who only a few hours earlier had been their masters. They were all the more astonished since nothing serious had happened in Leopoldville. The Thysville rising had been an isolated case.

65

La Roncière, had been ashamed, for he felt an instinctive solidarity with a vast military clan which included friends as well as enemies and in which no one had the right to behave like a coward.

Under the mocking gaze of the journalists, he had merely muttered:

"Disgraceful ... disgraceful. ..."

And now here was this Belgian behind him, all cock-a-hoop, as though one could be proud of having piled some stones one on top of another when one did not have the courage to defend them.

Therein lay the whole tragedy of the West: being able to build towns, but not loving them enough to be willing to die for them.

Fonts tapped him on the shoulder.

"Leo—I went there once or twice when I was at Brazza. Before what they too call the 'troubles,' it stank of money and complacency. The Belgians had done their best to overcome their small-nation complex in this part of Africa. They tried to make a good job of it. The buildings were huge and solidly built, but their work on the population was shoddy. In any case, whatever one does in Africa is shoddy. I'll tell you something. Africa doesn't like white people. From time to time she shakes herself and gets rid of them, like an old lion shedding its fleas."

Th plane had landed. The air hostess announced:

"Passengers for Leopoldville, please have your passports ready and fill in the police forms. For transit passengers, there will be a stop of about one and a half hours."

"One and a half hours if all goes well," said the Belgian behind them. "When you touch down here, you never know what's going to happen. It may well last three hours or even half a day. All it needs is for one of these smart-alecs to get a bee in his bonnet and the fun and games begin. The only advice I can give you is to keep calm whatever happens. Above all be very polite and don't argue; they're apt to beat you over the head."

Fonts turned round and saw that the Belgian had lost his swagger.

"And now," he said to la Roncière, as he rose from his seat, "the Negro circus show begins. Remember that anything may happen. Follow the advice of this half-wit behind us, it's quite sound. Be all the more polite to these buffoons, the more unbearably they may behave. Afterwards you'll always have the opportunity to settle accounts. ..."

Still half asleep, the passengers wandered like sheep to-

66

wards the N'Djili building, "the Plain," as the Belgians called it.

It was a huge structure consisting mostly of windows, above which fluttered the Congolese flag, white stars on a blue ground.

Fonts drew la Roncière's attention to four giant American Army Globemasters bearing the UN emblem.

"Some day or other we're liable to be saddled with them. At Gia Lam the Viets used to blow up our planes to put them out of action. We could do the same."

The crews in khaki flying kit went on placidly chewing their gum. This was a job to them like any other. They simply held themselves aloof from this seething mass of crazy Negroes, suffered from the heat and complained of the lack of white women.

All of a sudden a dozen Congolese soldiers in battle-dress, their helmets camouflaged with twigs, rushed towards the passengers brandishing their arms. Their teeth were filed to points and their big, mad eyes rolled in their sockets.

"This is it," said the Belgian. "They're already dead drunk. We're in for it."

Kreis had drawn closer to la Roncière, prepared to cover him. In cases like this he thought fast: perhaps he would have time to snatch one of these soldiers' submachine-guns out of his hand and hold the others up while the colonel and Fonts disarmed the rest of the gang. No, it was impossible, there were too many of them and they were too drunk. A drunk is always trigger-happy.

The soldiers scuttled past the Europeans as though they did not see them.

"What a stink of stale beer," said Fonts. "They must have had a skinful."

And tapping Kreis on the shoulder:

"Very unwise, what you thought of doing. In the first place it wasn't for us."

Shouting broke out behind them. The soldiers were kicking and belaboring with their rifle-butts a big black man in a navy-blue suit and homburg hat who was the last to have left the plane.

Having fallen on the ground, he had drawn up his knees to protect his groin and was desperately holding a black leather briefcase in front of his eyes.

"I say, it's Cléophas Batilatu," the Belgian calmly observed.

"Who's Cléophas Batilatu?" Fonts inquired.

"The local Minister of Public Works."

"In Lumumba's Government?"

"Not at all, in the present Government. On the contrary, he was one of Lumumba's opponents. But this gang of soldiers who are beating him up are probably Batetelas, from the same tribe as Patrice, and the minister's a Bakongo. Politics, as we understand them, have no bearing on this settling of tribal scores."

"We ought to do something," la Roncière objected in disgust. "They're going to kill him."

"Oh, no," the Belgian retorted. "A white man couldn't stand up to it, but that fellow . . . why, in three days he'll have nothing to show for it."

"How I love Africa!" Fonts exclaimed. "It's the only country where you can see a minister being given a hiding by the guard of honor detailed to welcome him."

A loudspeaker announced:

"Transit passengers, please proceed to gate number three."

From one end of the building to the other there stretched a huge streamer: "Lawlessness kills, peace gives life."

His Excellency Cléophas Batilatu, back from Brussels where he had represented the Congo at a conference of Public Works experts, was once more on his feet, his hat in one hand, his briefcase in the other.

Two soldiers hauled him off at a jog-trot towards the entrance of the airport. The others kept urging him on with kicks in the behind. One of them, holding his rifle by the barrel, swung it like a club to bring it down on his head, but lost his balance, missed the target and measured his length on the concrete with a metallic crash. A group of soldiers sitting in a circle by their kitbags burst into loud guffaws. The Batetela advanced on them in a threatening manner. One of the soldiers flung a bottle of beer in his face. The Batetela made as though to cock his rifle, then, thinking better of it, went off and rejoined his comrades, yelling insults over his shoulder.

"Those," the Belgian explained, "are Balubas. They can't bear the Batetelas."

In the transit waiting room the passengers, a score or so, sat down in deep armchairs. The leather had been ripped off the seats and the springs showed through. The ground was littered with spittle, crumpled paper and cigarette stubs.

A Sabena official crossed the room. La Roncière called to him.

"Could I have a fruit juice, please?"

The man looked at him in amazement.

"A fruit juice? But there's no one here to serve you, sir. The boys refuse to come to work before nine in the morning. The refrigerators don't work and there's no fruit juice. The other day a passenger who wanted some information or maybe fruit juice addressed a passing waiter as 'boy.' Force of habit, you understand? The fellow replied: 'Since independence there are no more boys in the Congo. I'm not a boy, I'm an air hostess.' "

The airport stank of stale urine and overflowing lavatories.

"What a stench!" Fonts exclaimed, holding his nose.

"Eight months ago it was even worse," said the Sabena official. "Not a pleasant sight, I can assure you. Men, women and children lying on the ground in hundreds, maybe thousands. I know some who waited two weeks before getting a seat on a plane. Yet we did all we could. Passengers were piled into Boeings two hundred at a time and the crews kept going on benzedrine, as in wartime. On the first day the lavatories were blocked. . . the water had been cut off. There was urine dripping down the stairs. That was eight months ago, but they haven't yet managed to unblock the lavatories."

"What can you expect, sir? The blacks don't want to work. If you've got a white skin, they refuse to obey you and if you insist they call you a 'dirty Fleming' and beat you over the head. I myself have been in prison five times since independence."

"But haven't the Africans got any men capable of running this airport?" la Roncière asked.

The Sabena man shrugged his shoulders.

"The blacks who are in charge of 'the Plain,' or anyway who are supposed to be, spend their whole time palavering in their offices or else copulating in every corner. This isn't an airport, it's a debating-hall and giant brothel."

"What about Katanga?"

"It seems it's not quite the same: they're still Negroes, of course, but behind them there are white men who pull the strings. That makes all the difference."

"I've had a bellyful of this lousy country," said Kreis. "When do we leave?"

Fonts whirled round on his heels.

"You've just arrived and you've signed a two-year contract. What did you do with your enlistment fee?"

"I banked it in Switzerland; I like reasonable people."

A group of policemen in gray uniforms, not too badly turned out and hovering between arrogance and timidity, entered the room. They were followed by a big, fat police commissioner with gleaming skin who kept opening his mouth as though he was drowning in his own sweat.

Fonts observed:

"I say, the circus show isn't over yet. But it's not so serious. These ones don't look as though they've drunk too much and they're unarmed."

After a sweeping glance at the passengers, the fat commissioner noticed a fair-haired young woman and went up to her at once.

The woman turned pale.

"Don't be frightened," he said in a thick voice, slurring his r's. . . . "You see, I'm responsible for the security of the free and independent Congolese people. Black and white, we're all friends together, so let's have a look at your passport."

Somewhat reassured, the young woman handed him her papers.

"Ah, you're Belgian . . . and you're going to Elizabethville? Why are you going to Elizabethville?"

"My husband works there."

"He's not a paratrooper, is he?"

"No, he works at the Union Minière."

One of his assistants butted in:

"That's not good, the Union Minière. The colonialists of the Union Minière want to get hold of our wealth."

A third joined them and, to lend weight to what he was about to say, ran his thick pink tongue round his lips.

"Lumumba himself said so: if the colonialists steal the mines from us, the Congolese will have to live on bananas."

The commissioner turned with a scowl on his subordinate.

"You shouldn't make thoughtless remarks. Patriots have no right to talk like babes in arms, otherwise we'll be the laughing stock of the whole world. All right, all right, that will do!"

And he handed the passport back to the young woman.

"Is that the end of that?" la Roncière inquired.

"There's never an end to anything in Africa!"

The door of the waiting room was suddenly flung open with a blow from a rifle-butt and the horde of Congolese soldiers adorned with twigs burst in with a great din, their hobnail boots clattering on the tiled floor. At their head was the big Batetela, a bottle of Polar beer in one hand, his rifle in the other.

"This place is full of spies," he yelled.

A Belgian, seated in one of the dilapidated chairs, was listening to the news on his transistor.

The Batetela pounced on him.

"What's that thing?"

The Belgian rose to his feet.

"A transistor."

"What are you doing with it?"

"I'm listening to the news."

"Don't you know it's forbidden to listen to the colonialist news?"

The Batetela put down his rifle, took a gulp of beer, gave a belch, then snatched the transistor from the Belgian who thought the incident closed.

"Monsieur le Commissaire," he called out, "this is a scandal. My papers are in order."

The commissioner had turned gray but, not wishing to lose face in front of the foreigners whom he believed he had impressed with his solemn tone, he feebly tried to intervene.

"Gentlemen, you mustn't make a *matata* here."

"What's a *matata*?" Kreis asked.

Fonts told him:

"That's what they call a row. In Brazza it's known as *poto-poto*. *Matata, poto-poto,* that's Africa for you. . . . But don't you go butting in now. These warriors are even more sozzled than before."

The commissioner had recovered his self-assurance and went on with his harangue.

"Because *matata* is anarchy . . ."

One of the soldiers, rolling his eyes fearfully under his helmet, cut him short.

"Who are you anyway?"

"I'm the Commissioner of Police."

"Me, I don't know the police, but I'm Corporal Joseph Kalikouko and I only take orders from Sergeant Amédée Bonuko and he isn't here."

Another soldier bellowed:

"All right, you white people, on your feet and take off your shoes!"

The commissioner scurried off, moving faster and faster the closer he approached the door.

"And it's with this lot you want to practice psychological warfare?" Fonts asked la Roncière ironically.

71

Kreis, with an ugly expression on his face, did not budge. He felt a blind rage welling up inside him and growled between his teeth:

"This rabble ought to be mowed down with a machine-gun."

Fonts gave la Roncière a jab with his elbow.

"Keep an eye on your Teuton, he's going to do something silly."

In Kreis, this big fair-haired fellow, the Batetela scented the hereditary enemy who, in his thick skull, came immediately after the Bakongo whom he despised, the Lulua whom he feared, the Baluba, the Bakete, the Mongo and the Mutwa; it was the Fleming.

He poked his rifle into his stomach.

"I told you to take off your shoes, you dirty Fleming."

Kreis controlled himself.

"I'm not a Fleming."

The Batetela snatched his passport out of his hand and flung it on the floor.

"I know what I'm talking about, I do . . ."

All the soldiers pounced on Kreis.

"You, you're coming back to the camp with us."

La Roncière caught sight of a UN Swedish officer who was witnessing the scene and asked him to intervene.

In extremely good English the Swede apologized:

"I'm frightfully sorry, sir, the UN can't intervene in the internal affairs of the Congo."

Just then another soldier, similarly bedecked and screaming some incomprehensible words, burst in through the door leading on to the runway.

All the warriors let go of Kreis and rushed for the door, yelling and brandishing their weapons.

Fonts asked a Belgian:

"What's going on?"

"The chap who's just come in told them in Swahili that a plane full of Belgian paratroops was about to land. So they've gone off to defend the Congo. Maybe it's a trick of the police commissioner's to get rid of them, or perhaps of the company agent."

The Sabena official arrived, snapping his fingers.

"Quickly, gentlemen, the plane for Elizabethville. This way, if you please . . . hurry."

La Roncière stiffly inquired:

"Is it always like this?"

The other man looked astonished.

"No, not every day."

3. Justin Pimuriaux's Little Schemes

The thick soggy carpet of the equatorial forest was succeeded by savannah country with its isolated trees and occasional round or square huts grouped into villages.

"We're flying too high," Fonts remarked, "too high and too fast. The green turns to brown and that's all. But we've just moved from one world into another. It's another climate and another human species: mankind has ceased to be crushed by nature. Farther on come the green hills of Africa . . . Rhodesia, Kenya, White Man's Africa. But I like the other Africa . . . stagnating on the banks of her lagoons, preserving her ancient ritual and monstrosity."

La Roncière, who was looking out of the porthole, turned round.

"My dear fellow, I always knew you had a taste for folklore and local curiosities: opium and child harlots in the Far East, hashish in Beirut and, I suppose, Circassian or Druse girls. And here, of course, Negroes on the rampage. The little scene we've just witnessed wasn't enough for you?"

"Those Negroes are ten or twelve centuries behind us, with social structures like those of the Goths or Visigoths. We turn up in their country with jets, frigidaires, fine principles, motor-cars, the UN and all the rest of it. Imagine our Celts, our Franks, all those ancestors of ours, if they'd been submitted to the same shock! And then there's the climate that devastates the blacks, a soil that may produce copper, uranium and diamonds, but as for daily bread . . . nothing or almost nothing, sweet potatoes and manioc."

"You can't blame them for being such clods . . . at least in the sense in which this word is understood by us, the

73

little geniuses of the jet and the atom! Because, in their own way, they're quite bright! I know what I'm talking about, I assure you! For instance, when it comes to a palaver—and a palaver is much the same as politics—they beat us hands down. . . . They have a natural gift for confusion and obscurity and can keep it up for days! My lecture has made me thirsty: will you stand me a drink?"

He turned to Kreis.

"And you, you Goth, Visigoth, Germanic Aryan, who invented the jet engine, the concentration camp, the rocket and the gas oven, what will you have?"

"A beer," said Kreis. "They have good beer here."

Justin Pimuriaux extracted his plump little body from the big black car that had brought him to the airport. Bakaya, his Baluba driver, held the door open, cap in hand.

"You wait here," Pimuriaux told him, "and when the plane lands, but not before, go and park at the foot of the steps. You understand?"

"Yes, Monsieur le Secrétaire-Général. Me understood."

"Repeat what I've told you."

"When the plane he land. . . ."

He rolled his eyes and repeated:

"When the plane he land . . . then. . . ."

Over his big flat face broke a gleaming smile that revealed all his teeth.

"Then, boss . . . me bugger off!"

"You blockhead. . . . No, you don't bugger off, you drive on to the runway and draw up by the steps. . . . And don't call me boss, but Monsieur le Secrétaire-Général."

"Yes, boss . . . Secrétaire-Général."

Pimuriaux shrugged his shoulders in despair.

"And they say the Balubas are the most intelligent! That's why the others try and wipe them out . . . because they're more intelligent than they are. . . ."

His bad temper evaporated when he turned round to look at the black Chevrolet which he had just been allocated. On the bonnet fluttered the red-and-green Katangese pennant adorned with four brass crosses, the same pennant as the ministers flew.

"This Chevrolet isn't really at all bad," he reflected. "Only eight days ago I was driving a Peugeot 403. I was not yet Secretary-General, only private secretary to the President. A private secretary is engaged and dismissed like a typist. But not a Secretary-General. . . . And yet Monette is still not satisfied!

"Women are insatiable! People think they resign them-

74

selves to being broke. It's not true! They go on wanting what they haven't got—luxury, attention—as violently as ever. But they bide their time. Oh yes, they know how to bide their time! They don't lose their appetite. Monette now wants me to ask the President for a bigger official residence and three extra servants. Just to overawe her girl friends, the ones who used to look down on her as a kind of Cinderella. She now wants to give big cocktail parties, with servants in white gloves . . . who help themselves to the drink, get sozzled long before the guests and insult any ministers who do not belong to their tribe."

It was unwise to make oneself too conspicuous. Kimjanga and his ministers, however advanced they might be, considered themselves the masters and did not like the white men in their service to make too much of a splash with their money.

What a tricky and difficult business it was to explain all this to Monette whose only thought was to pay back old scores!

Pimuriaux stepped into the hall of the airport building.

Decronelle came forward to greet him, deferent and familiar at one and the same time. He too was extremely pleased with himself.

"What news, Monsieur le Secrétaire-Général?"

For the last four months Bernard Decronelle had been representing the American news agency, Associated Press. Up to the time of independence he had earned a living of a sort in the press section of the Union Minière. His work consisted mainly of issuing visiting journalists with glossy hand-outs extolling the achievements of the company. The rest of the time he spent going to the airport to meet the directors, reserving hotel bedrooms for these gentlemen and organizing safaris for them. Independence had made him a real journalist who dispatched cables which were published by all the big papers in the world. Monsieur Van der Weyck, the Director of the Union Minière, no longer treated him like an underling! Now it was always: "My dear Decronelle. . . . Of course you'll keep your salary and your appointment, also your office . . . but not officially. And your villa . . . which seems rather too small to me. But the residence of one of our assistant directors has just fallen vacant. We'll see to that. Your assistant Purot will take your place . . . but you'll continue to be in control. . . . Incidentally, since you're always so well informed, I'd like to have a look at your cables. . . . Just in case you put a foot wrong anywhere. . . . I'm in close touch with Pimuriaux; he'll help you. . . ."

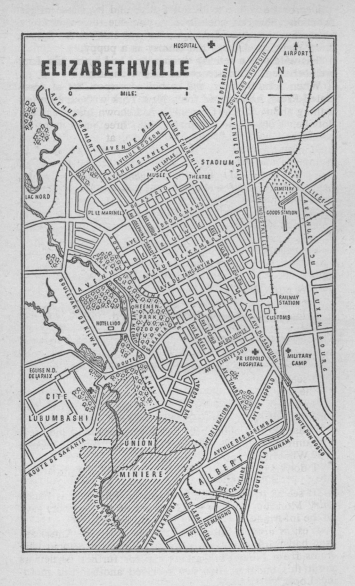

Decronelle was a toady by nature and by virtue of his functions. Slim, conscientious, paying due respect to every hierarchy and every principle, he was still, at the age of thirty-eight, as devoted and clumsy as a puppy.

His wife was a retiring woman and had borne him four well-behaved, albeit somewhat sickly, children.

When John Spencer, the special correspondent of Associated Press, had arrived from New York without knowing a thing about Africa, Decronelle had shown him round Jadotville, Kolwezi and Kipushi, the three great mineral-producing centers. All this, of course, at the expense of the Union Minière.

Spencer was looking for a local correspondent, a stringer who would not cost the agency too much, spoke English, had good contacts, knew the country well and was completely devoid of imagination. He was also very impatient to get back to Johannesburg where he had met a good crowd of poker players. Reckoning that Decronelle fulfilled these conditions, he engaged him.

Decronelle stuck to Pimuriaux like a leech.

"Really, Monsieur le Secrétaire-Général? No news at all?"

"No, none. . . ."

Pimuriaux was about to turn his back on him but, knowing Decronelle's vanity, changed his mind and leaned towards him:

"If I had heard anything, my dear fellow, you'd be the first person I'd tell. I've merely come to meet some French friends who are going to do a little big game-hunting and sight-seeing. . . . Since they don't know Katanga . . . since it's the first time they've set foot in the country. . . ."

Pimuriaux realized he was talking too much and abruptly fell silent, but Decronelle did not notice.

"What about Lumumba?" the novice journalist inquired.

"Lumumba? You've seen the official report, haven't you? What more do you want?"

"I don't know . . . a few additional details and particulars. . . ."

"It seems to me that in his press conference His Excellency Monsieur Bongo, our Minister of the Interior, gave all the information you could possibly want!"

"Yes, of course, but you know how it is: the Americans keep badgering me. Since yesterday I've received four telegrams from New York asking me for further particulars about this business. I've just received another this morning. Look."

Decronelle handed him the cable. Pimuriaux read it:

Ursule Salisbury reports Lumumba not killed during escape attempt but executed Elizabethville by Bongo on Kimjanga's orders stop Inform urgently stop Matter extreme importance stop Sending John Spencer with whom please collaborate closely stop Good hunting and regards stop Amélie

"What's all this nonsense about?" Pimuriaux asked. "And what does Madame Decronelle think of all these female relationships: Ursule . . . Amélie? . . ."

With a touch of condescension Decronelle explained:

"Ursule is the code-name of our competitors, United Press, in Salisbury. Amélie is my agency, Associated Press. As you see, they're taking a serious view of the Lumumba business."

Pimuriaux felt more and more ill at ease but now he could no longer break off the conversation.

"Your Americans have lost their senses. The transatlantic press has always had a morbid taste for the sensational. It didn't matter so much when América had no influence on world politics . . . but now she meddles with what's going on in Laos, Formosa, Guinea, Algeria and the Congo. The tendency of this press towards the sensational is consequently catastrophic . . . yes, catastrophic, my dear fellow!"

Decronelle was dumfounded by this violent outburst, for Pimuriaux had the reputation of being an extremely moderate man "whose tongue never runs away with him," as the Managing Director Monsieur Van der Weyck described him. All he could say in reply was:

"Well, you know . . ."

"Anyway, my dear fellow, I assume you're going to put things right promptly and clearly. Can you imagine the President and His Excellency Bongo perpetrating an assassination, the President ordering it and Bongo carrying it out? It's outrageous! You know how highly the President and I both esteem you. I think it's your duty to issue a most categorical denial of any rumors on this subject."

"May I quote you and say that you officially deny the report?"

Pimuriaux was caught in his own trap. He assumed a stiff, somewhat scornful manner.

"Come now, Decronelle, you're no longer a child!

78

You're quite capable of expressing an opinion yourself without relying on every Tom, Dick and Harry . . . and, of course, being responsible for the consequences."

"Monsieur le Secrétaire-Général, I assure you . . . I beg you to believe me . . . you misunderstood me. Let me explain. . . ."

"Perfect, my dear Decronelle, perfect. We knew we could count on you. My good friend Van der Weyck, with whom I'm dining this evening, said to me only the other day: 'Decronelle is worth his weight in gold . . . serious, industrious, methodical, devoted. He'll go far in the Union Minière. . . .' "

The loudspeaker crackled:

"The aircraft from Brussels, Rome, Kano and Leopoldville is about to land." Pimuriaux took this opportunity to escape from the journalist and made his way outside. He reflected:

"Luckily Decronelle can't see farther than his own nose. But the other fellow, Spencer, the American who's arriving . . . he doesn't give a damn about the Union Minière, Van der Weyck and our relationship with President Kimjanga."

Pimuriaux aimed an angry kick at an empty cigarette packet and almost fell over. Casting a furtive glance over his shoulder, he fancied the big Sabena agent was laughing at him behind his back; he only just prevented himself from calling him to order.

"Keep cool, keep cool," he reminded himself. "What a nuisance this business is, however! Why on earth did they have to go and bump off Lumumba? If only they had done it discreetly! Those idiots Ryckers and Van Beulans must have been behind it. It's obvious: Bongo's involved up to the neck. Maybe he attended the execution or even took part in it, reeling with alcohol and hemp, with blood up to his elbows. 'It's either his hide or mine!' he used to say, referring to Lumumba. So how can one not suspect him?

"This fellow Bongo's a dangerous lunatic, an absolute savage. He'd look better sitting naked in a lion-skin on the skull throne of his ancestor M'Siri than in black coat and striped trousers.

"But he's also the only one in the gang who's got any guts. Spencer's an utter idler and woman-chaser. He'll leave all the real work to Decronelle, and Decronelle will toe the line. As for women, we'll try and find him some. But all the others, good heavens, all the newspaper and agency correspondents who'll be turning up again just when la Roncière is landing with his acolytes. I hope his acolytes aren't too flashy. La Roncière was bamboozled by the journalists in Paris. . . . That's not serious, of course, but it all adds up. . . ."

The Boeing had come to a stop. Pimuriaux was pleased to see that his car was moving slowly forward towards the steps that had just been put in place. That idiot Bakaya had at least understood what he had told him.

He turned round and saw Decronelle who had followed him outside.

"Are you meeting someone too?" he asked.

"Me? No, I came to see if there were any other journalists on the plane."

"Félicien Dorat, for instance?"

"He's just gone back to France."

"But could always come out here again. I say, there's your old friend Pérohade. I'll leave you two together. . . ."

A thick-set man with a shiny face and hairy arms, wearing his shirt outside his trousers, came rushing up. He panted:

"I thought I wouldn't be here on time. Hello, Decronelle."

He had a south-western accent, was quick with his fists, drank heavily, and owned the Mitsouko, the only night-club in E'ville where you could find reasonably pretty girls, underdone steaks and wine that didn't come from Angola.

For all these reasons and because the Mitsouko had become the meeting-place of adventurers of every sort, ministers making merry and UN officers, because Marcel Pérohade had a sharp ear and made few financial demands, Félicien Dorat had made him the local correspondent of his paper. Pérohade took his job very seriously, which infuriated Decronelle. Moreover he addressed him as "tu"—"Since we're colleagues, what?"

Decronelle intended to hold himself aloof but forgot to do so in the face of his "colleague's" excitement.

"So you were notified by this bad penny here, were you?" Pérohade asked him, turning toward Pimuriaux to whom he gave a little bow. "Do you know his wife? What a shrew of a woman!"

"But what on earth's going on?"

"You're not going to tell me you don't know about the arrival of the French mercenaries? He's come to meet them. It seems there's a paratroop colonel or general in command of them. De Gaulle's sent them to Kimjanga to annoy the UN."

Decronelle broke into a forced laugh, because he couldn't laugh naturally.

"You're already drunk; it can't be true. Your story doesn't hold water. How do you think French mercenaries are going to arrive here without anyone knowing anything about it! Pimuriaux's here because he's meeting some friends. He's just told me . . . some big-game hunters."

"Yes, head-hunters!"

Decronelle assumed a paternal tone.

"Look, Pérohade, you know I'm always willing to help you. We're the only two full-time men in the place and it's in the interests of both of us to work in harmony. I've told you over and over again to check your sources. You're apt to pick up any bit of gossip you hear and cable it back. That's not the way to work. We have certain responsibilities, old boy. You understand? It's one thing to run a bar and another to be a journalist and keep the public informed."

"I say, why don't we go and ask Pimuriaux himself?"

"I wouldn't hear of it!"

"It was Paul who told me, and you know what Paul's racket is. It's an open secret. But look what's going on! Pimuriaux has gone aboard the aircraft, he's hustling three fellows out . . . and popping them into his car. There you are, it's off! No customs, no passport control, nothing. Did you ever see anything like it? Come on, we're going to follow them!"

"Do you think we ought to?" Decronelle asked, horrified.

"When you were eighteen, you must have still asked the girls for their permission before kissing them. Come on, jump into my car; yours is a dud and though you're Belgian you drive like a Swiss!"

"My wife's waiting for the car."

"What does it matter about your wife at a time like this? You're a journalist, aren't you? We have certain responsibilities, haven't we? We must keep the public informed!"

Sitting beside the driver, Kreis contemplated this country in which he was embarking on a new adventure. The climate had been a pleasant surprise to him. In Leopoldville the heavy clammy heat crept up his legs and beat down on the back of his neck: the same sort of heat as in Tonkin. Here it was cool: 10° or 12°C. perhaps.

"You'll see," said Pimuriaux, "Katanga's very pleasant; you need blankets at night, which is rare in Africa."

The rain had washed the trees and the savannah, and the sun had just pierced through the grey clouds. On each side of the surfaced road leading to E'ville there stretched a sort of plain. The tall, razorsharp grass that covered it revealed here and there a patch of swamp.

The driver hooted to pass a "bath-tub," a sort of semi-armored transport vehicle, painted white and equipped in front with mobile steel shutters like a machine-gun-carrier. Above the rear bumpers the letters ONUC were inscribed in blue. The soldiers jammed into it were very young. They had fair complexions and pale-colored eyes, wore sky-blue berets, and each was armed with a strange-looking weapon: a submachine-gun on to which was riveted a long bayonet.

"That armored car reminds me of something," said Kreis. "The Wehrmacht had vehicles like that."

"It's Swedish," Pimuriaux informed him. "They've got a dozen or so of these bath-tubs here and never stop driving them around."

"And who are those strange soldiers with complexions like cream-cheese?" la Roncière inquired.

"Our worthy UN friends. Also Swedish. ONUC stands for *Opération des Nations Unies au Congo*. I must say these Swedes aren't bad fellows. They're young lads who've finished their military service and enlisted for a year. The pay is good, they see a bit of the world and there's every chance they'll never have to fire a shot. They've really come to do a bit of sight-seeing. Look, each of them has a camera as well as his gun."

"Are the UN troops all Swedes?"

"No. The blue helmets are about fifteen hundred strong and include an Irish battalion as well. The Irish are a bit of a nuisance: they drink a lot, which makes them surly. But that's not the worst of it. They're white, you see, and in Africa white men are apt to stick together. What worries us far more is the arrival of the Indians and Ethiopians."

Kreis felt a kind of affection for the UN soldiers. They reminded him of the young recruits he had received in 1942, at Orel, just before the Battle of Stalingrad was launched. They were as young as these lads but in six months they had been turned into men and had lost their

clumsy fledgeling gait and manner. Good human material
if properly handled. He noticed that two soldiers had put
their weapons down on the floorboards of the vehicle. The
NCO in charge merely went on reading his paper. Very
slack!

La Roncière inquired:

"How do they get their supplies?"

"By air. The men, the equipment and even the basic rations are all flown in."

"Is this the only road into town?"

"Yes."

"Colonel," Kreis observed, "their set-up leaves them
wide open. All you need do is block the road and force
them back to the airfield. After which they can be
rounded up and crushed."

"You're right, Kreis. Five or six miles of road surrounded by savannah, the ideal ground for ambushes! One
could take cover anywhere behind those piles of yellow
earth. What are they, by the way?"

"Ant-hills," Pimuriaux explained. "They're as hard as
rock." He gave a somewhat forced laugh. "But, gentlemen,
I beseech you, don't fly off the handle. We have not yet
reached the point of fighting and I very much hope we'll be
able to avoid a show-down."

Fonts looked at Pimuriaux with interest. The fellow did
not inspire him with confidence; he was too fat, too excitable. Above all he looked ill at ease and was sweating profusely. Even the way he had met them at the airport was
strange. Pimuriaux had come puffing into the aircraft and
pounced on la Roncière. He spoke too loudly, like a bad
actor who cannot pitch his voice correctly. To the colonel's amazement he had started gabbling away.

"I'm so glad to see you again, my dear fellow. How's
your charming wife? In the best of health, I trust. You're
in luck: perfect weather for a safari. . . ."

La Roncière had been on the verge of retorting that he
could not see what his wife had to do with all this. He had
been divorced for ten years.

Fonts had given him a nudge and whispered:

"Keep your trap shut, Jean-Marie, there's something
funny going on."

Pimuriaux had hurried them down the steps and cata-
pulted them into his car. He went on talking more and
more loudly and did not begin to relax until the car was
on the road.

In an ostensibly detached tone Fonts remarked:

"I say, your reception parties out here are rather cursory. Colonel la Roncière promised us a band and a guard of honor. . . . I feel we've been diddled out of it!"

Pimuriaux did not know how to make up for this bad start. He was painfully aware of his "guests'" embarrassment which they tried more or less adroitly to conceal by asking questions that purported to be technical.

Eight days earlier things would not have happened like this. He resolved to be frank: one should always be frank, or at least appear to be, with soldiers.

"Gentlemen, I'm going to put my cards on the table, what I have to say being strictly confidential, of course. Patrice Lumumba is dead, as you probably know."

"Dead?" la Roncière asked. "Or executed?"

"I don't know, but it wouldn't make any difference. As a result of this unfortunate accident, the whole world now has its eyes fixed on Katanga. The UN patrols have suddenly re-emerged from their barracks to which they were confined. An investigation commission is arriving at Leopoldville. Maley, the Secretary-General's representative, who has never had a soft spot for us, is doing all he can to aggravate the situation."

"What's the next move?"

"As usual, when things aren't going well in Katanga, the UN start talking about the mercenaries."

La Roncière looked astonished.

"But the UN have been talking about these mercenaries for months!"

Pimuraux produced a sheet of paper from his pocket and handed it to the colonel.

"Only this time they're doing more than talk. Here's the resolution which the Security Council passed last night in New York:

RESOLUTION ADOPTED BY THE SECURITY COUNCIL AT ITS 942ND SESSION

The Security Council,

Having considered the situation in the Congo,

Having heard with deep regret the announcement of the killing of the Congolese leaders, Mr. Patrice Lumumba, Mr. Maurice M'Polo and Mr. Joseph Okito,

Deeply concerned at the grave repercussions of

these crimes and the danger of widespread civil war and bloodshed in the Congo and the threat to international peace and security,

1. Urges that the United Nations take immediately all appropriate measures to prevent the occurrence of civil war in the Congo, including arrangements for cease fires, the halting of all military operations, the prevention of clashes and the use of force, if necessary, in the last resort;

2. Urges that measures be taken for the immediate withdrawal and evacuation from the Congo of all Belgian and other foreign military and paramilitary personnel and political advisers not under United Nations command, and mercenaries;

3. Calls upon all States to take immediate and energetic measures to prevent the departure of such personnel for the Congo from their territories and for the denial of transit and other facilities to them. . . .

After reading it, la Roncière handed the paper to Fonts who whistled through his teeth:

"In other words, we've come at the worst possible moment!"

"It does look like it," Pimuriaux agreed. "It would be disastrous if the news of your arrival leaked out today, firstly for the President and secondly for me, because this resolution concerns me as well. Hence this cursory reception, which I'm afraid will not go unnoticed. There were a couple of journalists on the runway. . . . Luckily they're both from E'ville and we can handle them. But the others, the special agency and newspaper correspondents who are attracted by Lumumba's corpse, will be arriving in hordes. . . ."

"You've no means of keeping a check on the journalists?" the colonel asked.

"That's easier said than done, my dear fellow. What about you yourself in Paris? Incidentally, let me tell you, your press conference caused quite a stir. Maley immediately rang up the President to ask if it was true he had engaged you. Naturally the President denied it categorically. You put us in a difficult position, all the same!"

La Roncière had turned pale. That press conference kept being rammed down his throat! In his stiffest manner he replied:

"If you consider our presence undesirable after sending for us, we can go back at once!"

"Come now, Colonel, keep calm. After all the situation isn't as tragic as it may look. The first part of our plan is already achieved: I've just been appointed Secretary-General to the Presidency, which means I hold the strings. President Kimjanga is still extremely well disposed towards you. In fact he wants to see you at once. We're going straight to him. I merely wanted to remind you that we have to be extremely prudent."

Kreis had not listened to a word of this conversation. He sat gazing at the town which the car had just entered along the Avenue de Saio.

Behind some little bungalows surrounded by blue jacarandas which reminded him of the flamboyants in Indo-China, he saw a towering chimney-stack of blackened bricks. A cloud of smoke rose straight into the bright blue sky. Close by stood a huge slag heap.

He turned round to Pimuriaux.

"What's that contraption?"

Only too glad to change the subject, Pimuriaux became extremely long-winded and eager to please.

"That's the Union Minière, the chimney of the Lubumbashi copper works. That chimney is the very symbol of Katanga. Do you know what they say? When the Lubumbashi chimney is extinguished, there'll be no more Katanga. But, as you see, it's still smoking away. The blacks have a similar proverb: 'When Libimbashi broken, Katanga done for.' You see, the Congolese aren't able to pronounce the sound *u*, so the *U*N become the *I*N."

He then gave a hearty guffaw but la Roncière did not even smile.

The car had entered a broad thoroughfare, the Avenue de l'Etoile, flanked by four- or five-story blocks of flats. Under their arcaded galleries were shops. The town seemed to be well run: at every crossroads policemen in white gloves directed the traffic. Some of the café terraces overflowed into the road.

At eleven in the morning they were already full of Irish or Swedish soldiers drinking beer or day-dreaming as they watched pretty fair-haired girls in light dresses or skin-tight trousers walk by. But the girls pretended not to notice them.

"Don't those chaps ever do anything?" Fonts asked. "The girls aren't too bad!"

Primuriaux preened himself as though the compliment was addressed to him.

"Life's not dull in Elizabethville, you know. We often

have cocktail parties, dances . . . and there's also the swimming-pool. In Katanga law and order reign, the law and order which you have come to defend, gentlemen."

"I've never defended law and order," Fonts reflected.

"Nothing in common with what's happening in the rest of the Congo, where they're raping, killing, committing atrocities."

"There don't seem to be many Negroes about," Fonts observed.

"Out here, my dear Monsieur Fonts—that's your name, I believe—we call them blacks or natives. . . ."

"Then you're not very up to date. Throughout Africa the Negro's all you hear about these days, Negro civilization, Negro rhythms, Negro art. . . ."

"Well, these Negroes, as you call them, in order to be up to date, live in African cities which, moreover, are extremely well laid out and planned. These people, as you must know since you seem to be familiar with Africa, like to keep to themselves. There's the Hotel Leopold II where you'll be staying tonight: it's the best in town. They have a French chef. Look, over there to the left is the Mitsouko, a little night-club which isn't at all bad. I must ask you, for the time being, not to show your faces there. The owner prides himself on being a journalist and the Mitsouko is full of UN officers."

At the end of the Avenue de l'Etoile the car stopped at some traffic lights.

"On the left," Pimuriaux went on, "that long yellow two-story building is the Union Minière head office."

He leaned towards the colonel to make him realize that he alone was concerned.

"You'll be meeting the director, my great friend Monsieur Van der Weyck, at a dinner I'm giving for you this evening. He sees eye to eye with us."

"Tell me," said la Roncière, "for such a powerful firm, which can do more or less what it likes in this country, it seems to have singularly modest premises!"

"We Belgians in Katanga are serious-minded people. We don't try to play to the gallery. Not like those fellows in Leo, who build skyscrapers with our money! The directors of the Union Minière fulfill their mission here conscientiously; they do a proper job without trying to throw dust into people's eyes. They have made the country what it is today. The Director-General, Monsieur Van der Weyck, is in his office by six o'clock every morning . . . and often on Sunday as well."

"In other words, the Union Minière is God the Father!"

"You've never spoken a truer word, Colonel! In E'ville, who provides the running water? The Union Minière! Who maintains the roads and railways? The Union Minière! Who builds the cities? The Union Minière, as usual!"

The Baluba chauffeur, delighted to take part in the conversation, spluttered:

"Mignon Minière, he very good!"

"You see! Look, let me tell you a story. One day a school inspector asked a little black boy: 'Whom do you obey?' 'The master,' he replied. 'And your master?' 'The Head.' 'And the Head?' 'The Governor.' 'And the Governor?' 'The King.' 'Very good, and the King?' 'The Mignon Minière. . . .' Well, here we are."

The car turned to the right and stopped at a gate. A dozen Africans and Europeans were arguing outside, showing their papers to a harassed sentry who kept repeating: "No can do . . . no can do. . . ."

"Look, gentlemen," observed Pimuriaux, who had recovered all his dignity as Secretary-General, "it's like that all day long. The President is a real father to his people. . . . But, alas, he has to do everything himself . . . it's utter hell!"

The gate opened and the car drove up a ramp. The Presidency, formerly Government House, backed by a large garden surrounded by walls, was also a modest one-story building with an arcaded gallery.

The front door was guarded by two sentries in drill battle-dress, each armed with a Fal automatic rifle.

The two soldiers snapped to attention and presented arms, their rifles held flat in the British manner.

La Roncière saw that they were well turned out, which made a pleasant change after the trigger-happy members of the Force Publique he had seen during the stop at Leopoldville.

About two dozen people were waiting in the lobby, which was adorned with fading portraits of the former Belgian governors of Katanga. There were businessmen with briefcases crammed with papers on which they kept nervously drumming, and a few young Africans in coats and stiff collars, students who had finished their spell in Belgium and had come to ask for a job worthy of their newly acquired wisdom. In a corner, slumped in an armchair, sat an elderly Negro with white hair.

Pimuriaux rushed up to him.

"How are you, Chief? You've come to see the President? He knows you're here, I hope?"

The chief wore a crumpled, old-fashioned European suit with a hole in one elbow. The lapels of the jacket were speckled with grease stains. He had no tie and his scrawny neck emerged incongruously from a striped cotton shirt. On his knees he carefully cradled a filthy pith helmet adorned with cock-feathers.

The old man embarked with Pimuriaux on a tortuous palaver. Fonts, as inquisitive as ever, pricked up his ears. It was all about a woman, some goats and cases of beer, a malevolent witch-doctor and a great deal of money spent.

"He's one of our big hereditary chiefs from the north," Pimuriaux explained. "As you may know, we've had some trouble with the Balubas. This chief, a Baluba himself, joined forces with us. His support has been invaluable. He has five hundred warriors and ten rifles."

"What does he want?" Fonts inquired.

"Justice to be done. One of his relatives married last year. He paid the agreed price: four goats and five cases of beer. But since his wife hasn't had a child he wants to divorce her. His parents-in-law have died in the meantime. Well, the old boy agrees to return the goats but not the beer because it has all been drunk. The witch-doctor also sold him a potion which didn't work. It's all rather complicated."

"And to settle this silly business," la Roncière asked, "for the sake of five cases of beer and a potion which gave his nephew a stomach-ache, this chief demands to see the President . . . just when the whole Afro-Asian camp, the UN and the Americans are after his hide?"

"You'll understand later on: part of the President's great strength, besides his Western qualities as a statesman, derives from the support he receives from his hereditary chiefs. Because he neglected this support, Lumumba died, in spite of being backed by the Russians, the Chinese, the Ghanaians, the Guineans, the Indians and all the rest of them."

Pimuriaux opened a glazed door and stepped into a huge office. A smell of rice-powder and sweat made him wrinkle his nose. Two women, a blonde and a brunette, sat hammering away at their typewriters. Stacks of paper were piled high on their desks and the remains of a ham sandwich lay on a plate.

The two women, pretending not to notice Pimuriaux, went on tapping as attentively as ever on their keyboards.

He paused for a moment, gave a little cough, then turned to the brunette.

"Good morning, Madame Bruycker, would you please tell the President I'm here?"

The brunette typed out another paragraph, then raised her pointed nose. Her greasy hair was bedraggled and her dress had semi-circular stains under the armpits.

Germaine Bruycker was an exceptionally faithful and loyal secretary. She regarded President Kimjanga as a god and devoted her life to serving him. It was said that, to increase her hold over him, she organized exclusive orgies for him.

Her inside knowledge afforded her considerable influence. She was said to be able to make and break ministers and ruin public careers. She had a difficult character, with unpredictable moods, and was animated by a dual Belgian and Katangese chauvinism. She loved flags and parades and was on the best of terms with that lout Major Van Beulans. Very cleverly Van Beulans pretended to believe that her close relationship with the head of the Katangese state had no other aim than service to her country.

But Pimuriaux knew this old bitch delighted in it and that one had to be careful of rousing her morbid jealousy. Patient and sly, she was capable of any kind of underhand scheming and the Secretary-General was forced to admit, somewhat late in the day, that he had made a great mistake in not making an ally of her. He would have liked to ask her home to dinner but Monette had firmly refused.

"No, my dear. It's out of the question. Have you no consideration for me? Germaine Bruycker's just an old tart. Take her to the Mitsouko if it's necessary for your career: she'd be more at home there than in a decent woman's house."

"The President certainly won't be able to see you this morning," Germaine decided. "He's in conference with Major Van Beulans. It's important. After that he has several other appointments."

Realizing that fulsomeness would be of no avail, Pimuriaux assumed his most official manner.

"Dear madam, I have with me three people whom the President is expecting. It's extremely urgent. . . . The future of Katanga depends upon it."

"What is it?" Germaine inquired, without lifting her nose.

"If the President decides to discuss it with you, he will tell you himself."

Sensing there was a secret from which she was being excluded, Germaine shriveled up like an enraged octopus.

"We'll see. . . . But I happen to know that Major Van Beulans will be some time with the President. I'll let you know if the President thinks he'll still be able to see you and your three birds."

She resumed her typing energetically to make it quite clear to "Monsieur le Secrétaire-Général" that she had no time to spare for such an insignificant person.

Pimuriaux went out.

"A runt of a man," she said through clenched teeth, "a shady little lawyer who works for whoever pays him and for anyone else who might pay him later on."

"What about his wife?" said the blonde. "Do you know her? I saw her the other day at the hairdresser's. . . ."

"That will do," Germaine interjected. "We've got better things to do than sit here and chatter. How far have you got with that report on the pacification of the Balubas? Everything must be ready by lunch-time. I promised the major who has to take it to Consul Ryckers."

Germaine claimed for herself the monopoly of making mischievous remarks. All she demanded from others was to agree with her.

"The President will see you right away," Pimuriaux informed la Roncière.

A door opened behind them. There was a slight stir among those who were waiting and a big heavily built man with a red face, blue eyes and gray close-cropped hair came out of the presidential office. He wore a Belgian Army uniform, with belt and shoulder-strap. A heavy revolver was slung on his hip and his collar was adorned with the red insignia of a staff officer.

Pimuriaux rose from his seat and went up to him.

"Good morning, Major."

"Well, if it isn't Pimuriaux!"

The major gave a great guffaw.

"But, of course, you're now Secretary-General, aren't you? You're going to see the boss . . . with these three gentlemen . . . I understand he's expecting you."

Pimuriaux stammered with embarrassment:

"They're friends of mine who are passing through. They've come to see the President about some business matter. . . ."

Van Beulans decided not to leave; he smelled something fishy. Who could these "friends" of Pimuriaux's be? In la Roncière and Kreis he had immediately recognized regular soldiers, by the upright bearing peculiar to anyone who has worn uniform for any length of time. These two, especially the older man with the lean face and graying hair, did not look as though they would be friends of such a ludicrous figure as Pimuriaux. It was only because of these troubled times that this third-rate little meddler had been able to assume a semblance of importance. But everything would fall back into its proper place in due course.

Van Beulans could not wait any longer. He took his leave.

"Good-bye, gentlemen. If you're going to be in E'ville any length of time, do drop into my office, I'd be delighted to have a chat with you."

"Big game-hunting. . . ." Pimuriaux began.

"Well, I also hunt . . . and I think I know as much about it as our worthy Pimuriaux. You remember, Pimuriaux, don't you . . . that cow you mistook for a buffalo? Luckily you missed!"

When he had gone, la Roncière asked:

"Who's that fellow?"

"An idiot, Colonel, but very dangerous for our plans: Major Van Beulans, Chief of Staff of the Katangese Army. He's one of the people who helped the President to power in July. For several months he was in complete control. But he's in the process of being discredited: too flashy by half. And then he's committed any amount of blunders. Flemish heavy-handedness, you know!"

With a self-satisfied little laugh he went on:

"I can claim without bragging that I've put paid to him. He won't be hanging about Katanga much longer. You'll be replacing him, my dear fellow. And so much the better, I must say."

Germaine appeared through the glazed door with a sheet of paper in her hand.

"Would you please come in, the President will see you now."

Kimjanga was a tall, slightly corpulent man of thirty-five with a youthful face and the blackest of black skins. His deep voice had a solemn bell-like tone. He wore a well-cut dark suit, a white shirt, a spotted tie and a large diamond on his finger.

He had a child-like smile, but this smile, one could see, was assumed. He rose from his desk to greet his visitors and shook hands with them. Pimuriaux forthwith started bowing and scraping.

"Gentlemen," said the President, "I'm glad to welcome

you to Katanga, the land of law and order and liberty, and I thank you for coming here to help us save those Western values."

"He's going it a bit," Fonts said to himself, "but that's the style of the new Africa! It's amazing how much the West is being saved this year in every swamp and every savannah! Kimjanga is as sly as a peasant, and peasants all over the world are alike. He's got some old nag to sell us and is going to prove it's a thoroughbred."

La Roncière was waiting, on the defensive, watching the President's eyes which alternately narrowed, giving him a sharp expression, or opened wide, making him look as innocent as a child. He was young, of course, young enough to have audacity, a liking for new and original solutions, but also to be self-satisfied and open to influence.

The President turned to another black who was standing at the end of the room. He was extremely well dressed and wore sunglasses although it was dark inside. His close-cropped hair showed signs of incipient baldness and his fine features were frozen in a sort of grimace which was sulky and at the same time scornful.

"This fellow," Fonts decided, "is probably an aristocrat, whereas the President looks more like a cattle merchant who has done a good deal. . . . The one settles his problems by subtlety and subterfuge, the other by brutality . . . without hesitating to resort to poison and the knife. . . ."

Hesitating occasionally at the choice of a verb or adjective, all smiles and amiability, the President sang the praises of Monsieur Bongo, the Vice-President of the Government and Minister of the Interior.

"You'll often have occasion to work with him and there's no doubt in my mind that his collaboration will be fruitful!"

Bongo, impassive and expressionless as ever, never took his eyes off the three mercenaries. They would be "his whites." His ancestor, the great M'Siri, who had arrived with a few trading muskets from far-off Tanganyika, had carved out a kingdom as big as England. He had had up to ten thousand warriors under his orders, three thousand of whom were armed with rifles. He too had "his whites" who remained alive only because he allowed them to do so. Two of them, both Arabs, were his secretaries; a lovely Portuguese half-caste girl, Maria de Fonseca, was his concubine; and the rest of them were harmless missionaries.

Anyone else who ventured into his kingdom quickly realized, after witnessing an execution, that it was best to hurry out again. The victim was buried alive and left to die of hunger. Those who insisted on remaining simply disappeared.

Bongo summed up the three men at a glance: two of them were certainly soldiers, but a type which was fairly new to him. The colonel had something cat-like in his bearing. It's the panther whose hackles rise that retreats. When you think he has fled, that's when he attacks. The Frenchman was not like those swaggering overfed Belgian soldiers. He knew how to kill and fight. It was said he had a secret method of loosening tongues; he, Bongo, likewise had a secret method.

The lieutenant, the big fair-haired man, also knew how to kill, but like a charging buffalo which nothing can stop. Bongo had never seen eyes that were so pale and unblinking.

The third, the little dark man who could not keep still, disturbed him because he did not know in which pigeon-hole to place him.

Fonts had a sort of gift which enabled him to discern in primitives the instincts by which they were impelled— hatred, violence, friendship, greed—even before these instincts manifested themselves in gesture or speech.

He could sense Bongo's distrust and cruelty. Had his features altered at all when he killed Lumumba?—for he was now sure he had killed him with his own hands. No, his thick lips had perhaps curled back from his sparkling teeth, while a savage joy seared his guts.

Afterwards he must have made love with a woman whom one of his bodyguard had gone to fetch. Then he had dismissed her in order to start drinking again and the beer must have trickled down the front of his coat.

"Gentlemen," said the President, "we're going to do a good job together. Our cause is just. We are pacifists. We don't wish anyone harm. All we ask is the right to preserve our liberty and thus the welfare of the people of Katanga."

He raised his hands heavenwards like a priest in the course of his sermon.

"All I ask is to come to an understanding with Leopoldville but, with the exception of Colonel Mobutu, the people of Leo are all incapable and worthless. They're a lot of petty little bureaucrats, that's all. I'm a rich man, you know. I own farms, hotels, cows. I should be far happier if I were not in power. The Leopoldville ministers hang on to their positions because they want to drive around in big cars, drink whisky and sleep with . . ."

President Kimjanga stopped just in time. He was about to say: "With white women."

La Roncière felt that he ought to embark on his own speech.

"Monsieur le Président," he began, "we have come here to help you because we are convinced . . ."

The door opened. It was Germaine.

"I must remind you, Monsieur le Président, you have a luncheon appointment for half past twelve at the Chamber of Commerce. Which suit should I put out for you?"

The President lost his patience.

"It doesn't matter which: the navy blue. No, the gray striped."

"With a blue tie?"

"I don't care. No, a green one."

Germaine slammed the door shut after her.

La Roncière went on with his discourse:

"As I was saying, we're convinced of the justice of your cause. Today the world is dominated by the great powers who are trying to impose their law on the smaller nations. The Communists and Capitalists are trying to share the world between themselves. My comrades and I . . ."

Germaine reappeared; behind her were two black officers whom she was trying in vain to hold back.

Fonts chuckled with joy while la Roncière began to lose patience.

"Monsieur le Président . . ." Germaine and the first lieutenant began in unison.

They stopped short. The secretary assumed a prim expression but the two officers burst out laughing.

"Monsieur le Président," said Germaine, "your gray suit hasn't come back from the cleaners. Furthermore Major Van Beulans has just rung up: he urgently wants the decision he submitted for your signature about the Baluba prisoners. . . ."

"Van Beulans is becoming a nuisance," Bongo coldly observed. "It's not up to him to lay down the law here. Who does he think he is? Can't you see the President is busy?"

Stupefied, Germaine retreated towards the door.

The President called her back.

"Germaine, ask them to bring us some champagne, some Mumm Red Label."

She went out, assuming the air of an offended queen.

The taller of the two lieutenants went up to the President, shook him firmly by the hand and embarked on a voluble speech in Swahili.

"If this goes on," Fonts reflected, "he's going to get even more familiar."

The lieutenant continued his speech in French.

"This man," he said, indicating the other lieutenant who was idly kicking his heels, "is my friend, Lieutenant Bompaka. He passed out of Arlon School at the same time as I did. As he's a cousin of Tshikasa who married the wife of Kalato, we both thought we ought to come and see you. At headquarters there's an idiotic Belgian colonel who wants to send us away to fight the Balubas. Well, since we've just left Arlon School and are fully trained and know how to fight, it would be silly for us to get killed. We want to stay on in Elizabethville."

Pimuriaux had noticed the surprise, then the exasperation of the French colonel. He rose to his feet.

"Monsieur le Président, I see you're very busy; perhaps we could come back tomorrow morning."

"No, no, not at all. What about the champagne?"

Then, realizing that the two Katangese officers were on the point of sitting down, he gave them a flashing smile and ushered them towards the door.

"We'll see about it in the morning. . . ."

A servant in a white coat eventually appeared carrying the wine and some glasses on a tray.

The President insisted on uncorking the bottle himself. He raised his glass.

"Gentlemen, I drink a toast to the health of General de Gaulle, the great friend of Africa, who has sent you here to defend a small nation's right to independence."

Kreis, wide-eyed, glanced at la Roncière. The colonel hesitated no more than a second, then in his turn raised his glass and drank.

"Here in Katanga," Kimjanga went on, "we consider General de Gaulle one of the greatest statesmen in the West. He has granted independence to his African colonies and will soon put an end to the war in Algeria. He's a really great man," he concluded, politely raising his hand to his mouth as he belched.

"Algeria is a complicated problem," la Roncière began.

But Fonts interrupted him. He took another glass of champagne.

"Let us drink," he said, "to the two great statesmen whom we have the honor to serve: yourself, Monsieur le

Président"—he bowed toward Kimjanga—"and of course General de Gaulle."

"I like the French," Bongo declared. "They're not like the Belgians; the Belgians are racialists."

Then he sank back in his armchair.

"Racialists?" Fonts asked.

"Racialists. Those people haven't understood that Katanga is no longer a colony. They still want to behave like masters."

"Monsieur le Ministre," Pimuriaux cautiously ventured, "there are all sorts of Belgians, colonialists, of course, but also Liberals, whose one desire is to help you sincerely."

Bongo stuck to his idea.

"And also a lot of Communists. Take Spaak and the Socialists, for instance, they're Communists. Here in the Congo they wanted to destroy the traditional chieftainships. They thought of withdrawing authority from those who are naturally entitled to it, the chiefs, and hand it over to little clerks and civil servants. . . ."

"Like Lumumba," said Fonts.

Bongo thumped the table with his fist.

"That cur! Yet I warned him. . . ."

He gave an icy laugh, suddenly stopped, then went on less violently.

"I hate the Belgians because they have done us harm. At this very moment Brussels is making approaches to Leopoldville after giving us all sorts of promises. The Belgians have no sense of honor."

He took a gulp of champagne.

"You know they murdered my grandfather M'Siri, and my father died in their prisons."

Deeply embarrassed, Pimuriaux gazed attentively at a stain on the ceiling.

The President gave a loud guffaw.

"That's true," he said. "The Belgians have often played dirty tricks on us, but after all there are good Belgians and bad ones!"

For several minutes Fonts had been looking with amusement at a portrait hanging above the desk. The President noticed this.

"You see," he said with sudden vehemence, "that's the portrait of King Baudouin who had his sword stolen at Leopoldville. I wanted to have it taken down but Major Van Beulans said it would annoy the Belgians."

"Van Beulans is a racialist," Bongo began.

The President nodded his handsome head.

"It's true he's sometimes exasperating with all that heel-clicking. And then he carries a horsewhip. It reminds one of the lash. For the last few days, mind you, he's stopped carrying it. But I think that at heart he likes us; he was useful to us in the period of transition. . . ."

Not wishing to reveal his big guns, through an instinctive sense of distrust which in him took the place of caution, he stopped and turned to la Roncière.

"My dear Colonel, I've been very happy to meet you and your friends. After this long journey I imagine you would like to have a rest. I suggest you come and see me tomorrow at ten o'clock. We could get down to work. I'll leave you in the hands of our friend Pimuriaux who, I'm sure, will do all he can to make your stay as pleasant as possible. Needless to say, I'm at your disposal to give you anything you might need. All the same, be discreet and cautious. There's the UN, and the traitors who inform them. Good-bye, gentlemen."

Germaine poked her nose round the door.

"Monsieur le Président, your luncheon engagement!"

Holmer Van der Weyck, managing director of the Union Minière of Upper Katanga, had a heavy mustache and a lean brick-colored face. He smoked a pipe and apologized for this by negligently explaining that he had picked up this bad habit while serving as a squadron-leader in the RAF.

He spoke with a slight English accent, which he had kept since his Oxford days but, unlike some of his more uncouth fellow countrymen, he did not interlace his conversation with English words. He suffered, of course, as much as they did from being just "a nice little Belgian." But there was nothing in his manner to show this. His suits came from London, he played golf well, but was absent-minded at the bridge table and preferred beer to whisky.

He had a high forehead, graying hair, slender long-fingered hands. He was a good husband although he felt no more than a vague affection for his wife. Hortense Van der Weyck was a fat Brussels woman and by no means disagreeable. "We Belgians don't give ourselves airs," she would say somewhat too often for his liking. But she was the niece of one of the senior directors of the controlling company which supervised the governing board of the Union Minière. Fortunately Hortense did not come to Katanga very often, preferring to live in Belgium during the school year with her three children and spend the summer at Théoule, on the Côte d'Azur, where she owned a big villa.

Van der Weyck had arranged a select little dinner party. Only three people: Colonel la Roncière, Pimuriaux and himself. But Pimuriaux had advised him also to invite "that fellow" Fonts, the colonel's second-in-command.

The Secretary-General had added:

"I believe he's working as an observer for the Elysée. He even has a number of friends closely connected with the President of the Republic. The colonel told me something about it."

"This fellow Fonts—he's not really very fond of him," Van der Weyck had reflected while Pimuriaux was speaking to him on the telephone—also knew Africa well; he had even fulfilled certain diplomatic functions in Guinea.

Van der Weyck was both amused and intrigued by this unexpected character who disturbed the worthy Justin so deeply.

He ordered another place to be laid and regretted that darkness fell so early, which prevented him from going out for a round with Riverton. To anyone who voiced his surprise at seeing him so often in the company of the American Consul-General, he never failed to reply that they shared a passion for golf and that he was amused by his daughter Joan, that insolent and capricious red-head.

He clapped his hands to summon a servant and asked in Swahili for a Simba beer. Later on he would drink whisky or port. Lying back on a sofa, he kept relighting his pipe although it had not gone out, which he often did when he was deep in thought or day-dreaming. For the last two months Holmer Van der Weyck had been gently sinking into the calm waters of the dream world.

The people with whom he had to deal every day were dissolving into flimsy silhouettes blown about by the wind like clouds: Kimjanga, that artificially created President whose electoral campaign he had financed; cruel Bongo whom he had once got out of prison; that little puppet Pimuriaux whom he had used to get the French mercenaries out here; that idiot Major Van Beulans and that madman Patrice Lumumba who had tried to behave as though the Congo existed.

There would then appear a red patch which turned into a head of tawny hair, and very prudishly Holmer Van der Weyck would imagine that Joan Riverton was his daugh-

ter. She went golfing with him and at every hole sang a
little ditty that he had often heard as a child.

> Barbençon
> Mon mignon
> Le crispin
> Sur le pain
> Le bouvreuil
> Sur le seuil. . . .

He lit his pipe yet again and got up to have a shower.
His guests would soon be arriving.

Major Van Beulans had been unable to see Ryckers, the
Belgian Consul, until late in the evening, when the latter
was about to leave the office he used on the fifth floor of
the Société Générale. Ryckers, a small, placid man with
the artificial charm of a shop-walker, had at first tried to
appease the soldier's fury, but in vain.

"No, my dear Consul," the major kept saying, "we can't
yield an inch. The least concession would be taken for a
sign of weakness. I shall go on wearing uniform, and the
photograph of King Baudouin above his desk will continue
to remind the President that he wouldn't even exist if it
weren't for our king and his army."

"You must make allowances . . . spare certain people's
feelings. . . . It costs so little. . . ."

"And one fine day you find yourself booted out."

The major rose from his armchair.

"I don't know what it is . . . but there's something going
on at the Presidency. I've never seen Kimjanga so withdrawn, so evasive. . . ."

"He always has been."

"What's Pimuriaux up to?"

"Being very active so as to keep his head above water."

"Three Frenchmen arrived this morning and the President dropped everything to receive them together with that
blackguard Bongo. . . . When I think I might have had
that fellow's hide . . . for a hundred thousand francs. Pimuriaux was leading them around."

Ryckers pricked up his ears.

"Three Frenchmen?"

"Not the usual rabble we've seen passing through for
the last few months: adventurers of every sort, deserters
from the Legion. . . . No, these were substantial men, sure

of themselves . . . and the President was expecting them. . . ."

"Could you describe them?"

"I'm not a photographer. I made inquiries, they're staying at the Leo II. Two of them, I'd wager my right hand, are soldiers . . . or ex-soldiers. Their professions?"

Van Beulans gave a loud guffaw and took a piece of paper out of his pocket.

"Jean Dupont, engineer. . . . Thomas Marceau, foreman. . . . Charles Créash, technical assistant . . . all three working for the Pétro-Congo. . . . But Pimuriaux tells anyone who's willing to listen that they've come to hunt big game and discuss business with the President."

Ryckers, the Consular Agent of Belgium in Elizabethville—that was his "cover"—found that the major often misinterpreted the information he received: he saw a plot in everything. . . . But this time the particulars were disturbing. Ryckers was a man of little imagination but he was not lacking in memory or method. He opened his safe, extracted a file from it, and from the file a slip of paper. Attached to this slip was a photograph, a rather hazy one, cut out of a newspaper. He handed it to Van Beulans who studied it, pursing his lips.

"It bears some likeness to one of our three birds. Who is it?"

"Colonel Jean-Marie la Roncière, who commanded a parachute regiment in Algeria, one of France's leading specialists in psychological warfare. . . . Quite a number of discoveries have been attributed to him. . . .

"Two weeks ago he held a press conference in Paris at which he announced his departure for Katanga. It had a deplorable effect. We thought then that the operation was canceled for good. But are you sure he's our man?"

The major studied the photograph more closely.

"I'm not absolutely certain. Everyone looks alike in a newspaper photograph; everyone has the face of a murderer or a minister."

"Let's stroll round to the Leo II."

The old-fashioned but comfortable Hotel Leopold II was situated next to the Société Générale building, at the corner of the Avenue de l'Etoile and the Avenue du Kasai which had recently been re-christened the Avenue de l'Abbé Fulbert Youlou.

The furniture was of teak or mahogany. A few green plants made a vain attempt to brighten the dingy lobby. Low tables and old arm-chairs upholstered in black leather were arranged in front of the two pillars and at the foot of the staircase.

The major and Ryckers sat down behind one of the pillars close to the reception desk.

"Who'll be able to tell us?" Ryckers inquired as he lit a cigar.

"Albrecht, the Swiss hall-porter. He works for the UN but he knows that I know. So in order to keep out of trouble he gives me information as well. Germaine also rang me up."

"Ah!"

The waiter came to take their order.

"Tell the hall-porter I'd like to see him," said the major, "and bring us two beers . . . no, two whiskies. . . ."

Very formal in manner and rubbing his hands together like a parson, Albrecht appeared in his blue coat, its lapels adorned with two gold keys. He spoke in a low voice and the only features that moved in his pale waxy face were his lips.

"What can I do for you, Major?"

Van Beulans slapped his thigh.

"You old blackguard! You think you can get away with anything. You remember that spot of bother you had last year. . . . Luckily good old Van Beulans was there to help you."

"Sheer bloody-mindedness!"

"Anything new for me?"

"Just now, when they came to collect their keys, I heard the man with the German accent call the older one with gray hair 'Colonel.' The third, the little dark fellow, gave him a nudge, then he looked at me. Naturally I pretended I hadn't heard anything."

"Have you passed this on to Colonel Degger?"

"You know me!"

"Have you passed it on or haven't you?"

Albrecht raised his eyes to the ceiling as though to invoke a God in whom he had long since ceased to believe.

"Degger looked in just now. . . . He too had heard about their arrival. A Norwegian officer in his service happened to be at the airport. He noticed that three men whom Monsieur le Secrétaire-Général was meeting did not go through the customs or police formalities."

"What about their passports?"

"Brand new, all three of them . . . issued in Brussels on the same day by the French Consulate. . . . They're still in their pigeon-holes."

The major motioned him to disappear.

Ryckers had sunk back in his armchair. All that could be seen of him was his commonplace little head.

"Major," he suddenly declared, "this time it looks like serious business. If we don't counter-attack very soon, you may as well pack up and leave."

"You're joking. . . . Me, Major Van Beulans, who . . ."

"Are you going to the American Consul's cocktail party this evening?"

"Of course!"

"I'll see you there, then. Meanwhile I'll put a call through to Brussels. We must settle things with the President at once and, if necessary, demand that he sees us to-morrow."

Arnold Riverton tugged impatiently at his collar which was too tight for him. At E'ville he was putting on weight. Impossible to take any exercise in this damned country, apart from a few rounds of golf with old Van der Weyck. He was a bit of a snob, was Van der Weyck, but quite a good player, though easily put off his stroke and often absent-minded. At least he did not share the mania of his fellow-countrymen who kept trying to convince him of the stupidity of American policy.

Van der Weyck had apologized, saying he would not be able to come to the party. A pity! He lent this sort of gathering a little sparkle, and what fun it was to see all those Belgians bowing and scraping to him!

Arnold Riverton found it more and more difficult to put up with these cocktail parties at which he had to take care not to ruffle anyone's feathers, observe certain delicate social distinctions and, in spite of all his good resolutions, down a few glasses himself. A consul who does not drink is almost as suspect as a consul who drinks too much!

At the age of fifty Arnold Riverton was still a fine figure of a man; tall, slim, with a smooth face and graying hair, he had kept the athletic bearing of a former track champion. But he had to be careful: at E'ville one could not only lose one's waistline but also ruin one's career!

Before taking up his post he had been told by the head of the Africa Section:

"Arnold, you've made a fool of yourself, that's why you've been posted to my department. This may be your big chance. We're going to get busy in Katanga one of these days. If all goes well you'll have a legation. . . . If it doesn't work out you'll end up in an office in Washington. . . ."

Riverton had arrived four months earlier. Until then he had been Councilor in Djakarta and it was always with regret that he remembered the big Asiatic town and its smell compounded of vanilla and decay. At Djakarta, for the first time in his life, he had fallen in love like an adolescent, and with an adolescent's lack of caution. Sunnarti was unbelievably sweet and lovely; the skin on her lips had the firm texture of orange peel. One day the scandal had broken out and his wife Ethel had left him, making a great song and dance about his having preferred a "native girl" to her.

In this painful situation his daughter Joan had taken his side. He had been astounded by this. In his eyes all American women, from puberty to decrepitude, stood together against their menfolk. Yet Joan had abandoned the female clan and had followed him to Katanga. He was deeply grateful to her for this.

She was a damned pretty girl, was Joan, red-haired, with long legs, a freckled nose, blue-green eyes and a peculiar way of approaching people and things with the frankness of a boy . . . a somewhat badly brought up boy, moreover. . . .

Which made her gesture all the more incomprehensible. If she had been unattractive, he would have understood: it is easy for an unattractive and undesired girl to sacrifice herself to her father's career.

The consulate-general consisted of three long one-story buildings surrounding a lawn. To the right and left were the administrative offices. In the middle, the living quarters. The whole place had been whitewashed, but underneath the paint the leprous green of the old walls showed through.

The party was held in the big downstairs room. The buzz of conversation and tinkle of glasses which he could hear from the first floor reminded Riverton that he was on duty. He unbuttoned his collar, loosened his tie and slipped off his coat. If Ethel had been there he would not have dared to do this. She hated "sloppiness."

Riverton promised himself to drink no more than three dry martinis but as he made his way downstairs he already knew he would not keep his word.

A group of men in dark suits were gathered round Joan, who was dressed in gray to set off her flame-colored hair.

"What can she see in them?" the Consul-General wondered. "They all look alike and say the same things. The ones that aren't married want to marry her, and those that are still have hopes. . . ."

It was the fault of Allen, his assistant, whom she had rebuffed. He had spread the rumor that there was hot blood in the family.

Madame Van Beulans had just arrived, squeezed into a purple dress and wearing a hat like a lamp-shade. It was going to be hard going from the very start.

"I assure you, Joan," young Ravetot was earnestly saying—he was earnest about everything he said, everything he did, everything he hoped—"you ought to come with us. It will be a splendid safari. I was just saying to Dufermont: without Joan our expedition will be a washout!"

"It's true," Dufermont echoed.

His only purpose in life was to confirm what his friend said.

Since Ravetot was nevertheless one of the most presentable young men in E'ville, Joan had gone out with him several times. She had allowed him to kiss her, more out of kindness than from any feeling of attraction for him. Ravetot kissed reasonably well, but no more. It was insipid. When he had tried to go farther she had primly put him in his place. Since then he had fallen in love with her and was firmly resolved to marry her.

Three stout ladies bursting out of their flowered dresses—begonia, daisy and cornflower—sat drinking port, their little fingers extended.

Joan went over toward them, making her skirt whirl round her thighs, and, just for the fun of it, dropped them a deep curtsey, which left them flabbergasted.

The begonia seized a sandwich from a passing waiter and gobbled it down.

"That Riverton girl is a little slut . . ." she decided. "Always with an eye on the men. Fancy dressing like that. You watch, she'll end up by walking around stark naked!"

The daisy returned the ball.

"If her father doesn't marry her off quick he'll have a lot of trouble on his hands!"

But the cornflower could not hold out any longer and made a bee-line for the buffet.

The begonia went on feebly:

"Marry her off, but to whom? If they're all like her father in the family!"

She leaned forward.

"They've got ants in their pants. . . . Oh good evening, Consul. We were just saying how charming your daughter is!"

The cornflower came back with a plate of cakes in her hand.

"And so original!"

"What can she have done now?" Riverton wondered.

He caught sight of Major Van Beulans in civilian dress standing in one corner. The *miles belgicus gloriosus,* as Joan had called him, was deep in conversation with Ryckers, his consul, who was looking even more somber than usual.

Van Beulans kept glancing over his shoulder. Obviously he was anxious not to be overheard.

"Yet another open secret," Riverton reflected wearily, "or else some dirty trick they're preparing."

He took another martini and recovered his spirits.

"Well?" Ryckers asked the major.

"It wasn't easy. Luckily Germaine helped me. President Kimjanga will see us at nine o'clock tomorrow."

"Don't forget that we issue him with an ultimatum: it's Belgium or the French. And what's the UN attitude?"

"Through that old bungler Albrecht, I managed to put Colonel Degger wise. Albrecht told him la Roncière's true identity and gave him a few personal particulars . . . as much as I knew, anyway."

"I say, Pimuriaux hasn't turned up. He's probably with his mercenaries. He must be disappointed not being able to sport his brand-new title of Secretary-General at this party!"

"He's dining with our birds at the Union Minière, with the Managing Director."

"I beg your pardon?"

"Pimuriaux came to fetch them at the Leo II. Haven't you noticed, Van der Weyck isn't here either. . . . Yet he's very fond of Riverton . . . and also of his daughter. . . ."

"This business is getting more and more serious, old boy. Here's my wife. See you tomorrow. . . . Don't forget: if we fail, you pack your bags. . . ."

"Peter," said the fat lady in purple, "it's more than I can stand. Do you know what that Monette Pimuriaux has just said to me? Yes, she had the nerve to come alone. . . . That one had to keep up with the times . . . and that Katanga should get rid of its last traces of colonialism. Do you hear? Colonialism, after all we've done for them!

106

Look at Joan Riverton . . . a little bitch on heat. . . . And that husky voice she puts on when she talks to a man!"

Joan saw Jenny Ligget appear dressed once more in a horrible frock which did not succeed in spoiling her rather melancholy looks. Slacks suited her far better, the young American girl reflected. They accentuated her perfect figure. But she could not very well come to a cocktail party in slacks or let her thick black hair, which came down to her waist, hang free.

Joan went up to her and asked:

"How's the Ligget tribe?"

"All topsy-turvy, the kids, the garden, the husband, the dogs, the cats and the horses. Where's John Ligget?"

"He's not at the bar, so he can't have arrived."

Married to the British Consul and born in Rhodesia, Jenny lived outside Elizabethville in a villa surrounded by a big garden. She did not entertain much, read a great deal, loved music, flowers and horses.

Joan considered she had the charm of a "Southerner" or Creole, a graceful manner and a touch of melancholy, the melancholy of the condemned races, which is often accompanied by the mysterious gift of indolence.

She was her only friend; two or three times a week she went out riding with her and in her company recovered her schoolgirl spirits. Joan then dismissed from her mind all the men she had ever met; she could shed tears over a sunset or the death of a bird, then burst into fits of laughter; nothing ever surprised Jenny. Towards mankind in general she showed a tolerance which Joan on certain days suspected of being mere indifference.

She took Jenny by the arm and drew her aside.

"I'm bored," she said. "The men here this evening are even duller than usual . . . except, of course, your husband who never looks at me."

"He doesn't look at me either when he's drunk, which he is more and more frequently. . . ."

". . . And my father, but I can't talk to him, he's too strait-laced. How I wish he'd tell me about his affair with that pretty Indonesian girl. It cost him his wife and very nearly cost him his career. . . . I've found some photographs of her, I'll show you some day. The girl looks younger than myself . . . and—how can I put it?— extremely sexy. . . . It's hard to imagine one's father making love!"

"What about Maley?" Jenny asked.

"Maley's bearable when he's in form but he's got such a

107

damned difficult Irish character that most of the time you can't even approach him. He doesn't look at me either . . . and you know perfectly well why: he blushes when I mention your name . . . I feel he wants to give me a good spanking. As he's very badly brought up and utterly mad, he will do so one of these days! I've had a letter from Davis . . ."

"Davis?"

"That boy at the University with whom I . . ."

"Did you enjoy it?"

"No, but I had to go through with it. I didn't want to be held up to ridicule: a virgin in my third year, just imagine! . . . especially at Yale! His letter is a tissue of platitudes. Come on, let's go and bait Maley! When you're there he goes bright red in the face! Too late, my girl! Colonel Degger and Daddy Riverton have just joined him in a plenary session. All three of them have that irritating expression of men who believe they're doing something important! I've always dreamed of a man who would do something important but still look as though it amused him."

"Well?" Maley asked Degger. "Have you got any information on them?"

Degger had long, very fair hair and the manner of an elderly student. He exasperated Maley with his slow wit which was further accentuated by his hesitant speech:

"Er . . . er . . . sir . . . the most important of the three . . . er . . . appears to be a certain Lieutenant-Colonel la Roncière of the Paratroops and the Foreign Legion. . . . I went to see Musaille, the French Consul. He has a French Army List. Well, er . . . he has a very fine record, this fellow la Roncière, I might even say . . . er . . . an exceptional record. . . . Musaille will be here presently, you can ask him."

Maley switched easily from rage to hilarity but he could not be indifferent and he delighted in his contradictory nature. The son of a Sinn Feiner who had spent eight years in British gaols, he hated the English. But he always liked to have a few of them on hand, if only to remind them of the perfidy of their race and to tell them that the only great English writers were Irish. A good Catholic, he was only happy in the company of sinners and, though a woman-hater, was always falling in love. He was in love with Jenny, and his lively imagination suggested countless ways of conquering her which he would never put into practice.

The Belgians annoyed him with their ponderousness,

108

their self-satisfaction, their heartiness. He enjoyed the company of Paul Musaille, but since the Frenchman also had a bad temper they never stopped quarreling.

Furthermore, they were opponents in the party which backed the UN against the Katangese Government.

Maley tried to remember what stage he had reached in his relations with Musaille. Could he ask him quite openly what he thought of la Roncière?

A left-wing man and a liberal, Patrick Maley felt as soon as he arrived that the secession of Katanga had been provoked by the big Belgian and British economic interests which he abhorred. He was, moreover, convinced that this secession was harmful and prevented the creation of a proper Congolese State.

To him Katanga did not exist and had the semblance of a State only because all the power had remained in the hands of the Belgians. The Belgians were on the point of being driven out and now mercenaries of the most dangerous type were arriving: paratroops and legionaries from Algeria, connected with the extremist elements in that country.

"What do you think?" he asked Riverton.

The esteem he felt for the American had grown into friendship the day he had heard about the "blunder" he had committed.

"The arrival of these mercenaries is a flagrant violation of the latest UN resolution."

"What do you intend to do about it?"

"Protest officially in the name of the United States, as you will do in the name of the UN. Do you think it will be of any use?"

"No, none at all! As usual, Kimjanga will deny it and make promises that he won't keep. Twenty times over, since I've been out here, he has openly violated the written undertakings he has given. I'm building up a fat file against him. . . . The day when we've had enough, we'll be able to take action on a firm basis. This farce can't go on forever!"

"When are you seeing the President?"

"Tomorrow morning, and this time, on this specific question of the *mercenaries*, we'll be able to tackle him resolutely by waving the UN resolution in his face. Arnold Riverton, your harpy of a daughter is always making fun of me. You ought to teach her a good lesson!"

"Easier said than done!"

Patrick Maley got up quickly and left. With his black

109

hair falling over his forehead, his coat hanging open and a mischievous glint in his nut-brown eyes, he went over to Joan and Jenny:

"Jenny, one of these days I'm going to . . ."

"What, Patrick?"

"Nothing," he replied furiously.

A tree-trunk blazed in the big fireplace with its copper cowl. Silently a Baluba or Lunda or Bayeke servant—Holmer Van der Weyck no longer remembered which—in white trousers and a jacket buttoned up to the neck put a big silver tray with ice, sherry, whisky, a siphon and glasses down on a low table.

The firelight played on the boy's flat face, his thick lips and crinkly hair.

"He's a Bayeke," Van der Weyck reflected, "from the same tribe as His Excellency Bongo. But tribes no longer have any meaning. Slavery has made such a melting-pot of the various races!

"What makes a Baluba different from a Lunda, a Walloon from a Frenchman, a Fleming from a Dutchman? Nothing except that they believe in this difference. . . ."

He signaled for the lights to be put on, and the big room was suddenly all aglitter. On the wall hung the portraits of the two founders of the Union Minière: Jean Jadot, Governor of the Société Générale, and Sir Robert Williams, Chairman of Tanganyika Concessions Ltd.

"Those two didn't have any problems. They were convinced of the justice of their action when, from Brussels or London, they gave orders for whole populations to be displaced and subjected them to forced labor in order to build the railway or extract the copper. They went to church, kept a close watch on the education of their children, founded dynasties on the fragile basis (which they, however, considered everlasting) that Africa would never develop and that the world would continue to be run by bankers."

His guests arrived and Holmer Van der Weyck stepped forward to greet these mercenaries he had just engaged to defend Jadot and Sir Robert's tottering empire.

The managing director received them with the somewhat distant courtesy that he adopted towards people of a certain rank but who did not quite belong to his world.

"Rather like a general who's about to entrust you with a dirty job," la Roncière reflected. "Salan had the same expression when he summoned us to Combined Forces HQ at the time of the Battle of Algiers—cordial and slightly bored. . . ."

"This fellow looks like Dumont with his latest Elysée manner," Fonts thought. "Only Van der Weyck wasn't born like him in the gutter. Dumont, whatever he does, will always bear the mark."

Van der Weyck led them toward the fireplace.

"Welcome, gentlemen, to this house, one of the oldest in Elizabethville. It's called Tanganyika House."

Fonts pricked up his ears.

"I don't believe it! He's putting on an English accent! Dumont at least would never indulge in such fantasy!"

He strolled round, stopped in front of the big block of green malachite, the first block of copper ore to be extracted from the Etoile mine, glanced at Jean Jadot with his mustache, at Sir Robert with his butterfly collar, then sank into an armchair. With an exaggerated drawl he remarked:

"Very . . . very interesting house . . . really."

Van der Weyck frowned and peered more closely at this sharp-eyed little fellow who knew how to be insolent without going too far. Perhaps the moment had come to explain his English accent and recall the time when he was a squadron leader? But in front of these specialists in warfare he was liable to appear ridiculous. He desisted.

Towards Pimuriaux, Van der Weyck showed just the right amount of cordiality that was due to a subordinate.

"How's your wife, my dear Secretary-General? Your new duties are not too arduous, I hope? . . . A difficult job, but you're the man to do it, the right man. . . ."

"This fellow Fonts," he reflected, "is really impossible with that smile flickering in his eyes but all his other features motionless. . . . Just like his eldest son Edouard who was studying art in Paris, in other words doing nothing!"

It was a good meal but had nothing in common with the usual heavy business dinners which leave the guests bludgeoned: hors-d'œuvre of raw vegetables, chicken with mushroom, French cheeses and salad, fruit from Rhodesia . . . and, as the only wine, a vintage claret.

They discussed politics in an evasive manner so as not to offend anyone, and Africa, as they might have discussed it not in the heart of the continent itself but in a London or Paris drawing-room.

When coffee was served Van der Weyck felt it was time to get down to business.

"Gentlemen," he said, "I'm very glad to see you here. I should now like to talk to you about Katanga and the present situation."

"At last!" sighed la Roncière who had been bored by all these futile preliminaries.

"As you know, I represent a number of important concerns which are not all Belgian, but also Rhodesian, South African, English and French. These concerns must stand aloof—officially, that is—from all political action. In this house you are my personal guests, not those of the Union Minière. Tomorrow I shan't recognize you. Everyone will know, of course, that you dined here with me. . . . This is what I shall tell them: intrigued by your arrival, I asked my worthy friend Pimuriaux to bring you round here for a drink. In my position it's my privilege—and my duty—to be curious. Are we all agreed on that?"

Fonts and la Roncière acquiesced with a nod. Pimuriaux, disconcerted, hesitated. Should he agree? Of course . . . but he wished he could have manifested his reluctance. By adopting this line of action Van der Weyck made it quite clear that if things didn't work out properly—this was the expression he used when referring to enterprises doomed to failure—he would leave them in the lurch.

"Gentlemen," the managing director went on, "you have not come to Katanga to wage war. Colonel, if I asked Pimuriaux to contact you, it's precisely because you have done more than merely wage war. . . .

"I followed the events in Algeria with the greatest interest; especially those of May 13th which brought General de Gaulle to power. Among these events I was impressed by one incident in particular."

He stopped and motioned the butler to serve the liqueurs. The glasses clinked in the silence; the logs could be heard spitting in the fireplace.

Van der Weyck raised his glass of fine Napoleon brandy to them and, without touching it, put it down on the table.

"This incident was the fraternization in the Forum. It doesn't matter to me whether it was genuine or contrived. Personally, I'm inclined to the latter hypothesis. But this fraternization was admirably exploited: the whole world talked about it. At one moment it was possible to believe in a 'fraternal' solution to the Algerian problem. Translated into business jargon: a solution whereby the interests of France would be safeguarded.

"I wanted to get to know the men who promoted this movement and who knew how to make such good use of it.

112

You were one of them, Colonel la Roncière, and from that moment I began to take an interest in you. I thought at the time that you might render us great services in Katanga."

La Roncière interrupted him. His lean shrewd face was held slightly to one side.

"I'm not sure that I follow you."

Van der Weyck got up, went and warmed his hands in front of the fire and without turning round continued:

"Gentlemen, Katanga does not exist and this is unimportant. But we want people to believe it exists and this is important. . . . It's up to you to make them believe it by means of the methods you have already employed.

"I've approached you Frenchmen because Belgians are too conspicuous and also because it looks as if they're staying on here merely to defend a big mining company whose main office is in Brussels, 7, Rue de la Montagne du Parc. My fellow countrymen are often rather clumsy: you've seen how our soldiers swagger about in the corridors of the Presidency or in the streets.

"It's only too easy for the whole world to cry Colonialism or Neo-colonialism. General de Gaulle did a good job in Africa when he granted independence to all the French possessions. Soon he will grant it to Algeria. Then France will be completely clear. But not Belgium. . . .

"In Katanga you can take any action you consider necessary. Provided, of course, you don't offend local susceptibilities. You won't be grudged the necessary means, you'll have all the money you want. You won't be bothered by sentimental problems: the local settlers are not your compatriots. . . .

"What has prevented this country from lapsing into chaos like the rest of the Congo is solely the fact that the whites have stayed on. Now we need law and order so as to be able to work. But we also want the presence of the whites to be less conspicuous and to be accepted by the native population."

"Have you got a Forum at E'ville?" Fonts inquired.

"It's up to you to find one!"

"I think I understand," la Roncière slowly declared. "It's a question of giving the world this picture of Katanga: a country in which whites and blacks work together in a spirit of fraternity, hand in hand, with the same ideals in mind, and ready to die for those ideals."

"You're going even farther than I was, Colonel. In my mind there was no question of dying. But I think you're right. You're liable, on this last point, to have some difficulty in persuading my compatriots. . . ."

113

"This man is suffering from no longer belonging to a country whose people are prepared to die," Fonts reflected and for the first time he felt a vague affection for him. This did not prevent him from provoking him when, wishing to cut short this discussion, Van der Weyck asked:

"Do you play golf, Monsieur Fonts?"

"I'm not well born, you know. I play bowls."

In the car that took them back to the hotel Pimuriaux explained at great length that the managing director had given ample proof of his confidence by being so frank with them.

". . . I would say even cynical, but he's a sensitive creature, disconcerting at times, and perhaps, just to surprise you, he deliberately overdid the cynicism. . . ."

La Roncière interrupted him abruptly.

"No, Monsieur Pimuriaux, he didn't overdo it; he's exactly as I imagine those who have big interests to defend. He's a very worthy fellow. We had a few like him in Algeria and at one moment we thought . . ."

"What?"

"Of hanging them, Monsieur Pimuriaux, so as to make people really believe in that fraternization in the Forum. Only here, as Monsieur Van der Weyck pointed out, we shan't be bothered by sentimental problems. So we have no reason to make such a spectacular gesture!"

The Secretary-General started with alarm: he had suddenly come to realize that the colonel was a dangerous man. He was not only a mercenary who traded his life or his technique. To him money was only a secondary consideration. He was a monster of pride, a sort of mad scientist whom nothing would prevent from making use of the arms he had invented. His last laboratory had recently blown up; in Katanga he was being provided with another.

But, optimist by nature that he was, he reassured himself.

"I've drunk too much," he reflected. "The brandy was excellent . . . and when I drink too much I have an unfortunate tendency to dramatize. Perhaps la Roncière is only trying to impress me: soldiers are often showmen. They enjoy witty repartee. Monette's going to be in a bad mood because I didn't take her to the American Consul's cocktail party. . . . Women always place their little whims above political essentials!"

4. Gelinet's House

Kimjanga was suffering from migraine. He did not like getting up early and he had been obliged to come to his office at eight-thirty in the morning. With irritation he looked at Major Van Beulans sitting opposite him, red-faced and massive, squeezed into his uniform and wearing all his decorations. His belt creaked each time he moved. Prim as ever, Ryckers sat with his skinny buttocks resting on the very edge of his chair.

The President rubbed his eyes and forehead, then massaged his temples. He was trying to play for time . . . an old habit of his . . . but Van Beulans had cornered him and would not let him go.

"Monsieur le Président," he began, "I have come to say good-bye."

Kimjanga gave a start and was about to rejoice. But it was too good to be true, and what was too good to be true never happened so easily.

"Say good-bye, my dear Major? But whatever for? You're not leaving us?"

Ryckers interjected in a honeyed tone, as he examined his nails:

"Our friend Van Beulans feels that having lost your confidence it is his duty to resign. He has outlined his scruples to me at great length. The major is extremely sorry, of course, to have to leave this country for which he has worked with such devotion, but he feels that henceforth there's no place for him here. I must say I agree with his decision . . . that's to say I agree with it in my official capacity, as the local representative of Belgium."

This time the President was alarmed: he assumed an air of simplicity and smiled, as innocent as can be.

"Come, come, what's all this about? Why do you say the major has forfeited my trust?"

Ryckers gave a knowing smile.

"We heard yesterday that you had recruited a French colonel to command your army. Colonel la Roncière. He arrived at E'ville with a false passport under the name of Dupont"—he stifled a chuckle—"yes, Dupont, and accompanied by two other officers."

Van Beulans adopted the grand manner to which he was partial.

"I can but submit to your decision, Monsieur le Président, but I regard it as a sign of distrust towards me. My honor as a soldier obliges me to hand in my resignation."

"What luck it will be if he leaves without kicking up too much of a fuss!" Kimjanga reflected, but he assumed an air of consternation.

"My dear Van Beulans, you know how highly I myself and all my ministers regard you. Your departure would be a disaster for Katanga. But, of course, if your mind is made up . . ."

"I have to inform you," Van Beulans went on, "that I shan't be leaving alone. I discussed this problem last night with a number of my colleagues on the staff and in the training centers. They are resolved to follow me. I have good reason to think that the three hundred officers and NCOs serving with the troops will do likewise."

Van Beulans paused, stretched his legs and smoothed down his tunic with the flat of his hand.

"The trouble is, of course, that we'll probably have to call off the operations in the north against the rebel Balubas. I would not go so far as to say that you haven't any competent Katangese officers, since they were trained in our schools. But maybe they're lacking in experience!"

Kimjanga knew perfectly well that without European leadership his troops would disband forthwith. For the last five months they had been fighting an arduous campaign in the north against the Balubas supported by the Leopoldville Government. The Balubas were the cleverest but also the most cruel of all the Congolese, and there were a million of them! He tried to compose his thoughts. . . . But, at this unearthly hour of the morning, and with migraine, how difficult it was! The previous night had been exhausting! La Roncière might be requested to accelerate the arrival of the French officers. But he would need at least a month to take over. In a month the situation could become disastrous. Kimjanga pictured the

116

Baluba hordes descending on Elizabethville, the press of the entire world seizing upon the event and reporting a popular revolt against the régime. . . .

His grin broadened.

"Come now, gentlemen, let's not fly off the handle. I think there has been some misunderstanding. We've all known one another for a long time. You know that I'm always frank and open with you: it has never been my intention . . ."

"We've won," Ryckers reflected. "The fish is hooked but we mustn't let it get away: Pimuriaux can still throw it back."

"Monsieur le Président, I was in contact with Brussels last night. Your decision has caused great surprise at a high level and is interpreted as a hostile gesture not only towards Major Van Beulans"—he bowed towards the major—"but also towards the Belgian Government itself. As you are well aware, my friends and I have acquired strong support among political circles in Brussels, so strong that it was not unreasonable to hope for a *de facto* recognition of Katanga. Naturally our friends will now be somewhat hesitant . . ."

Kimjanga's headache grew worse and worse. As always happened when things were turning out badly, he felt an irresistible urge to slip away. He made a great effort.

"Gentlemen, gentlemen, please. As I was saying just now, it's a misunderstanding, just a little misunderstanding."

Once again, a broad grin. It was easier to grin than to talk, but he had to talk more and more, lull these two hostile men. . . . Later on he would examine the question more thoroughly. . . . Later on. . . .

"Katanga needs all the friends she has in the critical times through which she is passing. You and Major Van Beulans are two of her closest and most competent friends. The Frenchmen were recruited by Pimuriaux and you know his devotion to our cause. I thought he had spoken to you about it. According to him, they could be very useful. Well, you're the best judges of that."

"It's either la Roncière or myself," Van Beulans snapped.

"The fool!" Ryckers reflected. "We'd already won without any trouble, the President had saved face, and now this clumsy lout has to go and issue an ultimatum."

"Gentlemen," the President concluded wearily, "I think we'll be able to settle this little difference to the satisfaction of all concerned. Only, you see, I signed a little paper for those Frenchmen."

"A contract," Van Beulans thundered. "According to the agreement we made, those contracts are only valid if counter-

117

signed by me. You don't have to worry on that score, Monsieur le Président."

Van Beulans and Ryckers rose to their feet. They shook hands with the President with feigned cordiality.

As he reached the door, the major turned round.

"Monsieur le Président, I have to inform you that we're having a little difficulty over the delivery of the ammunition."

"What ammunition?"

"The grenades and rifle ammunition which we ought to send at once to Manono. As you probably know, your troops have more or less exhausted their supplies. If the Balubas attack they'll find themselves in a difficult position."

"Really? What should be done about it?"

"Three coach-loads have reached the frontier from Angola. But for some reason which escapes me they have been held up at Teixeira de Sousa. I'm going to see how I can settle this business."

Germaine poked her pointed nose into the room. Her hair was even more bedraggled than usual.

"Monsieur le Président . . . Maley, the UN delegate, has arrived for his appointment at ten o'clock."

"I'm not in. . . ."

Ryckers clicked his tongue.

"May I venture, Monsieur le Président, to give you a word of advice? See Maley, I don't think he's come to discuss anything very important . . . only this little business of the mercenaries. And there aren't any mercenaries any more!"

"That's true," Kimjanga bitterly observed, "there aren't any mercenaries any more. Only good Belgian officers who are ready to die for Katanga. Show Maley in, Germaine."

"You also have an appointment with those three gentlemen who came here yesterday with Pimuriaux," the secretary reminded him.

"Tell them I'll see them another day and ring up Monsieur le Secrétaire-Général"—he insisted on the title, which for the moment was the only display of independence in which he could indulge—"and say that I'm expecting him. . . . No, don't bother, he's bound to turn up presently."

As on the day before, a score of people were clustered round the gates of the Presidency, trying to get past the sentry. The same soldier, roaring with laughter, kept saying delightedly (for the game amused him):

"No can do."

"Listen," said a man of about fifty with the gentle intelligent face of a pastor or a priest, "I'm the rector of the University. The President has asked to see me. You must let me through, otherwise the President will be furious with you!"

"No can do," said the sentry. "You have no pass!"

"What do you mean, no pass? What do you think this is?"

From his inside pocket he produced a pink card which he waved in the sentry's face. The man gazed at it upside down for several moments.

"All right, you can come in."

The rector smiled amiably, went through the gate and carefully put away the precious document: a reduced-fare ticket on the Belgian railways that had been out of date for two years.

The rector was a man of high principles who had never told a lie or used false papers in his life. Africa had just taught him his first lesson in pragmatism.

Fonts and la Roncière arrived by taxi. La Roncière was carrying a heavy briefcase stuffed with documents. Fonts had his hands in his pockets. He raised his nose and sniffed the air in quest of a new smell: it was only the smell of any park in Europe: damp grass, moss, rotting wood.

La Roncière elbowed his way through the crowd and beckoned to the sentry.

"We have an appointment with the President at ten o'clock. My name is Dupont and this gentleman is Monsieur Thomas."

"No can do."

"Send for the guard commander."

The sentry guffawed with laughter.

"Guard commander he not here. Anyway you must all step back. It's forbidden to stand less than two yards from the gates."

The Belgians at once complied, grumbling under their breath. La Roncière maintained his composure and very stiffly, as though on parade, demanded:

"Where's the duty officer?"

The black in his astonishment adopted more or less a position of attention.

"Get a move on, man!"

"All right, boss!"

The sentry rushed off towards the house and came back a few minutes later with an African lieutenant.

"I have no instructions," said the lieutenant.

Fonts took a notebook out of his pocket, tore out a sheet and scribbled:

"Monsieur Pimuriaux's two French friends are waiting to

119

see Monsieur le Président with whom they have an appointment at ten o'clock this morning. Despite their efforts they have not been able to penetrate the fortress."

He handed the sheet of paper to the lieutenant.

"Here, Captain. Could you take this note to the President's secretary?"

Delighted at being addressed as "Captain," the lieutenant gave a broad grin and turned on his heels.

The sound of a horn made Fonts swing round. A long black car flying the blue-and-white UN pennant had just drawn up. At the wheel sat a magnificent Sikh in a turban, his curly black beard held in place by a thin silk thread.

"It's that dirty swine Maley again," said a Belgian. "I hope the President flings him out on his ear!"

"He knows what he's doing, the President," another grunted. "Maley won't last long here and we'll soon be rid of these UN vermin."

"Did you hear that?" Fonts asked la Roncière. "They don't seem to be very fond of these UN lads!"

"This is just the first stage. It's our job to urge them on to the second; then they'll begin to chuck stones. At the third, they'll open fire on them. It's just a question of conditioning them."

The gate was opened; the Sikh gently let in his clutch.

In the back sat a dark-haired man, with his legs crossed and his coat hanging open, tossing a silver dollar in his hand.

Fonts thought Maley bore a strong resemblance to his old pal Juan who had been with him in the Maquis. Juan had the same nervous tic, but his coin was a Spanish doubloon.

The young lieutenant came sauntering back to the gate at a leisurely pace.

"Well?" la Roncière asked.

"The President is too busy to see you this morning."

"It can't be true!"

Behind them the Belgians were sniggering.

"I tell you it's the President himself who arranged for us to see him this morning. Whom did you approach?"

"I gave the note to Madame Bruycker. She told me: 'No, the President is seeing some UN people at the moment.' "

By this time the Belgians were laughing out loud.

"You see," said one of them in a Brussels accent, "some people think they merely have to throw their weight around. . . ."

"And afterwards," said another, "they slink away with their tails between their legs."

Fonts took la Roncière by the arm.

120

"Look, Jean-Marie, there's something funny going on. Let's not stay here, we'll go back to the hotel and ring up Pimuriaux. We didn't come here to stand kicking our heels in front of these monkeys. How do you expect them to obey us later on?"

As he walked away Fonts trod on the foot of one of the Belgians and apologized politely.

"Terribly sorry, monsieur. . . ."

He trod on his other foot.

"I'm so clumsy!"

Outraged, the Belgian gazed at this dark little man with the dangerous smile and agile hand which was already drawn back to deliver a blow with the knuckles, gangster fashion.

"No harm done," he stammered.

In the stuffy telephone-box at the hotel Fonts was sweating profusely. The operator had already given him three wrong numbers. With a preoccupied air the hall-porter was consulting a directory by the door, his ears pricked. Fonts at last got Pimuriaux on the end of the line.

"Hello, my dear fellow," he asked, "how are you?"

"Lousy!"

"I beg your pardon?"

"There's something funny going on, that's what. My little pal and I went to the Presidency as arranged, but we weren't allowed in."

Pimuriaux burst out laughing.

"It's a misunderstanding, just a misunderstanding. The sentry couldn't have realized who you were."

"You can trust my little pal. He didn't take the sentry's word for it. . . . We sent in a note with the duty officer and it was the President's secretary who sent a message for us to come back another day."

"It was one of Germaine's tricks!"

"Listen, Pimuriaux, we're getting a bit fed up with all this nonsense. We land here on the sly, we hang around a gate with a lot of nitwits looking on, we get slanged by a lot of other louts and secretaries decide to cancel our appointment with the President. What sort of a set-up is this? I know we're in Africa, but you'd better not go too far!"

"Come, come, my dear fellow, calm down, do. I told you; it's a mistake. I'm going round to the Presidency at once. Wait for me at the Leo II with the colonel."

After a pause he added:

"I think it would be better if you stayed in your room. We

don't want you to be too much in the public eye. I'll be round in a few minutes."

Fonts hung up. He felt that Pimuriaux was a great deal more anxious than he wished to appear.

As he came out of the telephone-box he stopped in front of the hall-porter, looked at him in silence, then, in a confidential tone, inquired:

"I say, Dad, who are you working for?"

"I beg your pardon, sir? ..."

"It's dangerous, the work you're doing ... especially as you haven't mastered the technique ... I could see you from the telephone-box ... and when you haven't mastered the technique, you don't make old bones. You behave yourself! You've got a good job ... and you're not as young as you were!"

La Roncière was sitting in an armchair in the lobby, nervously puffing at his cigarette.

"Well?"

"Nothing. Just a lot of talk. Justin says it's a mistake, that he's hurrying off to the Presidency and will pick us up here. He asked us not to make ourselves too conspicuous."

"If this goes on, I'm clearing out of this bloody country!"

"Don't worry, it's only the Negro circus show. We'll go and have a quiet little game of poker in my room until our bird shows up. I'll send for Kreis. Does he play poker, that Hun of yours?"

And turning to the hall-porter, he added:

"Hey, Dad, have a bottle of champagne sent up to number 125!"

Pimuriaux arrived just as Kreis was uncorking the third bottle. He seized a glass and drained it in one gulp. The three men looked at him in silence.

"Well, come on, old man, let's have it," Fonts encouraged him. "What's all this nonsense about?"

Pimuriaux was white in the face. His hand shook as he put his glass down.

"I've just seen the President," he began. "A slight setback. This morning he was paid a visit by Van Beulans and Ryckers, who demanded your immediate departure. They threatened, if you took up your duties, to stop all Belgian aid to Katanga. It's sheer blackmail!"

"But damn it all, who runs the place?" la Roncière asked. "The President or Van Beulans?"

"Well ... the President, of course! But you see, at the moment he needs the Belgians. There's the question of arms supplies and training of his troops. Furthermore, the

122

Americans have heard about your arrival. I wonder how, incidentally. . . ."

"I'll give you three guesses," Fonts chipped in.

"This morning," Pimuriaux went on, "Maley went to the Presidency. He thumped the table a bit. The President was forced to swear that he didn't know anything about it. . . ."

When he was angry la Roncière spoke through his clenched teeth, almost inaudibly, and Pimuriaux had to listen carefully.

"As far as I can see, everyone's leaving us in the lurch. But Christ Almighty, what do you think you're up to? You come to Paris especially to recruit me and my friends, you give us fantastic contracts, and now you come and calmly announce there's nothing doing!" All of a sudden he started yelling, as though his voice had burst out of its prison. "Look here, old boy, do you take me for a bloody fool?"

"Colonel, please, don't shout so loud, they'll hear us!"

'I don't give a damn if they do!"

He snatched a sheet of paper out of his briefcase and waved it in Pimuriaux's face.

"Do you know what this is? It says here: Enlistment Contract, and at the bottom there's the President's signature. What do you make of that?"

Pimuriaux flapped his stumpy arms, raised his eyes to heaven and admitted pitifully:

"Van Beulans claims the contracts aren't valid because they're not countersigned by him."

Silence ensued. Pimuriaux had sat down in an armchair. His trousers clung to his thighs; he wriggled to loosen them.

With exaggerated care la Roncière grimly inserted a cigarette into his ivory cigarette-holder. Fonts was lost in contemplation of a fly buzzing round the room. The German, sitting stiffly in his chair, had his pale eyes fixed on him. Pimuriaux was frightened. He felt anything might happen: la Roncière merely had to make a gesture and this great lout would get up and hit him. Pimuriaux did not like fisticuffs. He had always lived in a world in which no one ever resorted to physical violence.

La Roncière took a deep puff at his cigarette. His voice was dangerously controlled.

"Look, Pimuriaux, we're not going to waste time arguing for hours. You've made a hash of things and you've been had for a sucker. I'm not the sort of puppet who can

123

be summoned to Elizabethville one day and then be told the day after that he's not wanted. The next plane for Brussels leaves tomorrow. You will kindly see that reservations are made for me and my two friends. As for our contracts, they're duly and properly signed by your President and I don't give a damn if Van Whatsisname has signed them or not. I shall institute legal proceedings and, if I didn't make good use of the press on one occasion, this time I think I'll put up a better show."

Pimuriaux was tempted to drop the whole business. His vanity alone saved him. If he allowed the three Frenchmen to leave, he would have to admit defeat and yield to Van Beulans and Ryckers. He would be dishonored and would have to leave Katanga: Monette would never forgive him for this humiliation, and Van der Weyck, on whom the ridicule would redound, would break him for ever.

With a sort of horror he pictured Antwerp, his native town, the crumbling old houses, the overcast sky full of soot and smoke. Opening a lawyer's office in Antwerp, trudging from door to door at the age of fifty, dealing with cases of dogs being run over, trespassing, and skivvies being wrongfully dismissed!

He made a final attempt to stop la Roncière.

"Colonel, I'm surprised to see a man like you surrendering so quickly. There's been a mishap, it's true. This situation is humiliating for you, I admit. But believe me, it's even more so for me. The position isn't hopeless, the President as good as said so; he would be most distressed if you left, but he had to take an immediate decision. Van der Weyck is backing us. He told you so quite clearly last night. Give me two weeks and I'm certain I'll be able to settle the matter."

La Roncière did not reply.

"Just two weeks, I beseech you."

"No."

The colonel rose to his feet to indicate that the interview was at an end.

"One moment," said Fonts.

La Roncière and Pimuriaux turned round.

Fonts drained the bottle of champagne into the glasses.

"At the price they sell it, it would be a shame to waste it."

He drew the curtains and looked out of the window.

"There's a storm brewing up, which makes everyone jittery."

124

"Yes," Pimuriaux foolishly agreed. "The clouds always appear about this time of day but an hour later it rains and everyone feels much better."

"I think we ought to grant our friend Pimuriaux the two weeks he requests. Nothing is ever finished in Africa. . . . Everything can start all over again . . . and in two weeks Pimuriaux will have time to get his little scheme under way once more."

La Roncière thumped the table, which made the glasses tinkle.

"I said . . ."

"Yes, you said . . ."

They glared at each other, then Fonts twirled round and gave a throaty chuckle.

"Can you see us arriving back in Paris? How they'll laugh, all those little pals of ours! They'll say it's another Munchausen exploit. I'm a sufficiently comic and unknown character for it not to make any difference. But for you, Jean-Marie, it's more serious! There's been enough muck-raising about your name already. I've still got friends; you no longer have the Army. Go on, give him a chance. What do you say, Kreis?"

Kreis shrugged his shoulders.

"I'm with the colonel. If he goes, I go; if he stays, I stay. But if I do go, I shall never join him again."

La Roncière acquiesced with a nod, then walked out without a word and went to his own room.

Flashes of lightning ripped across the gray sky. It started to rain, gently at first, then more and more violently. There was a sound of shutters banging to and fro.

Fonts slapped Pimuriaux on the back.

"There, you've got your two weeks . . . Monsieur le Secrétaire-Général. You can make use of the time to organize that safari about which there's been so much talk!"

Pimuriaux heaved a deep sigh.

"Thank you, Monsieur Fonts. . . . I think it would be advisable for you to move out of the hotel this evening. I'll come and fetch you and take you to a close friend of mine who supports our cause, Monsieur Gelinet, the owner of the brewery; he has a lovely villa with a swimming-pool and a good cellar . . . outside the town."

"And like that we'll be less conspicuous, eh? Is he married, this fellow Gelinet?"

"A charming wife . . . charming. . . . They even say . . ."

"Ssh! Careful now! There's Kreis looking interested. Come on, let's move out there at once!"

Gelinet's house was situated near the residential quarter of the Lido, beyond the golf course. It was a sort of big bungalow, with only one floor, surrounded like every other villa in Elizabethville with jacarandas and mango trees; it looked out on to a big *kikouyou* lawn sloping gently down to a sort of ravine with a stream flowing through it.

People in E'ville always lowered their voices when they mentioned Gelinet's house. So that when the news leaked out in the streets, bars and drawing-rooms, that the French mercenaries had taken refuge there, no one was surprised. Where else could they go except to Gelinet's house?

Bernard Decronelle, more self-important than ever, ran into Pérohade who, with his shirt outside his trousers, was prowling about outside the Hotel Leo II.

"They've left," Decronelle told him, feeling very pleased with himself.

Pérohade shrugged his shoulders.

"Do you think I didn't know? Old Gelinet rang me up just now to tell me they were staying with him, but to keep it dark."

"Do you know what it's all about?"

"Yes, vaguely. . . ."

"Well, my dear chap, I've got detailed information from someone who spent a long time with them the very evening they arrived. . . ."

"So what?"

"Only I'm not on very good terms with old Gelinet. I'll give you my information. In return, you tell me what's going on at Gelinet's. All right?"

"All right!"

"The men in question are Lieutenant-Colonel Jean-Marie la Roncière who used to command the Third Foreign Parachute Regiment, a lieutenant in that regiment called Kreis, of German origin, and a technical adviser, a civilian, called Thomas Fonts, an Intelligence expert."

"Is that all?"

"Monsieur Van der Weyck—but keep this under your hat—wanted to know what they were doing in Katanga, so insisted on Pimuriaux bringing them to see him. They had a drink together at Tanganyika House. He told me so himself. Do you want to know what else he said?

" 'These lads seemed quite interesting, but I have a feeling they've come to Katanga before the ground has been

126

adequately prepared . . . and without knowing exactly what they are going to do. The whole business seems rather slipshod.' "

"It certainly does," Pérohade agreed, slapping his thigh. "Your little UN pals don't want them here; the UN have just made an announcement: Pimuriaux has disappeared! I'll go round to Gelinet's this evening and see what I can pick up."

"But John Spencer, the Associated Press special correspondent, has just arrived. He wants some information at once."

"Then let him go out and get it, you're not his flunkey!"

"You could give me a ring when you've seen the mercenaries."

"Drop in at the Mitsouko tonight."

"At the Mitsouko?"

"Why not? . . . Ah yes, I see, the Managing Director of the Union Minière might hear about it. . . . But we have a very respectable crowd at the Mitsouko. UN people, the French Consul. . . . Even the American Consul's daughter has come there to dance with a couple of her boy-friends. Luckily no one knew who she was! There were a few chaps of the Gelinet type in the place, who aren't too fond of the Yanks—the sort Dorat calls the Old Guard of Katanga!"

"What time?" Decronclle asked reluctantly.

"Whenever you like. We close at two for people we know. After one o'clock come in by the back way. *Ciao!*"

Antoine Pérohade could not get away until late in the afternoon. He had to replenish his stock of whisky, by pouring contraband UN whisky into bottles bearing the customs stamp, see some receivers of stolen cigars and cigarettes and make some artificial lemon flavoring for the gin-fizzes and gimlets.

He also had to endure the jeremiads of Nathalie, who looked after the cash-desk, supervised the accounts and shared his bed. She was a good-natured and good-looking girl, a well-upholstered brunette, a hard worker with plenty of energy, and still quite young. But every so often she felt an urge to complain that Antoine did not have enough consideration for her, that's to say he refused for the time being to marry her.

Night was falling when he reached what Gelinet called "Gelinet House" in imitation of the Director of the Union Minière's "Tanganyika House."

On the veranda at the back he found the master of ceremonies sipping a whisky in his rocking-chair. Madame Gelinet, who was said to have the loveliest buttocks in E'ville and who, for that reason, was always in trousers, was reading a fashion magazine; Colonel la Roncière was gazing at the smoke rising from his cigarette into a sky that was turning purple. Kreis, sitting motionless in an armchair with his hands on his knees, was taking deep breaths of the cool air that came at night-fall. He looked like a good workman who, his day's labor over, was sitting on his doorstep while his wife was cooking dinner and the children were doing their homework.

But he had neither wife nor children and his job was waging war, dealing out death, and teaching others to deal it out with a minimum of losses.

Kreis once again felt the urge to march with men wearing the same uniform as himself. Tottering with fatigue, he would continue to advance, bent double under his kit-bag, his shoulder constricted by the strap of his rifle. But he would maintain intact inside himself a vast reserve of energy which at the moment of battle would make him nimble and agile, ready to run, scramble, fire and kill.

Kreis also felt the urge for a woman. He gazed at Madame Gelinet's rump which swelled when she held her hand out to the newcomer.

In the friendly tone of a publican addressing a group of regular customers, Antoine Pérohade greeted them:

"Good evening, gentlemen. How's life?"

"Who's this?" la Roncière asked.

Gelinet stopped rocking.

"Antoine's a journalist . . . at least that's what he says . . . but he's also a friend of mine, you can take my word for it."

"We can't see any journalists."

"He's an exception, Colonel. If we ask him not to blab, he won't blab . . . he's not like that little ass Decronelle. . . . Besides, he's a fellow countryman of yours . . . and I think he's got the same ideas as we have. Weren't you a paratrooper, Antoine?"

"Sergeant-major in the Second Battalion in Indo-China, dysentery, repatriated, demobbed. . . . Ran a pub in Brazzaville: there were too many pubs and not enough customers, so I crossed the river, but at Leo they take themselves very seriously, collars and ties . . . and poodle-faking. Not my line at all. . . . I heard things were different in E'ville.

. . . It's two years since I started the Mitsouko here and it's not doing so badly."

La Roncière was not entirely reassured.

"But how does journalism come into all this?"

Before Pérohade could reply, Gelinet chipped in, shaking his white mop which curled up at the back like a Hebrew prophet's.

"Antoine's a journalist from a sense of duty . . . he does it in order to serve our cause. . . . Whatever happens, there are bound to be journalists here. . . . So all the better they should be our own chaps. . . . What'll you have, Antoine, you old bugger? Whisky eh? . . . No, we'll drink some champagne. Because when we meet, it calls for a celebration. Madame Gelinet, go and tell the boy to bring us some champagne."

Without the slightest embarrassment Pérohade sat down in the chair that Hortense had just vacated. He knew that Gelinet was going to put on his act, as he always did in front of any new acquaintance. His experience of the world, his job, his Southern blood had taught him to be tolerant. He merely said to himself:

"One has to pay for one's drink one way or another. In a pub it often works out cheaper!"

"Good old Antoine!" Gelinet went on. "On July 7th, 1960, at the moment of independence, when the Army had mutinied in Massart Camp and the Balubas were marching on the town, all the civilians scampered over the border into Rhodesia . . . and quite a number of soldiers as well. Who stayed on? Major Van Beulans, who opened fire on the mob . . . and, among the civilians, Antoine who had got hold of an automatic rifle, and myself with my old elephant gun and a handful of chaps who would rather die than see their womenfolk raped. We held out on our own for three days, until the 11th, when the President came to power. Then we got rid of all those sods from Leopoldville. . . . We should have done so long before. . . . Now law and order reign. . . ."

He thumped the table.

"But when that lousy rabble came back from Rhodesia with their cars, their bedding, their squawling brats, after peeing themselves with fright—their pants were still dripping, weren't they, Antoine?—they tried to give themselves airs again. They need a good kick in the arse, those people . . . and the next time any of them runs away, up against the wall with him!"

Gelinet was choking with anger. His wife came back, a

129

lovely placid Flemish woman with a full bosom and gently swaying hips.

"She must be mad about men," Fonts reflected, ". . . and her husband's at least twenty-five years older than she is. He's a card, this fellow Gelinet. . . . Just like an Algerian Frenchman who went through May 13th . . . at least who believed he went through it. Everywhere it's the same old act, in darkest Africa no less than on the shores of the Mediterranean!"

Fonts was sitting on the floor, his knees drawn up to his chin. He had summed up Pérohade in a flash: a sound fellow, and sharper than he looked, capable of fighting if he felt his interests or friends were threatened, in the know about quite a number of things, thanks to his job, incapable of sorting out the information he picked up, ready to give the shirt off his back for the mere asking, but dying of boredom in this country which was so ill suited to his exuberant nature. Félicien Dorat, who realized this, had chosen him as a correspondent, but he, Fonts, was going to make him his accomplice.

Thereby, he would be following an old habit of his. In all the operations he had undertaken, he had always made a pub or nightclub his base: never a hotel, a brothel or an opium den, where the police were apt to have contacts. The Mitsouko would suit him nicely, for if Dorat had chosen it as his headquarters, it could not have been without good reason. Dorat's reasons often coincided with those of Fonts and his ilk.

The champagne was served, and Gelinet took this opportunity to drink a fulminating toast against all Belgian settlers, those gutless namby-pambies . . . ready to bolt like rabbits at the first shot.

"Why not stay to dinner?" he said to Pérohade.

"I can't. I've got to get back to the Mitsouko. . . . When I'm not there, there's too much dipping into the till! . . . Well, Colonel, what am I going to say about you?"

"Nothing."

"You don't mean it! Are you staying? Are you going back?"

Fonts rose to his feet.

"We'll think of something or other. We could perhaps issue a statement to the effect that we never even came here. I'll go back into town with our friend."

La Roncière reminded him that none of them was supposed to leave the house, that their presence was known everywhere and that police or spies in the pay of the President, the UN or the Belgians must be keeping watch on the premises.

"That restriction applies only to you, Jean-Marie," Fonts pointed out, "because you're well known, they've seen your photo. No one has the faintest idea who I am. Everyone's obsessed by the trio: la Roncière, Kreis, Fonts. . . . So I'm going on my own. I'll hide in the back of the car as we drive out. I say, we could even do the old Soustelle trick . . . under a rug. . . . We can't go on like this, without any information. . . . I want to have a sniff at this town and the people living in it. . . . I'm like a bloodhound, I follow the scent!"

The colonel shrugged his shoulders.

"After all, do as you like. I can see we've got off to a bad start. So what does it matter if you go on a bender or two before flying back to France . . . or if you have a few bits of skirt. . . ."

Fonts calmly sat down in the front seat beside Pérohade. When they had left the Lido quarter, he inquired where the French Consul, Monsieur Musaille, lived and asked him to drive him there.

"And if you have ten minutes to spare," he added, "please wait. Not in front of the door, of course, but at the cross-roads . . . I may soon be able to give you enough material for a good story."

Paul Musaille was just going out to dinner with Ryckers at the Belgian consulate, a dinner arranged for the benefit of the cause. The conversation, of course, would be largely about the arrival of the mercenaries, which was interesting; the food would be bad, which was less so; and instead of young girls there would be nothing but old hags.

Paris had notified him of the arrival of the mercenaries and also of the presence among them of Thomas Fonts who belonged to "the service" and was to be shown every consideration. Since then, nothing.

An old friend like Fonts might at least have got in touch with him, if only by telephone, even apart from service matters. For the first time in his life Musaille would not be forced to tell a lie when he said that he knew nothing about the mercenaries. In this position, a novel one for him, he felt ill at ease.

The door bell rang.

"Hello," said Fonts, thrusting aside the servant who was trying to prevent him from entering the drawing-room. "This is the residence of Paul Musaille, isn't it?"

"Make yourself at home," Musaille peevishly replied.

Fonts took him at his word.

Musaille was a swarthy, slightly paunchy man of forty; he liked good food and complicated situations. A native of Espalion, he would have been extremely rich had it not been for the war. His father owned a successful restaurant and brewery. Paul was only a consul and, at Espalion, they were not very proud of him: anyone can be a consul, his father would say to him, all you need are a few diplomas and some friends. To be a big restaurant owner, however, you have to belong to one of the three or four big Aveyron families, be thrifty and monogamous, have a sound business sense, be sober, a good psychologist and a hard worker, none of which is required of a consul.

"You're in a spot of bother again," Musaille observed as he handed Fonts a glass of whisky, "and you're going to drag me in as well; you can never work things out on your own. What do you want this time?"

"A little dough; I'm flat broke. Some information; we're completely in the dark. You'd also better notify Uncle Chaudey . . . of our discomfiture."

"Chaudey's easy. As for information, I have a copy of the report I've just sent, I'll let you have it. When you've read it you'll know as much as I do. . . . As for money . . ."

"Still as close-fisted as ever, you dirty Auvergnat! I'll write you a check on Paris."

"I wouldn't touch it with a barge-pole; your checks always bounce. I've already got three or four of them tucked away. . . ."

With a sigh Musaille went out and came back clutching a handful of Katangese banknotes.

"Will this be enough?"

"I don't know yet. What sort of racket do you run out here to make your expense account go farther?"

"It's quite simple. At the official rate the Katangese franc is on a par with the Belgian franc, on the black market it's worth no more than half . . . and, if things go on as they are, it will drop to a third . . . I draw my pay in Brazzaville."

"Your old man will be proud of you one of these days. Do you know Pérohade?"

"Antoine? . . . A very good fellow."

"He'll be our liaison agent."

"But you're being chucked out, my dear old boy, both you and your Colonel la Roncière! It's true, you're used to it!"

"It's not by any means certain!"

"Have you heard from Dumont?"

"Power doesn't suit him: he's become unbearable since having a police bodyguard. He was much more fun when those same policemen were on his heels. Oh well, one can't stay young forever. . . . Let's have that report of yours, I'll pass it on to la Roncière, he likes reading. He believes in paper-work. Since you've been churning it out you've put on weight."

"I'm so bored here."

"It won't be for long. Pérohade told me you were a pal of that UN fellow, Maley."

"He's the only one who hates the English as much as I do! But alas, in Katanga, the English are our allies against the UN."

"Take good care of little Maley; we'll be needing him."

"Who do you take him for? He's no fool and has long ago suspected what I'm up to behind his back."

"So long, old lad, I have a date."

Fonts poured himself out another swig of whisky and left.

Musaille rubbed his hands together. At last something was going to happen. To create havoc, he could always rely on his old friend Thomas Fonts.

Fonts was sitting at the bar opposite Nathalie. He had warned Pérohade:

"I'm going to get off with that girl of yours; it will keep me in countenance."

There were a dozen or so tables surrounding a minute dance-floor. On each table there was a lamp with a white lamp-shade on which the customers, according to local tradition, signed their names. A pick-up provided soft background music: blues and slow fox-trots punctuated by cha-cha-chas.

Dufermont, who was a bit sozzled, came and sat down next to Fonts.

Nathalie introduced them.

"Monsieur Thomas, a French tourist. Monsieur Dufermont, of the Upper Katanga Timber Company."

"What on earth are you doing here?" asked Dufermont. "I did hear correctly, didn't I . . . you're a tourist?"

"I've come to see some friends . . . have a good time. . . ."

"Have a good time in E'ville? But, Monsieur Thomas, in E'ville one can only have a boring time. Isn't that so,

133

Nathalie? I shall go on being bored for another quarter of an hour in the Mitsouko, then I shall go and be bored for an hour or two with my friend Ravetot . . . for Ravetot has become a dreadful bore since falling in love with that American girl. A whisky? . . . For me too, boy. . . . We shall discuss next week's safari over and over again. Have you ever been on safari? No? Well, it's very . . . very . . . very . . . boring. Maybe Jenny will be there with that drunken husband of hers. What do you think, Thomas? I could easily fall in love with Jenny. She's Joan's best friend. But Maley's already in the running. Everything's so complicated this evening!"

"I know," Fonts observed. "The gaping void between the fifth and sixth whisky, the depressing stage. Boy, make it two doubles."

Dufermont became merrier as the alcohol took effect. But in this state he could not bear to be alone, even for a minute.

"Why don't you come along with me?" he suggested to his companion. "A drink's always a drink, no matter where you drink it!"

Fonts gave Nathalie a wink and on the way out asked Pérohade:

"I've been picked up. Who is it?"

"The gilded youth of E'ville."

"Could you possibly nip over to Gelinet's? Just to drop this envelope. . . . It's for my little pal. He's liable to be short of reading matter this evening. Thanks."

Fonts slipped the report into Pérohade's pocket and followed Dufermont outside. At the age of twenty-four Dufermont had left Liège because he was bored there, and for the last two years he had been even more bored in Katanga.

Paul Ravetot lived behind the Lubumbashi works, in a staff villa, class F, for unmarried engineers with three years' seniority.

He had tried to give it a little personality by putting a few colored shawls on the sofas, some Negro statues in the alcoves and above the drinks table a pirogue paddle. The result was unfortunate: the place looked like a souk.

To wile away the time his guests were trying out cocktails: old-fashioneds on top of mint juleps, dry martinis followed by rumpunch. John Ligget was downing glass after glass. The alcohol seemed to have no effect on him, though he was beginning to go red in the face. Jenny, his wife, lay on a sofa beating time to a dance tune with her foot. Joan was dancing with Ravetot. She would have preferred to be alone, inventing steps as the fancy took her, instead of being encumbered with this boy pressed close against her.

She remembered the little urchin she had come upon one night in the south of Spain, dancing in the moonlight, perched like a goat at the top of a street climbing up to the stars. He was snapping his fingers and singing in a voice which had not yet broken and oscillated between gruff and shrill.

When he caught sight of her he had scampered off.

Ravetot was breathing down her neck.

"I'm tired," she said. "Let's stop."

Ravetot was a dead weight, and she did not like his smell. Abandoning her partner, she went and sat down next to Jenny.

"What are we doing here?" she asked her.

"Nothing, we're waiting."

"For what?"

"For John Ligget to get dead drunk, for Daisy to come back from her little stroll with that boy who works at something or other somewhere, for that Swedish captain to stop talking about his wife and children to Marcelle who's pretending to listen . . . for three o'clock in the morning to come round, so that we can go to bed . . . for whatever else you can think of. . . ."

Dufermont, followed by Thomas Fonts who was imitating his weaving gait, made his entry.

"I say, there's a new face," Jenny observed.

She sat up on her sofa.

"Really new . . . and not the sort of face you come across in E'ville."

"What's so different about it?"

"He doesn't look in the least bored!"

As Fonts walked by her, Jenny asked him:

"Are you from Mars, monsieur?"

"Of course, madam. I've been delegated by my planet to look into a plague that is sweeping the earth."

"What plague?"

"Mankind! In China the human race has proliferated to such an extent that we can no longer see the mountains through a telescope. It's a great nuisance; we've simply got to get rid of it."

"What treatment do you plan to use against this plague?"

"As usual, facilitate its self-destruction."

135

And he quoted the opening lines of a Shakespeare sonnet in an exaggeratedly declamatory voice:

"Devouring Time, blunt thou the lion's paws,
And make the earth devour her own sweet brood;
Pluck the keen teeth from the fierce tiger's jaws,
And burn the long-liv'd phoenix in her blood. ..."

Then, in a more natural manner, but with that touch of condescension peculiar to international bureaucrats, he went on:

"Our New York office informed us that in the Congo it was possible to find some extremely good viruses of discord, some excellent ferments of racialism, tribalism and cannibalism. So I hurried over; it's even better than I expected. ..."

"Who's this clod you've brought along with you?" Ravetot asked Dufermont in a sour voice.

"Clod indeed! I was slightly tipsy before coming here, so I let him drive. You should have seen him! He made my Chevrolet behave like a circus horse. That fellow can really put a car through the hoops ... stop it dead, turn it on its rear wheels, tires shrieking. ... It's amazing, he really must work in a circus!"

"Look at him now, the clown, playing up to Joan, and the little bitch, just to make me jealous, is deliberately encouraging him!"

Without paying any heed to the other guests, Fonts had squatted on the floor by the sofa where Jenny and Joan were sitting.

"Are you going to be with us for long, monsieur?" Joan asked.

"A few days, a few weeks. On my planet officials enjoy great liberty. They are entitled to indefinite leave when emotionally involved. In my next report I shall mention a red-head with a freckled nose and a dark-haired Creole who swings her leg as though she was in a hammock ... and I shan't have to give any further particulars on my mission."

"You've got nice people to work for," said John Ligget in a thick voice.

He drew a chair up to the sofa, tried to stroke his wife's foot, but received a kick.

"John Ligget, you're only affectionate when you're drunk. Let this gentleman from Mars go on describing his administrative problems."

John got up and went over to the drinks table.

"Are you Italian?" Joan asked. "Spanish? French? You've got a funny accent when you speak English. I can't place it. Let me guess what your job is. You work for the UN? The World Health Organization? UNESCO? They're usually people who live on Mars . . . they only understand one another. I'm Joan Riverton and my father is the American Consul in this lousy country. . . . This is Jenny Ligget, and the slightly tipsy man who was here just now is her husband, the British Consul. All the rest are local fauna: young unmarried engineers from the Union Minière, a few UN soldiers or civilians, secretaries who've come with them and who are all trying to get married."

Fonts's dark eyes were sparkling and this was what Joan noticed first of all: this sharp, mischievous, crafty look. Later on she was to call it "The Snare."

"Now tell me, who are you?"

"My name's Thomas Fonts," he said springing to his feet. "I was born in French Catalonia; I don't work for any of the big international concerns you've just mentioned. I'm a mercenary."

"You're a mercenary?"

"I belong to a slightly different sort than the ones you've seen hanging about the place. I don't personally use a sub-machine-gun. I hire myself out, sometimes for money, occasionally for my friends, but more often than not just for fun. . . ."

"Is it fun, waging war?"

"I choose my side and I don't cheat by sheltering behind high principles. Shall we dance?"

"Why not? I like people to be frank."

"I'm only frank with women who interest me. The others deserve nothing but lies: it saves so much time!"

Fonts was about the same height as Joan but he danced well and did not hold her too close. Why did he remind her of that urchin singing in the moonlight, who had suddenly scampered off? His hands were hard and dry: he must have been drinking but he did not show it. His chin was slightly stubbly.

She would never see him again. Being a mercenary was a job that could not be tolerated in this day and age and in the present circumstances.

When they stopped dancing, Fonts did not see her back to her seat. His lips were frozen in the sort of smile a child might have who is resigned to grown-ups never understanding him. Without saying good-bye to anyone he disappeared. Joan almost believed she had put him to flight like that urchin in the south of Spain. Creatures like that scampered off before one had time to know them or form an opinion of them; how annoying they were! Were they frightened of being slighted?

When Joan got back to the consulate, the light was still on in her father's study. She went in.

With his spectacles on his nose—he only wore them when working—and a glass of whisky in front of him, Arnold Riverton sat perusing a file.

"Did you have a good time?" he asked.

"No."

He took off his spectacles and tapped them against the papers he was reading. In the evening he often indulged in confidences but they always had some bearing on his work, his duties, never on Sunnarti, the young Indonesian girl.

"It's getting more and more complicated," he said. "You know some French mercenaries have just arrived: a colonel, a lieutenant, and also a certain Thomas Fonts. He's a particularly dangerous man. I've just been sent his file."

"He's only a mercenary, a poor wretch who sells his hide because he has nothing else to sell!"

Riverton looked at her in astonishment; he had no idea his daughter was so concerned about UN interests in Katanga.

"No, Joan, this fellow Fonts isn't for sale: he caused us a lot of trouble in Laos a year and a half ago, and our whole policy was affected; recently he was in Guinea, as a consul, with roughly the same rank as myself . . . and he's much younger. He's no mercenary. He serves his country and serves it well."

"What's he doing here?"

"Our worthy friends the French are up to their tricks again. Mind you, Joan, they're not always wrong. In Laos we should perhaps have listened to them. . . . They're at home in these rotten old countries, but as soon as one does listen to them they become unbearably vain and use our dollars to serve their political ends. As they're not always very sound, they make blunders where we only commit mistakes. I've been asked by the Department to keep a close watch on Thomas Fonts's activities."

"He's not particularly interesting."

"Have you met him? Already?"

"Only for a minute or two."

"Good-looking fellow?"

"Thomas Fonts is short, swarthy, ugly: he murders Shakespeare's sonnets when he quotes them."

Riverton knew she was lying. On the desk in front of him was a photograph of Fonts as a Laotian paratrooper, when he was helping a certain Kong-Lê, then an unknown captain, to seize Vientiane: the operation had not caused a single death. But, when the people whom the Americans were backing tried to retake the town, there had been thousands. Fonts had then taken up another post. The consul handed the photograph to his daughter and Joan blushed.

For some unknown reason she was glad that this swarthy little man was not an ordinary adventurer, that he had been in an official position and that so many people were taking an interest in him.

La Roncière lay on his narrow bed, reading the report that Fonts had just sent him. He did so with his usual gravity, underlining certain sentences, jotting others down in a little notebook that lay by his side. But this sort of work, which he generally accomplished with ease, today imposed a great effort on him. The fact was, he no longer believed in his Katangese venture.

He had to remind himself that it was always interesting to get to know a new country and study it, that one of these days Africa would become a vast testing ground for every method of subversive warfare. . . .

The report was marked in big red letters: "Top secret."

It was a mere formality, but this sign reassured la Roncière by reminding him that he still had access to secrets even if they were a lot of nonsense and that he still belonged to the governing classes of his country.

The report was only three days old, since it was datelined Elizabethville, 1 May, 1961.

It started by pointing out certain obvious facts and, first and foremost, that the Union Minière of Upper Katanga was at the root of the secession, that this secession could only last thanks to the Union Minière, and that without the support of the Union Minière President Kimjanga's régime would collapse at once.

This support manifested itself in two ways:

Financially, by the payment of dues to the Katangese authorities. These dues averaged twenty-six thousand million francs a year, representing before independence half the budgetary receipts of the Belgian Congo as a whole.

By investments in kind in what may be called "useful Katanga," that's to say the mining strip running along the Rhodesian border. The Union Minière runs the public services: electricity, water supply, railways, etc. It is solely because the Union Minière kept its staff on the spot at the time of the events which followed the proclamation of independence that Katanga did not experience the collapse and chaos witnessed in the other regions. The strength of the Union Minière amounts to twenty thousand employees, two thousand of whom are Europeans.

The Union Minière today refrains from participating in any way in the political life of Katanga. Its directors, in particular, most emphatically deny that they furnish any financial aid to the Kimjanga régime. They take refuge behind the following argument: we are paying dues, as we always have, to the Congolese State. The sums in question are deposited as usual with the authorities in Elizabethville. If, subsequently, the régime in power omits to hand over to the Central Government in Leopoldville the part that is due to them, this is a political problem which is not within the jurisdiction of the company and with which it is not concerned.

This explanation, of course, is not accepted by the opponents of the Kimjanga régime, that's to say the Central Government in Leopoldville and the United Nations. . . .

Like many officers brought up in the hard schools of the Resistance, the wars in Indo-China and Algeria, la Roncière had a childish idea of the capitalist world, its organization and the trusts which by interlocking with one another formed its texture. The officers discussed it among themselves, but without really believing in it, like myths on which one enjoys elaborating or those scarecrows that are brandished at public meetings. Not one of them could credit that in this day and age such outworn systems should survive and that the State should not have taken them over by entrusting their management to civil servants.

Without even realizing it, while believing more often than not that they subscribed to the opposite ideology, these officers had become Socialists.

La Roncière now discovered that these big businesses still existed, that they could decide the fate of whole nations, even afford the services of a hundred men of his sort. He suddenly realized the immense confidence trick to which he was being asked to subscribe. Even on the technical plane, this omnipotent presence of the world of finance could only impede him. How could one indulge in Socialism when in the service of the banks, or in psychological warfare in order to defend some mines? How create a nation to justify the privileges of a financial group? If I stay on, la Roncière decided, I shall use the Union Minière's money to make Katanga a Socialist type of country and immediately afterwards I'll nationalize the mines. Then Monsieur Van der Weyck will have all the time in the world to reduce his golf handicap.

Stimulated by the idea of betraying those who were employing him, which enabled him to remain true to a few of his principles, or rather his techniques, la Roncière went on reading.

The Union Minière had held itself aloof from all the agitation that followed the proclamation of independence in the Congo, leaving two Belgian groups, which it controlled behind the scenes, to grapple with each other in the limelight: those who could be called the "extremists" were headed by Major Van Beulans and the Belgian Consul Ryckers who had previously been in charge of Security.

One fine morning the blue helmets had landed at Elizabethville airport despite the opposition of the Belgians and Katangese, and this had changed the whole situation.

From then on it was impossible to go on maintaining Katanga as a protectorate in disguise. In their own way the directors of the Union Minière had questioned their consciences. They had then decided that in the eyes of the world Katanga should behave like an independent State since it was henceforth impossible to envisage its integration into Belgium. This solution of integration was obviously doomed by the increasing pressure not only of the Communists and Afro-Asians but also of the Americans who were always in search of customers to do down the Russians.

It was then the Union Minière had produced Pimuriaux, head of the Liberal rank and file, out of its hat. For several months he had already been on the company's secret payroll.

He had been made Secretary-General to the Presidency in spite of the violent opposition of Ryckers, who operated in the background, and of Van Beulans who had clumsily appointed himself "Political and Military Adviser" and consequently assumed complete control.

Supported from then on by the Union Minière, Pimuriaux, who only the day before was being accused of treason, had started nibbling at Van Beulans's prerogatives. But the task was beyond his powers, and his plan to replace the Belgians with Frenchmen had just ended in failure.

La Roncière suddenly heard a slight noise in the corridor: a rustle of silk skirts, then some muffled footsteps, the steps of a woman walking barefoot.

The blood rushed to his head at the thought of that woman padding by, feeling her way with the tips of her fingers along the walls, making for his room perhaps. . . . It was Hortense Gelinet, since she was the only woman in the house.

The footsteps went past his door and up the staircase. There was only one attic room on the first floor: the one Kreis had been given.

Kreis's door opened quietly, with hardly a creak. The German was sleeping with his window wide open and the pale moonlight fell on his finely chiseled face, his fair hair, his powerful torso that lay exposed.

Hortense watched him breathing, inhaling deeply and calmly. One of his arms hung over the side of the bed.

Kreis suddenly woke and, as he propped himself up on his elbows, revealed his naked body down to the groin.

In a dull voice he asked:

"Why have you chosen me in particular? Because I noticed straight away, with all those men round you, you could hardly bear it: you had to have a man and your husband's fat and old."

Hortense closed the door; her voice was quite calm as she said:

"Fonts doesn't attract me; I don't like dark little men . . . and besides, he talks . . . and men who talk too much . . . often do nothing else. Or else they're irresponsible children who make women unhappy. The colonel scares me. I knew a missionary in E'ville who had a face like his. . . ."

A gust of honeysuckle-scented wind blew the flap of her nightdress aside, revealing her legs and part of one thigh.

"Why me?" Kreis repeated.

"You're strong . . . and also it's convenient, the upstairs room. No one can hear . . . I arranged for you to have this room."

She slipped out of her nightdress, lifted the sheet, and

142

without the slightest shame ran her soft warm hand over Kreis's sexual organ before lying down on top of him.

In a whisper she muttered:

"Men don't give me any pleasure, but I enjoy giving it to them."

Never, not even for a moment, did Hortense lose her self-control, so exclusively did she concentrate on what she was doing.

Then she put her nightdress on again and, silently as ever, disappeared.

Kreis, without saying a word to her, had rolled over on his side as though he was sleeping. But he had promised himself that one day Hortense would find pleasure in his arms . . . because it wasn't tolerable that a woman should play the man's part . . . that she should give instead of receive, and remain independent.

La Roncière once more heard the steps padding along the corridor. His ears were buzzing. He felt like getting up, dragging Hortense into his room and flinging himself on her. But he restrained himself, gulped down a glass of water and forced himself to go on reading.

. . . At the same time Brussels was coming to the same conclusions as the Union Minière. Belgian political circles are still sympathetic to President Kimjanga's régime but they feel that Belgium can no longer recognize the State of Katanga without provoking violent reactions in the UN as well as in every chancellory. At the moment the policy of the Belgian Government is closely akin to that of the financial powers: to give the President the necessary aid to enable him to succeed but to undertake commitments only with the utmost caution.

I must point out that this Belgian tendency to "withdraw" has been badly received by the European population as a whole who regard it as a "weakness" if not a "betrayal." This population is still firmly attached to the traditional forms of the European presence in Africa; it has accustomed itself to the idea of a Katanga under a colonial régime and finds it impossible to understand that the trend is gradually towards genuine independence, even if the Europeans are more or less assured of maintaining their advantages and privileges.

"What's Fonts up to?" la Roncière wondered. "He hasn't come in yet." He looked at his watch: half past one in the morning. "Who gave him this report? Someone well informed, who enjoys great independence *vis-à-vis* the Union Minière and the Belgian Government, a foreigner almost certainly, but whose duties enable him to approach a great many people . . . it must be one of Colonel Chaudey's agents."

He perused a few notes concerning the organization of the Union Minière and presently came across a paragraph which immediately drew his attention.

It was about his future opponent: the UN. Now, la Roncière had one great quality: unlike many of his comrades, he never underestimated the enemy and always tried to study him closely.

"You don't dabble in physics without being perfectly conversant with the laws governing material bodies; you don't practice psychological warfare if you're incapable of identifying yourself completely with your opponent." This was how he had begun his lecture at Staff College to an audience of young senior officers, as thrilled and excited as though they were attending the first night of a play or a film.

Mr. Hammarskjöld's new representative in Katanga, Mr. Patrick Maley, an Irishman, took up his duties only four months ago.

He does not conceal his prejudice against Katanga and the régime of the President whom he affects to regard as "a man of straw" in the hands of the Belgian extremists.

Energetic and resolute, his avowed aim is to put an end to the secession and place Katanga once again under the authority of the Central Government of Leopoldville.

Mr. Maley asserts he has no wish to meddle in the internal affairs of Katanga and he never misses an opportunity to point out that he feels no hostility towards President Kimjanga. He defines his mission as follows: to put into effect the resolutions of the Security Council which provide for the re-establishment of the unity of the Congo and the departure of all the mercenaries.

Maley likewise asserts that he has no intention of using force to achieve his end. And indeed his whole policy is aimed at getting the Secretary-General's "go-ahead" signal to bring the secession of Katanga to an end.

Maley does not believe in the existence of a Katangese national sentiment. He reckons that a sufficiently substantial deployment of armed forces would be enough to bring the President to his senses.

At the moment Mr. Maley does not have sufficient forces at his disposal to embark on an operation of this sort without taking serious risks.

The Katangese Army numbers about ten thousand men. The UN have about seven thousand troops in the whole of Katanga, dispersed over a very wide area. Elizabethville is occupied by three battalions: Irish, Swedish and Indian. The Swedes and the Irish are clearly of no military value.

However, Maley is now calling for substantial reinforcements of Indian troops from Leopoldville, as well as arms and ammunition.

The size of the Indian contribution to the UN operations in the Congo has led to the appointment of an Indian officer, General Siddartha, as commander of the troops stationed in Katanga.

This appointment will almost certainly lead to a hardening in the attitude of the UN. General Siddartha does not conceal his intention of getting rid as soon as possible of the Belgian mercenaries and officials, for whom he feels a violent hatred. . . .

"The complex of the former victim of colonization," la Roncière at once reflected, "but also of the colored man in relation to the white, of the champion of the undernourished, disorganized 'third world,' for whom dreams take the place of ideas, against a clear-minded and contemptuous West overflowing with riches.

"If I were a Hindu or an Arab or an Indonesian, I would never stop trying to overcome this Western world. But this world is order and I am disorder, strength whereas I am weakness. So I would play on its disparity, its lassitude, its generosity, its guilt complex. . . . What a powerful lever such hatred could be! We people who have lost the art of hating are lost!"

At the end of the report came a brief reference to the Balubas:

. . . Although President Kimjanga's régime was strengthened nine months ago, it remains none the less extremely fragile, for it has not been able to settle this Baluba problem. Now, out of a population of

145

roughly, 1,800,000 inhabitants, Katanga numbers about 1,000,000 Balubas, all of them in revolt against the Elizabethville authorities. . . .

"The crux of the matter is to be found in this last paragraph," la Roncière at once reflected. "The first problem we shall have to settle is that of those million Balubas."

The colonel switched off his bedside lamp and tried to concentrate on what he had read. The memory of the footsteps and the rustle of silk prevented him. Whenever he remained chaste for too long, his imagination got the better of his reason and his work was affected.

Fonts, with his manners of a Neapolitan pimp, would be able to find him a woman. Of course, it would have been more convenient to have the lady of the house, but his pride would not allow him to share with Kreis.

La Roncière, Fonts and Kreis spent ten days kicking their heels in Gelinet's house.

Pimuriaux came and called on them twice: the first time, secretly, to impress upon them yet again the need for caution; the second time to tell them that the situation was improving and that "someone important from Paris" was arriving any moment. The Secretary-General seemed less worried. He had even driven up in an official car flying the Katangese flag.

"President Kimjanga," he told them, "has no intention of abandoning his plans. In fact, the Belgian settlers, seeing they're losing ground, have fabricated a plot as a last resort. . . . In this plot, all three of you are involved, gentlemen, together with the President of the National Assembly, Bongo the Minister of the Interior, and myself.

"Our aim: to assassinate Kimjanga and replace him with Bongo. It's so idiotic that it can only emanate from Consul Ryckers and Van Beulans. I thought so at once and I wasn't wrong."

"Wasn't this man Ryckers in charge of the Sûreté before becoming consul?" la Roncière inquired.

"How did you know?" Pimuriaux exclaimed in surprise.

The colonel made a vague gesture with his hand.

"Is it true?"

"Yes."

"He must have thought up this story with the help of his former agents."

"And you're hiding something from us," Fonts added.

"The President started by believing it was a genuine plot."

"But . . ."

"It's a disease of every African head of state: plotting . . . and very often they have every reason to suspect it. By using a few distorted principles of democracy we have turned them into what their predecessors were before the conquest: Negro kings enthroned for the duration of their lives. Plotting and assassination are the only remaining means of getting rid of them."

"I see, Monsieur Fonts," Pimuriaux retorted impatiently, "that you know Africa extremely well. It's true that at the beginning the President, who had been shown certain agents' reports, took fright. But Bongo got his hands on one of these agents and, in front of Kimjanga, he made him confess he was lying."

"How? . . ." Fonts innocently inquired.

"I'm not quite sure, you know . . . the minister can be quite brutal at times.

"Was it he himself who operated?"

"That doesn't concern us. The President now knows that they tried to trick him; he's furious with Ryckers and Van Beulans."

"Then let him turn them out: he has a good excuse."

"It's impossible . . . not yet. The arms, the Army instructors . . . the Balubas. . . ."

"Could you tell us something about the Balubas?" la Roncière asked.

Pimuriaux flung his little arms in the air.

"It's a very tricky problem, Colonel."

Fonts drew closer, his interest aroused. Anything to do with tribes, sects and minorities fascinated him. On this territory he felt at home: he knew what methods to use, while realizing that more often than not it was largely a question of the survivals of a past doomed by inexorable evolution.

"Didn't the Belgians ever deal with them?" la Roncière insisted, seeing that Pimuriaux was trying to avoid the issue.

"For the last five months they have. At the time of independence the whole of the north of the country and its entire population slipped out of our control."

"This population consists of how many Balubas?"

"A million."

"And the rest of Katanga without the Balubas?"

"Slightly less. But these Balubas, who are known as the Jews of Africa, are not natives of Katanga. They were im-

147

ported from the Kasai by Belgian employers, including the Union Minière. They're more intelligent, more advanced than the autochthonous people, they got hold of all the subordinate posts, all the jobs requiring skilled labor, which was bound to cause a certain amount of jealousy.

"At the time of independence we had to choose: support the Balubas or the other tribes. We chose the others. And the Balubas, who had appointed as their leader a certain Melchior Molanda, a friend of Lumumba's, rebelled."

"What did you do about it?"

"We dispatched the Katangese Gendarmerie, led by Belgian officers and NCOs, to restore law and order . . . I wouldn't tell anyone else but you, but the fact is, they went much too far. The whole of the north of the country slipped out of our control."

"A classical situation," la Roncière interjected. "In Katanga a majority, the Balubas, are unable to express themselves against a minority who seize all the power and all the jobs. If we can't win them over, we ought at least to put an end to this repression and offer them more or less honorary posts. These Belgian soldiers think they're back in the times of Stanley."

"Don't forget we're in black Africa," Fonts pointed out, "and that every problem is more complex, the outlines less well defined."

"There are elementary rules . . ."

"Africa swallows up everything, even your rules."

Pimuriaux, who knew how embarrassing the Baluba problem was for Katanga, behaved like the President: he dismissed it from his mind because he could find no solution to it.

"Monsieur Van der Weyck," he said, "asked to be remembered to you . . . I think that on his side he has made certain approaches to Brussels and indirectly to Paris. . . ."

A beaming smile came over Pimuriaux's pink face.

"You see, everything's working out all right. . . . You're well off here: fresh air, rest . . . and company. . . ."

La Roncière, ostensibly extremely relaxed, simply reminded him that in five days' time they were taking the plane for Paris and that if everything was going so well, he therefore had plenty of time to tidy up this mess.

Pimuriaux was walking back towards his car when Fonts called out to him:

"I say, my dear fellow, is it true the Indian General Siddartha, who commands the UN troops, declared yesterday evening, at a party at Maley's, that all the mercenaries ought to be rounded up, court martialed and hanged?"

"Siddartha had been drinking; he has a weak head. It's true, he loathes you . . . he loathes all white men."

"I've drafted an article which you'd do well to have published at once in the local rag and submit to the agencies. You can read it in the car, it will while away the time. My respects to Madame . . . and tell her to keep a closer watch on her tongue. . . ."

"I beg your pardon?"

"Your wife goes around telling everyone that I'm interested in Joan Riverton; it's not true. I've only seen her once in my life and we didn't get on at all well. If Monette goes on like this I shall be forced to teach little Ravetot a lesson, because he's the one, isn't he, who makes a point of telling her? It would be a shame, we're liable to need him one day."

Pimuriaux was so disturbed that he almost climbed into the front seat next to the driver. How could these bloody men be so well informed? Gelinet didn't know a thing, and all his wife ever thought of was having a tumble. Decronelle . . . no, out of the question. He came bleating to him every day for news about the mercenaries. Pérohade . . . was a Frenchman, had been a paratrooper, but he didn't have enough contacts . . . even though there was a lot of loose talk in the Mitsouko.

As his car drove off in the darkness to the Presidency, he took the article Fonts had given him out of his pocket. It was typewritten.

General Siddartha is extremely embarrassed by the presence of French mercenaries in Katanga. He is even considering having them hanged . . . if he manages to catch them. . . .

The general, who has already given proof of his strong personality by a series of monumental blunders while serving on an international commission in the Far East, fears that the secret instructions he has received from his government might be revealed.

Mr. Nehru is seriously considering transforming the Congo into a colonization zone for his fellow countrymen, who are overcrowded at home. But to put this plan into effect, it will first of all be necessary to drive out the whites. Hence this hatred . . . and this fear of the mercenaries . . . who exist, of course, only in his imagination.

Mr. Maley has been told about this plan in detail and does not approve of it.

Could it be that these two gentlemen do not see eye to eye?

As soon as he reached the Presidency, Pimuriaux rang up Decronelle.

"I've got some sensational information for you, old boy. . . ."

"Put on your glad rags, Jean-Marie, assume your best pensive warrior expression . . . features drawn, brow wrinkled, the air of having great projects in mind. . . . We've been asked to dinner at the British Consulate. Don't worry, the consul won't be there; he's wandering about somewhere in Rhodesia. We'll leave Kreis here. . . . You'd much rather stay, wouldn't you, Kreis, old boy. . . . By the way, tell Hortense to double her old man's sleeping-draught. She was screeching last night like a cat on heat. I'll let you know where you can contact us if anything happens."

Kreis got up and walked over to Fonts.

"Monsieur Fonts, I don't take orders or advice from you outside service matters!"

Fonts did not bat an eyelid.

"Kreis, I'm getting a bit fed up with you. Your little affair with Hortense . . . is a service matter, as you call it . . . because if old Gelinet hears about it he'll throw us out. And where would we go then? Make love to her as much as you like, but gag her first, and don't think you're so bloody clever just because you tumble a girl on heat."

Kreis raised his fist.

Fonts took two steps back, picked up a teak chair and, holding it with its legs pointing at Kreis's face, waited for the attack in a semi-crouched position.

Kreis, having recovered his temper, dropped his arm.

"Monsieur Fonts, you're very unwise. One day someone will put paid to you before you have time to pick up a chair or a bottle."

"There's always something ready to hand: a knife, a pistol, a grenade. The game's always on equal terms."

Fonts put the chair down and la Roncière, as though there had been no incident at all, inquired:

"Will there be any girls there?"

"Yes, two . . . and since there are two of us. . . ."

"Who told you about Siddartha?"

"Joan rang me up. I don't know how she got our number . . . 'I say, little Fonts, is it true they're going to hang you?' she said. 'Anyway that's what General Siddartha was saying last night. What a dismal end to your career! Jenny and I would like to have dinner with you first. . . . Bring along your friend, that colonel who made such an unfortunate name for himself in Algeria!' You see, one can't keep anything from those girls!"

"Who's Jenny?"

"Joan's best friend, the British Consul's wife."

"I hate that sort of frivolous woman."

"Not this one, you'll see. She's bored to tears, her husband drinks. . . ."

A little later, in the car that Gelinet had lent them, la Roncière asked Fonts:

"Who's this man Pimuriaux mentioned, who's going to come out here?"

"Chaudey in some sort of disguise or other. . . . Musaille, the Consul, told me he was expecting him."

"Do you know Musaille well?"

"Extremely well. . . ."

"Is he sound?"

"As long as he amuses himself and doesn't endanger his career. But he loves amusing himself . . . and guzzling. . . . Last night I had dinner with him, just the two of us. He cooked the meal himself. You should have seen him, with his sleeves rolled up, an apron over his paunch, coddling his undercut of beef. We ate in the kitchen. . . . He likes getting up from the table every two minutes to attend to his saucepans. You know his family are stinking rich?"

"What about yours?"

"My mother's rich, I'm not. It's a lovely property we have, at Elne. You know, you're lucky to have been born poor. You've no idea how hard it is to escape from money . . . when the money has been honestly acquired from the soil and the vines ripening in the sun. You daren't spend that sort of money. It's sacred, a mixture of earth, sun and sweat. You'll see, Jenny's an interesting girl. A pity that red-headed bitch Joan annoys me so much."

"What did she do to you?"

"She seems to think that men are only born for women's amusement. Now it's somewhere near here . . . left . . . then first right . . . a house on its own with a lot of dogs. There it is! Listen to them barking."

"You think it'll work out all right?"

"With the girls?"

"No, our operation in Katanga."

"I'm not sure . . . it's on the cards, but we ought not to hang on here too long. . . ."

"Why not?"

"In Africa swift action is what counts. Nothing lasts. Africa's like me and it suits me!"

The beam of the headlamps picked out a slender figure with red hair, wearing blue jeans and a light-colored shirt.

"It's Joan; you can't say she's dressed up for us!"

Joan came up to the door.

"Hello," she said in French. "We've just come in from riding. . . . But if you like we could put on evening dresses. Jenny will lend me one of hers. Perhaps it would be more proper to wear evening dress for the last dinner of two valiant warriors, who are going to be hanged at dawn by General Siddartha after first being sacrificed to Vishnu, Siva, Krishna and three or four other weird gods. Do come in, I'll lead the way."

Jenny was likewise in trousers and her long black hair hung down to her waist. Bashfully, feeling awkward and clumsy all of a sudden, la Roncière kissed her hand.

He envied Fonts's easy manner and studied insolence. He himself always behaved like an alien, hedged in with taboos and conventions. . . . Whenever he violated them he went too far and behaved outrageously.

"Colonel," said Jenny, "you are a colonel, aren't you?—for the first time there's something strange going on in Joan's life: a man who irritates her to such a point that she can't stop talking about him. I'm referring to your friend."

"You speak French very well!"

"My mother's second husband was a Frenchman. My father lives in Rhodesia. . . . We are—how shall I put it!—the *pieds noirs* of that country. The Algerian war fascinates him!"

"What about you?"

"What men do among themselves doesn't interest me, only what they do or don't do to women. No, don't misunderstand me. . . . What I mean is, if they are friendly or hostile to women."

"What about your husband?"

"Neither the one nor the other. He's English. Will you have a whisky? I would have made some cocktails . . . but I always get the proportions wrong!"

Joan appeared.

"Thomas Fonts claims that what's cooking in your

152

kitchen is a mess. He says he knows only one man who can put it right: Musaille, the French Consul. He's telephoning him now."

Fonts came back.

"Musaille wasn't in. . . ."

He took la Roncière aside.

"Musaille was in, of course; Uncle Chaudey has just arrived in Elizabethville. He's seeing the President tomorrow. As I said, it's on the cards. . . ."

Then he sat down on the sofa next to Joan.

La Roncière raised his glass to Jenny.

"You're not like any of the girls in Algeria!"

"In what way?"

"They're more earnest . . . less off-hand . . . less easy-mannered, if you prefer. They weren't capable of making us want to die for them!"

"And the women in Africa? The white women, I mean!"

"You're the first I've met . . . and I'm . . ." he dipped his nose in his glass ". . . deeply disturbed."

"I'm going to ring up my father and tell him the news: we've at last got some Frenchmen ready to die for Rhodesia!"

La Roncière was furious with himself for speaking so pompously. . . . This woman was making fun of him. He felt like teaching her a good lesson. But women were elusive creatures who had their own hierarchies and did not respect any others.

Joan was doing her best to offend Fonts.

"How many people were killed in Laos?" she asked him.

"I don't know, the war's not over yet."

"And you don't care?"

"Yes, I do. The Laotians were not cut out to fight. War suits them about as well as a feathered hat would a bishop! Really, it required an immense effort from everyone for them to start shooting one another instead of lapsing yet again into endless discussions punctuated with feasts!"

"But you began it all, Thomas Fonts! I know."

"Listen, my little quail. . . ."

"Little quail?"

"It's the name of a bird. In the autumn you see it on the moors. In Laos I had a pal from one of the northern tribes who was in a dilemma. . . . He wanted to take a town but didn't know how to set about it! I helped him a bit. . . . The town was Vientiane."

"And who was the man?"

"Kong-Lê."

"The result was splendid: Kong-Lê subsequently went over to the Communists. . . ."

"He'll leave them again or get killed, that's his own look-out! Such a well-planned operation! For once we had the Russians with us, off-stage . . . just to annoy the Chinese! I played the first hand, but others went on with the game and made a mess of it! Just remember that nothing is simple, and now let's talk of something else!"

"What did you come here for, Thomas Fonts? To defend the interests of the Union Minière? To die for the mines? It's pretty dismal! In the Renaissance, mercenaries fought to carve themselves out kingdoms, and the Conquistadors were looking for Eldorado."

"What did your father come here for? Just to represent the United States? Not a bit of it! To get hold of these mines for his government and the financial groups which that government protects!"

"We don't need copper!"

"But you do need cobalt. And we in France also need cobalt, in order to play the lone-wolf game between you and the USSR. From the depths of our past we sometimes still feel the urge to play at being a great power. That's not a crime!"

He took Joan by the arm.

"Let's go out into the garden. The condemned man ought to be entitled, before his execution, to have a final stroll in a garden on the arm of a pretty girl. But all he gets is a tot of rum . . . on an empty stomach and at dawn."

"Are you a romantic?"

"No, a realist. I've managed to avoid the tot of rum on several occasions . . . but only just. . . ."

"For the sake of cobalt?"

"No . . . for the sake of some friends."

"Have you got lots of friends? They seem to spend their lives racing around and meddling in everything!"

"One doesn't choose one's friends, they choose one!"

"Because one has something in common with them! I don't see you being a friend, as you say, of the people I like!"

"Are they such bores?"

"You're unbearable! Always showing off."

The wind was blowing, a gentle fragrant wind that brought with it all the warm secrets of spring, lawns wet with dew, roses, mango trees and jacarandas and, in the background, a faint whiff of sugar, decay and burning which came from the Equator and was the true smell of Africa.

"Not happy?" Fonts murmured, leaning towards Joan.

"Not very," she admitted. "I'm bored here and my father doesn't understand me."

"Are you engaged?"

"Of course. . . ."

She had just this moment invented a fiancé for herself, as a first line of defense.

"Doesn't he understand you either?"

"No, he doesn't . . . and the little quail, as you called me, is sad; but I'll get over it. . . ."

Fonts suddenly drew nearer to her and brushed her lips with his own. She was surprised she did not slap his face. . . . But how could she slap him for this kiss which was not quite a kiss . . . which was more like a proof of friendship or sympathy, a game. . . . This damnable man had a gift for putting you in a false position, where a show of temper was liable to be ridiculous. After kissing her, Fonts did not even take her in his arms, which was the natural thing to do and would have given her the opportunity to rebuff him. But he went on walking beside her, gazing at his feet. . . .

"Are you married?" she asked him.

"Why get married? It's like a visitor at vintage time who drinks a little glass of new wine, a little local wine. He finds it rather good; of course, it has just been made, it tastes fresh and smells of fruit. He forthwith buys a barrel of it, lays it down in his cellar . . . where the new wine turns to vinegar. . . ."

"The French are always malicious about women, but they're the most conventional men in the world. They often marry their mistresses."

"I've never had any mistresses, only girl-friends with whom I happened to sleep."

They went back into the house.

Jenny was in her favorite position: lying on a sofa, beating time with her leg. The colonel stood leaning against the chimney-piece, delivering a lecture.

"Look at la Roncière: the great specialist in sympathy and noble feelings. The result is he does more harm than I do!"

155

"Do you think so?"

"Everything depends on the tone in which one starts an affair. Afterwards you merely have to keep up the tone."

"And you are? . . ."

"A clown, of course! Jean-Marie, let me guess what you were talking to Jenny about: the Resistance, Indo-China or Algeria?"

"About women's role in modern warfare: this role is primordial. If you want to win, you must have the women on your side. In Indo-China and Algeria we didn't rely sufficiently on the women. We shall do so here. What do you think, Jenny?"

"I can't stand all those creatures who go around in uniform brandishing machine-guns or making speeches. . . . The lovely courtesans have always been more important than they are, even in politics. I demand the proclamation of the neutrality of all women!"

The telephone rang. It was for la Roncière; Kreis was on the other end of the line.

"Colonel, Pimuriaux's here . . . and also someone from Paris. You must come back at once!"

"I'm sorry," la Roncière apologized, "but we've got to go. Are you coming, Fonts?"

As he kissed Jenny's hand, he repeated:

"I'm really sorry. . . ."

Jenny saw them to the car, walking along with her lithe gait, not knowing yet if she was pleased or sorry at this hasty departure.

Fonts ran his hand through Joan's hair, drew her towards him, kissed her on the mouth, but she bit him.

He burst out laughing and disappeared into the darkness.

Hortense and Kreis were lying on their backs, side by side, but without their bodies touching.

"Go on," said Hortense.

"We called those units *Einsatzgruppen*. I was then in Group C which operated to the rear of the troops in the region of Kiev. We already had quite a lot of partisans fighting against us behind our lines.

"There was mud everywhere, and straggling telephone lines. . . . Operations of this sort were known as infiltrations. Every adult male was rounded up. Later on, the term 'adult' applied to younger and younger chaps . . . and 'partisans' even to women. . . . If they weren't bad-looking

156

we'd put them aside. . . . Sometimes these partisans were armed. . . ."

"Sometimes?"

"Sometimes, not always.* But there was always a chance of their getting hold of some weapons . . . or stealing them from us. . . .

"Kaufmann had worked out a swift method of getting rid of them. . . . One day I thought I would follow his example. I loaded them on to a truck—thirty or forty of them, Jews and Communists, jammed in together. I can't even remember a single individual face: they were all gray, filthy, unshaven. with staring eyes and Adam's apples bobbing up and down faster and faster in their throats.

"I fixed a piece of telephone wire round each one's neck, a fairly short piece, connected to a row of telegraph-poles with a long iron bar across them.

"The dirty swine had sabotaged some telegraph-poles in the night, yet they knew it was *verboten.* I signaled to the driver. He started off with a jerk. The wheels slithered in the mud, a mud that was almost white."

"And then?"

"All thirty of them, strung up simultaneously, hung twitching on the ends of their telephone wires. It was good material; not one of the wires snapped. The men, it's true, were not very heavy: they hadn't eaten much for some time."

"You're a sadistic monster, Karl."

"I had been given my orders . . . and a soldier who doesn't carry out his orders is shot. That's laid down in the rules. You know, Hortense, they weren't all twitching. There were some who had had their necks broken at once, mostly those who were in the front of the truck. Only when the truck skidded, it took longer. . . ."

"Shut up."

"That's all I ask. . . ."

Hortense stretched out her hand, ran it over his chest, dug her nails into his flesh and brought her face closer to his.

With a sudden jerk he was on top of her.

---

* SS General von Gottberg gives the following figures for Operation Cottbus which he directed against these bands:

Enemy dead: 4,500
Suspects dead: 5,000
German dead: 59
Arms recovered: 492

Quoted by J. Delarne: *Histoire de la Gestapo.*

At that moment the telephone rang.

"Quick," said Hortense, ". . . it'll wake my husband."

When Karl came back, Hortense was no longer there. All that remained was her scent. ,

The white mud? But was it white . . . or pink like toothpaste, that Kiev mud? More often than not Kreis had to invent certain details and include scenes of horror that had never existed. . . .

The story of the truck and the Jews was true, but he had paid no attention to those who were about to die. No, he was not a sadist, he took no pleasure in these executions. He had been given orders to hang them and Kaufmann was always going around bragging about his method; so he had tried it out.

Whether they were strung up on a telephone wire or rope, whether they stood on a chair or were jerked out of a truck, what did it matter about dirty swine like that? But what is a dirty swine? The chap who's not on your side, that's to say who doesn't fight as you would wish him to fight!

What is a monster? The hangman is a monster, but also the judge and the man above the judge, and the man who starts a war . . . whichever side he is on.

When you're fighting a war, you mustn't try to understand, you must simply obey. If you try to understand you start reasoning with the enemy and end up by coming round to his point of view. Then you're done for, because everyone has good reasons for behaving as he does.

In Algéria they had started reasoning far too quickly, and Algeria had been lost.

Kreis never wanted to think for himself. He obeyed, always obeyed, because it was so much simpler. All of a sudden he pictured Fonts twitching on the end of a telephone wire . . . or Colonel la Roncière; weren't they both therefore dirty swine?

Their business looked like being settled. But when it was all over in Katanga, where would he go? The Egyptians, it seemed, were recruiting instructors for their army . . . preferably Germans and paratroopers. Men would still go on fighting for years to come, not in the big countries any more—it was too dangerous, what with the atomic bombs—but in the small ones, in all the countries which believed that being independent entails first and foremost being a nuisance to others. . . .

Hortense would not come back again tonight. She was listening to her old husband snoring . . . the fellow who kept talking all the time about sex because he was no longer capable of it.

Hortense liked being told horror stories before making love. She then had the impression of sleeping with a beast, and this excited her.

Hortense was not a monster and no judge would have condemned her, she simply needed stimulation; whereas he, Kreis, through having obeyed his superiors, might have been in serious trouble after the war.

The Russians and French alone had proved to be realists; the French recruited for their Foreign Legion, the Russians for the police and army of East Germany.

But the Russians required a spell of political training, whereas all the French demanded was good health.

Ach! it was a fine thing, the Legion, especially in Indo-China. There was that camp just outside Hanoi which had been set up in the quarter formerly reserved for singers, dancers and prostitutes. There were any amount of girls who were not too expensive, Chinese merchants who allowed one to run up bills, and under the acetylene lamps one could sit down and have a bowl of soup so heavily laced with pepper and *ngoc-mam* that it seared one's throat.

Colonel Chaudey did not like traveling. He always caught cold in a plane and was frightened of losing his luggage. What was the idea—Dumont's idea—of sending him to Elizabethville to "put things right" and saddling him with a false name but a genuine movement order? What was he going to say to this President Kimjanga? That the French Government was displeased because Katanga was not using the mercenaries whom he, Kimjanga, had engaged and paid for . . . at a very high price, moreover?

Chaudey felt it would have been wiser to drop everything. This business had only added to the complications.

And yet Chaudey was here this evening, entrusted with the mission of putting things right. The interests which supported Katanga were decidedly very powerful!

A woman arrived, followed by Pimuriaux; she was carrying a tray with glasses and a bottle. High time too! Since his arrival in Elizabethville Chaudey had been dying of thirst . . . yet the weather was not very hot. This was bound to make him even fatter. Every time he traveled he put on eight pounds.

This girl was quite shapely, but she had strange eyes:

159

very prominent, with the pupil reduced to a pin-head, like a drug-addict's.

"She's a nymphomaniac," Chaudey reflected, "but who's the lucky man, I wonder? . . ."

He imagined la Roncière at grips with her.

"Monsieur le Conseiller," Pimuriaux began.

It's true he had been christened "Conseiller." Why not "Repairer of Broken Pots and Pans"? . . .

Chaudey gulped down a large glass of beer with satisfaction, then remorse.

"I'm at your disposal, Monsieur le Secrétaire-Général. . . ."

"I asked Colonel la Roncière and Monsieur Fonts not to leave the villa."

Chaudey wanted another beer, which made him impatient.

"Why? Were they prisoners?"

"Not exactly . . . but just to be on the safe side. Anyway, they're coming. . . ."

The colonel had intended to leave by the afternoon plane, immediately after seeing Kimjanga. But in these whimsical countries appointments were always postponed, which would oblige him to travel via Salisbury. At Salisbury there was bound to be someone who would recognize him, and in the embassies they had nothing better to do than gossip.

The gossip would eventually reach Paris and when he returned he would be viewed with disfavor at the Quai, as though he had betrayed a cause. He would need two weeks to get back into the saddle. In the meantime all sorts of "regrettable little incidents" would occur which would complicate his work and his private life.

He stretched out his glass.

"A little more beer, please, my dear fellow. That ham you gave me was really very salty."

La Roncière and Fonts came in. Fonts was wiping his lips with a blood-stained handkerchief.

"Do the girls bite in this country?" Chaudey asked him. "I'm told they file their teeth. Good morning, Colonel. This business has certainly got off to a bad start . . . but Monsieur Pimuriaux claims we'll be able to fix things!"

"How?" la Roncière inquired.

"As brittle as ever, this fellow," Chaudey reflected. "He finds it quite normal that I should come all the way from Paris to get him out of the mess he's in."

Chaudey had sunk into an armchair and, while rubbing

his chin with his finger-tips, was doing his best to assume the air of an old sphinx.

"Well now . . . I don't see exactly how I can intervene personally . . . France still does not recognize Katanga, and for the time being has no intention of doing so. Of course, there's that contract you've been given and which hasn't been honored. . . ."

"Precisely."

"I shall confine myself to a protest."

"That's all?"

"If Katanga doesn't honor this contract, she won't honor any other. In that case France will have nothing further to do with this country and we can switch to Leopoldville part of the aid we were planning to give President Kimjanga."

Pimuriaux waved his little hands in the air.

"That will be more than enough ⁄ . . . the President is completely won over to our ideas. All he's trying to find is a pretext to force Major Van Beulans to reconsider our friends' situation."

Chaudey rose to his feet and turned to Fonts and la Roncière.

"I also wanted to see if you were in good health. I say, la Roncière, I've heard from Julienne. Still in Italy. . . . It seems she's studying the mentality of the Piedmontese Army with the help of a strapping Bersaglieri colonel. . . ."

"If I go back to France, how do I stand?"

"You've handed in your resignation from the Army. . . . But don't worry, we would never allow a man of your caliber . . . to languish in Paris without a job."

"It would be quite right and proper to take that line with me."

"Let's say prudent. Fonts, will you come outside a moment? I've got something to tell you. I hope you don't mind Colonel, it's a . . . family matter."

The two colonels shook hands ceremoniously, both heels together.

"Well, Thomas?" Chaudey asked as soon as they were outside.

"The infant's not doing too well."

"I'd like to know what's going on in the north, with the Balubas. Why don't you go up and have a look?"

"If I'm staying out here!"

"You're staying all right. You'll have to decide afterwards if you ought to go on . . . Musaille's very worried.

161

Two of your friends in Guinea have just disappeared. The fruit wasn't ripe. You were wrong. Pity, it was a good idea. . . ."

"What's all this about Julienne and the Bersaglieri colonel?"

"I invented it. Julienne's in Paris. I wanted to see how la Roncière would react: he's only worried about how he stands. I don't like a man who has been Julienne's lover to lose interest in her so quickly!"

"You're an old romantic, Uncle Chaudey, and you'll remain in love with Julienne all your life. . . ."

Then, in a suddenly bantering tone:

"Brothers-in-law all! There must be quite a lot of us. One day I must look at the Army List and tot up the score!"

"Dumont told me you ought to write to your mother."

"Tell him to mind his own business! You know he sends the old girl a long screed every week."

"Really?"

"Yes, the poor bugger never had a mother. So he gets rid of his inhibitions with mine!"

"If he never had a mother, how was he born?"

Fonts shrugged his shoulders.

"He never does anything like anyone else!"

Chaudey realized he would never have access to certain secrets of the gang; he immediately back-pedaled.

"Be very careful, Thomas, when you go up north."

"I'm too skinny to interest the Balubas!"

"When are you going to stop leading this vagabond life, flinging yourself, just for the fun of it, into a series of more or less dangerous games, for I'm not even sure you like winning? Some men have neither the means, nor the position, nor the necessary contacts to allow themselves to stop, that's not your case.

"The trap that will close over you will be a girl. Anyway I hope so, it's a very pleasant trap. I say, you're still bleeding. Choose the girl carefully. When people like you experience a disappointment in love, just when they're at last ready for a woman, it's very serious!"

"Why?"

"They believe firmly in love, they have made it the last refuge of their illusions. If they fail, all that remains for them is to go on with their games and keep smiling as they grow older."

"Was it such a tiring flight, Colonel? A good night's

rest, rocked to sleep by Musaille and Pimuriaux, and you'll be a new man in the morning!"

The colonel pointed at Fonts's lips.

"A red-head, wasn't it?"

"How did you know?"

"I read in a book on eroticism that red-heads enjoy biting. Félicien Dorat's arriving in three days' time. According to his mood, he'll be for or against you. He's interested in two things: the death of Lumumba, and the mercenaries. . . . Good-bye, Thomas. . . . You need another success in order to get back in the saddle, since it seems you don't yet feel the urge to stop."

Colonel Chaudey trotted off to the car in which Pimuriaux was waiting for him.

Two days later Pimuriaux came back to Gelinet's house in a state of great excitement, with two bottles of champagne under his arm.

"From the President," he announced. "It's in the bag, at least almost. . . ."

He bowed to la Roncière.

"Colonel, tomorrow you take up your duties as Military and Political Adviser. . . . We can't yet give you Major Van Beulans's appointment and office officially, but it comes to the same thing. In a month from now Van Beulans will have packed up and left."

"I'm in charge of propaganda and the maintenance of law and order, that's to say, the Army, the Police and Information?"

"Not exactly, but almost. The President will give you all the necessary support, as he assured the friend who came to see you and whom he received with the greatest cordiality. Anyway I'll be beside you to give you a hand."

"I'd rather start from scratch. . . . We'll have to get down to work straight away. Once again we're going to be caught up in all sorts of intrigues. . . ."

"Be reasonable, Colonel. . . ."

"What appointment do I have?" Fonts inquired.

"It so happens your friend from Paris is extremely interested in the Balubas. When the President told him he was sending an investigation commission into the area, he suggested you join this commission. You'll accompany our Transport Minister, His Excellency Evariste Kasingo, with the appointment of technical adviser. . . .

"Keep your eyes and ears open and, as soon as you get back, let us know exactly what the position is. We're very

163

worried, you know, and Minister Kasingo is very liable to be carried away by his own optimistic nature. . . ."

"In other words, to turn a blind eye on everything. When do I leave?"

"You take tomorrow's plane for Albertville."

"It's important," la Roncière observed. "It's even one of the most urgent problems that we have to tackle. If, as I believe, the Belgian officers have committed blunder after blunder in this sector, it will give us the opportunity to get rid of the Van Beulans gang once and for all by saddling them with the responsibility."

Pimuriaux jumped to his feet.

"It's all Van Beulans's fault."

He modestly lowered his eyes.

"At least the President must be made to think so."

Fonts was enjoying himself.

"I see no one's forgetting his own little scores to settle!"

"Do I keep Kreis with me?" la Roncière inquired.

"Of course, he's immediately responsible to you, but perhaps it would be a good thing to send him for the time being to Tshiko Camp as an instructor. . . . Things aren't going too well between the African and Belgian NCOs. . . . We need a reliable man out there. . . . The camp's only two hours by jeep from E'ville. Anyway, Colonel, this camp is being placed immediately under your command."

Kreis and Hortense had glanced at each other: he would be only two hours away from her. . . . Pimuriaux opened a bottle of champagne.

"And now, to celebrate our success, we'll drink a toast to President Kimjanga and President de Gaulle. . . ."

La Roncière pulled a face; he was not fond of de Gaulle; this aversion dated back to 13 May, 1958, when he had tried to oppose the move to appeal to him.

In the evening Fonts went to the Mitsouko, where he found Pérohade in a state of great excitement; he had received a cable from Dorat announcing his arrival.

"Calm down," Fonts said. "You'll see, Dorat will cause you a lot of trouble. We two know each other well. Tell him I've gone off to the Balubas and that when I get back I'll give him something to work on."

"You're going up north?"

"Tomorrow morning. . . ."

"I've got a good friend up there, Wenceslas. He's a Pole from the Anders Army . . . a real tough and no mistake! I'm not sure what he's up to but he's working with the Katangese Gendarmerie; Wenceslas must be wiping out Balubas."

"Pacifying."

"It comes to the same thing. Every week he sends me down a truck which I fill up with beer and whisky."

"He's a nice chap, this Wenceslas?"

"Yes, but he flies off the handle easily."

"I want you to do me a favor . . ."

He produced a handful of banknotes from his pocket.

"Buy some flowers tomorrow morning. . . ."

"Are you off your head? There's enough here to buy up the whole shop."

". . . and have them sent to Miss Joan Riverton at the American Embassy . . . with this."

He brought out an old gold coin pierced with a square hole.

Nathalie, who had been eavesdropping from her cash-desk, now drew closer, pink in the face with emotion.

Fonts glanced from one to the other with his dark eyes, those eyes which could smile and threaten at one and the same time.

"And if you and your girl-friend here breathe a word to anyone . . . especially to that dirty rat Dorat, when I get back I'll come and blow this place to blazes. If by any chance this girl asks after me, tell her I went back to France."

And Fonts sauntered off, his hand in his pockets, a cigarette in the corner of his mouth.

Nathalie turned on Pérohade.

"Monsieur Thomas, at least, knows how to live and behave like a lord. You wouldn't ever have had an idea like that! You don't give a damn for sentiment. Just so long as I'm here to run your pub and go to bed with you when you feel like it!"

"Nathalie, if you go on being such a bore, I'm going to bugger off to the Balubas. But before I leave it won't be flowers you'll get, but a good slap across the chops!"

5. Wenceslas's Scarlet Poppies

Next morning Pérohade drove Fonts to the airport.

In the car he said to him, half in jest, half in anger:

"When you want to put on a romantic act like sending flowers, try not to do it in front of Nathalie: it gives her ideas!"

The aircraft was not ready, the minister had not arrived. The two men sat down in the airport bar and ordered coffee.

"Things aren't going so well up north," said Pérohade, "especially round Nyunzu, Kabalo and Kongolo."

"I don't even know where these places are. Have you got a map?"

"Wenceslas told me all about it in his last letter, but he often exaggerates to play on my pity: I allow him credit. Good heavens! There's Guillaume! He comes from up there. He used to have a plantation between Kabalo and Kongolo, on the way up to Kivu. He could give you the latest information."

"I'm pretty certain what I'm going to find up there, old boy: the bush abandoned, the villages empty, and more or less well-armed bands taking pot shots at one another: that's the new Africa. . . . She's trying to find her balance but where does that get her? Back to her old customs. The white man merely passed through."

But Pérohade had already waved to Guillaume, a careworn man with gray hair, wearing a straw hat and a shabby blue serge suit.

"Well, Guillaume, how are you?" said Pérohade. "We haven't seen anything of you for a month!"

Guillaume sat down at their table and ordered a beer.

"I went back north," he said. "They told me the glorious army of little Uncle Kimjanga had restored law and order. I wanted to see what was happening to my plantation . . . and I came away again; the cotton was rotting in the fields; there was no one to harvest it."

"Why not?" Fonts inquired.

"Because up there, monsieur, they're too busy killing one another. I must tell you a story, however. Mind you, Antoine, I've already given it to one of your colleagues, but maybe you could use it again!

"I was in a jeep, driving along a narrow track through the bush, the only one the floods had spared. I came across four Africans, beatnik type, the sort of Balubas who have worked in E'ville: in trousers and shirts, all filthy dirty, of course. One of them had a transistor which wouldn't work, the three others wore dark glasses dangling over their noses. They must have been members of the Balubakat.* 'Fambo,' they said, which means 'Good morning' in their lingo.

"I'd stopped to let them go past. 'Fambo,' I replied and let in the clutch.

" 'Is that all?' one of these apes asked.

" 'Well, yes, that's all. Fambo: good morning and good-bye.'

"Then I heard him say to his pals: 'This white man isn't at all polite. . . . We must kill him when he comes back.'

"Under their shirts they had knives and bicycle-chains attached to wooden handles like whips. So the cotton will stay unharvested and the Balubas will die of hunger, but it won't prevent old Uncle Guillaume from enjoying his nice cold beer. Because those sods . . . they cut my foreman's throat, and my two boys . . . crucified against a tree. They had seen it on the films . . . and they're mad about the films. They want to do everything just like the cinema. . . . No, it wasn't to make fun of the Church or the missionaries . . . it was to imitate the films! To your health!"

The aircraft was due to take off at eight-thirty; the minister turned up at eleven, in a big American car and accompanied by Pimuriaux, his private secretary and another African who had no official appointment but happened to be the cousin of the aunt or uncle of the husband of the sister of His Excellency Evariste Kasingo; he was taking this opportunity of having a trip in a plane.

"I must be off," Fonts said to Pérohade.

* A party comprising most of the Balubas in Katanga and enjoying the support of the Leopoldville Government.

He took his watch off his wrist.

"Here's a present for you; I have a feeling that in this country it's best not to know the time: it only irritates you. So long, old lad, and watch your step!"

Through gestures of this sort, which were spontaneous and at the same time calculated, Fonts made friends everywhere.

Pimuriaux introduced him to His Excellency Evariste Kasingo, a big black who wore all the trappings of his office: homburg hat, white shirt, light-colored tie, well-cut dark suit, polished shoes, gloves and a black leather briefcase.

"Your Excellency, this is Monsieur Thomas Fonts whom the President mentioned to you. He knows nothing about our country: your help and advice will be invaluable to him."

A broad grin came over His Excellency's somewhat grumpy face.

"Delighted, my dear fellow. . . . It's a good thing indeed, as Monsieur le Secrétaire-Général has pointed out, that the white men who come here to help the people of Katanga to defend their independence should get to know the psychology of the men of our Bantu country. . . . What about a beer? I think we have plenty of time."

And thus it was that the aircraft, an old Dakota, did not take off until eleven-thirty.

Albertville, situated on the edge of Lake Tanganyika, at the foot of the volcanic Mitumba Mountains, with its bungalows surrounded by gardens, its green lawns and trees, struck Fonts as being a town suitable for long week-ends, one of those old-fashioned resorts where one came to play tennis, fish, sail and recite poems to pale young girls.

Among the notables who had come to welcome Evariste Kasingo was a prefect called Something-or-other, the Chief of the Health Service—six months earlier he was still a medical orderly—the Chief of Police, a sort of hippopotamus with gleaming skin who was sweating so profusely that he seemed to have just emerged from his water-hole, and a young European who was introduced as the Assistant Director of Cotonka, the big cotton firm in the province.

Fonts fastened on him.

Edgar Mullens was twenty-six; he had graduated two years earlier from the Agronomical Institute of Brussels. But as a result of the disappearance or departure of most of the staff, he now found himself the only representative of the company.

He was a sturdy lad, with the square muscles of the mountaineer, close-cropped hair and a pink complexion, a sort of Scout Master to whom the series of outlandish incidents he had witnessed during the last year had given self-assurance and even a certain sophistication. He had seen the board of directors collapse in a matter of days and the lie given to all the dispensers of advice who had welcomed him with such self-satisfaction into the company.

In the car taking them from the airport to the Hotel du Lac, where a reception had been arranged, Fonts asked him:

"What's going on here?"

Mullens calmly shrugged his shoulders.

"Nothing, of course. A year ago there were a thousand Europeans in Albertville, there must be about a hundred left. The bush has been abandoned, all the settlers have gone, their farms have been looted, their crops destroyed. . . . In the depths of the forest they're again dancing to the sound of tom-toms and sacrificing human beings."

"I saw a fellow called Guillaume at the airport."

"Old Uncle Guillaume? We used to buy cotton from him. He must have told you his famous *Fambo* story. . . . Poor old boy, he still hasn't recovered from it! Guillaume could not adapt himself to the new Africa. He treated his workmen well but would never allow them to speak to him without first taking off their hats."

"What about you?"

"Me? I've just arrived. What shocks Uncle Guillaume doesn't bother me. But what a mess it is! What's your minister come here for? To palaver like all the rest of them? The minister of a government which, in this area, doesn't govern anything!"

A south-westerly wind ruffled the surface of the lake, alternately churning it up and flattening it within its circle of mountains, rending asunder and scattering big black clouds to the four corners of the sky.

"It's quite simple," Mullens went on. "On the other side of the water lies Sumbwa, in Tanganyikan territory. It's connected by fairly good roads to Dar es Salaam on the Zanzibar coast. In the old days it was the slave route, now it's used for smuggling arms. Everyone has a hand in equipping the Balubakat bands: Nasser, Somaliland, etc. In several places Indian and Ethiopian UN garrisons have been established. These garrisons support Leopoldville against E'ville, provide the rebels with arms and ammunition, shelter them and behave as though they were due to stay forever."

"Not a very healthy picture!"

"Though the arms get through, the convoys of ore and cotton that used to be sent from Dar es Salaam no longer use this route. The mines aren't being exploited any more, the cotton is rotting in the fields . . . and everyone's dying of hunger. Look, there's the hospital. There are still a few doctors and nursing sisters left. That column is a monument to Captain Jacques, the founder of the town. It was donated by the Anti-Slavery Society of Belgium. Three years running he fought against the Arabs who swarmed over the lake and came to supply themselves with ebony wood. During the 1914-18 War he was made a general and Baron de Dixmude. He was a splendid character and absolutely pig-headed. He at least enjoyed himself in Africa!

"Here's the Hotel du Lac: we're in for speeches and a glass of champagne. Africa, monsieur, boils down to a few fine speeches, delivered by parrots who use the language of the white man without understanding it, and champagne . . . more often than not shoddy stuff which the big firms unload on them and which is drunk lukewarm. . . . But the bush is reverting to savagery. Well, I've delivered my little speech. *Vidye uyukilé!*"

"What does that mean?"

"An expression they keep using all the time: 'God alone knows.' "

By half past four in the afternoon the minister and his suite were dead drunk. They piled into three jeeps, preceded by a truckload of soldiers, and headed in the direction of Nyunzu. Another truck brought up the rear, stuffed with cakes of soap and packets of cigarettes "for propaganda purposes."

Edgar Mullens took advantage of the convoy to inspect the thousands of acres exploited by the company. He took Fonts with him in his car.

African roads usually resemble columns of ants, along which men, women and children, laden with bundles or calabashes, keep moving up and down incessantly.

The Nyunzu road was deserted. The villages built in the clearings alongside had been burned down. Rain had transformed the charred vegetation into thick mud which exuded a smell of old ashes. Of the square huts all that

170

remained, more often than not, were scorched black skeletons.

Only once did the convoy come across a small group of blacks, who, wild with terror, scuttled off into the bush.

A few miles from Nyunzu the jeeps stopped at the first Baluba village that appeared to be occupied. His Excellency, who had been sleeping off his brandy, got out of his jeep, with his hat askew and his suit crumpled.

The palaver began.

The police commissioner with the gait of a hippopotamus led the way, carrying the gifts: cakes of soap wrapped in paper bearing a portrait of President Kimjanga, and a few packets of Belga cigarettes.

An old man came forward wearing a monkey skin round his waist with the tail hanging between his legs, while a few hundred yards farther off, emerging from their huts, the population assembled. . . . There were no adult males, only women clad in robes, doddering elders and naked children with emaciated limbs and swollen stomachs.

"Let's go and have a look," Fonts suggested to Mullens.

The envoy from the village took the gifts and went back to his fellow villagers, who forthwith started arguing and gesticulating.

"Where's the chief?" the minister asked.

"He's not here," the police commissioner replied, "the old man says he's left."

"What about all the men?"

"They've left as well."

"But where?"

"Into the bush."

"What for?"

"He doesn't know."

The village elder returned with the gifts and laid them down by the side of the road.

"This time," said Mullens, "it's not going at all well; they've refused the presents. What's the matter with them?"

The police commissioner seized the old man by the arm and shook him as he led him towards the minister.

"This old bastard . . . and all the bloody bastards in his tribe say that President Kimjanga's soap sends people blind and that the cigarettes are poisoned."

"Who's told them these lies?" Evariste Kasingo demanded in Swahili. Fanning himself with his hat, he was trying to assume an air of outrage.

171

"The Balubakat," the old man replied.

He started to whine.

"For six months there's been war all the time. Everyone is very bad. The Balubakats take everything there is to eat and then they go into the women's huts and make free with them. . . . President Kimjanga's gendarmes also come and eat, rape and kill, and . . . make free with the women . . . and then everyone is sick and then there is no more medicine. . . ."

The minister gave an impatient signal and the convoy drove on with the soldiers drumming frenziedly on their mess-tins, the ramshackle jeeps bouncing over the muddy pot-holes, and the "notables" clutching their hats and their briefcases.

"The enemy also have their propaganda," Fonts remarked. "It's rough-and-ready and therefore effective; the adults buggered off into the bush as soon as our arrival was reported; or else they're frightened or hostile . . . probably both. It's not by burning down villages that we'll win the Balubas over. They're all dying of hunger . . . those kids with bellies and edema in the ankles and wrists, those grotesque heads: and of course, no doctors, no nurses: they've all gone back to Brussels or Albertville. How far are we from Nyunzu?"

"About five miles or less."

"What will it be like fifty or a hundred miles farther on?"

"That's simple, there'll be nothing."

They began to drive through big fields of cotton that had not been picked.

"No cotton, no dough," said Mullens. "But no one wants to work in these fields; everyone's frightened."

"What of?"

"Everything . . . because the white men went off as soon as the first incidents started. They went off as fast as they could, my compatriots. . . . Had we hung on, a month later all would have been well. . . ."

At the entrance to the town they passed an old truck crammed with merchandise.

"That's Patandakis the Greek. . . . He runs a little trading business: he'd shave an egg to sell you the whiskers, but at least he stayed on. . . . He's really the only one, because even the Pygmies have buggered off. It's a disaster."

"The Pygmies?"

"A strange sort of commerce had established itself be-

172

tween the Pygmy hunters and the Baluba cultivators. The Pygmies were not allowed to enter the villages and the bartering took place on the edge of the forest: meat in exchange for manioc, seed, sweet potatoes, but above all money. With this money the Pygmies bought salt, knives, cotton stuffs. The land is no longer cultivated, there's no more money . . . therefore no more Pygmies. . . . Those little savages are out-and-out realists!"

"We must make them come back."

"Go ahead and try!"

Nyunzu, a little town of five thousand inhabitants, had only a few proper houses, the rest of the buildings being mud huts. The only white men there were two Belgian officers and Wenceslas Borojaweski, a mercenary and soldier of fortune, who had not drawn any pay for two months. . . . But this did not worry him at all. He bought on credit, and whatever he was unable to buy he took.

With his carbine on his shoulder, a bush hat on his head and jungle boots on his feet, he ambled up to the former residence of the Belgian administrator, now occupied by an African administrator called Cyprien Malwike.

In a strong Slav accent he asked:

"Another circus show?"

He caught sight of Mullens and shook his head.

"Well, is the cotton still rotting?"

Jerking his head at Fonts, he then asked:

"What's this chap doing here, with his lovely trousers and beautiful khaki shirt?"

"I've come to collect the money you owe Antoine Pérohade; I only take cash."

Wenceslas slapped the butt of his carbine.

"I pay with this!"

"Look, Wenceslas, a new crowd has just taken over in E'ville: a French colonel, who's a friend of mine, and his henchman. I know from Pérohade that you're pig-headed but also a good fellow. . . . So either I have you chucked out or else you toe the line. . . . Take your choice. And don't try and impress me with that gun of yours; it's badly maintained and the barrel's rusty!"

During his arduous life Wenceslas had learned to judge men and could tell when they were bluffing.

"All right," he calmly replied, ceasing to act tough. "How's Nathalie? What a divine creature!"

"She's well," Fonts replied. "Show us where you hang out. I'll go and see the notables later on. Meanwhile you're going to stand us a drink and tell us what's going on up here."

Wenceslas lived in a villa in the opposite direction from the administrator's and they had to cross the whole town on foot. The streets were filthy, filled with refuse and rubble; stray dogs with mangy coats and prominent ribs slunk away with a growl as they walked past. Most of the shops had their shutters down. Some of them had been looted and fragments of glass still sparkled on the pavement where mangoes lay rotting beneath swarms of bluebottles; others had been set on fire and their metal roofs were charred and buckled.

A stench of latrines, rotting vegetation and rancid palm oil hung over the dead town. A few Negroes went by, shifty-eyed and clad in shorts of indeterminate color, their shirts hanging in shreds on their naked torsos.

Wenceslas had fitted out a couple of rooms for himself on the ground floor of the villa. The walls were covered with photographs of naked girls cut out of magazines, and labels from beer or whisky bottles.

Above a false chimney-piece was a weapon-rack stacked with shotguns, big-game rifles, a Fal automatic rifle and a Mauser with telescopic sights.

The first room was furnished with a camp bed, surmounted by a mosquito-net, and a couple of tin trunks; the second with a table in walnut veneer, six chairs, a sofa covered in bright red cloth, a mirror peppered with revolver shots, and an ice-box.

"All this is just an act, my fine friend," Fonts reflected, "to make you forget that you're just an old wreck . . . swept up, as they say, by the tide of history; but you're hard put to keep your head above water. You spent the whole of last night thinking of the clothes you were going to wear to receive us, that's to say of the role you were going to play for our benefit. You've got a receding chin, but a high forehead and intelligent eyes . . . a dreamer and a bit of a mythomaniac . . . I've never pulled off a successful job with square-jawed types . . . only with chaps like you, whom one holds to their own lies . . . and whom one saves or kills. Funny, here I am already with a team: the little engineer, a realist, and the Pole, a slave to his self-deception and failure."

Wenceslas opened some cans of beer with a commando knife.

"Now let's talk," said Fonts. "Before going back to the

174

clowns we're with, I'd like to have a clearer picture! You've been here how long, Wenceslas?"

"Three months."

"What have you accomplished?"

"One job against the UN, two or three pot-shots at Balubas. The Katangese gendarmes won't move a finger; they say no one pays them. But if they were paid, they'd spend their time swilling beer and wouldn't be any more active than they are now."

"So you let them stew in their own juice? What's the administrator like?"

"Cyprien? You'd better ask Mullens here; he's the former secretary of the Belgian who was here before him. . . . The only time he bestirred himself was to take his place. Since then he spends his time sleeping, drinking and fornicating . . . and he's windy as hell . . . windy of having his balls cut off. He can't have much fun here with Justinien Balake, the captain who in theory commands the Army, that's to say the gang of thugs recruited from the riff-raff of E'ville and christened gendarmes. He's equally idle, sozzled and debauched; in theory I'm his military adviser. There are also three Belgian officers, at least there were, but now there are only two left. The gendarmes still obey them. Before independence Cyprien was an assistant PT instructor, and Balake a corporal. Both of them shiver in their shoes at the sight of Muto, the Mwata of Jenge: they go and suck up to him every day and grease the palm of his witch-doctor to keep on the right side of him."

"Who's Muto?"

It was Mullens who replied:

"A nasty bit of work but quite a character: one of the few Baluba chiefs who's come over to President Kimjanga in order to have money and arms and become a big boss by liquidating all his neighbors. . . . You'll see him tomorrow morning."

"Brought up by the priests, who wanted to make a seminarist of him," Wenceslas added. "You should see the result!"

"And the Balubas?"

"Apart from Muto, who has a firm hand on his area, all the Balubas are against us. . . . They shoot us up with whatever weapons they can find: pop-guns which they manufacture themselves: a wooden butt, a bicycle-frame tube stuffed with gunpowder and nails . . . poisoned arrows, pangas . . . but also, for the last two weeks, with machine-guns sold or given to them by Ethiopian soldiers.

. . . There are any amount of bodies rotting away in the bush and others have been eaten. And not only by animals. . . ."

"Any amount?"

Wenceslas mopped his brow.

"Fifty thousand perhaps. When the Katangese Army, led by Belgians, moved up to pacify them, they must have lined up about twenty thousand. Fighting among themselves and starvation have accounted for the rest. The Balubas still believe Lumumba's alive. I heard in E'ville that Bongo wanted to send them Patrice's head, nicely embalmed, and have it carried round from village to village. But even then they wouldn't have believed it. When the operations were over everyone went back to E'ville, except for the officers I mentioned."

"And why did you stay on?"

"I'm a Pole; I don't like doing what everyone else does."

"Have you developed a taste for African girls?"

"They can also be found in E'ville."

"You drink on credit?"

"In E'ville as well. I tell you, I'm a Pole and I must have a taste for low life. Dostoievsky talks about it in his books. By the way, what's your rank? I'm a lieutenant."

Fonts picked up Wenceslas's knife and aimed it at the door, where it landed quivering.

"I don't know yet; I'm hesitating between colonel and general . . . but I think I'm going to remain plain Thomas Fonts to my friends. . . . Mullens and I will doss down here tonight. Find us a couple of beds . . . and a typewriter."

"What's the typewriter for?"

"For waging war, of course. I'm going back to Cyprien's. You stay here . . . and don't get too sozzled. We still have a lot to discuss."

"But . . ."

"Either you carry out my orders or else you pack your bags and clear out. At E'ville you'll be put on board a plane for . . . wherever you like."

Wenceslas tired to save face.

"All right, Thomas, I'll take you on approval. . . ."

"And I'll cough up the two months' pay you haven't yet drawn."

Fonts burst into a loud guffaw, standing upright with his hands on his slim hips.

"Well, Wenceslas, do you like the way I laugh?"

Wenceslas gazed at the small dark man in amazement.

"Why?" he eventually asked.

"Because Dostoievsky said: 'I believe a man can be judged by the way he laughs and that if, at first sight, a stranger laughs pleasantly, then he is fundamentally sound.' I'm very sound fundamentally, Wenceslas. So long!"

He fingered the barrel of one of the rifles.

"You ought to clean your artillery."

Cyprien had made a supreme effort to receive the minister, but such was the slovenliness that had reigned for the last six months that it could not be effaced by a few strokes of the broom. The refuse had been swept into the corners. But the tables were still littered with empty beer bottles; and the crowd of women and parasites, after being half-heartedly driven away, had quickly regained possession of the Residency where they were in the habit of living.

All these people, barefoot and gaping, stood watching Evariste Kasingo, waiting for him to amuse them with a speech or some display of magic.

Cyprien was not very bright, but he knew what the men of his race were like, especially those who were given to palavering and politics.

Rather than having the gobs of spittle and patches of dust swept off the floor, which would have required an effort, he had chosen, in order to keep his job, to resort to a mixture of artful dodges, negotiation and brazen lies.

"This place is in a pretty filthy state," the minister declared, "it's more like a chicken-run than an official's residence. What can the whites think of us? That we're incapable of being independent!"

From the thirty people thronging the room there rose a cry of protest. Thus encouraged, the delegate embarked on his act. Cyprien loved the people of Katanga, who had suffered so much in the days of colonialism. He had wanted them to share with him all the privileges he derived from his lofty appointment. Because this at least was owed to the people.

But all he demanded, personally, was to be relieved of his duties. He did not have the means to carry them out: the Army never moved out of camp and did nothing but beat people up, get drunk and burn down huts: his car had broken down, the telephone was out of order and everyone was hungry.

He then referred to the Ethiopians who raped the

177

women, the Balubakats with their bicycle-chains, the risk he himself ran of being kidnapped and massacred whenever he went into the bush.

As he outlined these dangers, Cyprien gradually went gray with fear, began to sweat and tug at his collar and wring his hands, and kept buttoning and unbuttoning the coat of his grease-stained drill suit.

The minister leaned over to Fonts.

"It's true, my dear friend, Monsieur le Délégué has a very hard life here. . . ."

"He's scared stiff," Fonts retorted. "No one has ever seen him in any of the villages through which we passed."

The minister assumed an air of austerity and apostrophized Cyprien.

"Monsieur le Délégué, from what we have seen in the course of our tour of inspection, the pacification with which you are entrusted is not making headway. . . ."

Cyprien protested: law and order reigned in the whole zone north of Nyunzu; he had won over the paramount chief of Jenge to the Katangese cause, the Balubas who were still in the bush were going to come back. . . .

The women kept pressing against the minister; one of them, who was young and pretty, with firm breasts and a prominent rump, stroked his sleeve.

But in front of Fonts, Evariste could not allow himself to be distracted without losing face. In the evening his private secretary would bring the girl along to him.

How much easier it would be if there were only blacks involved. Blacks understand that a grand person like Evariste Kasingo is entitled to certain privileges. Exercising power means taking what one wants, and without hesitation.

The minister remembered he had been told about a Belgian captain in the area who was specifically responsible for operations against the rebel Balubas. Where was he, this fellow? He had kept away just to insult him. He tried to think of his name: Captain Ruyck. . . . The girl was now pressed against him as though she was being pushed from behind. The minister's thoughts grew confused, the blood rushed to his head. If he said he was feeling tired, he could leave straight away and amuse himself with the girl.

Evariste made another effort.

"Where's Captain Ruyck?"

Cyprien took his revenge on the Belgian.

"He's out on operations," he said, "because a village

178

was burned down and a white man killed. But lots of villages are burned down and he doesn't go and have a look each time. The blacks can die; the captain despises the blacks. He has never called on me even though, as delegate, I'm his senior."

"It's unforgivable. . . ."

Fonts had noticed what the girl was up to: Cyprien must certainly have given her orders to seduce the minister and she was going about it absolutely brazenly.

Evariste could not hold out much longer.

Fonts came to his rescue.

"Your Excellency," he said, "it's impossible to work in this fairground atmosphere. It's been an exhausting journey. . . . I'm going to get down to business with Monsieur le Délégué. I think there's a room ready for you: you could have a little rest. Tomorrow's liable to be equally arduous."

The minister agreed with alacrity.

"The report I have to draft for the President . . ."

He went out, followed shortly afterwards by the girl.

"His Excellency also loves the people," Cyprien observed with satisfaction.

"And I love facts and figures, Monsieur le Délégué. Come along here for a moment."

Fonts closeted himself with Cyprien in the former administrator's office. On the wall hung a large map of the district, half torn away. There were stacks of files covered in dust. The telephone was held together with sellotape. Everything smelled damp and musty. Clearly Cyprien hardly ever came into this room; maybe he felt ill at ease in it?

Fonts, after wiping the armchair with his handkerchief, sat down as a matter of course behind the big teak desk. Cyprien remained standing, shifting from one foot to the other.

"How many police have you got on your strength?" Fonts asked him.

"A hundred, but they're a worthless lot; they refuse to set foot outside their barracks."

"Really?"

"They say it rains too much and a policeman who is wet can't do his job properly, that they've only got one uniform and would have to go around naked while it dried: a naked policeman would be a laughing-stock! That they haven't enough to eat and that a policeman who doesn't eat needs a lot of sleep . . . that they never draw

179

their pay . . . but then neither do I. It's not good, all this. I went to talk it over with them and they tried to beat me up. . . ."

"What have they got in the way of arms?"

"Rifles . . . but there's no more ammunition. They sold it all to buy beer. . . ."

"You should have taken disciplinary action."

"They've still got their rifles, after all. And then the UN soldiers come and taunt them . . . and throw them tins of sardines. . . . The Indians come along with soldiers from the National Congolese Army who tell them they're a lot of bloody idiots to stay on our side while in the National Congolese Army there's plenty to eat, everyone's a sergeant . . . and sergeants have whisky to drink at every meal."

Fonts leaned back in his armchair, put both feet on the desk, lit a cigarette and amused himself by blowing smoke rings.

Cyprien watched him, fascinated and increasingly ill at ease.

"How many police have deserted?" Fonts inquired.

"Twenty perhaps . . . or thirty. . . ."

"And you did nothing about it?"

"It's not my fault. . . ."

Fonts burst out laughing.

"You didn't happen to put their pay in your own pocket, did you?"

"That's one of Captain Ruyck's dirty lies . . . the Belgian swine. He's hand in glove with the UN . . . I have documents . . ."

"You've been here six months, haven't you? What have you accomplished in that time?"

Cyprien was slowly losing his self-assurance under the white man's harsh sardonic gaze. He was no longer the delegate, only a vainglorious little nigger who had thought, because he was able to write his own name, that he was capable of governing a province.

"It's not my fault, boss! The Government never told me what to do. . . ."

"You received no instructions?"

"None. . . . All the papers are in the desk and they all date back to the time of the Belgians. . . ."

He collapsed.

"I want to go back to E'ville."

Fonts got up and gave him a slap on the back.

"Maybe we'll have to have you shot . . . the minister's not at all pleased. . . ."

From the room above them came the sound of a bed creaking.

"The minister's quite pleased at the moment!" Cyprien observed.

His flabby face had suddenly assumed an incredibly sly expression. He was no longer frightened of Fonts.

"Where does the Belgian captain live?"

"He's gone."

"You're going to take me to see him."

"Maybe he has come back!"

"Because he never went away at all, because it was you who never asked him to come and see you. . . . You made that story up to blacken him in the eyes of the minister. . . . Cyprien, the country's collapsing all round you, and you can only think of your own little grudges, eh?"

Fonts shook his head.

Cyprien knew what a family, a clan or a tribe was, he did not know what a country was; it needed centuries to learn that. Granted, by means of radio, television and every other form of propaganda and brain-washing, it was now possible to manufacture a country more quickly. But how long would this jerry-built structure last against rain, wind and sun? The minister thought first of all about sleeping with girls . . . and the delegate about drinking beer . . . nothing else mattered; it was all a lot of white man's nonsense!

Captain Ruyck was at table with his second-in-command.

Fonts introduced himself; the two officers did not even rise from their chairs but went on guzzling their sausages and cabbage which they washed down with great draughts of beer.

Fonts seized a chair and sat down astride it, with his elbows resting on the back. Very calmly he repeated:

"I've come up from E'ville with Minister Evariste Kasingo who's on a tour of inspection of the northern provinces. I'd like to know what you think."

"Which minister?" the captain asked.

The bones showed through his yellow skin, his hair was so fair it looked bleached, and his hand was shaking:

"Don't know of any minister, myself. I heard there was something that looked like a minister trailing about the place. But you know, I haven't been notified!"

181

"I know . . . your little pal Cyprien wanted to do you down."

"Cyprien's a shit. . . . They're all a lot of shits. Just savages. And the only way to make savages understand is to shoot them up. . . ."

The captain's second-in-command, a big hearty fellow, tried to smoothe things over.

"It's a funny sort of job we've been given, monsieur. It was only yesterday we found young Second-Lieutenant Marey."

The captain's hand was shaking more and more. He dropped his fork.

Fonts realized the man was on the verge of collapse. In a different tone he inquired:

"What about this second-lieutenant?"

The captain explained in a hoarse voice:

"He'd been missing for four days. I'd sent him out on patrol along a track leading to Tongo, with two jeeps and eight gendarmes. . . . They fell into an ambush set by the Balubas. The gendarmes took to their heels. Marey tried to defend himself. . . . He mowed down as many as he could . . . but he got captured all the same . . . alive, poor boy. . . .

"The Balubas cut off both his feet at the ankles; they hammered pieces of wood into the stumps and dragged him along from village to village, forcing him to walk on these stilts . . . just to show that a white man is no more clever or courageous than a Baluba.

"Then they cut off his ears, gouged out his eyes and all the rest, those fine Balubas the UN are defending. . . . They hacked his legs to pieces with bicycle-chains . . . there were only a few shreds of flesh left on the bones.

"So now pacification's going to consist of one heavy machine-gun mounted on a jeep firing to the right, another machine-gun on the following jeep firing to the left, and anything that moves gets mowed down."

"Did you wait until Second-Lieutenant Marey was killed, Captain, before starting your pacification with machine-guns?" Fonts gently inquired. "Isn't that the reason the Balubas committed such atrocities on him?"

"Have you been in this part of the country before, monsieur? No? Well, I've been here five years, I know it well. I'd like to see what you'd do if you fell into their hands. . . .

"Because you're a white man, and even though we don't like what you're doing here, I'll give you one word of advice: bugger off and let all these niggers fight it out among themselves."

The big·lieutenant interjected:

"That's what the Belgian administrator did, the one who was sent as Cyprien's civilian assistant. He didn't even stay a week. Before he came he was Police Commissioner in Luluabourg. His wife was raped, he himself had his epaulettes torn off in his own police station, his revolver taken away, his arse kicked . . . by one of his own inspectors, on the grounds that he was no longer needed. Since then he couldn't stand the sight of a nigger and never stopped drinking.

"He was put on board a plane and flown home. . . ."

Fonts did not attend the dinner given by Cyprien in honor of the minister. He preferred to leave the Africans to themselves and not force them by his presence to pretend to be what they were not.

The whole lot of them would drink like fish, guzzle meat stewed in palm oil and red pepper, roar with laughter, tumble girls, palaver for hours . . . wallowing in the present moment, oblivious of the past, reassuring themselves by addressing one another by pompous titles. The future was a lot of white man's nonsense.

He went back to Wenceslas's villa.

With a great effort he tried to put his thoughts in order, to work out the steps that would have to be taken straight away to arrest the rapid collapse of the province.

The first essential, of course, was to send home the two Belgian officers who with their "pacification" raids could only alienate the Balubas completely. The point was to win them over, not massacre them. The captain prided himself on having been in the area for five years. To all of them, therefore, he continued to represent Belgium and thus detracted from their brand-new independence. The agents of the Balubakat and the Leopoldville Government were thereby provided with a magnificent propaganda point.

"You Katangese call yourselves independent, but Captain Ruyck's still there with his cap, his revolver, his swagger-stick and Belgian badge . . . he's the one in command."

Little Second-Lieutenant Marey had paid for this psychological error with his life.

Cyprien would also have to be recalled at once. But who was to replace him? A black? . . . He would do no better. A white? . . . But it was essential he should not be a former Belgian official. I'm in a cleft stick, Fonts reflected. I'll have to take on the job myself. I'm the only one who can restore law and order and feed all these starving mouths.

Young Mullens, one could see, was suffering at the sight of his cotton rotting in the fields. Wenceslas, if handled firmly, could at a pinch replace the Belgians as head of the Gendarmerie.

Fonts found Wenceslas and Mullens dining together by the flickering light of a kerosene lamp. An electric-light bulb hung useless from the ceiling.

He accepted only a slice of bread, a hunk of dry sausage and a beer, then asked Wenceslas:

"What does Cyprien do with himself?"

Wenceslas made a gesture with his hand.

"He's in Nyunzu only two days a week. The rest of the time he spends with Mwata Motu, the Baluba chief. . . . Over there he doesn't feel scared, he gets all the beer and women he wants, he can preen himself and palaver with self-importance. . . ."

"In other words, the real capital of the province is no longer Nyunzu but Mwata's village.

"Mullens, what happened when you tried to get the cotton cultivation under away again?"

"Cyprien just gaped; the silly fool couldn't understand it was the key to pacification. What he saw was the money to be made. He asked me to give him some seed to distribute. . . . Distribute indeed! All he intended was to sell it . . . outside the province. He also wanted money . . . for a present for the Mwata.

"Captain Ruyck told me to go to hell. He wasn't here, he said, to indulge in agriculture. If he felt like gardening, he'd rather do it in Belgium. Second-Lieutenant Marey was the only one who seemed interested.

"You know what the Balubas did to him? He was the nicest of the lot. . . . He must have been nabbed because he tried not to open fire at once."

"Aren't you frightened of ending up like him?"

"Of course, but one always thinks one'll get away with it: sickness, old age, death happen to others, not to oneself."

Fonts retired to the room with the broken windows, where a camp bed had been set up, and tried to sleep. But for years he had slept badly, even when he was exhausted, and would lie on his back with his eyes open, his hands folded on his chest like a dying man, and review all the incidents in his stormy past. Sometimes it was unbearable. He would then get up and go out. Whenever he was in a town in Europe he would move from one night-club to another until dawn; when he was in the Far East he would take refuge in an opium den. In Africa he had the feeling he was rotting away, devoured by thousands of worms.

Tomorrow, when he had seen the Mwata, he would draft his report. All was lost unless he himself, invested with plenary powers and unimpeded by the Belgian officers and Cyprien, tried once again to force his luck.

But he knew that once more, as in Indo-China, the Sahara and what was formerly French Africa, he would be attempting to preserve with his one pair of hands a parapet of sand on which the tide was encroaching and which was already crumbling away.

Fonts always said this sort of experience amused him and that he enjoyed fighting a rearguard action, but it was not true.

A certain form of life had become necessary to him. Nowadays it consisted merely of an aimless and fruitless commotion, which still tried to justify itself by the implementation of some great project or other which was almost always doomed by the rapid evolution of the world.

Fonts remembered Joan and her red hair, her ungainly and touching would-be boyish manner, also her aggressiveness and the sprinkling of freckles on each side of her nose, just where her cheeks began.

He pictured the face his mother Antonia would pull if he brought the young American girl to Elne one day and said:

"I think I'm going to marry this girl and raise a family."

Antonia had already found him three or four local girls, all of whom owned land, knew how to bring up a child and run a house, danced the sardana and spoke to the servants in Catalan, which enables one to remain on friendly terms with them yet still make them obey one.

Joan would commit all sorts of blunders, and it would be great fun to see her, a girl who believed herself to be free, at grips with the ritual, customs and finer points of the old Mediterranean world.

Fonts vowed never to see Joan again. He knew only too well that if he made her his mistress or wife he would soon get tired of her, like all the other women he had known.

He did not get to sleep until an hour before dawn.

The Mwata Motu lived thirty miles to the north of Nyunzu, near the source of the Lufwango River; he controlled thirty thousand Balubas. When independence was declared, his subjects had shown a certain degree of restlessness but, thanks to the support of the witch-doctors who had been able to dispatch a few hot-heads to the other world, he had emerged from the ordeal with increased power.

He was a small man of about fifty, with lighter-colored skin than most Balubas; he spoke French fairly well and even knew a few words of Latin, for the priests who had brought him up had taught him to serve at Mass. He could no longer read, however; he had forgotten how to. But, being too vain to admit this, he pretended his eyesight was poor. He never had his spectacles with him and would hand the paper he had been given to a secretary who always stood behind him.

Motu was intelligent, but intelligent only as some Africans are: they are fully aware of the problems which concern them, they have a clear concept of them; but the rest of the world which begins at the threshold of their huts remains lost in the mists.

As soon as he had come to power, Lumumba had taken action against the hereditary chiefs. His avowed aim was to get rid of "this scourge which prevents Africa from developing."

The Mwata Motu had heard two or three speeches on this subject in Leopoldville. Then he had gone home and thereafter had laid aside European dress in favor of brightly colored robes, gold bracelets, the long staff with its ivory handle shaped like a monkey's hand, and a lion-skin.

Being a Baluba, he loathed the other races, whether they were Lundas from the same tribe as President Kimjanga or Bayekes like Minister Bongo. He felt he had to guard against the most immediate danger; this danger was Lumumba.

His death had given him intense joy, but he knew it would take several years to eradicate the false ideas sown in these thick black skulls.

Three months earlier Motu had sent emissaries to Elizabethville and after lengthy negotiation had obtained all he wanted from Kimjanga: the title of Minister of State, money, a few arms, and plenary power over the members of his tribe. The Belgians and the gendarmes would not concern themselves with the pacification of his

186

territory . . . but would attend more particularly to the neighboring hereditary chiefs.

In great pomp President Kimjanga had received him in Elizabethville and had driven him through the streets in his open car, while the Public Relations department flooded every editorial office in Europe with the account of this admirable adherence to the cause.

Motu had simply found in Kimjanga, and especially in Bongo, two men who thought as he did and who sought the support of the hereditary chiefs out of scorn and fear of the more advanced younger generation who rejected all traditional authority.

To receive the Minister of Transport and his escort, Motu had had some triumphal arches of plaited foliage erected on the road. As the convoys drove past, the inhabitants of the villages clapped their hands and waved palm fronds.

But he himself had not troubled to come and greet them. He waited at Jenge for Evariste Kasingo, a man of lowly birth who scarcely knew who his father and mother were. Was not he, Motu, also a minister and above all did he not wield the real power, the power that is rooted in Africa's ancient past and is endowed with all her magic?

Jenge was a big village of ten thousand inhabitants whose huts formed a square round a hard-wall house with a roof of corrugated iron sheets painted red. In the middle of a patch of open ground stood a pole on which fluttered the Katangese flag.

An imposing figure despite his short stature, seated on a wooden bench the sides of which curved upwards like horns, surrounded by his chattering court in all their finery, his warriors stripped to the waist and with their faces daubed in warpaint, his witch-doctors with their masks and coconut fiber robes, the Mwata Motu awaited his visitors.

Behind him stood his bodyguard, fifty warriors clad in tattered camouflage uniforms, armed with rifles of every make and caliber, grouped round the fetish which symbolized the Mwata's strength: a machine-gun on its tripod, with its ammunition belt clipped in.

This machine-gun had cost him a great deal of money, and so had Sergeant Baremko' Joseph, who had deserted, bringing the weapon and some ammunition with him. Motu had made him a captain, had given him a big hut, land, three young women and plenty of beer.

But he had not yet had an opportunity to use the gun

187

and dreamed of the day when the warriors of Bazungu, his tribal brother, would be mowed down like ninepins while the weapon went da-da-da-da-da, spitting flame.

Thousands of pink mouths were screaming, thousands of rumps undulating to the mysterious muffled beat of the big tom-toms, as the jeeps unloaded their passengers. Then only did the Mwata, with the assistance of two of his courtesans, rise from his seat and, with a stately gait, step forward to greet Evariste Kasingo. The lion-skin knotted round his waist flapped against his legs. On his head he wore a sort of diadem of white bark with red and black encrustations surrounded by feathers from which sprouted strings of white beads falling down to his chest. With a robe covering his loins, he walked barefoot, his big toes spread wide, his long staff in his hand.

"The old Africa is still holding out," Fonts reflected, "in certain places she's even rising from her ashes. All the same she's doomed. A pity from the picturesque point of view, a pity also for these millions of detribalized wretches for whom no new structure has been prepared.

"With his staff and lion-skin the Mwata Motu certainly has a different bearing from Evariste Kasingo. But Evariste knows that other worlds exist, that the fate of Africa is more often than not decided far away, that the great palaver center is neither in E'ville nor Leo but in New York, where the UN hold their sessions. Motu only wants to know about his own tribe and its problems."

Evariste Kasingo did his best to assume a lordly, and therefore preoccupied, air but he felt embarrassed by the crowd that had gathered in this huge clearing, by this man advancing towards him with his frozen expression, his fair skin, his features as fine as those of certain Ethiopians: a man who must know all sorts of secrets, including those of all the Baluba witch-doctors who believe in the great earth goddess, sun-worship and the spirit of the bush. To the Balubas, the souls of the dead continue to haunt the living; they hover within the chiefs' vicinity. Thus the Mwata was escorted by thousands of souls, whereas he Evariste, with his half-hearted Christianity, felt weak and bereft.

The two men came face to face and greeted each other solemnly.

Evariste had prepared a speech full of the high-falutin phrases which the blacks borrow from the whites, which they do not yet understand and in which the whites no longer believe. But he felt so ill at ease that he could not

188

remember a word. He therefore confined himself to saying:

"Mwata Motu, I bring you greetings from President Kimjanga and the people of Katanga."

Motu thanked him with a nod.

"What about the arms?" he asked. "Kimjanga promised me arms to defend myself against the Balubakat, against the UN, against the National Army, against that cur Bazungu. I want arms: not rifles that go pop-pop . . . but those that go da-da-da-da-da-da. . . ."

Disconcerted, Evariste turned to Fonts.

"The President has entrusted Monsieur Fonts here to investigate your arms and ammunition requirements."

The Mwata motioned Fonts to approach him.

"So you're bringing the arms, are you? When will you have them?"

"Next week," Fonts calmly replied.

In Africa time has no meaning and a week can equally well be seven days or a month.

Followed by his visitors, the Mwata led the way to the great guest hut while the big drums hanging from poles carried by naked men started booming slowly, then faster and faster.

Palm wine and millet beer were served in calabashes for the sake of tradition, bottled beer in glasses to assuage thirst.

"What has become of the Baluba chiefs?" Fonts asked the Mwata.

Cyprien had ceased to exist. He clung to the Mwata, bowing and scraping as though he found in him a shelter from all the dangers menacing him and the many more that existed only in his imagination.

"You answer that question," the Mwata said, pointing his staff at the delegate.

As though reciting a lesson, Cyprien rattled off his reply at top speed—the chiefs were a lot of cowardly swine but the biggest swine of all was Bazungu, who had stayed in his tribe only because he had UN soldiers to protect him.

"It's true," Motu confirmed. "Bazungu wants to be chief of all the Balubas in the north. He's a friend of Lumumba and the Communists. They have turned his head: it was easy, he's young. Twice Bazungu has tried to have me poisoned, but his witch-doctors are not as powerful as mine. Amen!"

Fonts almost laughed out loud. He learned subsequently that the Mwata, as a result of his religious education, always ended some of his sentences with "Amen," even when he was offering, according to custom, women to his visitors.

The Mwata then complained that the Belgian officers commanding the Katangese Gendarmerie did not show the respect that was due to him when they called, that they put up difficulties when he asked them for arms and ammunition to go and fight against Bazungu.

"They're for Bazungu and against me," he kept saying, "because Bazungu was a sergeant in the Force Publique. They don't realize he's a Communist."

The Mwata eventually retired, leaving the three men to have a little rest. A few minutes later a warrior solemnly brought in two extremely fine robes for the minister and the delegate. He bowed and disappeared.

"What are they going to do?" Fonts wondered. "Take off their coats and ties and be comfortable in native dress or continue to ape the whites and stew in their own juice? He's a clever fellow, Motu. If they wear robes, he'll be the big boss and take precedence over them!

"Cyprien is a mere puppet, but Evariste after all has a little more standing. It's important for the Mwata to put him in a position of inferiority and force him to meet him on his home ground, the Africa of tradition and ritual.

"The bush is abandoned or reverts to barbarism, while the National Congolese Army, preceded by gangs of beatniks armed with bicycle-chains, settles in without firing a shot, introducing even greater chaos. The Katangese Gendarmerie withdraw, firing at anything that moves.

"The Mwata alone holds out with his pop-guns and fetishes. But, to get anything out of him, we'll have to give him the arms he requests, puff up this petty chief into a sort of king.

"Isn't that repeating the very mistake we made, out of sheer facility, in Indo-China; the mistake of supporting Bao-Dai, the racial minorities and the sects; and, in Algeria, of inventing Bellounis and playing on racial differences? But in the Nyunzu district, apart from the Mwata, there's no one at all and time is pressing. Maybe it would be better to rely on the military . . . but Katanga never had an army and the African NCOs, despite their brand-new badges of rank, carry no more weight than the Congolese officers of the National Army."

Before leaving for Jenge, Fonts had insisted on visiting the Gendarmerie camp. Luckily Evariste had not come

190

with him: the gendarmes would have torn him limb from limb.

They were a wretched shoddy lot, dragging their rifles around by the barrel. They would no longer obey the Belgians because they were independent, nor would they fight because they were scared, especially since the rebel Balubas had made so free with little Second-Lieutenant Marey.

The only person they still seemed to obey was Wenceslas, maybe because they felt he was as worthless as themselves and also because, from time to time, he gave them cigarettes and a bottle of beer. Good old Wenceslas! He waged his own little psychological war with Pérohade's dough!

Evariste and Cyprien contemplated the robes, held them up against their dark suits and cast embarrassed glances at the white man.

"There's no choice, I'm backing the Mwata Motu," Fonts decided.

He went up to the minister and fingered the cloth.

"Your Excellency, it would have a very good effect on the population if you wore this robe. Nkrumah in Ghana and Sékou-Touré in Guinea, for big feast-days, don't hesitate to wear robes; which does not stop them wearing dinner-jackets the next day."

"I think you're right, my dear fellow," Evariste gravely agreed. "We have our own civilization, our own customs. . . . Many centuries ago the Bantus formed a great kingdom, with King Wotu who had brought fire . . . and the Minga Bengale who discovered salt. . . . We have no reason to be ashamed of our history. On the contrary, we ought to be proud of it. . . . The black race has given the world . . ."

Fonts, who was beginning to get bored with this sort of talk, interjected:

"Jazz, Your Excellency. . . ."

When darkness fell, some big fires were lit on the open ground. Pigs were placed over them on spits, and presently the smell of roasting meat dominated all the others.

Men and women, hollow-bellied with hunger and giddy from palm wine, chanted songs punctuated by shrieks and yells, and danced faster and faster: the men, with feathers in their hair, naked to the waist and brandishing their arms; the women, with bare breasts, shaking their hips.

One of the Mwata Motu's servants came to fetch the guests for dinner. The darkness was damp and heavy, pierced only by the glow of the fires; the smoke rose scarcely higher than the foliage of the tall trees, where it settled like a pall.

The whole of Africa loomed up before them with her lights, her rhythms and her smells. Draped in their robes, with an expression of deep content on their faces, Evariste and Cyprien succumbed to her, beating time to the music, recognizing the great collective soul of the Negroes.

Fonts was alone, strangely clear-headed, alien to the pagan joy emanating from all these dancing bodies.

The meal began with great libations of beer. Meanwhile, in front of the Mwata and his guests who were seated on cushions, dancers, accompanied by a tom-tom and a sort of kettle-drum, alternately went through the motions of fighting, hunting and love-making.

Fonts had seen a great deal of dancing in Dahomey, Togo and the Ivory Coast. It was imbued with more meaning and mystery than the uncouth evolutions he was now witnessing.

He was sitting next to the Mwata's secretary, the one who read for him "when he had forgotten his spectacles." Israel Bulodji was dressed in European style: trousers, shirt and espadrilles. He was a young man with a sharp expression and seemed only moderately appreciative of all this debauchery and nigritude.

"Don't you like it?" Fonts asked him.

"Not as much as the cinema," the secretary replied. "At the cinema there are horses, cowboys, sheriffs and beautiful blondes. . . . Everyone drinks whisky and there's a lot of shooting."

"What are you doing here?"

"I used to work in the Tourist Office in Leopoldville. I saw a lot of people, but then they started hunting down the Balubas. . . . So I followed the Mwata Motu, who needed someone because he can't read. He offered me a lot of money. There isn't any money; nor is there anything to eat, but as much beer and as many girls as one wants. . . . The Mwata alone has thirty girls all to himself!"

"Who's this man Bazungu?"

"A chief on the Lukuga River. He doesn't care for dancing and fetishes. He doesn't care for President Kimjanga and his gendarmes either, or for Lumumba and the Leo police, or for anyone else . . . even the Mwata. . . . He just wants to be left in peace. Only, as long as he's around, the Mwata won't be able to become a big chief."

"They say he helps the Balubakat."

Prudently the secretary became evasive.

"So they say. . . . The boss wants to speak to you."

Fonts went and sat down next to the Mwata, who offered him a charred hunk of pork. Straight away Motu asked him:

"What are we going to do about Bazungu?"

"I think," Fonts began, "that you ought to re-establish contact with the other Baluba chiefs who have taken to the bush, tell them that we wish them no harm, that it is not our intention to do away with the chiefs but on the contrary to strengthen their powers."

"We would also have to tell them they'll be given food. . . ."

"We shall give them food."

"That doctors will come to look after the sick. . . ."

"We'll send some up from Elizabethville with medicine."

"And injections?"

"And injections as well."

"Because injections are better than medicine. . . . And also that we'll give them money . . . and rifles to defend themselves against the Balubakat who don't want chiefs any more."

"We'll give them rifles."

"All the same they won't come back."

"Why not?"

"Bazungu will stop them: he doesn't want the chiefs to come back or to meet you."

With grease dripping from his mouth, Evariste, who was beginning to get drunk, made a sweeping gesture with his hand.

"Bazungu must be summoned to E'ville!"

"Bazungu doesn't obey anyone."

"All you need do is send some gendarmes to fetch him!"

"I can go and fetch him," Motu suddenly suggested. "Give me a few soldiers with a white man to lead them and the gun that goes da-da-da-da-da. . . . Afterwards all the chiefs will come back. . . ."

"Bazungu's a bloody nuisance," Evariste yelled. "Either he toes the line or else we lock him up."

Motu screwed up his little eyes. His pointed teeth bit into his lips.

"I'll go and fetch him, and you give me soldiers!"

"We might first send him a messenger," Fonts suggested, "with presents."

"He'll take the presents and fling the messenger into the

river for the crocodiles to eat. But if there are soldiers he'll be frightened!"

Fonts felt there was something fishy about the whole business. If Bazungu was firmly on the side of the Balubakat and the UN, Motu would not have asked for permission to seize him. No one ever asks for permission to fight an enemy! But Fonts had had a bellyfull of these palavers and complications. In his hand he held a trump card: the Mwata. He was not going to spoil it by inquiring into whatever personal scores he had to settle. After all, that was his own business.

"All right," he said. "Go and fetch Bazungu with some soldiers, and if he makes any fuss about following you, hit him over the head!"

The Mwata clapped his hands with delight.

"You at least understand very quick and you know how to tackle these curs. Some beer. . . ."

The feast went on with more and more frenzied dancing, more and more copious libations.

His Excellency Evariste had risen to his feet and, with a blank expression, started to dance, clapping his hands, shaking his head and shoulders, pawing the ground in time to the music.

The Mwata Motu looked at him with a curious smile on his face and without taking his eyes off him, gave some orders to the captain of his bodyguard, the man with the gun that went da-da-da-da-da, who had squatted down beside him.

Feeling tired, Fonts went back to the guest house. Shortly afterwards the Mwata's secretary set out to look for him, as he had something to tell him, but on the way he came across a bottle of spirits and drank from it until he passed out.

Next morning he had forgotten what he wanted to tell the white man.

His Excellency Evariste Kasingo left Fonts at Albertville, where he had decided to pursue his inquiries, and proudly returned with the report which the Frenchman had drafted for him. Without quite knowing what it was about, he had appended his signature to it, followed by a cross and the date, as he had been taught by the missionaries who had brought him up.

The whites drafted the documents, the blacks now signed them; the whites still built roads and bridges, but the blacks officially opened them; the whites manufactured motor-cars, the blacks drove them, and when they smashed them, complained that they were made of shoddy material. It was no longer the whites who were intelligent and strong but the blacks, and it was pleasant to be a black. That at least was the opinion of Evariste, who had always thought himself the cleverest of men.

Fonts had entrusted Edgar Mullens, who was going back to Elizabethville, with a personal letter for Colonel la Roncière, a letter in which he gave a forthright picture of the situation and suggested the few measures which at a pinch it would be possible to take.

My dear Jean-Marie,

It has taken me no more than three days in North Katanga to realize that all is lost, barring a miracle. But surely Africa is the land of miracles, when one sees a nincompoop like Evariste Kasingo become Transport Minister. Everything is collapsing and dissolving in the great nigritude.

It would be advisable, if not essential, for me to remain a month in this area with plenary powers. I could easily assume these powers since no one is particularly anxious to exercise them, but I should like to have a letter signed by the hand of the President.

Please have the two Belgian officers in command of the Gendarmerie recalled at once, also the African delegate. I shall easily find local replacements for them. The only man with a certain amount of influence up here is Motu, the Mwata of Jenge. Maybe he's a blackguard but he knows what he wants and, for reasons which have nothing to do with Katangese nationalism, he is a hundred per cent on our side. I've promised him a hundred rifles, but if we give him thirty, with six hundred rounds of ammunition, he'll be quite happy. Through him we could try to win over the other chiefs who have fled into the bush.

Do your best to send me some supplies as soon as possible: all the villages are dying of hunger. Edgar Mullens, whom you'll be seeing, is prepared to get the cotton cultivation under way again. We must never give food away for nothing, but demand in exchange some work even if this work is pointless. The African is only too ready to assume that everything is his due and falls quite naturally into the role of parasite.

The presence in this area of UN and Congolese National Army contingents represents a grave danger.

We must lure the population over to our side by forcing them into action against the UN troops. The ensuing reaction, which we could exploit psychologically, is liable to impel them not so much to join our ranks as to remain neutral, which they no longer are. They have several good reasons for not being, for the repressive measures that were taken were contrary to all common sense. But people quickly forget past misfortunes if further misfortunes stare them in the face.

I'd like you to send me a small group of three or four men—white men, of course—capable of undertaking three commando jobs, one against the Ethiopian post at the exit of Albertville, another against one of the boats that brings arms to the rebels across Lake Tanganyika, and the third against the railway. I want specialists, that's to say men who will leave no trace, so that the Katangese soldiers and loyal Balubas may then be accused of these raids. I also need a couple of mortars mounted on jeeps with which I can shoot up the UN camp, if only to remind the Indians that there's a war on, which they appear to forget. They may then stop sauntering around with their swagger-sticks under their arms and embarrassing us with their propaganda in favor of the Leopoldville Government.

Nothing can be worse for a defender of the peace and of the "third world" than to find himself forced to fire on colored men.

As I said before, the position in North Katanga is extremely precarious, but it's here that Elizabethville, its mines and its President must be defended.

Hang on to the banisters, otherwise I'll topple over.

Yours ever,
Thomas

Two days later Thomas Fonts received the following message from la Roncière:

Do as you see fit; you have full civil and military powers for the whole of the Northern Territory reoccupied by our troops, but impossible to give you a letter from the President. He can't compromise himself to that extent. The Belgians have been recalled; the delegate is to stay on. He has the support of Evariste Kasingo.

I'm trying to send you a convoy of foodstuffs, medical supplies and arms; impossible to find medical team; the Balubas have got too bad a reputation. I agree about the UN, but the specialists are lacking and so are the mortars.

I'm hanging on to the banisters, but there's a lot of jostling on the staircase. Dorat wanted to join you; it was easy to dissuade him by telling him what happened to Second-Lieutenant Marey. Keep out of the limelight. The Maley offensive against the mercenaries and Belgian instructors is intensifying day by day. A few interesting elements have been sent us from Rhodesia, but, alas, useless for your area. Nothing from France. A red-headed girl keeps asking after you and wears a chain with a gold coin round her neck. Make haste, I need you in Elizabethville.

The message was signed:

J. M. la Roncière, Political and Military Adviser to the President of the Katangese Republic,

and was addressed to:

Monsieur Thomas Fonts, Adviser, attached to Monsieur Cyprien Malwike, Delegate-General for the Reoccupied Territories.

Cyprien had just been promoted.

On the same day, under the protection of a strong Indian contingent, Melchior Molanda, chief of the Balubakat, appointed regional chief of North Katanga by the Leopoldville Government, landed at Albertville. Fonts saw fit to pack up as quickly as possible and made his way back to Nyunzu by road.

At Nyunzu Wenceslas was waiting for him together with the Mwata Motu's secretary Israel Bulodji, who in happier times had worked in the Tourist Office in Leopoldville.

Israel was gray with fright and Wenceslas kept saying over and over again:

"No, it's not possible . . . it's not possible. They can't be such bloody swine and such bloody fools!"

"What's going on?" asked Fonts, who scented real trouble.

Wenceslas pushed Israel forward.

"You tell him since you saw it."

Israel moistened his thick lips with his tongue.

"It's like this, boss . . . I looked for you the evening you were with the Mwata, to warn you . . . but I couldn't find you. . . . When you gave him permission, the Mwata told a dozen of his men to go and fetch Bazungu and take him to the minister, who would then fling him into prison. Bazungu and his followers, armed with cudgels, pitched into these men who had come to fetch him. . . ."

"And then?"

"You said, if Bazungu kicked up a fuss, to hit him over the head. The bush is now full of dead . . . thousands and thousands. . . ."

Wenceslas interjected:

"That bastard Motu, relying on Evariste Kasingo's support . . ."

". . . And yours . . . it was yours he needed most of all . . . attacked next day with all his tribe. Bazungu and his men were not expecting it. An absolute massacre!"

"The first total wars were tribal wars. No quarter given, complete extermination. We've got to put a stop to this at once. We'll go and see the Mwata right away."

Israel shook his crinkly head.

"You won't find anyone there; everyone's at war in the bush. War's a fine thing: warriors kill the men and make free with the women . . . even the youngest. They burn down the villages and take away whatever can be eaten: the millet, the manioc, the goats . . . Mwata's warriors have drunk a lot of palm wine and are absolutely wild."

"That's not all," Wenceslas continued. "The two Belgian officers you had recalled are accusing you personally of organizing the whole business. They left this morning for Albertville where they are due to take the E'ville plane. I'm pretty certain they're going to contact the UN representatives and you're going to find yourself accused of 'genocide' or something like that."

"We'll see about that later. Meanwhile pile as many gendarmes as you can into the three or four trucks that are still working and let's be off."

"It takes ten hours to get to the Lukuga River and the territory of Bazungu's tribe. It'll be dark in a couple of hours."

"We're going all the same. At least we shall be on the spot by tomorrow morning. It may be too late but it's our last chance. If the Baluba tribes start killing one another off. . . ."

"They always have. . . ."

"We're up here, therefore we'll be held responsible. . . . The only possible move is to rely on the traditional chiefdoms, win over the chiefs by guaranteeing their privileges, and be the first to do so. What do you think Melchior Molanda, the Balubakat chief whom the Indians have just installed in Albertville, is going to do? Exactly the same thing! Now that Lumumba's dead, and with him the craze for modernism, everyone's reverting to the old palavers and former customs."

Israel was wriggling with indecision; he had something else to say but he did not know if it was important; white men judged things in such an odd manner, they took unimportant details into account and overlooked what the blacks considered essentials.

"The Mwata," he said, "well, he's the cousin of the uncle of Melchior Molanda's father."

Wenceslas had difficulty in collecting some sixty gendarmes and piling them into trucks. Since the departure of the two Belgian officers, the gendarmes considered themselves their own masters and refused to do anything.

Fonts looked everywhere for Cyprien, but he was not to be found. Had he joined his old accomplice Motu and followed him on his manhunt? It was not characteristic of the delegate, who preferred palavering and scheming to the hazards and physical effort of war even if the reward was to be a young Negress held down by four men while a fifth raped her.

The little convoy, preceded by a jeep armed with a machine-gun, set off in the dark. Very soon the track narrowed. Wenceslas was driving the jeep. Fonts sat beside him chain-smoking and kept urging him on.

"Faster . . . faster. . . ."

Shaken about like a rag doll, Israel Bulodji merely whimpered, clutching on to whatever he could.

The track was often flooded, always full of pot-holes. Every now and then an animal could be glimpsed in the beam of the headlamps: an antelope or Derby elan. Wild boar scampered ahead of the beam before finding an opening in the two walls formed by the bush and vanishing into it.

Shortly before dawn a lean sleek cheetah leaped right across the track in a single bound.

"You also come across elephants," Wenceslas said, "but there are fewer and fewer of them: the Balubas and Pygmies hunt them for food and to sell the ivory. There's no one left to buy the ivory, and not enough elephants to provide food for everyone."

In the morning they reached the banks of the Lukuga, a sort of marshy river which in some places spread out into a broad black sheet, in others narrowed down into seething rapids.

Clouds of mosquitoes lurked beneath the trees, and a heavy putrid smell of decomposition floated in the atmosphere.

An overturned canoe went floating downstream. A little farther on they saw a village which was still on fire but showed no sign of life.

Fonts ordered the trucks to halt. In the main square lay twenty bodies, mingling with the brown earth. Some were horribly mutilated; children with their skulls split open, women impaled on stakes. Most of the corpses, which were already decomposing, were minus ears and, more often than not, minus hands and feet as well.

Carrion birds, which the arrival of the trucks had driven off, hovered just above them, flapping their wings. One of the gendarmes picked up a Fal automatic rifle and, roaring with laughter, fired a few bursts at them.

The sight of the bodies, their smell, did not seem to bother the Katangese soldiers. One of them turned over the rubble of a wrecked hut with his toe, another made some obscene remarks about the sexual organ of one of the dead.

Wenceslas leaned against a tree and vomited. Fonts handed him a flask of brandy which he had produced from his pocket.

"Here, have some of this. You mustn't let these fellows see you falter."

Wenceslas tried to excuse himself.

"Yet I was at Warsaw when the Russians just stood there and watched us being massacred by the Germans. But it wasn't as horrible as this!"

"In what way?"

"Here one has the feeling that they've left behind only those they weren't able to carry off and eat . . . because, as you may or may not know, they do eat one another. . . . Under the Belgians they did it secretly and if they were caught it meant the gallows."

"Are they really so short of meat?"

"Not at all! It's on religious grounds: by eating the liver

200

or kidney of an enemy, they believe they inherit his strength and courage. . . ."

The farther they went along the river the more numerous were the villages that had been set on fire, and also the corpses.

On two occasions a pop-gun opened fire on them, which gave the Katangese gendarmes the chance of loosing off their weapons in all directions.

"The resistance is getting organized," Fonts observed. "Today the fugitives from Bazungu's tribe are attacking us with old blunderbuses. Tomorrow the Balubakat or UN will give them proper weapons. They in their turn will kill off the Mwata's valiant warriors, who'll only have pangas to defend themselves with because they'll have used up all their ammunition."

Bazungu's village at one time numbered three or four thousand souls. It had been entirely destroyed by fire. A smell of charred flesh emanated from it, for Motu, to get the job over quickly, had burned alive all the inhabitants who had not had time to get away. Those who tried to escape from the flames had been mowed down by the gun that went da-da-da-da-da. . . .

The surrounding bush was still on fire.

A helicopter appeared in the sky, flying sideways like a dragon-fly.

It came closer and closer and hovered above the tops of the trees.

On board could be seen four men wearing dark glasses. Wenceslas tried to attract their attention.

"White men!" he cried with relief.

Since no one in the helicopter saw him, he took off his bush hat and waved it at arm's length.

The pilot eventually noticed him and motioned to the passenger sitting next to him. At once the helicopter rose abruptly and flew off.

"What's the matter with them?" Wenceslas asked.

"They saw your rifle . . . or something like that! Maybe they think we're the ones who did this job! It's not possible; it would be too idiotic!"

Yet it was because of this very misapprehension that Patrick Maley began to lose his self-control, thereby landing himself in all sorts of misadventures. He forgot he was merely an international official, responsible for making law and order reign in the name of somewhat vague principles and that he was not entrusted with the task of reconstructing the world by means of gunfire to make it suit his own principles.

Maley was thumping his knees with both fists. He was stifling in this plexiglass bubble. He had wanted to see with his own eyes the result of this River Lukuga massacre which had been the main topic of conversation in Elizabethville since the previous evening. But he did not know if it was Europeans, Belgians or mercenaries who had organized it. Now he had proof in the form of these two white men, one of whom was waving his hat, these trucks, these Katangese gendarmes calmly examining their handiwork: a village razed to the ground. A few minutes earlier he had heard them firing.

Maley yelled, waving his fist at the little figure below which went on waving at him:

"Murderers! Yes, my skin's white like yours, but that's no reason to become your accomplice! Dirty swine! Filthy Nazis! If I had a gun I'd shoot you down. You make me ashamed of being a white man!"

But the noise of the engine and whirr of the blades drowned his cries.

With a dry mouth he turned to one of the Swedish officers with him.

"They're going to pay for this . . . and a high price too!"

The Swede's composure contributed still further to his rage.

"Doesn't it matter to you, Captain, having such a foul sight before your eyes? Of course they're only blacks, so you don't give a damn! Only white people count for you! At Elizabethville, when you have a drink, it's with a white man; when you talk to a woman, she's a white."

Maley stopped: the quarrel he was picking with the Swede suddenly seemed pointless. . . . And yet one of the biggest worries of the chief UN representative was the attitude of some of the white troops who sided more or less openly with the Belgians. It was even said that some officers were in contact with the mercenaries, exchanging whisky, cigarettes and even women with them.

He pictured Lieutenant-Colonel la Roncière lurking in some office in the Presidency, lean, relentless and precise, establishing his network . . . a nimble spider, devoid of conscience, with no problems, thinking only of the web he was weaving. One thread culminated in this massacre and these burnt-out villages from which the smoke still darkened the sky, the other perhaps led to this Swedish officer who had needed only three months in Africa to remind himself that he belonged to a superior race.

The indolent Jenny had likewise been taken in. When he told her all he knew about la Roncière, his activity in Indo-China, the torturing in Algeria, she had laughed in his face.

"He's an extremely interesting man, my dear Patrick, who has learned about life elsewhere than in a university lecture-room. Don't forget that I'm Rhodesian . . . and that one day you're liable to be one of the people who'll drive me out of my country, whereas he at least will defend me!"

Once again Maley had lost his temper, which had not improved the situation. Clumsily he had tried to explain that the whites in Africa were condemning themselves by resorting to such defenders.

Jenny—and it was the first time she appeared to shed her indifference—had retorted with biting sarcasm:

"What do you know about Africa and the men living here, black or white, you damned Irishman? You read a few books, then come here and calmly settle this problem, deciding on what's good or bad in the name of extremely vague principles. I was born in the green hills of Africa . . . and I don't see in the name of what principles I should leave them . . . or become the fourth wife of my house-boy!"

Maley had never felt towards anyone such hatred as he felt towards the head of the French mercenaries. His personal feelings, his conception of the world, the traditions of the martyr nation to which he belonged, the idea he had formed of his mission, were all inextricably mingled together in his brain.

Sometimes too he had doubts about himself, about the value of what he was defending, especially when he discerned in his military assistant, the Indian General Siddartha, that blind hatred for the whites which was nothing but envy at not being able to be one of them. And there again he accused la Roncière.

General Siddartha wanted all the mercenaries and Belgian advisers to be hanged; it was utter madness and the best way of rousing all the whites, even the Americans, against the UN, as Arnold Riverton did not fail to point out; the operation of the blue helmets in Katanga should on no account turn into an anti-European pogrom. Without the whites there would be no more UN, for they alone

203

were able to make this unwieldy organization work and to pay their contributions.

On the other hand, if the mercenaries and Belgians were expelled, Katanga and her puppet government would collapse at once.

According to the latest information Maley had received, the Belgian officers and advisers numbered about three hundred, the mercenaries two hundred or two hundred and fifty.

Jenny was not yet la Roncière's mistress. Maley refused to believe otherwise; he was apt to put the women he loved on a pedestal and could not bear the idea of beauty in the arms of the beast. La Roncière merely exercised a sort of fascination over her which would cease when the colonel left Katanga. Jenny would soon forget him; she only noticed people in her immediate vicinity. She never spoke of anyone absent.

If he got rid of the military, the Belgian advisers and the mercenaries, of Major Van Beulans, Justin Pimuriaux and la Roncière, he would settle simultaneously his two most pressing problems: the secession of Katanga and Jenny.

Jenny Ligget came to see la Roncière every evening in the secluded little villa which Pimuriaux had taken for him a few hundred yards from the British Consul's.

Chance alone had dictated this choice. Jenny, who trusted a great deal to chance in her sentimental affairs, had found no particular reason to resist the French colonel's awkward advances.

From la Roncière's room she could see when the light went on in her husband's study. This was the sign he had just come in. He had opened the cupboard where he kept his whisky and poured himself out a drink, still sucking on his unlit pipe.

Then, taking her time, Jenny would have a shower, tidy her hair, smoke a cigarette, run her hand through the colonel's grey locks, before going home.

John Ligget never asked her where she had been, and this indifference, together with various other factors, was one of the reasons for her infidelity.

Since her husband had started drinking, Jenny had had a number of lovers to whom she had never attached much importance. She referred to them as partners, liked them to be affectionate and discreet, and never surrendered anything of herself to them.

One day, much to Joan's dismay, she had defined love as "a pleasant exercise which can only be performed by two people and which merely requires a mutually suited couple."

But with Jean-Marie la Roncière the exercise was getting more complicated and dangerous; the colonel kept questioning her, asking her the reasons for her slightest reactions, explaining his own, which made the game more confusing, of course, but also more fascinating.

Jenny discovered that a man whose jealousy has been roused gives all the more pleasure. If the human race in the course of the ages had invented love, its complications and deceits, and had proved so partial to the spice of life, it was not without good reason.

After their third meeting their relations had ceased to be limited to a simple exchange of physical effort, maybe because of the new spice with which the colonel seasoned their pleasure.

Jenny had invented a liaison with Maley because it was the first name that came into her head when la Roncière, refusing to believe that he was the only one, had insisted on knowing the names of her other lovers.

The colonel kept telling her about a certain Julienne with whom he had been in love, with whom many men had been in love, and who bore a close resemblance to her.

"One of these days I shall find myself involved in all sorts of complications," she reflected, "but I shall do what every other woman does and get away with it. Unless I become Maley's mistress as well, but the Irishman's becoming a bore and lives on his nerves; he's no fun at all. At the age of thirty one doesn't play at being Messalina: two children, four horses, one husband and one lover are ample to fill a woman's life."

When she got home Jenny found her husband more fuddled than usual and Joan Riverton in a state of great excitement. John Ligget made some excuse or other and left the room.

"I've had news of Thomas Fonts," Joan announced. "The Balubas haven't yet made mincemeat of him. A certain Mullens, who comes from North Katanga and is a friend of young Ravetot's, was singing his praises just now. Little Ravetot is wild with rage. There and then he presented me with an ultimatum: either I marry him or he goes back to Belgium."

"So what's going to happen?"

"I'm not marrying him and he's not going back to Belgium. Ravetot has a two-year contract with the Union Minière. Maley, whom I've just seen at my father's, was preparing to submit his seventeenth ultimatum to President Kimjanga in connection with the departure of the Belgian advisers and the mercenaries. More and more Indians are arriving at the airport. They're Gurkhas; they're not even Indians but Nepalese and serve as mercenaries in the army of that good apostle Nehru.

"I told General Siddartha, who's beginning to annoy me, that if he had to hang the mercenaries, he would have to hang his Gurkhas as well. He was furious.

"Don't you find, Jenny, that all these people are lacking in a sense of humor and take themselves rather too seriously? People without morals, like Fonts, are much more bearable!"

Jenny was lying on the sofa in her favorite position, one foot beating time to the music. She appeared quite detached from all these complicated affairs, of which she seemed to retain only what affected her personally.

Joan could not contain herself.

"Yesterday evening," she said, "a French journalist came to dinner at the consulate, a man called Félicien Dorat. He's a friend of Ferwell's, our ambassador in Leopoldville. They were out in Indo-China together. This journalist is ugly but intelligent, in that annoying way in which the French often are . . . like jugglers who can keep several balls in the air at the same time. At the time you're amazed, but afterwards you ask yourself: 'How many balls were there'?"

"She's also a juggler," Jenny reflected. "There's only one thing she wants: to talk to me about Fonts. I don't talk to anyone about the colonel, not even to Joan; I don't feel the need to, perhaps because I am still conscious of the smell of his skin, the fatigue of my loins. Joan is a young girl: she wants everyone to participate in her affair; I'm already an old woman . . . I keep things to myself."

"This man Dorat," Joan went on, "knew Thomas Fonts very well. To him he's the very model of a certain type of adventurer, a gambler who's never had any political ambitions, yet is extremely sharp and in the know about any amount of secrets.

"Thanks to a certain number of hazards and plots, men of his sort, most of whom were his friends or accomplices, have reached government rank in France with General de Gaulle. The adventure, according to Dorat, was aimed at the assumption of power and the seizure of a very rich and very old country. But Fonts was thrust aside, whereas his best friend, a certain Dumont, has it all his own way in the Elysée. I love the description that Dorat then gave of Thomas."

Sitting at the foot of the sofa, Joan tried to remember the journalist's very words.

'A little marquis without powdered hair, cruel, insolent and tender-hearted, this Catalan is too fond of mankind, scoffs at high principles and clings to his freedom. As a southern accent and southern exuberance are not highly regarded at the Elysée, he was made a vice-consul in Guinea. He got into trouble there, so he's just been sent to Katanga where he'll certainly get into further trouble."

"What did this man Dorat say about Colonel la Roncière?"

"He can't stand him. To him he's a technocrat of warfare, too sure of himself, the antithesis of Fonts. I went with Dorat to the Mitsouko where he had arranged to meet a group of journalists, Americans: they're all expecting a show-down. They saw Maley, who is firmly resolved to get the matter settled once and for all. It seems he's received encouragement from New York. The owner of the nightclub, Pérohade, kept winking at me as though we were accomplices. I didn't understand what it was all about until I learned it was through him that Fonts had sent me the flowers and the gold coin."

She fingered the coin which she wore attached to a chain round her neck and showed it to Jenny.

"Where could such a disreputable person have found this object? It's very old, you know. My father told me. Dorat claims he stole a sack full of them from a Chinese pirate and doles them out to all the women he knows. He has known so many that it's his last coin. Your husband seems odder than ever today, Jenny. What's wrong?"

Fonts did not catch up with the Mwata Motu and his gallant warriors till the following morning, in a little village into which they had just moved. The Mwata had spent all night watching Bazungu die, after stringing him up on a tree by his hands and feet. He himself had plunged the thorns into his young rival's naked body, now spattered with blood, and noticed how his skin quivered and his muscles alternately contracted and relaxed. Muscles are like snakes in a man's body.

Afterwards the witch-doctor had put his eyes out for

207

having betrayed the ancient rules of the tribe, and some young men had amused themselves by hacking his legs to pieces; they had taken such delight in this that they had not even noticed the moment that Bazungu died.

Then the whole council had assembled for a lengthy palaver. They had drunk beer, belched, weighed up the pros and cons, and two of the elders had driven off in the Mwata's car to Kabalo where, under a UN escort, the head of the Balubakat, Delegate-General of the Leopoldville Government for North Katanga, Melchior Molanda had just arrived. They brought presents with them, including Bazungu's transistor radio, and a personal message from the Mwata to the man who was at the same time his son and his father since he was the cousin of his mother's uncle.

Fonts halted the three trucks and the jeep at the far end of a big square patch of open ground in the middle of the huts. He ordered the gendarmes not to leave the vehicles and the drivers to keep their engines running.

He did not yet know what he was going to do; he did not even have the slightest idea. The main thing was to avoid being sucked into this seething mass of drunken Negroes and to keep his distance, as a weaker boxer holds off his opponent.

Israel slipped out of the jeep and made his way towards one of the huts into which streams of men kept pouring. Outside it stood his friend, the head of the Mwata's bodyguard, the man with the gun that went da-da-da-da-da. . .

Fonts, followed by Wenceslas, advanced towards Motu who was dressed almost completely in European clothes and, seated on his little bench, looked extremely pleased with himself.

"Have you brought the weapons?" he asked. "You know, the hundred rifles you promised me. Luckily the strength and courage of my warriors took the place of your rifles. . . ."

Fonts scented danger. The henchmen surrounding the chief were swaying about uncertainly, with vacant grins on their faces and the glazed eyes of drug addicts. The whole lot had been drinking spirits and smoking hemp.

They all had sly or hilarious expressions, and stank of sweat, blood and savagery. Not one showed the slightest sign of shame or fear. The Mwata was far too shrewd to be unaware of the situation in Albertville and the rest of the province. If he had taken the risk of exterminating the neighboring tribe, he must have obtained assurances not only from the Katangese side but the other side as well.

Behind him hung Bazungu's body with its flayed tibias. Motu had not even taken the precaution of hiding it. On the contrary, he turned round towards it several times as though calling it to witness.

Fonts waited for Wenceslas, who stood gaping with horror several paces behind him, and in a hurried whisper warned him:

"There's something fishy going on. Go back and get the jeep, train the machine-gun on the chief. Quick! Otherwise we're done for!"

"What was that you said?" Motu asked.

"The lieutenant wants to fetch your present: a rifle that fires with telescopic sights."

"Go and get it."

Wenceslas forced himself not to break into a run, not to start screaming, and walked back to the jeep with jerky steps, like an automaton.

The crowd of warriors with feathers in their hair, stripped to the waist or in singlets, their faces daubed with warpaint, or wearing old saucepans on their heads by way of steel helmets, brandishing pangas and makeshift rifles, crept silently towards the Gendarmerie trucks.

Fonts distinctly heard the rattle of breaches being loaded. A long burst, fired far too high, swept the trees. The jeep drove up and stopped thirty yards away from the Mwata and his court: the machine-gun was swinging round on its pivot.

Fonts heaved a sigh, leaped into the back of the jeep and trained the weapon on the Mwata.

"Motu, let us drive off or I'll open fire and mow down the lot of you, starting with you. Tell your savages to leave my soldiers alone."

Without budging, the Mwata pretended not to understand, playing for time until the trucks were surrounded.

Fonts fired a short burst which whistled over the chief's head. Motu took fright, because it was not only his men who were in danger of being killed but also himself.

He made a gesture with his hand: the warriors came to a halt ten yards from the trucks. He tried to resume the palaver with Fonts.

"It was Minister Kasingo who wanted me to go and fetch Bazungu . . . and Bazungu fought back and killed my soldiers. . . . He tried to set fire to my villages. . . ."

Fonts fired again, just over their heads, then lower and lower until they were all lying flat on the ground.

209

The noise of empty cartridge cases clattering down on the bodywork of the vehicle sounded louder at certain moments than that of the detonations.

Wenceslas looked at his hands trembling as they clutched the steering-wheel.

Some of the Balubas were hit; the others lay prone in the dust. The gendarmes also had started firing from the trucks, and bullets were flying in all directions.

"About turn!" Fonts yelled.

Wenceslas was surprised to find that his hands and his legs obeyed him.

Israel, running as fast as a greyhound and flinging his arms in front of him, clambered aboard as the jeep raced forward.

"Boss," he panted, "we had plenty luck! Motu was waiting for the head of the Balubakat. He wanted to hand you over for him to sell you to the UN. He now says you promised arms to Bazungu, who was working with you, and that's why he set off to make war on Bazungu. Me, he would have cut my head off, to silence me."

"What was there in the hut where the man with the machine-gun was standing?"

"Cyprien. But he's going to die," Israel replied with indifference. "His wives have already been shared out among the others."

Wenceslas wiped the dirty sweat from his face with a big spotted handkerchief and gave Fonts a nudge.

"No one can say you're lacking in nerve, Thomas. On my own, I should have been done for! If Motu hadn't signaled his fellows to stop, what would have happened?"

Fonts shrugged his shoulders; he felt neither hatred nor fear, nothing, only immense fatigue. He reflected:

"To me danger's just like an old mistress. I make love to her out of habit, but the pleasure's gone. Thomas Fonts, you're getting old and, unlike Dumont, you haven't even found another form of pleasure."

When they got to Nyunzu, in the middle of the night, the news they heard was even worse than they expected.

After Maley's tour of inspection, and on his orders, the UN representatives, civil and military alike, had thrown off their masks and intervened directly against the Katangese Government.

Melchior Molanda had been recognized as the only legal chief of the province, and the remnants of the Katangese administration and Gendarmerie were regarded as rebels.

The civil servants were being rounded up or done away with, and the military had been disarmed. Katangese troops were disbanding everywhere, the gendarmes were discarding their uniforms but keeping their rifles and ammunition to sell. More often than not the Balubas offered them money which they did not possess and, as soon as they had the rifles in their hands, killed them. But since they knew the value of bullets and retained a memory of the pacification operations, they preferred to use knives, bludgeons and bicycle-chains.

Edgar Mullens had come back from Elizabethville with a truckload of cotton seed, three cases of medical supplies and two sabotage packs like those used by the commandos in the Far East. They contained four charges of plastic, primer cord, a tube of detonators and time pencils, all wrapped up in canvas haversacks.

He also brought a message from la Roncière in a sealed envelope.

If our plan is to succeed, it will be absolutely necessary for you to hang on in the north by whatever means possible! The UN are crowing with delight; it's against the UN you must strike. I can't send you anything: neither men, nor vehicles, nor mortars.

But we must at all cost reply to Melchior Molanda's arrival at Albertville with some sort of action, and the more spectacular the better!

You have enough imagination to choose the target and organize the operation.

The President, the people of Katanga and myself are absolutely relying on you. . . .

Fonts crumpled up the letter and asked Wenceslas to pour him out another whisky. Then, glass in hand, he sank back on to his bed with his legs spread wide.

It was very hot; mosquitoes and moths kept fluttering round the oil lamp and every now and then one of them would come and singe its wings against the smoking glass. The smell of burning reminded Fonts of the foul stench of Bazungu's village: three thousand bodies burned, hacked to pieces or abandoned to the animals! He considered himself responsible for this, since he had allowed himself to be duped by the cruel and reactionary old chief. Luckily he had not let him have any arms, but this was only because he had not received any himself.

On the Mwata Motu he had wanted to base a policy of pacification and alliance with the hereditary chiefs. How absurd! Motu only lived in the past, with his hatred and old settlement of accounts. He would never forget the Balubas' resentment against the other races who occupied Katanga long before them.

It was not in Motu's interest to side with Katanga. He had wooed Elizabethville simply in order to be paid a higher price by the Leopoldville Government; he had taken advantage of the general confusion to assert his authority and get rid of a young rival.

Fonts suddenly felt like dropping everything and flying back to France. But he would never be able to forget the three thousand bodies; he had to exorcize their memory. Was he, for the first time in his life, going to take to his heels with his tail between his legs, like a mongrel puppy that had just been whipped? No, never!

Without putting down his glass he sprang to his feet. He had nothing to fight with except the two men who were there, a mythomaniac and a Boy Scout.

"We backed the wrong horse," he said slowly. "We've lost North Katanga without fighting as we ought to have done. . . ."

"All that remains is to pack up our bags and clear out," Wenceslas observed with relief.

Already he pictured himself swaggering around Elizabethville or leaning against the Mitsouko bar, flirting with Nathalie . . . dropping those casual remarks which enable one to lie without being caught out.

He would never again make the mistake which had obliged him to leave England, then France, and come to Rhodesia and involve himself in this horrible grotesque war.

Before Fonts's arrival life at Nyunzu had been easy, for nothing ever happened. Wenceslas would bluster loudly, carry out a few ostentatious patrols along some nice deserted tracks, and leave the dirty work to the Belgians. He would display his trophies and talk in a tone of disillusioned confidence about his glorious past—a past which he had largely invented.

To others, and even to himself, he had become the son of a cavalry colonel, a personal friend of Marshal Rydz-Smigly. At the age of nineteen, as a mere cadet, he had been in action, armed only with a lance, against the German tanks advancing across the great plains of the Vistula. Taken prisoner by the Russians, miraculously escaping the massacre at Katyn and the machine-guns of the NKVD, he had been released as a result of the agreement between the Soviets and the Allies. He then made for Persia and spent two months in Teheran, wandering about the streets and bazaars where part of the stolen American aid was sold at low prices.

Wenceslas would even describe how a moth-eaten merchant had proposed to let him have a Liberty ship moored in Khoramchar. As a lieutenant in the Anders Army he had fought in Italy, and he often spoke with great emotion and reserve of "the scarlet poppies of Monte Cassino," while whistling a well-known marching song through his teeth.

Usually he waited until he knew his audience fairly well before describing the dramatic night when he learned that Warsaw had risen against the Germans. Twenty officers, including himself of course, had been dispatched forthwith to England, taken in charge by some Polish pilots serving in the RAF and, against all orders, dropped by parachute two days later over the capital of Poland in flames.

Wenceslas had never been dropped by parachute over Warsaw; he had never been an officer, only a sergeant-major in charge of supplies. He was not the son of a cavalry colonel, but of a little tailor in Krakow. He had never been in action against the German tanks in the broad plains of the Vistula and, if he knew the bazaar in Teheran, it was because he had worked for three months in a Lebanese merchant's office.

Picked up at random during a snap raid, he had spent five months in a Soviet camp where he became the secretary of the commandant since he spoke Russian extremely well.

Wenceslas was not a mere mythomaniac. He had chosen to be a character other than himself, but this character had actually existed. He had come across him several times in the Middle East and in Italy. He was Captain Count Wenceslas Peresky, as handsome as a god, as stupid as a donkey, as brave as a lion. He had dropped into the furnace of Warsaw and had never been seen again. Wenceslas had gone so far as to borrow his Christian name but had not dared to appropriate his surname, thereby avoiding being taken for a common imposter.

In *emigré* circles the truth was soon discovered but, with a strange pertinacity, Wenceslas went on lying, with the result that he usually found himself obliged to leave the country where he was living.

He had been frightened that Thomas Fonts might involve him in some unpleasant situation, thus forcing him,

213

the hero of Warsaw, to show courage when he had never been courageous.

He asked again:

"When do we clear out?"

Fonts looked astonished.

"But there's no question of that! We've been fooled, I admit, but that's no reason for giving in! My dear Wenceslas, we both of us have our reputations to think of: you, the hero of Monte Cassino and Warsaw, must surely agree with me—we can't allow ourselves to be flung out without at least leaving our visiting cards! In Elizabethville, Maley is going round saying that he doesn't want to meddle in the internal affairs of Katanga, but here, because there are no witnesses, he makes no bones about it. . . . So he has the laugh on us. As for the President, the people of Katanga and that stinker la Roncière who takes me for a choirboy, I don't give a damn for any of them. . . ."

"Then why are you fighting?" Mullens asked.

"Because I'm small and I don't like being trampled on! Have you got a map of the area, Wenceslas?"

Wenceslas felt the trap closing in on him; he tried to struggle.

"A Michelin map, that's all."

"It will do. In France, during the Resistance, they were all we had. What about you in Poland?"

Fonts got up and came over to the table on which Wenceslas had spread out a fly-blown map. With his finger he followed the railway running from Albertville to Nyunzu.

"I say, Mullens, you must know this stretch of rail!"

"Like the back of my hand!"

"Does the line pass over a small metal bridge anywhere, a simple platform without an arch or, better still, along an embankment?"

"What do you want to do?"

"I'm asking you a simple question."

"The line runs along an embankment above the road for two hundred yards between Niemba and Nyunzu."

"That's all I wanted to know: that's where Wenceslas and I will wait for the arrival of the first train which the UN are bound to send up laden with troops to reoccupy Nyunzu. The UN are short of trucks and receive their equipment and reinforcements across Lake Tanganyika."

Fonts began pacing up and down, alternately disappearing and reappearing in the circle of light thrown by the lamp.

"What about the telephone?" he asked. "Does the telephone work between Nyunzu station and Albertville? Is the station-master at Albertville still a Belgian?"

"Of course," Mullens replied in astonishment.

"Do you know him?"

"Yes."

"Take the jeep, drive down to the station, ring him up and ask him if the UN intend sending a train tomorrow morning in the direction of Nyunzu. . . . Come back straight away."

"But . . ."

"It's not asking you much. Are you prepared to defend this country or do you want to have it taken over by the Indians, the Ethiopians, the Ghanaians and all the rest of them? Incapable of organizing it, capable only of looting it, they'll be forced to appeal to white men other than Belgians: Russians or Americans, depending on which way the wind is blowing. As they know nothing about the place or the people, they'll commit all the blunders which you Belgians have learned not to commit any longer."

Mullens hesitated. He had come to the Congo to grow cotton and not to wage war. He did not believe in the narrow nationalism of his forebears and felt more European than Belgian. But in this chaos and confusion he felt a sense of solidarity with men like Fonts who, without referring to high principles, merely talked about "visiting cards."

In any case nothing was important any longer, neither the cotton seed nor the well-fed Cotonkat shareholders. It was simply a question of helping some friends and doing something at all costs.

Mullens went off. Fonts had obtained what he wanted from him—an incipient commitment—but he derived no pleasure from this. With young men of his sort the most time-worn tricks always worked. A wave of naïvety was going to submerge the world when all this generation of young men between twenty and twenty-five reached adult age.

He still had to get a grip on this worthy lout Wenceslas, who almost died of fright on the Lukuga River and had never seen danger so close.

The Pole poured himself out another drink with a shaking hand.

"There's nothing very difficult," Fonts went on, "about derailing a train, because that's what we're going to do. You've done this sort of job before, I take it?"

"Well . . ."

"Silly of me to ask, of course. The only difficulty lies in acting quickly and keeping it secret. We can't allow ourselves to be caught, whatever happens, because the job must be attributed to the local population or the gendarmes."

"Everyone knows the niggers aren't even capable of lighting a firecracker."

"Everyone knows it, but it still remains to be proved!"

Edgar Mullens came back half an hour later with information: the UN delegate had requisitioned a string of coaches and an engine, but the train would not be leaving Albertville until the day after tomorrow for Niemba, where it would be joined by two armored cars and a company who had been moved up by truck.

"From Niemba to Nyunzu," the young man added, "it's about a hundred miles. The road follows the railway, and the two convoys will advance side by side. They seem to be frightened of something happening at Nyunzu. There's a rumor that reinforcements of Katangese gendarmes commanded by mercenaries have arrived."

"I hope you confirmed it! So it's no go between Niemba and Nyunzu if the trucks and train move up together. What about between Albertville and Niemba?"

"Immediately after Albertville the railway skirts the forest. Half-way, about ten miles out, there's a track branching off to Manono. Only it's a straight stretch and there's no bridge."

"Above all we need a line of withdrawal. We'll still manage to blow up the rails. Tomorrow you'll show us the spot. You'll drive out in your truck and we'll follow in the jeep. After that, you drop us and come back to Nyunzu with your cotton seed. All the little black planters are waiting for it, aren't they?"

"And how! Especially if I accompany it with free gifts."

"Before you get to the cotton fields you'll set fire to your truck . . . and then tell everyone it was the blue helmets who destroyed it because they want the Balubas to go on dying of hunger. After that you'll make whatever arrangements you can to rejoin us at Manono."

"At a pinch, I'm prepared to show you the way . . . but, for the seed, I'm responsible to my company!"

"Let me tell you a story, my little Edgar. It was in France, in 1940, during the great rush southwards of all our little soldiers who had 'discarded their weapons on the field of honor,' as Uncle Céline puts it.

"An ordnance captain refused to issue rations, equip-

216

ment and ammunition to one of the few units who were still prepared to fight, because no one had the necessary vouchers. He had even armed his clerks so that they could fire on what he called 'these runaways.' But he handed everything over to the Jerries, including the account books and inventories; then, with a clear conscience, he let himself be taken prisoner. He spent five years in an *Oflag*, happily playing bridge and learning Sanskrit . . . still with a clear conscience. I would have put a bullet in his head and so, I believe, would Wenceslas. But the officer confronting him had principles; he was a regular; he buggered off with his ragged warriors.

"So you see, old boy, I don't give a damn about your company. Your seed will never be planted, or else the cotton will rot in the fields. At least let it serve to sow a little disorder!"

"You're right, Fonts," Wenceslas agreed in a thick voice. "Only we shan't find a single nigger to accompany us on our expedition."

"We shan't need one!"

By the following morning Nyunzu had been evacuated by all its inhabitants. The rumor had spread about the arrival of the Congolese soldiers, and the Africans had fled into the bush, taking whatever they possessed with them.

The police and Gendarmerie barracks were deserted. Their inmates had all piled into whatever trucks were still working and driven off before dawn towards Elizabethville.

Some women who had tried to follow them had been beaten to the ground with rifle-butts, and one or two children had been run over.

Wenceslas had slept badly. Fear gnawed at his bowels. But still more than fear, he dreaded, after having lost his nerve, running into Fonts at Elizabethville and being asked by him to describe yet again his exploits in Poland and Italy.

His fatalism impelled him, moreover, to do nothing. Everything would be settled one way or another, for Fonts would never have the time or the means to blow up the train.

Fonts, Wenceslas and Mullens left Nyunzu about ten o'clock in the morning to hide out in an abandoned plantation near Niemba, where they had decided to wait until it was dark. Mullens himself drove his open Dodge, and Fonts was at the wheel of the jeep.

The three men concealed themselves and their vehicles in a shed on the edge of the forest which was once used

217

for sorting cotton. It was all that remained of the planta-tion.

Fonts dismantled the machine-gun and its tripod.

"It's too conspicuous," he explained. "Each of us keeps his carbine and grenades. We're merely peaceful Cotonkat planters. Planters don't need a machine-gun to defend themselves, they have their employers' gratitude and their own clear consciences!"

"We're not going to die for the sake of a visiting card," Wenceslas kept saying to himself. "It's not possible! Fonts will tell us presently that we're clearing out."

The heat made the grass crackle. Mosquitoes stuck to their forearms and faces; bluebottles—the flies of death, Wenceslas reflected—sucked at their sweat. When they crushed them their hands became sticky with blood.

The beer they had brought with them was warm—horse-piss, Fonts had called it. Lying stretched out on some wattles, their ears pricked, they waited for night to fall.

"Soon we'll be left in peace," Fonts promised. "The blacks don't like being out at night, whereas at this time of day you may suddenly find yourself face to face with a gang of Balubas who are bent on some sort of mischief. No point in firing, a grenade tossed into their midst has more effect . . . because everyone's hit at the same time, there's an explosion, shouting, surprise. You must have used grenades quite often, Wenceslas. . . . But why have you kept both ends of the pin bent back on that grenade you've got next to you? If the Balubas turn up, you'll never have time to release it. I can understand a youngster like Mullens not knowing this, but I'm surprised at an old hand like you!"

Mullens tried to come to Wenceslas's rescue.

"I met an American girl in E'ville who knew you," he remarked to Fonts.

"Oh really?"

Fonts took off his shirt, picked up a water-bottle and poured a thin stream down his skinny chest. A long scar ran from his right breast to his ribs; the heat and humidity made it more prominent.

"How did you get that?" Wenceslas asked.

"It's nothing. I tore myself on some barbed wire . . . I was in a hurry and I had to get through. What time is it?"

"Half past four. Why haven't you got a watch?"

"I gave it away."

Fonts rose to his feet, shook his dark, almost frizzy hair

218

which gleamed as though it had just been daubed with brilliantine, then suddenly asked:

"Wenceslas, what are you going to do with all the money you've made in Katanga?"

The Pole smiled bashfully, like a young girl confessing to her mother that she has misbehaved, though feeling no remorse about it.

"I'd like to bugger off to Tahiti."

Suddenly he became voluble.

"It's paradise out there, you know. You mustn't live in Tahiti itself, it's full of tourists, but on one of the smaller islands: Moorea, Bora-Bora or in the Tuamotu. Once you've settled, you don't need money any more: everything grows; the girls are forthcoming, the lagoons are full of fish. . . ."

"Did you ever see a country where you didn't need money, where the girls didn't ask you for money?"

"The main expense is the voyage: you're not allowed a one-way fare, you have to pay for a return."

"And you know why, Wenceslas? Too many old wrecks were washed up on Tahiti and the French Government had to send them home at its own expense: they're known as banana tourists!"

"But I wouldn't be a banana tourist."

"Do you know what's surprising about the Pacific? Those islands, separated by hundreds of miles, are all like concierges' lodges side by side in the Rue Mouffetard or the Rue de Buci. Everyone knows everything about everyone else."

"What do you know about it?"

"I spent three months in Tahiti after the war . . . I came back, I was so bored there. Nothing ever happens; it's Clochemerle in the tropics."

"That's what I call paradise: a place where nothing ever happens."

"But also a place where there's no curiosity, where people believe everything they're told without trying to check if it's a lot of lies."

"Anyway, that's what I think of paradise."

"The little Chinese girls are pretty. If we get out of this alive, if your passport's in order . . . and I can help you about that . . . I'll give you some girls' addresses. Now let's get down to work!"

"So we're really going to do this job?"

"Of course. You're not windy by any chance?"

"Me?"

"I was only joking."

Mullens had the feeling he was witnessing a boxing match between a professional and a wretched amateur. The champion was amusing himself by slowly demolishing his opponent: it was unbearable.

He made another attempt to enable Wenceslas to get out of it.

"I'll never be able to set fire to my truck . . . but I should like to remember one day that I blew up a train. Fonts, take me with you, and Wenceslas will see to the cotton seed."

Fonts looked at him in surprise.

"No, Edgar. To be a saboteur, you've got to be trained and not give a damn, like Wenceslas and myself. . . ."

With drooping shoulders Wenceslas walked over towards the jeep, with his grenade slung on his belt and his carbine in his hand.

Fonts seized Mullens by the arm.

"You're a brave little bugger!"

"He's frightened, Fonts."

"I know, he's always been frightened. Tahiti is a sort of cocoon, a refuge for everyone who's frightened of life, of war, of women, of cold, of hunger. Wenceslas only needs to stop being frightened, just for once, and bring off one successful job. Then it won't be a failure who sets off for Tahiti, but a man; maybe he won't even feel like going any more. You know, I've never set foot in Tahiti . . . but I can describe it pretty well, even realistically . . . as Wenceslas describes the fighting he's never seen! I'll bring a hero back with me to E'ville . . . and you'll see how silent he'll be. I had to keep pitching into him so that he shouldn't lose his nerve. You understand?"

"Yes, but I still don't think I'm going to set fire to my truck."

"What the hell do I care!"

"That American girl's eyes sparkled when I talked to her about you."

"Really?"

"I think I know why!"

Mullens led them through the forest along a series of bumpy tracks till they reached a sort of hunters' camp consisting of a round hut, the roof of which had caved in.

On the way they encountered two or three columns of Negroes, half-naked or in gray denims and filthy shirts. They merely waved at them and watched them drive past. They did not seem in the least frightened.

"They recognize the truck," Mullens explained.

Rusty tins of bully-beef lay scattered in the thick grass. A few moments of unbearable silence, then night fell with its noises.

"The railway is a hundred yards behind that row of trees," said Mullens. "A little path leads up to it."

The young Belgian waved an embarrassed farewell at the two men and drove off, crashing his gears.

"The youngster's in a hurry to leave, isn't he?" Wenceslas observed with an effort, for his mouth was painfully dry. "Do we start straight away?"

"No. At first light. You've checked the spare jerry-cans of petrol all right? We don't know how far we'll have to drive."

"Yes."

"Now we've got to be very careful: we're going to cut down some branches to hide the jeep."

Fonts opened one of the sabotage packs.

"They haven't done us very proud: old American equipment dating back to the war. The detonators work when they feel like it, the primer cord is rotten. . . . Mind you, it still does the trick occasionally. . . ."

Squatting down on the floor of the hut, with lizards and cockroaches scuttling all round them, they dined on a biscuit and tin of bully-beef each, washed down with beer followed by neat whisky.

"Don't worry, Wenceslas," Fonts said with sudden gentleness, "it's not as hard as all that to derail a train, and it's not the first time I've done it. Perhaps it won't do any good, but at least we'll have tried. Now I'm going to get some sleep. You take the first watch and wake me up when you feel sleepy."

Wenceslas remained alone, leaning against the mud wall, with his carbine between his legs, staring into the dank equatorial darkness, a darkness black as pitch and unrelieved by a single star.

The moment of truth that he was dreading had come, and he discovered that being brave and taking risks was infinitely easier than telling lies and then suffering in consequence.

Tomorrow, when the train had been blown up, he would confess to Fonts that he had never been in action, that he had merely hung about cook-houses and offices.

Then the little dark man would keep him with him. It was easy to live and be brave with a man like Fonts who appeared to regard death as a joke in bad taste. . . .

Wenceslas received the blast in the stomach, and the flash of the detonation, fired a few yards off, was such that he had the impression of standing in front of the mouth of an ancient cannon.

Two Balubas in warpaint accompanied the man who had fired the pop-gun: a bicycle-frame tube transformed into a rifle and stuffed with nails.

All three of them leaned over Wenceslas. There was a sound of firing and the glistening faces disappeared.

Fonts was now beside Wenceslas and he gently inquired:

"Did you fall asleep?"

He lit a match. The Pole's shirt, trousers, belly and gizzards were reduced to pulp.

Wenceslas would go on living for another hour or two before dying in utter agony . . . and there was nothing to be done on account of the gas gangrene which would set in straight away.

"I think you're going to get away with it, Wenceslas."

Fonts went off to fetch a bottle of whisky, came back and made the Pole take a long swig.

Wenceslas hiccuped.

"I thought that with a stomach wound one shouldn't drink!"

"Doctors' nonsense. It's only a scratch. I'm going to get the jeep, then we're off. There are too many Negroes wandering about the bush for us to stay here. Too bad about the train. . . ."

He disappeared, then Wenceslas heard him say in the affectionate, embarrassed tone one uses to an old friend who is on the point of leaving:

"Have a good trip to Tahiti . . . and give the girls my love."

Fonts fired and the bullet thudded into Wenceslas's skull.

"I hope," he reflected, "that I'll have a friend to do me the same favor when I have to embark for Tahiti!"

He took the hero of Warsaw's papers, wallet and weapons, got into the jeep and, with headlamps blazing, headed for Manono.

He had loosened the pin of the grenade lying on the seat beside him. If he was captured he would blow himself up with those who took him prisoner.

Just then he remembered Juan, the head of the Maquis who used to play with the gold doubloon and who had stu-

222

pidly blown his face off while tinkering with a German mine he had found in an abandoned dump.

Before dying he uttered these disillusioned words:

"The dead are all worth the same, Thomas, whether they're heroes or cowards, because once they're dead they're not worth anything."

Lieutenant Kreis was sent to Tshiko Camp, fifty miles outside Elizabethville, the day after la Roncière assumed his duties and moved into an office next to President Kimjanga's.

The colonel had told him what he wanted. His voice was stiffer and more precise now that he had an official appointment again:

"Quite a lot of things are in pretty poor shape, Kreis, especially the training of the Katangese Army. If we had to fight we couldn't count on a single decent unit, not even a battalion, not even a company. The Belgian officers in Tshiko Camp continue to train the gendarmes as though they still belonged to the Force Publique and were limited in their duties to dispersing a handful of demonstrators with rifle-butts. . . . Choose the best elements from the three thousand men in the camp, select them carefully. If you find your hundred that are suitable you'll be lucky. . . . These four hundred you'll turn into para-commandoes."

"We'll put them through a parachute course?"

"Where would we find the aircraft? No, we'll merely give them camouflage uniform, red berets and paratroop badges. The clothes often make the man, the white cap the legionary, and the camouflage uniform the paratroopers. . . . In two months, three at the latest, I want some men on whom I can rely. It's up to you, Kreis, to provide them from human material which isn't worth very much if you compare it with French recuits or our legionaries."

"Will I be on my own?"

"There are about a dozen foreign instructors in the camp and also a few Belgians. I'm putting them under your orders. You'll have trouble with both lots, but I'll be behind you. If you need me, send for me at once and I'll come. It's going to be a difficult job."

"I've only commanded German soldiers and legionaries; they were often the same. I've never commanded blacks."

"You'll learn. I should have liked Fonts to spend a couple of days there with you, but he's with the Balubas. Don't ever forget that the Negro is vain and touchy, given to fits of panic or irrational temper, but that it's possible, by playing on his vanity, to make an acceptable para-commando out of him, if not a soldier. Go!"

"I'm dropping into unknown territory, Colonel."

"One more word of advice, Kreis. I don't want to see any women in Tshiko. You know what I mean? If you get the itch, come into Elizabethville. It only takes an hour by car and I'm putting a vehicle at your disposal."

"Very well, Colonel."

Kreis, who was wearing a British uniform without any badges of rank but had retained his old green beret and French decorations, clicked his heels and marched out.

Tshiko Camp looked like any of the others which the Belgians had built in the Congo for their Force Publique. In the middle stood the barracks, consisting of long single-story blocks which formed a square around a somewhat more imposing building, the command post and administrative offices. Opposite these stood a flag-pole.

To the right, on a hill, the villas of the officers and European NCOs lay hidden among the foliage and grouped around the camp commandant's quarters. These were occupied by a Belgian major awaiting repatriation and whose duties were now non-existent.

To the left, in a hollow, was the Negro village where, in huts or hard-wall houses, the soldiers with their wives and countless offspring were quartered. The corporals and sergeants were entitled to larger huts and a small garden.

Since independence, a number of African NCOs had become officers but only three of them had come to live in the white men's village, Captain Joseph Nadolo and two lieutenants, Kiwe and Molobu.

Joseph Nadolo's promotion remained a mystery, even to the other Katangese soldiers. He was more or less illiterate, extremely unpopular and had a violent temper. But he was tall and strong, with a tough handsome face, and above all he belonged to the Bayeke tribe. He was said to be related to the family of the Minister of the Interior, Bongo.

Kreis, who had left Elizabethville at seven o'clock in the morning, drove into the camp two hours later.

At the entrance a sentry stood leaning against his sentry-box, his rifle lying on the ground near by. Although the car, a black Peugeot which had once been Pimuriaux's pride and joy, flew the Katangese flag, the man did not even straighten up as it passed.

A gang of prisoners were pushing a wheelbarrow, super-

224

vised by other soldiers who shared cigarettes and bottles of beer with them.

The administrative buildings were empty except for one office where two Belgian NCOs were busy filling in some big ledgers.

Kreis asked where the camp commandant was to be found.

"Which?" asked one of the NCOs. "The white one? Major Jacquet's packing his bags and I'm working out his accounts. The Negro? Joseph Nadolo got so drunk last night that he's probably still sleeping it off. He was celebrating Major Jacquet's departure. He's now the big boss here."

"No, he isn't. I am. Lieutenant Karl Kreis. The President has just sent me from Elizabethville."

The second NCO lifted his nose from the ledgers. A broad grin came over his apple-cheeked face.

"You'll have to argue that out with Nadolo. That fellow has no doubts about himself; he already sees himself as Commander-in-Chief of the Katangese Army! Only a few months ago he used to salute me from a distance of six paces, you know."

"Where are the other instructors?"

"Nine o'clock, they've knocked off for a snack. We Belgians feed in the officers' mess. There are eight of us left. The mercenaries mess together in one of the villas. You know, Lieutenant, there's not much contact between us Belgians and the other foreigners . . . because among your mercenaries what a lot of riff-raff there is, from every country in the world!"

"It's with that riff-raff from every country in the world that one of the best units in the world has been formed: the Foreign Legion!"

The NCO dipped his nose back into his books.

"Excuse me, but Major Jacquet is waiting for his accounts before he leaves."

Kreis was shown the way to the officers' mess, a big bright room with bay windows opening on to a glorious landscape of wooded hills. At the far end was a platform on which a microphone had been installed, in memory of better days when over fifty Belgian officers and their wives used to come here and dance.

Everything was covered in dust. The chromium-plated tubular chairs were no longer wiped clean, nor were the tables. Above the bar, a patch on the wall marked the place from which the picture of King Baudouin had recently been removed.

Two officers and four NCOs in battle-dress were dunking thick slices of bread into bowls of coffee and synthetic milk.

Kreis clicked his heels and very stiffly introduced himself:

"Lieutenant Karl Kreis, of the Third Foreign Parachute Regiment."

The Belgians turned round without acknowledging his greeting, without even rising to shake hands.

The oldest of them, a tired-faced captain, did, however, make an effort.

"I'm Captain Ardelles. We've been notified of your arrival. Being senior in rank and belonging to the Belgian Army, there's no question of my serving under your orders. You'll be in command of the foreign instructors. . . . We'll continue to deal with the administration of the camp. Our two offices are connected by telephone; I think that will be all?"

"Foreign Parachute Regiment," a young lieutenant inquired, "they're legionaries, aren't they?"

"Yes, they are."

"Kreis? You're German, aren't you?"

"I was."

"I don't like Germans."

Kreis went white in the face. If he had not had this mission to fulfill, a difficult mission for which his colonel was relying on him, if he had not been his own master, he would have given this young whippersnapper a good hiding.

If he had only been able, like Fonts, to reply with some biting retort, some allusion to the utter panic that had overcome all the Belgian officers at the moment of independence!

But he could think of nothing to say and turned on his heel.

There were only eight foreign instructors left. Two of them, finding life boring at Tshiko, had gone to seek their fortunes elsewhere; they had not been seen again.

Among those remaining were three former legionaries, and Kreis had no difficulty in taking them in hand. The fourth was a former paratrooper, soaked in alcohol like a sponge. Just after being promoted regimental sergeant-major at the age of thirty, Henri Buscard, who had a passion for gambling, had got into serious trouble in Indo-

China: he had gambled in Cholon with his battalion funds, which, in spite of his exceptional record, had caused him to be reduced to the ranks, repatriated and dismissed from the service.

Kreis's Légion d'Honneur and above all his Médaille Militaire, which showed that he was a former NCO, made an impression on him; he was the first to come over to his side and he promised him not to touch another drink as long as he was in the camp.

The remaining three, who wore beards, were vague about their nationality and past careers. They were inclined to be familiar. Kreis put them firmly in their place. One of them said to him:

"Rank doesn't mean a thing here, it's the individual that counts. Let's see if you're a man!"

Kreis struck him in the face with his clenched fist and, as the fellow was about to draw his revolver, hit him over the head with a bottle.

Kreis then bundled the trio into the truck which was leaving with Major Jacquet's kit and the portrait of King Baudouin. After that he went in search of Captain Joseph Nadolo.

He found him already installed in the camp commandant's office, with his shirt unbuttoned but his cap on his head, smoking a big cigar and leaning back in his armchair. .

Kreis saluted and removed his beret, according to regulations.

Flattered, Nadolo motioned him to be seated.

"Make yourself at home, my dear fellow. . . ."

He clapped his hands and an orderly came trotting in.

"Go and bring us some beer," Nadolo ordered him.

"Where from, boss?"

"The canteen."

"What about money?"

"Tell them it's for the camp commandant."

Kreis drew his chair up to the desk.

"President Kimjanga has made me responsible for training."

"That's fine."

"And has ordered me to form a unit of para-commandos."

"What on earth's that?"

Nadolo's smile had turned into a sly suspicious expression. He ran his tongue round his lips.

"I'm in command of Tshiko now. Dwaft me a weport

on these pawa-commandos . . . and I'll take a decision."

Kreis rose to his feet.

"I've got orders and I intend to carry them out."

"Major Jacquet twansferred his command to me. I've signed any amount of papers. You've no idea. . . ."

"I take my orders direct from my commanding officer, Colonel la Roncière, who takes his from President Kimjanga, and I carry them out."

"The army's not like that, in the army you have to have a hiewarchy. . . ."

"I've had seventeen years of the army and seventeen years of war . . . Captain. I was first an ordinary soldier, then an officer, then a soldier again, then an NCO, then an officer, and I know all about discipline and hierarchy."

Kreis marched out without saluting this sloppy puppet slumped in his armchair. He felt it would have been discreditable to do so.

Nadolo was mortified by this. He had always dreamed of commanding whites. With the Belgians it was difficult: they knew him and called him "Sergeant Stinker," but this fellow Kreis, since the Katangese Government was paying him, ought to obey him and show a little respect.

Seventeen years of war! That wasn't so difficult, seventeen years of war. He had also made war on everyone who refused to toe the line.

When the orderly came back with the two beers, Nadolo said to him:

"Put them down there . . . and have a drink with me. That white man who was in the office just now is a bad man, you know . . . maybe a spy. We'll have to keep an eye on him. What are the soldiers saying in their palavers?"

"That it's not good here at Tshiko, that it's better in Elizabethville, that there aren't any women . . . that the grub's not good, that the beer's too expensive. . . ."

"Me, I'd like the lot of us to go back to E'ville, but that Fleming they sent us says we've got to stay here, get down to work, go out on route marches and train, train, train . . . as we used to do before independence. He doesn't like blacks . . . and he refuses to obey me . . . me, the camp commandant. Tell all this to the soldiers."

"Very good, boss."

On the following day Kreis issued a number of orders which were not at all popular with the garrison. Everyone was confined to barracks for eight days during the take-over; there were inspections, exercises and parades. No one was allowed to loiter outside the administrative buildings; everyone had to move at the double. . . .

But it was not enough to issue orders, they also had to be carried out and accepted.

Kreis for the first time in his life was in a position of command; he was his own master. But the Katangese Army was not like the Legion, a perfectly geared machine, and the four Europeans he had under him could not do everything.

It was Henri Buscard, the former sergeant-major, who suggested a more suitable approach.

"In this place, Kreis, ever since independence and the abortive rising at Massart Camp, discipline has been replaced by palaver. You must palaver as well, to begin with. Your idea of para-commandos is a good one. They'll all want to dress up and play at big warriors. Once your choice is made, you isolate the para-commandos from the other men, which will lead to rivalry; you'll take advantage of this to restore order. The Belgians used to make use of tribal rivalry, they employed the Balubas to beat up the Lundas, the Lundas to beat up the Bayekes. We're going to create a completely new race—the para-commandos. That's Africa for you! But you'll see how difficult it is; what they learn one day they forget the next . . . they're not bad fellows, but easily influenced and willfully idle . . . unless they're kept amused."

During the first week Kreis kept them amused. The camp became a vast competition stadium. Kreis had decreed that whoever wanted to become a para-commando had to prove himself stronger, run faster, march longer without drinking, and be able to outdo the others.

A dozen uniforms had arrived from Elizabethville, and Kreis had issued these to the four instructors, his driver and three African NCOs who, alone of the whole mob, showed a semblance of authority.

From Elizabethville, too, had come Joseph Nadolo's notification of promotion to major.

Nadolo strutted about the camp displaying his new badges of rank. He now carried a swagger-stick under his arm and sneered at the soldiers who, in shorts or battle-dress, spent their time running, leaping and flinging dummy grenades to earn their red berets and camouflage uniform. He called them silly sods.

He was often to be seen with the group of Belgians; he even had nine-o'clock breakfast with them; they pretended to treat him as though he was one of them.

On two or three occasions, on the advice of Buscard whom he had appointed his second-in-command, Kreis had tried to approach him and interest him in what he was doing; he had asked him to attend the training periods and help in the selection of the para-commandos.

But the man's self-satisfaction and military worthlessness, his malevolence, his would-be insidious questions and meaningless remarks exasperated Kreis and made him lose his temper.

Seeing there was no solution and feeling hampered by Nadolo's nasty attitude, he rang up la Roncière to ask him to relieve the major of his command.

The colonel told him it was impossible. No matter what the cost, he would have to come to an understanding with Nadolo, who had valuable support in the Presidency and was considered to be an officer with a great future.

Kreis almost choked on the other end of the line.

"But he's a thoroughly bad hat, Colonel. He doesn't know a thing, he's undermining all my work by openly mocking what I'm trying to do."

"I'll come and see you next week. I'm sending you eight hundred camouflage uniforms straight away."

"The uniforms can wait . . . we haven't reached that stage yet."

"But I can't wait. . . ."

This conversation between Kreis and la Roncière was overheard by a Belgian NCO in charge of Signals and reported to Captain Ardelles who passed it on to Nadolo, exaggerating the remarks that Kreis had made about him.

Nadolo decided to take action at the first opportunity. Kreis, ill at ease with the blacks, too brutal, obsessed by the idea of rapid progress and hardening these flabby bodies, unable to laugh or joke, was unconsciously committing blunder after blunder.

For the last three days a hundred worthy frizzy heads had been wearing berets and camouflage uniform, swaggering about conceitedly, believing that the future of Katanga depended on them alone and that their former comrades were good for nothing.

Kreis wanted to induce a competitive spirit; it rapidly turned into rivalry. But this was complicated by squabbles over women or money.

It was then that the ammunition incident occurred.

One morning Kreis took it into his head to inspect the rifle ammunition of the company commanded by Lieutenant Kiwe, a close friend of Nadolo's.

Half the men had no ammunition, the other half only a fraction of what they had been issued.

Kreis first of all thought they had left their ammunition in their quarters so as to have less to carry. He sent them back to fetch it but they returned with their ammunition pouches empty.

One of them admitted that the ammunition had been lost . . . "not lost exactly . . . only sold here and there, so as to have money for beer, to some men who bought it for the blacks to fight in Angola against the Portuguese."

Summoned to account for this "criminal negligence," Lieutenant Kiwe retorted that he could not count his men's ammunition every day, that this was the sergeant-major's duty and the sergeant-major was on leave because his wife was ill.

Wild with rage, not knowing if the lieutenant was a complete idiot, utterly witless or simply making fun of him, Kreis went off to Major Nadolo to ask him to take disciplinary action against Kiwe and his soldiers.

Nadolo did not appear to consider the offense so reprehensible; he promised "to have a word with the men and tell them not to do it again." As for Kiwe, he was in no way to blame.

"You ought to put them in prison . . . court martial them," Kreis yelled, "and put Kiwe immediately under close arrest!"

Delightedly, Nadolo watched this "Fleming" fly off the handle, but he rejected the suggestion of disciplinary action—"which I alone can take," he pointed out—since Kreis was here only as an adviser.

Kreis realized that his nice Belgian friends had taken care to enlighten Nadolo.

On the following day he ordered the ammunition to be reissued so that each soldier had his full allocation, and two days later he held another inspection.

Everyone had his ammunition, but Kreis, weighing one of the rounds in his hand, noticed it was unusually light. He broke it open; there was no powder in the cartridge case.

Backed up by all his soldiers who were delighted to see their officer at grips with the Fleming, Kiwe asserted they had been issued ammunition without powder because, being Negroes, they were not to be trusted.

With a great effort Kreis managed to control himself, opened another lot of ammunition in front of Kiwe and reissued it.

On the following day he held another inspection: this

time the rounds were too heavy, the powder had been replaced by sand.

Driven into a corner, Kiwe asserted that his men had not sold the powder and that it was Kreis and the other mercenaries who had filled the cartridge cases with sand.

"The real ammunition," he said, "you give to the whites so that they can shoot at us."

The former legionary's fist smashed into Lieutenant Kiwe's self-satisfied face, sending him flying. Kreis summoned two para-commandos, who put the lieutenant back on his feet, and ordered them to haul him off to the guardhouse, which they did without a trace of astonishment.

In his office he found Buscard who with two fingers was typing out the para-commandos' training program.

Buscard had quickly become a close friend, the *Kamerad* that a man like Kreis was unable to do without. Girls can be found anywhere, the sort that go to bed with one for pleasure or for money or because they are bored.

Pals are more difficult to come by and, in war, they need to be loyal and true, so that you can get drunk with them or have a fight without the binge or the squabble having any consequence.

You risk your life for a pal, you hand over your girl to him, but if he gets killed you soon forget him; another takes his place.

"I think I've done something silly," Kreis said to Buscard. "I bashed Lieutenant Kiwe in the face, you know, over that ammunition business."

"I told you he had Nadolo and the Belgians behind him."

"I couldn't control myself, Buscard, I'm not used to this sort of thing."

"I say, listen! You've been had for a mug."

Kreis went up to the window: a horde of soldiers were gathering round Lieutenant Kiwe, who had not got as far as the guardhouse. More and more soldiers came rushing up, shouting more and more loudly, and were joined by others carrying their weapons.

"The only one who can calm them down is Nadolo," Buscard observed.

A stone shattered one of the office windows.

"Wait here, Kreis, and above all keep under cover."

Buscard looked in all the offices; they were empty, Nadolo's as well as the two Belgian officers'. But there was a smell of cigar smoke in both rooms: a few minutes earlier they had still been occupied.

When he came back Kreis was no longer there but outside, alone and unarmed, facing a mob of furious soldiers milling round Kiwe whose nose was bleeding and who kept yelling hysterically:

"They issued arms to the whites to fire on us; our cartridges were filled with sand to prevent us from fighting back. Brothers, they're out to massacre us. That dirty Fleming struck me because I'm a black."

"That's not true," said Kreis.

His first impulse had been to fling himself on Kiwe and frog-march him off to the guardhouse. But these raving Negroes, in the name of sudden racial solidarity, because he was white and therefore the enemy, would have lynched him. He felt quite calm, even-tempered, trying to see what steps he should take, not to curb these furious hysterical men, but to bring them to their senses. The old legionary methods were of no avail here: everyone at attention . . . a ten-mile march to cool off, then disciplinary action. . . .

He remembered one of Fonts's remarks: "Nothing is ever lost or won in Africa, everything is endlessly called in question," and what Colonel la Roncière had said: "The black is vain, touchy, prone to irrational fits of temper and panic. . . ."

The mob of soldiers kept increasing. A stone went whizzing over his head. .

"If I fall I'm done for," Kreis reflected.

He raised his hand.

"I'm alone against all of you, and unarmed . . . I can't escape. . . ."

He had his back to the wall of the administrative building and could feel the roughcast against his bare arms.

". . . But I'm not frightened, because I trust in your sense of justice, your common sense, your patriotism. . . ."

"And a grenade flung into their midst," he simultaneously reflected, "what effect would it have? A blood-spattered crater, red lips which would open in this seething black mass and then close in on me."

But a leader did not defend himself against his men with grenades, or else he was not worthy to lead.

Another missile whistled past him. Kreis had never imagined that he could die in this manner, stoned, torn to shreds by raving Negroes. It was his own fault, he had not been able to behave like a leader since he had given way to temper.

A leader does not lose his temper, or else he lays himself open to ridicule.

233

He raised his voice.

"You've been told I'm against you. That's not true, since it's the President, the leader of us all, who made me responsible for teaching you to fight against the UN soldiers who want to massacre your wives and children.

"You are now great warriors. . . . You'll all become para-commandos. . . . More uniforms will be arriving."

The mob was no longer milling round Lieutenant Kiwe. He had ceased to be the center of interest; the blacks now had other ideas to distract them: hunting down UN soldiers, in the uniform of para-commandos; parading through the streets of E'ville wearing red berets; drinking beer in the little cafés of the African city in camouflage battle-dress.

Kiwe tried to revive the riot.

"Why did you put sand in the ammunition?"

But the sand and the ammunition no longer interested anyone.

"Pipe down, you," one of his own soldiers ordered him. "Where are the uniforms?"

Kreis felt that he could still win the day.

"We shall issue them presently. But first of all, we must resume training. You are now all para-commandos. Fall in by platoons and companies to defend Katanga and President Kimjanga. . . ."

Kreis felt a certain sense of shame, of course. He had won the day, but by lying and palavering: never could he turn all these desperadoes into para-commandos, and there were no more than a hundred uniforms in the storeroom. But he also felt pride and joy: he had got himself out of a nasty situation, he had regained control of his men who only a few minutes earlier had been ready to kill him.

The soldiers dispersed, yelling loudly, and he found himself alone face to face with Kiwe who was wiping his bruised lips with his handkerchief.

Slowly Kreis turned his back on him and went back to his office. He had beaten Kiwe on his own ground.

But that evening he received a telephone call from la Roncière, ordering him to return to Elizabethville straight away.

"But why?" Kreis asked.

"You're absolutely mad: striking an African officer in front of his men! It's a wonder you're still alive! The President won't have anything more to do with you. It was all I could do to prevent him flinging you into jug. You'll probably be chucked out of the country!"

6. Rumpunch

Fonts lay, with his eyes closed, on a mattress on the edge of the swimming-pool of the Sporting Club. The sun made his skin tingle; a ball thrown by a clumsy hand splashed a few drops of water over him.

The voices, the sound of a diving body, the popular tune blaring from a loudspeaker, and the smell of disinfectant rising from the water reminded him of other pools, other beaches, other Sporting Clubs.

Every episode in his life was enacted in the same sort of place. He was swept up by a towering wave and, for weeks or months, had to struggle with all his might not to sink, floating at times on the crest of the wave, at others cast on to rocks or dragged down to the depths. Then, without any reason, the wave would deposit him on one of these strange shores, sheltered from the world and its storms: a stretch of sand, a green swimming-pool smelling of disinfectant, where men played with beach balls and girls oiled their skins and basked in the sun.

Yesterday he was twenty years old; today he was twice that age and nothing had changed except perhaps himself, who now resembled those bits of driftwood which the sea keeps washing up, which become increasingly smooth and fossilized until they eventually sink, completely waterlogged.

The reddish reflection on his closed lids grew dim: some object had come between him and the light. Grumpily he opened his eyes. It was Musaille, looking swarthier and hairier than ever in bathing trunks stretched tight over his little paunch.

The French Consul squatted down beside him.

"Hello, Thomas."

"Hello."

"You know, they're saying all sorts of things in town about your jaunt to the Balubas?"

"Such as?"

"That you're responsible for the Lukuga River massacre."

"That's put out by the two Belgian officers I had recalled from Nyunzu; it's untrue, I'll explain how it happened."

"Then you took to your heels, leaving Wenceslas in the hands of the Balubakat."

"Wenceslas received a blast of rusty nails in the guts."

"They also say you were going to sabotage the Albertville railway but lost your nerve."

"It was while we were preparing for the job that Wenceslas copped it. I spent a whole night with a thousand Balubas and National Army soldiers on my tracks, not to mention the Indians, alone in a jeep which kept slithering deeper and deeper in the mud. I thought I'd never get away with it."

"I personally believe you. So would anyone else who knows you. But you ought to be on your guard because in E'ville no one knows you. . . . You arrive here without your little halo. Maley has decided to make an investigation into what he pompously calls 'the Lukuga River genocide.'"

"He'll learn the truth: it's a settlement of old scores between tribes."

"Maley doesn't give a damn about the truth; what he wants is to involve the mercenaries in this massacre. A good pretext, in the eyes of the world, for intervening directly in Katanga and calling up the Gurkhas. He also needs this pretext to justify himself in his own eyes: Maley's a complex creature."

"When a fellow is mentally twisted or tells lies or behaves badly, they say he's suffering from a complex. . . . You know why psychoanalysts, who are more or less all crooks, have such success? Because in the name of these complexes they find excuses for everything anyone does. . . . Excuses and also justifications. You're a pederast, you play around with small girls or small boys, you have a morbid hatred of your country, you can't see a Frenchman, an Englishman, a Chinaman, a Russian, a Jew or a Negro without longing to bump him off, but it's all quite normal: at the age of seven you wanted to have sexual relations with your own mother! To hell with all that! Priests, at

236

least at confession, absolve but don't justify; they always give one a penance. You ought to send Maley off to see a priest. . . ."

"What's wrong with you?"

"I'm fed up with all these complications people think up for themselves. A man's responsible for his own actions. . . ."

"Who ever said he wasn't?"

"Supposing you buy me a drink instead of bending my ears back!"

"You're the one who does the talking! You haven't changed, Thomas. Each time things don't work out the way you want, you turn into a sea-urchin—you know, one of those black sea-urchins which are known in Algeria as Jews and which prick without having anything to defend: they're empty. I've seen la Roncière: he's taking himself very seriously!"

"He's always taken himself seriously."

"Where are you living?"

"With Gelinet, it suits me down to the ground."

"The house is under observation and if there's a snap raid. . . ."

"You want me to move in with you and guzzle your over-rich food?"

"No, you're too compromising. But I've found a nice little flat opposite the post office: two rooms, kitchen, bathroom and telephone."

Preceded by Pérohade, Félicien Dorat appeared, casting fleeting glances to right and left like a submarine revolving its periscope.

He stretched a limp hand out to Fonts.

"Hello, Thomas . . . Monsieur le Consul . . ."

And, pulling up a deck-chair, he sank back into it.

Pérohade went off in search of a waiter, who presently arrived with whiskies in which the ice was already melting.

Dorat raised his glass.

"To the health of the valiant mercenaries who, for five hundred thousand francs a month, have come to defend Western civilization in Elizabethville. I say, Thomas, do tell me what's going on in North Katanga!"

"Are you short of material?"

"Yesterday evening there was a lot of talk in the Mitsouko about the death of a certain Wenceslas. One fellow said he was a Soviet agent and had got what was coming to him."

"Wenceslas was just a nice ordinary fellow. He acted

237

tough, with the result that he died like a tough. . . . The cloak of Nessus. . . ."

"And you were the cloak? I'd like further details. . . ."

"This evening. But I shall need a lot to drink."

"Ten o'clock at the Mitsouko. . . . Does that suit you?"

Fonts dived into the pool, swam after a big blonde girl who uttered startled cries, played ball with some children for two or three minutes, then came back and dried in the sun without opening his mouth again.

Musaille went back with him to the changing-room and gave him the address and key of the flat.

"Ligget's a cuckold," he announced as he took his leave, "Jenny's having an affair with la Roncière."

"What's the outcome?"

"Nothing yet . . . no one knows about it. Gelinet's also a cuckold, but everyone knows about it: Hortense goes traipsing around everywhere with Kreis!"

"So what?"

"Nothing. Gelinet's been a cuckold for years!"

"Do you really enjoy all this tittle-tattle?"

"I like to know what's going on. Then, when I put a foot wrong, I at least do so consciously. You seem in a great hurry to leave, Thomas! You haven't got a date with the Riverton girl by any chance?"

"No, and I have no wish to see the Riverton girl. La Roncière's waiting for me: we're lunching together. Tell me: what about you, who do you sleep with?"

"Tarts! They're the least expense and the least trouble. People say: he sleeps with tarts . . . and that's all there is to it; no one gives a damn. Tarts are anonymous, faceless, devoid of interest. What fools people are!"

Colonel la Roncière had been brought all the papers that had just been flown in. He perused them carefully. An article signed by Félicien Dorat immediately caught his eye. It was entitled "The Terrors" and was datelined Elizabethville.

There is a night-club in Elizabethville called the Mitsouko where, in the old days, the Union Minière engineers and bachelors who enjoyed a certain standing used to bring their girl-friends. They danced there to tunes that had been popular in Paris twelve months earlier.

The Mitsouko has changed its management and also its clientele: it is now the meeting-place of the

238

'Terrors,' for this is the name given to the white mercenaries who have enlisted in President Kimjanga's army.

The Terrors do everything they can to justify their name; they never shave, they avoid soap and water, and affect an exaggeratedly virile manner, rather like Paris tramps who have been engaged as extras in a thriller film and swagger about clenching their jaws to show how tough they are.

How did they come by their name? I was told the following story to account for it:

Four months ago a dozen mercenaries returned to Elizabethville after a month of extremely arduous campaigning in the north against the rebel Baluba tribes. They were filthy dirty, unshaven, covered in sores and stank of stale sweat. They sat down at a café terrace and shouted for litres and litres of beer. A group of young ladies, freshly perfumed and powdered, were eating ice-creams at a neighboring table before going on to a cocktail party. They looked at these strange.men with disgust. One of them lisped: "But who are these creatures? They're absolute terrors!" One of the mercenaries rose to his feet. He was a Pole by the name of Wenceslas who had served in the Anders Army and been dropped by parachute over Warsaw at the time of the uprising, a sort of misfit hero. He marched over to her, snapped to attention and said: "Madam, my comrades and I are extremely grateful to you. We hadn't yet got a name. You have been good enough to find one for us. From now on we shall be known as the Terrors of Katanga."

Then he added: "We've just spent a month up north. We lost eighteen of our comrades who were hacked to pieces alive by the Balubas. I hope, if we ever clear out of here, the Balubas will do the same to you."

He bowed solemnly: "My respects, madam, from a Terror to a gaggle of silly little geese."

Needless to say, the Terrors never had eighteen of their comrades "hacked to pieces alive": all this is part of the exaggeration that is typical of these men; but it is true, however, that a number of them have lost their lives in North Katanga, often in horrible circumstances. Wenceslas himself was later killed by a blast of rusty nails in the stomach.

The Terror is never to be seen without an astonishing assortment of weapons: Colt revolvers slung low on the thigh in the manner of Western sheriffs, knives, grenades, submachine-guns. . . .

He wears his hair long, curling or hanging over his dirty shirt collar. A beard is compulsory: it may sometimes be accompanied by a sort of moustache.

All these men are incredibly loud-mouthed and aggressive. . . .

There is an extremely exclusive sort of club in Elizabethville: that of the mercenaries' ladies who keep to themselves and look down on the rest of the female world. The mercenaries' ladies consider they belong to a sort of élite: they are the mates of heroes fighting for the freedom of Katanga.

As a matter of fact, the Terrors do not appear particularly constant in their affections, and their ladies seem perfectly happy with this state of affairs. Exchanging women is a current practice.

Opinions differ widely as to the real importance of the work accomplished in Katanga by the mercenaries. The UN consider that without them President Kimjanga's régime would collapse in a few weeks. In Belgian military circles, on the other hand, the role of the mercenaries is said to be "highly exaggerated."

This attitude seems to be shared by the few regular French officers who have enlisted in the service of President Kimjanga. They reckon that the large-scale recruiting recently undertaken in Rhodesia, South Africa, Belgium and France itself has attracted to Katanga an excessive number of young adventurers without any real military value and whose presence here is pointless.

How many of these mercenaries, these Terrors, are there? Depending on the source of information, the number varies from nought to fifteen hundred. Officially, the Katangese Government denies the presence of a single mercenary. I have been assured more than once by government spokesmen that all the Terrors had been repatriated at the end of June, on termination of their contracts. This is manifestly untrue, since a mere ten-minute stroll through the streets of Elizabethville will reveal quite a handful of them.

La Roncière was not fond of Dorat, but he had to

admit that the journalist's description of the Terrors was for the most part accurate.

An hour earlier la Roncière had discussed this subject with Major Van Beulans. Despite all their differences, the two officers had come to a sort of working agreement, much to the anxiety of Pimuriaux who saw in everything a plot against himself.

They had drawn up a list of fifty particularly obstreperous and conspicuous mercenaries who would have to be expelled from Katanga forthwith. The rest would be dispatched to Jadotville or Kolwezi where the Union Minière would see to their board, lodging and transport, on condition, of course, that everything was done with the utmost discretion.

It was decided that mercenaries who came to Elizabethville in the course of their duties would not be allowed to carry arms or wear uniform. They would have to dress properly, avoid all scenes in public and refrain from mentioning their actual profession.

"Maley," la Roncière observed, "sees red when he runs into one of our picturesque characters. There's no point in provoking him still further by waving a red rag in his face."

By dispersing his mercenaries outside Elizabethville, by getting rid of fifty of them (the most harmful, whose names he planned to submit to the UN) la Roncière was taking precautionary measures.

President Kimjanga considered them pointless. La Roncière had not been able to convince him that Maley might attempt something or other.

The President had greeted him with his "friend to all the world" manner:

"Come now, my dear Colonel," he had said, spreading his arms wide like a priest at the *Dominus vobiscum,* "the UN can't do anything against us. On that score I have the most definite assurances from the French and British Consuls. Their Governments, and the US Government as well, would never allow the blue helmets to take direct action. The UN are obliged to confine themselves to a peaceful role. . . . Have you thought about my personal guard, Colonel?"

The President was obsessed with the idea of having a personal guard "like a real President of the Republic, like General de Gaulle," with plumed helmets, sabers and horses.

He clung to his guard like a child with its favorite toy and could not think of anything else.

"This will amuse Fonts," la Roncière reflected.

He promised the President that his assistant would make himself responsible for recruiting and equipping this guard as soon as he had recovered from his arduous jaunt to the Balubas.

"And what about Kreis?" the President had suddenly asked. "That fellow who had the audacity to strike one of my officers! To put things right, I had to promote Kiwe to captain and Nadolo to colonel."

"At the time I thought of having him expelled at once by the police, Monsieur le Président, because his action was unforgivable. I sent for him, I looked into the matter. He's guilty . . . . but less so than it would seem at first glance. Certain provocations on the part of the Belgian instructors. . . . In actual fact he has organized his two companies of para-commandos extremely well.

"I dictated a letter of apology for him to write to Captan Kiwe and . . . Colonel Nadolo. I've relieved him of his duties for a month. But we can't afford to dispense with anyone, especially someone who would be so sound in a crisis. I'm still waiting for the officers I selected in France, Monsieur le Président."

"They'll come. . . . They'll come. . . . Pimuriaux's seeing to it.

"I must have a word with Monsieur Fonts about the Katangese Guard . . . I want high black boots and close-fitting white breeches. . . ."

"I've also decided to move one of the two para-commando companies into E'ville and send the other to Jadotville. I trust you agree to this, Monsieur le Président? In the event of trouble it would be a good thing to have some reliable troops on the spot."

"My dear la Roncière, you're a pessimist!

"We have an army . . . of ten thousand men, and our dear Bongo has his tribes. Do as you see fit, do as you see fit but don't lose your head. . . ."

When he got back to his office after leaving the President, la Roncière found Fonts sitting back in a chair with his feet on the table, reading Dorat's article.

"Quite a bright idea of his," he remarked as he put the paper down, "to present Katanga as a sort of burlesque Wild West, just the sort of thing to blow our little schemes sky high!"

"Dorat's got his knife into us."

"Not really. What he sees, anyone else can see. . . . He simply seizes on an important detail, the absurdity of all these pseudo-toughs swaggering about the streets."

"I'm evacuating all those brawling mercenaries from Elizabethville."

"Splendid idea."

"We must now attend to the civilian population, starting with the whites. My experience in Algeria . . ."

"Wouldn't you rather forget it?"

La Roncière ignored the interruption.

"This experience has taught me that one can't launch a crowd into the streets until it is properly conditioned and directed.

"From the conditioning process we need a group of propagandists with slogans and specific instructions, each dealing with one particular section of the population.

"We're going to create a sort of movement like the ones we put to use at the time of May 13th."

"Why? Don't you think we had enough trouble with them?"

"Well, what do you suggest, then?"

"Our task is to make people believe that Katanga exists, which isn't true, that the population is united, which is likewise not true, that there's an army and a government, whereas in point of fact there's nothing.

"Why not also make them believe that we have a resistance organization embracing all the Belgians in Elizabethville who are ready to die for the independence of Katanga?

"It's just one more piece of bluff. Besides, since no one belongs to this movement, there'll be no internal squabbles, no personal enmities, no leakages. . . . The most secret resistance movement in the world, the only really secret one that has ever existed. We must find some initials for it: everything else about it, those silly sods will manufacture in their own heads. What do you think of MIR?"

"MIR? What does that stand for?"

"Nothing at all, that's the point. The MIR is on the watch. . . . The MIR executes traitors. . . . The MIR is behind you. . . . If you don't like it we can easily think of something else. . . ."

La Roncière was pacing to and fro, considering the question.

"I thought at first you were joking . . . but, properly worked out, this joke could become something serious. The MIR is yours, Thomas. You're its Chairman, its Secretary-General, its Political Office and only member."

243

"Also its Treasurer. You'll have to cough up some dough for my movement. But a bluff is only effective if it is backed by something definite. I've had a word with Uncle Gelinet and his gang of desperadoes: tradesmen, artisans, foremen and a few young engineers from the Union Minière. They're very enthusiastic and their morale is high.

"At the time of independence they were the ones who went out into the streets, and it was probably thanks to them that the military did not behave like their colleagues at Leopoldville.

"We can count on forty or fifty lads who could be trusted with weapons: also perhaps a couple of radio transmitters. I'll take charge of that as well."

La Roncière gazed at Fonts with something akin to admiration.

"You're just the same as ever, Thomas. Your setbacks, instead of disheartening you, act as a stimulant . . . as they did in Indo-China. You go out on a bender, put on a new suit and start all over again. . . ."

"Like a fly that keeps trying to force its way through a window-pane, just a silly fly, that's all. . . ."

"You couldn't have done anything else with the Balubas."

"Yes, I could. I could have kept out of it, since I knew there was nothing to be done."

"First of all let's remain masters of 'useful' Katanga, her mines and wealth; we'll return to the north later."

"When we abandoned the Thai territory in Indo-China, we also thought we'd be able to return.

"Where shall we have lunch?"

"At my place? Jenny will come and join us for coffee . . . and Joan too perhaps. It's a quiet little place . . ."

"Colonial adultery . . . siesta time. . . ."

"It's more than mere adultery."

"Eh?"

"We're united by the same cause, Jenny and I."

"You can't do anything simply, not even make love. . . . Everyone has to surround their simplest desires with all sorts of pretexts."

"What about you with Joan?"

"That girl excites me and irritates me. . . . Love and its pretexts or its justifications, I don't know. . . . You'd better have lunch without me."

"You're too difficult to handle. . . . Tomorrow, I hope, you'll have calmed down. Can I drop you anywhere?"

"Yes, at my new hide-out opposite the post office."

"Hide-out? We're not yet clandestine agents!"

"We shall be, and the sooner the better. I'm getting bored with all this!"

La Roncière jotted down Fonts's new telephone number in his notebook and stuffed a lot of documents into his briefcase. Fonts noticed they concerned various arms purchases and straight away wondered:

"Is Jean-Marie getting a rake-off?"

With his head resting on a cushion, Fonts had fallen asleep. Next to him, on a low table, stood a sandwich that he had barely touched, a bottle of beer, and a revolver that he had started cleaning before sleep overcame him: Wenceslas's revolver, marked with notches in memory of all the men he had not killed.

The telephone ringing roused him from a nightmare. It was Joan. Fonts realized she was furious because she assumed a honeyed tone.

"Thomas Fonts, I've just heard from Jenny that you're frightened of meeting me. . . ."

"Really?"

"Jenny's a bit of a psychologist. . . . She claims you're in . . . at least, that you have a soft spot for me. I find that rather funny: I can't see you having a soft spot for anyone, you're far too self-important—a complex peculiar to Latin men below average height!"

"What about the dignity of Latin men, you shameless red-headed hussy. . . ."

"What!"

"I was only joking. . . . When am I going to see you?"

"I'm very busy."

"What are you doing at six?"

"A round of golf with Holmer Van der Weyck . . . but you only play bowls, I hear. . . ."

"See you on the golf course."

"No."

"I've never seen a golf course in my life."

"You're lying, you're always lying . . . you're . . . exasperating. Always showing off . . . all this blood and thunder . . . other people's blood, of course. I hate you!"

"Jenny, who's a bit of a psychologist, would say . . ."

She hung up on him.

"Are you interested in golf, Monsieur Fonts?" Van der Weyck asked with a twinkle in his eye.

He was wearing a singlet, gray cotton trousers which

matched his hair, and thick-soled spiked shoes. He had a sort of half-glove on one hand which left his fingers free. Against the deep green of the turf he looked all the more elegant and distant, the symbol of a world and caste that seemed unassailable, defended by their privileges and wealth.

Fonts, tousle-haired, stood with his hands in his pockets and an unlit cigarette in the corner of his mouth. He produced a little booklet out of his pocket.

"I've just bought it . . . *Twenty Hints on Golf.* . . ."

"Would you like another hint?"

"I've been given so many!"

"You're an attractive fellow, with a somewhat . . . stormy past. Leave Joan Riverton alone . . . or else clear out. You could see her anywhere else but here. Please don't misunderstand me . . . I've got a son who's exactly like you. . . ."

"My father always avoided giving me advice . . . except on how to gut a hare or wild boar, train a dog, press wine and set an ambush. For the rest he trusted in my instinct. . . . But the last ambush he set cost him his life. . . . He was commanding a Communist Maquis, which did not prevent him from voting right wing and saying his rosary. He too was a mass of contradictions."

"The Communists allowed . . ."

"He was so efficient at his job that he was entrusted with any amount of things. Don't worry, I have a conception of women that I must have inherited from my father and which doesn't coincide at all with Joan Riverton's personality. She's more dangerous for you than for me!"

"What on earth do you mean by that?"

"The temptation of youth for those who have lost it without ever having known it!"

Van der Weyck felt embarrassed and cleared his throat.

"How old are you?"

"Twice twenty."

He burst out laughing.

"And you?"

"Once fifty."

"That's the whole problem."

"Excuse me, my partner's waiting for me to start; it's Arnold Riverton, Joan's father. She won't be long. Wait for her in the bar . . . and say that you're my guest: only members are served. . . ."

"Who's that chap?" Arnold Riverton asked.

"You know him by name at least, Thomas Fonts."

246

"I know him."

He drove off and his ball landed on the green. Van der Weyck's ended up in a bunker.

They strode off down the fairway.

Suddenly Arnold Riverton stopped.

"My dear Holmer, the attitude which the Union Minière has perhaps been forced to adopt has led your firm to make use of certain men whom the State Department consider dangerous. That's what my ambassador told me yesterday in Leo. . . ."

"I don't quite understand."

"I can see every reason for your encouraging the secession of Katanga at a time when you had no alternative . . . Lumumba was in power, and with him the Communists. Russian 'advisers' were arriving by the plane-load and we ourselves were extremely anxious. But times have changed. Adoula has replaced Lumumba and is recognized by the whole world; the Russians have packed up and left. . . ."

"A good thing too."

"The secession of Katanga, which was useful at that time, is now an embarrassment for all of us, for you as well . . . above all for you."

"The Union Minière has remained neutral; we pay our dues to the local Government."

"Please, Holmer, this is just between friends. Take a number-ten iron to get out of the bunker. For the Adoula Government to assert itself and overcome Gizenga, Lumumba's lieutenant in Stanleyville, it's necessary to put an end to this secession. If we don't put an end to this secession, he threatens to appeal, outside the UN, to the Afro-Asian group, which would only bring chaos, or worse still, the Communists, which America cannot tolerate. My Government is therefore resolved to support Adoula against Kimjanga.

"This secession, if you don't mind my saying so, is only maintained through you. If it's done away with, and if you continue to support the Kimjanga régime, you're liable to see all your employees expelled and your mines nationalized. Good shot, Holmer. . . . You ought to get down in two more."

Van der Weyck took three.

"Arnold," he suddenly asked, "has it ever occurred to you that our position here is not so simple? In Brussels they're tending to think as you do and, speaking for myself, I'm inclined to agree."

"Well, then? These arms purchases, these mercenaries,

247

these royalties you pay Kimjanga instead of paying them to the Leopoldville Government. . . ."

"If we stopped helping him, President Kimjanga would nationalize us straight away. He would find the necessary specialists to keep the mines turning over . . . in Rhodesia, maybe in France, certainly in England. Bongo, who's a madman, might easily blow up our plant in a fit of rage. A large part of my staff would be against me. I'm in a very difficult position."

"If Maley decided on a trial of strength, it's not impossible that Washington would back him. Take that into consideration, my dear Holmer."

"The British and the French would oppose it."

"What did they do at Suez? They climbed down!"

"If only they hadn't. What does your daughter see in Thomas Fonts?"

"He's not reasonable, which amuses her. . . . We are reasonable, which bores her . . . because you are reasonable, aren't you, my dear Holmer?"

"Thomas Fonts, what do you intend doing with your life? Don't look so startled. Just for once I'd like to talk to you seriously."

Fonts looked up at the sky.

"It's going to rain."

Joan wrinkled her freckled nose.

"No, it's not going to rain: you're trying to escape me again!"

With a certain ostentation she was doing her best to keep calm by maintaining the conversation on a lofty plane, which enabled her to avoid embarrassing subjects like the mercenaries, a subject which would have led them once again to argue and quarrel, part from each other in a rage and regret it immediately.

Although she was dying to hear about his jaunt to the Balubas, Joan had made up her mind not to ask him a single question about it.

Fonts had never found Joan so attractive; never had he been so deeply conscious of her charm. She was lying on her side in a chaise-longue, with her hands folded under her red hair, dressed in a shirt and trousers which accentuated her slender waist, narrow hips and small well-poised breasts.

Suddenly he no longer felt intolerant of her tactlessness and aggressiveness, her idleness and energy, her gravity and childishness, her guttersnipe manners, her high principles and the important position she attributed to her own small person in the organization of the world.

Her smell of soap and lavender water with just a hint of musk, that tantalizing fresh smell of young red-headed womanhood, disturbed him deeply.

Since he was still suffering from the effects of his setback and felt an even greater lassitude than usual, he wanted to go off with her on one of those aimless, purposeless journeys for which he had more than once felt an absolute necessity.

They would stroll among ruins on some sandy shore and, resting against warm stones worn away by wind and salt, would doze or wait for nightfall, culling snippets of history from a guide-book.

On some days they would feed on sandwiches, like impoverished students, on others appease their hunger with rich food washed down with resinated wine drawn from a barrel in the depths of a shady tavern.

They would go to Italy, to Yugoslavia, to Greece, to a country made for tourists. They would be just a couple of tourists themselves, but bohemian, free-and-easy and superior, playing truant from the agencies' itineraries and compulsory sight-seeing.

They would have one suitcase between them, in which their clothes would be mingled pell-mell with cheap souvenirs. The suitcase would be adorned at each hotel with a new label and, when they parted, they would burn it on the side of the road.

Fonts knew the whole world and its secret races: the Karens of Burma, the Hazareh Mongols of the Afghanistan frontier, the Méos, the red Thais, and the Sahara Jews who celebrate the New Year at Tamendit, the lepers who lived in that little valley in Yunnan and, in the Tibesti, the Tibbus with their spindly shanks and the Gorane women with pierced nostrils.

But he was almost completely ignorant of old countries as close and familiar as Italy, Greece or southern Spain, those countries which one must discover at the age of twenty, with empty pockets, playing at being in love with a girl of the same age. . . .

Joan and he would make up their minds to love everyone; they would be the ready and amused victims of guides, hall-porters and voluble, slightly dishonest head waiters.

He, Fonts, would submit to the whims of a demanding little female; he would abdicate his critical faculty and lucidity for her and perhaps feel immensely relieved in consequence.

"Answer my question," Joan insisted.

"What about going for a trip together to Greece, Italy . . . Spain. . . .

"Are you serious?"

"We'd quarrel the very first evening: you want a room with two beds and I want only one, a great big one. Leaving a woman one has just been making love to, in the middle of the night, and going to another bed . . . slipping away like a thief . . . out of the question."

"That's presupposing, Thomas, that I'd be willing to sleep with you!"

"You'd bore me stiff wanting to race round museums and attend cocktail parties given by all the consuls that Uncle Sam maintains in Verona, Florence, Rhodes and Candia."

"You don't know me, Thomas. I might be a very pleasant traveling companion who prefers café terraces and long siestas to the Sistine Chapel. I wouldn't see a single consul and I would dip into 'native' dishes full of anti-American microbes."

"We'll go to Spain, to Catalonia. My family lives on the other side of the frontier."

"Unbearable little dark men who eat together while their wives just stand and look on."

"They write poetry in ancient Catalan which no one else understands and meet twice a week in lovely old houses where they build a world of their own."

"What is that world like?"

"Exclusively Catalan: it hovers between earth and heaven, between France and Spain, in an indeterminate age. It is heedless of all economic, scientific and international contingencies. My cousin Miguel is always wracking his brains to give it a constitution which would be utterly unacceptable."

Joan had taken Fonts's hand and was squeezing it as though they were already strolling around together.

"Thomas," she asked, "where else could we go? I'm so happy you've made up your mind to leave Katanga."

Fonts appeared to wake from a deep sleep. He gazed in astonishment at the green turf, heard the click of balls being struck, withdrew his hand from Joan's and automatically smoothed down his jacket, as though he had just fallen down and got up again.

"I think I was talking a lot of nonsense, my little quail!"

"It was the first time you weren't!"

"The voyage is over, Joan, I'm staying in Katanga. I've got to get back to town: are you coming with me?"

Throughout the drive Fonts remained silent, gazing straight in front of him, answering Joan's questions in monosyllables.

She had thought she held him fast and once again he had escaped her. But she now knew what she wanted from him: that one day he would not withdraw his hand.

How fascinating and novel it all was, a man who rejects instead of pursuing you, whose weaknesses you anxiously fasten on in order to take possession of him and make him happy: for Fonts was unhappy and unstable, Joan had decided, and this was what made him so cruel and cynical.

Joan believed that all human beings were good, that only ignorance, lack of understanding and complexes for which they were not responsible made them seem bad.

As he got out of the car Fonts looked panic-stricken. He took her in his arms, kissed her gently on the temples, the forehead, the eyes, then the lips.

He held her closer, stroked her breasts and thighs. Joan had the impression of being invaded and pillaged, of being unable to defend herself and of not particularly wanting to. But at the same time she was furious at this lack of respect, at her own acquiescence and the weakness to which she surrendered in the face of this ardent, exacting little male.

She arched her back to thrust him away but at the same time offered herself to him and, in spite of herself, provoked him.

Her flexed thighs trembled and the blood ebbed from her body before sweeping back in thundering waves. One part of herself remained conscious and witnessed her own struggling.

"What's come over you, my girl? You're not going to let yourself be raped on the edge of a pavement?"

Fonts ventured a final caress, leaped out of the car, and made a vague gesture with his hand.

"Good-bye, my little quail!"

But he was pale, and Joan thought he looked more unhappy than ever. Thomas was that little boy in the south of Spain who had scampered off. He was angry with himself for being in love with her, and this was the reason why he was behaving so wildly and crudely.

Joan went back to the consulate and had a long cold

251

shower, then rubbed herself down with a horsehair glove until her skin tingled, until she regained control of her lips, her breasts, her belly and loins, which for the first time in her life she had lost.

Every ounce of womanhood in her had been betrayed. She had been the quivering acquiescent maiden and not the easy-going comrade who makes a brief gift of her body to a boy mad with desire, love and admiration, the condescending goddess who bends over him and, haughty and enigmatic as ever, draws him up to her own level.

In a fury she smashed a tooth mug.

"That unbearable man Thomas Fonts is going to make me believe that I can behave like a brazen hussy. I'll make him pay for this and it will be quite easy because, to have behaved so badly, he must desire me fiercely . . . to the point of losing his head!

"I'm going to turn that head of yours, my friend, and when you ask me to marry you, for it will come to that, I'll laugh in your face and go off with that insipid little fool Ravetot."

The new Katangese constitution was published.

This constitution, the brain-child of Henri Malard, the rector of Elizabethville University, was neither particularly good nor bad.

Like all constitutions, it proclaimed a few high principles in its introduction, while the rest remained obscure and open to interpretation.

Maley had exploded with rage. The very title, inscribed in capital letters before his eyes, was a provocation:

CONSTITUTION OF THE STATE OF KATANGA

It was also a personal setback for the UN representative in Elizabethville.

For the first time President Kimjanga was officially proclaiming to the world that Katanga was no longer a province of the Congo, but a sovereign and independent State.

For three months Maley had done his utmost to induce Kimjanga to go to Leopoldville and start negotiations to put an end to the secession.

Kimjanga had stalled and tried to play for time in his usual horse coper's manner. But he had never openly raised any objection.

Maley realized he would have to take countermeasures.

252

He decided to accelerate the launching of Operation Rum-punch.

The UN representative's residence, Villa des Roches, was a large white bungalow with bay windows. One side looked out on to the Avenue Fulbert Youlou, which the inmates of the villa privately called the "Avenue Vulgaire Filou." The Abbé did not have a good press with the UN and was supposed, not without reason, to be behind Kimjanga.

The back of the house opened on to a big swimming-pool surrounded by lawns sloping gently down to a water-fall.

Before the blue helmets arrived, the Belgians who owned it must have led a peaceful life here, an uneventful cozy family life, skimming the surface of the pool with butterfly nets to remove the leaves that fell into the water, and saying every half-hour or so: "How pleasant it is here!" while longing all the time to be off somewhere else.

That at least is what Maley claimed, for he had started off by loving the house and had then come to hate it because, he said, of the big fireplace with the copper cowl that adorned the living-room.

Maley was sitting at a small metal desk on which stood two telephones, a cheap ashtray, an engagement book and the inevitable little name-plate.

Behind him was a map of Elizabethville fastened by drawing-pins to a panel of plywood.

Through one of the open bay windows he could see some Swedish soldiers with tall fair-skinned bodies and flaxen hair bathing in the pool, splashing one another and shouting.

General Siddartha was announced.

With his blue beret in his hand and his swagger-stick under his arm, slim, clean-cut, wearing red tabs on the collar of his tunic, he came in, clicked his heels, gave a slight bow and sat down, crossing his legs carefully.

"A perfect British officer," Maley reflected, "distant, precise, well brought up." But he had a dusky complexion, the large dark eyes of figures in a Persian miniature, and despite all his efforts he spoke in a sing-song voice.

Intelligent, no doubt, and undeniably expert at his job, but blinded by his hatred of the whites, to whom he attributed, no matter what their nationality or political complexion, all the misery of the world and the distress of his own vast country.

Maley would have liked to be on friendly terms with

him, as he had been with his predecessor, a gluttonous, garrulous, francophile Ethiopian, who paid far more attention to the food at the Villa des Roches than to his soldiers' welfare.

Siddartha had refused to eat with him and had taken refuge behind a regulation which obliged him, he said, to mess with his officers.

He preferred to live on his disgusting tinned curry.

"At your orders, sir!"

The general reminded Maley of his presence in that impersonal voice which he had tried to model on that of his British instructors.

Maley picked up an official telegram from his "In" tray.

"Spaak is prepared to recall all the Belgian political and military advisers forthwith, General. In spite of pressure from the extremists, the Brussels Government have decided to back the unity of the Congo.

"We can now implement Resolution 942 of the Security Council on the immediate evacuation from the Congo of the 'Belgian military and para-military personnel and political advisers and those of other nationalities. . . .' Tomorrow morning we launch Operation Rumpunch. Three hundred Belgians belonging to the Army or the administration will leave within forty-eight hours. Consul Ryckers will be responsible for notifying them and arranging their transport by air. That doesn't concern us."

"I can well believe the Belgians will allow themselves to be shipped out like a lot of sheep, but what about the three hundred mercenaries and political advisers engaged by the Katangese?"

"You have a list of their names and addresses."

"Most of the names on our lists are false, so are the addresses. Do you remember the names of the fifty mercenaries who the Presidency told us had been dismissed? The day before yesterday we captured five of them who'd come back from Rhodesia under different names. Do you think a man like la Roncière hasn't got wind of the operation? There are no more mercenaries to be seen in town."

Maley shrugged his shoulders.

"Obviously! They've become delivery men, drivers, foremen or engineers of the Union Minière. It's up to you to winkle them out! You round them up, lock them up in a camp guarded by the Gurkhas and, as soon as we have the planes, we fly them to Kamina and from there to Leopoldville where we'll force them to take air tickets for Europe.

No question of letting them go to Rhodesia: they'd be back here the next day. I don't want any violence!"

"Among them, sir, there are utter criminals whom we ought to arrest and hand over to the Leopoldville authorities to be tried and sentenced to death . . . men like Thomas Fonts, who's responsible for the Lukuga River massacre."

"Not so easy. The man who benefited from this massacre, the Mwata Motu, has just come over to our side, and the Adoula Government doesn't seem particularly shocked by what it calls 'a mere tribal incident.'

"Calm down a bit. If we start arresting people indiscriminately to bring them up for trial, we'll be accused of white man-hunting."

"So what? Where's the harm in it? Who are responsible, if not the whites? If we want to settle the matter, it's not enough to expel the three hundred Belgian officials, the three hundred mercenaries, but also the fifteen thousand whites still living in Katanga."

"You're not serious, my dear fellow!"

"Every white man working in this country is an adviser and mercenary for Katanga. His work serves to strengthen the régime. No more whites, no more secession!"

"By whom would you replace the technical instructors? By Indian technicians? I always thought you were short of them! Do you want to starve the country?"

"The Katangese will be hungry, perhaps, but they'll be free. It was only a suggestion, sir."

"And I accept it as such. Take special care not to miss the three French mercenaries: Colonel la Roncière, Karl Kreis and Thomas Fonts. . . . As to certain public figures like Justin Pimuriaux or Rector Malard, I'd rather the Swedes attended to them."

Siddartha gave a prim smile. This smile was intended to show that he had no alternative but to acquiesce to this manifest collusion between Maley and the whites, of whom he was one.

The UN delegate was an excitable character. He thumped the table with his fist, which, to Siddartha, was a sure sign of low breeding.

"I don't want any incident with any country. It's not the job of the United Nations to create incidents but, on the contrary, to settle them for everyone's good. See what our Secretary-General has to say on this matter in his last note. Our aim is not to seize Katanga by force but, by withdrawing foreign support, to induce President Kimjanga to negotiate with Leopoldville."

Siddartha took a stubby pipe from his pocket, filled it carefully with English tobacco, lit it and, emitting a cloud of smoke, declared:

"I don't believe in negotiation, only in force. We shan't be able to put an end to the secession except by force. President Kimjanga will never go to Leopoldville and I'll tell you why he won't: he's one of the men responsible for Lumumba's assassination; he knows that some day or another he will be brought to trial."

Maley could not resist being sarcastic, although he knew Siddartha would be offended, but the Indian's self-satisfaction exasperated him.

"You want to put the whole world on trial: the mercenaries, the Belgians, the Katangese, the British as well, I suppose, and the French because of their war in Algeria, the Americans because of their racial segregation, the Russians because of theirs—because they too practice segregation in some of the outlying republics."

"We have our rights!"

"What rights?"

"The rights of exploited and downtrodden nations."

Maley rose to his feet.

"Judge not that ye be not judged. . . . I never quite understood that Kashmir business and the massacres that ensued. Be reasonable now, no incidents. You launch the operation at six in the morning. Half an hour later you must be in possession of the post office and radio station, and Bongo must be under house arrest and unable to set foot outside.

"Without Bongo, President Kimjanga is a body without a spine."

That evening, when la Roncière got back to his house, he found a big Negro there in a state of great excitement. He said he was a member of the staff of His Excellency Bongo, Minister of the Interior, and had been sent to escort him to the African city. La Roncière asked to see his papers; the Negro did not have any. He was about to fling him out when the telephone rang: it was Fonts.

"Jean-Marie. I'm at the French Consul's and I'm staying here tonight. The raid's for tomorrow morning. Kreis is already waiting for you in Bongo's shack. In the African city you'll be out of harm's way: the UN lads will never dare penetrate there: they're much too scared. At last we're in for some fun and games! The code name for their op. is Rumpunch."

Reassured, la Roncière followed the member of Bongo's staff who, in addition to his official duties, owned three cafés in the African city and appeared to be connected with the hemp business as well since he offered some to the colonel.

The Minister of the Interior was not there. He was staying in town, where he reckoned he had nothing to fear since only the mercenaries and the Belgians were threatened.

Bongo did not wish to abandon President Kimjanga to his own instinct, which was always to fly from danger and promise whatever was asked, there being nothing to stop him breaking those promises later.

The minister's shack, la Roncière was startled to see, had no telephone.

On 28 August, before dawn, Operation Rumpunch got under way with the UN troops moving into position. The post office and radio station, which were not guarded, were occupied without a shot being fired and Bongo's villa was surrounded.

Then, armed with lists, small Swedish, Irish and Indian detachments spread through the town, knocking on doors and calling out names, which was painfully reminiscent of certain Gestapo methods. But the Gestapo used to break the doors down, whereas the UN soldiers, when there was no answer, turned on their heels after leaving a summons.

Major Van Beulans, who had been notified by Consul Ryckers in the middle of the night, at once assembled the officers and NCOs who were quartered in Elizabethville and the outlying camps.

Still half asleep, the Belgian soldiers listened as their commanding officer, flanked by the consul, spoke to them about discipline and obedience.

"Gentlemen, the Belgian Government, as a result of extremely violent pressure from outside, has seen fit to recall us, abruptly interrupting our task in Katanga . . . long before it was finished. Whatever our personal feelings may be, we have to obéy . . . because . . . because . . . soldiers who don't obey are no longer soldiers.

"I must ask you not to leave your quarters until your departure. You will receive instructions from me and from no one else, you will have no contact with those UN gentlemen, who have no orders to give you."

Deeply moved, he stammered:

"I understand your great distress . . . I am also distressed, you know. Long live the King, long live Belgium, long live Katanga, long live President Kimjanga!"

Meanwhile a small group of officers, most of them young, who had gathered round a stern-faced captain, stood motionless and speechless, frozen in a position of attention.

The major felt there was trouble brewing and did all he could to avoid it.

"My friends, you have done a good job and, in the name of the King, I should like to congratulate you. . . ."

The major glanced at Ryckers for help.

The captain interrupted him.

"That's enough hypocrisy, Major! You're scuttling off with your tail between your legs; but personally, I'm staying."

"What's come over you, Gersaint?"

"We induced the Katangese to secede. We began by training them . . . and the day they really need us, we leave them in the lurch. I formed two companies. I told them: 'You can count on me, I shan't let you down.' And now I must go and tell them: 'We're off, so long, my lads!' "

"Gersaint! The Government's orders . . ."

"A government of rats who lose their nerve at the first threat from the UN thugs is no government for me. You're bolting according to orders because it's Brussels that doles out the pensions, medals and promotions. What about your sense of honor? What are you doing about it? . . . Stuffing it up . . ."

Purple in the face, Van Beulans bellowed:

"Hold your tongue, Gersaint, this is a refusal to obey orders!"

Without saluting, with a scornful smile on his lips, Captain Gersaint marched off, followed by a dozen officers.

Van Beulans spluttered:

"This isn't possible! This sort of thing isn't done in our army. Upon my word, one would think we were in France. . . ."

Rycker took him by the arm.

"I'll try to settle this matter with them, my dear Major. . . . In certain tricky situations diplomacy takes precedence over discipline. Above all, no scandal!"

"My sense of honor . . . stuffing it up!"

"Have you sent telegrams to all our officers and NCOs who are on operations outside E'ville?"

"I obey the Government, even Monsieur Spaak's government."

Ryckers leaned towards him and in a falsely distressed tone remarked:

"Poor old Pimuriaux's on the lists!"

Cheered up by this news, the major assumed a sorrowful tone which scarcely concealed his jubilation:

"It can't be true! He's not an official: he'll have difficulty finding his feet!"

"I managed to get an extension for his wife: just long enough to pack up the house."

"What about the Frenchmen?"

"Disappeared."

"My dear Consul, I'm going to be quite frank with you: in my heart of hearts I'm really quite relieved that it should end like this. Since la Roncière's arrival we've been heading for disaster. At least we shan't be held responsible for the serious blunders that are going to be committed. You feel the same way, don't you?"

"Kimjanga's still got some tricks up his sleeve!"

"Without us, what can he do? Maley's got him this time!"

Ryckers cleared his throat.

"I'm in a painful position all the same, you must admit, my dear fellow. After being, together with you, one of the partisans of the independence of this country, I'm being forced, with my own hands"—he held out his unkempt hands—"to destroy what I've done."

"The joys and miseries of service, my dear Consul!"

A score of soldiers and two Irish officers arrived at Gelinet's house with an official warrant from the United Nations Organization in the Congo. They had come to take in charge Jean-Marie la Roncière, Thomas Fonts and Karl Kreis, who were due to be expelled from the country.

An astonished Gelinet received them in pajamas and bedroom slippers.

"Those gentlemen aren't here any longer," he said.

He recovered his breath.

"And if they were, I wouldn't tell you!"

He buttonholed one of the officers.

"Aren't you ashamed of the job you're doing . . . you, a regular officer, I assume, and a white man to boot . . . hunting down honorable men, soldiers like yourself, and driving them out of this country, our country, so as to deliver us defenseless to hordes of raving Congolese!

"Hortense, come and have a look, because this must be

engraved on your memory . . . European officers . . . and I think you have even danced with one of them . . . putting themselves in the service of the Leopoldville nun-rapers. . . . You're a Catholic, I suppose, being an Irishman?"

The lieutenant tried to calm Gelinet down.

"Please, sir, we have to obey orders even if it isn't always pleasant! With your permission, may I have a look inside your house?"

"Come in, since you don't believe me. Hortense, show these gentlemen our bedroom and the attic and the cellar and the kitchen. Open all the cupboards and drawers. . . . Show them my big-game rifles! Let them take them away with them if they want. . . . Let them dole them out to the blacks for them to use against us!"

The second officer, who understood French better than his comrade and who was beginning to lose his temper, gently thrust Gelinet aside to enable three soldiers to enter.

Gelinet sank back into an armchair and, in his distress, used the hem of his pajama jacket to wipe the tears from his face: but it was only sweat.

In point of fact he was delighted with the incident, and all the more so because there was no one staying with him any longer; because that fellow Kreis with his taciturnity, his refusal to "chum up," his obsequious and at the same time distant manner, was beginning to get on his nerves. There was no one he hated more than the Germans, unless it was the Flemings.

He was glad to be rid of him; his wife obviously did not share this view, which added still further to his pleasure.

Hortense appeared in a diaphanous dressing-gown, holding one hand in front of her mouth to stifle a yawn. Under the impression they were guests, she held out her other hand to the two officers, which only increased their confusion.

"Hello, it's a long time since we've seen you. You must come and have dinner one of these days!"

"It's not a question of dinner," Gelinet bellowed. "These gentlemen are doing a police job and have forced their way into the house! It seems they're looking for mercenaries! I must ring up Pérohade and tell him the news so that he can put it in his paper! Am I allowed to use the telephone, officer?"

It was one of the regular customers of the Mitsouko, a

260

Swedish captain, who was made responsible for searching the premises of the night-club.

Gunthar Olugsen was all the more embarrassed because he had a soft spot for Nathalie and was fond of Pérohade who allowed him credit at the end of every month.

Pérohade flung his arms in the air.

"My dear fellow, are you dotty? Have you ever seen a night-club manager keep his customers on the premises after closing hours? The mercenaries, as you told me yourself, cleared out a week ago, except the tramps whom no one wants to have anything to do with . . . and they don't come in here.

"There's been no news of any of the Terrors with whom you used to booze: the Rhodesian, the two Belgians, the Frenchman and the Dane . . . unless you've had a letter from them?"

"All the same I've got to have a look!"

"Go ahead and look. You know, it's a lot of balls, all this; it's bad for business, bad for human relations. One of these days, because of public opinion—and public opinion counts in this racket—I shan't be able to serve you or allow you in here any more, you UN people.

"I was discussing it only the other day with the French Consul, Musaille, who knows what's what. . . . Incidentally, I must ring him up, my consul, to protest, because this search by a foreign army in an independent country isn't legal. Did you know that?

"I've been talking to you as a night-club proprietor; now I want to question you as a journalist: tell me, what's going on? Has Maley gone off his head? It's true that since he's been made a cuckold he can't think straight any longer! What time did it begin, this pogrom of yours? Was the President notified?"

"I don't know, Monsieur Pérohade, I'm simply obeying orders and I have to make sure you're not hiding anyone. I'm not going to go and wake Nathalie, you'd be only too glad to tell everyone I'd raped her! I'll take your word for it this time."

"You have it, Gunthar. . . . Excuse me, I must go and wake my special correspondent, Dorat, who must be snoozing away happily without realizing poor Maley is making a bloody fool of himself!"

Justin Pimuriaux was having breakfast with his family before going off to the Presidency. The coffee smelled good. His eldest daughter, Juliette, who wanted a new bathing-dress, had buttered his toast for him, and his wife Monette, who had just been given a servant who had worked for the former Governor, was sweetness itself.

Major Gustav Soderkün, who had been a guest of the house on several occasions, was ushered in by a servant.

"Have a cup of coffee, my dear Major," Monette Pimuriaux said. "What brings you here so early in the morning, belted and spurred as though you were going off to do battle?"

The major ignored the invitation.

"An unpleasant duty."

He turned to Pimuriaux.

"Monsieur le Secrétaire-Général, you're under an expulsion order decreed by the Security Council."

Pimuriaux put down his buttered toast.

"Me? An expulsion order?"

"I'm sorry. You have to leave by the evening plane for Brussels, on which a seat has been reserved for you. Madame Pimuriaux will be able to stay a week longer to put her affairs in order and see to the packing."

Monette was the first to recover her wits. The storm had broken in a sky that had never been so cloudless.

She had to say to herself over and over again: "They're throwing us out, that's what! That's what this great Swedish oaf is saying. Justin will be bundled on to a plane this evening without further ado, like a thief, a crook being expelled. I'm being given time to pack my bags. But what are they all doing, the President, the Union Minière and that unbearable snob Van der Weyck? He must be playing golf. He's the one who's got us into this mess. . . . What's to become of us, the villa, the servants, the Chevrolet . . ."

Her anger slowly got the better of her, without a trace of it appearing on her face. Gustav Soderkün was therefore all the more surprised when she rose to her feet, pointed at him and screamed:

"Get out of here, you ill-mannered oaf!"

Pimuriaux tried to calm her down, which only increased her fury.

"And you, you nitwit, just stand there and do nothing. . . . Because this gentleman, who comes from God knows where and murders every civilized language, tells you to go, you're going?"

Juliette was weeping into her napkin.

"Do something!" Monette screamed.

Their youngest son, Albert, a boy of fifteen, came in

followed by two big dobermanns who were prancing round him.

When Major Soderkün subsequently tried to explain the incident to Maley, he could only say:

"I didn't know what was going on, sir. It all happened so quickly!

"Madame Pimuriaux began by swearing at her husband who had sunk back in an armchair. He was holding the expulsion order which I had given him. She tore it out of his hand, flung it in my face, then burst into tears, calling me a Nazi, a murderer and Gestapo agent. At the time, I admit, I didn't quite understand what she meant. The son, thinking perhaps that I had insulted his mother, flung himself on me. I had no difficulty in overpowering him: a sickly highly strung lad! He then urged his dogs on. Hearing the rumpus, my soldiers burst in; they had their rifles in their hands.

"One of the dogs made as though to pounce on me. The first soldier rushed up and tried to drive it off with his rifle-butt. They were both young and inexperienced. They found themselves in this mad-house atmosphere, in the midst of these shrieks and yells and the barking of those silly dogs which were slobbering and trying to bite them. You know what those dogs are like, sir?"

"I hate them; they're the kind that were used to track down the Resistance fighters and guard the concentration camps!"

"One of the soldiers fired, probably without meaning to . . . a sort of instinctive reaction of defense."

"Which proves his rifle was loaded!"

"He must have cocked it when he heard the dogs."

"You might have taken some less trigger-happy lads with you!"

"To my mind, I was paying a social call on people whom I considered reasonable and with whom I was on the best of terms. Madame Pimuriaux began by offering me a cup of coffee. I almost accepted it, yet there she was a minute later screaming like a harpy and swearing at me . . . it was enough to send one mad!"

"Then what happened?"

"The bullet shattered the dog's skull and pierced a telephone directory lying on a table next to Monsieur Pimuriaux, with the result that he's now accusing me of attempted murder. I felt it was advisable to withdraw, after warning him that I would come and fetch him two hours before his plane was due to leave.

"When I went back, the place was stiff with journalists and press photographers. They were taking pictures of that damned telephone directory and the dog's dead body. Others were scribbling away in notebooks; I didn't know what was happening. But there was also a platoon of Katangese para-commandos, with their weapons trained on me.

"The African officer in command seemed in an unusual state of excitement. He threatened to 'settle my hash' unless I cleared off at once! I asked him where he got his orders from. He replied: 'The Minister of the Interior!'

"What do I do now, sir?"

"For the moment, nothing," Maley replied. "Yes, go and help yourself to a drink in the room next door. I'll deal with the matter. It's a regrettable incident, but incidents of this sort are now inevitable. Your worthy Belgian friends are hopping about like a lot of fleas, and behind them I fancy there are some resolute and unscrupulous men manipulating the strings!"

Maley felt exhausted, although he reckoned that Operation Rumpunch had been a success.

Out of six hundred people who were due to be expelled, only ninety-nine had slipped out of the net.

General Siddartha came in with a list of the missing men: ten Belgian officers who had refused to comply with the orders of their government, fifty-four Belgian volunteers, eleven Frenchmen, four Englishmen, one Pole, one Hungarian, one Dane, two Portuguese, one Swede, eight Italians, one South American, four Dutchmen and one New Zealander.

"We've rounded up almost all of them," he said to the Indian, who was puffing at his pipe with an inscrutable expression on his face.

"Yes, except for the big fish: we haven't got la Roncière, or Fonts . . . or any of the ten thousand civilians who have weapons hidden away in their houses.

"These ninety mercenaries whom we haven't been able to find were on our lists, but what about all the ones whom our Intelligence Service has not been able to trace? Where are they?"

"I must remind you, General, that we're not here to wage war but to work out a political solution. We have now found that solution. I've got Kimjanga in hand: he's sending away all the mercenaries and he's agreed to go to Leopoldville!"

Siddartha shrugged his shoulders.

"How many times has Kimjanga promised to send away the mercenaries and go to Leopoldville?"

"I tell you, I've got him in hand! If you had seen him just now, you'd have no doubt about it: he was peeing in his pants. What's more, he's just spoken on the radio."

"Where is he now?"

"He's gone home: I had no further reason to hold him prisoner!"

Siddartha quoted an old English proverb:

"A cat in gloves catches no mice."

At midday, after receiving the first reports on the operation, Maley had gone to the Presidency. He had asked to see Kimjanga immediately and had had to push past Germaine, his horrible secretary, who kept swearing, with tears in her eyes, that her boss was not in.

When he had crossed the threshold, without being announced, Maley found Kimjanga slumped behind his desk.

In a quavering voice and with a crucified expression Kimjanga had once again protested his good faith and eagerness to conciliate. But, alas, no one would believe him, he was being betrayed. . . .

Maley had had the painful impression of being faced with a worthy Negro, straight out of *Uncle Tom's Cabin*, who had just been whipped for a fault he had not committed.

But this time he was firmly resolved to have done with it and he had refused to content himself with promises.

"You talk of your good faith, Monsieur le Président. Prove it at once. Go to the radio station and from there broadcast an appeal for the population to keep calm.

"Then go to Leopoldville and have a meeting with Monsieur Adoula. I assure you no harm will come to you. We guarantee your personal security."

The President had promised to do this, and much more. At one o'clock, in a tremulous voice, he broadcast the following statement:

"I am renouncing violence. Recalled by their governments, the Belgian officers and NCOs are going home. All contracts with foreign advisers are declared null and void. . . . They too must go home. Those are my orders. . . ."

But he had said nothing about going to Leopoldville.

After this appeal Maley had gone off and personally seen to Bongo's release. The Minister of the Interior was pacing to and fro with the lithe gait of a caged panther.

"You got the better of me," he growled. "Next time I'll be more careful."

Since then the President had disappeared and Bongo had taken his place in the Presidency.

Maley had made a mistake in releasing this wild beast against the advice of General Siddartha who wanted to charge him with the assassination of Lumumba and send him, bound hand and foot, to Leopoldville. Bongo had forthwith reacted with brutality. On his own authority he had sent the para-commandos to Pimuriaux's house.

Maley summoned his driver to take him to the Presidency: he was resolved to tackle the beast in his lair, to bring him to heel and force him to withdraw the para-commandos.

But just as he was about to drive off, an officer came to warn him that the Katangese soldiers had just broken into the Belgian Consulate and molested Consul Ryckers.

Fortune sometimes delighted in playing ironical tricks.

At five o'clock a group of para-commandos had invested the premises of the Societé Générale to defend it, they said, against a crowd of Belgians who were about to invade it. The crowd was thin on the ground . . . fifty, perhaps a hundred demonstrators. They accused their representatives of "collaborating with the enemy," handing over the Belgian officers and not protesting against the attempted murder of Justin Pimuriaux.

At first the Katangese soldiers had behaved perfectly. But some bottles of beer had been distributed and, encouraged by the Belgians, they had made their way to the consulate. They had smashed the doors, torn down the Belgian flag, thrown the files out of the window and chased the skinny Ryckers from the premises, urging him on with kicks in the behind. Ryckers, who had never run so fast in his life, had taken refuge at the French Consulate where a hilarious Musaille had greeted him, overflowing with cordiality.

Among this crowd, next to two or three jouranlists, a short dark man answering to the description of Thomas Fonts had been seen inciting the populace. It was surprising, however, that, with a warrant out for his arrest, Fonts should not have left town.

Maley made up his mind, since he was responsible for the maintenance of law and order, to protest as well against the looting of the Belgian Consulate. It would be the funniest part of the interview. . . . He would be posing as the defender of Belgium.

Bongo received him in the office of the President, from whom, he said, he had provisionally taken over at his own request.

The man had any amount of faults—he was circumscribed, cruel, proud—but he was not lacking in courage, and Maley, who was impressed by this courage, began in a conciliating tone:

"Your Excellency, you cannot oppose the expulsion of the foreign advisers. The Security Council has decreed it and the Belgian Government has recognized the principle."

Bongo, his eyes blazing, had sprung out of his chair. He was wearing a shirt, and, since his tie bothered him, he tore it off and shouted in Maley's face:

"I don't give a damn for the UN, or for the Belgians. Pimuriaux is staying. I have the upper hand!"

"No. I not only have right on my side, but the upper hand as well!"

"What right? This isn't your country! What upper hand?

"We Katangese have a Gendarmie of ten thousand men, and you have two or three battalions of tourists!"

"What about the Gurkhas?"

"Gurkhas versus Bantus, we'll see!"

"We also have the Air Force!"

"Go ahead and try and use it, your Air Force!"

"Don't forget, Monsieur le Haut Représentant, that you are under our protection. You came to our country to prepare the way for the Communists, you want to put bandits in power. . . . You ought to be personally careful about what may happen to you!"

Maley had left in a rage, aware all the same that this threat was not an idle one. He had ordered Siddartha to dispatch a company of Gurkhas to Pimuriaux's residence straight away.

"What if we meet resistance?" Siddartha had asked him, in a voice that was no longer impersonal but vibrating with excitement.

"You open fire."

By the time the Gurkhas, supported by a couple of bath-tubs, had arrived, the para-commandos had disappeared. Justin Pimuriaux, in a state of collapse and carrying a small suitcase, had been driven to the airport with an escort disproportionate to his status.

Here again Maley had been worsted by the same intelligent and cynical opponents, who exploited his errors without even giving him time to correct them.

This time it was Fonts. During the interview between Maley and Bongo, he was standing in the room next to the President's office with his ear glued to the door. No sooner had the UN representative left than he came in.

"It's working out perfectly," he said, to Bongo's stupefaction. "It doesn't matter about Justin Pimuriaux, he's no longer of any use . . . or rather, yes, we can make use of him for the last time."

It was Fonts himself who had given the order, by telephone, for the para-commandos to withdraw forthwith to their barracks in Massart Camp.

"Your Excellency," he explained, "Maley will be using a steamroller to swat a fly . . . he's going to send troops and armoured cars to Pimuriaux's house. Pimuriaux will be a victim in the eyes of the population. The UN officials and soldiers will be held up to further obloquy and ridicule. All the press will be there.

"We're not yet ready for a show-down. . . . Our para-commandos would scuttle at the first rifle shot, and the departure of the Belgian instructors is going to leave a big gap."

Bongo had listened without reacting. Then he had burst into a strident cruel guffaw; he had just understood. But it had sent a shiver up Fonts's spine. Once again he had realized how dangerous it would be to leave this brute free to follow his instinct. He would not be able to let him out of his sight for a second.

"What's the President doing?" Bongo asked.

"As you know, he's in the African city with la Roncière, who's taking him firmly in hand. But in your bloody shack there isn't a telephone!"

Bongo curled his lips back from his teeth.

"Maley was frightened just now, I saw!"

"And no wonder!" Fonts reflected. "The main thing is to see if it's worth exploiting this fear. There are some men who become brave and have their reactions sharpened by fear, others who are paralyzed by it . . . they are usually the more imaginative ones, and Maley, being an Irishman, is probably one of those!"

At nine o'clock in the evening Maley remembered he had been invited to a cocktail party at the French Consulate—a purely formal invitation to which he did not propose to go.

But he felt an urge to defy public opinion, which he sensed was hostile because it was being whipped up

268

against him by methods which he considered underhand, the methods of gangsters.

There would be journalists at Musaille's; he would be able to defend himself and exploit to his own advantage, and on enemy territory, the incident at the Belgian Consulate.

Moreover, it was necessary to show all these people that he accepted personally the responsibilities and decisions. He was sure of Arnold Riverton's support. Perhaps Jenny would realize how much he needed her. A smile on her lips, a squeeze from her hand, would be enough to comfort him. Maley had little in common with his colleagues, whether Swedes or Indians. He was able to work with them, but found it hard to relax in their company. They had little sense of humor and none of the fantasy that makes life bearable.

He gulped down a couple of whiskies to raise his spirits, dressed somewhat more carefully than usual, and made his way to Musaille's alone.

In the garden of the consulate in the Avenue de Saio, Félicien Dorat stood gazing up at the sky as though lost in contemplation of the stars. Pérohade and Decronelle were doing their best to rouse his interest by exaggerating the dramatic aspect of the events through which they had just lived.

"If you had seen that dog," Decronelle gasped. "Blood all over the place . . . it was horrible!"

"I don't like dogs," Dorat declared. "The bigger they are the more stupid they are . . . I have a cat called Barbara, she's rather like me: she can't bear the sight of a dog."

Decronelle was dismayed that he should discuss this business with such levity. After all, the dog had belonged to Monsieur Pimuriaux who for some hours had figured as a martyr of the Katangese cause.

Pérohade saw fit to come to the rescue of the Belgian.

"They're bloody swine, those Swedes!"

Dorat grinned broadly and chuckled:

"This time, anyway, Maley got the better of you!"

"That's what you think. . . . They only rounded up fifty mercenaries, the useless ones who've been left here as bait . . . like goats. The statement Kimjanga made is a lot of eyewash. He didn't say anything about going to Leopoldville. Then he disappeared. . . ."

"To Rhodesia, wasn't it?" said Decronelle.

"Rhodesia, my arse! He's not as far away as that!"

Dorat, who was getting bored, summed up the situation:

"As far as I can see, you've won the war, and so has Maley. . . . Let's have a swig of that old skinflint Musaille's whisky to celebrate this double victory!"

Then, suddenly suspicious, he buttonholed Pérohade.

"I say, don't you provide him with some filthy hooch which he then decants into proper whisky bottles?"

Pérohade was injured in his professional pride, but only as a pub-owner. His pride as a journalist was more accommodating.

"My whisky, hooch? I get it from the UN fellows, who sell me their PX rations."

Maley's arrival introduced a chill. Ryckers, squirming with embarrassment, made himself scarce. John Ligget, the British Consul, mumbled a vague greeting and made his way to the bar though his glass was still full.

Maley looked round for Jenny: deep in conversation with Van de Weyck, she was again wearing her beastly spinach-green dress. Only Jenny could wear a dress like that without making herself hideous.

She gave Maley a half-hearted wave and appeared to forget him.

Musaille came up to him and led him aside.

"Well, things seem to be moving, my dear fellow! E'ville tonight is like an ant-heap that has just been stirred up!"

"Tomorrow the ants will calm down!"

"Do you think so?"

"On condition, of course, that certain people, of whom you are one, see to it!"

"Incidentally, a number of your compatriots slipped out of our net."

"My dear fellow, I have no idea what they're up to; they're not registered at the consulate; so I can't recognize them!"

"Does it still amuse you, this little game of hide-and-seek?"

"Talking about hide-and-seek, do you know where President Kimjanga is?"

"At home, I presume!"

Maley left Musaille, who kept grunting in an irritatingly knowing manner. He went off in search of Arnold Riverton, but neither he nor his daughter had yet arrived.

Dorat, still followed by Decronelle and Pérohade, buttonholed him as he went by.

"Are you satisfied with the operation, Monsieur le Haut Représentant?"

"Certainly, a complete success!"

Decronelle could no longer contain himself since his scale of values had been upset: that a man as important as Pimuriaux should be flung out like something unclean. . . .

"Are you aware, monsieur, of the responsibility you're taking in expelling all the European instructors from the Katangese Army? These savages won't have anyone to command them; they're going to descend on the town, rape the women, kill the men."

Maley assumed an innocent expression as he said:

"Savages? Are you referring to the Katangese? I thought there was such a marvelous understanding between the whites and the blacks . . . you know, the famous multi-racial community. . . ."

"You're a traitor to your race, you, a white man, bringing Gurkha mercenaries here to massacre Europeans."

"Monsieur Decronelle, if there are any massacres they'll be caused by over-excited, narrow-minded people like you and those for whom you work!"

A dozen or so guests had gathered round them.

"That poor dog," said a shrill woman's voice.

"I tell you, she was wearing a blue dress . . ."

"His name was Flash."

"No, it was Dick."

"Just like the Gestapo . . ."

"No, more like the OGPU . . ."

"Thirty of them, monsieur, there were thirty of them, all in handcuffs, and the Gurkhas was bundling them into the trucks . . ."

"I remember now, it was a mauve dress."

Tired of these people and their inane chatter, Maley felt that if he stayed much longer he would make a scene, which was not to be recommended in his position.

Before leaving he had to say good-bye to Musaille, even though he was scheming against him. It was what was known as a social duty.

He caught sight of the consul and began to move over towards him.

All of a sudden he stopped. A hard object was being pressed into his back. A voice curtly said:

"We'll get you one of these days, Maley. You see, it's not so difficult."

Maley turned round: there was no one behind him except a group of men and women munching olives and sipping dry martinis.

A yard away from him, a short dark man was telling a story to Joan Riverton who was in fits of laughter.

7. Prelude to Morthor

Three days later the mercenaries launched their counter-offensive.

Operation Rumpunch had caused no casualties, either dead or wounded, apart from Justin Pimuriaux's dobermann.

The counter-offensive led to bloodshed and provoked violent reactions throughout the world.

The demonstrations of 3 September heralded the era of violence and at the same time made certain measures appear acceptable which, until then, Maley had considered incompatible with the UN peace mission.

Further incidents continued to aggravate the situation and prompted him to take a firmer hand and eventually mount a vast military operation which was to put an end to the secession of Katanga forever. It was given the strange code-name of Morthor. Morthor is not the name of a Norse or Gaelic god, but means "to strike" in Hindi, the federal language of India.

It was the Indian General Siddartha who chose it.

Ever since Rumpunch la Roncière had not dared to leave his refuge, for he knew he was liable to arrest.

He had gone to ground in a little shack in the African city, behind the Lubumbashi works.

The colonel did not care for these rows of little houses standing side by side, with their brick walls, corrugated iron roofs and tiny unkempt gardens. It was a bad copy of the white man's town, a miniature copy. But the Negro pestilence had settled in with its filth, its swarming children, its refuse and its stench: the stench of pounded millet, sweat and sour beer.

The colonel, though by no means inclined towards the picturesque, would have preferred to live in the depths of the bush, in a hut, and to be kept awake at night by tom-toms rather than by transistors and loudspeakers.

If Maley or a UN envoy had offered him the opportunity of going back to France without any fuss, he would probably have accepted.

President Kimjanga, this time without an escort of outriders on motorcycles, had come to see him in the middle of the night, utterly demoralized and thinking only of dropping everything and taking refuge in Rhodesia.

In his panic-stricken state he was pitiful but at the same time exasperating, for what he wanted from la Roncière was a good pretext for taking flight.

The colonel likewise thought that there was hardly any hope for him, that events had moved too fast for him to be able to save the situation. Without its Belgian instructors the Gendarmerie no longer existed. The handful of mercenaries dumped at Jadotville or Kolwezi had neither the temperament, nor the ability, nor the discipline which might have enabled them to take the place of the Belgian civil servants and military.

Yet la Roncière took a certain pleasure in denying the President the excuse he wanted.

At great length he reminded Kimjanga of the supporters he still had all over the world, in France, in England, in Belgium, and in Africa itself: in Rhodesia, Brazzaville, South Africa. . . .

For their support to manifest itself, he merely had to give them a pretext.

It was then the idea occurred to him to organize a demonstration in order to proclaim the solidarity between the people of Katanga and their President.

With any luck—the crowd being sufficiently excitable—this demonstration could be turned into a riot against the UN.

The colonel omitted to suggest this last detail to Kimjanga. This was no time to scare him. He simply made him promise to go back to his residence and, in a few days, to deliver a big speech to the crowd gathered on the Place de la Grande Poste.

The more he forgot his fear, the more did the President remember his humiliation.

When, to persuade him to resist, la Roncière said to him: "What would your people think?" the argument prevailed. For Kimjanga attributed thought to his people,

274

more often than not confusing them with the few characters that constituted his intimate circle.

La Roncière felt that this time he would keep his promises, provided the effort was not too long and success not too distant.

The colonel slept extremely badly.

The walls of his bedroom were adorned with pictures of naked women cut out of magazines. The only reading matter was some children's picture books and some highly pornographic works, which gave a lofty idea of the preoccupations of the owner of the shack, His Excellency Bongo.

Never had la Roncière felt so dejected.

Jenny had asked him to spend a few days on her father's plantation at Fort Jameson in Northern Rhodesia.

She had even given him to understand that she would join him there.

"I might even be able to come with you . . . but my husband's very busy. In his own way, he is also defending Rhodesia. . . . I sometimes wonder if his way is not more effective than yours. It required no more than a thump on the table from Maley for all your mercenaries, bristling with grenades, to take to their heels."

Because of Jenny, in order to retain her affection and keep her interest in him alive, la Roncière had to do something.

The "human material" at his disposal was inconsistent, fluid and malleable.

But at the same time it was as unstable as nitroglycerine. A heavy crash had no effect on it, the slightest jerk would cause it to explode. Now, he was not acquainted with the laws that governed its reactions: perhaps there existed no other law than that of mere chance?

La Roncière had always dreamed of working out a number of formulae which would enable a mob to be perfectly conditioned. He believed he had succeeded in Algeria.

Never had he felt so solitary as tonight. When he was in the Army he could rely on the men under his orders or on leaders who were ready to shoulder certain responsibilities.

He merely had to pick up a telephone, call up on the radio, give a loud yell, for the machine to be set in motion, for officers to take action and troops to get under way.

Fonts turned up next day at nine o'clock in the morning, spruce and freshly shaven, dressed all in white as though for a game of tennis.

"Did you have a good time?" la Roncière sourly inquired.

"Not too bad. These worthy Belgians are beginning to get on my nerves. Pimuriaux's dog has become the first martyr of the Katangese cause. One has to start somewhere, I suppose!"

"What do you want to do with your Belgians?"

"Nothing. They're not yet ready. Anything coming from them would be badly received in any case. If you had seen Ryckers's face as he was being booted out of his consulate! For the moment I think we must confine ourselves to adding fuel to the flames here and there."

"We're going to organize a big demonstration against the UN."

"A thousand white men gathering outside Maley's house and hissing at him won't do any good. On the contrary, it will provide him with yet another argument to show that in Katanga it's the whites that count . . . since the Negroes don't make a move."

"Who said anything about whites? There are between a hundred and eighty thousand and two hundred thousand blacks packed into this district alone . . . and only ten thousand whites in the whole European city."

"We've got to get them moving, these blacks. Behind this pasteboard façade of an African city another town has come into being, grouped into tribes and families who obey their chiefs and witch-doctors.

"Maybe by making use of these chiefs and witch-doctors we could get some results. Bongo is longing for a scrap: he's absolutely wild. We take what we can find, witch-doctors or agitators, it doesn't matter which, provided we do something."

"Calm down, Jean-Marie."

"It's all very well for you: I'm stuck here. . . . There's not even a telephone, and my only company is a pub-keeper who calls himself a government official, who brings me food and drink but can't find me a sheet of paper or a newspaper."

"That's no reason for launching a horde of Negroes against the European city. You never know how far they'll go. Your demonstration might well turn into a massacre of all the whites. Imagine three thousand whites lying in the street with their guts ripped out."

"We can take precautions. If we don't reply to the UN, we may as well pack up and leave. Do you like the idea, Thomas, of being buggered about by a handful of Swedish tourists commanded by a little Irish professor who thinks he's Napoleon?"

"Go on. . . . To organize this demonstration we need a simple, straightforward pretext . . . so that our Negroes can get it into their thick skulls."

"UN atrocities."

"Eh? Look here, Jean-Marie, don't go too far! What atrocities have they committed, the tourists? A few glasses smashed in the pubs, a few brawls with civilians who tried to pick a quarrel, a few obscene compliments shouted at the girls . . . more often than not in a language which they couldn't understand. None of this nonsense affects the Negroes."

"The atrocities, the raping . . . we invent it all."

"Can you imagine a Swede trying to rape a fat-arsed Bantu woman stinking of palm oil?"

"You don't understand the first thing about psychological warfare! Rape is still one of the most powerful motives, not only for primitive people but also for certain civilized people; it's what impels them to war, repression, pogroms, massacres, man-hunting. What incident in the Congo had most effect on the masses? The raping more than the looting. . . . Remember Algeria and certain lynchings in America. A single case of rape often leads to a whole village being razed to the ground. . . ."

"Thanks for your little lecture. But I wonder what good the demonstration will do? Does it amuse you so much to draft a speech for Kimjanga to bray into a microphone?"

La Roncière was pacing to and fro in front of the wall covered with naked women, his eyes glinting, his features tensed, his teeth clenched on his cigarette-holder.

Fonts, lying back in an armchair with his feet on the table, asked once more:

"What good will this demonstration do, not counting the huge risks you'll be taking? You'll get three lines in the newspapers."

"Not if it causes a few deaths. I want the UN troops to open fire on this mob, preferably on the women and children."

Fonts whistled through his teeth.

"The Africans don't mean a thing to you."

"We shan't be assassinating those women and children, it'll be the UN, the defenders of law and order and of the colored people, the champions of the underdog and high-mindedness.

"Whatever happens, there are bound to be some people
277

killed if the soldiers of the Congolese Army land at Elizabethville in UN aircraft: women raped, children put to the sword, men hacked to pieces . . . and all for nothing. You watch, it won't even be mentioned!"

"You're resolved to take this risk?"

"Of course! I didn't know you were so squeamish, my little Thomas! Yet if my memory doesn't deceive me, in Indo-China and Algeria you had fewer scruples about dispatching mobs against machine-guns."

"I was only improvising. . . ."

"I beg your pardon?"

"Planning an operation of this sort in advance, systematically and in every detail, knowing exactly whom you'll be sending to their death, at what time they'll be struck down . . . that's what bothers me. We look as though we're planning an execution, like judges or prosecutors."

"That's where we differ: you improvise, which enables you to find an excuse. . . . Afterwards your little friends can shrug their shoulders and say: 'Thomas has been rather thoughtless again!' when you have filled the streets with corpses!

"But I look things square in the face and don't cheat. I kill for a specific reason, with a specific aim in view, the few men whose deaths seem to me necessary for the execution of my plans. And then they accuse me of being a war criminal!"

"Jean-Marie, you can kill and get people killed dispassionately, but I can't. I'm not in the least passionate about saving Katanga. Whether Kimjanga prevails or someone else . . . what the hell does it matter to me? It wasn't the same in Indo-China and Algeria. . . ."

"You argue like a woman, Thomas: I'm in love, I therefore have every right, even the right to kill . . . I'm not in love, so there's nothing doing!

"Katanga doesn't matter to me any more than it does to you . . . but I'm logical. I want to try out certain methods here. Furthermore, I'm conscientious: I was engaged to fight and therefore to win. . . ."

"Jean-Marie, you argue like a half-wit. Let's leave personal feelings out of it, if you don't mind. We don't have the same blood running through our veins: yours is cold, mine is boiling. This time you've got to work with Negroes, it's a new problem. Have you ever seen an African mob on the rampage?"

"No."

278

"I have, and it puts the fear of God in me . . . the sort of fear that claws at your guts. . . ."

"What about the mob we unleashed in the Forum? First the French Algerians, then the Moslems?"

"We had a firm grip on that mob, and also it had a miracle to believe in. The blacks we unleash in the streets of Elizabethville won't have any miracle to believe in. They don't give a damn about miracles, all they want is to win their freedom by killing and looting. . . ."

"Freedom from what?"

"Who knows? Freedom from being Negroes!"

"I have no choice. Here I am, shut up in this shack like a rat in a trap. The blue helmets now have the upper hand. I want to see them scuttling back into their holes. By launching this demonstration we'll frighten them . . . and if they open fire—and I want them to open fire—we shall discredit them in the eyes of the world.

"We didn't come here to play at Boy Scouts. Your little twinge of conscience has come a bit too late. We have barely a week left to retrieve the situation!"

"It's your look-out, after all. I'll bring Bongo to see you here this evening. What will my job be?"

"I don't want you to soil your lily-white hands. You deal with the press. It's for the benefit of the press we're putting on this show. You know what to do: don't leave your little pals out of your sight, and have them ready when the time comes. . . . When the blood begins to flow, rub their noses in it. I want them to be drenched in blood, those pen-pushers. . . . And the photographers, especially the photographers, and the newsreel and television cameramen. I want Monsieur Durand or Mr. Smith to be drenched in blood while sitting in front of their screens in Paris or London . . . that blood which the UN will have shed. I'll give you a minute-by-minute account of the rejoicing, from the speech up to the time of the riot. Tomorrow President Kimjanga will be back in the Presidency."

"About time too! People are beginning to wonder if he hasn't made off with the till. Maley will want to see him!"

"The President won't be able to receive him: he'll be very busy and he won't be in when the UN delegate calls. I have his word."

"Do you trust his word?"

"Bongo will be with him. Find me another hide-out with a telephone."

"Out of the question. Your photograph has been circulated everywhere and, since the Kimjanga Government is

279

so shaky, there are many people who wouldn't hesitate to hand you over . . . Belgian officials or officers who accuse you of not warning them of the roundup . . . mercenaries who wouldn't mind a reward, some of Kimjanga's ministers or police who are wondering if the time hasn't come to play the Leopoldville game."

"What about you, what do you do?"

"No one takes me seriously, I'm a civilian. Civilians don't worry the UN military . . . not yet . . . I hang around the bars, I go out with girls, especially the American Consul's daughter."

"Romance in Katanga! The secret agent who does himself proud! Have you heard from Chaudey recently? Do you still conscientiously draft your report every evening to the Elysée?"

"To hell with you, Jean-Marie la Roncière. I don't draft any reports. They attached me to you in order to stop you making a fool of yourself by following your bloody logic . . . and also to keep us both away from Paris or Algeria, where we might have had temptations!

"You're not my boss, I'm not yours. We're here to help each other. You're having first throw of the dice with your demonstration! I'm supporting you, and when it's my turn to throw, you won't let me down! I think it's just as well to thrash this out once and for all. From now on I'm at your orders, Colonel!"

"Where are you going?"

"To the swimming-pool."

"Is that all you can do?"

"I run into journalists there . . . I tell them a lot of lies and, since Dorat has given me a splendid build-up, they believe them. So long, Machiavelli!"

"So long, Fantasio!"

In the evening of 2 September all the African cities began to show signs of activity. The men gathered round certain cafés, certain houses which served as living quarters for chiefs, witch-doctors or even police, who were often either one or the other.

To begin with, the agitation confined itself to more or less heated palavers at which tempers imperceptibly rose as the crowds increased like swarms of flies on garbage.

The little cafés served beer, and for once the owners did not seem in a hurry to be paid for the drinks.

In the middle of each group an agitator in the pay of Bongo set to work, uttering yells punctuated by slogans:

"They're going to steal our country and our wealth." "The UN want to have our President Kimjanga assassinated." "Kimjanga needs us."

The audience repeated the slogans, growing drunk on them as on alcohol. Tom-toms started beating, big drums with a slow obsessive rhythm.

The rabble-rousers composed impromptu war-songs which the audience accompanied at first with murmurs, then with hand-clapping.

> Aou-a-haou-a!
> Kimjanga, you have called on us
> To defend our womenfolk
> And our babes in arms
> Against the wicked UN
> Who have come to cut their throats.

> Aou-a-haou-a!
> Kimjanga, you tell us to come
> And defend Katanga and her riches
> Against the wicked UN
> Who want to burn and loot our houses
> And rape our women.

> Aou-a-haou-a!
> With our pangas, with our rifles,
> With our cannon and our aircraft,
> We, the valiant Bantu warriors,
> Will drive off these evil white men
> And pursue them to Leo
> Where the Communists live.
> Aou-a-haou-a!

The worthy little Union Minière employees had exchanged their shorts and singlets for loincloths and animal skins.

The storeman Ologo Joseph, who used to be instanced as a model of sobriety and piety, had adorned his head with two horns and painted his torso in gaudy colors. But he kept his rosary in his pocket: an additional amulet.

The tom-toms never stopped beating.

The rumor ran from mouth to mouth. Tomorrow no one would report for work at the Lubumbashi factory, but the daily salary would still be paid.

There were thirty thousand Union Minière laborers

living in the African cities, and a hundred thousand parasites lived on them.

> Aou-ahaou-a!
> We will kill all those dogs
> With our hands, with our teeth. . . .

The women, who at first had kept to themselves, now mingled with the men and brandished their children, who uttered screams of terror.

Desire roused the males, who all wanted to appear as redoubtable warriors. Witch-doctors were busy selling amulets, as at the start of a war: a hundred francs, five hundred francs, a thousand francs, depending on whether they protected their owners from knife thrusts or bullets, whether they were made of frog skin, whether they had been dipped in bull's blood or in the blood of a blue helmet. Not a single blue helmet had been killed, but this did not prevent the witch-doctors from claiming that they had collected the blood of several of them.

Men emerged from their houses with barbed sticks, hatchets, pop-guns or old sabers.

Impassive, wearing a double-breasted jacket and a tie, Bongo lay in a deck-chair outside his shack. Emissaries would come and report to him, whisper in his ear, then disappear again into the darkness.

Leaning against a flaking wall, feeling alien and useless since Bongo insisted on taking control of everything, la Roncière, with a parched throat, listened to the anger, the lust for violence, blood and death, rising from black Africa.

"Everything's going well," said Bongo, displaying his gleaming teeth. "But they mustn't go to sleep tonight or have intercourse their wives. Otherwise they'll forget why they are so angry!"

Scared and sickened, the colonel locked himself up in his room and, with both hands clasped to his ears, tried not to listen to the sound of the tom-toms punctuated by savage cries.

At midnight an officer of the Swedish battalion, Captain Alterman, had to drive past the African city on his way back to the villa which he occupied with two of his friends. He heard the deep beat of the tom-toms, and the sound reminded him of a documentary film he had seen in Stockholm. Intrigued, he tried to make his way towards the center of the city, but he received a volley of stones on his car and straight away turned back, which probably saved his life.

The captain tried to ring up his immediate superior, Colonel Oste, but without success. Oste was spending the night with a dear little German tart called Trude, whose favors he shared with a Belgian officer and a Rhodesian mercenary with whom he was on the best of terms.

After many a hesitation, Alterman felt it was his duty to notify Maley himself.

Awakened with a start and in a very bad mood, the UN representative asked the captain not to drink so heavily and to leave the Negroes alone when they wanted to have a little innocent fun among themselves.

"It wasn't so innocent, sir," the captain pointed out. "They threw stones at me."

"You had no business to be in the African cities. I've forbidden all UN troops to enter them. We're in Katanga to maintain law and order and not to stir up trouble. We've been sufficiently accused, as it is, of meddling in what doesn't concern us."

Fonts had taken Joan to the cinema. She had absolutely insisted on seeing a French film, *Hiroshima, Mon Amour.* Its attempt at audacity and its pseudo-poetic verbiage had enchanted her, but had put Fonts in an extremely bad temper.

"I can only stand Westerns," he said, as they left the auditorium.

"You like shooting, sheriffs, Indians and outlaws? A sign of infantilism."

"Pacifism annoys me when it's so blatant: it's just snobbery, a technical trick. . . . Long live the sheriffs and the pioneers! There was a man I knew who used to say: 'Pacifism smells of slaughter from the sheep's point of view.' " *

"Was he a killer?"

"No, a doctor."

When Fonts said good night to Joan he kissed her on the cheek, as though he no longer felt any desire for her, only affection.

"Stay indoors tomorrow morning," he advised her.

"Why?"

But he had sauntered off, with his hands in his pockets, whistling an old cowboy song.

* Dr. George Wolfromm, *Courts-circuits* (Stock).

At the Mitsouko Pérohade was lecturing Kreis who sat drinking brandy at the bar.

"You may say it's none of my business . . . You may also say it's not the first time Mother Gelinet has had a fling, but between the two of you, you're going too far!

"Pawing her here in public, as you did just now, are you off your head? What if Uncle Gelinet hears about it? I'm very fond of Gelinet—he shoots his mouth off, but he's got guts!"

Kreis slowly rose to his feet and paid for his drink.

"To hell with you," he said, "to hell with the whole lot of you."

And he marched out.

Kreis was suffering from not having any pals with whom to spend the night drinking. A pal was more necessary to him than a woman, even if that woman was good in bed.

He was beginning to get bored with Hortense: she was now in love with him and fastened on to him like those shell-fish in Algeria known as *arapattes,* which can drill into solid rock.

Tomorrow he would report to the colonel, promise not to make a fool of himself again, and ask to be sent back to the para-commandos. Training men for war was his job. But in Katanga there would never be a war. Katanga was like a lump of sugar which melted under a few drops of water.

The next day, at eight o'clock in the morning, crowds began to gather in various parts of the town, waving childish or offensive banners:

"UN go home." "Liberty or death." "The UN are finished." "Katangese unite." "UN means Communism."

The men were brandishing rifles, clubs, pieces of piping, iron bars and hatchets.

What first struck la Roncière, as he ventured into the native cities with an escort of two black policemen, was the strident grating noise of thousands of pangas being sharpened on the pavements.

Most of the men were stripped to the waist and daubed with paint: the women were dressed in sacking. A pungent animal smell rose from this mob already drenched in sweat.

More than once la Roncière intercepted angry glances cast in his direction. He was white, therefore an enemy. Everything was becoming dangerously simplified.

284

As a precaution, he had posted two companies of para-commandos in reserve behind the post office.

Kreis, accompanied by a policeman, had reported to him at seven in the morning, snapping to attention and clicking his heels.

"At your orders, sir."

La Roncière, who had no time to lecture him, had told him to keep an eye on the para-commandos.

"Stick close to them, in civilian clothes, as though nothing was up, and if there's any trouble try to keep them in hand."

"Very good, sir. If the UN intervene, I intervene as well."

"Most certainly not. You're there to protect the whites. The rest's none of your business. You must deny the demonstrators access to the three avenues leading to the European quarters. . . ."

La Roncière was frightened that the demonstration might turn into a riot in the European town and that the police, gendarmes and para-commandos might side with their colored brethren.

But the die was cast, as Fonts said. It was too late to retrieve it. This mob that was about to stream into the streets had not been conditioned according to scientific methods, led by cheer-leaders responsible for making them shout out slogans. Bongo had spent the night whipping up its instinct for murder and pillage, its latent racialism, its hatred of the white man.

In an hour's time the flood-gates would be opened and these black savage waters might sweep everything before them, causing thousands of deaths. . . .

The evening before, Bongo had introduced Mandefu, a crafty old policeman who was steeped in every vice.

"Just tell him what you want: he's very clever . . . and he knows he can make a lot of money . . . or get into serious trouble."

La Roncière had taken the fellow into his room; he had spread out the map of the town and indicated the main post office.

"You know it?"

By way of laughter, Mandefu bared his yellow stumps.

"Have you a watch?"

The policeman had a big gold-plated chronometer on his wrist. He pulled back his scruffy shirt-cuff to display it.

"Now listen carefully. Everyone will be on the square outside the post office to listen to President Kimjanga's big

285

speech. He's going to speak from ten o'clock till eleven. You take charge of the women. They'll be on the left."

"All right, boss."

"At eleven o'clock the demonstrators will disperse. There will be only one way back to the African city, along the Avenue du Sankuru which will not be closed off. Sankuru, as you know, is to the right of the post office. Everyone will go that way. But not you. With the women you'll go down the Avenue Royale: there'll be a police roadblock there, but orders will be given for you to be let through. You understand . . . at eleven o'clock!

"You know the UN auxiliary hospital behind the post office? You'll halt your women outside it. You'll make them shout and fling stones. You'll stay there a quarter of an hour . . . but no longer. By then it will be eleven-thirty. You turn into the Avenue de Saio and start marching up it."

"What if a UN patrol tries to stop me?"

"You cut up rusty. Katanga's your own country. They're not going to fire on women and children. You shout very loud and you make the women shout . . . for the benefit of the journalists and newsreel cameramen."

Mandefu followed la Roncière outside and stopped in front of Bongo. The minister fished a bundle of hundred-franc notes out of his pocket.

"There are twenty, at least," Mandefu reflected. He had rarely seen so much money.

He stretched out his hand, but Bongo took the banknotes back and, to the old policeman's dismay, tore them in half.

"If you do well," he said, "you'll get the rest. If you do badly, nothing . . . except a load of trouble. Do you understand what the colonel told you? Repeat it!"

Mandefu repeated la Roncière's instructions accurately, scratched his groin and shambled off.

"So it's all set?" Bongo asked. "Are you happy? But what's the purpose of all this exactly?"

"We need a few people killed, Your Excellency. The idea is to engineer their killing. The mob that's going to demonstrate tomorrow will be whipped up to a frenzy, you must see to that. We select a thousand women and children out of this mob. They are led by Mandefu up to the hospital. Shouts, stones. The UN post takes fright and asks for reinforcements.

"According to my calculations, it will take these reinforcements ten or fifteen minutes to arrive. The only way they can come is along the Avenue de Saio. They are bound to run into the women and children still led by Mandefu."

"Everything's ready?"

"We have the powder barrel, all we need is the fuse and the match."

"The women must not be content with merely insulting the UN soldiers. They must grapple with them, try to dislodge them and seize their weapons. To incite these women, I want a few reliable and enthusiastic lads. Mandefu's too old; he'll be frightened. They are the fuse. Can you find them for me?"

"Easily. . . ."

"And now for the match: the trickiest bit of all. For this, I need a particularly able man on whom everything will depend. He'll be carrying a pistol when the trouble starts, he'll fire it. . . ."

"At whom?"

"Not at the UN soldiers. The blue helmets must not suffer any casualties. If this man is caught, especially with a pistol on him, the game's up."

Bongo did not bat an eyelid. He now regarded the colonel with a certain respect and it was in an almost confidential tone that he assured him:

"The man won't be caught and he'll never talk! He's from my tribe."

"Do you vouch for him?"

"He once did something much more difficult than what you want him to do, something that could have earned him a great deal of money if he had talked; he did not talk."

While the hatchets were being sharpened, la Roncière tried to recall the face of old Mandefu who, for two thousand Katangese francs, was to lead the women along the Avenue de Saio. All he could remember was a wrinkled face and lips curling back from yellow stumps. Who were the other blacks selected by Bongo to launch the women against the tanks? Who was the man who would fire the pistol? One of those men who never talk.

They were Bongo's killers, bound to him by secret rites, oaths, and exchanges of blood. Were they with him when he killed Lumumba?

So many hazards were liable to make his plan fail! Mandefu might forget that he had to stop no more than fifteen minutes outside the auxiliary hospital, the women

287

might fail to follow him, Bongo's killers might have stayed up all night drinking and still be sleeping it off in some river-bed.

But there was nothing he could do about it; the die was cast.

At nine o'clock ten thousand Africans emerged in vociferous columns and gathered outside the white post office building. A platform adorned with big Katangese flags had been erected in front of the entrance. President Kimjanga, Bongo and the principal ministers were standing there. Some of the press were busy taking photographs or plugging in microphones, others merely hung about gaping.

Dorat took Fonts by the arm.

"I say, it wasn't worth getting up for this show. This is just another of your wild-goose chases. Kimjanga's speeches, I can turn them out by the dozen, always the same. . . ."

President Kimjanga stepped up to the microphone, with a piece of paper in his hand.

"Katangese brothers," he said, in French, in his lovely deep voice, "we want peace, but at Leopoldville they want war. . . . The UN, in the service of the Communists . . ."

"To hell with this," said Dorat, "I'm off!"

Fonts held him back.

"Wait, for God's sake!"

Kimjanga went on:

"The Communists want to make slaves of us. The UN cannot tolerate that blacks and whites in this country are on such good terms. . . ."

"Very important," Decronelle brayed, "very important, this statement of the President's about the relationship between the blacks and the whites. . . ."

Dorat, who was feeling hot, growled:

"A lot of balls, as usual. Who do you think's interested in your multi-racial community? Your agency doesn't give a damn about it!"

"That's not true, Monsieur Dorat."

He rushed off to the post office to send off his first cable.

In the course of an important mass demonstration President Kimjanga once again confirmed the excellent relations that exist between the blacks and the whites in Katanga.

The President folded up his sheet of paper and broke into Swahili.

The crowd, which had gradually calmed down, now began to seethe, surge and struggle, as though they were in fetters and Kimjanga's words had just struck them in the face.

"We are being threatened," he said, wringing his hands, "our independence, our very life is endangered. Every day the UN bring in more mercenaries with orders to steep our freedom in blood, to massacre our women and children. They bring in guns and aircraft . . . but we shall defend ourselves, we know how to die, and the UN will understand . . . for we too have our weapons, our arrows, our knives . . . and also guns, aircraft. . . ."

"What's going on?" Dorat inquired, suddenly on the alert.

"The President is translating his speech into Swahili," said Decronelle who had just come back from the post office.

"Don't talk balls. It's not soothing words or slogans about friendship between black and white that are inciting all these people! Look at them, you idiot! They're brandishing clubs and rifles; a woman has started screaming. And all those apes waving hatchets!"

"There are white men who have come here to help us," President Kimjanga went on, "who will fight on our side, but there are also others who are traitors and who have only come to defend the wealth that does not belong to them but to us. . . ."

This was greeted by a prolonged howl. The drums began to beat. Big fat mammies with swinging breasts stamped their feet, clawed at their faces and slapped their thighs, while their vast buttocks undulated under their sacking dresses.

It was no longer the gentle President Kimjanga with the innocent smile of a child who stood yelling on the platform, half choking in his white tie. With bloodshot eyes, he raised his clenched fists in the air and harangued the mob in a series of hoarse rhythmic cries. The same slogans kept cropping up over and over again: "They want to kill us. . . . The UN murderers. The evil whites who are betraying Katanga."

Exhausted, hoarse and out of breath, he stepped back from the microphone. Bongo took his place to give the crowd instructions to disperse.

A score of journalists looked on in disappointment as

the black stream ebbed away. Nothing had happened. Words, nothing but words, as usual. Crowd scenes: they had any amount of pictures of them.

"You're losing your grip," Dorat said to Fonts. "You promised us something. Nothing, just a palaver, and it's already over!"

"No, old Fifi, it's only just beginning!"

"Where?"

He pointed in the direction of the hospital.

"If I were you I'd stay put; look at that herd of women who've just broken through the barrier. . . ."

Kreis had sidled up to the company of para-commandos. He gave an order. In two ranks the men deployed on each side of the war memorial denying access to the Avenue Royale and the Avenue de l'Etoile which led to the European city.

The mob turned on their heels, brandishing their spears, their rifles, their hatchets and finding the only way out was by the Avenue du Sankuru which led to the African cities, poured into it in a furious torrent.

But, according to his instructions, Mandefu had started up the Avenue Royale at the head of a group of seven or eight hundred women. Some men and children brought up the rear, all of them in a state of great excitement.

The women had powdered their faces with flour—a sign of mourning among the Bantus. This white paste, diluted by sweat, accentuated their thick purple lips and turned their faces into horrible grotesque masks in which their eyes showed like dark holes. Their bare breasts hung down to their waists. Abiding by an old tradition, as young women they had had the muscles supporting them cut through. Their hair, anointed with palm oil, was twisted into six-inch plaits.

The UN auxiliary hospital was installed in a former hotel. It's entrance, an ordinary swing door, was guarded by half a dozen armed Swedes.

At the sight of these wild women, and to avoid any incident, the sentries, on orders from the sergeant, withdrew into the hospital and barricaded the door.

Mandefu gesticulated, pointing at the big blue UN flag, then took a stone out of his pocket and flung it at a window. Three or four men who were with him also produced some stones and followed his example.

Glass tinkled down on to the pavement.

The Irish sergeant commanding the guard watched in horror from the first floor as the seething crowd closed round the hospital. A stone had already struck one of the patients, and an Italian doctor had been injured by a splinter of glass.

He realized that if the doors were smashed in, he could do nothing, not even open fire.

He called up Headquarters on the telephone and got through to the Swedish duty officer.

"Auxiliary hospital here. We're being attacked by a thousand women. . . ."

"Really? Lucky you!"

"A thousand women on the rampage, sir. They're hurling stones, they're going to break in, and maybe set the place on fire. I've got thirty sick and wounded. . . . The women have got hatchets . . . and sticks. They'll cut the patients' throats. . . ."

"You've got a guard post, we've even reinforced it."

"There are six of us . . . confronting a thousand Furies. There are also some men with them. Be quick about it, otherwise we're done for!"

From the sergeant's anguished tone the officer realized that this was no time for joking.

He rang up the Indian camp on the road to the airport and notified Dokkal Singh, the captain commanding the emergency company.

"The hospital's being attacked. Move in with two platoons. Take a bath-tub with you as well, that'll overawe them, and drive them away from the building. But no shooting, mind, they're all women!"

At the sound of the windows breaking, the journalists and photographers had rushed up. The photographers crept forward, took a couple of pictures, then beat a hasty retreat, while the journalists looked on from afar.

The old hands like Dorat, who were wary of mobs, kept a safe distance away and worked out a line of withdrawal.

"Is this all?" he asked Fonts. "For two hours I've been sweating it out, and all you provide is a student rag with two or three broken window-panes!"

"Well, go back to bed, then!"

"If you've organized anything else, tell me where it's going on."

"The women are going to march up the Avenue de Saio towards the Indian camp. It's along that avenue the blue helmets will be arriving. I'm going to make myself scarce. So long!"

At eleven-thirty Mandefu led his women off towards the Avenue de Saio. At eleven-forty they entered it and overflowed into the road, still accompanied by the journalists. Five minutes later Captain Dokkal halted his jeep fifty yards away from the screaming mob. Behind him were the Swedish bath-tub and four GMCs filled with Gurkhas.

Dokkal thought it degrading and absurd that an Indian Army captain and two platoons of Gurkhas, crack troops, should have been called out to disperse a few housewives. Those wretched Swedes had lost their heads again! Admittedly, they had not done much fighting since the days of Charles XII.

Dokkal stood up in his seat and, with his stick, motioned to the women to clear the road.

They continued to advance on the jeep; it was a swarming ant-heap, a river of mud flowing slowly, irresistibly. Dokkal tried to calm them down. He signaled to an African interpreter, a Baluba, who was sitting behind him, to translate for him.

"You must now go back to your homes. You must obey orders and let my detachment through. . . ."

The women, still advancing, shouted curses at him.

"What are they saying?" the captain asked the interpreter.

A broad grin came over the Baluba's face.

"That your mother is a whore and that we're all cuckolds and murderers."

"Tell them I give them two minutes to get back on to the pavements, otherwise, cuckold though I am, I'll run them down with my trucks."

The interpreter cupped his hands to his mouth but still could not make himself heard.

The women, advancing still farther, began stamping and clustering round the jeep.

Dokkal, seeing these thousands of open mouths with their pink palates and filed teeth, these faces distorted by hatred, began to take fright. A black hand seized him by the trousers. He freed himself with a blow from his stick and the woman started howling.

The interpreter clutched him by the epaulette. His face was gray and he stammered: "Sir . . . sir . . . look out."

The captain turned round. Behind him, the muddy stream had flowed right up to the trucks and the bath-tub and was swirling round them.

A man pointed at Dokkal and shouted:

"He's the one, I recognize him, he's the one who killed our brother Bonzogo yesterday!"

Dorat and Pérohade had climbed on to a balcony,

292

which provided cover and at the same time gave them a better view.

"They're going to turn really nasty," Pérohade remarked.

"That's exactly what your little pals want!"

"This is it: the women have come to grips with the Indian captain. Look at that fat mammy who's got hold of his swagger-stick, like the Negro who pinched King Baudouin's sword on independence day!"

Round the second truck some even wilder women began to clutch at the Gurkhas' legs in an attempt to drag them from the vehicle and had to be driven off with rifle-butts.

An NCO shouted an order and the soldiers cocked their rifles. From vehicle to vehicle the order was transmitted: "Prepare to open fire: one salvo in the air to disperse them."

"What? They're going to start shooting?"

"Can't you see? But in the air. Usually it has an immediate effect. But the bullets are bound to ricochet and there'll be some wounded again, you'll see!"

A little Gurkha, weighing barely seven stone, was tugged out of one of the vehicles by a fat Negress. The other women flung themselves on him and started tearing his uniform to pieces, while he shouted for help and struggled.

The sergeant gave the order:

"Fire!"

The salvo echoed down the street, but two revolver shots had accompanied it: a woman, the fat Negress, and a man, Mandefu, lay writhing on the ground, bleeding profusely.

"I don't understand," said Pérohade. "The Indians fired in the air, I saw it quite clearly, yet that old boy and that woman have been hit, and seriously at that!"

The women, who had begun to withdraw, now rushed forward again and, clambering on to the trucks, flung themselves on the Gurkhas' rifles.

Captain Dokkal gave orders for a second salvo to be fired in the air. But most of the Gurkhas had their rifles held fast by the women or pointing downwards, while others had lost their balance. Four bodies toppled into the street.

Dorat saw a child racing away and, struck by a bullet, bound in the air like a rabbit.

The women had been driven off the trucks. The Gurkhas reloaded and this time trained their weapons on the

mob. One of them pointed out the child, who had collapsed at the foot of a tree, and for one moment Dorat
thought that the man was proud of his shot.

The women were fleeing in all directions, their arms
flung out in front of them. Some of them, tripping over a
wounded body, fell down and looked as though they too
had been hit.

In two minutes the avenue lay empty in front of the Indian column, and Captain Dokkal, to his stupefaction,
counted ten bodies lying round his trucks.

From a distance of ten feet a photographer snapped
him standing next to the child's body.

"Clear off," he yelled, "I forbid you to take pictures!"

The photographer, who was an American, went red in
the face with rage.

"To hell with you, you goddam murderer. . . . Women
and children. . . . Clear off yourself!"

Other photographers and newsreel cameramen rushed
up.

"Why did you fire on the crowd?" a South African re-
porter demanded.

"We fired in the air," the disconcerted Indian replied. "I
give you my word as an officer!"

"Fired in the air indeed, you bloody liar! How do you
account for these dead bodies, then?"

"I must ask you to behave properly or I'll haul you off."

"Swine! Bugger! Sod!"

The ambulance sirens started wailing. On the balconies
men and women stood yelling: "Murderer, murderer!"

Dorat looked at the captain and was surprised himself
by the hatred he felt for this wretched puppet. He saw
him look for his swagger-stick, pick it up from beside a
dead body, then, reassured, as though nothing had happened, give the order to the convoy to move forward.

"This time I'm going to let these UN swine have it good
and proper. You see, Pérohade, our little pal Fonts wasn't
far wrong. . . ."

"I'll say he wasn't. It almost looked as though he was
expecting all this to happen!"

"That's what I don't like about this business . . . that he
was expecting it to happen!"

"What do you mean?"

"Nothing, old boy. . . ."

In the afternoon la Roncière drove through the African
city and skirted the Lubumbashi works so as to approach

Kasumbalesa, the frontier post, from the south. He had been told that by going this way he was not liable to run into a UN patrol. The blue helmets had not ventured into the city for some time.

The colonel felt calm and relaxed, as though he had just had a hot bath. Mysteriously his nerves were less strained, his headache had vanished. At last he had been able to leave that prison shack which had no telephone but in which he was deafened by the Negroes shouting and singing and the beating of their drums. He had escaped from those four yellowish fly-blown walls, from those overpowering photographs of naked girls, from the self-satisfied idiotic grin of his jailer-janitor, from Bongo who now regarded him as an accomplice. Did they not, both of them, have blood on their hands?

The city was in an uproar. Outside the little pink brick houses groups stood palavering and gesticulating. There were queues of men at every café, holding glasses of beer in their hands. The colonel realized that the same hostile glances were being directed at him as in the morning, when he had made his final tour of inspection. He had to drive slowly, bumping over the pot-holes. He remembered what Gelinet had told him:

"Be very careful with African crowds. If they get out of hand, it's terrible. . . . You're confronted with men whose only thought is to kill you, simply because you have a white skin."

La Roncière recalled the demonstrators that morning, with their warpaint, their animal smell and their hatchets. What would have happened if they had poured into the European town? The colonel dismissed this thought from his mind. His plan had succeeded: that was all that mattered. He reflected that in three hours' time he would be in Rhodesia, at Kitwe.

John Ligget, the British Consul, had arranged everything. John or his wife? What was the real relationship between them? Indifference? Complicity? Which was the cuckold? John Ligget or Jean-Marie la Roncière?

He remembered the Englishman who was to be seen, always drunk or drugged, in the stews· of Saigon and who used to say with a chuckle that he was a journalist. He was the cleverest, the most knowledgeable of the British agents. This wreck had shown what sort of man he was when they had fallen into an ambush together near Mytho. He had proved resolute, clear-headed and astonishingly tough. During the two hours the crisis had lasted he had stopped mumbling and revealed himself in his true colors: as a man who had sold his soul to his country . . . and had likewise sacrificed his body to her but who recovered, when he had to, all his soldier-like qualities. . . . For this drunkard had remained a soldier.

Who was John Ligget? Who was Jenny?

Two hours after the shooting Jenny had come to Bongo's hut with Fonts.

He had felt like taking possession of her on the camp bed, to efface the memory of his four days of prison in that damp over-heated atmosphere.

Jenny had darted an amused glance at the wall with its naked women, tidied the dirty sheet on the camp bed, then turned towards him.

"My dear Jean-Marie, you can't stay in Katanga any longer after what has just happened. Every UN Intelligence service is out to catch you at any price. . . . They mustn't catch you. Your consul and my husband are absolutely agreed on this point."

La Roncière was about to argue, but Fonts chipped in.

"Jenny's right. Ligget went to see the American Consul, and Musaille has received an extremely vehement telephone call from Riverton as well. Maley suspects he's fallen into a trap. Siddartha claims that if he catches you he'll know how to make you talk!"

"And what if he catches you?"

"There's no evidence against me. I haven't been out of the journalists' sight for the last three days."

"But where can I go?"

"Rhodesia," Jenny had said. "You'll be out of danger there for as long as it's necessary."

"I'm not in the habit, after . . . a little fuss and bother. . . . of scuttling off and hiding . . . like a common-or-garden hired killer . . . I set a trap, it's true. Maley fell into it, so much the better! I may have some blood on my hands, but he's drenched in it . . . from head to foot!"

Jenny had addressed him again by the familiar *tu*.

"Listen, Jean-Marie, forget your gentlemanly scruples. When you do a job like yours, you can't afford them. You keep talking to me about efficiency. Well, be efficient. . . ."

"It's not just a question of going into hiding," Fonts had explained. "You'll have work to do. The Rhodesians are very worried about the way things are turning out in Katanga. The last thing they want is to find, in six months' or a year's time, Maley installed in their own country!"

"And so?"

"Ligget thinks it might be a good thing if you established direct contact with them. The Rhodesians would like it and have told him so."

"Smith rang my husband," Jenny confirmed.

"Smith? Who's Smith?"

"You don't know him. He's been instructed by Sir Roy Welensky, the Rhodesian leader, to follow Katangese affairs; he pads about on the frontier. I think he's a sort of . . . what's it called in French? Someone engaged on clandestine activity . . . I know, a *barbouze*."

"I'm all in favor of this trip," Fonts went on. "You kill two birds with one stone: you drop out of circulation for some time and you get the Rhodesians to help us, which will be extremely useful if next time Maley brings his big guns to bear. That's more than likely to happen!"

La Roncière hesitated, but he knew Fonts was right: closer cooperation with the Rhodesians would indeed be extremely useful. All he wanted was to leave this stinking sordid shack, escape from this all-engulfing nigritude, from the uncertainties of a policy dictated by mood and whim like that of Kimjanga and his merry band.

But it meant abandoning Jenny just as she was revealing a fresh aspect of herself and becoming disconcertingly more attractive by promising to be the perfect mistress: the accomplice who tomorrow might turn into the enemy. . . .

"What about you, Jenny?" he asked. "Do you still intend going to Rhodesia for a rest?"

Fonts burst out laughing.

"My dear Jean-Marie, you have a very direct way of suggesting to a lady that she ought to join you."

Jenny hated this sort of remark. She put Fonts in his place.

"It's silly of you to laugh, Thomas. It so happens that I planned long ago to go and spend a few days at home near Fort Jameson. My father has a big tobacco plantation there. It would be very interesting for Jean-Marie to meet him!"

Fonts shook his head in despair.

"Even Jenny now takes herself for Lawrence of Arabia!"

"That's enough, Thomas."

Fonts gave him a military salute.

"Very well, Colonel. Let's get back to serious business. I suggest you leave this afternoon. You could spend the night at Kitwe, where there's a good hotel, the Royal. I think we could arrange for you to meet Smith tomorrow?"

He glanced at Jenny inquiringly.

"Yes. John's going to ring him up this evening."

"Good. Then everything's settled. I'm going to drive Lawrence of Rhodesia back to her house. After which I'll drop in on Kimjanga to see which way the wind's blowing!"

Jenny handed la Roncière a piece of paper.

"This is my father's address: Ralph Conway, Spring Falls Estate, Fort Jameson, Northern Rhodesia. I'll ring him up tomorrow to let him know you'll be arriving in the course of the week. You'll be warmly welcomed!"

"What I want to know is, when will you be there?"

Jenny gave him a sardonic smile but her eyes were sparkling.

"In three days perhaps. We'll go out riding in the hills. We'll go fishing together."

As he shook hands with la Roncière, Fonts added:

"Have a good rest, you're losing your grip!"

La Roncière looked him straight in the eye, then took Jenny by the arm.

"I'd very much like to meet a real consul some day. It doesn't matter what nationality he is . . . a consul whose sole job is consular affairs and whose wife looks after the children and does the cooking. Does such a thing still exist?"

Then he brushed Jenny's hand with his lips.

He waited until Fonts and Jenny had left, until the sound of their car engine had died away, then he climbed into a Peugeot which was parked outside the door.

A black driver handed him the keys and registration papers, saluted and disappeared.

The car belonged to the Union Minière, according to the documents.

La Roncière slammed on the brakes. Four men were blocking the way. The first, dressed in an apple-green nylon shirt and a sort of cowboy hat, leaned through the window.

"UN?" he asked.

La Roncière drew back, overcome by the violent smell of sweat mingled with sour beer.

"No," he said, "not UN, but adviser to the Katangese Army."

The black did not understand and grasped the colonel by the sleeve.

"Get out at once!"

A dozen men surrounded the car. Two fat mammies looked at the colonel and chuckled. Some children started picking up stones.

La Roncière slowly produced from his pocket the permit with the Katangese colors and President Kimjanga's signature. The man with the hat could not read but he at least recognized the colors of his flag. He shouted something in Swahili. In a second the atmosphere had changed: the two mammies rushed forward to shake his hand. The children, disappointed, dropped their stones and the men cheered with joy.

"That's all right then," said the man with the hat. "I'll come along with you."

"But where are you going? I'm going to Rhodesia."

"It doesn't matter. You can drop me off on the way."

He burst into a loud guffaw and added:

"I like driving about in cars. Besides, like this, I can go and see my cousin Boluto. You'll give me a lift, won't you?"

Reluctantly la Roncière let the man get in and drove off.

At seven in the evening he reached the Rhodesian frontier, after an hour of absurd and perpetually repeated argument. The policeman would not let him through. He had to have a special permit from Minister Bongo to leave Katanga, he said. So the document signed by Kimjanga was not valid? La Roncière had made the mistake of raising his voice, which had not improved matters. Luckily a gendarme intervened in his favor: he never discovered why—maybe to annoy the policeman and assert his own importance.

A hundred yards farther on was the customs office, an old wooden shack.

The head official was not there and his assistant, leaning over the barrier across the road, kept saying over and over again:

"Chief not here, you no go through."

When the chief eventually turned up he did not look at any document, did not even open the boot of the car, but asked the colonel to bring him some meat and cigarettes when he came back.

"It's cheaper over there," he explained, pointing at the Rhodesian frontier post.

On reaching Rhodesia la Roncière was invaded by a strange sense of well-being . . . as though he was waking from a nightmare. He had just rediscovered white law and

299

order after three months spent in the chaos of Katanga.

"This order may not be the best," he reflected all of a sudden, "it may even be unfair for the blacks, but, after all, it is my sort."

All the immigration officers and customs officials were Europeans, impecabbly dressed in white, freshly shaven and competent. The Africans, in khaki uniform and bush hats with the brim turned up on one side, were either drivers or clerks. When a white man spoke to them they snapped to attention and gave a regimental salute. Everything was done calmly and in silence.

The customs and police formalities were over in five minutes. The immigration officer waited until la Roncière had left his office before notifying his superior at Kitwe.

The colonel was now driving across a flat countryside punctuated by savannahs. Every ten or twenty miles stood the works of a copper mine.

Kitwe was a modern town built by the whites for the comfort of whites. The colonel reached it at eight o'clock in the evening.

Gentlemen in exaggeratedly long shorts, with tennis rackets under their arms, were strolling back from their club to dress before the first cocktail of the evening. On the terraces of the cafés fair-haired women in bright colored frocks sat sipping long drinks through straws.

At the Hotel Royal la Roncière found a message waiting for him. Mr. Smith apologized for not being able to meet him that evening. He was detained by an important meeting at Lusaka, the capital of Northern Rhodesia. He asked him to join him there the following afternoon to meet an "interesting person closely connected with Katangese affairs." He would expect him at the Hotel Peninsula any time after four o'clock.

The colonel sipped an ice-cold mint julep as he had his bath. The shooting that morning, the risks he had run in launching the blacks against the European city, the stifling shack, his attempts to organize a country which could never be organized, the Penelope's task that had to be started anew every day, all this had at last come to an end.

La Roncière dressed and went down to the restaurant. The food was better than he had expected. The South African wine was drinkable, as good as a Beaujolais-type whose grapes had ripened in the plains of Algeria. The customers conversed in undertones. He noticed two or three tall, fair-haired girls with long legs. Fonts had told him they had the reputation of not being too stand-offish.

A head waiter in a tail coat relentlessly turned back men who were not wearing ties.

After the meal la Roncière ordered a French brandy but was too tired to drink more than a mouthful of it. He decided to go up to his room.

As he was about to enter the lavatory, a hand came to rest on his shoulder. The head waiter was peering at him with a reproving air.

"But, sir, this is the native lavatory. The whites' is on the other side."

He suddenly realized he was addressing a foreigner, a Frenchman probably from his accent. He knew how extraordinarily indignant Frogs could be about this sort of thing. So he explained:

"It's not racialism, sir. It's simply a hygiene precaution."

Then, lowering his voice:

"Those fellows are all syphilitic."

Maley had spread thirty European and American newspapers out on his desk. Not one of them sided with him. They all repeated the same old facile myths and reassuring commonplaces. Kimjanga was once more the Father of his People, and the UN troops "savage aggressors" who had come to Katanga to sow disorder and hatred.

A Rhodesian paper referred to him, Maley, as the "butcher of Elizabethville" and "the murderer in the pay of Nehru." The Indian troops were compared to SS extermination squads.

This journal was a mere rag and its influence, outside Salisbury, more or less nil.

But all the big London papers were well nigh unanimous in condemning the attitude of the blue helmets in no uncertain terms.

Maley glanced through several of them spread out in front of him. Their front-page headlines read as follows:

"UN troops fire on African Women and Children."

"Massacre at Elizabethville."

"Savage Aggression against Unarmed Civilians."

The American press, although usually in favor of Maley's policy, attacked him unmercifully.

A well-known weekly, with one of the largest circulations in the world, featured a big photograph of Captain Dokkal standing upright in his jeep, his swagger-stick in his hand, his face ostensibly calm and serene. In the foreground, ten feet from the vehicle, lay the body of a child drenched in blood with one arm oddly twisted.

Underneath was the caption:

"An Indian officer restores law and order in Katanga."

The ten deaths caused by the demonstration of 3 September reduced three months of arduous work to naught. Throughout that time he had striven to undermine Kimjanga's supports.

Moreover, he was beginning to have some doubts about the accidental nature of the shooting.

Among the dead a certain Mandefu had been identified, whom Colonel Degger, the UN Security Chief, knew extremely well. He belonged to the Katangese Sûreté and from time to time, in exchange for a reasonable retribution, he brought the colonel interesting information. What was a policeman doing at the head of a demonstration of women? On his body had been found a bundle of banknotes cut in half.

Degger did not pay a lot, but he paid in whole banknotes.

Other witnesses reported the presence among the journalists of a small dark man in a light suit. It was Thomas Fonts. Ten minutes before the shooting started, he had been seen urging the journalists and cameramen not to return to their hotels but to go at the first sound of shouting to the auxiliary hospital and the Avenue de Saio.

Maley had several discussions with Captain Dokkal. Dokkal denied all responsibility in this affair. He stuck firmly to his story: his men, being threatened and finding themselves obliged to retaliate in self-defense, had fired in the air. If some demonstrators had been hit, he was sorry, but after all it was they who had started the rumpus.

Maley had then suggested to Siddartha that disciplinary measures should be taken against him and that he should be "posted back to the Indian Army." If only to appease public opinion.

Siddartha had curtly refused. Maley could still see him, sitting opposite him in his office, furiously striking the arms of his chair with his swagger-stick.

"No disciplinary measures will be taken against Captain Dokkal," the general shouted. "He's in no way to blame. In his place I should have done exactly the same. Those savages got what was coming to them!"

And he had added:

"It's not Dokkal who's responsible for this incident. The real guilty parties are those who are content with half measures and haven't the courage to put paid to Kimjanga and his gang of colonialists once and for all!"

302

Maley had asked:

"What do you mean, Siddartha?"

"You know perfectly well, sir. I warned you after Rum-punch that Kimjanga would come unstuck. For four days he was at our mercy. We could have made him capitulate and sent him by force to Leopoldville. You gave him time to recover and prepare his counter-blow. We're in a real mess now. I hold you responsible. A mere captain who did nothing but obey orders is not going to pay for your mistakes. I'm sorry, sir, but that's how I see it!"

After Rumpunch Maley had received a telegram from the UN Secretary-General congratulating him on his "energetic and splendidly effective action." The incident of 3 September had unleashed quite a different reaction in the glass skyscraper in New York. Maley still had in front of him the signal he had received the night before.

Secretary-General deplores regrettable incidents causing civilian casualties stop Requests you send immediate report explaining in detail circumstances of shooting and clearly establishing responsibility

It was not even signed by the Secretary-General himself but by some underling or other in his office. Maley was too well acquainted with the intrigues of the seraglio not to realize what this procedure meant: they were looking for a whipping-boy, and he was extremely liable to fill the role. He himself had tried to sacrifice Captain Dokkal. Siddartha had saved Dokkal's skin. Who would stand up for Maley in New York?

The telephone rang; it was Colonel Degger; the Security Chief sounded very excited.

"Sir, I have the autopsy report on the casualties."

"Yes," said Maley, "what does it say?"

"Very interesting! Of the ten bodies, only eight were killed by rifle bullets. The others were hit by bullets from a 7.65-caliber pistol."

"I don't give a damn if they were killed by shots from a pistol or an arquebus, it doesn't alter the fact that we have ten corpses on our hands!"

Degger's courteous voice assumed its most official tone. Degger disapproved of the senior representative's violence, verbal outbursts, bad behavior and lack of self-control. In his opinion a diplomat or an officer would have filled the post better than this excitable university professor who never stopped to think twice, acted hastily and fell blindly into the traps his opponents set for him.

"I beg leave to differ, sir. None of the detachment commanded by Captain Dokkal was carrying a pistol except for the captain himself. And he never drew his weapon from its holster, as can be proved by all the witnesses and all the photographs!"

Maley whistled.

"Then how? . . ."

"I personally think there's no doubt whatsoever: Mandefu and the woman were not killed by our soldiers. They were shot down by someone standing behind them, in the mob of demonstrators, that's to say by a Katangese. This proves . . ."

"I understand," Maley interjected. "Thank you, Colonel!"

Maley replaced the receiver. Someone had deliberately launched women and children against the blue helmets. This person wanted there to be casualties and, to make certain that the blue helmets would open fire, in cold blood he had instructed a killer to shoot down two of the demonstrators.

Maley thought of la Roncière's icy expression, Fonts's cynical smile and Bongo's face convulsed with rage.

He rang for his secretary.

"Georgia, get hold of Félicien Dorat. Tell him to come and see me as soon as possible, at any time that suits him."

Lying back in his armchair, Dorat watched the smoke rising from his cigarette. He was hot, and angry with Maley for arranging this meeting immediately after luncheon, when he usually had a snooze—an old habit of his that he had developed in the Far East.

If only the Irishman had had some sensational news to give him: his resignation, for instance. But, as usual, he had summoned him only to complain of his dear colleagues' attitude and his own. During the twenty years he had spent traveling all over the world, wherever there was any fighting, Dorat had witnessed the same scene a hundred times over: some bigwig, ambassador, resident minister, senior representative, general or delegate would begin by saying how much he despised the press and its methods, then ingratiatingly add: "But of course you're not like the others, my dear fellow. . . ."

The interesting part was what usually happened next:

either Dorat would be called a corrupt blackguard and be shown the door or else the bigwig would burst into tears and talk about the justice of his cause: this was still more embarrassing and lasted longer.

After twenty years of wars, conspiracies and revolutions Dorat no longer believed in the justice of causes. The "liberators" were often just as bad as the "oppressors." The "liberators," moreover, had the disadvantage of being extremely touchy and more often than not behaved exactly like the "oppressors," for, alas, there was only one way of managing the world: by being utterly unscrupulous. These methods had been codified by a perspicacious Florentine more than four centuries ago.

Maley, in a sarcastic voice, read out the article that Dorat had written:

Elizabethville, 3 September.

I have just taken a ten-year-old boy to hospital. He has two bullets in his shoulder, and his left arm, almost torn off, is hanging by a few shreds of flesh. He does not understand what has happened to him. He knows only one thing: some men in helmets and boots, bristling with weapons, belonging, they say, to the Army of Peace and responsible for the maintenance of law and order, fired on him . . .

Dorat interrupted him.

"Don't bother, I know it by heart!"

"I never knew you had such a taste for sensationalism!"

"I say that the UN Indians killed ten people, that two children were wounded, and that there was blood everywhere. Is it a fact or did I invent it?

"Damn it all, look at these photos. What do they show? Black women and children taking cover from bullets. Who are firing those bullets? Gurkhas with none too prepossessing faces, Nepalese who serve as mercenaries in the Indian Army and who, rightly or wrongly, have an established reputation for ferocity. I wrote what I saw; that's what I'm here for."

"But what did you see? An isolated incident which you have deliberately built up. You've done the same as all your colleagues. You've gone and paddled in the blood and splashed it all over your rag to overawe your readership of old women. But you haven't for a moment tried to explain the reasons for the incident. The whole world suddenly learns that some Indians massacred a defenseless

305

crowd because they were demonstrating in favor of Kimjanga. That's not the right thing to do, Dorat, believe me!"

Dorat suddenly lost his temper.

"No of course not," he said. "And I suppose you call shooting women and children the right thing to do! You're like anyone who's been given a little authority. You can't stand being contradicted. The slightest criticism makes you furious. If you want to avoid criticism, the best way is not to commit so many blunders. And I'll tell you something else. In this business I'm almost certain you've let yourself be duped like a choirboy!"

"My Intelligence service tells me that you're on the best of terms with certain mercenaries. . . ."

"I know several, it's true, and at least one of them is a friend of mine. They're just about as tolerant as you are."

Dorat lit another cigarette which, with his usual free-and-easy manner, he took from Maley's packet; then he looked at him artfully, like an old cat at last taking interest in a mouse.

"You know, Maley, you remind me a great deal of la Roncière?"

"You flatter me. . . . That filthy swine!"

"Both of you think that journalists are a harmful species that ought to be shot or at least flung into jail."

Dorat rose to his feet.

"And now, above all, don't talk to me about morality. . . . If you had been able to engineer that incident and it was favorable to you, you would have done so . . . in the name of your morality. La Roncière—because I'm certain it was his idea—acted in the name of his morality . . . or rather according to his technique. La Roncière's won, you've lost. Try not to spoil your last chances!"

The same day, la Roncière met Mr. Smith at the bar of the Peninsula Hotel at Lusaka.

Mr. Smith was a giant of a man, forty or fifty years of age, with slightly bloodshot blue eyes, cheeks the color of underdone beef, and a red handlebar mustache.

"You're partial to whisky," la Roncière reflected. But he did not deceive himself: Smith was an efficient and dangerous man. He had put on weight, he was sweating profusely, but he was the very model of those competent hard-headed agents that England had scattered all over the world to watch over the interests of the Crown.

Smith was admirably well informed about Katangese affairs. He understood Kimjanga's mentality perfectly.

"A rabbit disguised as a lion," he said. "Not so easy to work with those fellows, eh! We've also had a little fuss with our Negroes, but in Rhodesia we're still the masters. I can't help wondering for how long, though. It's convenient, being the master: one can always, when necessary, resort to the lash."

Mr. Smith had greeted the colonel most cordially.

"You've done a good job of work," he had said, squeezing his hand.

Then, with a wink:

"That demonstration trick . . . well done!"

"I beg your pardon!"

"Come, come now, my dear colleague, this is between ourselves: no need to make a mystery about it. I know how that sort of thing is organized. And this time it was really well done!"

La Roncière felt uneasy. That Smith should know the precise strengths of the UN forces and the Katangese Army was only to be expected. That he should be familiar with the difficulties the mercenaries encountered in accomplishing their task, that was somewhat more surprising! But how on earth did he know that it was he, la Roncière, who had engineered the incident on 3 September?

Ligget must have informed him! But Jenny alone knew of certain details, and these details seemed to be known to Smith.

Once again la Roncière wondered what game the young woman was playing when she had insisted on his immediate departure for Rhodesia. La Roncière had believed it was the anxious reaction of a woman in love. But Jenny's attitude was less simple. Perhaps she had other motives.

Mr. Smith drained his glass.

"It's time we were going. We have a meeting with Lawson at seven. After that, I hope you'll give me the pleasure of dining with me. He's all right, Lawson, you'll see; a bit of a snob, but he's all right!"

La Roncière preferred not to ask who Lawson was.

The car drove through a gate and drew up in front of a white colonial-style house.

Two sentries in blue drill tunics buttoned up to the neck stood on guard. A dozen cars, sporting pennants, were parked under the trees.

"This is Government House," said Smith. "Today there's a very important meeting being held in which Sir

307

Roy Welensky and Mr. Caldicott, the Federation Minister of Defense, are taking part. Lawson, whom you're going to see, is Caldicott's right-hand man."

Lawson was the opposite of Smith: pale-complexioned, he dressed with extreme elegance and tried to appear more British than the British. His Oxford accent was so affected that the colonel understood no more than half of what he said and, to his annoyance, he had to resort to Smith's help.

"Very pleased to meet you," said Lawson. "Smith told me what a remarkable job you've done in Katanga. You know we're following developments closely. Sir Roy has come to Lusaka with Mr. Caldicott to examine what measures must be taken to defend our frontier. That's why I was anxious to see you."

He lit a cigarette.

"What's the situation in Katanga?"

"As good as it can be," said la Roncière. "But I'm afraid there may be trouble. Maley's getting overwrought. You know how excitable he is. I think that if he receives the 'go-ahead' from the UN, he'll try to settle the problem by force."

Lawson quietly asked:

"What will happen then?"

La Roncière hesitated a second; he did not wish to put all his cards on the table before knowing his opponent's game. He replied:

"Maley will come up against a brick wall: we're strong enough to stand our ground. . . ."

"Bloody nonsense," Smith growled.

"Please, Smith," Lawson broke in. "Go on with your summary of the facts, Colonel."

"We're strong enough to stand our ground, provided we are helped," la Roncière went on. "That was what I was going to say when I was interrupted. I'd very much like, in my turn, to ask some questsions: if Maley takes action, what will you do for us? Is England prepared to come to our rescue?"

Lawson gave a little cough.

"The trouble is," he began, "we don't see the problem in exactly that light. You know how things are: to maintain good relations with her other African territories, England is prepared to soft-pedal on Katanga and probably even on Rhodesia."

"And so? . . ."

"And so it's on us Rhodesians you'll have to rely. Sir

Roy is firmly resolved to do anything to save Katanga. It's the necessary buffer between nigritude and our Rhodesia. I can tell you, in his name, that he is prepared to give you all the support you need.

"I am authorized to tell you even more: if Katanga is really threatened by the UN, we are resolved to send troops into Katanga, on condition, of course, that President Kimjanga requests them."

"I don't think that'll be necessary," la Roncière replied stiffly. "We're perfectly capable of defending ourselves!"

Smith had been wriggling in his chair for the last few minutes, dying to speak. He could not contain himself any longer.

"Look, sir, it's high time we faced the facts."

He turned to la Roncière.

"You know perfectly well, Colonel, that if the UN decide to bring their big guns to bear, you'll have no chance of holding out. The Gendarmerie will disband in a few hours. You'll be left on your own with your mercenaries.

"Do you think a hundred men can stand up against several battalions? You'll beat a hasty retreat because you won't be able to do otherwise. After which you'll go home and leave us to deal as we can with the savages on our frontier."

He thumped the desk with his fist.

"All this because you want to make Katanga a French game reserve. It's always the same with you people. You only think of your own interests."

La Roncière was beginning to be amused; he remembered that Jenny had pestered him at least ten times to know if it was true that General de Gaulle intended installing in Katanga the Frenchmen who sooner or later would be forced to leave Algeria.

Lawson made a conciliating gesture with his hands.

"Gentlemen, gentlemen, we're here to reach some agreement."

He turned to la Roncière and said in a confidential tone:

"I shan't be telling you anything new, Colonel, when I say that the Rhodesians have extremely close historic links with Katanga. Normally Katanga should have come to the Crown of England rather than King Leopold of Belgium."

To the Rhodesians, the problem was not only a political one—and la Roncière knew this—it was not only a question of creating a buffer-state between Salisbury and Leopoldville. Considerable economic interests were involved:

Katanga produced about eight per cent of the world's copper, roughly equivalent to the surplus which poured on to the market every year. These three hundred thousand tons made prices drop. If Rhodesia managed to get her hands on Katanga, she would at the same time take control of the copper and derive enormous financial advantages from the operation.

"I don't think we have yet reached the stage of needing your troops," the colonel went on. "Of course, if this should prove necessary, we would appeal to you. Meanwhile you could give us effective help without running too big a risk."

"How?" Lawson interjected.

La Roncière reflected for a moment.

"Firstly, facilities of communication. If we are attacked by surprise, we shall need supplies and munitions. It would be simpler to have these sent from Rhodesia."

"Agreed," said Lawson. "What else?"

"I think a deployment of troops on the frontier would make an impression on the UN."

Smith chipped in:

"That's already catered for. Tomorrow we're moving up three battalions, who are going to camp down opposite the frontier posts. We're also organizing air patrols."

"If the UN attack," la Roncière went on, "we'll need a bolt-hole, if only for Kimjanga's personal safety. The best thing would be to send him to Kipushi, which is only twenty miles from Elizabethville. Are you prepared to give him asylum?"

Lawson hesitated.

"It's rather compromising."

"Less so than sending your troops into Katanga."

"All right," Lawson sighed. "We'll agree on Kimjanga. What else do you want?"

"I'd like you to be less fussy about the transit of mercenaries in Rhodesia: several times my men have been bothered because their visas were not in order."

Lawson rose to his feet.

"Look, Colonel, I think you can settle all these details with Smith. I hope you're not deceiving yourself about your capabilities to resist. Anyway, good luck!"

He held out his hand.

"You're furious," la Roncière said to himself. "Things didn't turn out as you expected!"

On the landing he turned to Smith. To his great surprise

the giant was hilarious. He gave him a hefty slap on the back.

"You bloody Frog, you're as stubborn as a British bull-dog! I think we're going to do a good job together. Meanwhile let's go and have a drink!"

La Roncière knew that Smith was prepared to collaborate, until, of course, the interests of his country induced him to leave him in the lurch, if not actually put paid to him.

He was the sort of man he could understand.

La Roncière woke with a slight headache. The evening with Smith had dragged out till three in the morning and he had had to drink a great deal. The big Rhodesian had told him all sorts of stories about the tribes living astride the frontier, but the colonel no longer had a very clear memory of this ethnic muddle.

This morning he felt as though he was on holiday.

He asked for a bottle of mineral water to be sent up and telephoned Fort Jameson to let Jenny's father know he would be arriving about five o'clock.

Smith had advised him not to travel by road.

"Five hundred miles over bumpy tracks, old boy, we're too old for that sort of thing. Furthermore it's dreadfully dull country. Take a taxi-plane."

At a height of fifteen hundred feet the little Piper flew over a monotonous savannah landscape. Now and then the ground rose and the savannah gave place to denuded plateaus. There were very few villages to be seen.

"Not very rich, this part of the country," said la Roncière.

The pilot shouted to be heard above the noise of the engine:

"No. In Northern Rhodesia we've attended above all to the mines. Less than one per cent of the land is cultivated. The natives have settled in the copper belt or else migrated to Southern Rhodesia to work on the farms."

The plane made a big detour to avoid a flock of vultures.

"Dirty brutes," the pilot fumed. "The other day a pal of mine collided with one of these vermin: he almost crashed. You're going to Uncle Conway's, aren't you?"

"Yes. Do you know him?"

"Everyone knows him. He's one of the oldest settlers. He was born at Fort Jameson and has never moved. He has owned his tobacco plantation for thirty years. A splendid fellow. You don't find many like him these days."

"I know his daughter, Jenny. I met her in Katanga."

"Jenny? Damn pretty girl, eh?"

The pilot gave a wink.

"Seems she's pretty hot stuff, like her father. Do you know he has been married four times? The old hands out here say he's got bastards all over the place."

La Roncière settled back in his seat and fell silent. He knew that Jenny had had a number of affairs, but he did not like people to mention this in front of him.

The pilot throttled back and touched down on the laterite air strip. He brought the machine to a halt outside a modest hut which served as an airport. La Roncière alighted and took down his suitcase, somewhat surprised to find no one there to meet him. Conway was probably late. A Land-Rover came racing up, raising a cloud of red dust. It stopped in front of him.

"Good morning," said Jenny, as though it was quite natural that she should be here and that it was she who had come to fetch him.

"I'm so glad . . ."

He never managed to strike the right note when talking to her.

La Roncière was about to fling his arms round her, but he restrained himself in time: the pilot, who was walking back to his aircraft, gave him an ironical little wave.

Jenny was wearing short raw-hide boots, old khaki slacks and a man's shirt adorned with pockets. This uniform made her look like a young girl.

"I felt it was my duty," she said in a serious tone, "to welcome to my ancestral home the hero entrusted with the task of defending the wretched settlers who are being threatened. I took a plane yesterday from Elizabethville, and here I am."

She leaned towards la Roncière, brushed his cheek with her lips and whispered:

"I wish I could kiss your properly. But I'm a respectable woman. I have to think of my reputation!"

"I hope you're prepared to give it a few jolts?"

"Later on. Meanwhile get in. The plantation's twenty miles away and my father's impatient to see you. He's dying to give you his opinion on the future of Africa, the London politicians and the ridiculous pretensions of the Negroes to independence."

"Spare me," said la Roncière. "I don't even want to hear Africa mentioned, anyway for a few days."

"What do you know about it . . . about our Africa . . . the white man's Africa?"

The Conway estate spread over seven thousand acres. It was situated on a hill planted with jacarandas and frangipanis. The house itself was a big squat one-story building which must have been added on to several times.

"Africa at the time of the War of Secession," la Roncière reflected.

The blacks who worked in the vast tobacco and corn fields were stripped to the waist and wore shorts. They looked up and waved as the Land-Rover drove past.

"I know almost every one of them," said Jenny. "They live in two villages which depend on the plantation. Some of them were already working here in my grandfather's day."

"And before that?"

"They used to kill one another. The white man's peace . . ."

"And now the hatred of the white man . . ."

"*Uhuru* . . . independence . . . which in Swahili also means freedom. We ought to find another word. Independence and freedom have nothing in common."

Some servants dressed in white jackets with gold buttons, but barefoot, came and collected the luggage.

In a big living room with bare beams, reminiscent of an old Yorkshire manor house, a gaunt white-haired man of sixty sat sipping gin and reading a newspaper.

Ralph Conway unfolded his lean frame, kissed his daughter, held out his hand to la Roncière and forthwith exploded.

"Colonel, do you know what it says in this rag?"

He indicated the *Rhodesian Observer*.

"Elections in Kenya this year, do you hear? Those damned monkeys are going to vote! The Mau-Mau who used to burn down the farms and slit women's throats are going to elect other Mau-Mau, those who directed the revolt in secret in the towns! With Her Majesty's blessing, Jomo Kenyatta, who should have been hanged, will end up with a knighthood and the Order of the Bath!"

"Now then, Daddy, don't lose your temper: it's only six o'clock!"

"Don't you think it's enough to make one lose one's

313

temper? In Kenya they're voting. And here the Negroes are beginning to get restive."

"On your estate everything's quiet?"

"Call me Ralph, Colonel. Everyone calls me Ralph, Uncle Ralph, even my daughter. Everything quiet here? My Negroes know me, they knew my father. If those bastards from the towns didn't come and turn their heads, they'd be perfectly all right. The young ones get a bit worked up, but their elders calm them down." He chuckled. "Sometimes they even make them drink some devil brew which calms them down forever!"

Throughout the meal the old man never stopped ranting for a moment. La Roncière once again heard all the old arguments that had been dinned into his ears in Indo-China and above all in Algeria: "Independence will bring nothing but misery and the natives don't really want it, for they'll merely come under the yoke of other tribal chiefs in the guise of deputies or ministers. . . ."

Conway pointed at the plain outside.

"Growing tobacco's not so simple, Colonel. It's not just a question of scattering some seed on the ground. You've got to select the plants, then prick them out and . . . keep weeding, weeding all the time. Then there's the sorting, the drying. . . . We also go in for corn; vegetable crops, a little cattle-breeding.

"The Negroes, as I've learned to my cost, can't see farther than their own noses. They're incapable of any kind of work unless they're certain of immediate profit.

"When my father first arrived, it was nothing but bush. If the whites leave, it will relapse into bush and my tobacco plants and corn will disappear. *Uhuru* . . . why, they'll die of hunger. I'm very fond of my Negroes. What frightens me is not so much that they should be independent, but that they're incapable of organizing their independence. Incompetence and self-satisfaction!

"They think they know everything about economics, politics, agriculture. Economics indeed! If they have fourpence in their pockets, they go and buy pink chamber-pots and robes and spend the rest on drink. Politics they confuse with palaver. As for agriculture, they burn down a bit of forest, scatter a few seeds, and if anything comes up, so much the better! But the forest will cease to exist, the rains will carry off the soil. *Uhuru*. . . ."

"Conway drinks a lot," la Roncière reflected, "so he can't deplore this vice in his son-in-law. On the other

314

hand, he doesn't seem particularly pleased that this son-in-law is a diplomat from England."

"It's soldiers we want," old Conway kept saying, "not dandified Oxford graduates with a lot of silly ideas in their heads!"

Jenny, in a state of undress, calmly came and joined la Roncière in his bedroom.

"What if your father saw you?"

"Apart from tobacco and his bugbear called *Uhuru*, everything's a matter of indifference to him. We're . . . how shall I put it? . . . extremely tolerant about this sort of thing in white Africa. The houseboys will chatter away tomorrow. . . . But even if I hadn't come and joined you here, they would have said I had. . . ."

"They're used to it, aren't they?"

"We're a handful of privileged persons, hated and envied and surrounded by millions of blacks. Our bunker: a few hills in the center of Africa. Fidelity and jealousy can't withstand the atmosphere of the bunker, only certain traditions . . . such as dressing for dinner. We're eager to enjoy life and our last remaining privileges, because we're liable to lose everything in the coming months."

"You're very pessimistic!"

"Do you know how much the Conway plantation was worth five years ago? Nearly a million pounds. Nowadays my father wouldn't find a buyer at a hundred thousand because of *Uhuru*: the plantation's far from the town and requires a substantial labor force.

"Jean-Marie, in this country we understand the French in Algeria . . . the settlers, that's to say. We know why they hang on to their estates, why they are prepared to do all sorts of silly things, knowing that all is lost. Rhodesia will soon be lost to the whites, we can't do anything about it. However, I've persuaded John Ligget, whose children should inherit this plantation, to help us. You too will help us defend ourselves. . . . Before we leave, we in our turn will probably do all sorts of silly things.

"You don't know how beautiful it is, this white man's Africa! Tomorrow I'll show you Lake Nyasa at Bandawe, where we have a cottage. It's lovely: clear green water, blue mountains, sparkling sweet-scented air . . . too lovely for us to lose it!"

On 5 September Maley invited the local and foreign press to the Villa des Roches. The tension was progressively mounting, the relations deteriorating, between the UN soldiers and the local population. The correspondents hastened to the villa.

Maley made his entry accompanied by a man with a Terror-style beard and unkempt hair. The man had shifty eyes, a receding chin and appeared to be under the effect of a violent emotion.

"Gentlemen," said Maley, "I have very grave news for you: Colonel la Roncière and the French mercenaries have been planning to assassinate me and also General Siddartha. We have full proof of the plot. Here is the man who was entrusted with the task of preparing the outrage, a Frenchman from that gang, Captain Judet."

Maley heard someone say:

"What's the point of all this nonsense? To make people forget the deaths of September 3rd?"

He raised his voice.

"Does it surprise you? The French officers who've gone over to the OAS in Algeria show that they don't hesitate to resort to these methods. . . . The same breed is at work here. Here is Captain Judet. His job: a mercenary, as he will tell you. Ask him any questions you like."

In a low hesitant voice, which did not ring true, Captain Maurice Judet told his story.

Colonel la Roncière had sent him to the Minister of the Interior, Bongo, who wanted a reliable man for a very special mission. Bongo, who had received him in his house, had then asked him to prepare an attempt on the lives of Maley and General Siddartha. He had offered him five hundred thousand Belgian francs and had threatened to have him bumped off if he breathed a word or refused this mission.

Judet had therefore accepted but, as soon as he had been able to do so, had asked for asylum with the UN.

Maley interjected:

"Judet put himself under the protection of our troops at five o'clock yesterday. Two hours later I had a visit from the Public Prosecutor and an official from the Minister of the Interior, both of them Belgians, who were most insistent that I should hand Judet over to them.

"They accused him—listen to this carefully, gentlemen—of currency offenses. There's always some fiddling of that sort among that lot, but I detected something else. They were really too insistent. So I asked to see the fellow in person. Our Security services also had their doubts about him . . . I threatened Judet to hand him over to the

316

Katangese authorities, and he confessed everything to me."

Pérohade rose to his feet with an embarrassed air.

"May I say something?"

"Go ahead."

"Well, this Captain Judet of yours is well known to me. In the first place, he is not a captain but a sergeant; second, he's not French but Belgian. He's one of the tramps la Roncière got rid of."

There was a loud burst of laughter. Pleased with his effect, Pérohade went still farther. He turned to the pseudo-captain.

"I say, Mollard, you've got quite a lot on the slate at my place . . . it comes to, let me see now, five thousand francs!"

Maley tried to retrieve the situation.

"Gentlemen, please . . . Mollard or Judet, what does it matter? Everyone here has three or four different identities. The fact remains, this man has confessed that he was ordered to assassinate me, that Bongo wants to have me killed. He even threatened me in person. . . ."

The Associated Press correspondent, John Spencer, slapped the table with the flat of his hand and hissed through clenched teeth:

"Mr. Maley, it does matter if his name is Mollard or Judet. In the present circumstances, I don't believe this fellow's fantastic story, and I can't help wondering whether you haven't paid him yourself and whether this isn't a put-up job for your own unavowable ends!"

"You'd better keep quiet, Spencer. I'll have you . . ."

"What?"

Maley felt the blood ebbing from his head. All the journalists had risen to their feet and were gazing at him in silence. He suddenly felt as though he was a prisoner in the dock and, when they left the room one after another, he had the impression they were withdrawing to pronounce a verdict.

"What do I do now?" asked the false captain.

Maley eyed him with contempt.

"You'll be repatriated when you've told me the truth. To Paris or to Brussels?"

The man hung his head.

"Brussels."

On the following day the MIR gave the first signs of its existence. During the night a number of slogans were painted on the pavement or on the walls:

"The MIR is on the watch." "The MIR executes traitors and collaborators."

At the same time a number of Belgians—but also every consulate, which was the best means of reaching the UN—received some roneographed leaflets.

APPEAL TO THE FRENCH AND BELGIAN RESISTANCE ORGANIZATIONS OF THE '40-'45 WAR

Comrades,

The people of Katanga, both black and white, are at present experiencing what you had to endure during the dark years between 1940 and 1945. We are being unwillingly subjected to the worst Gestapo-like methods on the part of the UN mercenaries:

Arbitrary arrests, searches, identity checks, threats, summary executions, and what have you. . . .

EVERYONE HERE IS HAUNTED BY FEAR

The resistance which you VICTORIOUSLY offered the NAZIS during the last world war has dictated our line of conduct, for we are ready to die for the independence of our Country. Katanga is free and DEMOCRATIC. The troubles are provoked only by the presence of the UN mercenaries.

Comrades, we are issuing a vibrant appeal: DO NOT ALLOW YOURSELVES TO BE CRUSHED UNDERFOOT. Give us moral support and demonstrate in your villages and towns. Protest against our enslavement and murder!

LONG LIVE THE FRENCH, BELGIAN AND KATANGESE RESISTANCE FIGHTERS.
Colonel Alain,
O.C. MIR Clandestine Organization

Another leaflet was drafted in the following terms:

White Katangese,

The UN are proposing to search your houses in order to find out whether you have arms hidden away.

Be on your guard, do not yield!
Maintain complete trust in Katanga.
We shall be victorious because we are stronger.

MIR

The first pamphlet had been drafted by Fonts, who was not very proud of it but he had been pressed for time. The second by Pérohade who, on the contrary, was delighted with it: he had even pinned it up above the bar in his night-club.

The slogans had been painted on the walls by Katangese police, and the pamphlets roneographed in Gelinet's own office at his brewery.

The UN Intelligence services made an investigation and, since it yielded no result, they thought they were faced with a particularly well organized clandestine movement. In the drawing rooms of E'ville it became the smart thing to hint that one belonged to the MIR, as one belonged to the golf club.

The newspapers and press agencies showed an interest in the MIR. An interview was even published with the mysterious Colonel Alain, and a list of persons suspected of collaborating with the enemy. . . .

The disappearance, then the execution, of Albrecht, the hall-porter of the Hotel Leo II, who acted as an informer for the UN, was attributed to the MIR and led to a fresh investigation which once again yielded no result.

Bongo and his killers alone were responsible: Albrecht, who had a weakness for very young African boys—which had earned him the nickname of The Egyptian—was, it seems, lured into the African city, where he then had his throat cut. His body was found near the golf course.

Maley did everything to have Bongo arrested. He sent telegram after telegram to Headquarters in New York. A reply came, which was no reply:

Arrest Bongo but only if he's caught red-handed inciting racial warfare

"What's racial warfare?" Maley asked Siddartha.

For once the Indian showed some sense of humor.

"Why, sir, racial wars are those which the whites wage against colored people; the others are wars of liberation! So in no way can Bongo be accused of racial warfare but only of murder, theft, rape, peculation. . . ."

The managing board of the Union Minière made it known that they would be obliged to evacuate the women and children if the situation grew any worse as a result of the activities of the UN.

This announcement contributed a great deal to the general panic. Arnold Riverton rang up Van der Weyck to ask him what on earth he was up to.

"I've also got my extremists," the managing director replied.

"Could we meet?"

"It's rather tricky just now."

"The MIR is on the watch?"

"Above all, my collaborators are. In fact, for the last few days, they've been paying close attention to everything I do and they find that in these dramatic circumstances playing golf with the American Consul, or even just playing golf, is a provocation."

Van der Weyck was about to say something else but rang off.

A vigilance committee had just been formed at the Union Minière and the man behind it was that young fool Ravetot.

Van der Weyck now realized the mistake he had made in introducing the little group of French mercenaries into Katanga. Through their techniques, which paid no heed to political or economic realities, they were driving Katanga into civil war and perhaps the Union Minière to its downfall.

Justin Pimuriaux had screamed this to him over the telephone three hours before he was bundled on to the plane.

On 9 September President Kimjanga held a press conference and, in his turn, made a great song and dance about a plot.

Maley—he had proof of this but apologized for not yet being able to produce it—was planning to arrest him as well as Bongo, the Minister of the Interior, disarm the Gendarmerie and replace them in E'ville with the National Congolese Army, "the looters, drunkards and violators of Thysville Camp."

The Gurkhas still kept arriving by the plane load: in American Globemasters, which lent Kimjanga's words a certain degree of truth.

On 10 September some demonstrators flung some stones at the windows of the American Consulate, and an hour later at the post office. Fournier, one of Maley's assistants, was violently upbraided by a Belgian police commissioner.

On the morning of 12 September there arrived in Elizabethville a Tunisian by the name of Brahimi, a senior

UN official, assistant to the UN representative in the Congo.

Together with Maley, he forthwith called on President Kimjanga and summoned him to go to Leopoldville on the following day to meet the UN Secretary-General who was due to land there.

This time Kimjanga made no attempt to prevaricate. He curtly refused and referred to the right of nations to settle their own affairs.

Brahimi persisted, pointing out that this time the Secretary-General was determined to put an end to the secession of Katanga and that the President was being given his last chance to come to an honorable agreement with the Central Government of the Congo.

If he refused, the UN were resolved to resort to other methods.

Kimjanga asked Germaine to show "these gentlemen" out. He had not shaken hands with them; he had not asked them to sit down.

As they went off, Fonts's tousled head popped round a door, and Bongo, encountering them in the ante-room, pretended not to see them.

Kimjanga was being kept firmly in hand.

Brahimi then gave Maley five warrants of arrest signed by the Public Prosecutor of Leopoldville and issued against Kimjanga, Bongo, Evariste Kasingo and two other ministers, guilty of "torture and murder."

Though extremely put out by the manner in which he had been received, the elegant Brahimi, a wily diplomatist, advised Maley not to arrest Kimjanga immediately.

"The Secretary-General fervently hopes to avoid all bloodshed. He wishes you to force Kimjanga to capitulate, as on August 28th. It would be a good thing if he broadcast an appeal to the people to keep calm. Then you send him off to Leopoldville, where we'll see what ought to be done with him."

"What if he refuses?"

"Produce the warrant of arrest."

"What if he resists?"

The Tunisian spread his arms out.

"Do as you see fit. . . . Don't forget, however, that the Secretary-General's position is rather difficult these days, in fact extremely difficult."

"Are you giving me the 'go-ahead' signal?"

"You have the warrants of arrest. . . . However . . ."

He made an all-embracing gesture.

321

"If only it could be done quietly and not give rise to unduly lively reactions throughout the world! That shooting on September 3rd . . . embarrassing. . . ."

"It was the French mercenaries."

"Of course. I'm in a perfect position to know the unscrupulous but by no means incapable sort of men they are. Our wretched Secretary-General is due for re-election in a few months. We're all hoping he'll be re-elected. Strange that he should have made himself so unpopular with the Russians and the French as well. He's very anxious not to have the British against him."

"The French are also your enemies . . . Bizerta . . ."

"Let's say former enemies, which is a very different thing. There are some former enmities that in certain respects resemble friendship!"

At six o'clock in the evening Maley summoned General Siddartha.

"Morthor, four o'clock tomorrow morning."

A smile came over the Indian general's face.

Three years earlier Patrick Maley had been a young economics professor at Dublin University.

One fine morning he had felt an urge to escape from this hide-bound conformist world—conformist in that it was anti-conformist on principle—and consort with men who were not all grand ideas and petty spites.

His father, who was connected with a member of the Government by a long-standing bond of friendly hostility, had got him into Foreign Affairs. There were still the same petty spites, complicated by snobbery and self-satisfaction. On the other hand, grand ideas were unknown. There was still no sign of men. Where were they, then?

Maley put himself at the disposal of the UN, hoping that in this vast organization, in which every race rubbed shoulders, he would at last escape from the narrowness of national causes and encounter the men for whom he was looking. No sooner had he arrived at the Glass House in New York than he noticed that the UN officials had all the defects of the university staff as well as all those of the diplomatic corps, not to mention various kinds of national or ethnic touchiness.

But when he had obtained a responsible post in Katanga and at last had soldiers to command and important decisions to take, Maley discovered the drug known as action.

By pressing a button he had launched Morthor, and

322

General Siddartha's impassive countenance had altered. Colonel Degger had heaved a sigh as he fiddled with the buttons on his uniform, and he himself had ceased to be bogged down in all sorts of difficulties and worries. He had taken action. He had changed the world.

Maley drove round to the American Consul, Arnold Riverton, who had invited him to dinner.

"There'll just be the three of us, you, my daughter and myself, behind our broken windows."

Riverton was waiting for him, glass in hand; he was alone and slightly tipsy.

"Well, Patrick, how's everything going?" he asked.

Maley helped himself to a whisky and made the ice tinkle in his glass.

"It's coming to a show-down, my dear Arnold. And the sooner the better. We're in a false position, between intervention and non-intervention. We refuse to recognize the secession of Katanga, while addressing Kimjanga as 'President' and Bongo as 'Your Excellency.' We have nothing substantial against us except this handful of mercenaries. Law and order must be re-established, and very rapidly. . . ."

"What law and order?" Riverton asked. "The law and order of Leopoldville? That's disorder more than anything else! Well, it's disorder we've chosen. Here's yet another country, Katanga, where we're going to make ourselves hated!

"We've been backing the wrong horse all over the world . . . the 'Ugly Americans'. . . . Sometimes it's our own fault. . . . But more often it's the fault of history, which gives us, for the time being, the leadership of half the world.

"There were some Belgians among the Africans when they broke our windows. Is the multi-racial community going to be created by blaming us for everything? When the British and French governed the world, how easy it was to accuse them of unforgivable faults! So you reckon, my dear Patrick, that you have nothing against you but this handful of mercenaries? You've caught a few of them, the rest are in hiding."

"I don't give a damn about those pistol-toting bearded cowboy types that we bundled into our trucks! It's Colonel la Roncière I'm after, and that little gangster Fonts. . . ."

Joan came in just as Maley, who was striding up and down, exclaimed:

"They're murderers!"

Joan, with her eyes sparkling and her little nose tilted under its sprinkling of freckles, asked:

"Who are murderers, Patrick?"

"I'm talking about la Roncière and your little pal Thomas Fonts!"

"It's amazing the number of murderers there are! Everyone calls you a murderer as well! Even the American papers, yet I know you're not a murderer!"

"It's disgusting!"

"Meddling in other people's business, playing politics in other people's countries, is always a bit disgusting."

"You're not being indoctrinated by any chance, Joan?"

"I'm merely trying to preserve a little sanity in this mad-house. I'm very hungry; shall we go in to dinner?"

"Where have you been this evening?" Riverton asked her.

"I was at Jenny's. . . ."

She had just been with Thomas Fonts. Once again he had kissed her in the car . . . with a great deal of feeling. Joan wanted him to be adrift, and so persuaded herself that he was. Soon she would be the mooring-post to which he would fasten. Then, since men are so undecided, she would have to take a number of decisions for him and, since men are so lazy, solve a number of problems for him as well.

The mention of Jenny's name, the tormenting memory of her, had made Maley still more aggressive. Jenny had gone over to the enemy, and so had Joan, not from conviction but from absurd romanticism; women preferred outlaws to policemen, and he, the son of a Sinn Feiner, now found himself on the side of the police.

"What does Jenny think of it all?" he asked in a choking voice.

"Well, you know, her husband's English and I don't fancy the English agree with what you're doing. She herself is Rhodesian, and the Rhodesians agree still less!"

Since Maley was beginning to lose his temper, she tried to be even more offensive.

"She also feels a certain . . . how shall I put it? . . . affection . . . no, rather attraction and admiration . . . for Colonel la Roncière."

"Does she think he came to defend Rhodesia at Elizabethville? No, only to earn his pay, which must be substantial, indulge in a little racketeering—they all do—and try out one of his foul experiments on human material: it's called psychological warfare, Joan!"

"That's a rather hasty judgment, don't you think?"

"In my opinion, Thomas Fonts is even worse; he doesn't give a damn about Africa or Algeria, or even perhaps about his pay. That forty-year-old juvenile is bored. At the age of twenty he must have read one or two adventure stories: Malraux or Lawrence. Then he tried to build himself up, because he resented being so short. . . .

"The result, as you know, is three thousand massacred on the Lukuga River, women and children shot dead in the streets of Elizabethville . . . and a hotel hall-porter found yesterday with his throat cut by a pseudo-resistance movement called the MIR!"

"That's not true!"

"Go and ask him himself . . . because maybe you know where he is, even though my services and I don't?"

Joan flung her napkin down on the table.

"I'll go straight away. If you've lied to me, Patrick, I'll never forgive you. If Fonts has lied to me, I swear I'll make him pay for it!"

"Stay where you are," said Arnold Riverton. "This is no time to wander about the streets with your red hair proclaiming to all and sundry; 'I'm an American'!"

"Daddy, to me this is a serious business, *my business,* just as it's your business to put an end to Katanga!"

She went out, slamming the door behind her.

Maley had a lump in his throat. He apologized.

"I'm sorry, Arnold, I'm rather on edge . . . I'm extremely fond of Joan, and that fellow Fonts . . ."

"I'm not happy either to know that she sees that boy, especially in the present circumstances. But aren't you going a little too far? Your feelings are running away with you. . . ."

"Jenny has nothing to do with it!"

"You're as excitable as my daughter! I was referring to your political feelings; politics, so they keep telling me in the Department, should be divorced from feelings!"

Riverton produced a photograph from his wallet and handed it to Maley.

"Her name was Sunnarti, she was an Indonesian girl. For her, I almost ruined my career and my life . . . and today I can't think why!"

As he left, Maley said to him:

"Stay indoors tomorrow morning and stop your daughter going out. . . . After that, you'll see, everything will be much simpler."

"Good luck, Patrick!"

Joan went to the Hotel Leo II and rang up the number Fonts had given her.

"Hello, Thomas, are you at home? I must see you at once! No, I don't want to be seen in a dump like the Mitsouko and play 'the mercenary's lady,' as your friend Dorat puts it. Not at Musaille's either. At your place, why not? . . . Only I don't know where you live . . . where your hide-out, as you call it, is. It's very important, I tell you. . . . The big Société Générale building behind the post office, sixth floor, on the left. I'll be there in five minutes."

Joan rang the door bell. Thomas Fonts came and let her in. He was in shirt sleeves and had a book in his hand. As she glanced at the book he showed her the title: *Bantu Philosophy* by R. P. Placide, Tempels.

"You see my little quail, though you're convinced I spend every night firing pistols or tumbling girls, I'm working. What's wrong, Joan?"

Fonts seemed to be amused. . . . His eyes were sparkling, which exasperated the young girl. She had sworn to keep calm, however.

She sank back in an armchair and took a cigarette from a half-torn packet, but her lighter would not work, which put her in a worse mood than ever.

Fonts gave her a light.

"Thomas, I'm not in the habit of calling on boys at this time of night."

"It's a good habit, though!"

"I've no time for joking. I want to ask you three questions. Were you responsible for the River Lukuga massacre? Did you provoke the shooting in the Avenue de Saio? Are you this Colonel Alain who's directing the MIR and who had that poor Swiss hall-porter murdered?"

"How am I to answer these questions?"

"By a Yes or a No."

"I can't answer Yes or No, it's much too simple!"

"So you're guilty: Maley was right!"

Fonts's irony had suddenly given way to the sort of anger which is called white because it draws all the blood from a man's face.

"Joan, I don't owe you anything and I haven't promised you anything. If you think I'm a murderer and it shocks you, what are you doing here? I have no account to render to you. . . . I'm neither your lover nor your husband. And even if I were, I still wouldn't render accounts to you! In my country that's how it is!

"I'm fighting my war, Maley and your father are fighting theirs on the other side, and it's no less nasty than mine. You and I meet on neutral territory, so we don't talk about it.

"If you find this situation distasteful . . . take sides, assume a position, be as idiotic as all those women who are so anxious to meddle in what doesn't concern them. . . . That's the American style, I believe!"

Joan was choking with indignation. She leaped to her feet:

"I forbid you . . ."

"What, my little quail? To touch the American flag?"

"You're just a filthy brute, a poor unbalanced creature, a mental cripple. . . ."

"This doesn't work with me, my little quail: pity, womanly excuses for a man who's just a sick child. . . . No. It's like fashionable doctors, they say to a chap who has caught cold that he's seriously ill, that it's psychosomatic, that he ought to put himself in the hands of his physician. When the physician has got hold of him and anaesthetized him good and proper, he pinches his wallet. Women, however, want the fellow's skin!"

"You're absolutely crazy. To you the world is populated by female praying mantises, gangsters and crooked doctors. My poor Thomas, what men, what women have you come across in your life? I know men who live at peace with their consciences, who love their wives. . . ."

"Yes, but that sort are a bloody bore, my little quail, aren't they?"

Suddenly he addressed her by the familiar *tu*.

"Look, Joan, when a girl comes and raves at a man, anyway in France, it means she's either dotty or wants to go to bed with him."

"Oh!"

A sob rose to her throat and she burst into tears, tears punctuated by little hiccoughs which resembled the yapping of a dog.

"To you a woman is merely someone to sleep with, you can't imagine that there could be . . . something else!"

Joan had not even realized that she too was addressing him as *tu*.

All Fonts's anger had evaporated. He was now merely a big oaf of a man, embarrassed, not knowing what to do, full of tenderness and pity.

He took Joan by the shoulder and led her gently to the sofa.

"Calm down and have a drink, I beseech you. I'm going to drive you home."

As she dabbed at her nose with a ridiculous little handkerchief, Joan was made aware of the true weapon of all women: it was tears and not anger or indignation.

Though completely sincere at first, she now began to exploit it; it was so new to her . . . so easy and effective. Men's pride withstood blows, a few tears melted it away.

Still sobbing, but with a slight effort, she dipped her lips into the glass of whisky she held in both hands. Fonts had sat down at her feet. This time the child must not escape her, as he had in Spåin!

She put down her glass and stroked his hair, that thick rebellious curly mop.

He came closer to her, seized her by the shoulder again and drew her towards him.

It was Thomas who suggested:

"Let's remain on neutral territory a little longer!"

There was no trace of irony in his voice; it was almost a prayer. The child would not scamper off.

Thomas stroked the back of her neck, kissed her cheeks which were salty with tears, then her lips which were trembling. With a kick he sent the little bedside lamp flying.

Joan now realized she had always been waiting for this moment.

She never knew how she got into bed, how she found herself lying naked next to Thomas, barely covered in a sheet drenched with sweat.

When he had got up quite shamelessly to have a shower, a lean, hard figure with a pungent smell, she had not been shocked by what she had previously regarded as something extremely shocking.

For the miracle had happened: she had heard herself moaning and groaning, "dying of pleasure," for pleasure and annihilation were closely intermingled. She had discovered that a man's body could belong to her as though it was part of herself.

When Thomas withdrew from her, she had felt none of the disgust that made her flee from Davis on any pretext. She went on enjoying Fonts's smell and sweat and even the part of him which people called shameful. Drowsy and wonderfully relaxed, dismissing every problem from her mind, forgetting that he had not answered her questions, she said to herself:

"And to think I could have missed . . . this communion

of bodies. Here I am indulging in all the clichés from a five-cent love-story, the communion of bodies without which the other cannot exist. . . . What has Thomas got that is so different from the others . . . and why have I been so different?"

He was more adept at making love, he was attentive, but this was merely technique and did not explain that deep shameless inordinate joy that had welled up in her.

Thomas had told her a strange story. He was eighteen, it was the end of the Spanish Civil War. Five hundred thousand refugees, pursued by the *requetes,* were pouring out of Catalonia. Proud women and children in rags, men at their last gasp and covered in dust, throwing their arms away in the ditches.

Thomas had been on the frontier with his father to meet some relatives so that they should not be dispatched to the concentration camps at Argelès and elsewhere.

One old Spaniard, before entering France, had picked up a handful of earth, and it was with his fist clenched round this clod of earth that he crossed the frontier. A helmeted militiaman with a brutish face had chuckled as he made him drop this clod with a blow from his rifle-butt, and all the other militiamen had laughed heartily.

His father had prevented Thomas from flinging himself on the brute, and ever since that day the boy had felt a deep and lasting hatred for everything that represented law and order and that was symbolized by this militiaman, a hatred from which he had never recovered.

"But," he said, as he stroked her temple, "it's now my pals who are responsible for law and order in France; I can't get used to it. Disorder suited them so much better!"

Then he had taken possession of her once more, but why say it was he who took possession of her? She also took possession of him, and the miracle had begun all over again.

Just as Fonts had dispelled the image of the little Spanish boy scampering away, so she would dispel the image of the militiaman making the old refugee drop his handful of earth.

Then they would be happy. They would leave Katanga together, tomorrow, as soon as possible. . . . They would get married, because this made life so much simpler. Liberated from his hatred of law and order, Fonts would accept from his friends, who were responsible for law and order in Fance, an honorable post. He would merely have to tell them:

329

"I've forgotten the militiaman on the Spanish frontier; the proof is I've married a red-headed girl whose father is the American Consul."

Fonts lay asleep, with his hand near his head. She brushed it with a kiss, and, happy, satiated, vanquished and victorious at one and the same time, drifted into a deep sleep as warm and calm as a tropical lagoon.

8. Morthor

On 13 September, at four o'clock in the morning, a half-company of Gurkhas surrounded the main post office.

Fonts was roused from his sleep by the sound of hob-nailed boots, the clatter of rifle-butts and mess tins, against a background noise of muffled orders, running footsteps, roaring engines and squealing brakes.

To him these were familiar sounds, the sounds of troops preparing for a round-up in a big town. During the Resistance, on two or three occasions, he had escaped from this sort of round-up; in Indo-China and Algeria it was he himself who organized them.

He entertained no illusions as to the effectiveness of such operations; they were always too slow, too noisy, and, like an old fishing-net, left too many gaps.

What were they after tonight?

Was he in the net or outside it, fish or fisherman?

He opened his eyes; a girl with red hair lay asleep by his side, like all girls, selfishly withdrawn into herself, with her nose buried in the pillow and one fist clenched outside the sheet. The girl was Joan. He had just spent some extremely pleasant hours with her. Pleasure had been mingled with tenderness and even with a certain fantasy. But there was this clenched fist of hers. What was it holding?

And what about this noise of hob-nailed boots and rifle-butts? He realized all of a sudden that Maley had decided to take action, that his troops were investing the post office while other troops were simultaneously occupying all the strategic points in Elizabethville: Kimjanga's residence, the radio station, the railway underpass.

Fonts leaped out of bed, stood under the icy shower for three minutes, then woke Joan.

The young girl stretched as she thrust back the sheets. She was like some gorgeous plant, a red-tinted liana, with her flat stomach, long tapering legs and high-poised breasts. Joan smelt of pepper and fire. Her teeth were sparkling, and her lips full and shiny.

The rifle-butts clattered on the pavement, Joan's teeth clattered against his.

"You have an odd way of waking women," she said in a husky voice. "What time is it? What will my father say?"

She fumbled for the switch, but Fonts grasped her hands.

"Wait!"

A single shot had just rung out in the darkness, then a whole burst.

Joan felt it was no longer the same body crushed against hers; it was hard and tense. Her lover's rough hand was pummelling her own. And what were these shots? What was going on?

An armored car had taken up a position opposite the big doors of the post office. Captain Dokkal with a detachment of Gurkhas was creeping forward under cover of an arcaded gallery. General Siddartha had entrusted him with the task of seizing the building. He was full of gratitude towards his commanding officer who had supported him against the whites, the UN whites and all the others.

When Colonel Degger had questioned him, Siddartha had insisted on being present. In the mess he had deliberately seated him by his side.

General Siddartha was a gentleman under whose orders it was an honor to serve.

The Gurkhas, like all good soldiers, like the Dogras or the Sikhs, knew their job. No need to waste time making sure that orders were carried out. Dokkal was proud of commanding such men. The darkness was fading from the sky.

Two Katangese soldiers, rifles in hand, appeared in the open space in front of the post office. Dokkal noticed they were wearing that ridiculous camouflage uniform for which the French had set the fashion, and berets: not blue, but scarlet berets.

He motioned to the interpreter near him and told him twice over what he should say so as to make no mistake.

The latter put his megaphone to his lips and began in Swahili:

"Katangese soldiers, the UN have no hostile intentions towards you. We are your friends. Do not fire. We have not come to fight. Tell your officer to come and see me."

At the same time Dokkal and the interpreter stepped aside, revealing two Gurkhas lying behind their machine-gun.

Three other Katangese, in the same uniform, had joined the first two. One of them spoke. He may have been an officer or an NCO or just the spokesman of the gang.

"If you are friends, why have you come with armored cars and rifles? You want to seize our arms. But we shan't let you. We are para-commandos, we know how to fight."

Dokkal stepped forward into the open, followed by the interpreter with his megaphone under his arm.

"Tell them to send their leader to me!"

The interpreter translated:

"The UN commander says that he wishes you no harm. He merely wants a palaver between chiefs so as to reach some agreement."

On the Katangese side there was a lot of shouting and gesticulating.

Dokkal lost his patience. His orders were to be conciliating but firm, to seize the post office, get the job over quickly and, if necessary, resort to force!

"You'll see," Siddartha had told him, "the Katangese will be caught unawares and they'll climb down. . . . But if they start any nonsense, give them what for! They'll scatter like a flight of starlings!"

The Indian captain took the interpreter by the arm and pointed with his swagger-stick at the Katangese.

"Tell them I have orders and must occupy the post office. I want them to come out with their rifles slung. If they resist, I shall be forced to open fire."

The interpreter began to translate.

One of the Katangese interrupted him.

"That fellow talks while brandishing his lash like a white man who wants to whip us . . . us, the para-commandos!"

In a fit of excitement one of his comrades put his Fal to his shoulder and fired a single shot, then a burst. Hit in the chest and the head, Captain Dokkal fell, while the interpreter took to his heels, flinging away his megaphone.

Captain Dokkal reflected that he had shown exemplary conduct, even a British Guards officer could have found no cause for complaint in his attitude.

The machine-gun behind him opened fire in bursts of four or five rounds, well distributed according to regulations. The Gurkhas were really fine soldiers. Dokkal grasped his stick more firmly, then dropped it.

Caught in this murderous fire, the para-commandos began to fall like ninepins.

The armored car fired a couple of shells at the gates of the post office. A machine-gun loosed off a long burst. The Katangese returned the fire from the openings of the doors and windows. Giving a loud yell, the Gurkhas launched into the attack. The first hand-grenades exploded.

It was ten minutes past four.

Fonts had rushed to the window, followed by Joan who had wrapped the sheet round her. She was shivering with cold and fright.

"The fun and games are starting," said Fonts.

He listened carefully to the rifle shots and machine-gun bursts.

"Maley hasn't won yet. The Katangese are digging their heels in."

"Maley, Kimjanga, the UN and Katanga must fight it out between themselves, Thomas. It's none of your business!"

As though he had not heard her, Fonts walked over to the telephone and rang up the Presidency, which was engaged, then Gelinet.

"Who the devil is it, ringing me up at this unearthly hour?" the Belgian bellowed furiously.

"Fonts. Fighting has broken out at the main post office!"

"What's that you say? Have you been tanking up at the Mitsouko again?"

"The para-commandos and Gurkhas are knocking each other about! There's heavy firing!"

Fonts's voice was emphatic.

"For the moment you and your boys keep out of it, but tell them what has happened. They are to assemble at your place, but see that they arrive one by one, concealing their weapons, so as not to get nabbed by the UN patrols."

"All right, what next?"

"Warn Pérohade. . . . Tell him to wake Dorat. Dorat will notify all the other journalists. . . . That's a natural reaction in his profession. What time is it?"

"You still have no watch? A quarter past four."

Fonts dialed another number but Joan, who had come up to him, placed her hand on the receiver.

"I told you it's no business of yours."

334

Fonts thrust her hand aside and got through to Mus-aille. His voice was vibrating with excitement.

"You bloody Auvergnat doormouse, you were with a tart again. Fighting has just broken out . . . yes, at the post office. You must notify Paris and Brazzaville straight away. You have your contacts. Also wake Ligget . . . Sal-isbury must be informed at once!

"No, it hasn't got off to such a bad start. It looks as if Kreis is doing a good job with his para-commandos: they're standing their ground! You're surprised? So am I!"

He hastily donned trousers and shirt and started lacing up his shoes.

Joan stood watching him; the sheet she had wrapped round her had just fallen off.

Fonts raised his head and saw she was furious.

"What's wrong with you, my little quail?"

"Where are you going, Thomas?"

"I'm going to have a look round. Can't you hear? The firing's heavier and heavier. Listen! The para-commandos are using defensive grenades. The noise is sharper, there's more of a hissing sound than with ordinary grenades. . . . Because of the cast-iron fragments, you see. . . . So the Gurkhas have come to grips. They're trying to storm the post office, and the others are tossing grenades at them from the windows."

"Thomas, you stay here with me. . . . When all this din has died down a bit, we'll leave together. . . . We'll take the first plane for Europe. . . ."

Fonts was not listening to her.

"I say, the armored car gun is opening up again. The Gurkhas are being driven back!"

He took a revolver from a drawer, tucked it into his waistband with the barrel inside his trousers and seized Joan by the shoulders.

"You wait for me in this room without poking your nose out of the window. I'll give you a ring presently and come and fetch you. All right?"

Joan thrust him away.

"No! If you leave now, I'll never see you again. . . . Do you hear?"

"What's come over you? How complicated women are!"

"Don't you care about me at all or are you completely thoughtless? It needs only a few pistol shots for you to forget what has just happened!"

"What has just happened? Now listen, I have no time. . . . We'll discuss it later! My pals are being killed!"

"Your pals! A lot of bearded hooligans in fancy dress! Do they need you?"

Then she cried out:

"What about me? You spend the whole night telling me you can't live without me . . . and three hours later you're prepared to desert me in the middle of a riot . . . after 'having your fling.' Isn't that what you call it? Who the hell do you take me for?"

"Listen, my little quail, you're becoming a bore! I've got other things to do this morning than deal with your little whims! There'll be all the time in the world later on."

"Go and save Katanga, all on your own! Go and play at cowboys. . . . How ridiculous you are! It may impress the sort of girls you usually consort with, tarts, barmaids from the Mitsouko."

"They're good in bed and don't bother the clients afterwards! Some women could take them as a model."

"Get out of here, you dirty little killer! . . . Get out of here at once. . . ."

"So long. . . ."

Fonts lit a cigarette, took one puff and disappeared, slamming the door behind him.

Joan flung herself on the bed, sobbing with rage and clawing the sheets.

"Just like a bad film," she said to herself. . . . "All the essential ingredients, the rumpled sheets, the revolver, the cigarette . . . I, Joan Riverton, have just behaved like a gangster's moll! All that was missing was a slap in the face. It's not true; I'm Joan Riverton, a college graduate. . . . Before taking me out, boys used to send me orchids, even if they had to live on hot-dogs for the rest of the month!

"This dirty little tyke pulls on his trousers and, by way of thanks, says: 'You're a bore!' It's unbelievable. . . . But where have I read that? What's the point of putting on this act for me? 'My pals are being killed.' These little Latin men are too ridiculous! I understand now why they're always having revolutions in South America: just to pull on their trousers and impress women."

At the Villa des Roches Maley stood in front of General Siddartha, with his hands crossed behind his back, trying to keep calm. They had distinctly heard the two gun-shots.

The general replaced the receiver.

"It's at the post office, sir. A detachment of para-

336

commandos are digging their heels in there. The para-commandos are the best troops they've got. . . . But there's scarcely a company of them, a hundred and fifty men at the most."

He snapped his fingers.

"In an hour's time the Gurkhas will have liquidated them, together with Kimjanga and his gang. When day breaks, the secession of Katanga will be at an end. We're finishing the way we should have begun. Captain Dokkal has been killed. . . ."

"I'm sorry."

"A poor little Indian captain with very dark skin. What does it matter, eh?"

In a fury Maley swung round on his heels to face Siddartha, who was still sitting by the telephone.

"What's happening in the other sectors?"

"The operation is progressing according to plan. It's now four-forty. The Swedes, according to your instructions, must have invested the Presidency, Bongo's villa and the residence of the three other ministers. They have orders to arrest Bongo and the three ministers at five o'clock. My Gurkhas are at the radio station. The Irish at the Sûreté. All we need do is wait." .

"It's a slow business!"

"I hope this time you won't let Kimjanga slip through our fingers as you did after Rumpunch!" .

"This time I'll strike hard and fast. I'm going to make Kimjanga announce on the radio that the secession of Katanga has come to an end, and an hour later I'll bundle him on to the plane for Leopoldville."

"It may not be as easy as you think!"

"Once we've liquidated those para-commandos, who are probably led by mercenaries, the rest of the army will desert Kimjanga. The gendarmes have had a bellyful of speeches, parades and training camps. What they want is their pay, enough beer and an easy time, and above all no fighting!

"Colonel Degger has sounded them out and will tell you the same thing. As far as Kimjanga is concerned, it couldn't be simpler: he has no one left on whom he can rely, the Belgian instructors have gone back to Belgium, the mercenaries are dispersed, and he himself is trembling with fright!"

"He's still more frightened of going to Leopoldville."

"I'll give him an assurance that he'll be under UN protection . . . and furthermore, that he'll retain his post as head of the provincial Government!"

"You think he'll be able to retain it?"

"That's for Leopoldville to decide. I'm merely making a suggestion . . . that's all. . . ."

"But you'll promise him this?"

"How many times has he made promises to me which he hasn't kept?"

At four-forty President Kimjanga rang up. Siddartha handed the receiver to Maley.

"What on earth's going on?" the President inquired.

In an official tone, which did nothing to conceal his jubilation, Maley replied:

"The UN are taking action. The post office and radio station are occupied. Bongo and three of your ministers have been arrested. . . . Your residence is surrounded."

"I hear there have been some casualties?"

"Possibly. I'm sorry."

"The UN are committing a crime in attacking a defenseless people, and for no reason."

A conciliating, almost tearful note crept into his voice.

"Cease fire and let's examine the situation together: I've always been ready to negotiate!"

"Monsieur le Président, the days of prevarication are over. This time the United Nations are determined to see it through to the end. I must ask you to order the few troops still fighting to lay down their arms. Otherwise they'll be wiped out! Then you will deliver a speech on the radio, officially announcing the end of the secession of Katanga. In three hours' time you'll take the plane for Leopoldville and start negotiations with the Central Government."

"I don't want to go to Leo: those people there will kill me!"

"If you accept our conditions, I can assure you your safety will be guaranteed by our troops. The UN Secretary-General will be in Leopoldville in a few hours. He's expecting you. I want an immediate answer: Yes or No?"

On the other end of the line Maley heard the heavy breathing of the President, a stag at bay, a vicious and crafty stag who was not weeping but desperately seeking a means of escape.

"Well, what have you to say, Monsieur le Président? General Siddartha is here with me; he's waiting for my orders."

"Get it over!" Siddartha growled. "Finish him off!"

"All right, then! The operation will go on."

"Wait, Monsieur le Haut Représentant, I accept your conditions."

Maley was exultant.

"I knew you were reasonable, Monsieur le Président. For your own safety, I must ask you to spend the next few hours at my headquarters. I'm sending you a vehicle with two armored cars. Give orders for the cease-fire at once."

"I have your word of honor. . . . You guarantee my personal safety?"

Maley put his hand over the mouthpiece and turned to Siddartha.

"He has climbed down completely: total surrender!"

He withdrew his hand.

"I give you my word, Monsieur le Président!"

No sooner had the UN representative hung up than General Siddartha, in measured tones, gave his orders to an Indian major who had just come in.

"Take two bath-tubs and my personal car. Go and fetch Kimjanga. Take care when you reach the Presidency; the place is surrounded by the Swedes. Don't get yourself shot up like the last time. Bring Kimjanga back here at the double. Don't argue with him. If necessary, treat him rough. I want him back here in half an hour."

Maley protested:

"Don't do that. There's really no point!"

"Instead of a major, I should have sent a sergeant for him," said Siddartha. "That's all he's worth."

At five o'clock the battle was still raging at the post office. Bongo had disappeared, and so had two of the other ministers. Evariste Kasingo alone was under lock and key. He protested with great vehemence and invoked the League of the Rights of Man. He was not aware that it did not apply to him.

A great commotion was reported, however, at Massart Camp, which was occupied by the Katangese Gendarmerie.

At five-fifteen the two bath-tubs and General Siddartha's car came back without Kimjanga.

"What's going on?" yelled Siddartha, who forthwith lost his habitual composure.

In Hindi he cursed the major, who trembled like a leaf in the October breeze and stammered:

"When we reached the Presidency, we were fired upon."

"The Swedes?"

"There were no Swedes round the building, only the presidential guard."

"What happened then?"

"We returned their fire with a few machine-gun bursts. The guard, fifteen strong, surrendered at once. But no President. We searched the whole place!"

"Go on."

"A servant told us he had seen Kimjanga rushing off in a car belonging to a European. He was in pajamas and bedroom slippers, with an overcoat thrown over his shoulders."

The major waited and, since he was asked no further question, saluted and marched out.

Maley had gone white in the face. He seized the back of a chair and very slowly, emphasizing each word, declared:

"General, Operation Morthor was supposed to start by the sealing off of the Presidency; that was the most important point. You told me the Presidency was surrounded: the Swedes aren't there and Kimjanga has escaped in his pajamas!"

He burst out:

"What the devil do you think you're doing?"

Siddartha's face was ashen.

"Yesterday evening I issued my instructions in writing, in a sealed envelope, to Colonel Oste, the commander of the Swedish battalion. As an additional precaution, the message was coded and there was no other message with it. The Swedish battalion was supposed to be in position at four in the morning, before the post office was attacked."

"What do you think has happened?"

"Perhaps Colonel Oste did not approve of our plan!"

"What!"

"Sir, as you must know, Colonel Oste, like many other European UN officers, does not have a very clear-cut attitude to this business. Colonel Oste has given evidence of lack of discipline on several occasions. He has never concealed his sympathies for some of our most relentless opponents. You know he often used to see that Frenchman, Colonel la Roncière. They got to know each other on a Staff College course."

"To protect yourself, Siddartha, you dare to insinuate . . ."

"I'm not insinuating anything, I'm stating facts. Ask Colonel Degger! Admittedly, he's also very badly informed and secretly shares Colonel Oste's sympathies!"

340

"Go on!"

"Colonel Oste, like several other officers . . . Irish officers . . . has always struck me as being closer to Kimjanga's white mercenaries than to his UN Indian allies. I warned you about this. You didn't believe me. This war should have been fought by colored men. Once again the whites have shown a tendency to stick together!"

"Don't let's waste time on palavering. We'll settle our accounts later. For the moment the main thing is to catch Kimjanga. If he gets away, we're done for. All this business will be held against me, and against you as well."

"Catch Kimjanga! He's already safe in Rhodesia. Kipushi's only twenty miles from E'ville. It takes no more than half an hour to get there!"

"Find Kimjanga for me and summon Colonel Oste at once." *

At five o'clock in the morning Thomas Fonts drove into the African city at the wheel of Monsieur Perisson's car. Grumpy and unshaven, President Kimjanga sat beside him biting his lips.

"The best jobs," Thomas reflected, "are always due to chance!"

He was unable to get over his luck.

On parting from Joan to see what was happening, he had taken the precaution of leaving the building by way of the garage. There was heavy firing in the Place de l'Etoile.

Straight away he had wondered what on earth was happening at the Presidency, which was bound to be surrounded by a cordon of troops.

Fonts crept along the arcades skirting the Hotel Leo II, then crossed the Avenue de l'Etoile at the double, in a half-crouched position, expecting at any moment to receive a machine-gun burst. But the blue helmets seemed interested only in the para-commandos at the post office. Leaping from garden to garden, he reached the wall behind the park of the Presidency.

---

* Author's note: Strange though it may seem, two years after these incidents, the truth about this business is still not known.

Mr. O'Brien, then UN Representative at Elizabethville, admits in his book *To Katanga and Back* that he still does not know why President Tshombe's residence, in spite of specific orders, was not surrounded by the blue helmets on the morning of 13 September. However, Mr. O'Brien points out certain differences of opinion between Katangese Military Headquarters, under the command of the Indian General Raja, and Force Katanga B commanded by the Swedish Colonel Waërn.

The helmeted head of a Katangese soldier appeared on the other side.

"Where's the President?" Fonts asked him.

"President asleep. And you, what are you doing?"

Fonts, without pursuing the matter any further, made his way round the wall, still at the double, and eventually reached the guard post manned by a score of men wearing their caps askew and brandishing their arms.

"The UN are going to attack," said one of them.

"They want to kill our President. Where are the grenades?"

Fonts showed his pass, in which no one was interested, went through the deserted building and, taking four steps at a time, raced up to the first floor where Kimjanga had his quarters.

"Something amazing has happened," he reflected, ". . . a gap in the net exactly where the meshes should have been closest. My God, what an opportunity!"

He pushed open the door of the President's apartment: Kimjanga had just put down the telephone. Prostrated and gray with fear, wearing pink silk pajamas revealing his powerful torso, he had the innocent eyes of a child whom the whole world was taking pleasure in persecuting.

"What's wrong, Monsieur le Président?" Fonts inquired.

"All is lost, my dear friend! The UN are attacking everywhere. They're massacring my soldiers and I'm a prisoner in the Presidency!"

"Whose prisoner?"

"The UN's of course! The blue helmets are surrounding the government building, and Maley is sending an escort to fetch me. . . . Then he's sending me off to Leopoldville."

"How long ago did Maley ring up?"

"Just before you came in."

Fonts realized there was nothing but a spineless puppet before him: all Kimjanga wanted was to surrender.

He was not the first of this kind he had seen. Rare are the men who, wielding the reins of power, enjoying all the advantages that go with it, accustomed to having a swarming mass of officials and courtesans round them, do not collapse when they suddenly find themselves alone.

Fonts thought very fast.

"I've really got a winning hand. Why? We'll see later. When you play poker you don't ask yourself why you've been dealt four aces. You follow it up. . . ."

"Old Kimjanga's utterly demoralized. He really takes

the cake, this fellow! But I've got to get him out of here at once, pink pajamas and all.

"I have five minutes at the most, and he doesn't look as if he'll ever budge. How can I put some life into him? Say something . . . and, if that doesn't work, give him a good kick in the backside! Can't miss a chance like this. I'd never forgive myself for the rest of my life!"

"Nothing is lost, Monsieur le Président. The government building is not surrounded!"

"Eh?"

"But it will be in five minutes. Your troops are resisting magnificently. I've just come from the post office. You can't abandon the struggle when your soldiers are being killed!"

"What do I care? Maybe at Leopoldville my friend Kasavubu . . ."

"Kasavubu will have you bumped off . . . just as you did Lumumba!"

"It wasn't me, I didn't want . . ."

"Personally, I don't give a damn about Lumumba. There's only one thing that interests me: in four minutes we've got to be out of this building!

"I'll take you to the African city; you'll be safe there. Afterwards we'll see!"

"Let me think it over."

"No time for that!"

Fonts pulled him to his feet.

"We must be off at once."

"What about my clothes?"

Fonts went into the adjoining room and found a plastic raincoat, which he threw over Kimjanga's shoulders.

"Are you ready?"

"What about my shoes?"

"Let's get going!"

Tugging him by the arm, Fonts hauled him down the stairs. Kimjanga kept dragging behind. He had had enough of all these adventures; Maley had given him his word of honor that his life was not in danger and that he could even retain his appointment!

He, who never kept his word—giving one's word of honor is merely a method of embarking on a palaver—did not for a moment imagine, it seemed, that a UN representative, a white man, could show the same duplicity as himself.

This little dark man, on the other hand, was dragging

343

him into a painful adventure which might even be, indeed was sure to be, dangerous!

He tried to resist and stopped at the foot of the stairs, hanging on to the banisters:

"Let me go, it's no good. Your Colonel la Roncière promised me the UN wouldn't attack! But what are they doing at the moment? It's always the same with you white men! If it hadn't been for you, I might have come to some agreement with Leopoldville. Between Bantus, we always manage to settle our problems peacefully!"

Fonts fingered his revolver.

"Shall I knock him on the head or not? But if I knock him on the head I'll have to carry him: over fourteen stone of flabby flesh. And if a sentry saw me I'd be in for it! To lose all, because of Bantu stupidity!"

A burst was fired through the railings. Fonts saw his last chance.

"Here come the Gurkhas! They're going to kill you on the spot."

Kimjanga took fright, let go of the banisters and recovered the use of his legs. He followed Fonts as he raced across the park, and did not even need his help to clamber over the wall which was a good six feet high.

Awakened by the bursts of automatic weapons, Monsieur Perisson, the chief accountant of Premiot-Garnier & Co., hardware and chemical products, watched from his open window as these two men scrambled like thieves over the wall of the Presidency.

One of them was a black in pajamas, the other an unshaven white man who shouted to him as he jumped down:

"Is that your car outside the house?"

"Yes. Why? What's going on?"

"Chuck me the keys!"

"Are you off your head?"

Fonts climbed over the railings of the villa, drew his revolver and pointed it at Monsieur Perisson.

"The keys, or I shoot!"

"Yes," Monsieur Perisson reflected, "they're thieves who have tried to break into the Presidency." But he was more anxious to save his life than his car, which in any case belonged to his firm. He threw down the bunch of keys.

Perisson saw the fellow who had threatened him seize the African in pink pajamas by the arm, bundle him into the car and drive off at full speed.

It was not theft but kidnapping. . . . In these troubled

times it was wiser to keep out of this sort of thing. Perisson renounced his first idea, which was to call the police. Later on he would drop in at the station to report the theft of his car. Meanwhile he went back to bed.

Steering with one hand, Fonts placed the other on the President's knee.

"We're saved, we're entering the African city. You're out of danger. Where shall we go?"

"I don't know."

"Why not to Bongo's? I know the shack . . . maybe we'll hear some news."

"I also have a shack, as you call it. Turn right here . . . now left. There it is."

An old servant, who had to be awakened by kicking on the door, came and let them in.

President Kimjanga's shack was a modest house, slightly larger perhaps than Bongo's and equipped with a telephone.

On the ground floor, in the main room, stood a huge frigidaire. Kimjanga went straight over and opened it. It was chock-a-block with Simba beer. The President handed a bottle to Fonts and took one himself.

On the wall were some photographs of Kimjanga and a few cheap lithographs: Greuze's *Broken Jug* and *Sunset on the Bay of Naples.*

The armchairs were modern, made of tubular steel and garishly colored plastic. The table was made of cane but likewise painted an aggressive color. The general effect was cheap and hideous. Yet the President appeared to be more at ease here than in his official residence.

He kicked off his slippers.

"Can you give me a summary of the situation, Monsieur Fonts?"

"I say, he has recovered his breath," Fonts said to himself.

"You've made me run, Monsieur Fonts. I'd like to know where we're going!"

"To Rhodesia, Monsieur le Président. To Kipushi, on the frontier."

"What'll I do at Kipushi? If I leave Katanga it means I've lost."

"You'll become a symbol . . . like General de Gaulle in London. . . ."

Kimjanga sat up in his armchair; he felt better.

"Nothing is lost," Fonts went on. "On the contrary, we can still win the day."

"My army isn't strong enough to resist!"

"The problem is not only military but political. As soon as you've reached Kipushi you'll give a press conference. You'll tell the journalists that the blue helmets attacked you for no reason, just as you were preparing to start negotiations with Leopoldville."

"I told Maley I wouldn't go to Leo!"

"To surrender, but not to negotiate. You'll emphasize your desire to reach a peaceful solution. . . . When there are bullets whistling in the streets, it's always a good thing to talk about peace. . . .

"At the same time you'll give orders to all your troops to resist. On my side, I'll deal with the mercenaries and European volunteers."

"It's very good of you, but I'm not yet in Rhodesia!"

"That's easy to arrange!"

Fonts picked up the telephone and dialed John Ligget's number.

"Monsieur le Consul . . . yes, it's Fonts. How goes it? Not so bad! Kimjanga has slipped out of their clutches. I happen to have with me someone whose safety is extremely precious and who needs to cross the frontier. . . . You'll call me back in ten minutes? Fine. Here's my number. . . ."

The President went back to the frigidaire and took out another bottle of beer.

"Do you think," he asked, "that John Ligget understood you were referring to me?"

"I can assure you he did. Who commands the Katangese Army? An African officer, I suppose?"

"We had just decided to appoint . . ."

"Who's the most senior officer?"

"Colonel Nadolo."

"Is he the best you've got? We'll try and get hold of him!"

"Where's Colonel la Roncière?"

"It won't be long before we hear from him!"

"The UN are stronger than we are! What do you hope to do?"

"Wait three days for the reaction to develop throughout the world. In three days Katanga will appear in everyone's eyes as a poor little martyred country which has been savagely attacked . . . and for no reason, since you were anxious to negotiate . . . by a powerful army which claims to be a peace force. Katanga with her meager resources is holding out against the aggressor. . . . If Katanga is hold-

346

ing out, it means she exists as a nation. And is proving it with her life's blood! Afterwards we'll see!"

"That's all very well, Monsieur Fonts, but I'm hemmed in here and the UN will soon find the address of my . . . African residence."

The telephone rang. It was Ligget.

"I'm coming round to pick up your friend myself. It's simpler that way. I'll be with you in a moment!"

Gradually Kimjanga recovered his assurance, especially since knowing that the consul of a great country like England was handling his case. In a tone that was friendly, granted, but which nevertheless marked the distinction between them, he saw fit to thank Fonts.

"My dear friend, in these dark hours you have saved Katanga and her President. You have earned our eternal gratitude. We shall never forget you!"

"Gratitude from a head of state who has been caught in an unenviable position," Fonts reflected, "it's unheard of. When he feels better, Kimjanga will put paid to me . . . as he has to all the others. . . . But what you can never take away from me, my lad, is the fun I've had: witnessing the flight of a president in pink pajamas!"

"Thank you, Monsieur le Président, your gratitude is all I ask. Now we must find you something to wear!"

"I have some clothes here."

In the adjoining room, one side of which consisted of a big cupboard, twenty suits were lined up on clothes hangers. The drawers were full of silk shirts, ties, elegant socks and shoes.

The President dressed with the greatest care, and it was in a double-breasted blue suit, white silk shirt, spotted tie and polished shoes that he received John Ligget, with the sad smile of a well-brought-up martyr.

"I expected him to be more dejected," Ligget whispered to Fonts. "He can certainly take it!"

"No, it's the glad rags!"

"Eh?"

"A change of clothes has the same effect on him as it has on a woman. When you rang up, he was in a state of collapse."

"Very interesting! Shame we're in too much of a hurry to discuss it. Why didn't the Swedes surround the Presidency? Was it you?"

"No. What about you?"

"It wasn't me either!"

They went their separate ways, Ligget with the President, Fonts by himself, each convinced that the other was lying!

At six o'clock in the morning the Indian troops captured the post office. From Fonts's flat Joan witnessed some horrible scenes: Gurkhas flinging wounded para-commandos out of the first-floor windows. Three times she heard the thud of bodies crashing to their death on the cement paving. She also saw an Indian officer finish off a wounded man with a bullet in the head and repeat the gesture twice more.

Joan was so upset by this that she forgot her violent quarrel with Thomas and the caddish way he had behaved.

When he eventually rang her up, she described the end of the para-commandos before telling him once more that she had no wish to see him again.

"I'm sending Pérohade to fetch you in a car. He'll drive you home. Be ready at the front door!"

"I hate you!"

"And I adore you! I don't want anything to happen to you."

He rang off.

On leaving the President's "African residence," Fonts, not knowing quite where to go, dropped in at the Mitsouko. He had awakened Pérohade and ordered some coffee: the beer lay heavy on his stomach.

He was working out all sorts of plans, each one more audacious than the other, which he rejected immediately afterwards.

"Listen," he eventually said to the journalist-publican. "You heard what I said on the phone. . . . Go and collect Joan at my hide-out and, while you drive her home, get all you can out of her. She saw some Gurkhas pitching wounded para-commandos out of the window and an Indian officer finishing off a casualty.

"After dropping the girl, you dish up the story to Dorat and the other journalists. They're all at the Leo II and are probably awake by now. But above all don't say it was Joan who witnessed the scene!"

"It would be the hell of a scoop all the same: the daughter of the American Consul seeing the wounded Katangese being finished off as she looked out of her window!"

"You're taking to the job all right. You'll soon be as loathsome as our friend Dorat! Only the window she was looking out of happens to be mine. You'll have to think of something else. In any case other people must have witnessed the scene from their own windows! After that you go straight to Gelinet."

"He must be oiling his rifle!"

"You calm him down, and also the merry gang who are due to join him. Rendezvous at noon in Kenya City at Bongo's shack. Collect all the fellows who can be of any use. Meanwhile I'll go to Massart Camp and see what the valiant Katangese troops are doing!"

"They're doing bugger-all. They're palavering!"

"They have to do something!"

Pérohade was amazed by Fonts.

This cynical free-and-easy little man could risk his life in the most tricky situations, like that jaunt among the Balubas, and think nothing of it. He was also capable, when everything was collapsing, of improvising a plan, pouncing on an unexpected opportunity and exploiting it straight away. . . . He could snatch Kimjanga away in pajamas under the nose of the UN. Make use, for his propaganda purposes, of a lovely girl like Joan, to whom he must have sworn undying love in order to sleep with her. . . . Think of everything at the same time and be fresh and relaxed, joke with Nathalie, complain about the coffee and touch him for five thousand francs! The fellow was an absolute dynamo!

Fonts was only happy in an unexpected or dangerous situation. He at once forgot his difficulties, his aversions, his impending old age and the emptiness of his life. He forgot Joan. He no longer needed her. Finding his drug again, he became clearer-minded, more precise in his gestures, and overflowed with excitement, good temper and good fellowship.

A perpetual seducer, this time he was seducing men as well as women and felt all the better for it, perhaps because he was less sincere with men and used them for a definite end.

Before leaving for Massart Camp he reminded Pérohade:

"The journalists . . . I want them to be whole-heartedly on our side. They are our army. . . . Nothing else matters. Tell them I'll see them this afternoon."

"At Bongo's?"

"Are you crazy? If you tell them where I'm hanging out I'll have them round my neck all day. Apart from the fact that within a couple of hours the UN will know where our command post is! Let's say two o'clock in your back parlor. I want every newspaper in the world to be full of corpses . . . and of wounded being finished off!"

"They'll work in with us all right. But how can they send off their copy now that the post office is occupied?"

"Use your initiative, old boy. Requisition cars. The first properly equipped post office is at Ndola in Rhodesia. It takes four hours, driving fast. I'll ask the Rhodesians, through Ligget, for the cable office to be kept open all night. You organize a shuttle service of two cars a day to Ndola. Your pals spew out their copy and you see that it reaches its destination!"

"Is that all?" said Pérohade.

Fonts rubbed his hand together.

"Yes, old thing, that's all for the moment. Be prepared to do with very little sleep for the next few days!"

La Roncière did not know how to be happy, but for one week he experienced something closely akin to happiness. Forgetting his anxiety, his jealousy, he stopped asking questions and went out riding, sailing and fishing with Jenny. He even managed to forget Africa.

On the morning of 13 September he switched on the radio, tuned into some jazz, then into a boring talk on tilapia breeding. Tilapia did not enter into his present concerns. At last came the news. The impersonal voice announced:

"Fierce fighting broke out at four o'clock this morning in Elizabethville between UN troops and the Katangese forces. A number of deaths have been reported. President Kimjanga has left his residence. According to the latest information, fighting is still going on in the Katangese capital."

La Roncière rang up Smith, who merely said:

"An aircraft is waiting for you at Zemba. It will land you at Kipushi. Good luck. You'll need it!"

Fonts reached Massart Camp at ten in the morning. The camp was situated between the African city and the European town. It was a group of barracks forming a quadrilateral of over half a mile each side, surrounded by a high wall. Fifteen hundred men were stationed there, receiving military training of a bygone age.

Fonts had driven through deserted streets. No more shots could be heard, as though all resistance had ceased. But at the entrance to the camp he was greeted with shouts. A sentry, without challenging him, fired on the car.

He just had time to leap out of it and take cover in a ditch.

Now a dozen fellows started firing bursts of light machine-gun fire through the railings and from the top of the wall, transforming the Peugeot into a sieve.

When the shooting died down, Fonts made his way towards the gate, still under cover of the ditch. From a few yards off he shouted:

"Don't shoot. I'm a friend . . . I've been sent by President Kimjanga!"

A gendarme retorted:

"If you friend . . . put your hands up . . . step forward."

Fonts advanced slowly with his hands above his head, threatened by a score of rifles held by a score of frenzied and at the same time terror-stricken Negroes.

"To think that any one of these savages, depending on his mood, the state of his nerves or because a pal of his urges him on, can put an end to little Fonts's career in this grotesque country!

"There are more than a thousand of them behind these walls, with an absolute arsenal at their disposal, yet they tremble with fear at the sight of a white man arriving!"

Through the railings the gendarmes asked him for his papers but would not allow him to lower his hands to get them out of his wallet.

So, losing patience, Fonts deliberately put his hands on his hips.

"Where's the officer commanding this camp?"

"He's not here," said one of the gendarmes, contorting himself.

"The second in command? Any other officer?"

"No officer here, boss."

The gendarme staggered and clutched the railings to steady himself. Fonts then noticed that most of them were drunk.

Another one arrived, trailing his rifle.

"There are a hundred killed at the post office!"

Said yet another:

"We're off. The UN are arriving with tanks!"

They were all brandishing weapons and bottles of beer, yelling that it was the fault of the whites, that they ought to be killed because they were making war on the poor Negroes.

An NCO waved his rifle at Fonts.

"Get out of here, you, we don't want whites here! Get out of here or I'll kill you."

351

Without arguing the toss, Fonts made himself scarce. The roof of his car was riddled, the windows shattered by bullets, but the engine was still working. He roared off, hastened on his way by a few rifle shots.

"Nothing to be done with them," he said to himself. "Not a single officer in the camp. I can't rely on anyone but the whites to save Kimjanga and his régime. The Negroes don't give a damn about it!"

He left his car in a side-street and rushed up to his flat, four steps at a time. The front door was ajar. He was hoping for a message from Joan. There was nothing. Nothing but the unmade bed and some cigarette butts stained with her lipstick. The window overlooking the post office had been left open. The bodies of the para-commandos had been removed and the Gurkhas were now in position on the roof. There was not a sound. In the Avenue Royale a civilian, a Belgian of about fifty, stepped forward on to the edge of the pavement. He hesitated like a bird taking flight from its nest. One step forward, one step back. Suddenly, holding himself very upright, without looking, he advanced into the roadway. From the roof of the post office a Gurkha fired and the man doubled up. Rolling over and over, he sought the cover of the pavement. The Gurkha fired again and the body lay motionless.

"Bad," Fonts reflected. "Those sods of Gurkhas are now firing on anyone. Their officers must have told them that all the whites were armed. I'm cut off in this dump, there's no means of getting away. The car, in its present state, would betray me at once! On foot, it's out of the question! A Gurkha would select me as a target or else I'd run into a patrol! What the hell's going on in this bloody town? What do the UN hold? What are the others doing?"

He consulted the telephone directory. He had a map of the town in his pocket. With the directory on his knees, he began glancing through it:

"Monsieur et Madame Britton, 232 Avenue de Saio. That's in front of the railway underpass. The road that goes under the railway and leads to the Indian camp. It might be interesting!" He rang up the number.

"Hello, Monsieur Britton?"

"No, it's Madame Britton here."

The voice was extremely genteel.

"The MIR here."

"The MIR? What's that you say?"

"The resistance movement. . . ."

"Oh! The one mentioned in the leaflets. . . ."

352

"That's it!"

"You're Colonel Alain? . . . We're all with you. It's horrible, what's going on, people being killed all over the place! Gisèle . . . yes, you know, Madame Gigoule . . . told me the gendarmes were shot after being taken prisoner. . . ."

"That's right. From your window can you see the underpass?

"We're on the fourth floor: we can see everything, but it's rather noisy. I've often told my husband: "Hector, you ought to . . .' "

"Tell Hector again. What interests me is the underpass . . ."

"But Monsieur . . ."

"We want to save Katanga, help us to do so. . . ."

Fonts was about to ring off in a fury. He made a final effort.

"What is there in the underpass?"

"A lot of soldiers . . . whites."

"How many?"

"Thirty or so on this side. On the other side I can't see but there are some trucks parked inside the tunnel and a couple of those contraptions painted white, like milk vans.

"I can also see two of them on this side. The blue helmets have built some little houses with sandbags, and inside they've set up one of those big guns with bullets strung together in a long row, like sausages. . . ."

"Thank you very much, madam. I'll call you back. Meanwhile keep a close watch on every movement. Count the number of vehicles entering the town. Make a clear distinction between the trucks, bath-tubs and armored cars!"

"What sort of cars?"

"Armored. They're like tanks, but with heavy tires. Jot all this down in a notebook. I'll call you back. Good-bye, madam."

As a result of ten telephone calls Fonts learned that, in addition to the post office and underpass, the blue helmets had dug in at the Lido and at Clair Manoir, Siddartha's command post.

He even learned from a veteran in a great state of excitement that a couple of bath-tubs and an armored car had taken up a position outside the Villa des Roches, Maley's residence.

While trying to find out what was happening at the

radio station, he got through to Fournier, Maley's assistant.

"Monsieur Van Emmelrich?"

"No. Who's that speaking?"

"The MIR here."

"Eh?"

"Yes, the MIR. Haven't you heard of it?"

"Oh yes, quite often. Fournier here, assistant to the chief UN representative."

"They tell me you're a Frenchman, you shit! Aren't you scared your compatriots might come and bump you off?"

"Difficult at the moment: you're in a bad way! I'm occupying the radio station and . . ."

"Thanks for the information, that's all I wanted to know. See you soon, you sod!"

"So long, Thomas Fonts!"

By midday about thirty whites had assembled in Bongo's shack. There was not a single African there.

There was no news of the Minister of the Interior; it was only known that after being warned late at night he had just had time to escape from his house and take refuge with his tribe, the Bayeke.

A dozen men had collected round Gelinet, the stentorian brewer. Little Ravetot and two delegates from the Union Minière kept hovering between the Gelinet group and Kreis's gang. The German had rustled up a dozen mercenaries, including Buscard the former paratroop sergeant-major and the three legionaries from Tshiko Camp.

Standing well to one side was another group of civilians, ill at ease in mufti: the Belgian officers who had rallied round Captain Gersaint and refused to obey the repatriation orders.

It had required all Gelinet's vehemence to persuade them to attend this meeting. They formed an islet of hostility.

Fonts stood leaning against a wall next to Pérohade.

Colonel la Roncière came out of his room and at once took the floor.

"Gentlemen, two hours ago I was at Kipushi, where I had a meeting with President Kimjanga who is now safely there. He asks us to do all we can to save Katanga and has given me full powers to organize the resistance. Let us see what we can do."

"Just a moment, monsieur. . . ."

354

Captain Gersaint had insisted on this form of address and had stepped forward towards la Roncière.

"My comrades and I are Belgian Army officers. We have agreed, at Monsieur Gelinet's suggestion, to attend this meeting. But there can be no question of placing ourselves under your orders!"

"May I know the reason?"

"Your desire to eliminate the Belgians from this country, your methods. . . . We hold you responsible for what is happening today!"

"Ridiculous! If you had had more idea about how a subversive war should be waged, how an army should be trained, how a civilian population should be conditioned, we should have been more than a mere handful here today!"

Fonts interjected:

"We haven't assembled in this shack to create a unified command with a headquarters staff, nominal rolls and plans of action . . ."

La Roncière curtly interrupted him:

"It will be necessary all the same!"

"One can see you're not abreast of the situation, Jean-Marie! We have no troops or liaison or communications, only a few personal weapons and very little ammunition. In such chaos each man acts for himself!"

"Then we're done for!"

"No. This chaos is what saves us! We can be everywhere and nowhere, like a cloud of mosquitoes. The situation of the UN isn't as good as it seems. I don't know why the blue helmets aren't exploiting their initial success; they're losing valuable time. It looks as though they're hesitating to embark on a proper military operation! Now's the time to strike, everywhere at the same time. . . ."

"There are only thirty of us," Pérohade pointed out.

"Yes . . . but as you yourself told me, the UN convoys have been fired upon. Who fired on them? None of us here. So we have some people with us. We'll have to find out who they are!"

Then, addressing the Belgian officer:

"In a case like this, Captain, hierarchies and formalities go by the board! Could you get into Massart Camp?"

"Of course!"

"Well, I didn't manage it!"

"Because the gendarmes don't know you!"

"Would the gendarmes follow you and your comrades!"

"Certainly!"

"It's up to you Belgians, then, to deal with the African troops! I suggest we break up into small commando groups, four or five men at the most, each equipped with a bazooka or machine-gun mounted on a jeep.

"The groups will work independently of one another and will choose their target according to opportunity. What can we do? Harass the UN positions and attack their convoys. Isolate the various positions and cut their main line of communication from the airport. Above all we must put the wind up them. That's why we must be mobile. Turn up in one spot, open fire and pull out at once. Don't hesitate to make use of the civilians. They're with us at heart. Fire from the houses; occupy the roof-tops. Before the enemy can take cover, counter-attack and search the premises, you'll be miles away. Within twenty-four hours the UN must be given the impression that there are ten thousand men prepared to die on the spot in Elizabethville.

"One last thing: make sure there are always night attacks. Make as much noise as possible. You must prevent the blue helmets from sleeping. When they have had no sleep for three nights running, they won't be on their toes!"

"There's one thing I'd like to say, General," said la Roncière.

"You're not going to be as touchy as the Belgians, are you? Oh, these regulars!"

"We must organize two or three well-mounted . . . spectacular . . . operations. As to the rest, I agree with you: a cloud of mosquitoes. But, to begin with, two or three well-aimed blows!"

"Just a moment," said Captain Gersaint. "Monsieur Fonts's plan, or rather his lack of a plan, seems to me the only solution. Two or three isolated jobs which each of us undertakes as he sees fit, two or three more spectacular operations. That's all we can do. But with what aim in view? Where will it get us? We can't expect any military aid from outside. We have no reserves. It's highly improbable that the French or British will come and drop us arms and ammunition!"

"Our intention is not to wage war," la Roncière replied, "but above all to kick up a fuss so as to alert international opinion, to go on kicking up a fuss until we provoke a strong reaction from the French and British Governments. As you know, those two Governments are hostile to all armed intervention by the UN. The French on account of what overseas possessions they have left, the English on account of the Rhodesias and Kenya."

"How do the Rhodesians come into it?" Pérohade asked.

"They'll give us arms and ammunition. Sir Roy Welensky is even prepared to send us troops if necessary. On that score I have definite assurances!"

"But where is it going to get us?" Captain Gersaint repeated.

"If we can hold out a week, the UN Secretary-General will be obliged to call a halt."

"We'll never be able to hold out a week!"

"We can always try!"

"Even if the UN climb down this time, they'll begin all over again three months later."

"I agree with you, my dear colleague. We shall have gained nothing unless we obtain the evacuation of all UN troops."

"Do you think so?"

Little Ravetot felt it was time to put a word in:

"The blue helmets, a flight of sparrows . . . a few shots and they'll take to their heels!"

"As they did at the post office," Fonts remarked. "That's enough talk! Each of us does what he can, manages as he sees fit. Gelinet with his group, Gersaint with his and whatever gendarmes he can get to join him. I have a little expedition in mind for our friend Kreis. Let's say we meet again tomorrow . . . when we can, where we can!"

The smoky room slowly emptied. A man of thirty-five, with close-set eyes like a sparrow's and a diffident awkward manner, introduced himself to la Roncière. He had a strong Belgian accent.

"Excuse me, Colonel. I'm Lieutenant Berthot of the Belgian Air Force."

"Yes, well?"

"I pilot one of the two Fouga Magisters which France delivered to Katanga."

"I beg your pardon! France has delivered some Fougas? But I would have known about it: I'm the President's military adviser. He would have told me!"

Fonts jokingly observed:

"He's a little slyboots, our Kimjanga. He likes to have secrets from everyone!"

"It's incredible!"

357

"It's Negro."

"Berthot, how did the Fougas arrive here?"

Berthot looked astonished.

"In cases, Colonel. Three weeks ago, by the Union Minière railway which ends in Angola. Though I had a hell of a job to collect those cases! The Union Minière fellow wouldn't hand them over. He said I had to have a document signed by Pimuriaux!"

"How does Pimuriaux come into it?"

"It was he who arranged for the purchase of the Fougas and engaged me with a team of mechanics. I saw him at the President's. He said he had an agreement with France and could get them cheap!"

Fonts whistled.

"It looks as though our Justin didn't leave here with empty pockets!"

"As you can well imagine," Berthot went on, "a pilot without a plane doesn't cut much ice. With some pals of mine I managed all the same to pinch the cases from the Union Minière, and we assembled one Fouga."

La Roncière interrupted sharply:

"What the hell's the good of your Fouga? A five-hundred-mile-an-hour jet is no better than a wheelbarrow to us. As it's a training plane, it isn't armed!"

"Well, you see . . . my pals and I managed to fix two machine-guns and four rockets on her. It seems to work all right!"

"The UN fighters will shoot you down in five minutes!"

"The UN haven't any fighters . . . only transport aircraft."

"What's that?"

"Not a single fighter!"

"How long would it take you to get to Kolwezi?"

"Five hours by road."

"Too late to do anything about it today. But tomorrow morning, first thing, start off by shooting up the airfield. Then circle over the town. Do a little hedge-hopping over the post office, UN headquarters and the Indian camp."

"If I see a UN plane coming in to land, do I shoot it down?"

La Roncière hesitated.

"No. It's too great a risk. Destroy the aircraft on the ground. For the rest, loose off a few bursts, but to one side. They'll be frightened, turn tail and spread panic in Leopoldville."

"I'm going to enjoy myself, Colonel."

He saluted, raising his hand to his straw hat, and marched out.

"So here we are with an air force," Fonts observed, "just because Justin Pimuriaux felt like making a little dough on the side and this worthy Berthot wants to fly. . . . We're lunching at Gelinet's. I want to tell you about a little job I've been working out for Kreis and his gang!"

Since the launching of Morthor, Gelinet's house had come to resemble a partisan command post more than the residence of a peaceful brewer. The kitchen was busy all day long: beer and sandwiches were available at all hours. Gelinet was blissfully happy, uttering loud curses which frightened no one and issuing orders which everyone was careful not to follow.

Fonts took la Roncière and Kreis aside.

"I'm seeing the journalists at two o'clock. I'll have a lot to tell them, of course, maybe they'll listen to me, maybe they won't. But at three o'clock Maley is holding a press conference at the Villa des Roches. They're sure to listen to him. The Villa des Roches is protected with a couple of bath-tubs and an armored car. During this press conference, Kreis, I'd like you to set about destroying this armored car or the bath-tubs!"

"I have two bazookas with ten shells. They've just been dug up. They were buried in a garden."

"What about the men?"

"Buscard, my legionaries. Utterly reliable . . . I may well pull it off."

"A quarter past three?"

"That'll be all right!"

La Roncière congratulated Fonts, not without a trace of bitterness in his voice.

"Very good. Maximum psychological effect. I must admit, when it comes to improvisation, you show something amounting to genius. But afterwards?"

"Afterwards? That's up to you, Jean-Marie."

Gelinet had switched on the radio and was seething with anger.

Radio Katanga was announcing in Swahili that President Kimjanga had surrendered to the UN and ordered his troops to arrest and disarm the European officers and mercenaries.

He translated this for the benefit of la Roncière.

"Just imagine it, the sods!"

"What does it matter, my dear Gelinet?"

"One can see you're a recent arrival in Africa. The gendarmes all listen to the radio and believe everything they're told! At this moment Captain Gersaint and his officers are trying to win them over. They may easily be killed!"

"All we need do is blow the radio station sky high!"

"Easier said than done!"

"I'll see to it. Kreis, detail four or five of your chaps to come with me . . . and bring some plastic charges. Since we can't hold the radio station, we may as well blow it up!"

Fonts grasped him by the shoulder.

"Well done, Jean-Marie, you're waking up. We're going to cause real havoc in this town! Gelinet, what about some whisky? I drink to disorder and chaos, to everything that startles or makes a big noise, to the fun and games we're going to have, to the fright we're going to give those pale-faced Swedes and gray-faced Indians!"

Maley's press conference began a few minutes late. Everyone was waiting for General Siddartha who was due to arrive with the latest news.

In order to get into the Villa des Roches the journalists had to pick their way through a maze of sandbags and barbed wire. The presence of the armored car and two bath-tubs reminded them painfully that the "political" operation which had been dinned into their ears was turning into war.

The television reporters had set up their cameras, the radio reporters their microphones, the press photographers were busy taking flashlight pictures of an extremely nervous Maley.

Siddartha finally turned up with his swagger-stick under his arm. He leaned towards Maley, whispered something in his ear, then sat down.

"Gentlemen," Maley began in a voice which he tried to keep calm, "I have asked you here to sum up the situation. At four o'clock this morning the UN forces went into action in accordance with the Security Council resolution of February 21st. All the objectives were occupied by seven-thirty without our troops encountering any serious resistance. At the moment calm has been restored in the town, where the UN are ready to co-operate with the local authorities in order to assure the safety of the population. . . ."

Pérohade interrupted without letting Maley go any farther.

"Assure the safety of the population? But your troops stationed at the post office are firing on anyone who ventures outside! This morning two civilians were killed while making their way to the chemist's."

Siddartha interjected:

"That's not true. My men only fired in self-defense. They were replying to the fire of a mercenary who was shooting them from the Belgian Consulate!"

"What do you mean, it's not true? I was there myself when the two civilians were killed. They were unarmed. I tell you, they were going to the chemist's to get some medicine."

A gigantic Rhodesian asked:

"An ambulance was machine-gunned by the Swedes at ten o'clock. How do you account for that?"

"The ambulance was carrying a mercenary armed with a bazooka. He attacked an armored car, and the ambulance was destroyed by counter-fire."

"Can you show us the ambulance with the bazooka?"

"No. The mercenaries evacuated it straight away!"

Dorat then chipped in.

"For the last five minutes you've mentioned nothing but mercenaries. Who have you got confronting you: Katangese soldiers or mercenaries?"

"The Katangese surrendered almost at once, except when they were commanded by mercenaries."

"That's a lie!" Decronelle cried in a shrill voice. "The post office was held by a detachment of Katangese paracommandos who fought right up to the end. The Gurkhas finished off the wounded while they were still alive by flinging them out of the windows."

Siddartha sprang to his feet.

"I forbid you! . . . You're lying! It's sheer provocation."

Maley intervened:

"Gentlemen, I beg of you. Calm down! It's an undeniable fact: mercenaries took part in the fighting at the post office. The civilian population of Elizabethville and the Katangese authorities must understand that they are taking a great risk in allowing the mercenaries to prolong the fighting. It's difficult to avoid accidents in this sort of operation. If they occur, the civilians have only themselves to blame!"

Pérohade:

"You mean to say it's normal for UN troops to embark on military operations against the civilian population?"

Maley:

"I repeat, the UN troops went into action only after exhausting every means of settling the problem by peaceful methods. They are acting according to a resolution passed by the Security Council!"

Dorat:

"You say the secession of Katanga has come to an end. What does President Kimjanga think of that?"

"The President has accepted all our conditions. He admits that the secession must come to an end and he is prepared to announce it on the radio."

"Have you seen him?"

"I spoke to him on the telephone at four-forty this morning. It was then he informed me of his acceptance."

"And since then?"

"I'm expecting the President at any moment."

Dorat felt that Maley was losing his footing. In a gentle voice he went on:

"Radio Brazzaville announced at two o'clock this afternoon that Kimjanga had taken refuge at Kipushi, in Rhodesian territory, and that he had launched an appeal for total resistance."

Maley hesitated a moment. Then he took the plunge.

"I heard that rumor, which has not been confirmed by our Intelligence service. It is possible the President may have strayed and that his European advisers are trying to urge him on into a thoughtless action. I hope . . ."—he smiled in a knowing way—"I have good reason to believe that the President will realize that continued resistance would be sheer folly. We have the situation well in hand. The Katangese troops, many of whom are far from being unreservedly in favor of the régime, have laid down their arms. Our material superiority is overwhelming. . . ."

"The Nazis were also stronger," cried Decronelle, "but they were unable to beat the Resistance!"

"Kindly have that gentleman removed," Maley simply said.

Siddartha intervened with violence, striking the table with his swagger-stick:

"Katangese resistance is shattered! If my troops were attacked, either by mercenaries or European civilians, I should take decisive steps."

362

"Hostages, you mean?" asked Spencer of Associated Press.

Maley had no time to intervene.

The first bazooka shell exploded in the middle of the bath-tub on the left. A dull thud was heard, then a huge flame spurted out. The second shell merely damaged the other bath-tub, which its occupants, Swedes, abandoned at the double.

The armored car fired burst after burst. Suddenly it blew up. After a moment's stupor the photographers rushed to the windows and, taking cover behind the recesses, set to work with their cameras.

The wail of an ambulance siren in the distance grew progressively louder, reaching a deafening pitch as the vehicle approached.

Maley was white in the face. Dorat went up to Siddartha.

"Katangese resistance is shattered?"

"It's only a question of time . . . and means."

Kreis had approached the Villa des Roches on foot, bent double creeping up through the adjoining gardens. He led the way. Behind him came Buscard with the bazooka, then a legionary carrying five shells hanging from a strap, and, in close order, another legionary covering them with his Fal rifle.

Forty yards away from the bath-tubs and armored car, they had taken cover behind a low wall.

Kreis had slithered forward, then signaled Buscard to join him with the bazooka.

A young Swede sat in the turret behind the twin machine-guns, reading a paper. The remainder of the crew were eating their rations.

Not a breath of wind. The UN flag drooped like a rag on its pole. One of the legionaries took the shells out of their cardboard case.

Kreis placed a hand on Buscard's shoulder.

"Start off with the first bath-tub."

"Why not the armored car?"

"Not from here. Your shells would land in the conference hall. It's full of journalists."

"What do we care?"

"We're not waging war . . . Henri . . . but psychological warfare. That's what Fonts and the Colonel never stop telling me. . . . Those are the orders. Then shoot up the second bath-tub. . . . After which I'll take your blunderbuss, move forward twenty yards and have a go at the armored car!"

"You'll be out in the open!"

"Only for a moment, just long enough to fire."

"Off we go, then!"

Buscard fired the first two shells, while Kreis crouched beside him with the third projectile in his hand. He seized the bazooka, loaded it, appeared at the other end of the wall and, drawing himself up to his full height, with the bazooka resting on his shoulder, took careful aim, as though on an exercise, selecting as his target the turret from which the machine-guns kept firing without stopping. Then, dropping the weapon, he plunged into a flower-bed.

Each man had to get back as best he could, taking advantage of the general confusion.

One of the legionaries, who had been wounded in the leg, was about to be captured by an Indian patrol, but he waited for his pursuers with a grenade in his hand and blew himself up with them.

The rumor consequently went round that the mercenaries never allowed themselves to be caught alive, which added to the fear and confusion in the UN ranks.

"My Gurkhas finished him off," Siddartha told Maley a little later.

"But it was the mercenary who put paid to your Gurkhas!"

Maley was furious with himself for feeling proud of the wretched fellow's courage, because he was a white man like himself.

The attack on the radio station had been fixed for five o'clock.

La Roncière wanted them to make a quick job of it: occupy the building for a few minutes, long enough to place the charges, and withdraw immediately afterwards.

At half past four he was notified that fighting had already broken out at the station. Captain Gersaint with thirty Africans had just attacked it.

The broadcasts in Swahili had demoralized all the troops in Massart Camp. Old Gelinet was right: this kind of propaganda in a native tongue was difficult to combat.

The gendarmes had manhandled one of the Belgian officers. Gersaint was not lacking in courage: without being familiar, he had always proved fair and was the only officer who had retained all his prestige with his men.

He felt mutiny was imminent. Already he pictured the

364

fifteen hundred gendarmes, dead drunk, sweeping through the European city and massacring the whites, like the mutineers of Thysville. Thysville was a stain on the honor of Belgium; it was not to be repeated. He, the deserter captain, would know how to prevent it and would at the same time teach a good lesson to the arrogant French colonel and to that professional revolutionary without laws or traditions, Thomas Fonts.

Gersaint managed to persuade thirty men to join him, bundled them into an old half-track and a truck, then headed for the radio station, a long building in the middle of a lawn, situated between Clair Manoir and the President's residence.

Over-excited, the gendarmes had lost all their military bearing; the driver of the half-track was sporting a forage cap, others were wearing red scarves and brandishing pangas. One of them kept fingering an amulet under his shirt.

For the first time Gersaint forced himself to joke with his men, who gazed at him in amazement.

A hundred yards from the radio building, he made them disembark and issued his orders.

"Half of you to the left, the other half to the right, and don't budge. You mustn't be seen. When I fire the bazooka at the door, then you all rush forward behind me, shouting as loud as you can. Once inside, you break the place up.

"Don't finish off the wounded, you're not savages like the Gurkhas. You disarm the prisoners and boot them outside! Then we set fire to the place. All clear?"

It had worked perfectly. The men had surrounded the building all right without being seen. But Gersaint had had an unpleasant surprise: it was not the Swedes who were occupying it but the Gurkhas, with the flat faces and huge calves of mountain Sherpas.

Too late to withdraw.

It was then one of the gendarmes, either drunk or over-excited, fired a burst at the windows of the building. All was lost unless immediate action was taken. Gersaint snatched the bazooka from an NCO's hands and, hugging the wall, crept forward. On emerging from the lane which sheltered him, he dropped down on one knee to fire. But a machine-gun burst sliced him in two and made the shell in the tube explode.

The gendarmes disbanded and rushed back to the half-track and the truck, leaving four dead on the ground. Their blood stained the asphalt red.

A quarter of an hour later la Roncière moved into position behind the radio station with two 81-caliber mortars and started spraying the building and the immediate surroundings.

A shell fell right on the guard post, killing one Gurkha and wounding two others. Another destroyed the aerial, a third set fire to the truck.

Believing that a general assault was to follow, Fournier ordered the detachment occupying the building to fall back on Clair Manoir, while shells continued to rain down on the corrugated iron roofs.

Pérohade joined Fonts in the African city at five o'clock.

"How did Maley's press conference go?" Fonts asked him.

"Couldn't have been better. Maley was beginning to lose his grip. The bath-tubs and armored car went up at the very moment that big oaf Siddartha was announcing that all resistance had ceased!

"I wish you could have seen the shambles. They had at least a dozen killed. Maley was white in the face. What worries me slightly is that Siddartha seems determined to carry out reprisals. He said that if any of his chaps were killed he would hold the civilian population responsible. And now bullets are flying in all directions!"

"Who's firing?"

"No one knows exactly: mercenaries, Gelinet's gang, of course, but everyone's involved. A lot of noise but not much damage. It's a bit of a nuisance!"

"Why?"

"Siddartha might start shelling the town. He also has mortars. And E'ville is full of women and children!"

"We can't do anything about it, old boy. The civilians, women and brats included, are in the same boat as ourselves. There's no time for tender feelings."

"Don't you think you're going a bit too far?"

"We're forced to fire on the UN, otherwise we're done for. If the blue helmets fire on the civilians, they'll be in an unenviable position!"

"But, good God, don't you realize the civilians won't hold out! I know the Belgians. Apart from fifty or so who are prepared to take risks, the others will climb down at the first sign of danger. They've started already: cars are pouring out in the direction of Rhodesia!"

"Oh, to hell with it! We can't do everything at once! Not so good, the civilians taking to their heels. Rats leaving the sinking ship. . . . We ought to put up road-blocks."

"Go and tell that to Nathalie. She's absolutely mad, she

wants to pack her bags and take refuge at the French Consulate!"

"Beware of Musaille. He's a fast worker when it comes to seizing an opportunity!"

"He hasn't the time. He keeps driving all over the place with a big tricolor flag on his car. He got himself shot up and went off delighted to protest to Maley."

"In his usual unscrupulous way he probably claimed it was an attempt against his person!"

"Musaille says the blue helmets are in the hell of a mess."

"Not enough of a mess! You told me there was a make-shift transmitter somewhere."

"Yes, hidden away among some cases in one of the Lubumbashi warehouses. Hermant knows about it."

"Who's Hermant?"

"A Radio Katanga technician. He's one of Gelinet's gang."

"Put him to work. Tell him to get the transmitter and install it in the African city. I want a French announcer and a Swahili announcer. First broadcast at seven tomorrow morning. We must restore the Belgians' national pride. We'll begin with a tribute to Captain Gersaint."

"A hell of a fellow!"

"I'd rather have him dead than alive!"

"A hero."

"That's why. In this sort of game heroes are the last thing we want! I prefer cut-throats. What about your journalist pals?"

"Money for jam! I've laid on a car to take their copy to Ndola in half an hour's time. It will be at the post office four hours later. They're working double shifts over there. Tomorrow morning the articles will appear in Paris, London, Brussels and New York. What a shindy there'll be!"

"I certainly hope so! Without that shindy, we're done for!"

"Eh? But everything's going fine."

"Don't you believe it. If the blue helmets decided to bring up their big guns, we couldn't last an hour! But they won't dare, because of the shindy. Have another car ready to take their cables at noon tomorrow. Between now and then I hope there'll be some news."

"What?"

"You'll see. Is the Mitsouko open?"

"Of course, you go in by the back door. I've put up a notice: 'Out of bounds to foreign military personnel in uniform.' The blue helmets are the only ones in uniform. I'm in order and not liable to have any bother! You have to have your wits about you in the pub business!"

"You've got the gift of the gab!"

"So I've always been told."

"You wouldn't like to talk on the radio, would you?"

"I don't like being made a fool of, but I've got just the chap for you. A Union Minière accountant. He longs to. He's already got a pseudonym. Guess what? Bayard!"

"Who's this Bayard?"

"A chap who has an urge to talk before giving up the ghost!"

Shortly before sunset a UN convoy consisting of two GMCs and a jeep left the Indian camp and headed for the post office.

In each GMC were eight young Swedes, rifle in hand, sitting on cases of rations and ammunition boxes. Two of them still had their cameras with them. In the empty streets hordes of dogs of every breed and color went scavenging among the brimming dustbins.

Young Ravetot was extremely excited. Contrary to the regulations issued by Fonts that very morning, he was wearing a paratrooper's camouflage uniform and jumping boots.

With his pistol at his side, he paced up and down his friend Dufermont's living room on the third floor of a big block of flats in the Avenue Fulbert Youlou. Dufermont lay back in an armchair, drinking beer and sighing:

"Do you think the Rhodesians are going to help us? And what about the British? What does Radio Brazzaville say?"

"What does it matter what the British and Rhodesians are going to do?" Ravetot broke in. "It's up to us to show what sort of men we are. If every Belgian in E'ville seizes a rifle, you'll see how all those vermin will run!"

"It's all very well to talk. You're too fond of talking! You told us that you slept with Joan. Fonts, on the other hand, says nothing!"

"Fonts is a bluffer! He's all talk. He fled from the Balubas, leaving his pal Wenceslas to get killed in his place. And what's he doing here? Giving idiotic orders and hiding out among the Negroes!"

"Well, what have you done so far? All dressed up as a paratrooper without ever having been one! You've brought a Fal with a bag full of magazines here. You might have kept it at your place!"

"So you're windy, is that it?"

"No more than you; I show it more, that's all!"

"You've never been a man, Dufermont. All you can do is booze in the Mitsouko."

The jeep leading the convoy drove past in the street below.

Ravetot snatched up the Fal leaning against a wall and crept up to the window.

"Those sods again! They ought to be mowed down, the whole lot of them!"

"You who claim to be such a man, let's see how you'd set about it!"

Dufermont sprang from his armchair, shouting:

"Ravetot, don't be a fool!"

It was too late, the burst had been fired. The second GMC had slammed on its brakes. The Swedish soldiers were scattering in all directions. A body lay writhing on the road. In the truck a wounded man with his camera slung round him was raising his hands.

Ravetot, with a dazed expression on his face and his rifle still in his hand, kept saying in a tearful tone:

"Oh God . . . oh shit!"

Dufermont seized him by the arm.

"Of all the bloody fool things to do! In five minutes the blue helmets will be sending reinforcements. We're done for!"

"I didn't mean to do it!"

"You did it all the same. We've got to get out of here!"

"Where shall we go?"

"To Gelinet's. I never imagined you'd get up to such tricks!"

And Ravetot fancied there was a certain admiration mingled with the anger in his friend's voice.

The night of 13-14 September was punctuated by incidents. Instead of spreading through the town and pursuing their operations, the blue helmets confined themselves to holding the positions they had occupied during the day. Small posts stood on guard behind their sandbags.

"Either they're mad or else they're preparing something!" declared Spencer of Associated Press, as he drank a glass of beer with Dorat in the Mitsouko.

"Neither one nor the other," Dorat replied. "UNO is a vast machine with no proper command and split up into clans. Each decision involves an infinite number of moves . . . a ripple which spreads out and loses all its power by

369

the time it washes up against the Glass House at New York. The blue helmets won't do a thing. The others haven't a card in their hands, but they're kicking up a fuss and are liable to cause Maley and Siddartha a lot of trouble."

The Mitsouko was the only place open that night. Curtains were drawn across the windows; the door was locked. Only the initiates knew that there was a way in round the back.

All the customers displayed the self-important and falsely easy manner that men assume when they believe they are taking part in a great historical event. They were under orders not to make themselves too conspicuous, but they would have been distressed had they passed unnoticed.

There were no women, except for Nathalie at the cashier's desk; only grenades lying on the tables beside the glasses, and Fal rifles leaning against the chairs or the walls.

The first bandages and field dressings—indispensable adjuncts, whether genuine or false, to every revolution—began to make their appearance.

Voices were raised. . . .

"Those three Gurkhas, old boy, with one burst . . . money for jam! The grenade exploded right on the truck, absolute slaughter. They took to their heels with their tails between their legs. I tell you. . . ."

Irritated but cautious, Dorat leaned across to Spencer.

"These jokers think they're in Warsaw or Budapest!"

"You couldn't have described it better: Radio Brazzaville announced this afternoon that E'ville was a new Budapest!"

Pérohade joined the two journalists at their table and offered them a drink. Dorat remarked:

"These heroes of yours are knocking it back all right! War's good for business!"

"Not at all! Since being able to display their pop-guns they've stopped paying for their drinks! Your copy has gone off to Rhodesia."

He dipped his lips into a glass of whisky, then left them to greet some other customers.

"You see, Spencer," said Dorat, half closing his eyes as though he was talking to himself, "Siddartha is denying the journalists access to the post office because he's convinced of his rights and wants to assert his position. 'We'll see about it later,' he said, waving his swagger-stick.

"My little pal Fonts, who has never believed in anyone's rights, is performing all sorts of acrobatics to get our copy through!"

"He has a weakness for journalists!"

"No. He's intelligent. If it was in his interest to do so, he'd go out of his way to see that our cables did not arrive. But he'd be quite capable of standing us a drink and telling us frankly: 'It's all in the game. If you were in my shoes, old Fifi, what would you do? You'll get the better of me one of these days and, when you do, I'll have to accept that it's all in the game.'"

"A real sportsman. . . ."

"Yes and no. But his sort appeals to us. We've had enough of the others, with their high principles and fine feelings."

"Do you believe in this Katangese resistance?"

"I need a few colorful stories for my paper; so do you. Fonts has promised to show us the other side of the barricades! It's up to us to judge."

"Do you think he'll come?"

"I'm certain he will!"

"Why?"

"The UN have battalions of Swedes, Irishmen and Gurkhas, munitions, supplies and money. La Roncière and Fonts have nothing, apart from us! This handful of mercenaries is fighting for our benefit alone. The least we can do is play in with them."

"I don't get it."

"This entire show has been put on solely for the benefit of the journalists! Captain Gersaint and Legionary Peruski were killed for us."

"Interesting, but what we want are facts, not personal theories. I say, here comes your little pal now!"

Fonts had just strolled in, smiling and easy-mannered, greeting people at various tables.

"Well, what's cooking?" Spencer asked him.

"We're off on a little jaunt in town. You go with this big fellow; he's Uncle Gelinet. He'll show you round with his gang."

"What are they up to?"

"Sniping from the rooftops, while their wives tear up old rags to make bandages. You can question whomever you want and go wherever you please! I'll take old Fifi with me; we're an old married couple, he and I. Ever since we've been at each other's throats! Let's be off!"

"Where are we going?" Dorat inquired as the car raced

371

through the deserted town at seventy miles an hour. "To crash into a UN road-block?"

"There aren't any. I've checked."

"Why not?"

"Go and ask the blue helmets. Since this morning I don't understand what's going on: they allow Kimjanga to get away and don't put up any road-blocks!"

"Silly sods!"

"There must be something behind it. You can say what you like about Siddartha, but he's a good soldier. And Maley's anything but a fool. They've made a hash of the first part of the plan . . . and they daren't go the whole hog and beat up this town, where they're being held in check by a mere handful of desperadoes. . . . Yet that would enable them to retrieve their error! They're frightened of the smoke. They don't know what lies behind it."

"What does lie behind it?"

"Nothing!"

"What on earth do you plan to do, then?"

"Make more smoke, still more smoke!"

Fonts stopped the car in a courtyard on the corner of the Avenue de Saio, a hundred yards from the railway underpass. He took a little canvas bag out of the boot and led Dorat off.

"Let's go and see what the Irish are up to!"

Dorat, feeling somewhat apprehensive, growled:

"The Irish? What they're up to? When they're not in church they're drinking whisky!"

"We'll have some fun!"

"You have an odd idea of fun sometimes!"

"Come on, old boy, there's no danger. I promised Chantal to bring you back alive!"

"She doesn't give a damn in any case. If I die she'll get the insurance: twenty million."

"Keep your head down all the same as you cross the avenue."

Fonts raced forward ahead of him, bent double. Furious, but not daring to go back alone, Dorat followed. In any case he did not have the keys of the car and disliked walking.

Fonts entered a lane bordered by little gardens. The electricity was cut off; all the houses had their shutters closed.

They crossed the railway line. Dorat tripped over a sleeper and cursed.

"Playing silly buggers like this, you're going to make me break my leg!"

"Shut up!"

Dorat struggled to his feet.

"Look, I've had enough of this. I'm going back to the hotel!"

"Shut up! We're a hundred yards from the Irish, they fire on sight and will mow us down!"

Petrified, plunged all of a sudden into an unknown and dangerous world, Dorat mechanically followed Fonts as he crept forward, hugging a wall. He was out of breath and felt he was making a hell of a noise. Furthermore his leg was hurting. But he could do nothing else but follow this madman. Fonts stopped, hugged the wall more closely, and motioned to him to keep out of sight. Scarcely able to believe his eyes, standing in the middle of the lane, Dorat saw him open the canvas bag, take out a grenade, remove the pin, toss it over the wall, take out another and repeat the performance. Two flashes, followed by two violent explosions, pierced the darkness. Fonts raced across the lane, clambered over a wall and shouted:

"Follow me, keep your head down!"

To his great surprise, Dorat found himself on the other side of the wall. His ankle no longer hurt. Heavy firing broke out.

"Bugger!" he said.

Fonts chuckled.

"For two years, my dear Fifi, you've been describing war while swigging whisky safely back at base. Tonight at last you're seeing what war is really like!"

Dorat felt oddly elated. He was sheltered by a tree which looked fairly solid. For the first time in his life he had taken part in a dangerous action.

"People make too much of heroes," he said to himself, "it's not as hard as all that!"

Fonts's sardonic voice roused him from his euphoria.

"Let's get out of here, old Fifi! If a patrol winkles us out, it's curtains!"

Dorat had to run all the way back to the car.

He was furious once more with Fonts and refused to go and have a drink with him. Back in his own room, he seized his whisky bottle, took a gulp and, with all his self-assurance restored, sat down at his typewriter.

"I have just been out on night operations with a commando of five mercenaries who, under a hail of

373

fire, launched a grenade attack on one of the UN key positions: the railway underpass . . ."

Dorat pricked up his ears. With satisfaction he noted that the firing in the direction of the Avenue de Saio was still going on.

Four sloppily dressed Katangese gendarmes sat with their rifles between their knees, as though the place belonged to them, in the big sitting room of the Gelinet house. One of them had his feet on a small marquetry table, another was scratching himself under his shirt, the third was gazing at his empty bottle, the fourth was roaring with laughter.

"Hortense," Gelinet shouted, "bring our friends some beer!"

"I'd rather have whisky," said Spencer.

He was amazed at the presence of these four Negroes in the home of this rich brewer who was said not to be kindly disposed towards colored men.

Hortense came in. He noticed that she glared at the "guests" with manifest displeasure. Putting the tray down some distance away from them, she disappeared.

The firing in the Avenue de Saio broke out.

"Those are our boys," Gelinet remarked deliberately. "Soon it'll be our turn."

"Your boys . . . the mercenaries?"

"Don't dish that UN propaganda up to me. In this war for the defense of our common fatherland we're all united, blacks and whites. Look at these fellows! Eh, Massiba! Those shits are taking a good pasting!"

Massiba bared his teeth.

"It's good, boss!"

"You see, Monsieur Spencer, all the Katangese are on our side. These four fellows came and joined me of their own accord. They had formed a commando and put themselves at our disposal. Eh, Massiba! Everyone volunteering to protect our President Kimjanga!

"I'm taking them out on a little operation. If you'd like to come with us . . . you can judge for yourself that it's not always mercenaries who defend the Katangese flag! I must warn you, it might be dangerous."

Spencer shrugged his shoulders. He was fed up with all this propaganda. He sensed it was a show put on for the journalists. But the four Negroes might be interesting.

374

There had been no mention of Negroes since the start of this business.

La Roncière came in, dressed in drill trousers and shirt, unarmed. Gelinet rushed up to him.

"My dear fellow . . . you know Spencer, an American journalist?"

"I'm being formally introduced," the American reflected.

"Pleased to meet you," la Roncière curtly replied without shaking hands. "Is everything ready?" he asked.

"Yes," said Gelinet, "we'll drive you there straight away."

Spencer realized from Gelinet's eagerness to please, from the commanding tone of the man who had just come in, that he was a mercenary . . . but not just any mercenary, a leader. He alone interested him.

In a gentle voice he asked la Roncière:

"Well, how are things going this evening?"

"Everything's going very well."

"What are your plans?"

Gelinet chipped in.

"I was just thinking of taking Monsieur Spencer to see an operation mounted by Katangese troops."

"Good idea. Maybe the Americans will at last understand what's going on here!"

"Above all I want to have an overall picture!"

"Go ahead! Go and ask Monsieur Maley for information."

"You seem pretty well informed."

"I'm in a hurry. Good-bye, Gelinet!"

"Good-bye. . . ."

La Roncière went out. There was a sound of a car driving off.

"Who was that?" Spencer inquired, more and more interested.

"Oh, a friend. . . ."

"Is he Belgian? He hasn't any accent."

"He's a Walloon, you know!"

Spencer followed Gelinet and the four gendarmes. They moved into position on a terrace overlooking the post office, and in a few minutes, without taking aim and from a great distance, fired off all the magazines they had brought with them. It was a splendid fusillade.

"No result," Spencer noted. "Just a lot of noise!"

As he left them, one of the gendarmes to whom he had given a packet of cigarettes asked him:

"Happy, boss?"

"Yes," said Spencer. "And you?"

"I'm happy. When the war's over, all the whites will bugger off!"

The mortar was concealed behind a garden wall, the jeep near by was ready to move off. A mercenary was on watch at the top of the lane.

La Roncière set the sights approximately: a thousand yards was the range at which he estimated Clair Manoir to be. Direction . . . by judgment. . . .

He suddenly felt like a St. Cyr cadet again. Since those days he had worked out any amount of fire plans but had never done the actual firing himself. He was no longer sure how to calculate the trajectory and could not remember the range of the boosting charge.

He anxiously reflected:

"Let's hope the projectiles land on Siddartha and not on the Belgians. An error of one degree, a slight breeze, and I'll be shooting up the villa next door. Ah, well, that's war! The bomber pilots in 1944 or '45 didn't worry unduly over details like this! If there's a hitch we can always claim it was the blue helmets that fired. Everyone will believe it."

Seven out of ten shells landed on Clair Manoir, but caused more noise than damage; the three others exploded in the park.

After the attack on the Villa des Roches Maley had taken refuge in Clair Manoir. He now felt as though he was being tracked. He remembered the voice at the French Consulate that had said: "We'll get you . . . you see, it's only too easy."

Siddartha dispatched a patrol in the direction from which the firing had come. The Gurkhas came back with a few empty shell-cases.

9. Failure of Morthor

On her return from Rhodesia, Jenny gave asylum to three English families who lived near the post office with their servants and countless children. They had preserved, to the point of mania, the ritual, conventions and jokes of the Old Country.

It required all her tolerance to endure them. She could not picture herself living in England in the company of a John Ligget caught up once more in the conformity of his social background: five o'clock tea, pipes and tweeds, cricket matches. . . . Yet that was what awaited her if Rhodesia was lost.

After driving la Roncière to his plane she had had a drink with Smith. He had said to her:

"The situation's deteriorating throughout Africa. In Kenya the old Mau-Mau bands are being recreated and the Kikuyus are drawing up lists of those who tracked them down. The Rhodesias will go up in smoke any day. . . . What's happening in the Congo is lucky for us!"

"Lucky? What do you mean?"

"It's proof positive that Negroes left to their own devices are capable of every sort of stupidity. The African leaders are furious with this business, which discredits them. Consequently in Kenya, as in Rhodesia, our local politicians are soft-pedaling on their outrageous claims. But the Congo will soon be forgotten and they'll be demanding the departure of the whites all the more violently!"

"What do you think of Colonel la Roncière?"

"An interesting fellow, Jenny. . . . But he's only a mercenary. He puts into practice a few ideas which he believes to be new and revolutionary but which have nothing new about them: psychological warfare and intoxication of the masses—it's England who set the best example of that by the way she administered India. An entire nation, that's to say its upper classes, intoxicated by British snobbery!

"What's new about la Roncière is his phraseology. He wants to justify whatever shocking aspects his methods might have by scientific argument. All these new champions of revolutionary warfare strike me as having guilty consciences. The Indian Civil Service did the same job; they soiled their hands just as much, but they had a healthier attitude. They frankly admitted they were serving their country and defending the Empire by every means at their disposal.

"Apart from that, he's a very remarkable fellow, la Roncière: tenacious, clear-headed, and with quick reactions . . . but out here he's only an employee of the Union Minière, a specialist in a somewhat particular field who is lucky enough to be also serving his country. The Indian Civil Service knew all there was to know about India; la Roncière doesn't know the first thing about black Africa."

Joan spent a sleepless night. When she woke on the morning of 14 September and looked at herself in the mirror, she considered herself hideous and blamed Fonts for this.

Her father had not reproached her in any way. He did not even refer to her absence. But at breakfast, when she was trying to put a good face on it, Riverton said:

"I'd like you to stop seeing that fellow for a bit, however fascinating he may be. It so happens we're not on the same side of the fence."

"I have no intention of seeing him again."

"That's just as well . . . for the sake of my career, let's say . . . and your own peace of mind. I was very worried this morning when I found you weren't in your room . . . terribly worried. I think you ought to go back to America. . . . The situation's liable to deteriorate very quickly. You could take the plane."

"When?"

"Let's say tomorrow. Maley will get you a seat on a UN machine since the normal services have been discontinued."

"So soon?"

Arnold lowered his eyes.

"Yes. You're not looking well. The climate?"

"Yes, of course, the climate."

378

The Union Minière factory chimney loomed up straight ahead of him, emerging from the clouds. Lieutenant Berthot went into a dive, steadied the Fouga at fifteen hundred feet and began to circle over the town. Beneath him the streets were almost deserted. There were only a few UN vehicles parked in the middle of the roadway. Their occupants had abandoned them when they heard the aircraft overhead. They were probably firing at him now, but he heard nothing. All of a sudden a succession of red and orange fiery dots rose slowly towards him. The blue helmets had just opened up with an anti-aircraft machine-gun. One round in five was a tracer. Berthot thought with amusement of the autoroute he used to take from Brussels. He would hold his car right on the center of the yellow line, with the speedometer set at a hundred miles an hour. The little yellow dots rose to meet the windscreen with the same fascinating slowness as these machine-gun tracer bullets.

Berthot banked steeply, stepped on the gas and headed straight for the airport. The runway appeared on his left.

Two UN DC4s, painted white, were parked in front of the airport buildings. A fatigue party were unloading ammunition boxes. Berthot had time to see that some long wooden cases were being taken off one of the aircraft. They were coffins.

The fatigue party heard the noise of the Fouga too late. Berthot had already started a long dive. The air whistled past the cockpit. The first DC4 was right in his sights. Down below, soldiers in camouflage uniform were scattering in all directions.

One of them, a young lad, was carrying a case in his arms. Berthot could distinctly read the lettering on it: "Carlsberg." The fellow was paralyzed with fear and incredulity. His mouth was wide open as though to shout, but the pilot felt sure there was no sound coming from it. He launched his first rocket, which went off singularly slowly. At first nothing happened. Then a wisp of smoke ran along the wing of the DC4 and the whole machine vanished in a sheet of purple flame. Berthot turned. A column of black smoke was rising straight into the sky. He fired his second rocket. The second DC4 collapsed, its landing gear damaged, and likewise caught fire.

Berthot burst out laughing: the laugh of an urchin who has just carried out a good practical joke.

He was extremely pleased and so would his pals be when they heard their handiwork had held together, that there had been no trouble with the rockets or the machine-guns.

As he flew off, he fired a short burst at the control tower and called out on the radio:

"Control tower, hello, control tower! So long, lads, this was just a little courtesy visit. I'll come back tomorrow with the whole squadron. Have a good time!"

"You dirty filthy sod!" an English voice bellowed into the receiver.

Berthot switched off the radio and flew slowly back towards the town. He sighted the railway station, then the post office, and followed the Avenue de Fromont in the direction of Clair Manoir. He had two rockets left and half a belt of machine-gun ammunition.

The square building loomed up in front of him. Banking steeply, he dived straight down. The first rocket burst on the roof. The second overshot it and exploded in the garden. Berthot climbed swiftly and headed back for Kolwezi. His tanks were rapidly exhausted. At a low altitude he used a great deal of fuel.

Maley straightened up and struggled out of the trench in which he had been sheltering, brushing the mud off his knees with his hands. He was white in the face but felt he had not behaved too badly. Some UN officers and civilian employees were still crouching at the bottom of their hole.

The trench had been dug after the mortar attack on Clair Manoir.

Never had Maley imagined it would serve as an anti-aircraft shelter. He could hardly believe what was happening. They had just been attacked by a plane. Kimjanga, a puppet on the run, had jet fighters at his disposal, which even the UN did not have. Nothing had worked out as he had hoped, and he knew already that he had lost the battle. For the last two days he had been living on Indian Army rations, heavily spiced with curry, and he had a stomach-ache. He had complained to Siddartha, but the general had gruffly pointed out that this was hardly the moment for culinary concerns. Maley had eventually arranged to be served plain rice without curry. The first time the plate of snow-white rice had been placed before him, Siddartha had asked:

"You don't like Indian food?"

By which, of course, he implied:

"You don't like Indians!"

Maley had been on the verge of losing his temper; he had almost risen from the table and told this spiteful

380

touchy Indian what he thought of him. Just because Maley was white, Siddartha could not resist the temptation, by means of gesture, attitude and innuendo, of blaming him for everything—Captain Dokkal's death, the inexplicable error of the Swedish battalion and its colonel, the incidents during the night, the counter-attack by the mercenaries, and the blue helmets' withdrawal from the radio station.

Two soldiers who were hoisting an ammunition box up on the roof blundered into him without apologizing. They gave off a pungent smell of unwashed bodies. The water supply had been cut off by the first mortar bombardment. The electricity had also ceased to function.

Bombarded by mortar for the first time at eleven o'clock at night, Clair Manoir had again been attacked at four in the morning.

"They have only two guns," Siddartha had claimed, "but they keep switching them from one position to another, so it's impossible to pin-point them!"

Each time they went out on patrol, the UN troops picked up nothing but empty cases and were shot up by civilians concealed on the roofs.

The morale of the blue helmets had fallen considerably after these twenty-four hours of confused fighting. The young Swedes, who had not come to Katanga to make war, gave unmistakable signs of weakening. Many of them had allowed themselves to be taken prisoner without offering any resistance.

Maley's office at Clair Manoir was a dingy cubby-hole furnished with a deal table and a collapsible bed. The window was half blocked by a parapet of sandbags. Maley kicked aside a pile of cigarette butts in disgust, lit a fresh cigarette and picked up the report he had been reading when the warning sounded.

The document consisted of a dozen pages of typescript and was entitled "Military Situation." It was signed by Colonel Degger, head of the Security services.

Three factors characterize the situation:

1. The renewed activity of about fifty European mercenaries who, after escaping from the Rumpunch round-up, have come back to Elizabethville. They have regrouped into small commandos which harass our troops without respite while carefully avoiding a direct engagement.

2. The reorganization of certain elements of the Katangese Gendarmerie which had disbanded at the

381

start of our action. Some Belgian officers have succeeded in regaining control of an effective strength which can be estimated at about three hundred men.

3. The civilian population of Elizabethville is providing active assistance to the Katangese forces. A number of civilians who are in possession of firearms fire at our troops from the rooftops. All our troop movements are noted and forthwith reported.

Maley flung the report down on the table and picked up another, which was marked in capital letters STRICTLY CONFIDENTIAL. It was entitled, "Note on the Morale of our Troops."

The difficult conditions in which the fighting is taking place and the relatively heavy losses suffered by our troops are beginning to affect the morale of some of our units who are not seasoned to war and are therefore unprepared for this sort of operation.

According to information from Baluba sources, some of the mercenaries and European civilians are at the moment trying to establish contact with UN officers and soldiers to induce them to end the fighting and surrender to the Katangese forces.

Since six o'clock that morning a clandestine station had started operating: Radio Free Katanga.

Broadcasts were given in French and in English. It had required only one soldier to tune into it for everyone else to listen in forthwith. All the white soldiers had transistor sets. These could not, after all, be confiscated. It would create such a deplorable impression!

Maley had a copy of the second broadcast of the morning:

. . . President Kimjanga has placed himself at the head of his troops and is moving substantial forces towards the capital to liberate it.

At Elizabethville the UN troops are suffering heavy losses. Two hundred killed have already been counted. Our air force is attacking enemy units without respite and several aircraft have been shot down. Supplies are being held up and the soldiers have only a few days' rations and ammunition.

The entire Katangese nation is standing firm against barbarism. Hundreds of innocent civilians, including women and children, have been massacred in cold blood by the Gurkhas, those soldiers who belong to one of the most savage and primitive people on earth.

The President appeals to the UN soldiers to put an end to the fighting and lay down their arms. He assures them that they will be well treated, that no harm will come to them and that they will be released immediately after the cease fire. . . .

If the blue helmets persist in their crimes, he will no longer be able to protect them against the population's legitimate desire for vengeance.

Siddartha stormed into the room, his face contorted with fury.

"I've just had a call from the airfield. The Fouga has destroyed two aircraft on the ground. I've been forced to cancel all flights."

"Is it serious?"

"No. I have enough men and supplies to hold out for a couple of weeks, but it will have a disastrous effect on the troops. An army never likes the sensation of being cut off from its main base."

"You'll soon be getting some Ethiopian fighters!"

"Damn it all, they should have been here this morning! They took off from Addis Ababa yesterday afternoon. Since then, not a word about them. I wonder what has happened?"

Siddartha sat down on Maley's bed and filled his pipe, making an effort to recover his composure.

"Sir, the moment has come to take serious decisions."

Maley heaved a sigh and looked up at the ceiling.

"We can't go on like this," the general continued. "Communications with the airport are getting more and more difficult. The four points we hold in the town are isolated and we're having great trouble in supplying them. We keep being fired upon from the windows."

"What do you suggest?"

"Do something, by God, anything!" the general exploded. "We can't go on receiving blows without replying to them. My Gurkhas are getting out of hand. . . ."

"Yes," Maley chipped in, "the Red Cross reports they're even firing on ambulances and civilians."

"That's not true!"

"Allow me to go on," Maley curtly broke in. "I haven't finished yet. I gave you strict orders: no violence and no unnecessary bloodshed. Yesterday one of your officers took five Belgian hostages and bundled them into an ammunition truck so as not to be fired upon. Can you imagine the reactions of the population?"

"So what? Two Gurkhas had been killed five minutes before by those self-same innocent civilians firing from their windows. You see no harm in my colored men being killed, but not a hair of any of these worthy people must be touched: they have white skins!"

"I don't want to listen to your excuses, Général. I'm giving you an order: I don't want any more of this sort of thing!"

General Siddartha's eyes narrowed.

"You must understand, sir, that I'm responsible for the lives of my men and I'm in charge of military operations. For the last twenty-four hours we have had proof that the white population has taken up arms. My soldiers are killed brutally without being able to defend themselves. This town is in a state of open revolt; I shall bring it to heel!"

"You'll bring it to heel? How?"

"I'll give orders to fire back with heavy weapons each time there's a shot from a house. I shall dispatch mixed patrols of armored cars and bath-tubs throughout the town. At the first shot my men will fire back with machine-guns and cannon. I've set up several mortars. If we're fired upon, I'll spray the town. Ten shots to one!"

The general thumped Maley's table with his stick.

"I'll show them. . . ."

"No, you won't," said Maley.

"What do you mean? Who's going to stop me? You?"

The Indian defied him with his glare.

"No, Siddartha, not I but the UN Secretary-General. He has been in Leopoldville since yesterday. I don't know what's going on but I can assure you 'our initiative' has not been approved. Our good friends in the Hotel Royal are leaving us in the lurch! And this is the moment you choose to embark on total war!"

"I can't believe . . ."

"You'd better read this; it has just arrived!"

The message was brief and to the point:

By order of the Secretary-General, I am giving you the following instructions:

1. The Secretary-General is appalled that you should have exceeded your instructions and started military operations in Katanga without his agreement.

2. The Secretary-General is making every attempt to find a rapid political solution to the crisis.

3. The Secretary-General gives you categorical instructions to cease all offensive action and confine yourself exclusively to defensive measures so as to ensure the safety of your troops.

4. You are requested to take all necessary steps to avoid casualties among the civilian population.

"It's sheer madness!" Siddartha bellowed. "They're absolutely off their heads! If we don't act, the others will hack us to pieces!"

"Yes, apart from the fact that no steps can be taken against Kimjanga. At this rate the cease-fire will be signed in three days' time, and twenty-four hours later Kimjanga will enter his capital in triumph. Everything will have to be started all over again."

"But we must do something, sir. The Secretary-General can't be aware of the situation. We ought to tell him that nothing is lost. If he gives me a free hand for twenty-four hours, I'll clean up this town and the secession will be squashed once and for all."

"Read right through to the end and you'll see that it's too late. The UN authorities don't even recognize that we launched Morthor on their orders, that the 'go-ahead' was given us in this very place by the second-in-command to our representative in the Congo, Monsieur Brahimi!"

Siddartha was holding the Secretary-General's orders in his hand, but he found it hard to believe that anyone could climb down like this!

During the early hours of 13 September the UN forces embarked on a fresh operation to arrest the foreign mercenaries in the service of Katanga. While they were engaged on this operation, a fire broke out in a UN garage. As the troops were making their way towards it, some shots were fired at them from a building in which a number of foreign officers were quartered. Other shots were fired at our troops as they were advancing towards essential objectives in the town or going to relieve the posts which were guarding important installations.

"It's a stupid lie," he declared, "stupid and dishonorable! We attacked because we received orders to do so . . . and to obey those orders, men have been killed."

385

Siddartha pictured the journalists rushing about the corridors of the Royal, with their copy in their hands. He imagined the headlines: "Without Orders the UN Senior Representative in Elizabethville, Mr. Maley, and the Indian General Siddartha Launch War on Katanga."

The two men avoided each other's eyes.

"We're done for," Maley eventually observed. "Not only are we being left in the lurch but we're being held responsible."

Siddartha raised his head.

"As far as I'm concerned, I'm going to call a halt. I don't want my men to get killed for nothing. I'll confine myself strictly to defensive measures. But I may as well warn you that we ought to act quickly. I've got my Gurkhas well in hand. They've had a bellyfull, but they won't move unless they're provoked. But the Swedes' morale is very low. The whites are urging them to surrender and there are some I know who would like nothing better."

He rose to his feet with a sigh.

"As I see it, we're going to go down on our knees. In these conditions, the sooner the better!

"I must tell you, sir, that the Jadotville garrison is cracking up."

Maley raised his head.

"They're the Irish, aren't they?"

"Yes. We sent a company up to Jadotville on the 13th, shortly after Morthor was launched. This company was surrounded by about five hundred Katangese gendarmes. They are isolated in their camp and dare not set foot outside. The water has been cut off and they have hardly any supplies. The Katangese are now commanded by European mercenaries who are demanding an unconditional surrender."

"It can't be as serious as that! Do something to get them out. Why haven't you sent reinforcements?"

"I've tried. I dispatched fifty Gurkhas with a couple of armored cars. They were attacked a few minutes ago by the Fouga. The two armored cars were set on fire and most of the vehicles are out of commission."

"Their situation's really desperate?"

"Desperate? No, not for real soldiers. All they need do is make a determined break-out and they would disengage themselves on their own. . . ."

"Well, then?" Maley interjected.

Siddartha pursed his lips.

"Well, they've got the wind up and don't want to fight.

According to the signals I've been getting from their commanding officer, Major Keller, his men's morale has been reduced to nought. Here's his latest message:

> Situation extremely serious. Enemy pressure increasing hour by hour. Have received ultimatum demanding surrender nine hundred hours latest. Request reinforcements otherwise impossible withstand assault.

"A few minutes ago that bloody Bayard who speaks on Radio Katanga announced that if the Irish did not surrender within the next forty-eight hours they would all be massacred. I'm under the impression we're soon going to lose a company of valiant warriors. . . ."

Siddartha paused, then added:

". . . Who haven't fired a shot in anger. They were pretty poor soldiers, but I suppose they'll make very fine prisoners of war."

The general sprang to attention and saluted.

"My respects, sir."

Maley sank back in his chair without acknowledging the salute. He watched with sightless eyes the clouds floating low over the tree-tops. His office smelt of dust and smoke. He lit another cigarette, produced a bottle of whisky out of a cupboard and took a long swig from the neck of the bottle.

If the Irish were killed or wounded, they would never forgive him in Dublin. Any more than they would if the Irish were taken prisoner.

Kreis arrived at Jadotville the next day, on orders from la Roncière. He had brought with him Buscard, two South African mercenaries who after the operation against the Villa des Roches had chosen him as their leader, and a Hungarian called Max whose real name was so complicated that no one was able to pronounce it.

Since his return from France Max had been one of the main attractions at the Mitsouko where, for a brandy or two, he would be only too willing to describe his adventures. He did so with great deliberation and a completely straight face, much to the delight of his audience.

Max, a Hungarian refugee from the last war, had worked as a waiter in Paris, in a big restaurant in the Boulevard Saint-Michel. He was as pleasant as could be, married, with four children. His employer had eventually made great friends with him, after growing accustomed to what he called his "whims."

Once a month—at the turn of the moon, according to Monsieur Ruchet, who did not underestimate the great influence which this heavenly body has on the behavior of human beings—Max would come and see him. He would put down his tray.

"Monsieur Ruchet," he would say, "something's giving way up here!"

He would point to his head.

"I feel like breaking something!"

Monsieur Ruchet, who, to his cost, had some experience of these "whims," would then give him a thousand francs in exchange for his apron.

"Where shall I go?" Max would ask him, still as calm as ever.

Ruchet would indicate a rival establishment, preferably one in the immediate vicinity so that he would be able to witness the scene, and then, with his podgy little hands folded over his paunch, he would sit back and wait.

Max would order a drink at the bar and two minutes later, never longer, would start a row on a variety of pretexts.

Chairs would be sent flying, glasses and trays would be smashed.

Ruchet would look at his watch.

"I say, the police have taken three minutes longer than last time to turn up!"

The policemen would rush in and pounce on Max. This was the moment Monsieur Ruchet was waiting for.

Max would stop and produce from his wallet a veteran's card. He had been seriously wounded in the head during the Resistance, in an absolutely genuine engagement and the doctors admitted he was liable to be seized unexpectedly by furious fits, albeit of short duration. It was not sufficient reason to lock him up.

With great care the policeman would haul Max off and release him an hour later.

The next day he would resume his job and Monsieur Ruchet, like an enlightened amateur, would discuss his latest performance with him:

"You weren't in good form yesterday, eh! You've got a black eye."

The Veterans Association would settle the damage after the usual delay.

Max enlisted for Katanga on his employer's advice.

"You'll have a high old time," Monsieur Ruchet had told him. "And afterwards you'll have nothing to worry about for two or three years at least!"

He was posted to North Katanga. Max was far from pleased. He did not like the job he had been given, asked for his return ticket, got it and rejoined his wife and children in Paris.

But after a week he felt bored and had no money left. With great care he went over his accounts and concluded that he had not been paid all that was due to him. One morning, accompanied by his entire family, he turned up at the Katangese Delegation in the Avenue Henri Martin. It was one of his "whimsical" days, but he was not aware of this. With extreme politeness he asked a secretary if it was possible for him to see Monsieur le Délégué.

"He's not in," the secretary replied without lifting her nose from her papers.

Max drew a pistol.

"We'll see!"

Pushing the secretary, his wife and four children ahead of him, he forced his way into the office of Monsieur Thomaris, an immaculate African who did his utmost to emulate his idea of the perfect diplomat.

Monsieur Thomaris gave a shrill scream. The military adviser, a retired French major, rushed in. Max waved his revolver in his face and lined him up in the courtyard together with the secretary and the delegate. The children looked on, quietly holding hands. Madame Max had produced a little mirror from her bag and was busy powdering her nose.

"What about showing them your card?" she suggested.

Max got everything he wanted, even an air ticket for Katanga.

His "whim" was over; he put his pistol away, bade a polite farewell and went home.

Eight days later he landed at Elizabethville, a week before Morthor was launched.

Max fascinated Fonts, who enjoyed whims of this sort, and also Kreis, who recognized him as a pedigree soldier, conscientious and reliable, who did not lose his head when confronted with the unexpected.

La Roncière had said to Kreis:

"I don't quite know what's going on at Jadotville. It seems some hot-heads have fired a few shots at the Irish company stationed there. They're probably your para-

389

commandos. The Irish are cut off, without communications, and they're scared. I'm counting on you to transform this circus show into a proper military operation. You realize what a psychological effect it would have if they surrendered!

"Do as you see fit, I know I can rely on you and your gang. I want prisoners but no casualties. Congratulations on the Villa des Roches job. Maley has moved out."

"Thank you, Colonel. I had to make up for . . ."

"For what?"

"My stupidity at Tshiko Camp. I think I understand now!"

"I'm glad to hear it . . . because at Jadotville it's Colonel Nadolo who's theoretically in command and you'll be dealing with him again."

It was indeed the para-commandos, led by four or five mercenaries, who were hemming in the Irish.

Lying flat on a terrace overlooking the camp, through his binoculars Kreis observed the UN Sikorsky cautiously preparing to land. The helicopter had first circled over the camp at a high altitude and the Irish were now waving frantically at it from below. The Katangese had opened fire but Kreis, with a great bellow, had restored peace and quiet.

Without much difficulty, within twenty-four hours, Kreis and his gang had regained control of the para-commandos, much to the disgust of Colonel Nadolo. Since his arrival here he had not issued a single order to his men, except to fire away at random.

The helicopter landed gently in a cloud of dust raised by its blades. Some Irish soldiers in sweat-stained uniforms rushed towards it.

Still watching through his binoculars, Kreis saw the pilot, a tall, lean, fair-haired Swede, jump down. Straight away he was surrounded by a gesticulating mob. The Swede looked astonished. He spread his hands in a gesture of impotence. Three men stepped forward. Kreis recognized Major Keller, the officer commanding the Irish battalion. He was a giant of a man with a ruddy complexion and close-cropped gray hair. He was very partial to whisky and Kreis knew him to be extremely pious. Every Sunday he insisted on his men attending Mass, which was said by Padre Maughan.

An Irish fatigue party started to unload the machine. Kreis counted four dozen cases of rations and three barrels, probably water. The men looked disappointed. A young soldier pounced on one of the barrels and tried to open the bung. A sergeant sent him flying with a blow from his fist. The soldier slowly collapsed in the dust and lay motionless.

Major Keller led the pilot back to his command post: a shack surrounded by a wall of sandbags.

Kreis heard a shout behind him. He sighed and slowly rose to his feet. Colonel Nadolo had arrived, gesticulating, in jumping boots and camouflage uniform. He was accompanied by four guards in steel helmets, armed with Fals. Kreis turned to Buscard.

"Another circus show. Here come the clowns!"

Nadolo screamed:

"It's treachery! Why are you allowing them to land supplies? You've taken advantage of my absence!"

"I've issued orders," Kreis calmly replied. "You were having a snooze when the helicopter arrived. You must take your choice: either snooze or fight!"

"Why did you tell them not to fire? Because you didn't want them to fire on whites, eh? Without you we should already have taken the camp. Now you let them receive water and rations! It can't go on like this. I shall make a report to President Kimjanga; I'll have you shot for treachery!"

Kreis glared at Nadolo. He had a wild urge to bash his face in with a rifle-butt. The colonel took a pace backwards and his bodyguard raised their Fals.

Kreis managed to control himself.

"Colonel, I've explained the situation to you a dozen times. In the first place, you know I take my orders from President Kimjanga himself. You know our plan: we don't want casualties, only prisoners. The Irish must surrender."

"Why do you allow the helicopter to bring them water? You cut off the water supply when you arrived, well and good. Since then they've had nothing to eat or drink. Now they are able to drink."

"I don't want to shoot down a helicopter; it would cause too much of a shindy. Three two-hundred-liter barrels for two hundred men makes about three liters a man, which is hardly worth drinking. They'll be even thirstier afterwards. We'll prevent the helicopter from taking off. The Irish will realize they have no further opportunity of getting supplies, which will destroy their morale!"

The pilot of the helicopter was walking back to his machine, accompanied by Keller. Kreis seized a Fal and took careful aim at a point ten feet ahead of the Swede. He fired a short burst. The bullets kicked up the dust. Keller and the pilot flung themselves flat on the ground. Some Irish soldiers opened fire at random.

Kreis waited a few minutes. The firing ceased. Keller and the pilot had half risen to their feet. Bent double, they made a dash for the helicopter. They were only thirty feet from it when Kreis fired another burst. The two men fell flat once more. Then they withdrew, slithering back on their stomachs.

Kreis picked up his loud-hailer.

"Major Keller," he shouted, "listen to me. The helicopter is grounded. Don't let the pilot attempt to take off, otherwise we'll shoot him down. You've received six hundred liters of water for your men. We'll let you keep it for humanitarian reasons. At the first sign of an attempt at hostility we'll riddle the barrels. Look."

He fired, and the bullets landed with a thud on the upper part of a bung. Five jets of water spurted out. The liquid made a dark patch in the dust, then disappeared, absorbed in a matter of seconds by the parched ground. Keller and his two hundred men stood, with their eyes on stalks, watching the water stream down the canister.

Kreis took up his loud-hailer again.

"Your health, Keller. You can give your men a drink. When you get too thirsty, remember you only have to say the word. You know our conditions: if you surrender, we guarantee your safety and we'll have the water switched on again at once."

Kreis slept in the big room which Monteil, the Union Minière director at Jadotville, had put at his disposal. He was uncomfortable. The heat was intense and the sheets stuck to his skin. He had a shower, then poured himself out a glass of iced water. He suddenly thought of Major Keller. He had no particular feelings about this big, red-faced Irishman. They were both fighting, each on his own side. Both of them had mediocre human material at their disposal. Both of them were in Katanga to do a job for which they felt no enthusiasm. Kreis was obeying orders and so was Keller, that was all.

To Kreis's great surprise, his renewed contact with Colonel Nadolo had been less stormy then he had feared. He had found the colonel in a sumptuous villa which he had requisitioned as his command post. The floor and tables were littered with empty beer bottles. When Kreis had come in, Nadolo was drinking and palavering with a dozen Katangese officers. He had greeted him cordially and poured him out a huge tumbler of luke-warm champagne.

Kreis had realized at once that Nadolo was apprehensive. His first question had been:

"Do you think we'll be able to hold out?"

"Of course," Kreis had replied. "At Elizabethville it was hard going the first day, but now we have the situation well in hand."

"But President Kimjanga has taken refuge in Rhodesia, hasn't he?"

"He hasn't 'taken refuge in Rhodesia,' he has fallen back on a secret command post so as not to be arrested by the UN. From Rhodesia he's directing the resistance."

Nadolo did not seem convinced. Kreis thought of Fonts. He resorted to diplomacy.

"The President asked me to tell you that he was counting on you to bring off a striking victory at Jadotville. He sent me to put myself at your orders and to help you if necessary."

Nadolo gulped down half the contents of his glass and belched with satisfaction.

"The Irish won't face facts," he eventually said. "I surrounded their camp and launched an attack against them yesterday morning. But they fired back as hard as they could. There was a big battle and my men were unable to cross the barbed wire."

"Did you have any casualties?" Kreis inquired.

"Oh, not many. Two wounded, but the UN had at least fifteen killed."

"Not fifteen, fifty," declared a lieutenant, who added with satisfaction:

"Soon they'll all be killed. They can't hold their position much longer."

"I see how it is," Kreis reflected. "No one really attacked. The Katangese merely loosed off magazine after magazine. The others did the same. Result: a few wounded on both sides. At this rate it could go on for a month!"

He repeated for the benefit of Nadolo and his officers:

"What we want is the capitulation of the Irish. We must force them to surrender. President Kimjanga made it quite clear that he wished to avoid casualties. It's psychological warfare, you understand?"

"That's good, psychological warfare," Nadolo had proudly declared, pouring Kreis out another tumbler of champagne.

Kreis had started by cutting off the Irishmen's water supply, then he had reinforced the blockade. His instructions: to prevent the enemy from breaking out but to do the utmost to prevent casualties.

Then, with the help of the Union Minière, he had set up some powerful loudspeakers which broadcast the bulletins of Radio Katanga.

He had made a point of addressing Keller and his officers by name over the loud-hailer. He had discovered their identities almost at once, thanks to information supplied by the Union Minière agents.

It was an old trick which he had learned to his cost in Russia. In 1942, after the disaster of Stalingrad, his battalion had been completely surrounded. All night long the Soviet artillery had pounded away at the exhausted troops. Kreis was the only officer still alive. At first light, shortly before dawn, the firing had stopped and from the opposite side some Russian loudspeakers had called out, addressing him by his name and rank:

"Lieutenant Karl Kreis, it's useless to wait for help. The German Army is in full retreat. Don't prolong the fighting pointlessly. Surrender and you'll be treated as prisoners of war. If you resist, you will all be wiped out!"

The first time Kreis had raised the megaphone to his lips, Keller had given a start, them fumbled for his pistol, while his face went bright red.

Kreis had had the same sensation in Russia. When the enemy addresses you, you always think he's going to say something shameful about the people you are fond of.

Keller had raised his fist and cursed him at the top of his voice; Kreis had likewise yelled curses at the Russians.

To drown the voice of the loudspeakers, the Irish major had ordered his men to make as much noise as possible by hammering on their mess-tins. Kreis had sent to Elizabethville for some records of bagpipe music, which had put a stop to the mess-tin nonsense. Kreis was quite fond of the bagpipes but preferred the fife.

Now, when the loudspeakers started up or when Kreis spoke over the loud-hailer, a great silence hung over the Irish camp. The men, parched and demoralized, listened. Then small groups of soldiers lying in a patch of shade would discuss the news. The officers were slow to take action. The first day, they had tried to shake the men out of their apathy, but their heart was not in it. The evening before, at Kreis's request, Radio Katanga had broadcast an ultimatum; the garrison should surrender on the following day, at ten in the morning, otherwise the attack would be launched.

Kreis looked at his watch: two o'clock in the morning. He switched off the light and fell asleep again at once.

Someone was shaking him violently: it was Monteil, out of breath and stammering with excitement:

"This is it," he said, "we've got them! Keller wants to speak to you."

A slow smile came over Kreis's face.

"Where is he?"

"He turned up at the Katangese post opposite the main gate of the camp and asked to see the white commander. The Katangese have manhandled him slightly."

"Shit! I hope they won't get up to their tricks again! They'll spoil everything!"

Kreis hastily dressed, buckled on his belt, checked his grenades and went out.

He heard the shouting when he was still a hundred yards from the post and quickened his pace. Three soldiers stood with their rifles trained on Keller, who was lined up against a wall. There was a livid mark on his left cheek and his mouth was bleeding. A blow from a rifle-butt, no doubt.

"Take your shoes off, you dirty Fleming, or we'll kill you," Sergeant Lundula was screaming.

Kreis registered the scene at a glance: the ground was littered with empty beer bottles. Lundula was drunk and could barely stand upright. Lined up against the wall, Keller maintained his composure. He was frightened of these incomprehensible creatures who were threatening him but at the same time he was wild with rage that he, a regular officer of the Irish Army, should be treated like this by a lot of drunken savages.

Kreis felt instinctive sympathy for the Irishman. Like him, he was a white man and a soldier. He could not help being on his side.

He would have liked to draw his revolver and fire into this horde, but he remembered just in time that these Negroes were his own men and that Keller was the enemy. Calmly stepping forward, he tapped Lundula on the shoulder.

"Well done, Sergeant," he said, "good work. It's a fine capture, you'll be decorated!"

"You filthy swine," Keller hissed, "aren't you ashamed . . ."

"Shut your trap," Kreis interjected.

Then he added rapidly between his teeth and in English:

"Shut up, I'm trying to get you out of this hornet's nest. If you open your mouth, you're done for. They'll bump you off on the spot and I shan't be able to do anything about it."

"We're going to shoot this white man," Lundula shouted. "He has refused to obey a Katangese NCO."

He gave a belch and took a big gulp of beer.

"Let's have a swig," Kreis asked.

The German drank without putting the bottle to his lips.

"We'll shoot him later," he explained. "First of all, I'll have to question him. There are secrets he knows. I'm going to take him into the shack next door."

Kreis and Keller now found themselves face to face by themselves. The Irishman took a cigarette from his packet and lit it without offering Kreis one.

"Are you in command of these savages?" he began. "Congratulations, they're a fine army."

"Listen, Keller, I'm not here to listen to speeches from you. If you have anything to tell me, go ahead. Otherwise I'll hand you over to the Negroes!"

"But, good God, you can't behave like this! For the last two days you've been telling us we'll be treated as prisoners of war and that we had nothing to fear!"

"Am I to understand that you're surrendering?"

"I never said anything of the sort; I'm responsible for my men and, before taking any decision, I want an absolute assurance that they'll come to no harm!"

"Tell me," Kreis abruptly asked, "are you in command of soldiers or choirboys?"

"I'm in command of lads who have never done any fighting in their lives, who came out here because they were told it was for the sake of justice and peace. I don't want them to be hacked to bits by your savages!"

For the last few minutes Keller had been eyeing Kreis's green beret. His gaze now fell on the grenade.

"You were in the French Foreign Legion?"

"Lieutenant Kreis, of the Third Foreign Parachute Regiment."

"German?"

"I was. Now I'm a Frenchman in the service of Katanga. But what has that got to do with it?"

"Nothing at all," said Keller. "I'm only thinking that we're both of us regular officers. We are prepared to die, even for a lot of nonsense, but those boys back there"—he gestured in the direction of the camp—"have nothing to do with this business. I think it's too silly that they should die in Katanga, for God knows what reason!"

Keller held out his packet of cigarettes to Kreis. There was a long silence.

"All right," Kreis went on, "this is what I suggest. Tomorrow, at ten o'clock, you'll surrender, as agreed. You'll give me your signature and you'll lay down your arms. You'll stay in camp. I'll insure your protection personally."

Keller looked Kreis straight in the eye.

"I have your word that my men's safety will be guaranteed?"

Kreis hesitated no longer than a second.

"I give you my word!"

Keller rose to his feet and rubbed his face listlessly.

"Good! Well, that's fixed!"

He ventured the ghost of a smile.

"Don't forget to turn the water on again!"

"You'll have the water back five minutes after surrendering!"

Kreis looked at his watch.

"It's now four o'clock. I'll be outside the main gate of the camp at a quarter to ten. See to it that your men behave and everything will be all right!"

Kreis escorted Keller back to the Irish camp. The two men walked slowly side by side without speaking. They passed close to the small post, but the Katangese soldiers appeared not to notice them. Dead drunk, Lundula lay snoring, and Kreis had to make an effort not to kick his face in.

Kreis shook hands with Keller. He watched as the Irish major, with drooping shoulders, made his way towards the barbed wire entanglement.

Then he went back to Monteil's villa.

"Well?" said the Belgian.

"It's done. They're surrendering this morning, at ten o'clock, but I'm afraid we'll have some difficulty with the Katangese. I'm going to send a message to Elizabethville."

Kreis sat down at a table and began slowly to write:

Urgent stop Surrender Irish garrison arranged stop Fear serious difficulties with Katangese troops and threats to prisoners' lives stop Request immediate dispatch Katangese official with authority over Nadolo stop Kreis

The surrender took place without incident. Colonel Nadolo was present, sporting a brand-new uniform and a number of decorations of his own choice. He even insisted on inviting Major Keller to lunch, but the Irishman politely refused.

The Irish had handed over their weapons without any fuss. They appeared to be unaware of the situation and kept begging for water. When Kreis gave orders for the supply to be turned on, the soldiers dashed for the taps and the NCOs had to restore order with shouts and blows.

The first incidents started at one o'clock in the afternoon. A Katangese gendarme tried to confiscate the watch of one of the Irishmen, who refused to let him have it. The Katangese cursed and swore at him in Swahili. The Irishman's comrades gathered round him and a rubicund sergeant tried to reason with the Katangese. He found himself on the floor, laid out by a blow from a rifle-butt.

In a few minutes a crisis had occurred.

The Katangese had seized their weapons and trained them on the prisoners. Sergeant Lundula kept screaming:

"All the whites have to obey orders! They are prisoners! They must hand over their money and their watches!"

Rolling his eyes fiercely, he seized a young lieutenant by his lapel.

"Give me your watch!"

With a flick of his hand the lieutenant made him let go. Confronted with this unarmed white man, the sergeant felt an irresistible urge to strike him. He quietly put down his rifle, raised his enormous fist and lashed out. The lieutenant collapsed, with a broken nose. Immediately a dozen Katangese, jostling one another and screaming curses, pounced on the prostrate man and started hammering him with their rifle-butts.

A shot rang out. No one ever knew who fired it. A young Irish soldier lay writhing on the ground. A red stain spread from his brown uniform.

Kreis was lunching with Monteil when he heard the shot.

He flung his napkin down on the table.

"Those savages . . . they're always up to something or other. . . ."

He dashed out of the door. In the courtyard a dozen or so men lay snoozing in the shade of their vehicles. Buscard and Max were with them: they were the most reliable material he had been able to find at Jadotville. He had turned them into a sort of operational commando as well as his personal bodyguard. The others were Belgian volunteers. A mediocre lot, but good enough for dealing with Irish blue helmets or Katangese gendarmes.

"Get going!" Kreis shouted. "Make for the camp. I'll take the first jeep. Buscard, follow ten yards behind with the machine-gun, loaded. The rest of you get into the Dodge. No nonsense, mind! Don't fire except on orders from me, but when I give the order don't hesitate. It's our own lives we're fighting for, not only those of the Irish!"

Then he turned to Monteil.

"Send this message to Leo Command Post at once: 'Incidents broken out in prisoners camp stop Send help urgently stop Signed Kreis.'"

Kreis entered the camp without being challenged. There was no one in the guard post. All the Katangese had pounced on the quarry. In the center of the courtyard the Irish formed a vast terror-stricken group. The men were white in the face. The gendarmes, screaming and brandishing their arms, struck out at random with their rifle-butts and kicked the whites who had fallen down unconscious.

Kreis halted his jeep twenty yards from the group. One of the Dodges drew up on his right, the other on his left. Kreis darted a glance at his men. They were quite calm.

"Maybe we'll get away with it," he said to himself.

Silence had fallen. The Katangese were gazing at the mercenaries, as though spellbound. Kreis was standing next to the jeep, stiff and inscrutable, with his hand on the butt of his pistol.

Nadolo advanced towards him, dragging the semi-conscious Major Keller by his collar. Keller looked at Kreis, lowered his gaze and spat on the ground.

"What are you doing here?" Nadolo demanded in a thick voice.

He was still stinking drunk.

Kreis made an effort to speak quietly.

"I've come to make sure the prisoners are being guarded!"

"I'm responsible for that. There's nothing for you to do here."

Kreis lost his composure as he saw Keller's bruised and swollen face. A dozen Irishmen were lying on the ground, as inert as puppets.

"That's enough, Nadolo," he burst out. "You dirty savage! These men are prisoners and you have no right to strike them. Those are President Kimjanga's orders. I order you and your clowns to leave this camp at once."

Nadolo reached for his revolver. He did not have time to finish the gesture. Kreis had buried his fist in his face. The colonel tottered forward. Kreis caught him by the wrist, twisted him round and, with an arm lock, held him fast. Nadolo was panting with hatred and fear.

"Listen to me, all of you," Kreis shouted to the soldiers. "If one of you makes a move I'll bump off your colonel, and the machine-gun will open fire on you."

Buscard trained his weapon on the gendarmes. The other mercenaries had deployed on each side of Kreis, ostentatiously loading their submachine-guns.

"Keller," Kreis shouted, "tell your men to move off and fall in against the barrack-room wall.

"Nadolo, get your men out of the camp at once."

He turned to Buscard.

"At the first suspicious movement, let them have a burst in the guts."

The gendarmes hesitated; there was a momentary wavering.

Kreis, pressed against Nadolo, said to him through clenched teeth:

"Tell them to be quick about it; I'll give them a minute, then I'll fire."

He tightened his grip and Nadolo bellowed with pain.

"Move off, all of you," the colonel shouted. "Fall in outside the camp!"

For five seconds no one moved. Then a big Katangese headed for the gate, dragging his rifle by the barrel; a dozen others followed him. The rest started running. In less than a minute the courtyard was deserted.

Kreis heaved a sigh of relief. He turned to Nadolo.

"You stay with us. If I have any nonsense from your thugs, I'll bump you off myself."

He seized the colonel by the sleeve, dragged him towards the nearest barrack-room, opened the door with his foot and heaved him inside.

"You stay there. I'll have some beer sent in to you."

Major Keller came up to him.

"Thank you," he said. "That was a pretty close shave for all of us. Before we sailed from Ireland, a missionary came to bless the battalion and remind us that the Negroes

400

were our brothers! He'd better not try and deliver the same sermon today! What's going to happen, Kreis?"

"I don't know. For the time being tell your men to return to barracks and stay there. There's no point in provoking the Negroes. We'll attend to the wounded."

Three hours later a little single-engined plane touched down at Jadotville airport. Minister Bongo alighted from it, as elegant as ever, his eyes protected by his eternal dark glasses. Notified by a signal from la Roncière, Monteil was waiting for him with a car. Throughout the drive to the camp the Minister did not unclench his teeth. Monteil drew up beside Kreis's jeep.

Kreis snapped to attention and saluted the Minister.

"Where's Colonel Nadolo?" Bongo asked.

"Your Excellency, the colonel is extremely tired, he's resting in that barrack-room."

A shadow of a smile came over Bongo's face.

"Yes," he said, "yes. He must be very tired. Let's go and see him!"

Kreis pushed open the door. Nadolo was stretched out on a camp bed with his uniform unbuttoned. He was snoring loudly and trickles of sweat poured down his naked chest. As the two men came in, he struggled to his feet with a dazed expression. Recognizing Bongo, he darted a glance of triumph at Kreis.

"I must speak to you alone, Monsieur le Ministre. Something utterly unforgivable has happened. . . ."

"Colonel Nadolo," Bongo chipped in, "I bring you the warmest congratulations from the Government for the splendid victory you have won over the UN troops. President Kimjanga asked me to tell you that you have been promoted to the rank of general as from today and that you have been appointed to take command of the Katangese Army."

A large smile came over Nadolo's heavy countenance. Kreis stepped forward.

"Allow me to congratulate you, General!"

Nadolo took a pace backwards.

"You'll pay for this," he screamed, "you have struck a general!"

"Just a moment, General," said Bongo, raising his hand. "Your valiant troops are needed in Elizabethville. Fall in your men and move off at once. You will halt six miles from the capital. There, you will receive fresh orders!"

He turned to Kreis.

"You are responsible for guarding the prisoners. See to

it that nothing happens to them, otherwise you'll be in serious trouble!"

"But I wasn't the one who . . ." Kreis stammered in dismay.

"That'll do. You have your orders. Carry them out. As to our accounts, we'll settle them later!"

Bongo took Nadolo by the arm and ushered him into his car. The Katangese soldiers assembled at the gates gave him a great ovation.

Buscard could not stop laughing.

"Well, I must say!" Kreis said to him, "I give up!"

Colonel la Roncière had received Kreis's first message, announcing the capitulation of the Irish, at eight o'clock.

"Kreis has done a good job," he said to Fonts, as he handed him the signal.

"Yes, but this good job is liable to boomerang against us. If the gendarmes slit the Irishmen's throats, we'll be in a fine mess. No one will ever say the Negroes were responsible, they'll blame it on the mercenaries! The Negro is sacred in this heyday of the 'third world'!"

"Kreis can look after himself!"

"With fifteen chaps, while there are more than three hundred Katangese commanded by that half-wit Nadolo?"

"It's serious, then?"

"Since the River Lukuga massacre I take Negro folly extremely seriously. At E'ville we had quite a job preventing the prisoners from being hacked to pieces. So at Jadotville! . . ."

"Very annoying, but what can we do?"

"Why not send Bongo to Jadotville?"

"Bongo? Are you crazy? He's even more of a savage than Nadolo. If he goes there it'll be to order all the Irishmen to be killed!"

"I'm not so sure. He's a brute, but a clever brute! He doesn't give a damn about humanitarian considerations. If you go and sob in his lap about the poor little Irishmen, he'll send you packing! That's not the way to go about it. Go and see him; tell him the prisoners are a political trump card. We must show all the UN soldiers that if they surrender they run no risk! That's the sort of thing he can understand. . . . After that, if he likes, he can make mincemeat of them. Meanwhile he'll have calmed down."

Bongo was the only minister who could have taken the risk of returning to Elizabethville since the start of the fighting. He ran a shuttle service between the mercenaries and Kipushi, where Kimjanga had taken refuge.

Maley was right. Of the whole gang, Bongo was the only one who had any guts. Kimjanga had collapsed like a rag-doll. As for the other ministers, they were incapable of doing anything except palavering at a safe distance from the shooting, waiting meanwhile for a handful of white men to enable them to rest their arses in their armchairs!

Bongo had reacted exactly as Fonts had foreseen. Thumping the table with his fist, he had interrupted la Roncière.

"What the hell do I care if some of your Irishmen are killed? They're war criminals. The UN fire on women and children, shell hospitals and ambulances. Now you come and kick up a fuss just because a few Irishmen might get bumped off? Why did they come out here in the first place?"

La Roncière had patiently explained. At first Bongo had refused to understand.

"The Katangese," he had asserted, "are disciplined troops. They would never commit any reprehensible act. Colonel Nadolo is one of our best officers and I don't believe a word of this story. I'm sure that fellow Kreis is merely trying to get his own back by tarnishing the honor of a Katangese soldier!"

La Roncière mustered all his patience and embarked on his theme.

"Your Excellency, it's a very delicate business. I don't care any more than you do about the comfort of the prisoners who, as you say, are war criminals. But that's not the point. These two hundred Irishmen are going to enable us to bring pressure to bear on the UN. The Dublin Government will take fright. All our friends will set to work to see that the fighting is brought to an end. We'll send some journalists to Jadotville to take photographs."

"You see," the colonel pointed out, "it will be the same as in the case of the September 3rd incident. Throughout the world it will be said that, despite the savage aggression of which she is the victim, Katanga is a civilized country which respects the rules of warfare!"

The allusion to the 3 September business had won the day.

Bongo grinned broadly.

"All right. I'll go to Jadotville myself to settle the incident and I'll put paid to Nadolo. I'm beginning to get a little tired of that loud mouth of his!"

La Roncière had been obliged to calm the minister down.

"I don't think that's a good solution, Your Excellency. Colonel Nadolo is the most senior officer in your army. It would create a very bad impression if you relieved him of his command!"

Surprised, Bongo had shrugged his shoulders.

"Then what do you suggest?"

La Roncière pondered a moment.

"The simplest thing would be to bring the Jadotville garrison back to Elizabethville in order to reinforce our troops. Kreis and his men can easily undertake the guarding of the prisoners."

"That's right," said Bongo with a ghost of a smile, "and your Kreis then becomes the liberator of Jadotville!"

La Roncière hesitated a moment.

"On the contrary, Monsieur le Ministre, I suggest that we announce to the press that Colonel Nadolo has been victorious at Jadotville. Kreis won't breathe a word, I can vouch for that. I even think we could decorate Nadolo!"

"Or make him a general."

"Why not? You need a general. He'd be as good as anyone else. . . ."

Kreis's second message had reached la Roncière towards fifteen hundred hours. The colonel went off again to see Bongo. He found him at home, having a nap. Bongo had jibbed at first but had then fallen in with the plan. Half an hour later la Roncière escorted the minister to the little auxiliary airfield on the Kipushi road. A Piper was waiting for them, with its engine already warmed up.

La Roncière watched the little plane take off and disappear towards the west.

Arnold Riverton, the American Consul, decided to evacuate the wives of two of his subordinates who were showing undue signs of nervousness. He asked his daughter Joan to accompany them as far as Salisbury, from where she would be able to take a plane for New York.

Thanks to Radio Katanga, no one, either African or European, was unaware that it was American aircraft that had flown in the reinforcements without which the blue helmets would not have been able to launch Morthor.

A further incident had roused the population's anger, this time against Riverton himself.

The Katangese Government had summoned not only

the press but all the consuls to the Queen Elizabeth Hospital to show them some civilians who had been wounded by the blue helmets; all the diplomats and journalists had attended this invitation, with the exception of Arnold Riverton who had refused "to lend himself to this propaganda scheme."

With great composure and equal ill-grace he had replied to Decronelle who kept importuning him:

"My dear sir, General Siddartha gave me his word of honor as an officer that none of his soldiers fired on any civilians. I cannot but believe him!"

"What about the para-commandos who were finished off by the Gurkhas?"

"General Siddartha also gave me his word that this was untrue."

Bayard, the Radio Katanga announcer, never referred to Arnold Riverton except as "General Siddartha's word of honor." Some of the consulate staff had received threatening letters; a number of shopkeepers refused to serve them.

"I hope I'll breathe more freely in America," Joan had said. "Here everyone tells lies, including you. You dare to support the contention that there were no para-commandos finished off by the Indians, whereas I saw it happening with my own eyes; you claim that civilians were not fired upon, whereas Madame Martineau who does the consulate washing received a bullet in the shoulder. The others are also lying, of course, but is that any reason to follow their example?"

"Lies engender lies! Your little pal Thomas Fonts has no scruples about lying. He has invented everything, even a Katangese resistance movement, even a Katangese State. What else is he going to invent, I wonder?"

"I don't know anything about that, Daddy, but the UN are being beaten and the Irish garrison has just surrendered at Jadotville, and you still insist on lying! You know how a journalist started off one of his articles in the *New York Herald?*

"'According to the latest information—information which is certainly reliable since it is confirmed by a denial from the representatives of the UN and the USA . . .'"

"Joan, I'm under orders and I carry them out."

"I'm beginning to have a liking for people who don't carry out orders!"

"The Thomas Fonts and la Roncières of this world. . . ."

"Leave Fonts out of this, it's a matter between him and myself; it's settled; I shan't be seeing him again. Anyone can make a mistake. You made a mistake over Sunnarti, your Indonesian girl. Which doesn't stop you regretting the good time you had with her . . . any more than it stops me forgetting that Thomas Fonts was not an ordinary creature. . . . Unlike so many men, he at least was a real person."

Arnold Riverton lost his temper.

"Do you think the only people who are real are unstable hot-heads who turn somersaults on the stage and fire pistols in the air? They're not: even Fonts, in spite of all the gifts he may have! It was he who made Morthor fail by whisking Kimjanga away, and if you had held him back a few minutes longer Maley wouldn't be in such a mess now. Thirty men, not even fifty, trained rather than commanded by Fonts and la Roncière, are now inflicting a humiliating defeat on the United Nations. The United States have decided to finish with Kimjanga and his gang. We're going to give the UN the arms and the means they lack. America needs the UN. Therefore she can't leave them in the lurch at a moment like this!"

"Are the Marines going to land?"

"No. We're going to swallow the pill, as we did after Pearl Harbor. But we'll be back! The result will be still more innocent people killed and wounded. The world has become serious; it no longer tolerates mercenaries or soldiers of fortune! Those days are over. Maybe it's a shame from the point of view of the picturesque, but how much more reassuring for people who want to live in peace!

"Let's go on talking about Fonts, but in relation to you. It's easy to be free-and-easy with women and even to behave like an oaf. As far as I can see, that's how he has behaved. You can overawe a woman for a few days, especially if, like you, like your mother, she has always been worshiped and adulated. But you couldn't stand a man like that beside you for any length of time; your dignity is worth more than a few fleeting emotions!"

"You know that French expression about 'having a man under one's skin.' That was all it was with Thomas, just like you with Sunnarti. My luggage is packed!"

"You're a grand girl, Joan!"

"Don't you believe it. If you only knew how I longed to see him again, that odious fellow, how frightened I am something may happen to him . . . and how I hate myself when I think of him! You know why I hate him?"

She gave a little sob, like a hiccough.

"He taught me that I was first and foremost a woman, not the sort of statue which American men make of their women. Tell Patrick Maley I'm very sorry for him, and tell Jenny I'll write to her. And what shall I say to Mummy? . . ."

"That when one has been brought up to worship statues it's sometimes disturbing to meet warmer creatures . . . but that I'm sorry."

Riverton kissed his daughter; he was dreading the idea of being alone.

Fonts was at Gelinet's when Pérohade rang him up.

"Thomas, I've just got back from Kasumbalesa. They say your American girl and two women from the American Consulate have just been attacked on the Rhodesia road."

Fonts felt he was going to faint: a hand clutched at his heart and stopped it beating. On hearing that a close friend had been wounded or killed, he always felt rage or pain, but never anguish like this which numbed and paralyzed his throat. He realized all of a sudden that he loved Joan. What he felt towards her was not only desire and tenderness, mingled occasionally with irritation. Without his knowing it, Joan had become part and parcel of himself, she had occupied a vacant space and in the process had broken through a doorway which age alone had rusted away.

"Who by?" he asked. "The gendarmes?"

"No, one of those little bands of looters which have just made their appearance."

"Where?"

"Twenty miles from the frontier."

Fonts rang off.

"Are you coming?" la Roncière said to him. "We have to meet that Swede at Trude's. Just imagine, if the Swedes in their turn decide to surrender!"

"Shit!"

"What's wrong, Thomas? You look distraught!"

"Joan has just been kidnaped on the Rhodesia road. To hell with your Swede, Kimjanga and all the rest of them!"

"Is this really you talking?"

"A man can change!"

"Meaning?"

"That if I don't find Joan safe and sound, I'll drop

407

everything, even you, Jean-Marie . . . because, you see, that little red-head . . . I'm keen on her!"

Fonts collected some grenades, a submachine-gun and magazines, and leaped into a jeep.

"Wait for me," said old Gelinet.

"Fonts will never do anything worth while," la Roncière reflected, "especially now that there's this girl.

"Yet he would be useful in dealing with the Swede, considering that dangerous gift he has for making anyone accept anything. Thanks to him, a surrender is made to seem something unimportant . . . perhaps because, to Fonts, nothing really has any importance except the importance that is attached to it at the moment. The Communists had the Anarchists shot in Spain. Fonts is an Anarchist of the most dangerous sort . . . an Anarchist by instinct, without theories. . . . I must see what I can do on my own. If the Swedish battalion surrenders, we've won!"

But la Roncière was unable to forget Fonts.

"What would I have done in his place," he asked himself, "if Jenny had been in Joan's shoes?"

An hour later Fonts had reached the sixty-mile stone. The American Consulate car was parked on the side of the road. It had been looted. The driver, a Baluba, had been badly knocked about. The blood was drying on his forehead and cheeks. But he seemed to have recovered extremely quickly.

Fonts poked his revolver into his stomach.

"Wait," said Gelinet.

He questioned the driver in Swahili and translated the reply:

"There were three of them on the edge of the road, young lads without weapons, and a fourth lying on the ground holding his stomach. They were waving wildly; I wanted to drive on but the red-haired lady told me to stop. We got out of the car to see what was wrong. Whereupon the fourth man sprang to his feet and they all fell on us. They had pieces of lead piping under their shirts. They knocked me out."

"What tribe?"

"Balembas, local men. My head hurt but I heard them. Two of them wanted to take nothing but the suitcases, the two others nothing but the women. They hit me over the head again."

"What are the Balembas like?" Fonts asked with a frown.

"Neither better nor worse than the others. There are

408

some Balembas living in a village a couple of miles away. . . . but we can only reach it on foot. I know the chief."

"What are we waiting for?"

The village, situated in a clearing, consisted of about thirty huts. It was in ferment. Women were scurrying to and fro; children and dogs were howling. The men had assembled round the chief's hut.

"Don't lose your head," Gelinet said to Fonts, who was loading his submachine-gun. "If the harm's done, it's too late. It happened straight away on the side of the road. In any case we'll have to palaver. Chief Ngomwe is an old man and he's no fool!"

"Get going, for heaven's sake!"

The two of them plunged into the black horde. In his pocket Fonts clutched a grenade.

The old chief was sitting with his back against the door of his hut, holding his staff surmounted by a monkey's hand.

"Hello, Ngomwe," said Gelinet, clearing a place beside him with his elbows.

Fonts slipped in between them and pointed his weapon. The vociferating crowd drew a few feet back.

"Are they here?" he asked in a trembling voice.

Gelinet translated the chief's reply.

"Yes, the women are here in the chief's house. No, nothing serious has happened to them, at least so far as he knows. But what does he consider serious? Raping a woman is merely having a game with her. They're a bit shaken, that's all. The older one had a nervous breakdown. But the youths of the village say that the women belong to them and they want them. The chief says that's not good, but for the last few weeks no one has obeyed him much. He suggests a palaver. Maybe in exchange for ten cases of beer . . . but above all, don't fire! There are about a hundred of them, you'll bump off three or four, then they'll massacre us and have the women just the same!"

Words were exchanged to a monotonous rhythm between the chief and Gelinet. The blacks began to howl and the circle drew closer.

Gelinet seized Ngomwe by the arm.

"Tell them I'm the big beer boss, that I'm the one who makes it at E'ville, that I'll give them ten cases for each of the women and they can keep whatever is in the suitcases.· . . . We shan't send the gendarmes to hang them! Because, if they lay hands on the women, the village will be razed to the ground and everyone will be hanged."

The chief spoke at great length, tracing circles in the ground in front of him with his stick.

At last he stopped.

"They want twenty cases for each of the women." Ingenuously, he added: "That's rather a lot, eh, boss? You must bring them straight away, those cases. The other white man can stay with the women, but he must hand over his gun. As for you, everyone knows you!"

"All right," said Fonts. "I still have my grenade. Be quick about it before they change their minds, and tell old Riverton everything's fixed."

"Not yet!"

"Whatever happens, it's fixed. If they start any nonsense, I'll blow myself up with the women. Tell the old man to let me into the hut."

The three American women, with their clothes torn and their hair disheveled, sat pressed close together. Joan was the only one who had retained her composure.

"There you are at last," she said to Fonts, stifling a sob. "Because, of course, you're in command of these savages as well!"

"No, there'll be four of us for them to lynch instead of three if old Gelinet doesn't get back here quickly with his cases of beer. Each of you is worth, this evening, twenty cases of beer!"

"Thomas, what's wrong with you, you're trembling?"

She thrust aside one of the women who was clutching at her skirt and pressed herself against him:

"I was very frightened . . . you know. Their dirty black hands fingered me, nothing more. So as not to cry out, I thought of you. But you're not going to faint, are you, Thomas?"

"Impossible," Maley said over the telephone to Riverton. "All the troops are cut off . . . I'm worried to death, Arnold. . . . Maybe it's the mercenaries who kidnaped them. . . . That would be less serious. They're whites, after all . . . and they must know that one of their leaders has, shall we say, a soft spot for your daughter. You say it's some uncontrolled African elements? But who made them lose their control if it wasn't Radio Free Katanga station which broadcasts all this propaganda in Swahili?

"Try to contact Fonts through Musaille, the French

410

Consul. He's one of their accomplices. Or through Ligget, he's another! I'm terribly sorry. At the moment General Siddartha has no troops whatsoever at his disposal."

Maley replaced the receiver.

Siddartha had been far more outspoken.

"It's true," he had barked. "I have no troops and no means of communication. In any case it's too late. What a fuss you make when it's white women who are involved!"

Gelinet returned in his beer truck with a dozen mercenaries he had rustled up. To them a white woman was still something extremely important.

"I loathe Africa," said Joan as she got back into her car.

"Why?" Fonts asked. "You're like the mountaineer who curses the mountain because he has been caught in an avalanche."

"Are you going back to Elizabethville?"

"I want to be in at the kill!"

"You've risked your life to save me and now you're leaving me!"

"And you're in such a great hurry to take the plane for New York?"

"What are you suggesting?"

"What can I give you? A holiday. . . . If by chance I don't succeed in curing myself of you, we'll prolong the holiday. . . ."

He kissed her on the temple, leaped into his jeep and disappeared, followed by the truckload of mercenaries.

"Strange, that boy. Very Latin, isn't he?"

Mrs. Sutton, the vice-consul's wife, who had at last recovered from her emotion, was able once again to take a condescending view at the world and the creatures in it.

"Yes," said Joan, "an unstable hot-head who climbs on to the stage and fires pistols in the air. . . . A boy who's condemned by this serious world of ours. . . . But this serious world easily forgets about women who fall into the hands of Negroes on the rampage!"

Michael Fenner, the Irish Minister at Leopoldville, leaned forward.

"Sir, I have been instructed by my department to inform you of the extreme anxiety which the Irish Government feels about the fate of the Jadotville garrison. Our Minister of Foreign Affairs urgently requests that measures be taken forthwith to insure the safety of our soldiers."

The UN Secretary-General drew his hand listlessly

across his face: he was exhausted, and deep lines furrowed his brow.

"I shouldn't like to be in his shoes," Fenner reflected.

The Irish Minister, not without a vague feeling of pity, compared this careworn man with the tall, astonishingly youthful Nordic he had seen in New York in 1953 as he climbed on to the UN platform to take his oath after being elected.

With a gesture that had become a habit with him, the Secretary-General picked up a beautifully bound book lying on the table: the works of St.-John Perse.

"I venture to think your anxiety is somewhat exaggerated, Mr. Fenner. There is no reason to think those men's lives are really in danger!"

"That's not what the press says, however. Several statements have been made by leading Katangese to the effect that any blue helmets who are taken prisoner will be treated as war criminals!"

Fenner went on in his most official tone:

"Sir, my government expects a definite answer. Public opinion in Ireland is anxious to be reassured. I must add that my government does not approve of the continuation of military operation in Katanga and declares itself to be in favor of negotiation."

"The situation is going to develop rapidly," the Secretary-General promised. "Important decisions are going to be taken within the next twenty-four hours. I shall not fail to keep you informed."

After Fenner had left, the Secretary-General went over to the bay window in his office, situated on the sixth floor of the Hotel Royal. The Royal was an immense building of ten stories, with a commanding view over Leopoldville. The UN had installed their Congo headquarters there. Opposite, on the other side of the river, stood some low villas half concealed in the foliage: Brazzaville.

The Secretary-General glanced at the clock on the mahogany table. Once again he reflected: Sunday, 17 September, nine o'clock in the morning. It was almost unbelievable; he had arrived at Leopoldville on 13 September, confident and optimistic. Before leaving New York, he had been informed by a top-secret signal of the imminent launching of an operation which was to put an end to this cancer of secession. Maley's reports, confirmed by headquarters in Leopoldville, were explicit: the fruit was ripe; Kimjanga, abandoned by his troops, would submit to the Central Government. The whole affair would be over in a few hours and the entire world, faced with a *fait accompli*, could not but congratulate the UN and its leader on a rapidly executed operation without bloodshed.

Then everything had gone wrong: Kimjanga, after taking refuge in Rhodesia, had launched an appeal for total war. The blue helmets, on the defensive everywhere, were obliged to engage in active combat. The peace army had to fight; world opinion was up in arms against the Secretary-General and his advisers. To crown everything, the surrender of the Jadotville garrison constituted a heavy blow against the prestige of the UN. The Dublin Government was about to embark on a violent campaign against the continuation of the operations. Fenner, this time, had been fairly discreet but there could be no mistake about it: if a cease-fire did not occur very soon, Dublin, with the support of the British and the French, would launch a violent attack against him.

For this was what it came to: the Secretary-General found himself on the horns of a dilemma. He had the choice of intensifying the war in Katanga, which was hardly possible, or accepting a humiliating cease-fire. The UN Secretary-General found himself obliged to negotiate, which would be a real capitulation, with this fellow Kimjanga whom he despised, this man of straw supported by big international financial interests!

The day before, at midnight, he had received a message from his representative in Katanga: Kimjanga had suggested to Maley that he should meet him on the following day at Bancroft, in Northern Rhodesia. The excitable Irishman had forwarded the message to Leopoldville, accompanied by a biting comment: "I feel that in no circumstances can I go to Rhodesia, a country which has sided outright with the enemy. If Kimjanga wishes to engage in negotiations, it is up to him to come here. I propose arranging a meeting at my command post in Elizabethville."

The Secretary-General had hesitated for a long time. His first reaction had been to agree with his representative. Then he had thought it over. It was Kimjanga, not Maley, who held the trump cards. It was then he made his decision. Maley, who was too impulsive and had quarreled with Kimjanga, would never settle anything. It was up to him, the United Nations Secretary-General, to take the matter in hand. Kimjanga, he believed, would not dare to oppose him.

At three o'clock in the morning the Secretary-General

had sent a message to Kimjanga, informing him that he was prepared to meet him personally in order to put an end to hostilities and find a peaceful solution to this conflict. The message specified that this meeting could not take place until Kimjanga had ordered his partisans to cease fire.

The Katangese President's reply would certainly arrive in the course of the morning. All he could do was wait.

The Secretary-General opened St.-John Perse at random.

We shall not dwell for ever in these yellow lands, our pleasance . . . The Summer vaster than the Empire hangs over the tables of space several terraces of climate. . . .

He closed the book. He felt exhausted. For the last four days he had scarcely slept at all; he had kept going on coffee and benzedrine tablets. Four days of endless conferences with his civil and military collaborators! He had had to reassure the ministers of the Central Congolese Government who demanded total war, while the representatives of the great powers kept harassing him ceaselessly to arrange for an end to hostilities.

The English had been the first to open fire. On 15 September Lord Landsdowne, Minister of State at the Foreign Office, had landed at Leopoldville. Landsdowne had straight away put his cards on the table: "Her Majesty's Government informed the United Nations Secretary-General that it was considering publicly condemning the operation undertaken in Katanga unless a cease-fire was arranged within a short space of time."

The French had followed suit. Everything pointed to the fact that it was a joint maneuver. Their ambassador at Leo had been extremely outspoken: "My government has most decided reservations on the Katanga operation. It feels that the United Nations Secretary-General has exceeded his mandate and that the military operations launched in Elizabethville constitute a violation of the charter assigned to him by the mission to impose law and order, security and peace."

The attitude of the French had not surprised him. Since General de Gaulle had come to power, Paris affected to regard the UN with contempt. Bizerta had not improved matters. The Secretary-General had not forgotten the humiliation to which he had been subjected by the French paratroops between Tunis and Bizerta, when they had forced him out of his car to search him.

British reaction was still more worrying. The Secretary-General could not stop making the same calculations over and over again. In a few months' time the problem of his re-election would crop up. Against him he had the Russians, the French and the Belgians. The Americans would vote in his favor. If he also rubbed the British up the wrong way, he was very liable to be defeated!

The British had not confined themselves to threats. At Entebbe, in Uganda, they had seized the four jet fighters of the Ethiopian Air Force which would have put the Fouga out of action and enabled the air bridge between Leopoldville and Elizabethville to be re-established. The Secretary-General had protested to the British Ambassador. Sir John Lowpett had pleaded technical reasons. Meanwhile the one and only Fouga Magister of the Katangese Air Force calmly pursued its bombing raids and kept the UN transport aircraft grounded.

Encouraged by the attitude of London, the Rhodesians had come out openly against the United Nations. From Salisbury Sir Roy Welensky kept denouncing the "crimes of the UN" and accusing the Secretary-General of placing himself under the orders of "African imperialists controlled by Communist countries." The Rhodesians had gone even farther; they were giving asylum to Kimjanga and furnishing direct aid to the Katangese: arms, ammunition and food supplies. Maley asserted that groups of Rhodesian volunteers were fighting by the side of Kimjanga's mercenaries.

A good lad, Maley, but somewhat impulsive. . . .

Brahimi, one of the Secretary-General's two representatives in the Congo, entered the room with a somber air, holding a sheet of paper in his hand.

"Sir, it's intolerable! Kimjanga is going too far! It's an absolute insult to the dignity of the United Nations."

The Secretary-General peered coldly at this swarthy, over-excitable, over-garrulous Tunisian whom he suspected of having urged Maley into this mad adventure.

He held out his hand.

"Is that Kimjanga's reply? Let's have a look."

The Secretary-General donned his spectacles and read:

The President of the Katangese State is prepared to meet the United Nations Secretary-General tomorrow at Ndola, in Northern Rhodesia.

415

He is ready to accept an immediate cease-fire on the following conditions:

1. The UN troops will remain in camp and not move outside on any pretext.

2. No reinforcements will be sent to Katanga.

"It's an absolute ultimatum," Brahimi exclaimed. "Kimjanga's behaving as though he has won a military victory!"

The Secretary-General raised his eyes.

"Has he not won a victory?"

"But, sir, it's solely for humanitarian reasons that our troops have not cleaned up Elizabethville. General Siddartha maintains that if you give him the 'go-ahead' he can easily deal with it in twenty-four hours."

"You know perfectly well, Monsieur Brahimi, that I can't give him the 'go-ahead!' "

"Sir, you're confronted with this choice: if you accept Kimjanga's conditions, you destroy all the work we have been doing in the Congo for the last year. Maley is absolutely right: Kimjanga has been prompted by the extremists in Katanga. He will not put an end to secession unless he is compelled to do so by force. We have launched a military operation which may still succeed. If you decide to negotiate, the group of Afro-Asian nations which I represent will regard this move as sheer treachery."

The Secretary-General removed his spectacles and flung them down on the desk.

"Monsieur Brahimi, may I remind you that Mr. Maley and you yourself have deceived me. . . ."

"Sir . . ."

"You have deceived me," the Secretary-General repeated with vehemence. "If I gave my agreement to Morthor, it's because you assured me that the operation would be carried out without bloodshed. Look where it has got us now! Into active warfare, which the whole world condemns!"

"The Afro-Asian countries don't condemn it in any way!"

"But all the big powers except Russia do! Well, then?"

"I beg of you. We have reached the point at which we can't withdraw without dishonoring ourselves!"

He rose to his feet.

"In the name of my government and the *bloc* of Afro-

Asian nations, I ask you to authorize General Siddartha to put down the Katangese rebellion by force!"

The Secretary-General pressed the button on the internal line.

"Ask General Callaghan to come to my office at once."

Callaghan entered in the midst of a heavy silence. The Commander-in-Chief of the UN troops in the Congo was also an Irishman, burly and tall, with extraordinarily blue eyes. He wore a number of decorations, but had never done any fighting.

"What's the situation?" the Secretary-General inquired.

Callaghan shrugged his shoulders. For the last four days he kept being asked the same question, to which he always made the same reply.

"At Elizabethville our troops are everywhere on the defensive. They are ceaselessly harassed by commandos of mercenaries aided by armed civilians. The air bridge is cut; we have no fighter cover to protect our aircraft. The food and ammunition supplies are beginning to run out in an alarming manner."

"Is it possible to retrieve the situation?"

"Obviously not, if we are forbidden to attack!"

"What do you suggest?"

"You mean from a strictly military point of view?"

"Yes."

"Siddartha tells me—and I agree with him—that we can win the battle of Elizabethville!"

"How?"

"Simple. We are confronted by about five hundred mercenaries, plus five thousand armed civilians whose military worth is about nil. All we need do is destroy the resistance strongholds with mortars and open fire on the houses when the civilians fire on our troops."

"How long would it take to clean the place up?" Brahimi asked.

"Between twelve and twenty-four hours."

"Are you quite certain of this?"

"Absolutely certain!"

"There you are, sir!" Brahimi was triumphant. "Two experienced generals like General Callaghan and General Siddartha can't be mistaken! Give the order to attack, and victory is ours!"

The Secretary-General hesitated. Two minutes earlier he had felt the situation was hopeless. Kimjanga's insolent ultimatum had nettled him. Supposing the whole business

417

really could be settled in twenty-four hours! Could he take this risk?

Callaghan went on:

"I'm afraid I haven't made myself clear; I gave my reply from a purely military point of view. Now, it's difficult to confine oneself to this point of view alone . . ."

"Why?" Brahimi chipped in.

"Street fighting always leads to heavy casualties. I reckon that in Elizabethville we'll have to be prepared for several hundred killed, most of them civilians. It's a risk which, to my mind, the UN can't take!"

Callaghan paused for an instant and added:

"I must inform you, sir, that as far as I'm concerned, I refuse to give the order to attack Elizabethville. If you proceed with it, I shall be forced to hand in my resignation. I have received explicit instructions from my government. I must see about saving the lives of the two hundred Jadotville prisoners. You know what will happen if we attack? My men will probably be killed out of hand. That is a possibility I cannot envisage at any price!"

The Secretary-General rose to his feet.

"Thank you, gentlemen. I must ask you to leave me now. I shall think it over and let you know my decision."

At twelve-thirty the Secretary-General called for his secretary.

"Sylvia, have this message sent off at once."

In the cypher room Brahimi leaned over the shoulder of the cypher clerk and read:

From the Secretary-General,
To Mr. Maley, UN Representative, Elizabethville.
Please inform Kimjanga that the Secretary-General cannot accept his proposal to meet in Rhodesia and categorically rejects the conditions imposed for the conclusion of a cease-fire.

The Secretary-General had a hasty lunch with General Callaghan and Brahimi. The three men exchanged no more than a few words and parted with relief.

At two o'clock the Secretary-General went up to his room and lay down on his bed. He tried once more to read a few poems of his beloved St.-John Perse, but found he could not concentrate on them.

Immediately after sending his message to Kimjanga, he had felt relieved. But now he again lapsed into gloomy depression. He had rejected the Katangese President's conditions, but what should he do now? Impossible to launch a general offensive, against Callaghan's wishes. France and Great Britain would never forgive him for the hundreds killed which the operation might entail. If the Irishmen in Jadotville were executed, and Kimjanga was quite capable of giving orders for this to be done, his responsibility would be overwhelming. Well, then? There remained only capitulation. The Secretary-General looked at his watch: half past three.

He picked up the telephone and rang up his ADC.

"Lundqvist? Have my aircraft prepared. Take-off at five o'clock. Destination Ndola."

He rang for his secretary.

"Sylvia, take a message for Maley. Ask him to inform Kimjanga that I shall be at Ndola late this evening. Tell him to stay in Elizabethville and wait for my instructions there."

"Am I coming with you, sir?"

"No, Sylvia. You're worn out, you wait here. Take this opportunity of having a little rest. You need some sleep!"

Sylvia burst into tears. She was one of those female colleagues, infinitely more valuable than a man, who devote themselves heart and soul to serving their employer. The Secretary-General yielded.

"All right, Sylvia. I'll take you with me."

At half past four the Secretary-General arrived at the airport. The crew of four men, all Swedes, were already at their posts in the fuselage of the white DC6. It was General Callaghan's personal aircraft. Sergeant Harold M. Julien, a former American Marine who had become head of the UN Security services, was methodically searching the plane. As usual, he was carrying a huge Smith and Wesson slung low on his thigh. Two young Swedish blue helmets were to serve as bodyguard to the Secretary-General.

The pilot, Captain Hallonquist, personally checked that all was in order in the cockpit. The Secretary-General sat in front with his secretary beside him. Sergeant Julien and the two Swedish soldiers were seated behind. Seven harassed UN officials accompanied the Secretary-General. Counting the four members of the crew, there were sixteen people on board.

The Alvertina took off at five o'clock, gained height rapidly and disappeared towards the west. A few minutes later Captain Hallonquist leaned across to the Secretary-General:

"We shan't fly over Katangese territory, so as to avoid any risk of encountering the Fouga. We're going to make a detour eastwards as far as the Tanganyika frontier. Then we'll head for Ndola, flying over Northern Rhodesia."

"What time are we due to arrive at Ndola?"

"Midnight, local time."

The Secretary-General settled back in his seat, read a few verses of the Bible and, overcome by fatigue, fell asleep.

Lord Cornwell stroked his gray temples several times, a nervous habit of his whenever things were going too badly or too well, which frequently came to the same thing.

"We have only one hour longer to wait," he said to President Kimjanga. "The UN Secretary-General's aircraft is due to arrive at midnight."

Kimjanga, in a dark suit and with his hands behind his back, tried to assume the indifferent manner of a great politician who has won an unexpected victory.

The sky was clear, studded with stars, cool and at the same time still. The Ndola control tower looked like a huge lantern, and its big windows reflected the blue of the nocturnal sky.

The guard of honor stood stamping their feet; there was an occasional clatter of weapons.

Kimjanga could hardly breathe, so deep was his delight. It constricted his throat and chest, numbed his legs and loins. If he had been alone he would have emitted the old triumphant war-cry of the Lundas. He would have shouted his joy to the darkness, like a beast being driven out of a sick man by a witch-doctor, before padding off alone.

But walking beside him was the British High Commissioner for the Rhodesias, Lord Cornwell. In a short while the UN Secretary-General, that powerful man who had tried to create a World Government, would come and bow the knee before him.

Five days earlier he, Kimjanga, had fled from his residence in pajamas, urged on, almost threatened, by that fellow Fonts. A nasty moment, which he would prefer to forget! But once Fonts had left, who would remember it? Men of that sort are useful only in certain exceptional circumstances, the rest of the time they are an embarrassment! They have no respect for hierarchies, and hierarchy, as the Belgians had never stopped dinning into his ears from his early childhood, is the foundation of any organized nation!

Kimjanga would never have believed it possible. La Roncière had induced him to send an ultimatum, to demand that the Secretary-General should come to him, and to arrange for the meeting to be held at Ndola, in Rhodesian territory.

Confronted by this colonel with his lean face and disturbing eyes, he had done his utmost to resist. It was impossible, he had maintained, to inflict such a humiliation on the man who represented the United Nations, the most powerful force in the world. Moreover, the Secretary-General would never accept the terms but, on the contrary, would pursue the war in Katanga and order his tanks and mortars to fire on Elizabethville.

The colonel had rejected all his arguments, pulling them to pieces one after another, as though shelling peanuts. What he said had sounded so logical at the time, the Frenchman's enthusiasm and power of persuasion had been such, that he had allowed him to send this ultimatum.

On receiving the first reply from Leo, informing him that the Secretary-General refused to come to Ndola, Kimjanga had collapsed!

At that moment he was prepared to swear that his hand had been forced, that la Roncière had sent the signal without orders!

At the Secretary-General's refusal, the colonel had shown not the slightest emotion.

"Just as I thought!" he said in his sharp voice. "You didn't really expect the fellow to yield at the first punch in the face! Hold on! Anyway it's too late to withdraw now!"

La Roncière, he had realized with concern, was taking an intense delight in this mad game of poker. What was he risking? He had nothing to lose, and this was not his country! On the contrary, he was amusing himself. Kimjanga would have dismissed him had he dared, but he was reduced to nought, to a mere plaything, a card in the hands of this inscrutable maniac. Seated in his chair opposite him, la Roncière watched the smoke rising from his cigarette. He did not drink, did not sweat, he was a solid wall against which one broke one's nails!

At six o'clock in the evening the second message arrived, and Kimjanga was dumfounded. The thin sheet of yellow paper trembled in his hands.

As coldly as ever, la Roncière had said:

"Just as I thought! The fellow's begging for mercy.

421

We've won the first round, but we haven't yet won the second!"

Breathing heavily, the President had asked:

"What more do you want?"

"The evacuation of all UN troops stationed in Katanga."

"That's impossible. The Secretary-General would never agree to that!"

La Roncière had shrugged his shoulders.

"Monsieur le Président, you didn't believe me when I told you he would come to Ndola; you still refuse to believe me! If you don't obtain that evacuation, the round we have won today will be lost tomorrow!"

Kimjanga knew about men like this, who are never content and drive one to ruin. But he, the clever merchant, the crafty black peasant, was a sage, a politician who was able to appreciate the bounds of the possible!

To get rid of the colonel, he had made vague promises.

"Naturally, we'll broach the subject with the Secretary-General!"

"No, you won't. You'll thump the table and you'll say: 'First of all, I demand the evacuation of all the blue helmets.'"

Kimjanga, accompanied by la Roncière who had not stopped harassing him, had made the short flight from Kipushi to Ndola on board his personal aircraft. His ministers followed in another plane.

Lord Cornwell had greeted him on landing like a real chief of state and had addressed him by his official title, "Monsieur le Président."

Kimjanga glanced round him with satisfaction. About thirty officials had assembled on the tarmac of Ndola airport.

Kimjanga pictured the scene that would take place in an hour's time. Strolling slowly over towards the Secretary-General, he would politely shake him by the hand, while making him feel, however, that he was greeting a vanquished enemy! He would not forget to inquire after his health; one always inquires after the vanquished's health since he must be feeling unwell. One never inquires after a victor's health. He was sorry that Lord Cornwell had forbidden the journalists access to the airport.

He, Kimjanga, knew that it was neither la Roncière and his obstinacy, nor the handful of mercenaries who were fighting against the blue helmets in E'ville, who had brought the big white man to his knees. The colonel and his lot were indulging in white men's illusions! The Secretary-General's *muntu,* his vital force, was slowly dripping away from him, while it was invading the massive body of the President of tiny Katanga—tomorrow perhaps President of the great Congo!

The gods alone decided on a man's *muntu,* it was one of the great secret laws of the Bantu world.

Kimjanga was a Protestant and believed, of course, in Christ, but also in many other gods, infinitely closer to men, who were forever concerned about their destiny, their simplest everyday actions, what they were in duty bound to do and what was forbidden them.

They it was who made the millet and grass grow, hid metals away in the mountains, made the rain fall or fail. They were the dispensers of the vital force, *muntu.* The man who lost his *muntu* fell sick and eventually died.

Nor should one forget the *bavidjes,* the dead ancestors, and "all those who know and who started everything."

God Almighty was resting, listening to His angels reporting the palavers of the living, exploiting to the full His power and glory without bothering about the affairs of mankind, which would have disturbed His serenity.

It was all the little gods and all the dead, beloved of the witch-doctors, susceptible to sacrifice, tolerant and sensitive, who endowed men with *bangwa* which the whites in their simplicity called luck, without paying heed, the fools, to those who granted it!

The British High Commissioner was coughing. Engrossed in his thoughts, Kimjanga had forgotten to answer him. He had to force himself back to this hollow unsubstantial world of the whites.

"This evening," he said, with the emphasis of a local politician, "we are celebrating the victory of the forces of justice and civilization over the powers of evil. The Katangese people have won this splendid victory thanks to their indomitable courage, but above all because they had right on their side."

Lord Cornwell hated long tirades as much as sweet wine, and could hardly bear Negroes.

He had done his best for a long time to understand them, trying to discover the laws and motives that ruled their lives. Incomprehensible and disconcerting, these people respected none of the laws which had enabled a tolerable world to come into being. To them a man's word of honor did not exist: a lie was not reprehensible. The more highly developed of them were sometimes prone to fits of madness, like a faulty loudspeaker which suddenly goes wrong and emits strange noises.

This African, this fellow Kimjanga who kept babbling beside him, embarrassed him. The loudspeaker was transmitting audible sounds, but Cornwell discerned behind them those little scratchy noises which showed that the machine was going to break down at any moment.

The High Commissioner deplored this strange epoch, in which a British peer found himself obliged to treat a man like Kimjanga on an equal footing. It was not the color of his skin that bothered him, nor his smell, but his manners, which were not those of a gentleman.

The Foreign Office demanded it. London felt it was necessary to give the Katangese President a modicum of assistance. To tell the truth, his own person did not count at all. The main thing was to maintain an independent Katanga to act as a buffer between the Rhodesias and the rest of Africa. Kimjanga, it had to be admitted, played his part well. Lord Cornwell felt one should always credit a leader with what his subordinates had done. Was it not he who had taken the risk of choosing them?

But he found it distasteful to be by Kimjanga's side this evening, witnessing the defeat of a man like the UN Secretary-General who could not be reproached for anything except a Utopian view of the world and perhaps certain secret leanings which were shared by a number of British gentlemen.

"I think," said Smith, "that the occasion calls for another whisky."

La Roncière made a vague gesture of refusal, but the Rhodesian insisted.

"Come on, old boy, let your hair down! We've played our cards well and we've won. This calls for a celebration!"

The two men sat down at a bar, away from the officials.

"A curious job, ours," Smith observed. "We do all the work and, when it's over, we're asked to disappear. We become an embarrassment. So one has to know how to slip into the wings and keep one's trap shut, while listening to a spate of ineptitudes being spouted on stage."

With a jerk of his thumb over his shoulder, he indicated the notables assembled on the tarmac.

"Just look at them: a lot of antiquated puppets. They've done nothing these last four days and now they're congratulating one another on how they planned everything, fore-

saw everything and settled everything, thanks to their political acumen!"

"What's wrong with him?" la Roncière wondered. "He
must have had one or two whiskies too many. Unless . . ."

He smiled.

Smith had no doubt had the same difficulties with his
superiors as he had with Kimjanga.

The colonel raised his glass.

"Let's drink, my dear Smith, to the puppets' health.
They're the people who rule the world. At least they think
so! Why deprive them of their illusions, while we still ma-
nipulate the strings?"

Smith burst out laughing.

"You're right! Let's drink to our success. For once we
were on the same side and we've done a good job together!"

"Yes," said la Roncière. "Unfortunately my own job is
far from finished. The hardest part is still to come!"

"What on earth are you talking about?"

"I'm afraid Kimjanga might slip through my fingers!
He's bursting with pride because the Secretary-General is
crawling on all fours to him. Just imagine, here's the in-
carnation of the white world going down on his knees to a
fellow who fifteen months ago was merely a bankrupt
merchant. Two weeks ago Kimjanga was doing a flit in his
pajamas, urged on with kicks in the backside from one of
my assistants. . . ."

"To inflate an empty bladder, to create a king, isn't that
what you wanted to do?"

"Yes, but it's not enough! Kimjanga may not know it
himself, but he's shivering in his shoes at the thought of
confronting the Secretary-General. If the other fellow
plays his cards cleverly, he can overturn him completely.
In his place, that's what I would do!"

"What would you do?"

"I'd begin by flattering him and overwhelming him with
compliments. After which I'd knock him cold by making
him feel that he's only a little gang leader who can be
crushed with a flick of the wrist. I'm sure Kimjanga
couldn't withstand that sort of treatment!"

"Has he confidence in you?"

La Roncière hesitated, for he had no idea. He had noticed that Kimjanga constantly veered from one extreme
to the other. The President always came round to the opinion of the man who had spoken last. One believed one

had convinced him, yet two hours later he was subscribing to the opposite argument. It was exhausting!

"I don't know if he has confidence. What I do know is that I've embarked on this business and I'm not going to have it sabotaged just when victory is ours!"

Smith rattled the ice in his glass. He spoke slowly.

"May I give you a word of advice, my dear Jean-Marie?"

"Go ahead!"

"I know this country well, I've spent forty years of my life here. I think you're soon going to be in a difficult position."

"Why?"

"You're a white man and you've won a victory for a Negro. This Negro will never forgive you for that. Even a white man would find it difficult to do so. Each time Kim sees you, he'll remember that you forced him to take decisions by kicking him in the backside, which is liable to be dangerous for you."

"I think you're exaggerating! Kim, as you call him, needs me. He knows perfectly well that without me and my mercenaries he would now be in the shit. When the Secretary-General's message arrived, he almost embraced me. I assure you he looked quite sincere!"

"Don't be so sure!"

The Rhodesian drained his glass.

"I say," he said, "it looks as if things are moving. Let's go and see!"

All of a sudden the blue landing lights on the runway had all come on. Everyone stopped talking, as though the first rocket of a firework display had just been let off. The director of the airport came and notified Lord Cornwell:

"The Secretary-General's aircraft. It has just established contact with the control tower!"

Kimjanga raised his head and peered towards the east, trying to discern the plane's lights among the stars. The stars remained motionless, like the wisdom of the blacks. The little stars of the whites, attached to the wings of an unstable machine, never stopped blinking, green, red . . . unnerving, menacing . . . like the empire of the whites, which every day lost a little more of its *muntu*. The whites were losing the taste, therefore the urge, to live.

The faint hum of the engines grew louder. The outline of the DC6 could be seen distinctly against the pale sky.

The aircraft flew over the airport and headed west.

"What's he doing?" Kimjanga asked. "Why isn't he landing?"

"Everything's all right, Monsieur le Président," the director of the airport replied. "The plane is going to turn round about ten miles from here and come into land, facing east."

He looked at his watch.

"It's ten past twelve. He'll be on the runway in ten minutes."

The notables had gathered round Kimjanga and Lord Cornwell. The officer commanding the guard of honor verified his men's dressing. There was a crunch of hobnailed boots and a clatter of rifle-butts on the tarmac.

Kimjanga glanced nervously at his watch. Twelve-twenty, and still the aircraft was not in sight. Lord Cornwell glanced at the director of the airport.

"What's happening?"

The director looked worried.

"I'll just go up to the control tower."

He came back ten minutes later, white in the face.

"It's very odd, sir, the control tower has lost contact with the aircraft. We've been calling it for twenty minutes without getting any reply. The last message was received at ten past twelve, just as the plane was flying overhead."

"What did it say?"

"It asked for permission to land. The controller reported the atmospheric pressure and instructed it to come down to six thousand feet. The pilot acknowledged the signal. Since then, nothing."

"It's very odd," Lord Cornwell agreed. "What do you think has happened?"

"I don't know, sir. Maybe it turned round farther off than expected, but that still doesn't explain the radio silence!"

"Maybe," said Lord Cornwell. "Let's wait and see!"

He looked at his watch: it was twenty to one. Kimjanga, with clenched teeth, still had his eyes fixed on the spot where the aircraft was due to appear.

At one o'clock in the morning the director went back to the control tower. He reappeared immediately afterwards.

"Well?" Kimjanga asked nervously.

"Still nothing!"

"Monsieur le Président," said Lord Cornwell, "I think it's pointless to wait any longer. The Secretary-General has probably changed his mind. I imagine he has given up the idea of landing at Ndola and is making for Elizabethville.

427

I think it's odd he didn't have the courtesy to inform us!"

Kimjanga could no longer contain himself. To inflict such an affront on him, in front of these white men who were laughing up their sleeves! All the whites were in league, all over the world. The President was choking with rage. This brutal humiliation, after so much hope, made him feel sick. Raising his fist to the sky, he fumed:

"The dirty swine! The filthy sod! . . . I'll have my revenge. I'll make him pay for this. . . . To do such a thing to me, me of all people!"

Lord Cornwell intervened:

"Monsieur le Président, I suggest you go back to your hotel. I shall let you know as soon as I have any news."

Dazed, almost staggering, Kimjanga made his way to his car. La Roncière walked over towards him, but the President turned his back on him and climbed into his Cadillac.

Lord Cornwell, in spite of the complications which the Secretary-General's change of attitude was bound to cause him, was not displeased with the lesson that Kimjanga had just been taught.

"What do you think happened?" Smith asked la Roncière.

The colonel shrugged his shoulders.

"What do you suppose? Your boss is probably right. The Secretary-General changed his mind!"

"Why did he change his mind? Are there any fresh developments?"

"I don't know at all, old boy. I only hope the plane didn't crash. Because we're bound to be accused of having shot it down!"

For the last few minutes the colonel had begun to feel vaguely uneasy. He knew that, after settling the problem of the Irish prisoners at Jadotville, Bongo had gone to Kolwezi where the Fouga was kept. Had he given Berthot orders to shoot down the Secretary-General's aircraft? Bongo had been kept out of the negotiations with the UN because Kimjanga, like a good politician, wanted to enjoy his triumph by himself. Did he perhaps know that his minister was firmly opposed to any form of negotiation? With Bongo anything was possible! But no, he was intelligent, he would surely not take such a risk!

"Are you certain your Fouga isn't flying tonight?" Smith inquired in an even voice.

La Roncière gave a start.

"Don't talk balls!"

428

He realized he was almost shouting. On the tarmac several people had turned round and were looking at him in surprise.

"If there has been an outrage," he continued in a low voice, "it might just as well have come from your extremists, Smith, as from mine. You have no shortage of settlers who served in the RAF and who are not particularly well disposed to the Secretary-General. They certainly have friends among the pilots. One of them might have stolen an aircraft . . . and landed it again. . . ."

"Impossible, our pilots are more disciplined than yours and less adventurous. That's one of the reasons why Rhodesia will never become another Algeria! When I've had one or two drinks, I sometimes regret it! It's excusable. I was born out here."

La Roncière left Smith abruptly and got into his car. It was half past one. The lights on the runway had just been switched off. Ten miles away, at the very spot above which the pilot was required to make his turn, the scattered remains of the DC6 were blazing in the bush.*

* The inquest established that Mr. Hammarskjöld's plane crashed ten miles to the west of Ndola airport between thirteen and fifteen minutes past midnight on 18 September, 1961. The remains of the plane were spotted by another aircraft on the same day at ten minutes past three in the afternoon.

The exact circumstances of the accident have never been elucidated. Several courts of inquiry were held by the Katangese Government and also by the UN. None came to a satisfactory conclusion. A number of theories have since been advanced:

The DC6 might have been shot down by the Fouga Magister. The Katangese authorities officially denied this. The experts assert that the Fouga's range was not sufficient to enable it to fly from Kolwezi to Ndola, shoot down the Secretary-General's aircraft and return to base. However, as from 18 September, President Tshombo ordered the Fouga to remain grounded.

The accident to the DC6 might have occurred as the result of a fight on board between Mr. Hammarskjöld's bodyguard and a mercenary who had slipped into the aircraft and tried to force the pilot to land at the Katangese base of Kamina. This hypothesis is based on the fact that bullets were found in several of the bodies.

The ballistics experts do not agree on this point: some of them reckon that the bullets might have exploded when the aircraft caught fire, others declare that this is impossible.

The aircraft—and this is the most feasible theory—might have had a mechanical fault, the pilot might have been taken ill, unless, according to the criteria of Bantu theology, Mr. Hammarskjöld's *muntu* had run out and his *bangwa* had deserted him.

10. Nadolo the Victorious

On 20 September, in the last broadcast from Radio Free Katanga, Bayard, the valiant announcer, declared with bated breath, as though speaking of the greatest wonder of the century, that on the following day, at five o'clock in the afternoon, President Kimjanga was going to make his solemn entry into the Katangese capital.

He asked the whole population, European and African alike, to give an enthusiastic welcome to "Kimjanga the Liberator" and to the Commander-in-Chief of the Army, "Nadolo the Victorious," who at the head of his troops had saved the country and put to flight the barbarian hordes of the blue helmets.

Bayard indicated the route which the procession was to follow: coming from the direction of Kipushi, it would cross Heenen Park, go up the Avenue de l'Etoile as far as the Avenue de Saio and continue towards the Presidency along the Avenue de Tanganyika and the Avenue Albert Premier.

From three o'clock onwards, the Europeans who had played or, more often, thought they had played a part in the events, had piled into a fleet of cars and driven off to meet the "Liberator" and the "Victor." These cars were flying large Katangese flags and kept blowing their horns without stopping.

"Just like a Jewish or Lebanese wedding," Fonts observed.

He was finishing dinner alone with Musaille, but had barely touched the dishes which the consul had, however, cooked himself.

"What's wrong, Thomas?" Musaille asked him. "You ought to be delighted. With your little pal la Roncière and a handful of desperadoes, you've brought off one of the best bluffs in the world! You've brought the UN to their knees and transformed that puppet Kimjanga into a real head of state! What a victory!"

Fonts put down his napkin.

"A victory? Surely you're not going to indulge in this collective hysteria!"

He got up and went over to the big bay window over-looking the Avenue de Saio. Then, after pouring himself out another glass of wine, he started pacing up and down the room like a caged squirrel.

"There has been no victory, Paul! Or else this victory is very much like this war: empty wind!"

"Kimjanga is returning in triumph to his capital, the Secretary-General's second-in-command Brahimi has signed a cease-fire agreement in his boss's name, the blue helmets are no longer allowed to leave barracks . . . what more do you want?"

"But the blue helmets haven't yet evacuated Katanga! They never will!"

"Maley has been recalled."

"Siddartha's staying and is preparing his revenge! Maley will no longer be by his side to hold him in check. You can say what you like about Maley, at least he was a white man . . . it would have tortured him to give orders to fire on other white men. Siddartha doesn't have those problems! You know I saw Riverton again?"

"No, where?"

"At Ligget's. It was rather a joke! Riverton did not conceal the fact that the Americans, reassured by the anti-Communism of Leopoldville, were this time resolved to go the whole hog and finish with Katanga."

"France is also having a change of heart. I don't quite know what's going on in Paris, but we're toeing the line with Washington. I've received fresh instructions: we continue, of course, to manifest our active sympathy with Kimjanga, but it's all over as far as men and material are concerned. You know what I've been asked to do? Make every attempt to persuade Kimjanga to come to terms with Leopoldville. Three months ago it was the very reverse!"

Musaille produced a sheet of paper from his pocket.

"This is the best part. Just listen:

The department would recommend that the French Consulate at Elizabethville holds itself aloof with regard to the mercenaries of every nationality who, contrary to the decisions adopted by the Security Council, took service in the Katangese Armed Forces.

Fonts chuckled.

"The mercenaries of every nationality, like la Roncière and myself, were sent out here with the blessing of the Elysée. They're going it a bit! Tell me, old boy, it wasn't you by any chance who said something to Riverton about my being recalled?"

"I might have mentioned it. . . ."

"You didn't tell him as well, did you, that I was being reintegrated in our honorable brotherhood of secret-service consuls? That I was going to spend three months in Vientiane before coming back to this bonny land of Africa and resuming my little schemes with Sékou-Touré at Konakry?"

"Come now, you know me well enough!"

"Old Riverton seemed to be very well informed."

"A father's understandable concern for his daughter's welfare."

"Put on another tune!"

"Let's talk about dear old Kimjanga, who is at this very moment making his triumphant entry. But he doesn't know he is lost, deserted on all sides! And all those Belgians applauding him and making a hero of him! Those worthy creatures aren't aware that their government at Brussels has likewise come to terms with Leopoldville!"

"Oh, come off it!"

"What do you care? What does it matter to you now? You've finished your performance, you're going off. But I'm staying. I now have to do the opposite of what I've been doing for the last three months!"

"We're beginning to get used to it, eh, Thomas? You remember May 13th, in Algiers, when Big Charles told the Algerians he understood them? We were in a good position, both of us, to know what that meant. Just a short pause to wash our hands, then we set sail for Paris."

"Here's Pontius Pilate having remorse!"

"Don't you have any?"

"To hell with you! As though you didn't know! No, of course I'm not easy in my mind: I'm afraid of seeing certain pals of mine again. If they spat in my face, I think I'd turn the other cheek!"

"Go and join them in Algeria!"

"They're going too far. You'll see the same thing in Katanga, but on a less dramatic level . . . corrected by the nigger-boy aspect of the Africans!

"I'm beginning to get fed up with all these schemes, these grandiose plans and projects which our bosses draw up and which we try to put into effect by cheating, by lying like dirty little pimps!"

"Young Joan has infected you with her clean conscience."

"You leave Joan out of this."

"Take my advice: it's time you settled down! Marry Joan, sire a few children and give up all this nonsense."

"I'd be bored to tears; I'm too young or too old to change. We've had some fun this week, all the same!"

"So you're going to marry?"

"I'm going off for a week with Joan because I find the girl attractive, that's all. But I must tell you something; it'll make you laugh. This morning, at Kipushi, I went to say good-bye to Kimjanga! He made me wait for an hour in the anteroom. Then, on the pretext that he was busy, he granted me no more than a couple of minutes. In great haste he grudgingly expressed his gratitude. Not to me, of course, but . . . wait for it! . . . to the French Government who supported him in his cruel ordeal! He still has no idea that France is dropping him!

"I gave him a more realistic view of the situation by doing this"—and Fonts made the gesture of counting out money—"and I swear he was shocked. . . . All the same he handed over a wad or two!"

"Were you in need of money?"

"I always need money!"

He burst out laughing.

"I didn't give a damn about the money, it was the gesture that counted. At least Kimjanga won't be sending a telegram of thanks to the Quai, which would cause even more trouble! He won't hold it against me for having saved his stake. Africa's a small place and we're liable to meet again."

"No one can say you're lacking in nerve! Look, Thomas: here come Pérohade and Nathalie. I asked them to drop in for coffee. Nathalie has managed to make herself hideous with that sort of turd she has stuck on her head by way of a hat. And Pérohade in a coat and tie, stiff as a ramrod! They're coming on an official visit. How ugly they are! They want something out of me!"

Pérohade and Nathalie sat down on the edge of their chairs. Fonts put them at their ease.

433

"Pour out the coffee," he said to Nathalie, "and take off that hat!"

She replied primly:

"Monsieur le Consul asked us to come and watch the procession from his balcony."

Fonts was once more bubbling over. His black eyes sparkled.

"What's wrong with you?" he said to Pérohade. "Are you pregnant or something?"

"We came to say good-bye. You see, Thomas, we always knew you weren't one of those layabouts, like poor old Wenceslas. . . . You're a sort of official!"

"You feel more reassured about me because I have a national insurance card?"

"Of course not, as you know perfectly well!"

Blushing with embarrassment, Pérohade put his coffee cup down and turned to Musaille.

"Monsieur le Consul. . . . Oh, balls to this! It's Nathalie who told me to put on these airs. Anyway, in this business, it's not the consul that matters to me. It's the Auvergnat I'm interested in, and the Auvergnat I call Musaille. Listen, I want some advice. A Rhodesian has offered to buy the Mitsouko from me, in cash and in sterling, payable in a Swiss bank."

"A very good price too," Nathalie added. "But perhaps this isn't the moment to sell?"

"Sell," said Fonts, "sell at once. Make hay while the sun shines! In a few months' time the Katangese franc will be worth about as much as the Congo franc, that's to say bugger-all!"

Musaille stroked his cheek.

"I think Thomas is right. Buy a business in France, Pérohade, in Paris, in a new district, or else in the country, in a town that's developing. I'll give you a word for my father: go and see him at Espalion. He'll find you what you want! If you're hard put for ready money, he might even be able to help you."

Fonts slapped his thighs.

"Old man Musaille will lend you money at a usurer's rates, Pérohade, but you'll become a game reserve for the Espalion gang. They'll watch over you and your morals."

"Thomas is exaggerating. My father's a businessman, I don't say he's disinterested. But who's disinterested in politics, in the Army, or the Government? The end in view is different, that's all!"

"As far as morals are concerned, Thomas is not far

434

wrong. At Espalion they like things to be aboveboard, and your particular status . . ."

"Will I have to marry?" Pérohade asked in amazement.

"The police can put the screw on an unmarried couple too easily. Police mean riff-raff, and at Espalion we don't like any connection between pub-keeping, which is a serious business, and that sort of . . . how shall I put it? . . . uncertain, dangerous world. That's what gives the Auvergnat his strength, compared to the Corsican!"

Nathalie was triumphant but could not help going too far:

"You see, Pérohade, even Monsieur le Consul says so. France isn't the Congo! In any case, either you marry me or I leave you."

"Do you want a good slap in the kisser?"

Old accomplices that they were, Fonts and Musaille glanced at each other with delight.

The procession appeared, preceded by three motor-cyclists who had supplemented their uniforms with red scarves, and their helmets with camouflage netting and branches.

Then Kimjanga came into sight, standing upright in his open car, waving his hat at the mob. By his side, stiff as a ramrod, in full-dress uniform, stood General Nadolo, the conqueror of the blue helmets. In another car came Bongo, somber and enigmatic as ever, and Evariste Kasingo looking extremely uneasy. During his captivity he had lent a ready ear to some of Maley's proposals, and he knew that Bongo knew this.

On the pavements a crowd composed almost exclusively of whites screamed and shouted at the top of their voices. Children waved flags.

Monsieur Perisson took his wife by the arm and assumed a solemn tone.

"You know, Geneviève, if it hadn't been for me the President wouldn't be where he is today! When he said to me, 'Perisson, I'm done for!' I replied, 'Monsieur le Président, we are all with you,' and handed him the keys of the car."

Geneviève retorted sourly:

"The car didn't belong to you!"

"Never mind!"

"And what about that gangster with the revolver?"

"You never understood what I told you. Women are always the same!"

"Did he have a revolver or didn't he?"

435

"Shut up, Geneviève! At the time I couldn't tell you the whole story. On account of our children, I had to take every precaution. Just imagine if the blue helmets had arrested me. There was never any gangster! One day I'll go and remember myself to the President. Look, Geneviève, what a bearing! And what about General Nadolo? A splendid licking he gave those UN lads!"

"Edouard, mind your language! Licking indeed!"

"That's what war does to a man, my dear!"

"And what about the mercenaries?"

"A mere handful! Above all, they made a lot of noise. It's the whole Katangese nation, united behind the President, that rose against the oppressors!"

"Yet they say . . ."

"Geneviève, kindly hold your tongue! On a day like this I will not have you calling in question the sacrifices of the Congolese Resistance!"

"Now you're talking like Bayard!"

"I'm sorry for la Roncière," said Fonts as he sipped his brandy.

"Why?" Musaille asked.

"He's losing his head. He, too, is indulging in a little fit of auto-intoxication. He wants to believe that it was solely his methods of psychological warfare that prevailed over the blue helmets. Tomorrow, you wait and see, he'll bring out a little book about it . . . or else a series of lectures at Staff College. When I went to say goodbye to him I felt quite moved, but he began spouting at me. For two pins he would have accused me of treachery. And at the same time he was intensely relieved, like everyone else, to see me go. We embraced, however, for the sake of the memories we have in common. . . . Do you know what I like about Joan? Unlike so many people, she faces facts; she doesn't cheat."

"My word, Thomas, you're also suffering from auto-intoxication! Joan is no different from any other girl. You're attributing to her the finer feelings which all of a sudden you're missing."

"Paul, your brandy's filthy. You've decanted some hooch into an old bottle!"

Musaille burst out laughing and raised his glass.

"To the end of Thomas Fonts! My brandy's genuine and you know it. But you no longer are. I'll be your best man all the same . . . even if you don't want it . . . even if I have to pay my own air fare."

"I'd rather die than see your ugly mug that day!"

"It'll be there, above a morning-coat. I can just see it. Dumont, who'll have become a minister by then, the Deportees and Resistance Fighters Association, and, well to one side, the new lords of the régime, your little pals, the Companions of the Liberation!"

"What about shutting up?"

"I'll drive you to the airport. You take off in an hour's time. You watch, Thomas Fonts, I'll be the only one to see you off; there won't even be a member of Kimjanga's cabinet!"

At the airport there was also Kreis, stiff and ill at ease.

"What are you doing here?" Fonts asked him. "Who sent you? La Roncière?"

"No, I came . . . of my own accord. In the Legion we know how to recognize a man, even if he isn't our sort of person! When he leaves, we give him a bit of a send-off."

"What's going to become of you?"

"I have a job, I draw my pay. I have pals like Buscard and Max. We're all right, because we stick together. I'm better off here than I was in Paris when the colonel picked me up at Weber's."

"Hortense, eh?"

"That's all over."

"Because of Gelinet?"

"No. She bores me to tears. Women are all right for love, but they never take the place of pals. Buscard has a soft spot for her, I think I'm going to hand her over to him!"

"You're a sentimentalist in your own way. Keep your eye on Nadolo, all the same!"

"I'm in no danger . . . not with my pals to help me!"

"You bloody old German! If you had winged me in the war you would have finished me off!"

"You would have done the same to me. But beforehand you would have had to preach at me: I wouldn't! . . ."

"Is there anything I can do for you?"

"Nothing."

Kreis clasped him by the hand, gave it a hearty squeeze and went off to join his pals.

The procession had made a détour in order to drive past the American Consulate. The Stars and Stripes fluttered at the masthead but all the windows were shattered.

"Another martini, Patrick?" Riverton suggested to Maley. "We are today's defeated!"

Maley went up to the window.

"Look at this masquerade, Arnold. In the space of half an hour I received a telegram from the UN Secretariat-General recalling me to Elizabethville, another from my government informing me that I was no longer at the disposal of the United Nations. They might have waited a week. In any case I'm handing in my resignation to the Foreign Office!"

"Kimjanga got the better of you in the secret agreements signed at Ndola with Brahimi."

"Kimjanga's a silly fool, he didn't even demand the evacuation of the blue helmets. All he could think about was how much he hated me. It made him forget the essential!"

"Are you sorry?"

"To leave this dung-heap? No!"

"I mean sorry you didn't go the whole hog, Patrick, and give orders to fire on the civilian population, as Siddartha wanted."

"I'll have to consider that question; I'll have time enough in Ireland."

"Are you feeling bitter?"

"Yes, about being sacrificed for nothing. In his fright the Secretary-General lied . . . God rest his soul . . . so did Brahimi . . . but he seems to the manner born! I've covered everybody, for the sake of an order which was never carried out! Tomorrow we'll have to begin all over again. . . . Morthor. . . . There will be far more people killed, for do you know how many deaths this terrible battle caused? No more than twenty . . . and about a hundred wounded."

"Pointless deaths and wounds all the same. It's too costly!"

"Less than certain impostures. My mistake was trying to behave like a man of honor, when I was confronted by creatures without faith or law like those French mercenaries!"

Riverton toyed with his glass.

"If you had had them on your side! . . ."

"La Roncière represents everything I hate: contempt for human beings, their regimentation, racialism, fascism, deportation camps, war. . . ."

"He's also a cool-headed, brave and efficient man, extremely useful when he's kept firmly in check. We have

438

officers like that in our Marines, but we have forbidden them ever to think!"

"Is it true, Arnold, that Joan's going to marry one of these mercenaries, that fellow Thomas Fonts?"

"It's not true. She's not marrying a mercenary but Thomas Fonts, the French Consul at Vientiane. Furthermore, he himself doesn't yet know he's going to marry her, but Joan has made up her mind."

"Aren't you shocked?"

"Patrick, you have an extraordinary . . . professorial attitude to politics. To you there are only the good and the bad. You forget all the others. If you had persevered in this career, you would have learned how to accommodate yourself to lies and compromises by hanging on to the only thing that matters, when all's said and done: your country and her interests!"

"A nationalist profession of faith?"

"No, a realistic one!"

"I'm an Irishman, the citizen of a very small country without planetary ambitions. I can't make myself American; so it's impossible for me to understand!"

"What's Siddartha doing?"

"He's gnawing his nails with rage . . . but he's staying on, so he's not defeated!"

"I'd rather like to give a farewell cocktail party for you . . ."

"Pointless provocation, Arnold. Politics is a serious business, as you once told me yourself; feelings don't come into it. But if you like we could drink our heads off this evening, just the two of us! Since hearing that I'm due to leave, my dear colleagues are doing their best to avoid me. They scuttle away. It's revolting."

"Maybe they think that bad luck, like leprosy, is contagious! An old administrative disease."

"One day, perhaps, I'll write it all down and get it off my chest!"

"Pointless, your book will appear too late. No one will remember Morthor any longer, except a few initiates who, from being indifferent, will become hostile!"

"I could have won. . . ."

"You'll be blamed for not having won, and still more for saying that you could have won and that it was the others who prevented you!"

Baron Pieret, the Chairman of the Société Générale de Belgique, was a neatly built little man with a courteous

439

manner and an even, soothing voice. He was responsible for all delicate negotiations, and his arrival at E'ville left no illusions in Van der Weyck's mind as to what to expect: his recall.

But at the same time the managing director felt a certain relief. Such an important figure as Pieret would not have been sent all the way to Africa merely to explain to an employee, however exalted his position, that his presence was no longer needed in Katanga.

"My dear fellow," said the baron, rubbing his hands together, "our situation is getting more delicate every day! Definitely, we cannot go on supporting the Kimjanga Government. The whole world is against him. I don't mean the Communist countries or the underdeveloped nations, but also the Americans. . . . There's not much enthusiasm in Paris either. As for London? To please the Rhodesians, London is still helping Kimjanga, but not to the point of falling foul of the rest of Africa. . . ."

"In that case the Union Minière merely has to pay its dues to the Central Government in Leopoldville. No more money, no more Kimjanga!"

Van der Weyck rose from his armchair and drew his visitor's attention to the big map which covered one wall of his office: it indicated all the Union Minière installations in Katanga.

"But also no more mines! Today Kimjanga is victorious and drives about Elizabethville in an open car in the midst of his cheering subjects! All my European employees clap as he drives past. If we stopped paying the dues, the Katangese Government would nationalize us."

"The United Nations have offered to insure the security of our mines."

"My good friend the American Consul mentioned something about that but, like me, he recognizes that it's impossible! The blue helmets are not thick enough on the ground and the Katangese—who have the support, don't forget, of all our European staff—would soon sabotage our installations!"

"My dear Van der Weyck, our government, under the influence of Monsieur Spaak—and with reason, it seems—has decided to back Leopoldville and the unification of the Congo. It is extremely embarrassed about the position that the Union Minière has taken out here . . . I admit we could not have done otherwise. We must think of something if we want to keep the mines! Go on supporting Kimjanga, of course . . . while at the same time taking certain precautions. When Kimjanga had disappeared, we shall have to deal with the Congolese Central Government."

"What precautions?"

"Were you in Belgium or in France during the occupation?"

"No, in England."

"You were lucky, it was far easier! But you are not unaware how certain big concerns were able to . . . shall we say 'work' with the enemy . . . without incurring any reproach at the Liberation.

"The directors of these concerns accepted all the Germans' conditions and abided by them scrupulously. But first of all they demanded a requisition order, properly drawn up and signed. This requisition, if it was not properly carried out . . . at least this was what was written down . . . in some clause or other of the Military Code of Law . . . could entail the deportation and even the death of anyone contravening it. Everyone was more or less in the game, of course!"

"Kantanga is occupied only by Katangese!"

"From now on you had better ask your staff to demand requisition orders for anything that is given to the Katangese Government . . . money, equipment, rolling stock. Tell the more excitable of our employees that it's necessary for the sake of our accountancy, explain to the more sober-minded that we have to keep an eye on the future. All these requisition orders are to be sent forthwith to Brussels!"

"How long do I have, Monsieur Pieret, to explain our new accountancy methods to my staff?"

"One week. Don't get angry, Van der Weyck! Among other things, there have been some regrettable incidents at Jadotville! Our local director, Monteil, has shown a lack of discretion. We have received a very nasty note from the UN on this subject. He put his telephone system, trucks and living quarters at the disposal of the mercenaries. He even had one of them staying with him in his own house. Then, in Elizabethville, there was that Vigilantes Committee of young Ravetot's! Monsieur Van der Weyck, you are responsible for what your subordinates do. It was you, furthermore, who arranged for those French mercenaries to come out here!"

"I carried out the decisions of the Board of Directors."

"No. You interpreted their suggestions! My dear fellow, you haven't been dismissed, but, to satisfy the UN, the

Americans and the Leopoldville Government at one and the same time, we're recalling you to Brussels . . . to a more important post that's waiting for you!

"Freed from all external pressures, replaced here by an executive who will not be allowed to act on his own initiative, better informed on the general situation, you will continue to direct our beloved company in the Rue de la Montagne du Parc! Furthermore, you'll retain your appointment as managing director!"

"What will my role be in Brussels?"

"First of all, to reorganize the company's affairs. But discreetly . . . Monteil must be recalled, but with the utmost courtesy . . . Ravetot as well, and probably a few others."

"And after that?"

"These mercenaries—I refer to the leaders, of course —you must advise them to go back to France, and to continue, by means of reliable intermediaries, to maintain friendly relations with those who are staying on. . . ."

"To avoid acts of sabotage, I suppose?"

"What's so delightful about you, my dear Van der Weyck, is your subtlety! Another thing: in Brussels we cannot receive any . . . shall we say 'interested' visits from Katangese ministers. You will take charge of them and make them see reason!"

"And then?"

"In three or four months' time you might make a trip to Leopoldville with those requisition orders in your pocket. You yourself will explain, in person, all the difficulties you had with the Katangese authorities."

"Katanga is well and truly lost. We're being dropped by everyone. And that poor wretch Kimjanga, parading in the streets! Not a bad fellow, Kimjanga! With him one could always come to an agreement!"

"We may well have to come to further agreements with him!"

"There's only one man who frightens me: Bongo . . . the Minister of the Interior. He's primitive, a realist and violent, there's no knowing what he might do."

"We could invite him to Brussels. Maybe in a more relaxed atmosphere . . ."

"Whom are you sending out here to replace me?"

"It's up to you to choose your successor, so as to make sure he never forgets that he still depends on you. Which shows, my dear fellow, that we're not so displeased with your services! If you have the opportunity, thank the

American Consul, Arnold Riverton. Through his reports he has been extremely useful to you. You live alone here? Don't you get bored?"

"A lot of work . . . and an occasional round of golf . . . with Arnold Riverton."

"Very astute: no one could have any complaint to make about these contacts! I'd like to have a look at this procession, my dear fellow!"

"It's just a circus show . . . at least I imagine so!"

"With Negroes in lion-skins?"

"No, in top hats! I'll tell my driver to take you to the Belgian Consulate. A very fine view from the balcony, and you'll meet our representative, Ryckers, who's also feeling none too easy!"

Van der Weyck stayed behind, alone in his office, alone in the administrative building now deserted by his employees. The factory chimney had not stopped smoking throughout the September fighting. It would go on doing so.

In a week's time Van der Weyck would be back in his big flat in Brussels, with his wife and children, with the noise and commotion, all the little household problems which more often than not turn family life into hell on earth!

He would no longer wake to the clear African mornings, hear the sound of golf balls on the deserted greens of E'ville, or see that speck of red which sometimes appeared through the trees, Joan, always in revolt and as biting as ever, Joan whom he had loved without expecting anything from it. It was one of those deep melancholy loves known only to men in the autumn of life, a love to which they devote the best of themselves—all that they had not known in spring and summer!

He hummed the little ditty of his childhood:

> Barbençon,
> Mon mignon,
> Le crispin,
> Sur le pain,
> Le bouvreuil
> Sur le seuil . . .

Then he opened his safe and took out two files, the personal files of Monteil and Ravetot.

La Roncière left the procession as it drew level with the Presidency. The cars were hemmed in by a hysterical mob. Kimjanga, with a smile on his face, clasped the hands stretched out towards him.

The colonel could not stand this din and masquerade any longer. He wanted to be alone, so he went home.

The living room smelled of dust and fug. Cockroaches scuttled across the kitchen floor. Panga, the house-boy, must have taken advantage of his absence to go off on a few days' holiday.

La Roncière had a shower and poured himself out a whisky. No ice in the refrigerator, and the water in the tap was lukewarm and nauseating. The colonel opened a book at random and flung it down again after a few minutes. After a moment's hesitation he picked up the telephone and dialed Jenny's number.

"Jean-Marie! What a surprise! I am pleased to hear you. John and I were talking about you only at lunchtime! We wondered when you were coming back to E'ville!"

Jenny's voice did not sound natural; it was too cordial, too expansive. Usually, when he rang up the villa, she answered demurely, with affected courtesy. She never mentioned her husband's name to her lover.

"I'd like to see you, Jenny."

"Yes, of course, delighted. When?"

"Now."

Jenny hesitated.

"Well, you see . . . I'm giving a dinner this evening, an official do, and I'm a bit pushed for time. Never mind, I'll come. I'll be a little late, that's all. Where do you suggest?"

"My place? But it's in a terrible mess. Some quiet spot?"

"I'd like to have a little fresh air. I haven't been out all day. All the boys have skipped off because of the procession, and I have this dinner on my hands! We could meet at the Sabena Guest House, on the road to the airport. I'll be there in a quarter of an hour."

Jenny arrived half an hour later, dressed in a light blue frock which la Roncière had never seen her wear before. The colonel felt ill at ease; this seductive young woman was not the one he used to know. He remembered Jenny at Bandawe, on the banks of Lake Nyasa, in slacks and shabby sandals. That was on 13 September. It was now the 21st. La Roncière felt these eight days had separated them forever. A thread had broken somewhere in the weaving, an invisible thread, and all the other threads and knots were coming loose.

444

"Jean-Marie, how good it is to see you again! I'm so happy; we've won the battle. Here we are, victorious! You have no idea! Since yesterday my children have been completely out of hand, hopelessly over-excited. Denis has taught his sister the Katangese anthem and they keep bawling it all day long. They went off at four o'clock to attend Kimjanga's arrival. I haven't seen them since. . . ."

"Very touching," la Roncière interjected, "but I'm afraid all this joy is far from justified!"

The young woman looked surprised.

"Why not? The UN have capitulated and accepted Kimjanga's conditions. Maley is discredited and has been recalled. What more do you want?"

She leaned towards la Roncière.

"Come on now, Jean-Marie, stop being such a Cassandra! You've done a magnificent job. Only today John was saying: 'La Roncière has got us out of a nasty mess, and Smith thinks so too.' "

"I don't care what John Ligget thinks. I tell you Katanga is done for. Alas, I'm in a position to know . . . as well as your friend Smith!"

Jenny gazed in amazement at la Roncière's withdrawn expression, at his clenched jaw and hard eyes. She stiffened in her chair.

"What's wrong with you, Jean-Marie? What sort of tone is this? If you were going to be so unpleasant, it was hardly worth ringing me up!"

La Roncière was furious with himself, furious for behaving like a lovesick schoolboy green with jealousy. The last flickers of love often take the form of jealousy. How could he explain to Jenny that he could not bear to hear her talk about her husband and children, about all that part of her life which escaped him? She had always taken care to keep it to herself. Of the fine tapestry there remained only a few loose threads.

With an effort he managed to smile.

"I'm sorry, Jenny, I'm rather tired. These last few days have been exhausting!"

Jenny relaxed and patted la Roncière's hand.

"Tell me all about it!"

He felt like asking her:

"Was it your husband who sent you? Has he a report to make? Or was it Smith?"

But he controlled himself. After all, why not tell her the truth? So much the better if she warned Ligget, Smith and

445

the Rhodesians of the errors which the Katangese were in the process of committing.

"I spent three days begging Kimjanga not to surrender, to refuse to meet the UN Secretary-General except in Rhodesian territory."

"Well, he listened to you!"

"Yes, but not on the essential point. Kimjanga didn't demand the immediate departure of the UN forces."

"Don't you think, Jean-Marie, you want to have too much too quickly?"

"No, Jenny, I'm sorry to see that no one seems to understand what's happening, yet it's simple enough; Kimjanga held trump cards in his hand, which he will never hold again. The Secretary-General was at the end of his tether. We were lucky that he was killed. . . ."

"Jean-Marie, please!"

Like most women, Jenny accepted the fact, and without the slightest compunction, that men should be killed to serve the cause, but she could not bear it being mentioned.

"Listen, Jenny," la Roncière went on, "I'm talking about a political situation. Feelings don't come into it. It's a fact that the Secretary-General's death was a good thing for us. My job is to make a cool assessment of facts like that."

Once again la Roncière felt irritated, and, at the same time, he found Jenny less intelligent. He discovered she was just like any other woman, with her little problems, her little projects, her refusal to face facts.

He went on with a touch of irritation in his voice.

"As I was saying, the Secretary-General's death served our cause. We held other cards in our hand: an Irish company that surrendered in Jadotville, the Swedes in Elizabethville on the point of doing so. We merely had to give them a nudge."

La Roncière thumped the table with his fist.

"With all these trumps in our hand, we could have demanded the total evacuation of the UN troops. I went down on my knees to that idiot Kimjanga and begged him to demand it. He didn't listen to me. Now he's done for!"

"I don't understand: Kimjanga signed an agreement with Brahimi forbidding the blue helmets to reinforce their effective strength in Katanga. He even obtained a specific assurance against an attack from the Leopoldville troops. The UN have recognized his rights to defend himself against all aggression launched from outside!"

"But don't you understand, Jenny, that he has been

446

hoodwinked? The UN will never keep their promises, even if Brahimi was a man of his word. In a couple of weeks all the Afro-Asian countries, with Russia's support, will start a fresh campaign against Katanga. In a month's time they'll be shouting for a second military operation. You know what's going to happen? I don't give you three months before the UN embark on another Morthor. But this time it won't be a laughing matter! That's the fine job your brilliant Kimjanga has done!"

Jenny was aghast, but she resented la Roncière for being right and for treating her in such a cavalier fashion! Before coming to this meeting she had decided to break with him. She was all the more furious to find him hostile and ready to make this break more easy. She attacked him.

"You're the only one who understands the situation: Kimjanga is an imbecile who has been hoodwinked like a child! But who says he hasn't obtained any definite assurances? Are you sure of being in every secret?"

La Roncière shrugged his shoulders impatiently. He sometimes had the impression that he was reporting to one of those agents who were used during the Resistance and who were known as "live letter-boxes."

"Naturally, Kimjanga has obtained assurances or, to be more exact, certain promises! I can even tell you what: Brahimi has been very clever, he has lauded him to the skies, he has told him that the UN were mistaken about him, that they wished him no harm, that Africa needed him. To finish up, he dangled the carrot in front of him: Adoula was proving a disappointment to certain high-level authorities. Kimjanga could be the providential man, the man who was destined to save the Congo. He merely had to make his peace with the United Nations, co-operate with them, and not only would he be retained in his position but he would shortly be installed in the presidential chair in Leopoldville! He swallowed it all, the fool!"

"Who says that's what's going to happen?"

"No one, but I know it. I'll tell you why: Brahimi, I'm certain, has no intention of keeping his word. Kimjanga had a barrel of dynamite in his hands. Brahimi removed the fuse and now Kimjanga is at his mercy."

A long silence ensued. La Roncière and Jenny felt they had no more to say to each other. Both of them wanted to leave, but neither of them dared take the first step. Jenny was the first to make up her mind.

"I must be going, Jean-Marie, my guests are waiting for

me. I must also tell you I'm flying out the day after to-morrow with my children. Yes, I'm going to spend a few months in England with my husband's family. The doctor says Denis needs a change of air."

La Roncière rose to his feet.

"All right, Jenny. So it's good-bye!"

"Good-bye, Jean-Marie!"

She hesitated a moment.

"Jean-Marie, I'd like us to remain good friends."

La Roncière took her hand and lifted it to his lips.

"Yes, Jenny, good friends, even accomplices perhaps . . . another time!"

Jenny walked away slowly at first, but at the corner of the street she broke into a run.

La Roncière thought of Julienne, who was such a good listener and so understanding when a man was disappointed or unhappy. Julienne, the refuge!

Dorat got back to the Leo II in a state of exhaustion. It was time to "knock off" an article on Kimjanga's return, to describe the collective hysteria of the Europeans and also to make people aware of how fragile Kimjanga's victory was.

There was a knock on the door. Spencer, the Associated Press correspondent, came in.

"I say, you haven't a spare bottle of whisky by any chance? All the boys have buggered off to the fiesta. Impossible to find anything to drink in this dump!"

Spencer switched on the transistor which he carried around with him. Bayard's voice erupted:

". . . And so it's a final solemn warning that the Katangese people give to the Communist Maley, to the ignoble Siddartha, the butcher of Elizabethville, and to the infamous Brahimi, who tried to turn our capital into another Budapest. . . ."

"The man's off his head," Dorat observed.

Spencer put a finger to his lips. Bayard, having recovered his breath, was now in full flight.

"All these UN sub-humans came out to Katanga in order to kill, loot and rape for a handful of American dollars. For back at home, in Ireland, India and Tunisia, they were dying of hunger! All these wretched outcasts of humanity were starving beggars and murderers!"

"Well, I never!" Spencer exclaimed. "You know one of the clauses of the agreement signed yesterday between Brahimi and Kimjanga specifies that the Katangese radio should abstain from all propaganda hostile to the UN?"

"Whatever happens, no one has any intention of abiding by this agreement! Apart from that, I find this sort of propaganda unbearable! Mind you, it's the whites who are responsible for it. I'm convinced the Negroes would be less stupid!"

By eight o'clock Dorat had finished his work. He read through his copy with satisfaction. Seven pages, two thousand words. It was rather long but the subject was worth it. He gave his article to a colleague who was leaving for Ndola.

Dorat was woken by someone thumping on his door. He got up with an effort. A hilarious bell-boy handed him a telegram and a letter.

"For you, boss. You see, the UN have gone, so the post office is working!"

Dorat read:

Article far too long impossible publish stop Consider Katanga affair finished stop Request your immediate return for subsequent posting to Algeria stop Notify date arrival stop Greetings Rubichon

"That silly sod Rubichon hasn't understood a thing!" Dorat reflected.

Spencer came in.

"Well, are you hunting for news? We're trying to see Kimjanga!"

"It's all over for me! To hell with Katanga. I'm hunting for a seat on a plane!"

"Where are you off to?"

"Paris, then Algeria!"

"I see. The same old story, but a different place!"

When October came, la Roncière found himself on his own, rid of Thomas Fonts and his insolence. But he no longer had anyone with him to facilitate his contacts, to enliven the atmosphere by a good or a bad joke.

His pride gloried in this solitude, but his solemn demeanor and that biting manner he had of predicting misfortune did not endear him to Kimjanga and his cronies.

Ingenuously the President believed in the promises Brahimi had made and, when the UN abused the Ndola agreements, he assumed a knowing air. Kimjanga was convinced that the Tunisian was scheming behind the scenes to install him in Adoula's place as head of the Congo Government.

The fruits of victory were to be had for the picking, and how juicy they were! The President was recovering his taste for lengthy binges "between friends," for the very special parties that Germaine organized for him with easy-going people who were not bothered by questions of color.

Kimjanga gave receptions, opened bridges which had been open for some time, and barracks which were re-christened, according to the whim of the day, either military camps or education and selection centers. Champagne flowed, parade succeeded parade, and the army of Nadolo the Victorious, instead of carrying on with its training in camp, ambled about the town. The para-commandos alone, under the influence of Kreis and his "pals," retained a modicum of fighting spirit. But they used it more often than not in scuffles and brawls with the other members of the Katangese Army.

La Roncière was worried: the blue helmets were systematically reinforcing. Siddartha was operating with discretion: no movements in the capital, everything happened outside.

To his urgent demands "to do something or take precautions," the President replied with an evasive wave of his hand.

"Be reasonable, my dear Colonel. We have defeated the blue helmets. They can't do anything more. The entire population is behind me. If Siddartha's troops were to make a move, the town would bristle with blockhouses. At every window a rifle would emerge, behind every tree in the bush a bow and arrow!"

He found this phrase so satisfying that he repeated it several times on the radio, believing he had done enough to keep la Roncière happy and dissipate the vague dangers threatening him.

The President kept pestering the colonel about his personal guard. He wanted a mounted guard with peaked caps, gauntlets, long boots and black dolmans with red lapels, "like the Republican Guards of the President of the French Republic!" And also bugles, he added.

In his exasperation la Roncière sent a long telegram to Fonts who, "still on holiday with Joan," was then in Paris.

Urgently need twenty complete full-dress Republican Guard uniforms with all accessories stop Am asking this as final favor stop Please send by first plane to Salisbury stop Katangese Delegation Paris putting all funds at your disposal stop Fate of Katanga and mood Kimjanga depending on this stop

Thomas Fonts was living with Joan in a left-bank hotel. The windows of their bedroom overlooked the Seine.

At nine o'clock in the morning, in a litter of newspapers and magazines, with the telephone on the bed, they rang for breakfast and, nibbling toast and sipping black coffee, embarked on a new day. Joan knew in advance that it would be chaotic and nothing would happen as she expected! She had a different conception of happiness, but for a few months this sort of life was not without its charm.

A waiter brought up a telegram, which delighted Fonts. He handed it to Joan, then seized the telephone.

"Whom should I ring?" he asked. "Does the Republican Guard depend on the Minister of the Interior or of War? I can't leave old Jean-Marie in the lurch, after all! The fate of Katanga depends on these twenty costumes!"

"Are you going to wake up a minister or private secretary for this nonsense? Only yesterday Dumont was saying you really lacked a sense of administrative and political decorum!"

Fonts reflected.

"You remember, Joan, that fellow we saw the other day who's something to do with the cinema? Barrette, that's it. I must have his card somewhere.

"Hullo, Barrette, how are you? Fonts here, yes, Thomas Fonts. I have a problem . . . I'm going in for film-making . . . I'm putting on a super-production in black Africa, in Katanga . . . entirely financed by the Union Minière. In 'scope, of course . . . and natural color! The title? That's unimportant. I need twenty Republican Guard uniforms. No, no, it's not a big historical piece, just burlesque. You say I need only ring up Cor de Chasse and mention your name? Fancy dress and uniforms of every type, thanks. There's no shortage of actors. A director? I have one on the spot. If anything crops up for you, I'll let you know, of course; all expenses paid!

"Hello, Cor de Chasse. Cooperscope Productions here. We're making a film in Katanga. We badly need twenty Republican Guard uniforms with all accessories, helmets, swords, boots. What size? Give me an assortment. Which century? Is the Republic as old as that? We're firmly in

451

favor of the Fifth Republic style. You say it's the same as the Third or the Fourth? You want a reference? Ring up the Katangese Delegation in Paris, mentioning my name, and ask for the delegate, Monsieur Thomaris . . . the delegate producer, if you prefer! He'll make you out a check. Good-bye, monsieur."

He replaced the receiver and rolled over on-top of Joan.

"Let's go out and buy you some dresses, my little quail!"

"Hmm!"

"You have no idea how you change when a dressmaker wraps you up in a piece of cloth. You twist and turn in front of the mirror, you stretch out a leg or an arm, you extend your neck. Out of the corner of your eye you beg me to buy you this piece of cloth for a fortune. Since you still have a few principles left, you feel embarrassed. But then you think of Chantal, who'll die of jealousy, and all you principles vanish, you little hussy!"

"You delight in perverting me, you little wretch! What does this telegram from la Roncière mean?"

"That Negro madness is at its height in Elizabethville. And that unless he participates in it, which is not at all his sort of thing, Jean-Marie will soon be coming back to France to learn that old Uncle Chaudey has played him one of his tricks!"

"What trick?"

"La Roncière still believes that he'll be able, when he likes, to rejoin the Army in his present rank. He hasn't a chance. He'll be appointed full colonel, but in the Reserve!"

"Meaning?"

"That the Army has finished with him, my love, and he'll have to look for a job . . . like all his little pals coming back from Algeria!"

"Do you love me?"

"Of course not. I'm far too happy when I'm with you."

The Katangese Supreme Defense Committee, consisting of President Kimjanga, His Excellency Bongo, Minister of the Interior and Defense, the Chief of Staff and Commander-in-Chief of the Katangese Forces, General Nadolo, and Colonel la Roncière, military and political adviser, held its first meeting at Government House on 5 October, 1961.

In a room, the door of which was guarded by two fully armed para-commandos, la Roncière had adorned one wall with a huge map of Katanga marked with red arrows and those cabalistic signs that are in evidence in every headquarters. A curtain enabled it to be concealed. On the other side was a blackboard. Opposite the map stood a big table with four blotting-pads and four blocks of Defense Committee writing-paper bearing in red letters the legend "Top Secret."

Karl Kreis acted as secretary.

Kimjanga arrived in a bad mood. He was bored by military problems; he therefore regarded them as unimportant. He also had a crashing hangover and was trying, but in vain, to remember what on earth he had promised a little Czechoslovakian tart who had taken advantage of his drunkenness to get all sorts of promises out of him. Luckily he never kept them!

Bongo attended less and less to the problems of defense, allowing his cousin, General Nadolo, a free rein, and more and more to anything concerned with the Union Minière.

He indulged in the following simple argument:

"With money, we shall always have soldiers and arms. What matters, therefore, is money! Where does it come from? From the Union Minière. Now on that side nothing has been happening since Van der Weyck's recall. They haven't even sent out another Managing Director to replace him! The Union Minière is on a new tack and backing Leo. If I don't take action, we are lost!"

He had therefore decided to make a trip to Brussels three days later and considered this Supreme Defense Committee pointless. It was yet another white man's idea! He felt that la Roncière, like all his kind, talked too much and was only too ready to regard the Negroes as imbeciles because they knew nothing about logistics. . . .

What was the point in knowing about logistics if one had enough money to hire white men who knew about it?

Nadolo came in, swagger-stick in hand, his uniform jacket with its big pockets bisected by a shoulder-strap, his thick lips curled back into a pout under his gold-edged cap adorned with four brass flames.

La Roncière realized at once that Nadolo was determined to contradict him on every point. The general barely saluted him, sniffed scornfully at the map, tapped the table several times with his swagger-stick and treated Kreis like a mere orderly.

He was extremely proud of his first standing order to the Katangese Army, which he had spent hours in drafting with his Staff-Major Kiwe. Both of them felt that this doc-

ument would be a notable contribution to military litera-
ture in the French language.

Germaine, the President's secretary, had on her side
contributed a few improvements to this masterpiece. She
had just handed him the text, typed in triplicate—one
copy of which, she specified, was for the archives.

Nadolo could hardly wait to declaim this grandiloquent
prose to his army. So he was eager to escape as soon as
possible from this formal Defense Committee chore. He
could not prevent himself from taking the standing order
out of his pocket to savor it.

Officers, NCOs and Soldiers,

To the Government's appeal, you unanimously replied by fighting heroically for the defense of our
land.

Your faith and will to conquer remain unshake-
able.

President Kimjanga, the Head of State, has asked
me to congratulate you for the courageous work you
are accomplishing, giving the whole world proof of
the quality and superiority of our army.

General Callaghan, the commander of the blue helmets in the Congo, in a public statement, has tried to
give the impression that our army is divided, disorganized, at the end of its tether.

To these odious lies we shall reply as we have done
since the outbreak of hostilities. General Callaghan
should not confuse our soldiers with those of Leopoldville. In Katanga, the Army is not given to politics. It recognizes only one commander, the President
of the State.

My soldiers are disciplined and they have given the
whole world proof of their courage and fortitude in
action!

Of course, General Callaghan believes himself to
be in a strong position with his American aircraft
that are able to bombard and savagely machine-gun
the peaceful inhabitants of our cities. But, believe me,
I should be curious to see the results of a military engagement between the UN mercenary troops and
those whom I have the honor and privilege to command. Fighting with equal armaments, I have no
doubt as to what would happen to the UN Army. It
would quickly be annihilated. And yet, even though

454

the armaments are not equal, I am convinced that the fighting would nevertheless end in this manner.

The blue helmets would be wiped out by the valiant sons of Katanga, who at least know why they are fighting. They know that, behind President Kimjanga, they are fighting for the defense of Christian civilization against Communist servitude. My soldiers are the last bulwark in Central Africa against Soviet penetration, the prelude to a new form of colonialism which has nothing in common with the one from which we have just emerged!

My soldiers have embarked on a magnificent campaign, a campaign in the service of liberty and human dignity against barbarism.

As my elders used to say in Europe a quarter of a century ago, when the Christian West was struggling against another form of barbarism, I too shall say: "NO, THEY SHALL NOT PASS!"

May God protect Katanga and grant her final victory!

This is not only a hope, it is the deep conviction which the whole Government and I myself entertain at this time, which, for our people defended by an army of valiant fighters, heralds a glorious tomorrow!

General Nadolo

Elizabethville, 5 October, 1961

Drafted and presented in the French language by Major Kiwe of the Katangese Forces.*

The more he thought about it, the more pointless and even insulting did this Defense Committee appear to Nadolo, for, by creating it, la Roncière was trying to limit the attributions of the Commander-in-Chief.

Katanga had no need to saddle herself with white officers of this sort. They had been to military academies, but he, Nadolo, who had attended none, had defeated the blue helmets commanded by officers who had likewise been to military academies. Personal valor and courage was what counted, nothing else. The strength of the Ban-

---

* We have taken the liberty of transcribing here, without modifying anything except a few names, an official document published on 12 December, 1961, which is due to the inspiration of the valiant General Muke, "former sergeant in the Force Publique," and to the pen of Major Selamani of the Katangese Forces. We thank them for this collaboration.

tus was greater than that of the Irish, the Swedes, the Indians and the Belgians!

Nadolo knew that la Roncière was once more going to say that the UN were preparing a fresh attack. Never would Siddartha dare, or else all his soldiers would be massacred!

But the colonel kept saying the same thing, so as to be kept on and continue to draw his pay. The money doled out to the mercenaries would be better employed in the pockets of Katangese officers, who had difficulty in making two ends meet on their miserable pay.

La Roncière went over to the map and embarked on his theme.

"Gentlemen," he said, "the UN are not abiding by the Ndola agreements!"

With a ruler he pointed to North Katanga.

"In this region, in particular, the Congolese National Army is continuing to fly in reinforcements with a view to occupying the country. Here in Elizabethville the situation is even more serious. Contrary to these agreements, the blue helmets have not only left the positions in which they were supposed to remain confined, but have also . . ." La Roncière paused, "re-occupied the airfield, which enables them to land men, arms and equipment."

Kimjanga yawned behind his raised hand, Nadolo gazed at a buzzing fly. Bongo alone listened.

"If we do nothing about it, in a month's time we'll be at war again!"

"What do you suggest?" Kimjanga asked in a listless voice.

"Let's take the problems one by one: in the north we must first of all bring the National Army to a halt by launching a number of raids. . . ." He took up the ruler again, ". . . against Albertville, Kongolo and also against the Kamina base which is controlled by the UN and the Congolese forces.

"But we are short of troops in that area!"

Nadolo sprang to his feet.

"That's not true: I have just recruited two battalions, which my officers have taken over."

"Two battalions! And a fine lot they are, General! A collection of tramps and layabouts who have enlisted for a square meal! No ordnance: they're badly clothed, badly armed, badly fed, and disband as soon as the smallest unit of the National Army appears!"

"What do you know about it?"

"Lieutenant Kreis, who is here, has just inspected them. Ask him what the officers are worth. Nothing! They're not interested in anything but girls and beer. . . ."

"Kreis doesn't like Negroes, he's a racialist. He struck me!"

Kreis shrugged his shoulders.

"The battalion commander can't even read," he said. "A captain blew himself up on a mortar shell while trying to see 'how this contraption worked.' Another sold his company's weapons. . . . None of them wants to fight. That's all. I submitted a report to General Nadolo. I don't think he read it! I asked for disciplinary action to be taken."

"It's Elizabethville that interests us," Bongo broke in. "Let's leave the north for the moment, Colonel!"

"We ought to be able to deny access to the airport at any moment. It's easy: we need only install two or three batteries of mortars equipped with high-velocity shells at a range of fifteen hundred yards. After a few shots the runway would be out of commission."

Nadolo sneered.

"Ah, perhaps the colonel doesn't know, or else he has forgotten, that the regulation for an army in action says: no mortar should be sited like that in open country without being defended. Mortars ought to serve as support weapons, sited behind an infantry force attacking after artillery preparation."

"Absurd, General. We're not at Verdun now! It's a question of putting the runway out of commission, not fighting a classic battle to take an airfield!"

"The way Negroes fight isn't the proper way, I suppose? . . ."

"The conditions are different, and the art of strategy lies specifically in being able to adapt oneself to every condition. We are no longer short of material. The equipment I ordered from Europe has at last arrived. . . . But this material has remained in its cases. On your orders, General. We have received three hundred transmitters, new jeeps, bazookas, recoilless 75-mm guns, 60-mm and 81-mm mortars all in cases. . . . How can one instruct with equipment in cases?"

Nadolo bellowed:

"The colonel wanted to issue all this equipment to the mercenaries, not to the Katangese troops . . . to the mercenaries, who are whites, just to defend the whites!"

"Of course I wanted to issue it to the mercenaries, so

457

that they might instruct each unit, because they're the only ones who know how to use it!"

Nadolo spluttered with rage:

"They say in E'ville . . . that the mercenaries and their leaders are on good terms with the Union Minière . . . that they say it's the Union Minière who gives the money and that it's for money that they themselves fight!"

Bongo had pricked up his ears; Nadolo's accusations were filed away in his mind.

"One day perhaps," Nadolo went on, "the mercenaries will be here solely to defend the mines . . . even against us! Those mines are our flesh and blood, they are part of our land." Pathetic and grotesque, sweating like a pig, he pointed to la Roncière. "This man has come to rob us!"

La Roncière went white in the face.

"How stupid! Monsieur le Président, tell this fellow to hold his tongue and, since you need a general, give him some medals, put some plumes on his head, but above all don't let him take any action or deal with anything, otherwise you're lost!"

He turned to Bongo.

"I'm sorry, Your Excellency, that I advised you to make this puppet a general, whereas he should have been put in a zoo."

"Calm down," the President repeated, "calm down, we have grave decisions to take instead of flinging insults at one another. The same faith, the same ideal unites us all. . . ."

Nadolo was trembling with fury, appealing alternately to the President and to Bongo.

"He called me a monkey, he said it was he who made me a general, me, the victor of Jadotville! . . . Even Kreis can tell you that!"

"The meeting is closed," said Kimjanga, who was very thirsty and wanted to lie down. "Our work is progressing nicely. Thank you, Colonel. Do your best. What about my personal guard?"

"The uniforms are on the way. . . ."

"Very good, very good. . . ."

"But we've done nothing, come to no decision, Monsieur le Président. The blue helmets are going to attack and we're not prepared. . . ."

"We have brave men, arms, world opinion behind us. Long live Katanga, gentlemen!"

He withdrew, followed by Bongo. Nadolo hesitated a moment; he wanted to tell the French colonel that he would put paid to him. But an instinctive caution restrained him. In Katanga Nadolo was at home, in his own country, and he had plenty of time. The other man was merely someone who was paid. But, surrounded by his fetishes—the maps, the blue and red pencils, the blackboard—the colonel overawed him.

Nadolo spat on the floor and marched out.

The colonel sat down on the table.

"Well, Kreis?"

Kreis came and sat next to him.

"I remember, Colonel, the advice you gave me before I went to Tshiko."

"I know, Kreis . . . but these idiots don't realize how serious, almost desperate, the situation is, only ten days after what they regard as a victory."

"What can we do?"

"This victory was won exclusively by the whites. We must go on relying on the whites. They're our only hope."

"The Belgians are beginning to believe in Kimjanga, but the mercenaries think they're being too easily forgotten . . . Not one of us has received a word of thanks. . . . Oh well, so long as the pay keeps rolling in!"

Three days later some gendarmes, equipped with a requisition order signed by Nadolo, seized la Roncière's car while it was parked in front of the Presidency.

La Roncière rushed in furiously to see Kimjanga. The President canceled the requisition order. The colonel took advantage of this to ask him to give the necessary instructions to set up a field headquarters in the African city equipped with every means of communication: radio, telephone, etc.

"If the UN attack, we should then have a concealed signals center between all the units."

"Excellent idea," the President agreed. "There must also be blockhouses, sandbags and barbed-wire entanglements. We could show it to the journalists: the symbol of the Katangese people's spirit of resistance!"

"That's the last thing we want to do, Monsieur le Président. . . . We must keep the command post secret."

The President looked disappointed.

"Really? Oh, very well, I'll give orders to General Nadolo."

Nadolo never stopped scoring points. He obtained permission for all the mercenaries to be withdrawn from the Katangese units in which they were in a position of command, and formed into little independent groups based on Marinel near Kolwezi.

La Roncière could do no more than arrange for these groups to be commanded by Kreis. And even in this he would have failed had the mercenaries themselves not requested it.

The mercenaries received none of the new weapons and kept their old vehicles. The gendarmes drove around in brand new jeeps equipped with transmitters which they did not know how to use. Proudly they brandished their recoilless guns, which they did not know how to work, and their bazookas with electric firing mechanisms which were devoid of batteries.

Every day the colonel reverted to the subject of constructing a command post in the African city; every day the President promised the work would be started on the morrow.

La Roncière eventually realized that Nadolo was making things drag out as long as possible. The "hero of Jadotville" was afraid that if trouble broke out, the colonel, with a radio and telephone at his disposal, might resume command of the Army, as on 3 September. His prestige would never withstand such a blow.

He went around saying:

"Radio's pointless. It's a bit of useless junk . . . it goes di-di-di. Warriors don't need that sort of thing in order to fight."

But he broke three sets in an attempt to make them work.

La Roncière was now the only European in the President's immediate circle who was still concerned with military questions. But he had the greatest difficulty in getting the information he needed, whether it was about arms consignments, the military situation in the north, or the location and training of the units of the Katangese Army.

On several occasions he reported to Headquarters, but General Nadolo had always just gone out on a tour of inspection when he arrived.

"Where to?" la Roncière would ask.

"That's a military secret," Major Kiwe would reply with a chuckle.

The Supreme Defense Committee had ceased to meet after the first session. La Roncière had resumed contact with Gelinet and was beginning to set on foot a sort of secret army, about which there was nothing secret but its name. With the utmost difficulty he organized a system of street, district and block commanders. But the Belgians did not think the UN would venture on a new operation. Like the Negroes, moreover, they believed that they could make mincemeat of the blue helmets. They manifested supreme indifference, failed to turn up at the meetings and pooh-poohed the colonel's warnings. La Roncière had some arms and uniforms issued with the help of some Union Minière agents who acted as receivers. Young Ravetot was extremely useful to him for this sort of operation.

But more often than not the arms and the uniforms remained locked away in cupboards and only served to overawe wives, children and girl-friends.

"I'm short of men," la Roncière said to himself, "but I have the radio at my disposal."

Bayard, who had wisely resumed his duties as a technical adviser, made a come-back. The announcer excelled himself. He spoke about five thousand armed civilians perpetually on the watch, equipped with the latest weapons and radio communication, and prepared to die for the cause, about cellars transformed into blockhouses, about night marches and executions of traitors.

The MIR was given a fresh lease on life.

There were reports of a girl who had had her head shaved for having slept with a Swede.

"That's silly," Trude said to la Roncière.

The only comfort which the colonel, alone and friendless, could find was with the little German tart.

Trude was gentle, self-effacing, neat and tidy about the house and in her person. But she was extremely touchy in her relations with the girls who pursued the same profession as herself.

It was at her place that la Roncière had met a major from the Swedish battalion, who was disgusted with Operation Morthor and who at one moment had thought of surrendering.

Trude had established a clientele among the UN officers, but, since Bayard's threats, she no longer dared entertain the blue helmets. She relied a great deal on the colonel to protect her.

In her arms la Roncière experienced a certain pleasure, the pleasure of degrading himself. With her he indulged in certain caresses which his Protestant upbringing forbade him with other women. Sometimes he got drunk and beat her, which she passively accepted.

One night, just for fun, he asked her for some money.

She produced it, but la Rónciere flung the banknotes in her face.

Maley had been replaced by a ludicrous prim character, Edwin Davidson, who let Siddartha act as he wished and confined himself to saying, as he sucked on his pipe with a pensive air:

"Interesting. . . . Really, extremely interesting!"

He never felt at ease except with his consul, John Ligget, with whom he shared a liking for pink gin.

General Siddartha pretended to attach great importance to Colonel Degger's reports on the para-military organization and recruitment of the civilians of Elizabethville, even though he believed only partly in the value of these reports. He knew the Swede's lively imagination and his taste for sensational information. Degger's network was considerably reduced and many of his agents worked for the Katangese when they were not being used to intoxicate the UN services.

Siddartha had only one idea in his head: to redeem the humiliating defeat he had suffered in September. He wanted war, and this time he meant to win it without being hampered, as he had been during Morthor, by cautious or humanitarian instructions from the Secretariat-General. It was to these instructions, to the indecision and scruples of Maley, that the Indian attributed the failure of Morthor. For the last month, therefore, in all his reports he had deliberately exaggerated the military strength and organization of the enemy. This time he was certain of success: the Ethiopian fighters which he had so sorely lacked in September had now arrived. He had at his disposal several light Canberra bombers of the Indian Air Force and he had even received some heavy 120-mm mortars which would enable him to bombard the town from beyond the range of the Katangese weapons.

Siddartha had asked Colonel Degger for a general report on the situation. He had it in front of him now.

Under the command of French mercenaries trained in revolutionary warfare technique, the European population of Elizabethville is completely organized. The town has been divided into a number of districts and sectors under their respective leaders.

According to certain documents which have fallen into our hands, each leader has a specific mission:

To keep the Katangese High Command informed of our troop movements.

To organize barricades at key-points with petrol drums filled with sand, vehicles, barbed wire and various other obstacles which are already assembled in disused garages.

To turn cellars and premises overlooking certain important positions into blockhouses made of sand-bags or even cement. In these blockhouses positions have been installed for machine-guns, bazookas and recoilless guns.

In each of these sectors the civilians have been issued with uniforms, personal weapons and grenades.

The number of Belgian civilians recruited into this organization may be estimated at five thousand. . . .

Colonel Degger made much of unconfirmed information, according to which Katanga was alleged to have received a considerable number of mortars and even pieces of artillery and had at her disposal an embryonic air force stationed in the Kolwezi district.

After a few technical details he concluded:

The town, thus organized, constitutes a redoubtable fortress capable of successfully withstanding an assault launched by any infantry force which is not directly supported by artillery and from the air.

General Siddartha underlined certain passages in red pencil, then sat down at his desk and started writing:

Top-Secret Report for the Secretary-General, United Nations, New York.

Quoting Colonel Degger, he described at great length the Katangese military preparations. He simply omitted to point out that the information about the Katangese Air Force and artillery was not in any way confirmed and derived rather from the realm of fantasy. Then he summed up as follows:

The accumulation of war material and the organization of Elizabethville confirm my previous reports to the effect that the Katangese forces are preparing to launch a fresh attack against the blue helmets.

The strength of the enemy in Elizabethville henceforth precludes our reducing it by simple police operations or infantry raids, which would mean exposing our troops to very heavy losses.

In these conditions, and in the light of the September fighting, the High Command of the UN Forces in Katanga requests the Secretary-General for permission, in the event of an armed conflict breaking out, to resort if necessary to artillery and aircraft in order to reduce the fortified positions held by the Katangese Army and the armed civilians.

General Siddartha rose to his feet, went out on the balcony of Clair Manoir and, puffing at his pipe, gazed at Elizabethville and the smoking Lubumbashi chimney. The tall smoke-stack had become in his eyes the final symbol of the power of the whites in Africa. He was determined to flatten it.

The Gurkhas, Dogras and Rajputanas were out for revenge. No one, among the Indians, had forgotten how Dokkal had been summarily killed outside the post office by drunken Negroes.

Nor had he. But instead of blaming the Negroes for this, he attributed the responsibility to the capitalists of the Union Minière, the mercenaries in its pay, and all the whites in possession of the power, energy and wealth of the world.

Colonel la Roncière's troubles had not come to an end. One night, because he had nothing better to do, and also out of curiosity, he took Trude out to one of the little dives—semi-restaurant, semi-night-club—that had recently opened on the outskirts of the European city. Working-class whites and Africans with a little money to spend were beginning to meet there.

Without quite understanding the reasons, which must have dated back several months, Trude picked a quarrel with a mulatto girl who was as self-effacing as herself. The two women came to blows. The Belgian who was with the mulatto saw fit to intervene. La Roncière could not but do the same.

There ensued a confused mêlée, and everyone was hauled off to the police station.

Extremely conscious of his own importance, the African police commissioner interrogated all the witnesses and understood nothing. Since he kept hearing the word "protect" being used, he assumed the Belgian and la Roncière to be the "protectors" of these ladies.

In spite of the colonel's protests, he kept them all in prison until the morning. Only then did he ring up the Presidency, where he was ordered to release the prisoners at once.

The incident delighted Kimjanga, who asked to see the report on it. The lean-faced colonel was referred to as "the protector of a woman of easy virtue."

The President repeated the story to everyone and it thus came to the ears of Nadolo. It was easy for the general to get hold of a copy of the report. This police interrogation was the basis for the rumors which began to spread through the European town.

The French colonel was accused of indulging in arms smuggling, which was commonplace, but also of investing vast sums which he had made in this manner in a number of more or less questionable business deals.

He was charged with being the owner of all the night-clubs in the outskirts, of a number of brothels and dance-halls, and of living on the immoral earnings of girls of easy virtue who had to pay him huge sums to keep out of trouble with the police, the mercenaries or the MIR.

In no time la Roncière became the head of a vast racket which embraced the whole town. He had separated from Trude, who was really too foolish and too compromising. Outraged in her vanity, the girl had asserted that she had regularly given the colonel money to ensure his protection.

"One day, since I didn't have enough, he flung it back in my face," she said one evening at a table in the Mitsouko.

The rumor reached the ears of Musaille, who was first of all amused by it, then saw fit to warn the colonel. La Roncière was wild with rage.

Three days later, on orders from Nadolo, the colonel's villa was requisitioned as quarters for "a senior officer of the Katangese Army." La Roncière had to struggle all morning to obtain a cancellation of this requisition order from the Presidency.

Nadolo was informed that part of the weapons destined for his troops had been held back on arrival to be issued to the civilians, and this on la Roncière's orders, with the complicity of the Union Minière.

Nadolo screamed about a racial plot against Katanga and decided to take steps himself to have la Roncière arrested before he could get round the President with his lies. The prisoner would be hauled off into the bush; then an accident would happen to him while trying to escape.

The President would kick up a fuss, after which everything would be settled.

Kimjanga was in raptures over his personal guard, accoutered in the fancy dress dispatched by Cor de Chasse. Since he did not yet have any horses, he paraded his guards standing to attention in jeeps with drawn swords.

Kimjanga had no time to deal with the troubles of a mercenary who was of no further use to him and who kept boring him to tears with his complaints and alarming predictions. Bongo was still in Brussels and, to be on the safe side, had appointed no one to take his place at the Ministry of the Interior and Defense.

La Roncière had gone home about nine o'clock in the evening, after spending a couple of hours with Gelinet.

The old fellow was becoming inordinately over-excited. If he had been given a free hand, he would have gone off to attack the Indian Camp or Clair Manoir. The colonel had seen fit to advise him to keep calm, which had not pleased the brewer at all.

Some bitter words had been exchanged. Since la Roncière could not come to blows with the fellow who was his last support, he had to endure some extremely distasteful allusions to his "other rewarding occupations."

He now knew that the Belgians accused him of having had people killed pointlessly during the September fighting, while carefully sparing his mercenaries. He was blamed, among other things, for the death of Captain Gersaint.

How revolting and stupid it all was!

Tomorrow he would go to see Kimjanga and give him the choice: break his contract or get rid of Nadolo.

There was a crash of rifle-butts against his door. For the last two nights la Roncière had been on the alert; he had noticed figures prowling round his villa. The kitchen door had been forced and his new house-boy had disappeared.

He slipped a pistol into his belt and picked up a grenade. Then he flung the door open. A gendarme tumbled into the room with all his equipment.

Behind him stood Major Kiwe, who had just been invested with the title of "Head of Military Security," and four other gendarmes.

"I have orders to arrest you," said Kiwe, "for plotting against the State. I am to take you to Tshiko Camp, where

you will be detained until a court martial has been set up.
. . ."

La Roncière went through the motions of releasing the
pin of his grenade and stood up as though to fling it.

"Stand back," he shouted, "or I'll blow the lot of us
sky-high. Jump to it, Kiwe, or I'll spread your guts all
over the street. Get back into your truck with your ba-
boons. Tell Nadolo you failed to find me!"

Kiwe was frightened and tried to shield his face with his
hand. He blurted out apologies.

"General Nadolo says you're selling weapons to the
whites."

La Roncière immediately realized the gravity of the
charge, which would serve as an excuse to have him assassinated, as Lumumba and many others had been.

His last chance was to get to John Ligget's villa, the
lights of which he could see through the trees, then to
make tracks for Rhodesia.

"Jump to it," he said.

Kiwe and the five gendarmes climbed back into the
truck. La Roncière flung himself into the ditch and drew
his revolver. The truck drove off with its headlights blazing.

The British Consul was drinking by himself and, undis-
mayed by the appearance of the colonel, out of breath and
with a revolver in his hand, asked him to join him.

"Pink gin or whisky?"

Slowly la Roncière recovered his composure. He did not
want to cut a poor figure in front of this alcoholic gentleman whose wife he had seduced. Putting his revolver
down on the sideboard, he replied:

"Whisky, please. . . . No soda, just a little ice. May I
use your telephone to ring up my consul, Monsieur Musaille?"

Twenty minutes later Musaille arrived with his car and
driver. He looked anxious.

"You're to leave at once for Rhodesia," he said to la
Roncière. "Your luggage? I'll take care of that. They're
looking for you all over town, and Kimjanga, of course, is
not at home! The gendarmes will be back. Since they have
an odd conception of diplomatic immunity, it's best for
you to be out of here!"

"But I can't very well . . ."

"Please, Colonel, I feel responsible for your safety.
Furthermore, your prompt return is eagerly awaited at a
high level. My driver is familiar with the road. When

467

you're back in Paris, if he's still there, remember me to Thomas Fonts."

He hustled him into the car.

"What will you have to drink, Paul?" said Ligget when the colonel had disappeared.

"Same as you, John."

"You think these savages would have killed la Roncière after all he has done for them?"

"Almost certainly. They might have regretted it afterwards, when they found themselves in a *matata*. They become very realistic when they receive a good slap in the face."

"An odd place, Africa, eh, Paul?"

"Another gin, John Ligget. You know those strange, fantastic, composite beasts with a woman's breasts and a goat's body? The front paws are a lion's, the rear ones a griffon's, and the tail a serpent's? . . ."

"You mean chimeras?"

"We white men have populated Africa with chimeras. We've tried to impose our gods, our ideologies, our techniques on this country. . . . That's what la Roncière was trying to do with his revolutionary warfare! Africa, this vast belly, gobbled it all up. And what emerged? These monstrous composite beasts! What remains of the ideologies which were considered irrefutable, like Communism? Thomas Fonts, who knows Guinea very well, would have told you: a few catch-phrases like 'human investment' . . . 'deviationism,' 'capitalist exploitation,' 'the support of the masses,' etc. . . . which are used to season the old palavers like some new condiment.

"And what remains of our techniques, of which we are so proud? A few do-it-yourself hints. Our gods with their sublime thoughts have become irascible, gluttonous, sensual, idle and fanciful—real Negroes, in fact!

"We're furious to recognize in these black chimeras a few distorted, denaturalized vestiges of those notions, those techniques, those gods which we tried to impose on Africa!"

"Paul, have another drink. You're indulging in metaphysics, to which we English are extremely partial! But we conceal it, just as we conceal being jealous or sentimental. Do go on!"

"We cry treachery, we say we never meant it, but the Negroes don't give a damn, they're enchanted to let their new chimeras take flight. They launch them occasionally

468

against whites like la Roncière who have helped them to manufacture them. . . ."

In the Union Minière head office, 6 Rue de la Montagne du Parc, Brussels, Comte de Bertezène, the President, sat down at the conference table. Baron Pieret took his seat on his right and Van der Weyck on his left. Bertezène had the affable and faintly distant manner of a man accustomed to juggling with billions.

On the other side of the green baize-covered table, Bongo, slumped in an armchair, appeared to be dozing. He hung his head. His eyes could not be seen behind his usual dark glasses.

"He's either drunk or he has been up all night," Bertezène reflected.

After darting an inquiring glance at Van der Weyck, he gave a little cough and opened the meeting.

"Your Excellency, we have studied the note you submitted to us with the greatest interest. Some of your . . . er . . . suggestions are most interesting. But I must say that several of your requests seem somewhat hard to meet. I don't think you have been sufficiently well informed of the technical and financial dictates which prevent us from giving you complete satisfaction. Believe me, we deeply regret it!"

Bongo did not move. Bertezène went on:

"My collaborators, Monsieur Pieret and Monsieur Van der Weyck, whom you know very well, will explain the situation to you. I'm certain that once you hear our arguments you will agree with our reasoning. It's in the interests of all of us to understand one another!"

Baron Pieret recalled at great length the bonds of friendship which united the Union Minière to Katanga. He tactfully insinuated that President Kimjanga's régime could not have come into being and imposed itself, had it not been for the active support of the company. Then he summed up:

"You are well aware, Your Excellency, that every employee of our company has shown complete devotion to Katanga. That's why we were somewhat . . . shall we say, surprised . . . at the tone of your note. Our interests are linked together. We need a stable régime in Katanga. You need a company like ours, which is capable of making the best of your wealth and contributing to your resources. If we entered into conflict, what would happen? The copper would no longer be exploited and Katanga would soon go

469

bankrupt. I am sure, Your Excellency, that this is not what you want!"

Baron Pieret was satisfied with his speech. The President gave a nod of approval. Yet he fancied that several times there had been the ghost of a smile on Van der Weyck's lips.

"Now," said Baron Pieret, "I shall hand over to Monsieur Van der Weyck, who will explain certain technical aspects of the problem."

Bongo raised his hand.

"Gentlemen," he said in a calm voice, "all this is very interesting, but it seems to me we're wasting time!"

Bertezène and Pieret gaped at him. Van der Weyck went on scribbling on the sheet of paper in front of him.

"But your Excellency . . ." Bertezène began.

"Just a moment, please. I think there is no point at all in Monsieur Van der Weyck explaining, as you put it, the technical aspects. I'm not interested in technology. What I'm interested in is money!"

Bertezène gave a forced laugh. Pieret followed suit.

"Ah, Excellency, you will have your little joke!"

Bongo was not laughing. He went on:

"In the memorandum I submitted to you I asked for three things: an increase in production, an increase in the royalties which the Union Minière pays Katanga, and the prompt payment of these monthly dues, that's to say at the moment the copper leaves Katangese territory. I want to be satisfied on those three points. I want an answer: Yes or No."

Outraged, Bertezène and Pieret both started talking at the same time. Van der Weyck interrupted them. He still had a curious smile on his face.

"I think, gentlemen, it would be as well to ask Monsieur Bongo what he intends to do if our answer is in the negative."

There was a moment's silence.

"It's quite simple," said Bongo. "I shall nationalize your company!"

"Ridiculous! You can't do that. It's contrary to our agreements. After all we've done for President Kimjanga. . . ."

"You haven't done anything for Kimjanga," Bongo chipped in. "You've supported him because it was in your interests to do so. You have exploited Katanga as much as you could, and for years we have collected nothing but the

470

crumbs. Today the situation is reversed: if you want to keep your mines, you must pay for them!"

There was another silence.

"Monsieur le Ministre," Bertezène began, "you're playing a dangerous game which is liable to turn against you. If the Union Minière ceased its activity in Katanga, which it can do—our group, thank heaven, is strong enough to bear this sort of loss—the disadvantages would be infinitely greater for you than for us."

He cast a knowing glance at his two acolytes. Pieret and Van der Weyck indicated their approval with a nod.

"I don't think so," said Bongo. "I take this opportunity to inform you that my government has decided to cancel your company's privilege of exploitation."

He suddenly gave a loud guffaw.

"Yes, indeed, other financial groups are very interested in the Katangese mines. The South Africans, the Rhodesians, the Swedes and even the British are making offers. They feel they can produce a far greater quantity of copper and cobalt from our subsoil."

This time Bertezène spoke curtly.

"There's one thing you forget: we can also indulge in this sort of blackmail. Supposing we come to an agreement with Leopoldville and pay the dues direct to Adoula instead of handing them over to you? We have extremely interesting offers on that side! This isn't a threat. We don't envisage doing it. I simply want to show you that if we couldn't come to an agreement we hold other cards in our hands!"

Bongo's face was distorted with rage.

"He must have looked like this when he had Lumumba killed," Van der Weyck reflected.

The Katangese thumped the table with his fist.

"You hold no cards in your hands!" he yelled. "I know perfectly well that you're in the process of betraying us. But I tell you this. . . ." He gave the table another thump. "If you pay the dues to Leopoldville, I'll blow all your installations sky-high! The plan is all ready. I have the necessary men and explosives. One move from you and the whole lot goes up! Now I'm leaving, I've wasted enough time listening to your speeches. I go back to Elizabethville tomorrow. I want an answer tonight!"

Bongo almost tore the handle off the door as he went out, bumping into a secretary who had rushed up at the sound of the raised voices.

"Do you think he would do it?" Bertezène asked Van der Weyck.

"As certainly as you saw him stamping his feet in front of you, Monsieur le Président-Directeur Général!"

"What do you advise?"

"Within the next few months independent Katanga will have ceased to exist and our company will soon have to deal with the Leopoldville authorities. I think we ought to establish contact with them straight away . . . secretly, of course!"

"This time we can plead good faith, talk about constraint, stress this discussion with Bongo. Let's take advantage of the next meeting of the Security Council, where we shall be violently attacked, to issue a press statement pointing out that the Union Minière does not indulge in politics, that we pay our dues to a *de facto* authority which has the means of forcing us to do so. The people in Leo are no more anxious than we are for the mines to be blown up."

"Excellent, my dear Van der Weyck, you would have made a good diplomat! When could you leave for Leopoldville? In a week . . . which would give us time to prepare them for your arrival! Here you have a job commensurate with your talent! That fellow Bongo is really an unbearably circumscribed creature!"

Van der Weyck went on smiling.

"Bongo, Monsieur le Président, is one of those elementary characters who make martyrs, killers, dictators or big heads of State."

Dorat had met la Roncière at Julienne's, where the colonel seemed to have resumed his old habit of dropping in. The latter had been more cordial than usual, almost friendly. Dorat quickly realized why: la Roncière had failed and, as always happens, was accusing everyone in the world except himself. He had therefore decided to write a book about his experiences in Katanga, but did not quite know how to set about it and wanted Dorat to give him some technical assistance.

The colonel was bitter. On his return from Elizabethville he had been greeted coldly. The press had scarcely mentioned him. Colonel Chaudey had given him to understand that it would be better to wait before applying to rejoin the Army.

"Don't be so impatient. You have enough to live on, I believe," Chaudey had added.

In return, he gave Dorat some first-rate information on the situation in Katanga.

"I was right. I was always right," he had asserted. "The UN are going to take action at any moment, and this time it will be serious. The Europeans are absolutely off their heads. They think they're going to crush the blue helmets. It's terrifying!"

"Aren't you slightly responsible for their madness, Colonel?"

Dorat had rushed round to his office. He had no wish to go back to Algeria, where his cynicism and outspokenness had got him into serious trouble with certain members of the OAS and "parallel" police organizations, who were, however, old acquaintances.

He had explained to the editor of his paper:

"Fifteen thousand whites, cut off, deserted by everyone, right in the middle of Africa, and believing they're able to defy the whole world. It's too good a subject to miss! What we must show is how they intoxicated themselves with their own propaganda!"

"We're reverting to the problem of the Algeria settlers!"

"Yes, but with so much more freedom to discuss it! In Katanga the settlers are Belgian."

The editor had agreed.

"I give you two weeks, Dorat, but not a day longer. Approach the problem solely from the settler's angle. Katanga in itself is of no interest to anyone. The Quai d'Orsay is basically against Kimjanga, and at the Elysée they won't hear his name mentioned. Dumont, in front of me, referred to him yesterday as 'Monsieur Cashbox.' "

That very morning Dorat had come upon an agency telegram:

At Toulouse a former "Terror" called Fermantier has been arrested for trying, by means of advertisements in the local press, to recruit fresh mercenaries.

Dorat arrived at Elizabethville at ten o'clock on 23 November by the UAT DC8. He drove straight to the Hotel Leo, then went out for a tour of the town.

The streets were adorned with thousands of portraits of Kimjanga and posters proclaiming "Katanga is my country." Dorat noticed at once that there were very few blue helmets in the town.

He heard some shouts. A hundred men rushed past him.

One of them was bawling: "Everyone to the Belgian Consulate!"

Dorat followed them. Outside the consulate building close on a thousand people had collected, shouting slogans such as "Spaak to the gallows," "Long live Kimjanga!"

A group of youths chanted in unison "Re-cog-nize Katan-ga!" Others accompanied the chant on motor-horns.

In the first row, Dorat noticed a big man in shirt-sleeves, red in the face and streaming with sweat, who was shouting louder than the others: it was Gelinet. He tried to elbow his way towards him, but the crowd was tightly jammed. Before he could get to the brewer, a score of youths had started flinging stones at the windows of the consulate. Consul Ryckers stepped out on to the balcony, signaling with his arm to request silence. The noise died down for a moment. Ryckers opened his mouth. A young man standing next to Dorat produced a tomato from a beach-bag and the fruit burst on the consul's forehead. An absolute bombardment ensued: tomatoes, potatoes, rotten mangoes flew through the air. Dorat even fancied he saw a huge pineapple.

"Extraordinary," Dorat reflected. "The Algiers method has been followed everywhere. The next time they'll seize the consulate by force!"

He grasped Gelinet by the arm; the brewer looked round in surprise.

"So you're here, are you. When did you arrive? You've come just at the right moment!"

"In whose honor are these festivities?"

"Against that swine Spaak. The Belgian colony has decided to demonstrate. Just imagine, yesterday Spaak said on the UN platform in New York that the Belgian Government hoped for the reunification of the Congo and disapproved of the Katangese secession. It's sheer provocation!"

The crowd began to disperse. Young men went round issuing orders. Three trucks of African police drove up at a leisurely pace. The demonstrators, peaceful citizens once again, went home to lunch.

"All this looks extremely well managed!" said Dorat.

Gelinet smiled proudly.

"We do what we can, you know! It's not only you people in Algeria who are capable of organizing spontaneous crowd movements, you know! By the way, are you free for dinner tomorrow?"

"Yes."

"Come to my place. There'll be a few friends who might interest you!"

He slapped Dorat on the back.

"Mind you, several of them are not very fond of you. Your last articles weren't very nice! Let me give you a word of advice, old boy: think twice before you open your mouth. The people here aren't patient and you might get into serious trouble!"

"The same situation as in Algeria," Dorat was on the point of saying, "and the same words of advice which resemble threats! Luckily they're a softer lot in Katanga. But after a few years of conditioning, as la Roncière calls it. . . ."

That evening he went to the Mitsouko. The décor of the bar was still the same but the atmosphere was utterly different. Pérohade and Nathalie were in France. There were no more bearded mercenaries in the place, only self-satisfied Belgians quietly drinking beer. Everyone seemed blissfully happy.

The night-club, which had been bought by a Rhodesian, had been given to an Italian to manage. The champagne was sugary, it came from South Africa and cost twice as much as in the journalist-publican's day.

Dorat recognized the Italian. He had met him several times in September, disguised as a paratrooper and for ever talking about massacring all the blue helmets.

He asked him over to his table, an invitation which the man accepted without further ado.

"Where are all the blue helmets?" Dorat asked. "There are none to be seen in the street, except in groups or on duty. Don't they come here any longer?"

"They daren't go out into the town alone because they're afraid of being beaten up. Every so often they take the risk: they disappear and they're never seen again!"

"No reaction?"

The manager slapped his thighs.

"What do you expect them to do? The blue helmets know that if they make the slightest move they'll get a good hiding!"

He gave a wink.

"It's not like the last time, this business! We have ultra-modern equipment, aircraft, armor. General Nadolo certainly knows his job!"

Hortense Gelinet was wearing an extremely low-cut pink dress, which accentuated her curves.

"I wonder what has happened to Kreis," Dorat said to himself, "the lady's ex-boy-friend?" La Roncière had told him he was stationed at Kipushi and had stayed on because of the pay. He had discerned in the colonel a certain envy, not to say resentment, in regard to his former subordinate, perhaps because he had not left Katanga at the same time as himself!

Gelinet was affable, but the other guests had been reserved, almost cool.

"I'm in for the 'misunderstood patriot' act," Dorat reflected.

Nadelle, the new rector of the University, started attacking as soon as the whisky began to circulate.

"Monsieur Dorat, we're not going to take things lying down! This morning's little demonstration will give Spaak food for thought. All the Europeans are united and prepared to die for Katanga. The other day it was the Italians who paraded in the street, because Rome had put a dozen planes at the disposal of UNO. They almost throttled their consul!"

"Yes," Madame Nadelle lisped, "I could have died laughing! The wretched Parelli had to take refuge with the gendarmes, who put him through it good and proper."

"Aren't you afraid this sort of demonstration might eventually turn everyone against you?" Dorat asked.

Gelinet looked surprised.

"What an idea! I can't think why it should. Everyone is for Katanga, from General de Gaulle to Queen Elizabeth. Even Kennedy has changed his policy!"

I don't quite follow you. It seems to me that, on the contrary, Kennedy takes exception to Kimjanga. As for France, I can assure you she's backing Leopoldville wholeheartedly against Elizabethville."

Rector Nadelle gave a prim smile.

"I think, Monsieur Dorat, you're letting yourself be deceived by appearances. Believe me, we know what's going on out here."

"You're not afraid of being carried away by your own propaganda?"

Everyone burst out laughing.

"Journalists are odd creatures," Hortense Gelinet observed. "They always think they know better than anyone else! Isn't that so, Maître Herbont?"

The lawyer she addressed had razor-sharp features and wore gold-rimmed spectacles.

"The face of an intellectual extremist," Dorat reflected.

Maître Herbont declared:

"Things have changed a great deal since September. This time we're organized. There are five thousand men here who would die rather than yield an inch. Our army has been completely reorganized. If the UN venture on a trial of strength, this time they'll be heading for disaster!"

"We have more than fifteen aircraft," said Nadelle.

"But the UN also have fighters and bombers!"

Herbont smiled.

"They'll never be able to take off. You've seen the hills all round Elizabethville? They're stuffed with batteries of artillery. At the first shot, the airport would be pulverized and the UN aircraft grounded."

Dorat was fascinated by the unawareness of these men. Gelinet ran one of the biggest businesses in the town. Before coming out to Katanga, Nadelle had been the head of one of the greatest faculties in Belgium. Herbont, a legal expert of repute, had written several books which were highly regarded. Yet they all entertained a completely false picture of the situation. For instance, they believed in the existence of those batteries of artillery. Four days earlier la Roncière had told him what they amounted to: nothing. The colonel had suggested to Nadolo that three mortars should be sited in the vicinity of the airfield, but even this had not been done. Yet the three non-existent mortars had turned into "batteries of artillery." As for the Katangese Air Force, it consisted of three Piper-Cubs and two old Harvards hastily equipped with machine-guns. They would not stand a chance against the UN jet-fighters. There were certainly a dozen Fougas drawn up on the Kolwezi air strip, but they were machines made of lath and canvas to deceive the enemy.

"Even the children are fanatically determined," said Madame Herbont.

She was quite an attractive blonde, with big blue eyes, but she spoke in an affected parrot-like voice and insisted on keeping the little finger of her right hand extended.

"My son is eleven years old. He came back from Belgium a week ago. Do you know the first thing he said to me? 'Mama, don't forget to let President Kimjanga know I'm back.'"

"You see, Monsieur Dorat," the rector went on, "we've given the problem a great deal of thought. We have all come to the same conclusion: we must get it over now, once and for all. We can no longer tolerate the presence of the UN in Katanga. Brahimi didn't keep his word.

477

We're once more being threatened. Believe me, we're convinced pacifists, but now our patience is at an end. The UN are compelling us to resort to force. So much the worse for them."

"You mean you hope for war?" Dorat asked.

"Exactly, monsieur. My friends and I have questioned our consciences. Our duty as men and as Katangese is to liberate our country, once and for all."

"Forgive me, but I think it's madness. If you attack, Siddartha will flatten you with his mortars and aircraft. I saw Colonel la Roncière in Paris just before leaving. He reckons you don't stand a chance!"

Madame Herbont sneered.

"Naturally, a man who was paid by the UN to sabotage the Katangese defenses and who made a packet out of dealing in arms . . ."

"And in women," Hortense Gelinet added.

"One thing is certain," Nadelle sighed, "and this is that Colonel la Roncière and his French mercenaries have done the greatest harm to our cause. . . ."

"It was the fault of the French that fighting broke out in September," his wife added.

Dorat left the party early, excusing himself on the grounds that he had an article to write. He could no longer stand these people. Their obstinate stupidity made him feel sick.

"It's extraordinary all the same," he reflected. "They want war, without realizing that they're falling straight into Siddartha's trap. He's only waiting for a move to massacre them. When it turns out badly, they'll be the first to take to their heels, while denouncing the crimes of the UN and crying out that the West is deserting them!"

Dorat was disturbed. It was not the first time he had noticed this phenomenon. In situations like this it was always the intellectuals who lost their common sense and proved the most susceptible to the most elementary propaganda. In Indo-China, the Vietnamese intellectuals had believed right up to the end that the Vietminhs were not Communist. In Algeria, the French doctors and lawyers persisted in believing that the Army would come over to their side. In metropolitan France, the left-wing intellectuals were doing their best to maintain that once the war was over the Algerians and the French would become the best friends in the world.

He heaved a sigh and went back to his hotel.

The situation developed rapidly towards the end of November, as though the Katangese, both black and white, had made a pact with General Siddartha to enable him to avenge himself on Elizabethville and destroy the proud copper city with every appearance of justification.

The men who had unleashed this madness were no longer there to control it. In any case, even if they had wanted to control it, they would not have been able to do so. The fate of king-makers is to be hanged by the kings whom they have placed on the throne. Those who rouse the mob and launch it at the barricades are more often than not declared traitors and strung up on lamp-posts.

On 24 November the Security Council passed a fresh resolution, which gave full powers to the Secretary-General to deal with the problem of the Katangese secession by force.

This resolution was a triumph for all President Kimjanga's opponents.

Kimjanga retorted with an extremely violent declaration, in which he launched an appeal for total war to repel any attempt at invasion. Under the influence of his minister Bongo, who had just returned from Brussels, he threatened to carry out a scorched-earth policy and blow up all the Union Minière installations. "We shall reply to violence with violence, even if the entire population has to perish and if our entire economic structure is overthrown!"

On the following day Bayard began to broadcast instructions from Radio Katanga: "Attention, Katangese! The enemy is threatening you. To each man his blue helmet."

On 28 November Edwin Davidson, Maley's successor, went to a party given by Arnold Riverton in honor of an American senator who was passing through.

Just as his car flying the UN pennant was driving past General Nadolo's residence some para-commandos stopped the vehicle, crying out: "Death to the UN!" A sergeant slapped Davidson in the face and a soldier gave him a blow with his rifle-butt, which split his temple. The delegate managed to break free and made a sensational entry at Arnold Riverton's. Ten minutes later two jeeps crammed with gendarmes drew up outside the consulate with a screech of brakes. A dozen soldiers came storming in, shouting:

"There's a UN spy in here. He's carrying arms. He insulted us!"

Davidson tried to get away, but he was knocked down at

once. Four gendarmes started kicking him and then dragged him outside like a sack of potatoes. They flung him into a jeep and drove him off to General Nadolo's headquarters. Arnold Riverton, who had tried to intervene, was lined up against the wall with a rifle trained on him. It was not until an hour later that he managed to contact Kimjanga. Davidson was released straight away, with apologies, but he had three cracked ribs, a broken nose and deep cuts on his face.

During the night General Siddartha organized some patrols of blue helmets. Four Gurkhas driving in a jeep lost their way and strayed into the African city. Before being able to defend themselves, they were swamped by a score of Katangese who disarmed them and beat them up. Two horribly mutilated bodies were discovered next morning two hundred yards from the Presidency. The two other bodies were never found.

On 2 December the Katangese gendarmes began to set up road-blocks on the outskirts of the town to prevent the UN vehicles from moving. Gelinet's men began to make their appearance in camouflage uniform and carrying weapons quite openly. At the Mitsouko Dorat was slapped in the face by a Belgian because he doubted a decisive victory. In the African city poisoned darts made by the Bayekes were distributed on Bongo's orders.

Several incidents occurred at the road-blocks between the blue helmets and the Katangese gendarmes. Kimjanga held more and more press conferences, accusing the UN of preparing "genocide." Each time, he underlined his desire to safeguard peace and appealed to international conscience. Siddartha, busy in his headquarters, remained invisible. He refused to meet Kimjanga, demanding, before any negotiation, the lifting of the road-blocks which impeded the freedom of movement of his men. Kimjanga held yet another press conference to explain that the road-blocks were purely defensive.

On 4 December a UN helicopter flying at a low altitude over a Katangese road-block was shot down by a burst of Fal. The five men on board were savagely beaten up. One of them, an Indian lieutenant, was forced to cover half a mile at the double under a hail of blows from his guards. Since he had received two bullets in the stomach, he died on his arrival at the camp.

General Siddartha reinforced his patrols but gave orders to his men not to fire unless they were attacked. He demanded the restoration of the helicopter, and his demand was met.

On 5 December, in the morning, three UN Swedish officers got into their white Volkswagen to make a tour of inspection in the town. They drove through two road-blocks without undue difficulty. At the third road-block a Katangese NCO ordered them to get out of the car and confiscated their weapons. A soldier slapped Captain Aqvist who replied with a punch. A few seconds later there was a burst of machine-gun fire; the three officers were mowed down.

Siddartha heard the news almost at once. He called for his second-in-command, Colonel Kharma, and calmly told him:

"Operation Revenge. For 1200 hours today."

Colonel Kharma smiled.

"*Ach-cha,* they've fallen into the trap, sir!"

"Yes, we've got them now, Kharma. This time I'll put paid to them!"

At one o'clock in the afternoon several light columns of UN troops, preceded by some bath-tubs, moved in on the town. The first came from the airport. A second tried to pass through the railway underpass near the railway station. The third advanced from the west. The blue helmets were greeted by withering fire. The Katangese gendarmes had hastened to block the avenues and loosed off magazine after magazine. The one and only Katangese mortar in commission lobbed its shells at random in the general direction of the enemy. All the civilians had brought out their weapons. There was an extraordinary expenditure of ammunition. That night General Siddartha's men withdrew, then made two further attempts to advance without managing to break through the Katangese defenses.

At the Presidency, Kimjanga remained optimistic. To the two hundred journalists who had flown in from all over the world, he declared:

"Our country has been unjustly attacked, but every son of Katanga is ready to die to defend her liberty!"

The situation remained unchanged until 9 December. That morning the observers could not make out what Siddartha's tactics were. Why didn't he attack?

Dorat sent an article to the *Quotidien* which began as follows:

What a strange war, and what a lot of noise! On both sides there is ceaseless firing but no one is really

481

fighting. Up till now I have not witnessed a single attack. At this rate the war can go on for a year. General Siddartha's plan, assuming he has one, remains incomprehensible. He confines himself to moving his men a hundred yards or so forward twice a day. The Katangese unleash a withering fire, then the blue helmets withdraw. . . .

Every evening Siddartha read the operational report of the day.

"We've got them, Kharma," he would say, as he filled his pipe, "we've got them!"

Contrary to what Dorat believed, Siddartha knew exactly what he was doing. His appreciation of the situation was simple.

"If I advance," he explained to his second-in-command, "the Katangese will take to their heels, as they did in September. Kimjanga will go off whimpering and take refuge in Rhodesia. The French and British will demand a cease-fire."

"Yes, sir, but we must do something some time!"

"As a first step, I'll demonstrate that all my reports were accurate. We're being held in check in front of an absolute fortress, stuffed with blockhouses, in which the Europeans have openly joined battle. This time no one will be able to deny that the whites are fighting on Kimjanga's side.

"As a second step, I'll obtain permission from New York to bombard the town by mortar and use the Air Force. When I've obtained the 'go-ahead,' I'll strike and put paid to all these swaggering toughs. At the same time I'll round up the mercenaries and lock up the armed civilians."

"There'll be heavy casualties!"

"They asked for it!"

"When do you think you'll get the 'go-ahead'?"

Siddartha smiled.

"I still discern some resistance in the Glass House, but they'll yield eventually. It won't be long now!"

Nadolo stood in front of the President with an obstinate expression on his face.

"Come now," Kimjanga said, "don't you think it would be wise to call up those hundred mercenaries who are just sitting in Jadotville and twiddling their thumbs?"

"No, Monsieur le Président, we don't need those fellows to beat the blue helmets!

"In the first place, my soldiers don't like them! They're always shouting orders and making *matatas* everywhere.

Then, when they've finished shouting, like that man Kreis, they go off and drink beer and don't give a damn about anything. Afterwards they go around saying they are the ones who won the war."

"You're sure you can manage on your own?"

"Monsieur le Président, the UN are frightened. We fire a few shots and they scuttle off like rabbits. We don't need the whites any longer."

Nadolo jammed his cap on his head, saluted, squared his shoulders, clicked his heels and marched out, forgetting his swagger-stick. He came back, in a great flurry, to fetch it two minutes later.

Kimjanga was pensively fingering the little piece of leather-bound bamboo. He reflected with a certain regret that he would have liked to have la Roncière or Fonts by his side.

La Roncière had warned him so many times that the UN would not keep their word—and Brahimi had not kept his—that the blue helmets would not attack, and the blue helmets had attacked!

Fonts had already got him out of a nasty hole.

He handed Nadolo back his stick, was tempted to order him to call up the mercenaries, but he was afraid of hurting his pride and the pride of the entire Army.

General Nadolo had assumed considerable importance lately. He drove about all day in a big black Chevrolet, preceded and followed, in a wail of sirens, by jeeps crammed with members of his bodyguard. In every unit he visited, he embarked on lengthy palavers with the officers and even with the private soldiers.

The palavers quickly assumed the form of a chorus, of which Nadolo was the leader.

"We Katangese soldiers are as strong as lions," he would say.

"Strong as lions," the soldiers echoed.

"We don't need the whites in order to fight!"

"We shall fight alone!"

"With our guns and our rifles."

"With our planes."

"With our fists, with our teeth . . . "

"Even our children will fight . . ."

"I, Nadolo, say so."

"Nadolo who defeated the whites at Jadotville!"

"The whites need a lot of machines to make war!"

"But we Bantus have our own strength!"

The transmitters still lay unused in their cases, and the

wind gradually tore away the canvas of which the Fougas at Kolwezi were constructed and laid bare their wooden frameworks.

Siddartha obtained the "go-ahead" on 9 December, at ten o'clock in the morning. One hour later a light Canberra bomber of the Indian Air Force dived on the post office right in the middle of Elizabethville and machine-gunned it.

At three o'clock in the afternoon the heavy 120-mm Indian mortars began to pound the capital. The first shells landed all round the Presidency. Then the firing extended to the whole town. Some hospitals were hit. The shells pierced the thin corrugated iron roofs, exploded inside the villas and caused dozens of casualties. The inhabitants of Elizabethville could not make out what was happening. It took them several hours to realize, after seeing ambulances racing at full speed through the streets and coming back to the hospitals with mutilated bodies.

Panic ensued. Everything collapsed all at once.

The Katangese soldiers started to withdraw in disorder and took refuge in the African city. The civilians, filled with warlike ardor only the evening before, were transformed in a few hours into ashen-faced terrorized creatures. They buried their arms and uniforms in their gardens and, as in September, tried to escape to Rhodesia. But at the gates of the town they ran into inflexible Katangese road-blocks. Bongo had given explicit orders:

"The whites will stay here with us!"

He had added with a cruel smile:

"We're all in the same boat. There's no reason, when things turn out badly, why the whites should calmly go off and take refuge in Rhodesia, while the Negroes get killed."

On 12 December Elizabethville received three hundred mortar shells.

The Canberra machine-gunned the Katangese positions at the railway underpass, and the Swedish Saabs dived on Massart Camp in a scream of jets. Panic-stricken Katangese soldiers were seen crossing the town in the direction of the African city, dragging their rifles. Dorat questioned a sergeant whose head was muffled up in a red scarf.

"Well, boss," he said, "things don't look too good. We're going home. Our wives are waiting for us and besides, the UN are very unpleasant. It's not a good thing, war!"

Three hours later there were scarcely three hundred

gendarmes who still stuck to their positions. They went on firing fiercely in every direction, but it was obvious that they would take to their heels with their hands in the air at the first fairly serious attack.

Nadolo had lost his self-assurance. At the railway underpass he had struck a Katangese lieutenant who was pulling out with his men, but the lieutenant had retorted by jabbing him in the stomach with his revolver and the soldiers had threatened to kill him.

"You just stop buggering us about, with your loud mouth and swagger-stick," an elderly NCO had said to him. "You think you're a white, but the whites know what to do with guns and planes!"

Nadolo, crouching behind a truck with his head in his hands, tried to think. Absurd little snippets of military regulations kept cropping up in his mind:

"The hourly halt on a route march must be ten minutes every hour . . . but on a forced march this halt may be reduced. . . . Dismantling and assembling of the Fal rifle . . . first movement. . . . Training grenades . . . the individual issue of field rations. . . ."

Everything was muddled and confused in his mind.

He arrived at the President's at the double. His massive chest was heaving like a bellows.

"They're all running away," he exclaimed, "because of the aircraft and mortars!"

He was a sergeant again, waiting for someone to decide for him. Kimjanga realized this and gave him his orders.

"Get a message off to Kolwezi at once. Only the mercenaries can get us out of this mess!"

"Very good, Monsieur le Président."

"Tell Kreis to come as soon as possible with all his men. Install a command post in the African city straight away, as Colonel la Roncière suggested."

"Very good, Monsieur le Président."

"Tell Kreis to contact you. . . . Put yourself at his disposal."

Bongo arrived and, in Swahili, like a chief addressing a slave boy, added:

"And if you're told to peel potatoes, Nadolo the Victorious, then peel potatoes . . . and if you're told to go and fetch beer, you'll go and fetch it, and if they tell you to drop dead, you drop dead. . . ."

Nadolo's power had evaporated now that his soldiers had disbanded. But Bongo, whose power came from the depths of time and did not rely on bluff and palaver but

485

on what endures—the secrets of the bush, the blood ties—retained his *muntu* intact. Nadolo was frightened of him and gazed at the old Africa, in gray suit and black tie, with eyes full of fear and submission.

The shells continued to rain down on the town throughout the afternoon, and the last black troops disbanded. Elizabethville was now defended by no more than a dozen men of the Gelinet group who had been joined by a handful of mercenaries.

They split up of their own accord into small commandos of three men each, seized some vehicles, mortars and automatic weapons abandoned by the Katangese, and began to fire back, trying to remember what Fonts and la Roncière had taught them.

Three men would hoist a mortar onto a truck, set it up in the middle of the street, fire a dozen shots, pack up their equipment and repeat the drill a little farther on. Gelinet had mounted a 12.7-mm machine-gun on a jeep. He would creep up along a wall, fire a long burst at the positions held by the enemy, then drive off again.

The blue helmets did not move, did not advance. In the evening the town was deprived of electricity and water, and food supplies began to run short.

Musaille checked the store of tinned food that he had hoarded and saw that half of it had disappeared with his house-boys. He realized they were frightened, but he was furious that they had chosen the foie gras and left him nothing but baked beans. He stuck some candles into a big silver candelabra and, melancholily, in his kitchen, cooked himself a ratatouille. But his stomach was quaking. Fonts was no longer there to turn this dismal massacre into an adventure full of unexpected fun.

The Quai had instructed him not to show his face and to concentrate exclusively on the safeguarding of French interests.

Trembling with fright, Trude, who had no consul to whom to appeal and who believed herself to have many enemies, came and took refuge with him. He shared his beans with her, then made love to her, which was the best way in which to await future developments.

Kreis entered Elizabethville on 13 December, at dawn, after making a long detour to approach the capital from the south, thus avoiding the road-blocks and positions held by the blue helmets.

Out of a hundred mercenaries, only forty had remained

with him. Twenty of them had refused to toe the line. They had no wish, they said, to risk their lives for Negroes like Nadolo who, once the danger was over, would thank them with a kick in the arse. Finally, on the way, twelve of them deserted, with their weapons and their vehicles, and took refuge in Rhodesia.

Kreis found Nadolo in the African city; he was asleep. No sentries, no road-blocks. A UN patrol could have nabbed him in bed.

He shook the general without further ado and realized at once, by the way he sat up and put his hand to his face, that he was reduced to a mere puppet. Nadolo had lost his splendor; all he wanted was to take refuge in something he knew how to do well, something that had occupied ten years of his life: the role of a NCO.

"What's going on?" Kreis inquired.

Nadolo shrugged his shoulders.

"They're running away!"

"Take me to headquarters at once . . . at least wherever the transmitter is."

"This is headquarters."

"Where's the transmitter?"

"There isn't any. . . ."

"So you've done nothing . . . you silly sod . . . in spite of all Colonel la Roncière said! We're in a fine mess now: attacked on all sides and without communications! Nadolo, I'm taking command, do you understand?"

"Very good, boss."

Nadolo had not even thought of resisting; on the contrary, he looked relieved.

"This is what you're going to do: collect twenty soldiers—you must be able to find twenty—good types on whom you can rely. Go out on patrol with them and round up all the gendarmes who are hiding in the African city. Shoot some of them . . . at least bash their faces in, and send them back into the fighting line."

To Kreis's great surprise, Nadolo, who was incapable of being a general or even a lieutenant, was a good sergeant-major. He started by knocking down a few thugs, and urged the others into action with kicks in the backside, recovering all of a sudden a sort of coarse truculence which delighted the troops.

Later on, Kreis used him as a runner to carry his orders to various little groups which gradually got under way, and Nadolo the Victorious, in this new occupation, showed a certain degree of courage.

Kreis had had the bazookas and mortars unpacked and issued them to the mercenaries. Now there were about fifty whites fighting in Elizabethville. He adopted the same tactics as Fonts had done in September. His men worked in small independent groups, carried out a raid and disappeared immediately afterwards. But the results were by no means so good. The blue helmets no longer ventured into the town. To attack the UN, one had to slip into No-Man's Land and approach strongly fortified positions. On their way back the commandos were liable to be fired on by the Katangese. Kreis lost four men on the first day. Having no illusions, he knew perfectly well that if the UN attacked he would be forced to pull out.

The only definite instruction he had given his men was to withdraw if the blue helmets advanced and rendezvous with him at the exit to the town on the Kipushi road.

Kreis could not make out why Siddartha did not order his troops to attack.

"It's like butter," he said to Buscard. "Siddartha can slice through Elizabethville as though it was butter and I give him less than two hours in which to take the whole town!"

"Maybe, Karl, the blue helmets want to do as the Americans did in the last war: crush the town before entering it so as not to have casualties!"

The mercenaries drank a great deal, which revived Max's "whims." Since arriving in Katanga he had been free of them. He underwent an attack in the lobby of the Hotel Leo II. Just as Dorat was going into the telephone booth he flung himself on him, dragged him out by force and knocked him down with the butt of his rifle, shouting: "He's a spy. He's ringing up the UN to tell them our positions. I'll put paid to him!"

Dorat was rescued by Buscard who, without losing his head, knocked Max out with a right to the chin.

The first reactions of xenophobia were noted among the African population. The Katangese in the cities had no more money or food. They came up to loot the European town. Many of them were killed. Some Katangese gendarmes turned against the whites. They arrested passers-by and searched them. Others denied the Belgians access to the two food shops that were still open, crying: "The food's not for the whites. They can go home!"

After 14 December the situation of the civilians became even more difficult. The water and food supplies were exhausted, people were killed while going out in search of something to eat. The mortars continued to rain down at random. The hospitals were full and the corpses had to be buried in the gardens. The Gurkhas opened fire on the ambulances, and the wounded lay in agony for hours because it was impossible to take them off.

Candles were harder and harder to come by and became valuable objects; they had been rationed to two per person per day.

A house-boy, whom his mistress had sent to "collect her ration," was denounced to some gendarmes who beat him to death "because light was now for the blacks."

Kreis realized he would have to react at once. He sent off his "runner" Nadolo, who bashed in a few faces without quite knowing why.

Kreis would have been amazed if anyone had told him that he was utterly happy in the knowledge that the defense of the town depended on him and "his pals."

He became more human as a result, he smiled, he joked, and the man he spoke about most often was not la Roncière but Fonts.

"You remember," he would say to Buscard, "when Thomas took that big slug of a journalist Dorat with him and made him toss some grenades into the Irish camp? And when he got Kimjanga out of the Presidency by booting him in the arse?"

On 17 December Musaille came to see Kreis in the African city.

"My dear Kreis," he said, "this time I think we're done for: France and Great Britain have given up the idea of calling a halt to the UN. Siddartha won't stop until he has flattened Elizabethville. Kennedy has sent a message to President Kimjanga urging him to go to Kitona, near Leopoldville, in order to negotiate with Adoula. Kimjanga has asked my advice and also Ligget's. What do you think?"

Kreis felt flattered: this was the first time he had had an opinion to give on such a serious matter.

"We're cracking everywhere," he said. "We haven't a chance of holding out!"

The consuls of France, Belgium and Great Britain, representing the countries which were said to be in favor of Kimjanga, all advised him to reply to President Kennedy's message in the affirmative.

Kimjanga tried to prevaricate, however. In the hope of gaining time, he sent a reply to Washington saying he was prepared to meet Ferwell, the American Ambassador, on condition that the UN troops ceased fire and Ferwell came to Elizabethville.

He sent for Kreis to ask him his advice, but Kreis was not la Roncière. He replied that war, not diplomacy, was his profession. He was hanging on in Elizabethville, because the blue helmets did not attack him!

Ferwell's reply, for there was no further message from Kennedy, was extremely curt. The ambassador rejected the conditions laid down. He was waiting for Kimjanga at Ndola with his personal aircraft and vouched for his safety. As for the cease-fire, it would not take place until after Kimjanga's departure for Kitona.

On this last point Siddartha had proved intractable.

Arnold Riverton, who considered this mortar bombardment of a defenseless town revolting, had obtained permission from his government to suggest an immediate truce.

He had gone straight away to the Indian general to inform him of what the Government of the United States and every other government that had an interest in the Congo was hoping for: an immediate cease-fire.

Siddartha had lost his temper.

"The answer is no, sir. You want a repetition of the September nonsense? This town is still stuffed with blockhouses, crammed with snipers and mercenaries armed to the teeth! If we agree to a cease fire now, Kimjanga will again find the means of getting round it and in three months' time we'll have to start all over again. No, sir, I shall cease fire only when Kimjanga is safely tied to his seat in the aircraft taking him to Leopoldville!"

"The whole world is appalled by the number of civilian casualties!"

"We are also suffering casualties! Snipers, who haven't even the guts to wear uniform, are shooting our men in the back. Bazookas and mortars are being moved in ambulances. And you come and talk to me about pity!"

Siddartha had abruptly cut short the interview.

"Excuse me, sir, I have work to do. I must finish this off, once and for all!"

Davidson, the UN delegate, likewise asked for a cease-fire, but Siddartha, pleading orders from New York, had rejected his request.

"I think," Davidson had said to Riverton, "that our friend Siddartha is making the Belgians and mercenaries an excuse to settle an old score with us British. But he doesn't know it. . . . He will never be satisfied, even if he blew the whole of Europe sky-high. . . . On that day he

490

would feel so desolate that he would commit suicide on the ruins! A pink gin, Arnold?"

At five o'clock in the afternoon five Swedish Saabs attacked the Union Minière installations with rockets.

In spite of Kreis's instructions, the gendarmes had set up a Bofors anti-aircraft gun outside the Lubumbashi works. The reconnaissance Canberra had spotted it at once. The gun did not even have time to fire. The crew took to their heels as soon as the first fighters started their dive.

Max had got hold of a jeep on which he had mounted a heavy machine-gun. He happened to be opposite the railway underpass just when the Saabs attacked the Union Minière. At the Leo II the journalists had treated him to several whiskies, then some iced beer, to get him to repeat his story of his re-enlistment and his "whims."

After which he had gone off "to shoot something up."

Everything was quivering before his eyes.

"My God, I've got the whims again!" he said.

All of sudden he was seized with intense rage against the whole world: this town, the Negroes, the whites, and these three aircraft buzzing about like mosquitoes in the blue sky.

He drew up right in the middle of the street and started firing belt after belt at the Saabs, which were over two miles away. He kept screaming:

"Come on, you shits, come on!"

Lieutenant Singh, the pilot of the Indian Canberra, was circling quietly three thousand feet above Elizabethville while the Saabs finished off their job. Below, everything was calm. Suddenly, in a split-second, Singh noticed the flash of a machine-gun in front of the railway underpass. Banking steeply to the left and pushing his joystick forward, he dived on the machine-gun. In front of him he saw the jeep, drawn up in the middle of the road, loom up towards him. A man was sitting behind the gun firing at him. Singh thought of returning his fire, then gave up the idea. Pointless to waste ammunition on a single individual. He climbed steeply away.

"Shit! Coward! Sod!" Max screamed, clutching his machine-gun.

The Canberra made a complete turn and came back towards the tunnel. The madman below was still firing. So much the worse for him. Singh dived straight on the jeep.

"It's my turn now," Max yelled. "It's my turn, you sod.

491

Come on, you swine. Come on and I'll blow you to smithereens!"

The aircraft loomed up with incredible speed in his sights. He fired frantically.

The lieutenant pressed a button and his six machine-guns fired simultaneously. Riddled with bullets, Max was hurled against the opposite wall.

The Canberra headed for the Union Minière. The Saabs flew back to base, dipping their wings. Singh started taking photographs. A thick cloud of smoke rose into the sky.

General Siddartha observed it through his field-glasses. He felt that the lesson was not enough: the chimney had to stop smoking. On the following day, 18 December, at four o'clock in the morning, a violent mortar bombardment flattened the Lubumbashi works. At five o'clock the Ethiopian battalion went into the attack. The last defenders, a dozen mercenaries and a score of gendarmes, abandoned the position.

By seven o'clock in the morning Elizabethville was practically surrounded, except for the Rhodesia road which could be blocked at any moment.

Kimjanga capitulated. He announced that he would leave for Ndola in the afternoon. Once again he asked for the UN to cease fire at once.

Kreis tried in vain to see the President. Nadolo himself did not know where he was. The European civilian advisers were packing their bags and rushing off.

Finding no one, Kreis ventured as far as the French Consulate to ask Musaille what he ought to do.

"I don't know at all," the consul replied. "Kimjanga is capitulating yet again, and yet again he'll come out of it fairly well. But if you and your men are captured, you're liable to be in serious trouble. General Siddartha boasted in front of me that he would shoot all the mercenaries who fell into his hands! There's no point in your staying here any longer!"

"But I haven't received orders to withdraw!"

Musaille lost his patience.

"Well, for once in your life, use your own initiative. If you absolutely insist on an order, I'll give it you!"

Kreis saluted and marched out without saying a word. Half an hour later the last mercenaries had evacuated the center of the town and gone to ground on the edge of the bush near the Rhodesia road. The Katangese capital was no longer defended by anyone. The UN troops were expected to enter it at any moment. Yet the night went by without Siddartha making a move.

On 19 December, at half past seven in the morning, at Ndola, President Kimjanga boarded the aircraft that had been placed at his disposal by Ferwell, the American Ambassador at Leopoldville. The evening before, he had had a three-hour conversation with the representative of the United States. The President had retained a faint hope right up till then. Perhaps he would be able to discuss, bargain, demand guarantees, impose conditions. Ferwell, in an icy manner, had left him no illusions: it was a complete capitulation that was demanded of him. The ambassador had made it quite clear.

"I didn't come here to argue with you. I'm neither a negotiator nor a mediator. My aircraft is at your disposal to take you to Kitona and bring you back to Ndola. My personal role is to see that nothing happens to you during your sojourn on Congolese territory. Now, you are perfectly free to go to Kitona or not; that doesn't concern me. If you refuse, I shall leave at once and the UN troops will resume their offensive to occupy your capital. In that case, of course, I shall not be responsible for your safety."

Arnold Riverton had tried to soften Ferwell, but the ambassador had replied:

"My dear fellow, it's not up to the defeated to lay down conditions. Kimjanga either capitulates or he's crushed! That's all there is to it."

At ten o'clock in the morning Siddartha launched two armored columns towards the center of the town. There had been no firing since the previous evening. The Swedish bath-tubs, followed by armored cars and GMCs crammed with Gurkhas, advanced slowly up to the Presidency, then turned round. A bath-tub drew up outside the Hotel Leo II. The men trained their weapons on the front of the building. A young lieutenant got out and went up to the door leading into the lobby.

Dorat was standing there, with a grumpy expression on his face.

The lieutenant and the journalist looked at each other for a long time in silence. Dorat felt the anger welling up inside him and, since he could think of nothing else to do, stuck his tongue out at the Indian. The lieutenant produced a camera, took photographs of the astounded Dorat for ten seconds, then turned on his heel and marched off.

The first mortars burst in front of the Leo II at half

493

past eleven. The UN vehicles had got back to base a quarter of an hour earlier. A salvo of five shells followed immediately afterwards, shattering the hotel windows and smashing the parked cars to pieces.

Dorat, who was walking back from the French Consulate, received a few splinters in the arm. All the civilians who were out of doors rushed for the shelter of the Leo II lobby. The bombardment increased in intensity. Women screamed with fright and panic-stricken dogs yelped without stopping.

"The dirty swine!" Dorat shouted in Spencer's ear, though the latter could hear nothing. "All this just because I stuck my tongue out at one of those silly Indian sods. . . ."

"Eh? You did what?"

"Stuck my tongue out . . ."

Furious, reckoning he had a personal score to settle, Dorat, who was not in the least frightened, sat down at his typewriter.

This morning General Siddartha exceeded the limits of abjection. Although the cease-fire has been concluded since seven-thirty, although there is no longer a single Katangese gendarme, a single armed mercenary in Elizabethville, the commander of the blue helmets has launched a fresh bombardment of hitherto unparalleled violence.

Between half past eleven and a quarter to twelve more than a hundred mortar shells landed right in the middle of the town within a radius of a hundred yards. There can be no justification for the bombardment of an unarmed civilian population. It is a deliberate act of terrorism. There is only one explanation: before implementing the cease-fire, the UN are trying to impose a final punishment on the whites of Katanga who have defied them!

When the first shells landed, Buscard, whom Kreis had ordered to collect some papers in his room at the Leo II, rushed out of the lobby.

He headed south, crouching, springing up again, bending double as he crossed the dangerous zones. Eventually he ran into Gelinet who was driving off in his Peugeot in search of news.

"Quick," Buscard shouted, "take me to the city!"

"What's going on?"

"Those silly sods are lobbing shells on to the Leo II!"

"What? Are they our mortars firing?"

"Yes. We had three hundred shots left. Instead of evacuating them, Kreis told me to bung them on to the blue helmets massed behind the railway line. The range-finder must have gone wrong. They're firing two hundred yards short!"

Gelinet slammed on the brakes. Buscard leaped from the car shouting orders to the mercenaries who, with the help of some Africans, were manning the five mortars.

"Stop, for God's sake! Where's Fernand?"

"I've taken his place," said Felton, a big placid Rhodesian with a red mustache.

"Well, what the devil are you up to? You're firing two hundred yards short! You're lobbing your stuff right on to the center of the town!"

"I'm just doing what Fernand told me," said Felton. "He said: range two thousand. I'm firing at two thousand yards!"

"Fernand never said two thousand yards, but two thousand meters, you half-wit!"

Felton stopped the firing and in a calm voice said:

"Why don't these bloody French abandon the metric system? English measures are so much simpler!"

Kreis and his forty men established headquarters in a farmhouse on the Kipushi Road, about twelve miles from Elizabethville. At E'ville the first patrols of blue helmets were beginning to appear, accompanied by Katangese police in gray uniforms but without weapons.

One of the Union Minière directors, Monsieur Derrycks, was murdered by the Ethiopian blue helmets, and so were his eighty-year-old mother and his house-boy. Several women were raped by the defenders of order and civilization. Four Union Minière employees who tried to enter the company premises in broad daylight were mowed down in cold blood. On the airport road, under five inches of earth, the body of Monsieur Olivet, the delegate of the International Red Cross, was found, together with those of one of his assistants and a young nursing sister who was with them.

A week earlier their ambulance had received a direct hit from a bazooka fired from a position held by the Gurkhas.

On 21 December, late in the evening, President Kimjanga entered Elizabethville, dejected and defeated. A few hours earlier, at Kitona, he had been forced to capitulate on every point. He renounced the independence of Katanga and recognized the unity of the Congo. He ceased to contest the authority of the Leopoldville Government and placed his troops under the command of General Mobutu.

At Clair Manoir, General Siddartha celebrated his victory with his officers. At the end of the meal he raised his glass in the direction of the extinguished Lubumbashi chimney:

"Gentlemen, I drink to the self-sacrifice of the brave UN soldiers who have fallen in Katanga for the cause of justice and liberty! Thanks to your courage, to your devotion, to your exemplary conduct, the Katangese secession is definitely shattered, and with it colonialism in Africa!"

But the next day, taken in hand by Bongo, Kimjanga held a press conference and declared he had only signed the Kitona agreements under constraint.

A little later he was to assert that he had never signed those agreements at all.

On 23 December Kreis was summoned by Kimjanga. The President was once again smiling and self-assured. He started off by thanking Kreis for the job he had done with his mercenaries, then gave him his orders.

"You must disappear for a bit. I'm going to play a tricky game with the UN. I have no intention of abiding by the Kitona agreements. But I want to appear to yield on a number of points. For instance, the UN demand the immediate departure of all the mercenaries. I promised to give them satisfaction. I must ask you to assemble your men at Marinel Camp, near Kolwezi. Sort them out. I want two hundred reliable fellows who know their job. You'll be in command of them. You'll organize them as you see fit. Don't make a move. Don't make a sound. But be ready to take action as soon as I say!"

Musaille, notified by Kreis who had now fallen into the habit of dropping in on him, could not prevent himself from exclaiming:

"What an extraordinary fellow Kimjanga is! An absolute rubber ball. He bounces back, but he's finished all the same!"

"He's still paying me, Monsieur le Consul!"

"Good old Kreis, you belong to a dying race—the race of conscientious mercenaries!"

11. The Kolwezi Road

On 10 January, 1963, Dorat found Kreis in position with his mercenaries astride the road thirty-one miles from Kolwezi. He still had forty-six men, who had been joined by a dozen Africans—all that remained of General Nadolo's army. Swedish fighters and UN observation planes flew over the road incessantly. The mercenaries would raise their fists and curse them, but they did not fire. An Indian brigade, supported by armored cars and equipped with the latest material, was advancing by small stages on the mercenaries. Its advance party was only six miles away.

Dorat found Kreis in splendid form, calm, precise, efficient; he seemed to have assumed a great deal of authority. His men obeyed him without a murmur, without any recrimination.

Kreis handed him the field-glasses.

"Look at your little pals nosing about!"

Dorat took the field-glasses. The road ran dead straight across gently undulating country. About two miles away, the turret of a tank stood out against the sky-line. Dorat distinctly saw a blue helmet likewise observing through his field-glasses.

Kreis smiled.

"Don't bother, he won't shoot. What's the point? It's all over!"

An ambulance arrived from Kolwezi with supplies. Dorat happened to notice it was also carrying ammunition. On the coating of laterite dust covering the white paintwork, someone had inscribed: *Ave, Kimjanga, morituri te salutant!* and underneath, in huge letters:

Effective Strength: 200 mercenaries
Present in Katanga: 65
In Action: 46

"What has happened to Thomas Fonts?" Kreis asked all of a sudden.

Dorat looked at him in astonishment.

"You're more interested in him than in Colonel la Roncière?"

"You remember a man like Fonts, you're merely a temporary colleague with la Roncière!"

"Our friend Thomas has finally married his American girl. What a wedding! They almost came to blows!"

"Fonts and his wife?"

"No, the guests. The two clans of the same gang found themselves united. The victors and the vanquished of May 13th. Fonts enjoyed himself immensely. He has just been sent as consul to Cuba. Splendid choice. He's bound to appeal to Castro. In that romantico-Marxist mad-house he'll be as happy as a fish in water."

A Rhodesian mercenary called out to Dorat. He wore a Scottish bonnet adorned with a pheasant's feather and was noisily munching a croissant washed down with chocolate. The froth trickled down his dirty uniform.

"Well, how are things in Elizabethville?"

"The UN occupied it two days ago, everyone's fraternizing. The civilians sit and drink with the blue helmets."

He added mischievously:

"And the girls are beginning to get off with the handsome Swedes!"

"Oh, the little bitches!" the Rhodesian swore. "I'd like to go and toss a few grenades at them!"

"Yes," a Belgian went on. "Besides, those girls deserve to have their heads shaved!"

"That's enough nonsense," Kreis interjected. He shrugged his shoulders. "You're not going to do anything, so shut your traps and get back to your posts!"

"What for," said the Rhodesian, "since we sit here and do nothing? The others are advancing and we're not even trying to stop them. We might as well all contribute to buying them a bunch of flowers!"

Kreis took a step towards the Rhodesian.

"Shut up, Felton. Those are orders, so don't argue the toss!"

"What's going on?" Dorat asked.

"It's rather complicated; every day I receive contradictory orders. First of all I'm told to blow up all the Union Minière installations. Then it's called off. Three days ago they told me to counter-attack. We approached in the dark, which enabled us to surprise the Indians when they

498

were fast asleep. We gave them a good hiding! Whereupon a complete change of tactics. Now I have to keep the blue helmets at a distance and withdraw towards Kolwezi as they advance. No firing, unless they come too close and bother us. A complete balls-up, that's what it is!"

"What about the Delcommune dam?" Dorat inquired. "Are you blowing that up?"

Kreis looked amazed.

"The dam? Oh, that's another question: a political problem. That doesn't concern me."

Dorat knew Kreis was lying. Deserted by everyone, with his army routed, Kimjanga had only one card left in his hand: the huge Delcommune dam which overlooked the Kolwezi mine and works. The mine alone produced half the Katangese copper. If the dam went up, a mass of water, forty times larger than the one that ravaged Fréjus, would pour down on Kolwezi, flatten the town, engulf the mine and cause thousands of deaths. Since the start of the military operations Kimjanga had repeatedly said: "If the blue helmets continue their advance, I'll blow everything up!"

This was his trump card. Had it not been for this threat the UN troops would have occupied Kolwezi in forty-eight hours and everything would have been over long ago. This card Kreis now held in his hand.

Before his defeat the previous year and his capitulation at Kitona, President Kimjanga had appeared to be finished. Yet he had miraculously managed to survive, thanks to his usual methods: lies, prevarication and double dealing. With his hand on his heart, opening his eyes wide like an astonished child, he had proclaimed that he wanted to come to terms with his "brothers of Leopoldville." He had lauded "his dear UN friends" to the skies. He had been seen, during an official ceremony, exchanging a blood oath with General Siddartha. The two men had nicked their wrists and mingled their blood. Then they had embraced each other.

But Kimjanga had not yielded on a single point. Once again he was merely playing for time. Then he had started reorganizing his army. When he thought it was ready, he had broken with Leopoldville, asserting that it was impossible to come to terms with corrupt men whose "only thought was to drive around in big American cars and drink champagne with women."

Six months after the defeat of September 1961, Kimjanga seemed more firmly established than ever. All the work patiently accomplished by Maley, then by Siddartha, had to be started all over again. Dorat had paid a short visit to Elizabethville at the time. He had suddenly found himself carried back seven months. General Nadolo, more triumphant and more stupid than ever, asserted that in the event of an attack the blue helmets would be wiped out to the last man. The Europeans were clamoring for another war, which this time would be decisive!

And yet Kimjanga no longer stood a chance! At New York the new UN Secretary-General had been persuaded to resort to sweeping measures and eliminate the President. In Leopoldville the Americans had taken the matter in hand. Ambassador Ferwell had assured Adoula:

"This time we'll be responsible for the conduct of the war!"

A US Army general, entrusted with a mission in the Congo, had spent several days in Elizabethville. Officially, he was studying the requirements of the Congolese Army, but his real task was to draw up a plan of campaign for the final thrust.

In November giant Globemasters of the American Air Force started landing trucks, armored cars and guns at Elizabethville airport. A large part of this equipment still bore the white star and a stenciled inscription "US Army, Chateauroux."

In December things began to speed up. As in the previous year, Nadolo had fallen stupidly into the trap. He had set up road-blocks in Elizabethville, preventing the blue helmets from moving. The incidents had multiplied. Finally, when he had found his pretext, the Ethiopian General Ghebou, Siddartha's successor, had launched the attack.

On 28 December the Indian Brigade seized Elizabethville in four hours. No defense had been planned. The gendarmes disbanded at the first shots and rushed off into the bush. The mercenaries, still encamped at Kolwezi, were called up, but by the time they arrived the capital was firmly held. They withdrew towards Jadotville and blew up the bridges.

Events repeated themselves: Kimjanga fled to Rhodesia, but this time the Salisbury Government made it known that he was undesirable. He moved with his ministers to Kolwezi, the principal mining center in Katanga, two hundred and twenty miles west of the capital.

On the 30th the Ethiopians pushed towards Kipushi, which they seized without opposition.

On the 31st the Indians, masters of the capital, started to advance in the direction of Jadotville.

Kreis's men, cut off, insufficiently supplied, deprived of information, did what they could, but there were too few of them to contain the stream of assailants. They were constantly under fire from the Swedish and Ethiopian jet-fighters. Having remained inactive for a year, some of them had grown soft. Their pay came in at irregular intervals. A score of men had not drawn a penny for three months. Out of two hundred, about half deserted. They were to be seen swaggering about in the bars of Ndola.

Kreis notified Kimjanga that if the pay was not forthcoming within twenty-four hours he would stop fighting. Three hours later he saw the President's private secretary turn up with a briefcase stuffed with dollars. In the name of Kimjanga he begged Kreis to hold out at least three days. Kreis acquiesced with a nod and issued the dollars.

On 3 January the blue helmets entered Jadotville. Kreis cut the bridges to the west of the town and embarked with his meager forces on harassing tactics. The blue helmets' advance faltered, then stopped.

It was not this handful of mercenaries that held up General Ghebou. He had the means to wipe them out in a few hours. For him as for Davidson, the civilian representative, the problem was to see if Kimjanga would blow up the dam.

Davidson had come round to Arnold Riverton's opinion. He did not think Kimjanga would do it. To his mind, Kimjanga was a statesman and businessman. He would recoil from a gesture that would ruin his country. Apart from the fact that by destroying Kolwezi he would lose all hope of concluding a treaty with Leopoldville and pursuing a political career in the Congo.

But there was Bongo. Since the last UN attack, a blind hatred had seized him. The Delcommune dam, the Kolwezi mine and works had become the symbol to him of the power and arrogance of the whites. The whites had come to Katanga to steal her wealth and to humiliate him, Bongo, the descendant of the great M'Siri. With or without Kimjanga's agreement, he would blow everything sky-high!

Should he blow up the dam if he received orders to do so? For the last three days Kreis had been tormented by the question. For the first time in his life he found himself faced with this problem: can a soldier break his word and,

501

without failing in military honor, disobey the orders he has received?

Life had seemed so simple as long as he remained within the military framework. He retained a bitter memory of his brief sojourn in Paris where he had been left to his own devices after leaving the Legion.

What would he do if Kimjanga or Bongo ordered him to blow up Delcommune? Everything was ready. Some "extremist" engineers and specialists of the Union Minière had set the charges themselves. There remained one gesture to be made, and in less than a second it would all be over. Eight days earlier he would not even have hesitated.

But everything had grown unbelievably complicated. First of all Dessinges, the director of the Kolwezi mine, had summoned him to his office. He had started off by assuming a haughty manner:

"My dear fellow, you know the value of the installations for which I am responsible. You can't destroy them on a thoughtlessly issued order. I hope we see eye to eye: the demolition, assuming it comes to that, will be done only on my instructions."

Kreis had put the man in his place.

"I take my orders from the Katangese Government. I don't know you. If you have anything to say, go and see the President!"

Dessinges had climbed down.

"Don't lose your temper. We're a handful of whites in a country that has gone mad. We must keep cool and work together. We're all defending the same cause."

"Are you sure of that?" Kreis had asked. "Bongo claims you're betraying Katanga and have only one thought in your head: to hang on to your precious installations!"

"You know Bongo's a dangerous lunatic. Do you really think you'll be working for Katanga by destroying a mine which represents half her wealth?"

This argument had convinced Kreis, but not to the point of preventing him from carrying out orders. Now, Bongo seemed firmly resolved to go the whole hog. A few days earlier Kreis had had a terrible row with him. It was after the entry of the blue helmets into Jadotville. Before the town fell, Kreis had received contradictory orders: "Demolish, wait, blow everything up. . . ."

Dellemet, the director of Jadotville, had said to him:

"Don't bother, everything's ready. I'll see to the demolitions!"

The instructions had arrived four hours before the entry

of the blue helmets. Kreis, who was already falling back on Kolwezi, heard a series of explosions.

Three days later he stood to attention in front of a fuming Bongo.

"You have betrayed us, you're a dirty white like all the others! The Union Minière bribed you not to sabotage their installations. You'll pay for this, you dirty . . ."

Kreis had brought his fist down on the minister's desk.

"That's enough! What's all this nonsense about? I passed your orders on to Dellemet and I heard the explosions."

"Dellemet hoodwinked you! He blew up, for form's sake, a few transformers and part of the cobalt factory control-room. Everything will be repaired in a couple of weeks."

Bongo had reflected for a few minutes in silence, then, in a calmer tone, had said:

"It's just as I thought: the Union Minière are leaving us in the lurch. They're trying to deceive us by negotiating behind our backs with the UN. The same thing mustn't happen at Kolwezi. Go off and occupy the dam and the Union Minière works at once. Round up all the gendarmes still capable of bearing arms that you can find in town and put them under the orders of your mercenaries. Clear out all the European civilians and open fire if they don't jump to it quickly enough!"

Bongo was shaken by a new fit of rage. He stamped his feet:

"The dirty swine! I'll blow everything up, everything, do you hear, and if Dessinges lifts a little finger, I'll have him shot!"

On 12 January, Kolwezi, one of the big production centers of the Union Minière, afforded the very special aspect of a town to which a tottering government and the remnants of its army have just moved.

The ministerial documents were contained in a few cases piled up in a room. The colonels slept in the bathrooms, and the ministers on sofas.

Kimjanga had settled with Bongo and Nadolo on the outskirts of Kolwezi, in a big villa overlooking a garden. Opposite was a cross-roads, on each side a street. Nadolo had set up some barbed-wire entanglements and spiked iron fences. Kimjanga still had about a dozen of his personal guards and a few gendarmes with him.

Automatic weapons were sited in firing positions, and the vehicles parked under cover of the walls.

Kreis still had forty-six men, but ten of them, under Buscard's command, were detached nineteen miles away to defend or blow up, no one yet knew which, the dam which sealed off Lake Delcommune.

The lake, a stretch of extremely clear water, was nineteen miles long and nine wide; it was fed by the Lualaba River, punctuated by rapids.

When Buscard leaned over the parapet which crowned the concrete arc, he could see, over two hundred feet below, a stream of water glinting at the bottom of the gorge.

An electric mechanism enabled the whole lot to be blown up from a little building situated on the bank upstream.

Buscard merely had to pull a lever and the three million cubic yards of water—half the capacity of the Lake of Geneva—would drown the mines and sweep everything before them: workshops, control-rooms, the Marinel dam, towns and villages.

Before leaving him, Kreis, who had driven him to the dam, had seized him by the shoulders and looked him straight in the eye.

"Henri, I trust you as I would trust myself. If I personally give you the order to blow up the dam, you do it. Don't take any notice of anyone else, either Bongo, the President, Nadolo or even the hotheads of the Union Minière. Don't let anyone come near, either black or white. The game's up, but we still have this last surety. It's worth a lot to everyone. To us it's our lives saved, our arrears of pay, peace and quiet for months; to Kimjanga, maybe the opportunity to start his circus show all over again. If I get killed, it's up to you to decide."

Chaos reigned in Kolwezi. Four or five hundred gendarmes had eventually rejoined, most of them without their weapons and in tattered uniforms.

No arrangements had been made to feed or house them. They helped themselves, starting off by looting the houses in the African quarter and moving gradually up towards the European town. Several cars were stolen. When the owners tried to recover their vehicles, the gendarmes beat them up. Two European women were almost raped. Terrified, the Belgians asked the mercenaries for protection. Kreis, overwhelmed with work, at first refused, then organized a few patrols which took to driving slowly along the deserted streets.

The gendarmes got drunk on beer in the bars and indulged in savage brawls. Kreis ordered all the cafés to close at five o'clock. This measure proving insufficient, he forbade the sale of all alcoholic drinks.

Supplies began to run short. They usually arrived by road or rail from Elizabethville. The Union Minière sent their trucks to fetch food from Rhodesia, but the gendarmes looted them. Fully loaded trucks disappeared into the bush. The Europeans in Kolwezi had built up an absolute arsenal of weapons bought for a song from gendarmes thirsting for Simba beer. They had only one hope left: that the blue helmets would arrive soon to rid them of this riff-raff!

On 14 January the managing director of the Union Minière, Holmer Van der Weyck, arrived at Kolwezi from Rhodesia. Three days earlier he had been in Leopoldville. The head of the Congolese Government, Monsieur Adoula, had not concealed the fact that he wanted the Kolwezi installations to be saved at all costs.

"Kolwezi is my handiwork," Van der Weyck had replied. "The dam was started in 1950; I had just come out; the electricity works in 1953.

"I'm afraid of Bongo, he's on the spot. As far as Kimjanga's concerned, let the UN do as they like. Like all liars, he easily believes in the lies and promises of others. I'll leave for Luanda tomorrow. From there I'll get to Kolwezi by a company aircraft."

The local director of the Union Minière, Dessinges, came and asked Kreis whether he would be prepared to come to the Bonne Auberge and meet someone who was anxious to see him.

Dessinges had assumed the obsequious tone of a majordomo, and Kreis immediately realized he was referring to an important member of the company.

The Bonne Auberge, with its English prints, its armchairs covered in tartan cloth, its big fireplace and hunting trophies, tried to resemble any rest-house or club in Kenya or Rhodesia.

The cooking, luckily, was not English.

Sitting at the back of the bar, Van der Weyck rose to his feet as Kreis arrived, preceded by Dessinges. He motioned him to sit down and, at an imperceptible sign from the managing director, Dessinges made himself scarce.

"We don't know each other, Monsieur Kreis," Van der Weyck began, "but I've often heard about you from my directors and my staff. You came out to Katanga with Colonel la Roncière and Monsieur Thomas Fonts, didn't you?"

"That's right," said Kreis, unfolding his legs.

"In the midst of this chaos and confusion, you and your men represent the only reliable and coherent element. You have proved it by personally assuming control of the Delcommune dam."

Kreis waited.

"I believe you realize that this time Kimjanga is finished, the Katangese secession has been crushed. In a few hours the blue helmets could be masters of the whole country!"

"I know . . . but there's the dam!"

"I came here, Monsieur Kreis, to ask you to give me your word of honor not to blow up the dam but actually to defend it."

"I only obey those who pay me. They alone are entitled to give me orders. If President Kimjanga orders me to blow up Delcommune, I shall obey him . . . because obedience is one of the clauses in my contract . . . so long as I am paid."

On his way here, Van der Weyck had thought of offering Kreis and his mercenaries a very large sum of money in dollars and Swiss francs, the mercenaries' currencies. But he now saw this would be a tactless move; this fair-haired giant had an elementary clear-cut conception of what he called his honor, and he would not be bought. Van der Weyck was even liable to get his fist in his face!

Trying desperately to think of the arguments which would prevent him, Van der Weyck, if he was in Kreis's shoes, from blowing up the dam, he went on:

"Without thinking twice, you'll press a button, you'll destroy one of the finest achievements of the whites in Africa, simply because a Negro adventurer at bay orders you to do so. . . ."

"I'm a soldier; I'm not paid to think. All my comrades in Algeria and elsewhere who tried to think came in for a lot of trouble and suffered twinges of conscience."

"Have you seen the dam, the workshops, the power plant? Have you listened to the alternators roaring and the water being forced through the conduits? Three-quarters of the hydro-electric energy of Katanga!"

"I've seen it; it's magnificent. The walls are solid, the houses of the foremen and laborers are clean . . . but if I receive orders, the dam will go up."

"Ten years ago it was nothing but bush, pebbly scorched bush. I went over it in every direction with my engineers. Kreis, if you press the button, it will revert to bush. It's to defend all this work I'm so fond of that I came back to Kolwezi. You are prepared to submerge it under millions of cubic yards of water!

"For a rather . . . shall we say, primitive . . . conception of honor you'll ruin the economy of the country, you'll fling it back into the seething absurd world of the Negroes with their hysterics and fetishes. You'll impoverish the white world, for it's the white world that benefits and will continue to benefit from this wealth. But the Negroes, who have done nothing, benefit from it as well!

"We didn't come to Africa to enslave the blacks. A slave is a bad worker, he has no needs, therefore yields no output. We came here to transform this inhospitable country into a land where men, white and black alike, can live!

"Press the button and you become the accomplice of all those who, like Bongo, want to retain the old laws, the chiefdoms, who dream of a cruel bloodthirsty xenophobic Africa, and hope in their heart of hearts for the return of barbarism . . . because in the days of barbarism their ancestors were absolute despots!"

"All my life I've obeyed orders, Monsieur Van der Weyck, in Russia in the German Army, in Indo-China and Algeria in the Legion."

Kreis rose to his feet and suddenly leaned towards the managing director.

"And you know why I decided to obey? So as never to be confronted with problems of conscience. If I start wanting to choose, to decide for myself, I'd be caught up in the works and would lose my peace of mind! I eat well, I drink my fill, I sleep well, I'm not frightened, because I have no choice . . . I want to go on living like this!"

Van der Weyck realized he had won: Kreis had lost his composure. He would no longer have peace of mind, but the dam would not be blown up.

The managing director watched him as he weaved his way through the tables, and almost pitied him.

From the gendarmes who were ambling about the streets of Kolwezi, Bongo had succeeded in recruiting about forty belonging to his tribe, the Bayeke. He had found weapons for them and had taken them firmly in hand.

During the night of 15 January he sent thirty of them, led by one of his henchmen, to seize the dam and drive out the mercenaries.

Through a policeman in his pay, Bongo had learned about the meeting between Kreis and Van der Weyck at the Bonne Auberge. In Bongo's mind there was no further doubt: Kreis had been bought. But even without money, Bongo knew, Kreis would not have blown up the dam because he was a white man and the dam was yet another chain with which the whites had fettered Africa.

Bongo hated the whites and the dam.

His men surprised Buscard and Felton while they were having a nap, but made so much noise beating them up that the other mercenaries were alerted and opened fire.

The Bayeke gendarmes forthwith disbanded, taking with them their two prisoners.

One of the mercenaries managed to get through to Kreis on the telephone and notified him that the Katangese had attacked the dam and that Buscard and Felton had disappeared.

No sooner had the prisoners, urged on with kicks and punches, entered the room where Bongo was waiting than headlights flashed all round the villa.

Three jeeps, each armed with a 12.7 machine-gun, had just moved into position at the crossroads.

"Go and see," Bongo said to Nadolo.

President Kimjanga appeared in pajamas, yawning and rubbing his eyes. He was tired and in a bad temper. Jerking his chin at the mercenaries, strung up like sausages with telephone wire, he asked:

"Who are these two men?"

"Traitors, they're going to die!"

The presidential guard retreated in disorder towards the villa after tearing up the spiked fences. There was a sound of breeches being loaded.

Nadolo went down to the gates of the villa. Kreis got out of a jeep and came towards him.

The general felt ill at ease. Since December 1961, each time he encountered Kreis, he had to stop himself from snapping to attention. This time again he had to make an effort.

"Nadolo," Kreis shouted, "I give you five minutes to hand over Buscard and Felton, two of my men whom Bongo's thugs have just taken prisoner. If they're not out within five minutes, and in good shape, I'll open fire on the villa with three machine-guns."

Three minutes later, tottering in the beams of the headlights, Buscard and Felton came out, their clothing torn, their faces bearing the marks of blows.

508

In the cellar, to gratify his temper, Bongo was personally killing another mercenary, a Rhodesian pilot whom his men had brought in and who was accused of having given information to the UN.

He took pleasure in making him die slowly, and insulted him as he died. Then he gave orders for the body to be flung into Lake Delcommune.

The Rhodesian lived alone, apart from the other mercenaries, maybe thinking himself a superior species because he could pilot a plane. Since he had no friends, no one bothered about his disappearance. Two days later his body was found; his eyes had been gouged out. He was buried in a ditch.

On the following morning Nadolo turned up at the mercenaries' headquarters. President Kimjanga wanted to have an important discussion with Lieutenant Kreis and asked him to come and see him immediately.

Kreis had himself escorted by three jeeps, which ostentatiously moved into position round the villa. Then he went in, with a revolver at his side.

"My dear friend," the President said, shaking him warmly by the hand, "by a lamentable mistake two of your men were taken prisoner. As soon as I heard, I immediately gave orders for them to be released."

Bongo, still in his dark glasses, went up to the window and drew back the curtain. The three jeeps were there, with a mercenary behind each loaded machine-gun.

He turned round and went up to Kreis.

"Why won't you blow up the dam?"

"It's pointless, and I don't like the idea, Your Excellency."

"What if the President orders you to do so?"

"The dam will not be blown up."

"What if our troops attack it?"

"I shall defend it. Anyway you no longer have any troops."

"You're a traitor!"

Kimjanga intervened.

"Come now, calm down . . . nothing is lost yet! I can understand, Kreis, that you have certain scruples about destroying Delcommune, which is part of the industrial heritage of Katanga and of Africa. . . ."

The orator turned all of a sudden into a sly, crafty horse-coper.

"I never wanted Delcommune to be blown up, it's only

509

a card that I want to negotiate at a high price in Elizabethville. But I need you; I want your men to go on putting up a semblance of resistance on the road. Spread it around that if the blue helmets advance you'll blow everything sky-high . . . that only from me will you accept orders to the contrary!"

"What do you want to negotiate?" Bongo burst out. "There's nothing more to negotiate. Let's blow up the dam and go on with the war in the bush!"

"No," said Kreis, slapping the holster of his revolver.

"No," said the President, ". . . I have assurances from the UN. . . ."

Bongo tore off his dark glasses and tie and trampled them underfoot.

"I'm going back to the bush, back to my Bayekes. I shall resume native robes and the lion-skin. All whites are traitors, and also all those who want to be like whites!"

He yelled something in Swahili. Two or three of his men rushed up and followed him outside.

Kimjanga turned to Kreis and, as though nothing had happened, said: "So that's agreed, my dear friend?"

"But afterwards everything must be done in the proper manner, Monsieur le Président!"

"Of course, my dear Kreis!"

Two hours later Kimjanga flew off in a light aircraft and landed near Elizabethville. A UN car drove him to the new headquarters of the blue helmets, in the big concrete carcass of a half-built hospital.

Davidson, the Chief Representative, and Ghebou, the Ethiopian general, were waiting for him.

On 17 January Kimjanga signed his capitulation. He recognized yet again the end of the Katangese secession and submitted to the authority of the Central Government in Leopoldville.

The UN troops would enter Kolwezi on 21 January. This entry would be undertaken in a peaceful manner and no demolitions would be carried out.

In exchange, Kimjanga would remain President of the Provincial Government. Davidson, like Brahimi, gave him to understand that his political acumen and experience qualified him for an important post at Leopoldville.

Davidson personally thought it would not be a bad thing, but he knew that this time they had made up their minds to get rid of him, once and for all.

He lied without an effort, as only a gentleman can.

On the 20th, in the morning, back at Kolwezi, Kimjanga instructed Kreis to pull out during the day with his mercenaries and hand the dam over to a small unit of blue helmets who would come to occupy it at five in the afternoon.

"First of all let's settle our accounts," Kreis quietly said. "I shall hand over the dam only when everything is in order!"

"Meaning?"

"Belgian passports for all my men, an air ticket for their country of origin, two months' arrears of pay, three months' pay in advance!"

"I have everything with me."

"Of course, Monsieur le Président, during those three months you pay us in advance, we remain at your disposal. I'll load up the heavy equipment and arms for storage in Angola. I'll keep a dozen men with me. I know where to contact the others and how to make them come back!"

"I'm relying on that!"

Kimjanga suddenly burst into a loud guffaw, baring all his teeth.

"Because we haven't finished yet, Kreis!"

"Three months, Monsieur le Président . . . I give you three months. On the very day those three months are up, if we have not been paid, we'll be free to look for other employment."

Kreis snapped to attention and saluted.

"My respects, Monsieur le Président!"

The mercenaries left at six in the evening for Angola by the Union Minière train. They took all their equipment with them.

Dorat, who arrived with the blue helmets, rushed round to Kimjanga's. Before Dorat had time even to open his mouth, the President asked him:

"I say, Monsieur Dorat, there hasn't been much mention of Katanga in the press this time! A hundred Africans, a hundred Negroes were killed, yet not a word about it! Oh, I was forgetting those two white women who were murdered by the Indians and made the headlines in every paper in the world. But, of course, they were white!

"Katanga was in the news in September and December nineteen-sixty-one because some whites were killed or wounded! Aren't Negro casualties worth anything, Monsieur Dorat?"

"And the mercenaries, Monsieur le Président, what is to become of them?"

"The mercenaries? A mere detail! That's all they ever were."